A TREASURY OF AMERICAN HORROR STORIES

A TREASURY OF AMERICAN HORROR STORIES

Edited by Frank McSherry, Jr., Martin H. Greenberg
and Charles G. Waugh

BONANZA BOOKS • NEW YORK

Published 1985 by Bonanza Books, distributed by Crown Publishers, Inc.
225 Park Avenue South, New York, New York 10003.

Printed and bound in the United States of America.

Library of Congress Cataloging in Publication Data
Main entry under title:

A Treasury of American horror stories.

1. Horror tales, America.   I. McSherry, Frank D.
II. Greenberg, Martin Harry.   III. Waugh, Charles.
PS648.H6T74   1985   813'.0872'08   85-21269

Book design by June Marie Bennett

ISBN: 0-517-48075-1

h g f e

Acknowledgments

Grateful acknowledgment for permission to reprint material is hereby given to the following:

"Being," Copyright © 1957 by Richard Matheson. Reprinted by permission of Don Congdon Associates, Inc.

"One Happy Family," Copyright © 1983 by John S. McFarland. Reprinted by permission of the author.

"A Return to the Sabbath," Copyright © 1957 by King-Size Publications, Inc. Reprinted by permission of Kirby McCauley, Ltd.

"The Autopsy," Copyright © 1980 by Michael Shea; reprinted by permission of the author and the author's agent, Virginia Kidd.

"The Believers," Copyright 1941; copyright renewed © 1968 by Robert Arthur. Reprinted by permission of the agents for the author's estate, the Scott Meredith Literary Agency, Inc., 845 Third Avenue, New York, New York 10022.

"A Teacher's Rewards," Copyright © 1980 by Robert Phillips. Originally published in *The Land of Lost Content* (Vanguard Press). Reprinted by permission of the author.

"Chico Lafleur Talks Funny," Copyright © 1985 by Suzette Haden Elgin. An original story, used with permission of the author.

"The Legend of Joe Lee," Copyright © 1964 by John D. MacDonald. Reprinted by permission of the author.

"Seventh Sister," Copyright 1943 by Arkham House Publishers, Inc.; copyright renewed © 1971 by Arkham House Publishers, Inc. Reprinted by permission of Arkham House Publishers, Inc., Sauk City, Wisconsin.

"One Man's Harp," Copyright 1943 by Street & Smith Publications, Inc.; copyright renewed © 1970 by The Conde Nast Publications, Inc. Reprinted by permission of Davis Publications, Inc.

"The Smell of Cherries," Copyright © 1982 by TZ Publications, Inc. Reprinted by permission of the author.

"Away," Copyright © 1985 by Barry N. Malzberg. An original story, used with permission of the author.

"Twilla," Copyright © 1974 by Tom Reamy; copyright © 1979 by the Estate of Tom Reamy; reprinted by permission of Virginia Kidd, Literary Agent.

"His Name Was Not Forgotten," Copyright 1943 by the Curtis Publishing Company; copyright renewed. Reprinted by permission of Winifred W. Rogers.

"The Children of Noah," Copyright © 1957 by Richard Matheson. Reprinted by permission of Don Congdon Associates, Inc.

"The Man Who Collected Poe," Copyright 1951; copyright renewed © 1979 by Robert Bloch. Reprinted by permission of Kirby McCauley, Ltd.

"Pickman's Model," Copyright 1927; copyright renewed © 1955 by Arkham House Publishers, Inc. Reprinted by permission of the Scott Meredith Literary Agency, Inc., 845 Third Ave., New York, New York 10022.

Contents

CONTENTS

CONTENTS

The Monster Tour

Welcome aboard.

May we take your ticket and your comfortable feeling that evil—supernatural evil—will not happen to you?

The monster tour of the United States is about to begin. This volume carries fifty-one stories of horror, one set in each state of the Union and a bonus story set in the District of Columbia. But it is a monster tour in ways other than just geography. . . .

The land was green on the horizon when an English fleet under Sir Richard Grenville arrived in 1585 to found the first permanent settlement in that part of the New World later to become the United States. The weather was lovely, the natives friendly, the rich dark loam fertile; Grenville set up the town of Roanoke, Virginia. More settlers landed the next year; the town's first child, Virginia Dare, was born. In 1590 a third, delayed expedition arrived—to find Roanoke silent, its stockade gates swinging open in the breeze, the buildings empty. No bodies, not even any signs of violence—but there was no trace of human life. It was as if everyone there had decided to walk out of the town—and into thin air. Only one clue was found, a strange word, carved on a tree: "Croatan."

Thus American history began with a touch of horror, a red thread stitching through its colorful fabric. American literature picked up that thread and wove it into its soul; from Poe to Faulkner, almost every major American writer has made the tale of horror a part, and sometimes a major part, of his work.

Indeed, beginning in the 1920s with Howard Phillips Lovecraft, the scholarly recluse of Rhode Island, and culminating with Stephen King, the most widely read and commercially successful horror writer of all time, American authors have produced a surging wave of work that has swept them to world dominance of the genre.

The monsters we have chosen are varied, for each is the product of the people, the place, and the period that formed it. On this tour you'll meet the alien monstrosity out of space that appears in the Church of Starry Wisdom in Providence, Rhode Island, where an evil and ancient worship is not dead; a bloody nature god living under a huge field of golden corn that waves gently under a hot and windless Nebraska sky; a monstrous survival from prehistoric times still living among the massive mesas of New Mexico; the gaunt, burning-eyed actor in that modern Babylon, Hollywood, whose mere appearance in his Dracula-like roles brings heart-stopping fear to his fascinated audiences; and many more. The stories are written by such masters of terror as H. P. Lovecraft, Robert Bloch, and Stephen King; such masters of suspense as John D. MacDonald; and such virtuosos of science fiction as Isaac Asimov, Frederic Pohl, Richard Matheson, and William F. Nolan.

Nor are all the horrors supernatural; there are other kinds. As the Devil points out in Stephen Vincent Benét's classic "The Devil and Daniel Webster," when Webster tries to break a contract for a soul by claiming his client is an American and cannot be forced into servitude under a foreign prince: "Foreign? . . . When the first wrong was done to the first Indian, I was there. When the first slaver set out for the Congo, I stood on her deck . . . to tell the truth, Mr. Webster . . . my name is older in this country than your own."

Thus we have included tales of psychological horror, including, for example, one about a spy about to hang in Civil War Alabama; of social horrors, such as Whitley Streiber's gripping tale of a millionaire reduced to beggary by the Depression who encounters a pain-worshipping cult in a dusty Texas town, set against the greater horror of poverty in the Great Depression; of slavery and prejudice and bigotry in pre-civil rights Mississippi; and one of a dreadful tomorrow, when nuclear war comes to America.

The stories in this book include famous classics of American horror fiction; stories that were once famous but more recently have been overlooked, such as the tragic "Desiree's Baby"; modern masterpieces of fantasy and the supernatural; and new stories written especially for this volume by such authors as Barry N. Malzberg and Bill Pronzini.

Join us in this all-American monster tour of the night side of our nature, the dark side of the mind, a world alive with the dead. . . .
Bon voyage!

The Editors

A TREASURY OF
AMERICAN
HORROR
STORIES

ALABAMA

An Occurrence at Owl Creek Bridge
by Ambrose Bierce

A MAN stood upon a railroad bridge in northern Alabama, looking down into the swift waters twenty feet below. The man's hands were behind his back, the wrists bound with a cord. A rope loosely encircled his neck. It was attached to a stout cross-timber above his head, and the slack fell to the level of his knees. Some loose boards laid upon the sleepers supporting the metals of the railway supplied a footing for him and his executioners—two private soldiers of the Federal army, directed by a sergeant, who in civil life may have been a deputy sheriff. At a short remove upon the same temporary platform was an officer in the uniform of his rank, armed. He was a captain. A sentinel at each end of the bridge stood with his rifle in the position known as "support," that is to say, vertical in front of the left shoulder, the hammer resting on the forearm thrown straight across the chest—a formal and unnatural position, enforcing an erect carriage of the body. It did not appear to be the duty of these two men to know what was occurring at the centre of the bridge; they merely blockaded the two ends of the foot-plank which traversed it.

Beyond one of the sentinels nobody was in sight; the railroad ran straight away into a forest for a hundred yards, then, curving, was lost to view. Doubtless there was an outpost further along. The other bank of the stream was open ground—a gentle acclivity crowned with a stockade of vertical tree trunks, loopholed for rifles, with a single embrasure through which protruded the muzzle of a brass cannon commanding the bridge. Midway up the slope between the bridge and fort were the spectators—a single company of infantry in line, at "parade rest," the butts of the rifles on the ground, the barrels inclining slightly backward against the right shoulder, the hands

1

crossed upon the stock. A lieutenant stood at the right of the line, the point of his sword upon the ground, his left hand resting upon his right. Excepting the group of four at the centre of the bridge not a man moved. The company faced the bridge, staring stonily, motionless. The sentinels, facing the banks of the stream, might have been statues to adorn the bridge. The captain stood with folded arms, silent, observing the work of his subordinates, but making no sign. Death is a dignitary who, when he comes announced, is to be received with formal manifestations of respect, even by those most familiar with him. In the code of military etiquette silence and fixity are forms of deference.

The man who was engaged in being hanged was apparently about thirty-five years of age. He was a civilian, if one might judge from his dress, which was that of a planter. His features were good—a straight nose, firm mouth, broad forehead, from which his long, dark hair was combed straight back, falling behind his ears to the collar of his well-fitting frock coat. He wore a mustache and pointed beard, but no whiskers; his eyes were large and dark gray, and had a kindly expression which one would hardly have expected in one whose neck was in the hemp. Evidently this was no vulgar assassin. The liberal military code makes provision for hanging many kinds of people, and gentlemen are not excluded.

The preparations being complete, the two private soldiers stepped aside, and each drew away the plank upon which he had been standing. The sergeant turned to the captain, saluted and placed himself immediately behind that officer, who in turn moved apart one pace. These movements left the condemned man and the sergeant standing on the two ends of the same plank, which spanned three of the cross-ties of the bridge. The end upon which the civilian stood almost, but not quite, reached a fourth. This plank had been held in place by the weight of the captain; it was now held by that of the sergent. At a signal from the former the latter would step aside, the plank would tilt, and the condemned man go down between two ties. The arrangement commended itself to his judgment as simple and effective. His face had not been covered nor his eyes bandaged. He looked a moment at his "unsteadfast footing," then let his gaze wander to the swirling water of the stream racing madly beneath his feat. A piece of dancing driftwood caught his attention, and his eyes followed it down the current. How slowly it appeared to move! What a sluggish stream!

He closed his eyes in order to fix his last thoughts upon his wife and children. The water, touched to gold by the early sun, the brooding mists under the banks at some distance down the stream, the fort, the soldiers, the piece of drift—all had distracted him. And now he became conscious of a new disturbance. Striking through the thought of his dear ones was a sound he could neither ignore nor understand, a sharp, distinct, metallic percussion like the stroke of a blacksmith's hammer upon the anvil; it had the same ringing quality. He wondered what it was, and whether immeasurably distant or near by—it seemed both. Its recurrence was regular, but as slow as the tolling of a death-knell. He awaited each stroke with impatience and—he knew not why—apprehension. The intervals of silence grew progressively longer; the delays maddening. With their greater infrequency the sounds increased in strength and sharpness. They hurt his ear like the thrust of a knife; he feared he would shriek. What he heard was the ticking of his watch.

He unclosed his eyes and saw again the water below him. "If I could free my hands," he thought, "I might throw off the noose and spring into the stream. By diving, I could evade the bullets, and, swimming vigorously, reach the bank, take to the woods, and get away home. My home, thank God, is as yet outside their lines; my wife and little ones are still beyond the invaders' farthest advance."

As these thoughts, which have here to be set down to words, were flashed into the doomed man's brain rather than evolved from it, the captain nodded to the sergeant. The sergeant stepped aside.

II

Peyton Farquhar was a well-to-do planter, of an old and highly respected Alabama family. Being a slave-owner, and, like other slave-owners, a politician, he was naturally an original secessionist and ardently devoted to the Southern cause. Circumstances of an imperious nature which it is unnecessary to relate here, had prevented him from taking service with the gallant army which had fought the disastrous campaigns ending with the fall of Corinth, and he chafed under the inglorious restraint, longing for the release of his energies, the larger life of the soldier, the opportunity for distinction. That opportunity, he felt, would come, as it comes to all in war-time. Meanwhile he did what he could. No service was too humble for him to perform in aid of the South, no adventure too perilous for him to undertake if consistent with the character of a civilian who was at heart a soldier, and who in good faith and without too much qualification assented to at least a part of the frankly villainous dictum that all is fair in love and war.

One evening while Farquhar and his wife were sitting on a rustic bench near the entrance to his grounds, a gray-clad soldier rode up to the gate and asked for a drink of water. Mrs. Farquhar was only too happy to serve him with her own white hands. While she was gone to fetch the water, her husband approached the dusty horseman and inquired eagerly for news from the front.

"The Yanks are repairing the railroads," said the man, "and are getting ready for another advance. They have reached the Owl Creek Bridge, put it in order, and built a stockade on the other bank. The commandant has issued an order, which is posted everywhere, declaring that any civilian caught interfering with the railroad, its bridges, tunnels, or trains, will be summarily hanged. I saw the order."

"How far is it to the Owl Creek Bridge?" Farquhar asked.

"About thirty miles."

"Is there no force on this side of the creek?"

"Only a picket post half a mile out, on the railroad, and a single sentinel at this end of the bridge."

"Suppose a man—a civilian and student of hanging—should elude the picket post and perhaps get the better of the sentinel," said Farquhar, smiling, "what could he accomplish?"

The soldier reflected. "I was there a month ago," he replied. "I observed that the flood of last winter had lodged a great quantity of driftwood against the wooden pier at this end of the bridge. It is now dry, and would burn like tow."

The lady had now brought the water, which the soldier drank. He thanked her ceremoniously, bowed to her husband, and rode away. An hour later, after nightfall, he repassed the plantation, going northward in the direction from which he had come. He was a Federal scout.

III

As Peyton Farquhar fell straight downward through the bridge, he lost consciousness and was as one already dead. From this state he was awakened—ages later, it seemed to him— by the pain of a sharp pressure upon his throat, followed by a sense of suffocation. Keen, poignant agonies seemed to shoot from his neck downward through every fibre of his body and limbs. These pains seemed to flash along well-defined lines of ramification, and to beat with an inconceivably rapid periodicity. They seemed like streams of pulsating fire heating him to an intolerable temperature. As to his head, he was conscious of nothing but a feeling of fulness—of congestion. These sensations were unaccompanied by thought. The intellectual part of his nature was already effaced; he had power only to feel, and feeling was torment. He was conscious of motion. Encompassed in a luminous cloud, of which he was now merely the fiery heart, without material substance, he swung through unthinkable arcs of oscillation, like a vast pendulum. Then all at once, with terrible suddenness, the light about him shot upward with the noise of a loud plash; a frightful roaring was in his ears, and all was cold and dark. The power of thought was restored; he knew that the rope had broken and he had fallen into the stream. There was no additional strangulation; the noose about his neck was already suffocating him, and kept the water from his lungs. To die hanging at the bottom of a river!—the idea seemed to him ludicrous. He opened his eyes in the blackness and saw above him a gleam of light, but how distant, how inaccessible! He was still sinking, for the light became fainter and fainter until it was a mere glimmer. Then it began to grow and brighten, and he knew that he was rising toward the surface—knew it with reluctance, for he was now very comfortable. "To be hanged and drowned" he thought, "that is not so bad; but I do not wish to be shot. No; I will not be shot; that is not fair."

He was not conscious of an effort, but a sharp pain in his wrists apprised him that he was trying to free his hands. He gave the struggle his attention, as an idler might observe the feat of a juggler, without interest in the outcome. What splendid effort!—what magnificent, what superhuman strength! Ah, that was a fine endeavor! Bravo! The cord fell away; his arms parted and floated upward, the hands dimly seen on each side in the growing light. He watched them with a new interest as first one and then the other pounced upon the noose at his neck. They tore it away and thrust it fiercely aside, its undulations resembling those of a water-snake. "Put it back! put it back!" He thought he shouted these words to his hands, for the undoing of the noose had been succeeded by the direst pang which he had yet experienced. His neck ached horribly; his brain was on fire; his heart, which had been fluttering faintly, gave a great leap, trying to force itself out of his mouth. His whole body was racked and wrenched with an insupportable anguish! But his disobedient hands gave no heed to the command. They beat the water vigorously with quick, downward strokes, forcing him to the surface. He felt his head emerge; his eyes were blinded by the sunlight; his chest expanded convulsively, and with a supreme and crowning agony his lungs engulfed a great draught of air, which instantly he expelled in a shriek!

He was now in full possession of his physical senses. They were, indeed, preternaturally keen and alert. Something in the awful disturbance of his organic system had so exalted and refined them that they made record of things never before perceived. He felt the ripples upon his face and heard their separate sounds as they struck. He looked at the forest on the bank of the stream, saw the individual trees, the leaves and the veining of each leaf—saw the very insects upon them, the locusts, the brilliant-bodied flies, the gray spiders stretching their webs from twig to twig. He noted the prismatic colors in all the dewdrops upon a million blades of grass. The humming of the gnats that danced above the eddies of the stream, the beating of the dragon-flies' wings, the strokes of the water-spiders' legs, like oars which had lifted their boat—all these made audible music. A fish slid along beneath his eyes, and he heard the rush of its body parting the water.

He had come to the surface facing down the stream; in a moment the visible world seemed to wheel slowly round, himself the pivotal point, and he saw the bridge, the fort, the soldiers on the bridge, the captain, the sergeant, the two privates, his executioners. They were in silhouette against the blue sky. They shouted and gesticulated, pointing at him; the captain had drawn his pistol, but did not fire; the others were unarmed. Their movements were grotesque and horrible, their forms gigantic.

Suddenly he heard a sharp report, and something struck the water smartly within a few inches of his head, spattering his face with spray. He heard a second report, and saw one of the sentinels with his rifle at his shoulder, a light cloud of blue smoke rising from the muzzle. The man in the water saw the eye of the man on the bridge gazing into his own through the sights of the rifle. He observed that it was a gray eye, and remembered having read that gray eyes were keenest, and that all famous marksmen had them. Nevertheless, this one had missed.

A counter-swirl had caught Farquhar and turned him half round; he was again looking into the forest on the bank opposite the fort. The sound of a clear, high voice in a monotonous sing-song now rang out behind him and came across the water with a distinctness that pierced and subdued all other sounds, even the beating of the riples in his ears. Although no soldier, he had frequented camps enough to know the dread significance of that deliberate, drawling, aspirated chant; the lieutenant on shore was taking a part in the morning's work. How coldly and pitilessly—with what an even, calm intonation, presaging and enforcing tranquility in the men—with what accurately measured intervals fell those cruel words: "Attention, company.—Shoulder arms.—Ready.—Aim.—Fire!"

Farquhar dived—dived as deeply as he could. The water roared in his ears like the voice of Niagara, yet he heard the dulled thunder of the volley, and rising again toward the surface, met shining bits of metal, singularly flattened, oscillating slowly downward. Some of them touched him on the face and hands, then fell away, continuing their descent. One lodged between his collar and neck; it was uncomfortably warm, and he snatched it out.

As he rose to the surface, gasping for breath, he saw that he had been a long time under water; he was perceptibly farther down-stream—nearer to safety! The soldiers had almost finished reloading; the metal ramrods flashed all at once in the sunshine as they were drawn from the barrels, turned in the air, and thrust into their sockets. The two sentinels fired again, independently and ineffectually.

The hunted man saw all this over his shoulder; he was now swimming vigorously with the current. His brain was as energetic as his arms and legs; he thought with the rapidity of lightning.

"The officer," he reasoned, "will not make that martinet's error a second time. It is as easy to dodge a volley as a single shot. He has probably already given the command to fire at will. God help me, I cannot dodge them all!"

An appalling plash within two yards of him, followed by a loud rushing sound, *diminuendo*, which seemed to travel back through the air to the fort and died in an explosion which stirred the very river to its deeps. A rising sheet of water, which curved over him, fell down upon him, blinded him, strangled him. The cannon had taken a hand in the game. As he shook his head free from the commotion of the smitten water, he heard the deflected shot humming through the air ahead, and in an instant it was cracking and smashing the branches in the forest beyond.

"They will not do that again," he thought; "the next time they will use a charge of grape. I must keep my eye upon the gun; the smoke will apprise me—the report arrives too late; it lags behind the missile. It is a good gun."

Suddenly he felt himself whirled round and round—spinning like a top. The water, the banks, the forest, the now distant bridge, fort and men—all were commingled and blurred. Objects were represented by their colors only; circular horizontal streaks of color—that was all he saw. He had been caught in a vortex, and was being whirled on with a velocity of advance and gyration which made him giddy and sick. In a few moments he was flung upon the gravel at the foot of the left bank of the stream—the southern bank—and behind a projecting point which concealed him from his enemies. The sudden arrest of his motion, the abrasion of one of his hands on the gravel, restored him, and he wept with delight. He dug his fingers into the sand, threw it over himself in handfuls and audibly blessed it. It looked like gold, like diamonds, rubies, emeralds; he could think of nothing beautiful which it did not resemble. The trees upon the bank were giant garden plants; he noted a definite order in their arrangement, inhaled the fragrance of their blooms. A strange, roseate light shone through the spaces among their trunks, and the wind made in their branches the music of aeolian harps. He had no wish to perfect his escape, was content to remain in that enchanting spot until retaken.

A whizz and rattle of grapeshot among the branches high above his head roused him from his dream. The baffled cannoneer had fired him a random farewell. He sprung to his feet, rushed up the sloping bank, and plunged into the forest.

All that day he travelled, laying his course by the rounding sun. The forest seemed interminable; nowhere did he discover a break in it, not even a woodman's road. He had not known that he lived in so wild a region. There was something uncanny in the revelation.

By nightfall he was fatigued, footsore, famishing. The thought of his wife and children urged him on. At last he found a road which led him in what he knew to be the right direction. It was as wide and straight as a city street, yet it seemed untravelled. No fields bordered it, no dwelling anywhere. Not so much as the barking of a dog suggested human habitation. The black bodies of the great trees formed a straight wall on both sides, terminating on the horizon in a point, like a diagram in a lesson in perspective. Overhead, as he looked up through this rift in the wood, shone great golden stars looking unfamiliar and grouped in strange constellations. He was sure they were arranged in some order which had a secret and malign significance. The wood on either side was full of singular noises, among which—once, twice, and again—he distinctly heard whispers in an unknown tongue.

His neck was in pain, and, lifting his hand to it, he found it horribly swollen. He knew that it had a circle of black where the rope had bruised it. His eyes felt congested; he could no longer close them. His tongue was swollen with thirst; he relieved its fever by thrusting it forward from between his teeth into the cool air. How softly the turf had carpeted the untravelled avenue! He could no longer feel the roadway beneath his feet!

Doubtless, despite his suffering, he fell asleep while walking, for now he sees another scene—perhaps he has merely recovered from a delirium. He stands at the gate of his own home. All is as he left it, and all bright and beautiful in the morning sunshine. He must have travelled the entire night. As he pushes open the gate and passes up the wide white walk, he sees a flutter of female garments; his wife, looking fresh and cool and sweet, steps down from the veranda to meet him. At the bottom of the steps she stands waiting, with a smile of ineffable joy, an attitude of matchless grace and dignity. Ah, how beautiful she is! He springs forward with extended arms. As he is about to clasp her, he feels a stunning blow upon the back of the neck; a blinding white light blazes all about him, with a sound like the shock of a cannon—then all is darkness and silence!

Peyton Farquhar was dead; his body, with a broken neck, swung gently from side to side beneath the timbers of the Owl Creek Bridge.

ALASKA

Lost Face
by Jack London

IT WAS the end. Subienkow had traveled a long trail of bitterness and horror, homing like a dove for the capitals of Europe, and here, farther away than ever, in Russian America, the trail ceased. He sat in the snow, arms tied behind him, waiting the torture. He stared curiously before him at a huge Cossack, prone in the snow, moaning in his pain. The men had finished handling the giant and turned him over to the women. That they had exceeded the fiendishness of the men the man's cries attested.

Subienkow looked on and shuddered. He was not afraid to die. He had carried his life too long in his hands, on that weary trail from Warsaw to Nulato, to shudder at mere dying. But he objected to the torture. It offended his soul. And this offense, in turn, was not due to the mere pain he must endure, but to the sorry spectacle the pain would make of him. He knew that he would pray, and beg, and entreat, even as Big Ivan and the others that had gone before. This would not be nice. To pass out bravely and cleanly, with a smile and a jest—ah, that would have been the way. But to lose control, to have his soul upset by the pangs of the flesh, to screech and gibber like an ape, to become the veriest beast—ah, that was what was so terrible.

There had been no chance to escape. From the beginning, when he dreamed the fiery dream of Poland's independence, he had become a puppet in the hands of fate. From the beginning, at Warsaw, at St. Petersburg, in the Siberian mines, in Kamchatka, on the crazy boats of the fur thieves, fate had been driving him to this end. Without doubt, in the foundations of the world was graved this end for him—for him, who was so fine and sensitive, whose nerves scarcely sheltered under his skin, who was a dreamer and a poet and an artist. Before he was dreamed of, it had been determined that the quivering bundle of sensitiveness that constituted him should be doomed to live in raw and howling savagery, and to die in this far land of night, in this dark place beyond the last boundaries of the world.

He sighed. So that thing before him was Big Ivan—Big Ivan the giant, the man without nerves, the man of iron, the Cossack turned freebooter of the seas, who was as phlegmatic as an ox, with a nervous system so low that what was pain to ordinary men was scarcely a tickle to him. Well, well, trust these Nulato Indians to find Big Ivan's nerves and trace them to the roots of his quivering soul. They were certainly doing it. It was inconceivable that a man could suffer so much and yet live. Big Ivan was paying for his low order of nerves. Already he had lasted twice as long as any of the others.

Subienkow felt that he could not stand the Cossack's sufferings much longer. Why didn't Ivan die? He would go mad if that screaming did not cease. But when it did cease, his turn would come. And there was Yakaga awaiting him, too, grinning at him even now in anticipation—Yakaga, whom only last week he had kicked out of the fort, and upon whose face he had laid the lash of his dog whip. Yakaga would attend to him. Doubtlessly Yakaga was saving for him more refined tortures, more exquisite nerve-racking. Ah! That must have been a good one, from the way Ivan screamed. The squaws bending over him stepped back with laughter and clapping of hands. Subienkow saw the monstrous thing that had been perpetrated, and began to laugh hysterically. The Indians looked at him in wonderment that he should laugh. But Subienkow could not stop.

This would never do. He controlled himself, the spasmodic twitchings slowly dying away. He strove to think of other things, and began reading back in his own life. He remembered his mother and his father and the little spotted pony, and the French tutor who had taught him dancing and sneaked him an old worn copy of Voltaire. Once more he saw Paris, and dreary London, and gay Vienna, and Rome. And once more he saw that wild group of youths who had dreamed, even as he, the dream of an independent Poland with a king of Poland on the throne at Warsaw. Ah, there it was that the long trail began. Well, he had lasted longest. One by one, beginning with the two executed at St. Petersburg, he took up the count of the passing of those brave spirits. Here one had been beaten to death by a jailer, and there, on that bloodstained highway of the exiles, where they had marched for endless months, beaten and maltreated by their Cossack guards, another had dropped by the way. Always it had been savagery—brutal, bestial savagery. They had died—of fever, in the mines, under the knout. The last two had died after the escape, in the battle with the Cossacks, and he alone had won to Kamchatka with the stolen papers and the money of a traveler he had left lying in the snow.

It had been nothing but savagery. All the years, with his heart in studios and theaters and courts, he had been hemmed in by savagery. He had purchased his life with blood. Everybody had killed. He had killed that traveler for his passports. He had proved that he was a man of parts by dueling with two Russian officers on a single day. He had had to prove himself in order to win to a place among the fur thieves. He had had to win to that place. Behind him lay the thousand-years-long road across all Siberia and Russia. He could not escape that way. The only way was ahead, across the dark and icy sea of Bering to Alaska. The way had led from savagery to deeper savagery. On the scurvy-rotten ships of the fur thieves, out of food and out of water, buffeted by the interminable storms of that stormy sea, men had become animals. Thrice he had sailed east from Kamchatka. And thrice, after all manner of hardship and suffering, the survivors had come back to Kamchatka. There had been no outlet for escape, and he could not go back the way he had come, for the mines and the knout awaited him.

Again, the fourth and last time, he had sailed east. He had been with those who first found the fabled Seal Islands; but he had not returned with them to share the wealth of furs in the mad orgies of Kamchatka. He had sworn never to go back. He knew that to win to those dear capitals of Europe he must go on. So he had changed ships and remained in the dark new land. His comrades were Slavonian hunters and Russian adventurers, Mongols and Tatars and Siberian aborigines; and through the savages of the New World they had cut a path of blood. They had massacred whole villages that refused to furnish the fur tribute; and they in turn had been massacred by ships' companies. He, with one Finn, had been the sole survivors of such a company. They had spent a winter of solitude and starvation on a lonely Aleutian isle, and their rescue in the spring by another fur ship had been one chance in a thousand.

But always the terrible savagery had hemmed him in. Passing from ship to ship, and ever refusing to return, he had come to the ship that explored south. All down the Alaskan coast they had encountered nothing but hosts of savages. Every anchorage among the beetling islands or under the frowning cliffs of the mainland had meant a battle or a storm. Either the gales blew, threatening destruction, or the war canoes came off, manned by howling natives with the war paint on their faces, who came to learn the bloody virtues of the sea rovers' gunpowder. South, south they had coasted, clear to the myth land of California. Here, it was said, were Spanish adventurers who had fought their way up from Mexico. He had had hopes of those Spanish adventurers. Escaping to them, the rest would have been easy—a year or two, what did it matter more or less?—and he would win to Mexico, then a ship, and Europe would be his. But they had met no Spaniards. Only had they encountered the same impregnable wall of savagery. The denizens of the confines of the world, painted for war, had driven them back from the shores. At last, when one boat was cut off and every man killed, the commander had abandoned the quest and sailed back to the North.

The years had passed. He had served under Tebenkoff when Michaelovski Redoubt was built. He had spent two years in the Kuskokwim country. Two summers, in the month of June, he had managed to be at the head of Kotzebue Sound. Here, at this time, the tribes assembled for barter; here were to be found spotted deerskins from Siberia, ivory from the Diomedes, walrus skins from the shores of the Arctic, strange stone lamps, passing in trade from tribe to tribe, no one knew whence, and, once, a hunting knife of English make; and here, Subienkow knew, was the school in which to learn geography. For he met Eskimos from Norton Sound, from King Island and St. Lawrence Island, from Cape Prince of Wales, and Point Barrow. Such places had other names, and their distances were measured in days.

It was a vast region these trading savages came from, and a vaster region from which, by repeated trade, their stone lamps and that steel knife had come. Subienkow bullied and cajoled and bribed. Every far journeyer or strange tribesman was brought before him. Perils unaccountable and unthinkable were mentioned, as well as wild beasts, hostile tribes, impenetrable forests, and mighty mountain ranges; but always from beyond came the rumor and the tale of white-skinned men, blue of eye and fair of hair, who fought like devils and who sought always for furs. They were to the east—far, far to the east. No one had seen them. It was the word that had been passed along.

It was a hard school. One could not learn geography very well through the medium of strange dialects, from dark minds that mingled fact and fable and that measured distances by "sleeps" that varied according to the difficulty of the going. But at last came the whisper that gave Subienkow courage. In the east lay a great river where were these blue-eyed men. The river was called the Yukon. South of Michaelovski Redoubt emptied another great river which the Russians knew as the Kwikpak. These two rivers were one, ran the whisper.

Subienkow returned to Michaelovski. For a year he urged an expedition up the Kwikpak. Then arose Malakoff, the Russian half-breed, to lead the wildest and most ferocious of the hell's broth of mongrel adventurers who had crossed from Kamchatka. Subienkow was his lieutenant. They threaded the mazes of the great delta of the Kwikpak, picked up the first low hills on the northern bank, and for half a thousand miles, in skin canoes loaded to the gunwales with trade goods and ammunition, fought their way against the five-knot current of a river that ran from two to ten miles wide in a channel many fathoms deep. Malakoff decided to build the fort at Nulato. Subienkow urged to go farther. But he quickly reconciled himself to Nulato. The long winter was coming on. It would be better to wait. Early the following summer, when the ice was gone, he would disappear up the Kwikpak and work his way to the Hudson's Bay Company's posts. Malakoff had never heard the whisper that the Kwikpak was the Yukon, and Subienkow did not tell him.

Came the building of the fort. It was enforced labor. The tiered walls of logs arose to the sighs and groans of the Nulato Indians. The last was laid upon their backs, and it was the iron hand of the freebooters of the sea that laid on the lash. There were Indians that ran away, and when they were caught they were brought back and spread-eagled before the fort, where they and their tribe learned the efficacy of the knout. Two died under it; others were injured for life; and the rest took the lesson to heart and ran away no more. The snow was flying ere the fort was finished, and then it was the time for furs. A heavy tribute was laid upon the tribe. Blows and lashings continued, and that the tribute should be paid, the women and children were held as hostages and treated with the barbarity that only the fur thieves knew.

Well, it had been a sowing of blood, and now was come the harvest. The fort was gone. In the light of its burning, half the fur thieves had been cut down. The other half had passed under the torture. Only Subienkow remained, or Subienkow and Big Ivan, if that whimpering, moaning thing in the snow could be called Big Ivan. Subienkow caught Yakaga grinning at him. There was no gainsaying Yakaga. The mark of the lash was still on his face. After all, Subienkow could not blame him, but he disliked the thought of what Yakaga would do to him. He thought of appealing to Makamuk, the head chief; but his judgment told him that such appeal was useless. Then, too, he thought of bursting his bonds and dying fighting. Such an end would be quick. But he could not break his bonds. Caribou thongs were stronger than he. Still devising, another thought came to him. He signed for Makamuk, and that an interpreter who knew the coast dialect should be brought.

"Oh, Makamuk," he said, "I am not minded to die. I am a great man, and it were foolishness for me to die. In truth, I shall not die. I am not like these other carrion."

He looked at the moaning thing that had once been Big Ivan, and stirred it contemptuously with his toe.

"I am too wise to die. Behold, I have a great medicine. I alone know this medicine. Since I am not going to die, I shall exchange this medicine with you."

"What is this medicine?" Makamuk demanded.

"It is a strange medicine."

Subienkow debated with himself for a moment, as if loath to part with the secret.

"I will tell you. A little bit of this medicine rubbed on the skin makes the skin hard like a rock, hard like iron, so that no cutting weapon can cut it. The strongest blow of a cutting weapon is a vain thing against it. A bone knife becomes like a piece of mud; and it will turn the edge of the iron knives we have brought among you. What will you give me for the secret of the medicine?"

"I will give you your life," Makamuk made answer through the interpreter.

Subienkow laughed scornfully.

"And you shall be a slave in my house until you die."

The Pole laughed more scornfully.

"Untie my hands and feet and let us talk," he said.

The chief made the sign; and when he was loosed Subienkow rolled a cigarette and lighted it.

"This is foolish talk," said Makamuk. "There is no such medicine. It cannot be. A cutting edge is stronger than any medicine."

The chief was incredulous, and yet he wavered. He had seen too many deviltries of fur thieves that worked. He could not wholly doubt.

"I will give you your life; but you shall not be a slave," he announced. "More than that."

Subienkow played his game as coolly as if he were bartering for a fox skin.

"It is a very great medicine. It has saved my life many times. I want a sled and dogs, and six of your hunters to travel with me down the river and give me safety to one day's sleep from Michaelovski Redoubt."

"You must live here, and teach us all of your deviltries," was the reply.

Subienkow shrugged his shoulders and remained silent. He blew cigarette smoke out on the icy air, and curiously regarded what remained of the big Cossack.

"That scar!" Makamuk said suddenly, pointing to the Pole's neck, where a livid mark advertised the slash of a knife in a Kamchatkan brawl. "The medicine is not good. The cutting edge was stronger than the medicine."

"It was a strong man that drove the stroke." (Subienkow considered.) "Stronger than you, stronger than your strongest hunter, stronger than he."

Again, with the toe of his moccasin, he touched the Cossack—a grisly spectacle, no longer conscious—yet in whose dismembered body the pain-racked life clung and was loath to go.

"Also the medicine was weak. For at that place there were no berries of a certain kind, of which I see you have plenty in this country. The medicine here will be strong."

"I will let you go downriver," said Makamuk; "and the sled and the dogs and the six hunters to give you safety shall be yours."

"You are slow," was the cool rejoinder. "You have committed an offense against my medicine in that you did not at once accept my terms. Behold, I now demand more. I want one hundred beaver skins." (Makamuk sneered.) "I want one hundred pounds of dried fish." (Makamuk nodded, for fish were plentiful and cheap.) "I want two sleds—one for me and one for my furs and fish. And my rifle must be returned to me. If you do not like the price, in a little while the price will grow."

Yakaga whispered to the chief.

"But how can I know your medicine is true medicine?" Makamuk asked.

"It is very easy. First, I shall go into the woods——"

Again Yakaga whispered to Makamuk, who made a suspicious dissent.

"You can send twenty hunters with me," Subienkow went on. "You see, I must get the berries and the roots with which to make the medicine. Then, when you have brought the two sleds and loaded on them the fish and the beaver skins and the rifle, and when you have told off the six hunters who will go with me—then, when all is ready, I will rub the medicine on my neck, so, and lay my neck there on that log. Then can your strongest hunter take the ax and strike three times on my neck. You yourself can strike the three times."

Makamuk stood with gaping mouth, drinking in this latest and most wonderful magic of the fur thieves.

"But first," the Pole added hastily, "between each blow I must put on fresh medicine. The ax is heavy and sharp, and I want no mistakes."

"All that you have asked shall be yours," Makamuk cried in a rush of acceptance. "Proceed to make your medicine."

Subienkow concealed his elation. He was playing a desperate game, and there must be no slips. He spoke arrogantly.

"You have been slow. My medicine is offended. To make the offense clean you must give my your daughter."

He pointed to the girl, an unwholesome creature, with a cast in one eye and a bristling wolf tooth. Makamuk was angry, but the Pole remained imperturbable, rolling and lighting another cigarette.

"Make haste," he threatened. "If you are not quick, I shall demand yet more."

In the silence that followed, the dreary Northland scene faded from before him, and he saw once more his native land, and France, and once, as he glanced at the wolf-toothed girl, he remembered another girl, a singer and a dancer, whom he had known when first as a youth he came to Paris.

"What do you want with the girl?" Makamuk asked.

"To go down the river with me." Subienkow glanced her over critically. "She will make a good wife, and it is an honor worthy of my medicine to be married to your blood."

Again he remembered the singer and dancer and hummed aloud a song she had taught him. He lived the old life over, but in a detached, impersonal sort of way, looking at the memory pictures of his own life as if they were pictures in a book of anybody's life. The chief's voice, abruptly breaking the silence, startled him.

"It shall be done," said Makamuk. "The girl shall go down the river with you. But be it understood that I myself strike the three blows with the ax on your neck."

"But each time I shall put on the medicine," Subienkow answered, with a show of ill-concealed anxiety.

"You shall put the medicine on between each blow. Here are the hunters who shall see you do not escape. Go into the forest and gather your medicine."

Makamuk had been convinced of the worth of the medicine by the Pole's rapacity. Surely nothing less than the greatest of medicines could enable a man in the shadow of death to stand up and drive an old woman's bargain.

"Besides," whispered Yakaga, when the Pole, with his guard, had disappeared among the spruce trees, "when you have learned the medicine you can easily destroy him."

"But how can I destroy him?" Makamuk argued. "His medicine will not let me destroy him."

"There will be some part where he has not rubbed the medicine," was Yakaga's reply. "We will destroy him through that part. It may be his ears. Very well; we will thrust a spear in one ear and out the other. Or it may be his eyes. Surely the medicine will be much too strong to rub on his eyes."

The chief nodded. "You are wise, Yakaga. If he possesses no other devil things, we will then destroy him."

Subienkow did not waste time in gathering the ingredients for his medicine. He selected whatsoever came to hand such as spruce needles, the inner bark of the willow, a strip of birch bark, and a quantity of mossberries, which he made the hunters dig up for him from beneath the snow. A few frozen roots completed his supply, and he led the way back to camp.

Makamuk and Yakaga crouched beside him, noting the quantities and kinds of the ingredients he dropped into the pot of boiling water.

"You must be careful that the mossberries go in first," he explained.

"And—oh yes, one other thing—the finger of a man. Here, Yakaga let me cut off your finger."

But Yakaga put his hands behind him and scowled.

"Just a small finger," Subienkow pleaded.

"Yakaga, give him your finger," Makamuk commanded.

"There be plenty of fingers lying around," Yakaga grunted, indicating the human wreckage in the snow of the score of persons who had been tortured to death.

"It must be the finger of a live man," the Pole objected.

"Then shall you have the finger of a live man." Yakaga strode over to the Cossack and sliced off a finger.

"He is not yet dead," he announced, flinging the bloody trophy in the snow at the Pole's feet. "Also, it is a good finger, because it is large."

Subienkow dropped it into the fire under the pot and began to sing. It was a French love song that with great solemnity he sang into the brew.

"Without these words I utter into it the medicine is worthless," he explained. "These words are the chiefest strength of it. Behold, it is ready."

"Name the words slowly, that I may know them," Makamuk commanded.

"Not until after the test. When the ax flies back three times from my neck, then will I give you the secret of the words."

"But if the medicine is not good medicine?" Makamuk queried anxiously.

Subienkow turned upon him wrathfully.

"My medicine is always good. However, if it is not good, then do by me as you have done to the others. Cut me up a bit at a time, even as you have cut him up." He pointed to the Cossack. "The medicine is now cool. Thus I rub it on my neck, saying this further medicine."

With great gravity he slowly intoned a line of the "Marseillaise," at the same time rubbing the villainous brew thoroughly into his neck.

An outcry interrupted his play acting. The giant Cossack, with a last resurgence of his tremendous vitality, had arisen to his knees. Laughter and cries of surprise and applause arose from the Nulatos, as Big Ivan began flinging himself about in the snow with mighty spasms.

Subienkow was made sick by the sight, but he mastered his qualms and made believe to be angry.

"This will not do," he said. "Finish him, and then we will make the test. Here, you, Yakaga, see that his noise ceases."

While this was being done, Subienkow turned to Makamuk.

"And remember, you are to strike hard. This is not baby work. Here take the ax and strike the log, so that I can see you strike like a man."

Makamuk obeyed, striking twice, precisely and with vigor, cutting out a large chip.

"It is well." Subienkow looked about him at the circle of savage faces that somehow seemed to symbolize the wall of savagery that had hemmed him about ever since the Czar's police had first arrested him in Warsaw. "Take your ax, Makamuk, and stand so. I shall lie down. When I raise my hand, strike, and strike with all your might. And be careful that no one stands behind you. The medicine is good, and the ax may bounce from off my neck and right out of your hands."

He looked at the two sleds, with the dogs in harness, loaded with furs and fish. His rifle lay on the top of the beaver skins. The six hunters who were to act as his guard stood by the sleds.

"Where is the girl?" the Pole demanded. "Bring her up to the sleds before the test goes on."

When this had been carried out, Subienkow lay down in the snow, resting his head on the log like a tired child about to sleep. He had lived so many dreary years that he was indeed tired.

"I laugh at you and your strength, O Makamuk," he said. "Strike, and strike hard."

He lifted his hand. Makamuk swung the ax, a broadax for the squaring of logs. The bright steel flashed through the frosty air, poised for a perceptible instant above Makamuk's head, then descended upon Subienkow's bare neck. Clear through flesh and bone it cut its way, biting deeply into the log beneath. The amazed savages saw the head bounce a yard away from the blood-spouting trunk.

There was a great bewilderment and silence, while slowly it began to dawn in their minds that there had been no medicine. The fur thief had outwitted them. Alone, of all their prisoners, he had escaped the torture. That had been the stake for which he played. A great roar of laughter went up. Makamuk bowed his head in shame. The fur thief had fooled him. He had lost face before all his people. Still they continued to roar out their laughter. Makamuk turned, and with bowed head stalked away. He knew that thenceforth he would be no longer known as Makamuk. He would be Lost Face; the record of his shame would be with him until he died; and whenever the tribes gathered in the spring for the salmon, or in the summer for the trading, the story would pass back and forth across the campfires of how the fur thief died peaceably, at a single stroke, by the hand of Lost Face.

"Who was Lost Face?" he could hear, in anticipation, some insolent young buck demand. "Oh, Lost Face," would be the answer, "he who once was Makamuk in the days before he cut off the fur thief's head."

ARIZONA

Being
by Richard Matheson

IN darkness hovering. A soundless shell of metals glistening pale—held aloft by threads of anti-gravity. Below, the planet, shrouded with night, turning from the moon. On its black-swept face, an animal staring up with bright-eyed panic at the dully phosphorescent globe suspended overhead. A twitch of muscle. The hard earth drums delicately beneath fleeing pawbeats. Silence again, wind-soughed and lone. Hours. Black hours passing into grey, then mottled pink. Sunlight sprays across the metal globe. It shimmers with unearthly light.

IT WAS like putting his hand into a scorching oven.

"Oh my *God*, it's hot," he said, grimacing, jerking back his hand and closing it once more, gingerly, over the sweat-stained steering wheel.

"It's your imagination." Marian lay slumped against the warm, plastic-covered seat. A mile behind, she'd stuck her sandled feet out the window. Her eyes were closed, breath fell in fitful gasps from her drying lips. Across her face, the hot wind fanned bluntly, ruffling the short blond hair.

"It's not hot," she said, squirming uncomfortably, tugging at the narrow belt on her shorts. "It's cool. As a cucumber."

"Ha," Les grunted. He leaned forward a little and clenched his teeth at the feel of his sport shirt clinging damply to his back. "What a month for driving," he growled.

They'd left Los Angeles three days before on their way to visit Marian's family in New York. The weather had been equatorial from the start, three days of blazing sun that had drained them of energy.

19

The schedule they were attempting to maintain made things even worse. On paper, four hundred miles a day didn't seem like much. Converted into practical traveling it was brutalizing. Traveling over dirt cutoffs that sent up spinning, choking dust clouds. Traveling over rut-pocked stretches of highway under repair; afraid to hit more than twenty miles an hour on them for fear of snapping an axle or shaking their brains loose.

Worst of all, traveling up twenty to thirty mile grades that sent the radiator into boiling frenzies every half hour or so. Then sitting for long, sweltering minutes, waiting for the motor to cool off, pouring in fresh water from the water bag, sitting and waiting in the middle of an oven.

"I'm done on one side," Les said, breathlessly. "Turn me."

"And ha to you," Marian sotto voiced.

"Any water left?"

Marian reached down her left hand and tugged off the heavy top of the portable ice box. Feeling inside its coolish interior, she pulled up the thermos bottle. She shook it.

"Empty," she said, shaking her head.

"As my *head*," he finished in a disgusted voice, "For ever letting you talk me into driving to New York in August."

"Now, now," she said, her cajoling a trifle worn. "Don't get heated up."

"*Damn!*" he snapped irritably, "When is this damn cutoff going to get back to the damn highway?"

"Damn," she muttered lightly. "Damn damn."

He said no more. His hands gripped tighter on the wheel. *Hwy. 66, alt. rte.*—they'd been on the damn thing for hours now, shunted aside by a section of the main highway undergoing repair. For that matter, he wasn't even sure they were on the alternate route. There had been five crossroads in the past two hours. In speeding along to get out of the desert, he hadn't looked too carefully at the crossroad signs.

"Honey, there's a station," Marian said, "let's see if we can get some water."

"And some gas," he added, glancing at the gauge. "*And* some instructions on how to get back to the highway."

"The damn highway," she said.

A faint smile tugged at Les's mouth corners as he pulled the Ford off the road and braked up beside the two paint-chipped pumps that stood before an old sagging shack.

"This is a hot looking spot," he said dispassionately. "Ripe for development."

"For the right party." Marian's eyes closed again. She drew in a heavy breath through her open mouth.

No one came out of the shack.

"Oh, don't tell me it's *deserted*," Les said disgustedly, looking around.

Marian drew down her long legs. "Isn't there anybody here?" she asked, opening her eyes.

"Doesn't look like it."

Les pushed open the door and slid out. As he stood, an involunary grunt twitched his body and his knees almost buckled. It felt as if someone had dropped a mountain of heat on his head.

"*God!*" He blinked away the waves of blackness lapping at his ankles.

"What is it?"

"This *heat*." He stepped between the two rusty handled pumps and crunched over the hot, flaky ground for the doorway of the shack.

"And we're not even a third of the way," he muttered grimly to himself. Behind him, he heard the car door slam on Marian's side and her loose sandals flopping on the ground.

Dimness gave the illusion of coolness only for a second. Then the muggy, sodden air in the shack pressed down on Les and he hissed in displeasure.

There was no one in the shack. He looked around its small confines at the uneven-legged table with the scarred surface, the backless chair, the cobwebbed coke machine, the price lists and calendars on the wall, the threadbare shade on the small window, drawn down to the sill, shafts of burnished light impaling the many rents.

The wooden floor creaked as he stepped back out into the heavy sunlight.

"No one?" Marian asked and he shook his head. They looked at each other without expression a moment and she patted at her forehead with a damp handkerchief.

"Well, onward," she said wryly.

That was when they heard the car come rattling down the rutted lane that led off the road into the desert. They walked to the edge of the shack and watched the old, home-made tow truck make its wobbling, noisy approach toward the station. Far back from the road was the low form of the house it had come from.

"To the rescue," Marian said. "I hope he has water."

As the truck groaned to a halt beside the shack, they could see the heavily-tanned face of the man behind the wheel. He was somewhere in his thirties, a dour looking individual in a tee shirt and patched and faded blue overalls. Lank hair protruded from beneath the brim of his grease-stained Stetson.

It wasn't a smile he gave them as he slid out of the truck. It was more like a reflex twitching of his lean, humorless mouth. He moved up to them with jerky boot strides, his dark eyes moving from one to the other of them.

"You want gas?" he asked Les in a hard, thick-throated voice.

"Please."

The man looked at Les a moment as if he didn't understand. Then he grunted and headed for the Ford, reaching into his back overall pocket for the pump key. As he walked past the front bumper, he glanced down at the license plate.

He stood looking dumbly at the tank cap for a moment, his calloused fingers trying vainly to unscrew it.

"It locks," Les told him, walking over hurriedly with the keys. The man took them without a word and unlocked the cap. He put the cap on top of the trunk door.

"You want ethyl?" he asked, glancing up, his eyes shadowed by the wide hat brim.

"Please," Les told him.

"How much?"

"You can fill it."

The hood was burning hot. Les jerked back his fingers with a gasp. He took out his handkerchief, wrapped it around his hand and pulled up the hood. When he unscrewed the radiator cap, boiling water frothed out and splashed down smoking onto the parched ground.

"Oh, fine," he muttered to himself.

The water from the hose was almost as hot. Marian came over and put one finger in the slow gush as Les held it over the radiator.

"Oh . . . gee," she said in disappointment. She looked over at the overalled man. "Have you got any *cool* water?" she asked.

The man kept his head down, his mouth pressed into a thin, drooping line. She asked again, without result.

"The hair-triggered Arizonian," she muttered to Les as she started back toward the man.

"I beg your pardon," she said.

The man jerked up his head, startled, the pupils of his dark eyes flaring. "Ma'm?" he said quickly.

"Can we get some cool drinking water?"

The man's rough-skinned throat moved once. "Not here, ma'm," he said, "but . . ."

His voice broke off and he looked at her blankly.

"You . . . you're from California, ain't you?" he said.

"That's right."

"Goin' . . . far?"

"New York," she said impatiently. "But what about—"

The man's bleached eyebrows moved together. "New York," he repeated. "Pretty far."

"What about the water?" Marian asked him.

"Well", the man said, his lips twitching into the outline of a smile, "I ain't got none here but if you want to drive back to the house, my wife'll get you some."

"Oh." Marian shrugged slightly. "All right."

"You can look at my zoo while my wife gets the water," the man offered, then crouched down quickly beside the fender to listen and hear if the tank were filling up.

"We have to go back to his house to get water," Marian told Les as he unscrewed one of the battery caps.

"Oh? Okay."

The man turned off the pump and replaced the cap.

"New York, haah?" he said, looking at them. Marian smiled politely and nodded.

After Les had pushed the hood back down, they got into the car to follow the man's truck back to the house.

"He has a zoo," Marian said, expressionlessly.

"How nice," Les said as he let up the clutch and the car rolled down off the slight rise on which the gas pumps stood.

"They make me mad," Marian said.

They'd seen dozens of the zoos since they'd left Los Angeles. They were usually located beside gas stations—designed to lure extra customers. Invariably, they were pitiful collections—barren little cages in which gaunt foxes cringed, staring out with sick, glazed eyes, rattlesnakes coiled lethargically, maybe a feather-molted eagle glowered from a dark cage corner. And, usually, in the middle of the so-called zoo would be a chained-up wolf or coyote; a straggly woe-be-gone creature who paced constantly in a circle whose radius was the length of the chain; who never looked at the people but stared straight ahead with red-rimmed eyes, pacing endlessly on thin stalks of legs.

"I hate them," Marian said bitterly.

"I know, baby," Les said.

"If we didn't need water, I'd never go back to his damned old house."

Les smiled. "Okay ma," he said quietly, trying to avoid the holes in the lane. "*Oh.*" He snapped two fingers. "I forgot to ask him how to get back to the highway."

"Ask him when we get to his house," she said.

The house was faded brown, a two-story wooden structure that looked a hundred years old. Behind it stood a row of low, squarish huts.

"The zoo," Les said. "Lions 'n tigers 'n everything."

"Nuts," she said.

He pulled up in front of the quiet house and saw the man in the Stetson slide off the dusty seat of his truck and jump down off the running board.

"Get you the water," he said quickly and started for the house. He stopped a moment and looked back. "Zoo's in the back," he said, gesturing with his head.

They watched him move up the steps of the old house. Then Les stretched and blinked at the glaring sunlight.

"Shall we look at the zoo?" he asked, trying not to smile.

"No."

"Oh, come on."

"No, I don't want to see *that.*"

"I'm going to take a look."

"Well . . . all right," she said, "but it's going to make me mad."

They walked around the edge of the house and moved along its side in the shade.

"Oh, does that feel good," Marian said.

"Hey, he forgot to ask for his money"

"He will," she said.

They approached the first cage and looked into the dim interior through the two-foot-square window that was barred with thick doweling.

"Empty," Les said.

"Good."

"Some zoo."

They walked slowly toward the next cage. "Look how *small* they are," Marian said unhappily. "How would *he* like to be cooped up in one of them?"

She stopped walking.

"No, I'm not going to look," she said angrily. "I don't want to see how the poor things are suffering."

"I'll just take a look," he said.

"You're a fiend."

She heard him chuckle as she stood watching him walk up to the second of the cages. He looked in.

"*Marian!*" His cry made her body twitch.

"What *is* it?" she asked, running to him anxiously.

"*Look.*"

He stared with shocked eyes into the cage.

Her whisper trembled. "*Oh my God.*"

There was a man in the cage.

She looked at him with unbelieving eyes, unconscious of the large drops of sweat trickling across her brow and down her temples.

The man was lying on the floor, sprawled like a broken doll across a dirty army blanket. His eyes were open but the man saw nothing. His pupils were dilated, he looked doped. His grimy hands rested limply on the thinly-strawed floor, motionless twists of flesh and bone. His mouth hung open like a yellow-toothed wound, edged with dry, cracking lips.

When Les turned, he saw that Marian was already looking at him, her face blank, the skin drawn tautly over her paling cheeks.

"What *is* this?" she asked in a faint tremor of voice.

"I don't know."

He glanced once more into the cage as if he already doubted what he'd seen. Then he was looking at Marian again. "I don't know," he repeated, feeling the heartbeats throb heavily in his chest.

Another moment they looked at each other, their eyes stark with uncomprehending shock.

"What are we going to do?" Marian asked, almost whispering the words.

Les swallowed the hard lump in his throat. He looked into the cage again. "Hel*lo*," he heard himself say. "Can you—"

He broke off abruptly, throat moving again. The man was comatose.

"Les, what if—"

He looked at her. And, suddenly, his scalp was crawling because Marian was looking in wordless apprehension at the next cage.

His running footsteps thudded over the dry earth, raising the dust.

"*No,*" he murmured, looking into the next cage. He felt himself shudder uncontrollably as Marian ran up to him.

"Oh my God, this is *hideous,*" she cried, staring with sick fright at the second caged man.

They both started as the man looked up at them with glazed, lifeless eyes. For a moment, his slack body lurched up a few inches and his dry lips fluttered as though he were trying to speak. A thread of saliva ran from one corner of his mouth and dribbled down across his beard-blackened chin. For a moment his sweaty, dirt-lined face was a mask of impotent entreaty.

Then his head rolled to one side and his eyes rolled back.

Marian backed away from the cage, shaking hand pressed to her cheek.

"The man's *insane,*" she muttered and looked around abruptly at the silent house.

Then Les had turned too and both of them were suddenly aware of the man in the house who had told them to go and look at his zoo.

"Les, what are we going to do?" Marian's voice shook with rising hysteria.

Les felt numb, devoured by the impact of what they'd seen. For a long moment he could only stand shivering and stare at his wife, feeling immersed in some fantastic dream.

Then his lips jammed together and the heat seemed to flood over him.

"Let's get out of here," he snapped and grabbed her hand.

The only sound was their harsh panting and the quick slap of Marian's sandals on the hard ground. The air throbbed with intense heat, smothering their breath, making perspiration break out heavily across their faces and bodies.

"Faster," Les gasped, tugging at her hand.

Then as they turned the edge of the house, they both recoiled with a violent contracting of muscles.

"*No!*" Marian's cry contorted her face into a twisted mask of terror.

The man stood between them and their car, a long double-barreled shotgun leveled at them.

Les didn't know why the idea flooded through his brain. But, suddenly, he realized that no one knew where he and Marian were, no one could even know where to begin searching for them. In rising panic, he thought of the man asking them where they were going, he thought of the man looking down at their California license plate.

And he heard the man, the hard, emotionless voice of the man.

"Now go on back," the man said, "to the zoo."

After he'd locked the couple in one of the cages, Merv Ketter walked slowly back to the house, the heavy shotgun pulling down his right arm. He'd felt no pleasure in the act, only a draining relief that had, for a moment, loosened the tightness in his body. But, already, the tightness was returning. It never went away for more than the few minutes it took him to trap another person and cage him.

If anything, the tightness was worse now. This was the first time he'd ever put a woman in one of his cages. The knowledge twisted a cold knot of despair in his chest. A woman—he'd put a *woman* in his cage. His chest shuddered with harsh breath as he ascended the rickety steps of the black porch.

Then, as the screen door slapped shut behind him, his long mouth tightened. Well, what was he supposed to do? He slammed the shotgun down on the yellow oil-clothed surface of the kitchen table, another forced breath wracking his chest. What *else* could I do—he argued with himself. His boots clacked sharply across the worn linoleum as he walked to the quiet, sun-lanced living room.

Dust rose from the old arm chair as he dropped down heavily, spiritlessly. What was he supposed to do? He'd had no choice.

For the thousandth time, he looked down at his left forearm, at the slight reddish bulge just under the elbow joint. Inside his flesh, the tiny metal cone was still humming delicately. He knew it without listening. It never stopped.

He slumped back exhaustedly with a groan and lay his head on the high back of the chair. His eyes stared dully across the room, through the long slanting bar of sunlight quivering with dust motes. At the mantlepiece.

The Mauser rifle—he stared at it. The Luger, the bazooka shell, the hand grenade, all of them still active. Vaguely, through his tormented brain, curled the idea of putting the Luger to his temple, holding the Mauser against his side, even of pulling out the pin and holding the grenade against his stomach.

War hero. The phrase scraped cruelly at his mind. It had long lost its meaning, its comfort. Once, it had meant something to him to be a medaled warrior, ribboned, lauded, admired.

Then Elsie had died, then the battles and the pride were gone. He was alone in the desert with his trophies and with nothing else.

And then one day he'd gone into that desert to hunt.

His eyes shut, his leathery throat moved convulsively. What was the use of thinking, of regretting? The will to live was still in him. Maybe it was a stupid, a pointless will but it was there just the same; he couldn't rid himself of it. Not after two men were gone, not after five, no, not even after seven men were gone.

The dirt-filled nails dug remorselessly into his palms until they broke the skin. But a woman, a *woman*. The thought knifed at him. He'd never planned on caging a woman.

One tight fist drove down in futile rage on his leg. He couldn't help it. Sure, he'd seen the California plate. But he wasn't going to do it. Then the woman had asked for water and he suddenly had known that he had no choice, he *had* to do it.

There were only two men left.

And he'd found out that the couple were going to New York and the tension had come and gone, loosened and tightened in a spastic rhythm as he knew, in his very flesh, that he was going to tell them to come and look at his zoo.

I should have given them an injection, he thought. They might start screaming. It didn't matter about the man, he was used to men screaming. But a woman . . .

Merv Ketter opened his eyes and stared with hopeless eyes at the mantelpiece, at the picture of his dead wife, at the weapons which had been his glory and now were meaningless—steel and wood without worth, without substance.

Hero.

The word made his stomach turn.

The glutinous pulsing slowed, paused a moment's fraction, then began again, filling the inner shell with its hissing, spumous sound. A flaccid wave of agitation rippled down along the rows of muscle coils. The being stirred. It was time.

Thought. The shapeless, gauzelike airbubble coalesced; surrounded. The being moved, an undulation, a gelatinous worming within the shimmering bubble. A bumping, a slithering, a rocking flow of viscous tissues.

Thought again—a wave directing. The hiss of entering atmosphere, the soundless swinging of metal. Open. Shutting with a click. Sunset's blood edged the horizon. A slow and noiseless sinking in the air, a colorless balloon filled with something formless, something alive.

Earth, cooling. The being touched it, settled. It moved across the ground and every living thing fled its scouring approach. In its ropy wake, the ground was left a green and yellow iridescence.

"*Look out.*"

Marian's sudden whisper almost made him drop the nail file. He jerked back his hand, his sweat-grimed cheek twitching and drew back quickly into the shadows. The sun was almost down.

"Is he coming this way?" Marian asked, her voice husky with dryness.

"I don't know." He stood tensely, watching the overalled man approach, hearing the fast crunch of his boot heels on the baked ground. He tried to swallow but all the moisture in him had been blotted up by the afternoon heat and only a futile clicking sounded in his throat. He was thinking about the man seeing the deeply-filed slit in the window bar.

The man in the Stetson walked quickly, his face blank and hard, his hands swinging in tense little arcs at his sides.

"What's he going to do?" Marian's voice rasped nervously, her physical discomfort forgotten in the sudden return of fear.

Les only shook his head. All afternoon he'd been asking himself the same question. After they'd been locked up, after the man had gone back to his house, during the first terrifying minutes and for the rest of the time when Marian had found the nail file in the pocket of her shorts and shapeless panic had gained the form of hoping for escape. All during the time the question had plagued him endlessly. *What was the man going to do with them?*

But it wasn't their cage the man was headed for. A loosening of relief made them both go slack. The man hadn't even looked toward the cage they were in. He seemed to avoid looking toward it.

Then the man had passed out of their sight and they heard the sound of him unlocking one of the cages. The squeaking rasp of the rusty door hinges made Les's stomach muscles draw taut.

The man appeared again.

Marian caught her breath. They both stared at the unconscious man being dragged across the ground, his heels raking narrow gouges in the dust.

After a few feet, the man let go of the limp arms and the body fell with a heavy thud. The man in the overalls looked behind him then, his head jerking around suddenly. They saw his throat move with a convulsive swallow. The man's eyes moved quickly, looking in all directions.

"What's he *looking* for?" Marian asked in a shaking whisper.

"Marian, I don't *know*."

"He's *leaving* him there!" She almost whimpered the word.

Their eyes filled with confused fear, they watched the overalled man move for the house again, his long legs pumping rapidly, his head moving jerkily as he looked from side to side. Dear God, what is he looking for?—Les thought in rising dread.

The man suddenly twitched in mid-stride and clutched at his left arm. Then, abruptly, he broke into a frightened run and leaped up the porch steps two at a time. The screen door slapped shut behind him with a loud report and then everything was deadly still.

A sob caught in Marian's throat. "I'm *afraid*," she said in a thin, shuddering voice.

He was afraid too; he didn't know of what but he was terribly afraid. Chilling uneasiness crawled up his back and rippled coldly on his neck. He kept staring at the body of the man sprawled on the ground, at the still, white face looking up sightlessly at the darkening sky.

He jolted once as, across the yard, he heard the back door of the house being slammed shut and locked.

Silence. A great hanging pall of it that pressed down on them like lead. The man slumped motionless on the ground. Their breaths quick, labored. Their lips trembling, their eyes fastened almost hypnotically on the man.

Marian drew up one fist and dug her teeth into the knuckles. Sunlight rimmed the horizon with a scarlet ribbon. Soundlessness. Heavy soundlessness.

Soundlessness.

Sound.

Their breath stopped. They stood there, mouths open, ears straining at the sound they'd never heard before. Their bodies went rigid as they listened to—

A bumping, a slithering, a rocking flow of—

"Oh, *God!*" Her voice was a gasping of breathless horror as she spun away, shaking hands flung over her eyes.

It was getting dark and he couldn't be sure of what he saw. He stood paralyzed and numb in the fetid air of the cage, staring with blood-drained face at the thing that moved across the ground toward the man's body; the thing that had shape yet not shape, that crept like a current of shimmering jellies.

A terrified gagging filled his throat. He tried to move back but he couldn't. He didn't want to see. He didn't want to hear the hideous gurgling sound like water being sucked into a great drain, the turbid bubbling that was like vats of boiling tallow.

No, his mind kept repeating, unable to accept, no, no, no, *no!*

Then the scream made them both jerk like boneless things and drove Marian against one of the cage walls, shaking with nauseous shock.

And the man was gone from the earth. Les stared at the place where he had been, stared at the luminous mass that pulsated there like a great mound of balloon-encased plankton undulating palely in their fluids.

He stared at it until the man had been completely eaten.

Then he turned away on deadened legs and stumbled to Marian's side. Her shaking fingers clutched like talons at his back and he felt her tear-streaked, twisted face press into his shoulder. Unfeelingly, he slid his arms around her, his face stiff with spent horror. Vaguely, through the body-clutching horror, he felt the need to comfort her, to ease her fright.

But he couldn't. He felt as if a pair of invisible claws had reached into his chest and ripped out all his insides. There wasn't anything left, just a cold, frost-edged hollow in him. And, in the hollow, a knife jabbing its razor tip each time he realized again why they were there.

When the scream came, Merv slammed both hands across his ears so hard it made his head ache.

He couldn't seem to cut off the sound anymore. Doors wouldn't shut tightly enough, windows wouldn't seal away the world, walls were too porous—the screams always reached him.

Maybe it was because they were really in his mind where there were no doors to lock, no windows to shut and close away the screaming of terror. Yes, maybe they *were* in his mind. It would explain why he still heard them in his sleep.

And, when it was over and Merv knew that the thing had gone, he trudged slowly into the kitchen and opened the door. Then, like a robot driven by remorseless gears, he went to the calendar and circled the date. Sunday, August 22nd.

The eighth man.

The pencil dropped from his slack fingers and rolled across the linoleum. Sixteen days—one man each two days for sixteen days. The mathematics of it were simple. The truth was not.

He paced the living room, passing in and out of the lamplight aura which cast a buttery glow across his exhausted features, then melted away as he moved into shadow again. Sixteen days. It seemed like sixteen years since he'd gone out into the desert to hunt for jackrabbits. Had it only been sixteen days ago?

Once again he saw the scene within his mind; it never left. Him scuffing across late afternoon sands, shotgun cradled against his hip, head slowly turning, eyes searching beneath the brim of his hat.

Then, moving over the crest of a scrub-grown dune, stopping with a gasp, his eyes staring up at the globe which shimmered like a light immersed in water. His heartbeat jolting, every muscle tensing abruptly at the sight.

Approaching then, standing almost below the luminescent sphere that caught the lowering sun rays redly.

A gasp tearing back his lips at the circular cavity appearing on the surface of the globe. And out of the cavity floating—

He'd spun then and run, his breath whistling as he scrambled frantically up the rise again, his boot heels gouging at the sand. Topping the rise, he'd started to run in long, panic-driven strides, the gun held tautly in his right hand, banging against his leg.

Then the sound overhead—like the noise of gas escaping. Wild-eyed, he'd looked up over his shoulder. A terrified cry had wrenched his face into a mask of horror.

Ten feet over his head, the bulbous glow floated.

Merv lunged forward, his legs rising high as he fled. A fetid heat blew across his back. He looked up again with terrified eyes to see the thing descending on him. Seven feet above him—six—five—

Merv Ketter skidded to his knees, twisted around, jerked up the shotgun. The silence of the desert was shattered by the blast.

A gagging scream ripped from his throat as shot sprayed off the lucent bubble like pebbles off a rubber ball. He felt some of it burrow into his shoulder and arm as he flung over to one side, the gun falling from his nerveless grip. Four feet—three—the heat surrounded him, the choking odor made the air swim before his eyes.

His arms flung up. "*NO!*"

Once he had jumped into a water hole without looking and been mired on the shallow bottom by hot slime. It felt like that now, only this time the ooze was jumping onto him. His screams were lost in the crawling sheath of gasses and his flailing limbs caught fast in glutinous tissue. Around his terror-frozen eyes, he saw an agitating gelatine filled with gyrating spangles. Horror pressed at his skull, he felt death sucking at his life.

But he didn't die.

He inhaled and there was air even though the air was grumous with a stomach-wrenching stench. His lungs labored, he gagged as he breathed.

Then something moved in his brain.

He tried to twist and tried to scream but he couldn't. It felt like vipers threading through his brain, gnawing with poisoned teeth on tissues of his thought.

The serpents coiled and tightened. *I could kill you now*—the words scalded like acid. The muscle cords beneath his face tensed but even they couldn't move in the putrescent glue.

And then more words had formed and were burning, were branding themselves indelibly into his mind.

You will get me food.

He was still shuddering now, standing before the calendar, staring at the penciled circles.

What else could he have done? The question pleaded like a groveling suppliant. The being had picked his mind clean. It knew about his home, his station, his wife, his past. It told him what to do, it left no choice. He had to do it. Would anyone have let themselves die like that if they had an alternative; would *anyone?* Wouldn't anyone have promised the world itself to be freed of that horror?

Grim-faced, trembling, he went up the stairs on feeble legs, knowing there would be no sleep, but going anyway.

Slumped down on the bed, one shoe off, he stared with lifeless eyes at the floor, at the hooked rug that Elsie had made so long ago.

Yes, he'd promised to do what the being had ordered. And the being had sunk the tiny, whirring cone deep into his arm so that he could only escape by cutting open his own flesh and dying.

And then the hideous gruel had vomited him into the desert sands and he had lain there, mute and palsied while the being had raised slowly from the earth. And he had heard in his brain the last warning—

In two days . . .

And it had started, the endless, enervating round of trapping innocent people in order to preserve himself from the fate he knew awaited them.

And the horrible thing, the truly horrible thing was that he knew he would do it again. He knew he'd do anything to keep the being away from him. Even if it meant that the woman must—

His mouth tightened. His eyes shut and he sat trembling without control on the bed.

What would he do when the couple were gone? What would he do if no one else came to the station? What would he do if the police came checking on the disappearances of eleven people?

His shoulders twisted and an anguished sobbing pulsed in his throat.

Before he lay down he took a long swallow from the dwindling whiskey bottle. He lay in the darkness, a nerve-scraped coil, waiting, the small pool of heat in his stomach unable to warm the coldness and the emptiness of him.

In his arm the cone whirled.

Les jerked out the last bar and stood there for a moment, head slumped forward on his chest, panting through clenched teeth, his body heaving with exhausted breath. Every muscle in his back and shoulders and arms ached with throbbing pain.

Then he sucked in a rasping breath. "Let's go," he gasped.

His arms vibrated as he helped Marian clamber through the window.

"Don't make any noise." He could hardly speak he was so tired from the combination of thirst, hunger, heat exhaustion and seemingly endless, muscle-cramped filing.

He couldn't get his leg up, he had to go through the rough-edged opening head first, pushing and squirming, feeling splinters jab into his sweat-greased flesh. When he thudded down, the pain of impact ran jaggedly along his extended arms and, for a second, the darkness swam with needles of light.

Marian helped him up.

"Let's go," he said again, breathlessly and they started to run across the ground toward the front of the house.

Abruptly, he grabbed her wrist and jerked her to a halt.

"Get those *sandals* off," he ordered hoarsely. She bent over quickly and unbuckled them.

The house was dark as they hurried around the back corner of it and dashed along the side beneath the moon-reflecting windows. Marian winced as her right foot jarred down on a sharp pebble.

"Thank God," Les gasped to himself as they reached the front of the house.

The car was still there. As they ran toward it, he felt into the back pocket and took out his wallet. His shaking fingers reached into the small change purse and felt the coolness of the extra ignition key. He was sure the other keys wouldn't be in the car.

They reached it.

"*Quick,*" he gasped and they pulled open the doors and slid in. Les suddenly realized that he was shivering in the chilly night air. He took out the key and for the ignition slot. They'd left the doors open, planning to close them when the motor started.

Les found the slot and slid in the key, then drew in a tense, shuddering breath. If the man had done anything to the motor, they were lost.

"Here goes," he murmered and jabbed at the starter button.

The motor coughed and turned over once with a groan. Les's throat clicked convulsively, he jerked back his hand and threw an apprehensive look at the dark house.

"Oh God, won't it start?" Marian whispered, feeling her legs and arms break out in gooseflesh.

"I don't know, I hope it's just cold," he said hurriedly. He caught his breath, then pushed in the button again, pumping at the choke.

The motor turned again lethargically. Oh God, he *has* done something to it!—the words exploded in Les's mind. He jammed in the button feverishly, his body tense with fear. Why didn't we *push* it to the main road!—the new thought came, deepening the lines on his face.

"*Les!*"

He felt her hand clutch at his arm and, almost instinctively, his gaze jerked over to the house.

A light had flared up at a second story window.

"Oh Jesus, *start!*" he cried in a broken frenzy and pushed at the button with a rigid thumb.

The motor coughed into life and a wave of relief covered him. Simultaneously, he and Marian pulled at the doors and slammed them shut while he gunned the engine strongly to get it warm.

As he threw the gears into first, the head and trunk of the man appeared in the window. He shouted something but neither of them heard it over the roar of the motor.

The car jerked forward and stalled.

Les hissed in impotent fury as he jabbed in the button again. The motor caught and he eased up the clutch. The tires bumped over the uneven ground. Upstairs, the man was gone from the window and Marian, her eyes fastened to the house, saw a downstairs light go on.

"*Hurry!*" she begged.

The car picked up speed and Les, shoving the gears into second, jerked the car into a tight semicircle. The tires skidded on the hard earth and, as the car headed for the lane, Les threw it into third and jerked at the knob that sent the two headlights splaying out brightly into the darkness.

Behind them, something exploded as they both jerked their shoulders forward convulsively as something gouged across the roof with a grating shriek. Les shoved the accelerator to the floor and the car leaped forward, plunging and rocking into the rutted lane.

Another shotgun blast tore open the night and half of the back window exploded in a shower of glass splinters. Again, their shoulders twitched violently and Les grunted as a sliver gouged its razor edge across the side of his neck.

His hands jerked on the wheel, the car hit a small ditch and almost veered into a bank on the left side of the lane. His fingers tightened convulsively and, with arms braced, he pulled the car back into the center of the lane, crying to Marian,

"Where *is* he?"

Her white face twisted around.

"I can't see him!"

His throat moved quickly as the car bucked and lurched over the holes, the headlights jerking wildly with each motion.

Get to the next town, he thought wildly, tell the sheriff, try and save that other poor devil. His foot pressed down on the pedal as the lane smoothed out. Get to the next town and—

She screamed it. "*Look out!*"

He couldn't stop in time. The hood of the Ford drove splintering into the heavy gate across the lane and the car jolted to a neck-jerking halt. Marian went flailing forward against the dashboard, the side of her head snapping against the windshield. The engine stalled and both headlights smashed out in an instant.

Les shoved away from the steering wheel, knocked breathless by the impact.

"Honey, *quick*," he gasped.

A choking sob shook in Marian's throat. "My head, my *head*." Les sat in stunned muteness a moment, staring at her as she twisted her head around in an agony of pain, one hand pressed rigidly to her forehead.

Then he shoved open the door at his side and grabbed for her free hand. "Marian, we have to get *out* of here!"

She kept crying helplessly as he almost dragged her from the car and threw his arm around her waist to support her. Behind him, he heard the sound of heavy boots running down the lane and saw, over his shoulder, a bright flashlight eye bobbing as it bore down on them.

Marian collapsed at the gate. Les stood there holding her, trembling impotently as the man came running up, a forty-five clutched in his right hand, a flashlight in his left. Les winced at the beam flaring into his eyes.

"Back," was all the man said, panting heavily and Les saw the barrel of the gun wave once toward the house.

"But my wife is *hurt!*" he said. "She hit her head against the windshield. You can't just put her back in a *cage!*"

"I said get *back!*" The man's shout made Les start.

"But she can't walk, she's unconscious!"

He heard a rasping breath shudder through the man's body and saw that he was stripped to the waist and shivering.

"Carry her then," the man said.

"But—"

"Shall I blast ya where ya stand!" the man yelled in a frenzied anger.

"*No.*No." Les shook nervously as he lifted up Marian's slack body. The man stepped aside and Les started back up the lane, trying to watch Marian's face and his footing at the same time.

"Honey," he whispered. "Marian?"

Her head hung limply over his left forearm, the short blond hair ruffling against her temples and brow as he walked. Tension kept building up in him until he felt like screaming.

"Why are you *doing* this?" he suddenly blurted out over his shoulder.

No answer, just the rhythmic slogging of the man's boots over the pocked ground.

"How can you do this to anyone?" Les asked brokenly. "Trapping your own kind and giving them to that—that God only knows what it is!"

"*Shut* up!" But there was more defeat than anger in the man's voice.

"Look," Les said suddenly, impulsively, "let my wife go. Keep me here if you have to but . . . but let *her* go. *Please!*"

The man said nothing and Les bit his lips in frustrated anguish. He looked down at Marian with sick, frightened eyes.

"Marian," he said. "*Marian*." He shivered violently in the cold night air. The house loomed up bleakly out of the flat darkness of the desert.

"For God's sake, don't put her in a cage!" he cried out desperately.

"*Get back*." The man's voice was flat, there was nothing in it, neither promise nor emotion.

Les stiffened. If it had been just him, he would have whirled and leaped at the man, he knew it. He wouldn't, willingly, walk back past the edge of the house again, back toward the cages, toward that *thing*.

But there was Marian.

He stepped over the thrown-down shotgun on the ground and heard, behind him, the grunt of the man as he bent over and picked it up. I have to get her out of here, he thought, *I have* to!

It happened before he could do anything. He heard the man step up suddenly behind him and then felt a pinprick on his right shoulder. He caught his breath at the sudden sting and turned as quickly as he could, weighed down by Marian's dead limpness.

"What are you—"

He couldn't even finish the sentence. It seemed suddenly as if hot, numbing liquors were being hosed through his veins. An immense lassitude covered his limbs and he hardly felt it when the man took Marian from his arms.

He stumbled forward a step, the night alive with glittering pinpoints of light. The earth ran like water beneath his feet, his legs turned to rubber.

"*No*." He said it in a lethargic grumble.

Then he toppled. And didn't even feel the impact of the ground against his falling body.

The belly of the globe was warm. It undulated with a thick and vaporous heat. In the humid dimness, the being rested, its shapeless body quivering with monotonous pulsations of sleep. The being was comfortable, it was content, coiled grotesquely like some cosmic cat before a hearth.

For two days.

Piercing screams woke him. He stirred fitfully and moved his lips as though to speak. But his lips were made of iron. They sagged inertly and he couldn't move them. Only a great forcing of will would raise his leaden eyelids.

The cage air fluttered and shimmered with strange convections. His eyes blinked slowly; glazed, uncomprehending eyes. His hands flopped weakly at his sides like dying fish.

It was the man in the other cage screaming. The poor devil had come out of his drugged state and was hysterical because he knew.

Les's sweat-grimed brow wrinkled slowly, evenly. *He could think*. His body was like a massive stone, unwieldy and helpless. But, behind its flint, immobile surface, his brain was just as sure.

His eyes fell shut. That made it all the more horrible. To know what was coming. To lie there helpless and know what was going to happen to him.

He thought he shuddered, but he wasn't sure. That thing, what *was* it? There was nothing in knowledge to construct from, no foundation of rational acceptance to build upon. What he'd seen that night was something beyond all—

What day was it? Where was—

Marian!

It was like rolling a boulder to turn his head. Clicking filled his throat, saliva dribbled unnoticed from the corners of his mouth. Again, he forced his eyes open with a great straining of will.

Panic drove knife blades into his brain even though his face changed not at all.

Marian wasn't there.

She lay, limply drugged, on the bed. He'd laid another cool, wet cloth across her brow, across the welt on her right temple.

Now he stood silently, looking down at her. He'd just gotten back from the cages where he'd injected the screaming man again to quiet him. He wondered what was in the drug that being had given him, he wondered what it did to the man. He hoped it made him completely insensible.

It was the man's last day.

No, it's dumb imagination, he told himself suddenly. She didn't look like Elsie, she didn't look at all like Elsie.

It was his mind. He *wanted* her to look like Elsie, that was what it was. His throat twitched as he swallowed. Stupid. The word slapped dully at his brain. She *didn't* look like Elsie.

For a moment, he let his gaze move once more over the woman's body, at the smooth rise of her bust, the willowy hips, the long, well-formed legs. Marian. That was what the man had called her. *Marian*.

It was a nice name.

With an angry twist of his shoulders, he turned away from the bed and strode quickly from the room. What was the *matter* with him anyway? What did he think he was going to do—let her go? There had been no sense in taking her into the house the night before last, in putting her in the spare bedroom. No sense in it at all. He couldn't let himself feel sympathy for her, for anyone. If he did, he was lost. That was obvious.

As he moved down the steps, he tried to remind himself once more of the horror of being absorbed into that gelatinous mass. He tried to remember the brain-searing terror of it. But, somehow, the memory kept disappearing like wind-blown cloud and he kept thinking instead of the woman. *Marian.* She did look like Elsie; the same color hair, the same mouth.

No!

He'd leave her in the bedroom until the drug wore off. Then he'd put her back in the cage again. *It's me or them!*— he argued furiously with himself. I ain't going to die like *that!* Not for anyone.

He kept arguing with himself all the way down to the station.

I must be crazy, he thought, taking her in the house like that, feeling sorry for her. I can't afford it, I *can't* . She's just two days to me, that's all, just a two-day reprieve from—

The station was empty, silent. Merv braked the truck and got out.

His boots crunched over the hot earth as he paced restlessly around the pumps. I *can't* let her go! he lashed out at himself, his face taut with fury. He shuddered then at the realization that he had been entertaining the thought for two days now.

"Why wasn't she a *man*?" he muttered to himself, fists tight and blood-drained at his sides. He raised his left arm and looked at the reddish lump. Why couldn't he tear it out of his flesh? *Why?*

The car came then. A salesman's car, dusty and hot.

As Merv pumped gas in, as he checked the oil and water, he kept glancing from under his hat brim at the hot-faced little man in the linen suit and panama hat. *Replace* her. Merv wouldn't let the thought out yet he knew it was there. He found himself glancing down at the license plate.

Arizona.

His face tightened. No. No, he'd always gotten out-of-state cars, it was safer that way. I'll have to let him go, he thought miserably, I'll *have* to. I can't afford to . . .

But when the little man was reaching into his wallet, Merv felt his hand slide back to his back overall pocket, he felt his fingers tighten over the warm butt of the forty-five.

The little man stared, slack-jawed, at the big gun.

"What *is* this?" he asked weakly. Merv didn't tell him.

Night brushed its black iced fingers across the moving bubble. Earth flowed beneath its liquid coming.

Why was the air so faint with nourishment, why did the atmosphere press so feebly in? This land, it was a weak, a dying land, its life-administering gasses almost spent.

Amidst slithering, amidst scouring approach, the being thought of escape. How long now had it been here in this barren place? There was no way of

*telling for the planet's sun appeared and disappeared with insane rapidity,
darkness and light flickering in alternation like the wink of an eye.*

*And, on the ship, the instruments of chronometry were shattered, they were
irreparable. There was no context any more, no customed metric to adjust by.
The being was lost upon this tenuous void of living rock, unable to do more
than forage for its sustenance.*

*Off in the black distance, the dwelling of the planet's animal appeared,
grotesquely angular and peaked. It was a stupid animal, this brainless beast
incapable of rationality, able only to emit wild squawking cries and flap its
tendrils like the night plants of his own world. And its body—it was too hard
with calciumed rigidity, providing scant nutriment, making it necessary for the
being to eat twice as often so violent an energy did digestion take.*

Closer. The clicking grew louder.

*The animal was there, as usual, lying still upon the ground, its tendrils
curled and limp. The being shot out threads of thought and sapped the sluggish
juices of thought from the animal. It was a barbaric place if this was its
intelligence. The being heaved closer, swelling and sucking along the winds-
wept earth.*

*The animal stirred and deep revulsion quivered in the being's mind. If it
were not starving and helpless it could never force itself to absorb this twitching, stiff-ribbed beast.*

*Bubble touched tendril. The being flowed across the animal form and
trembled to a stop. Visual cells revealed the animal looking up, distended eyed.
Audial cells transferred the wild and strangling noise the dying animal made.
Tactile cells absorbed the flimsy agitations of its body.*

*And, in its deepest center, the being sensed the tireless clicking that emanated
from the dark lair where, hidden and shaking, the first animal was—the animal
in whose flaccid tendril was imbedded the location cone.*

*The being ate. And, eating, wondered if there would ever be enough food to
keep it alive—*

—for the thousand earth years of its life.

He lay slumped across the cage floor, his heartbeat jolting as the man
looked in at him.

He'd been testing the walls when he heard the slap of the screen door and
the sound of the man's boots descending the porch steps. He'd lunged down
and rolled over quickly onto his back, trying desperately to remember what
position he'd been in while he was still drugged, arranging his hands limply at
his sides, drawing up his right leg a little, closing his eyes. The man mustn't
know that he was conscious. The man had to open the door without caution.

Les forced himself to breathe slowly and evenly even though it made his
stomach hurt. The man made no sound as he gazed in. When he opens the
lock, Les kept telling himself—as soon as I hear the door pulled open, I'll
jump.

His throat moved once as a nervous shudder rippled through him. Could the man tell he was faking? His muscles tensed, waiting for the sound of the door opening. He *had* to get away now.

There would be no other time. *It* was coming tonight.

Then the sound of the man's boots started away. Abruptly, Les opened his eyes, a look of shocked disbelief contorting his features. The man wasn't going to open the cage!

For a long time he lay there, shivering, staring up mutely at the barred window where the man had stood. He felt like crying aloud and beating his fists against the door until they were bruised and bleeding.

"No . . . *no*." His voice was a lifeless mumble.

Finally, he pushed up and got on his knees. Cautiously, he looked over the rim of the window. The man was gone.

He crouched back down and went through his pockets again.

His wallet—nothing there to help him. His handkerchief, the stub of pencil, forty-seven cents, his comb.

Nothing else.

He held the articles in his palms and stared down at them for long moments as if, somehow, they held the answer to his terrible need. There *had* to be an answer, it was inconceivable that he should actually end up out there on the ground like that other man, put there for that thing to—

"*No!*"

With a spasmodic twitch of his hands, he flung the articles onto the dirt floor of the cage, his lips drawn back in a dull cry of frightened outrage. It can't be real, it has to be a dream!

He fell to his knees desperately and once more began running shaking fingers over the sides of the cage, looking for a crack, a weak board, anything.

And, while he searched in vain, he tried not to think about the night coming and what the night was going to bring.

But that was all he could think about.

She sat up, gasping, as the man's calloused fingers stroked at her hair. Her widened eyes stared at him in horror as he jerked back his hand.

"Elsie," he muttered.

The whiskey-heavy cloud of his breath poured across her face and she drew back, grimacing, her hands clutching tensely at the bedspread.

"Elsie." He said it again, thick voiced, his glazed eyes looking at her drunkenly.

The bedspread rustled beneath her as she pushed back further until her back bumped against the wooden headboard.

"Elsie, I didn't mean to," the man said, dark blades of hair hanging down over his temples, breath falling hotly from his open mouth, "Elsie, don't . . . don't be scared of me."

"W-where's my husband?"

"Elsie, you look like Elsie," the man slurred the words, his blood-streaked eyes pleading, "You look like Elsie, oh . . . *God*, you look like Elsie."

"Where's my husband!"

His hand clamped over her wrist and she felt herself jerked like a flimsy doll against the man's chest. His stale breath surrounded her.

"*No*," she gasped, her hands pushing at his shoulders.

"I love ya, Elsie, I *love* ya!"

"*Les!*" Her scream rang out in the small room.

Her head snapped to the side as the man's big palm drove across her cheek.

"He's *dead!*" the man shouted hoarsely, "It ate him, it *ate* him! You *hear*!"

She fell back against the headboard, her eyes stark with horror. "*No*." She didn't even know she'd spoken.

The man struggled up to his feet and stood there weaving, looking down at her blank face.

"You think I wanted to?" he asked brokenly, a tear dribbling down his beard-darkened cheek. "You think I *liked* to do it?" A sob shuddered in his chest. "I *didn't* like to do it. But you don't know, y-you don't know. I was in it, I was *in* it! Oh God . . . you don't know what it was like. You don't *know!*"

He sank down heavily on the bed, his head slumped forward, his chest racked with helpless sobs.

"I didn't want to. God, do you think I *w-wanted* to?"

Her left fist was pressed rigidly against her lips. She couldn't seem to breathe. No. Her mind struggled to disbelieve. No, it's not true, it isn't true.

Suddenly, she threw her legs over the side of the bed and stood. Outside, the sun was going down. It doesn't come till dark, her mind argued desperately, not until dark. But how long had she been unconscious?

The man looked up with red-rimmed eyes. "What are ya doing?"

She started running for the door.

As she jerked open the door, the man collided with her and the two of them went crashing against the wall. Breath was driven from her body and the ache in her head flared up again. The man clutched at her; she felt his hands running wildly over her chest and shoulders.

"Elsie, Elsie . . ." the man gasped, trying to kiss her again.

That was when she saw the heavy pitcher on the table beside them. She hardly felt his tightening fingers, his hard, brutal mouth crushed against hers. Her stretching fingers closed over the pitcher handle, she lifted . . .

Great chunks of the white pottery showered on the floor as the man's cry of pain filled the room.

Then Marian was leaning against the wall, gasping for breath and looking down at his crumpled body, at his thick fingers still twitching on the rug.

Suddenly her eyes fled to the window. Almost sunset.

Abruptly, she ran back to the man and bent over his motionless body. Her shaking fingers felt through his overall pockets until they found the ring of keys.

As she fled from the room, she heard the man groan and saw, over her shoulder, the fleeting sight of him turning slowly onto his back.

She ran down the hall and jerked open the front door. Dying sunlight flooded the sky with its blood.

With a choking gasp, she jumped down the porch steps and ran in desperate, erratic strides around the house, not even feeling the pebbles her feet ran over. She kept looking at the silent row of cages she was running toward. It's not true, it's not true—the words kept running through her brain—he lied to me. A sob pulled back her lips. He *lied!*

Darkness was falling like a rapid curtain as she dashed up to the first cage on trembling legs.

Empty.

Another sob pulsed in her throat. She ran to the next cage. He was lying!

Empty.

"*No.*"

"*Les!*"

"Marian!" He leaped across the cage floor, a sudden wild hope flashing across his face.

"Oh, *darling.*" Her voice was a shaking, strengthless murmur. "He told me—"

"Marian, open the cage. Hurry! It's *coming.*"

Dread fell over her again, a wave of numbing cold. Her head jerked to the side instinctively, her shocked gaze fled out across the darkening desert.

"Marian!"

Her hands shook uncontrollably as she tried one of the keys in the lock. It didn't fit. She bit her lip until pain flared up. She tried another key. It didn't fit.

"*Hurry.*"

"Oh God." She whimpered as her palsied hands inserted another key. That didn't fit.

"I can't find the—"

Suddenly, her voice choked off, her breath congealed. In a second, she felt her limbs petrify.

In the silence, faintly, a sound of something huge grating, and hissing over the earth.

"Oh, *no.*" She looked aside hurriedly, then back at Les again.

"It's all right, baby," he said. "All right, don't get excited. There's plenty of time." He drew in a heavy breath. "Try the next key. That's right. No, no, the other one. It's *all* right now. There. No, that doesn't work. Try the next one." His stomach kept contracting into a tighter, harder knot.

The skin of Marian's lower lip broke beneath her teeth. She winced and dropped the key ring. With a gagging whimper, she bent over and snatched it up. Across the desert, the wheezing, squashing sound grew louder.

"Oh, Les, I can't, I *can't!*"

"All right, baby," he heard himself say suddenly. "Never mind. Run for the highway."

She looked up at him, suddenly expressionless. *"What?"*

"Honey, don't stand there for God's sake!" he cried. *"Run!"*

She caught the breath that shook in her and dug her teeth again into the jagged break on her lip. Her hands stopped shaking and, almost numbed, she tried the next key, the next, while Les stood watching her with terrified eyes, looking over her shoulder toward the desert.

"Honey, don't—"

The lock sprang open. With a breathless grunt, Les shoved open the door and grabbed Marian's hand as the lathing sibilance shook in the twilight air.

"Run!" he gasped. "Don't look back!"

They ran on wildly pumping legs away from the cages, away from the six-foot high mass of quivering life that flopped into the clearing like gelatine dumped from a gargantuan bowl. They tried not to listen, they kept their eyes straight ahead, they ran without breaking their long, panic-driven strides.

The car was back in front of the house again, its front bashed in. They jerked open the doors and slid in frantically. His shaking hand felt the key still in the ignition. He turned it and jabbed in the starter button.

"Les, it's coming this way!"

The gears ground together with a loud rasp and the car jerked forward. He didn't look behind, he just changed gears and kept pushing down on the accelerator until the car lurched into the lane again.

Les turned the car right and headed for the town he remembered passing through—it seemed like years before. He pushed the gas pedal to the floor and the car picked up speed. He couldn't see the road clearly without the headlights but he couldn't keep his foot up, it seemed to jam itself down on the accelerator. The car roared down the darkening road and Les drew in his first easy breath in four days as . . .

the being foamed and rocked across the ground, fury boiling in its tissues. The animal had failed, there was no food waiting, the food had gone. The being slithered in angry circles, searching, its visual cells picking at the ground, its sheathed and luminous formlessness scouring away the flaky dirt. Nothing. The being gurgled like a viscid tide for the house, for the clicking sound in . . .

Merv Ketter's arm jerked spasmodically and he sat up, eyes wide and staring. Pain drove jagged lines of consciousness into his brain—pain in his head, pain in his arm. The cone was like a burrowing spider there, clawing with razor legs, trying to cut its way out of his flesh. Merv struggled up to his knees, teeth gritted together, eyes clouding with the pain.

He had barely gained his feet when the crashing, splintering sound shook the house. He twitched violently, his lower jaw dropping. The digging, gouging fire in his arm increased and, suddenly he knew. With a whining gasp he leaped into the hall and looked down the dark stairway pit.

the being undulated up the stairs, its seventy ingot eyes glowering, its shimmering deformity lurching up toward the animal. Maddened fury hissed and bubbled through its amorphous shape, it flopped and flung itself up the angular steps. The animal turned and fled toward

the back steps!—it was his only chance. He couldn't breathe, air seemed liquid in his lungs. His boot heels hammered down the hall and through the darkness of his bedroom. Behind, he heard the railings buckle and snap as the being reached the second floor, bent itself around into a U-shaped bladder, then threw its sodden form forward again.

Merv flung himself down the steep stairway, his palsied hand gripping at the railing, his heartbeat pounding at his chest like mallet blows. He cried out hoarsely as the pain in his arm flared again, almost making him lose consciousness.

As he reached the bottom step, he heard the doorway of his bedroom shattered violently and heard the gushing fury of the being as it

heaved and bucked into the backstair doorway and smashed it out to its own size. Below, it heard the pounding of the fleeing animal. Then adhesiveness lost hold and the being went grinding and rolling down the stairway, its seven hundred feelers pricking the casing and scraping at the splintering wood.

It hit the bottom step, crushed its huge misshapen bulk through the doorway and boiled across the kitchen floor.

In the living room Merv dashed for the mantel. Reaching up, he jerked down the Mauser rifle and whirled as the distended being cascaded its luminescent body through the doorway.

The room echoed and rang with sharp explosions as Merv emptied the rifle into the onrushing hulk. The bullets sprayed off its casing impotently and Merv jumped back with a scream of terror, the gun flung from his hands. His outflung arm knocked off the picture of his wife and he heard it shatter on the floor and, in twisted mind, had the fleeting vision of it lying on the floor, Elsie's face smiling behind jagged glass.

Then his hand closed over something hard. And, suddenly, he knew exactly what to do.

As the glittering mass reared up and threw its liquidity toward him, Merv jumped to the side. The mantel splintered, the wall cracked open.

Then, as the being pulled itself up again ahd heaved over him, Merv jerked out the pin of the grenade and held it tightly to his chest.

Stupid beast! I'll kill you now for—

PAIN ! !

Tissues exploded, the casing split, the being ran across the floor like slag, a molten torrent of protoplasms.

Then silence in the room. The being's minds snuffed out one by one as tenuous atmosphere starved each tissue of its life. The remains trembled slightly, agony flooded through the being's cells and glutinous joints. Thoughts trickled.

Vital fluids trickling. Lamp beams giving warmth and life to pulsing matter. Organisms joining, cells dividing, the undulant contents of the food vat swelling, swelling, overpowering. Where are they! Where are the masters who gave me life that I might feed them and never lose my bulk or energy?

And then the being, which was born of tumorous hydroponics, died, having forgotton that it, itself, had eaten the masters as they slept, ingesting, with their bodies, all the knowledge of their minds.

On Saturday of the week of August 22nd, that year, there was a violent explosion in the desert and people twenty miles away picked up strange metals in their yards.

"A meteor," they said but that was because they had to say *something*.

ARKANSAS

One Happy Family
by John S. McFarland

DR. ELLISON'S eyes burned. He squinted into the darkness, into the low-lying mist on the desolate gravel road ahead of his car, and it seemed the harder he concentrated on avoiding the gullies and potholes that regularly appeared out of nowhere, the sleepier he became. His vision was becoming more difficult to focus after each blink of his eyelids, and he realized that for several moments he had been mesmerized by the white mists drifting through the beams of his headlights. He rolled his window down a few inches and turned off the heater. This never made him less sleepy; it just made his physical discomfort more important for the time being than his sleepiness.

Three-twenty a.m. Babies, of course, always come in the middle of the night. Probably seventy-five percent of all children he'd delivered in the past six years had been born between midnight and five a.m. If Mrs. Knoss was as far along as her husband had described on the phone, then maybe hard labor would start soon. After all, she'd had four other children. This one would probably come a little quicker than the last, and the last had, as Mrs. Knoss had told him, been an easy, fast birth. If this were over by six, he could get home and get a couple of hours sleep before he had to be at the office—no, hospital. Tomorrow was the day he had to reinforce Mrs. Lupke's cervix. Later in the day, he would remove and insert IUDs, check for tiny heartbeats through the taut skin of swollen bellies, and possibly deliver another baby. Mrs. Grasse was due within the week, and she was always unpredictable. Hysterical and unpredictable. You'd think that after eight kids she wouldn't fall apart every time, but she'd been raised that way: to think of her labor as her "sickness," and to scream during delivery whether she really needed to or not. Ellison was sure that Mrs. Grasse's mother had

45

been the same way, and her grandmother, and he knew that she would teach
her own girls to think of themselves as inferior to their brothers, to regard
sex as a distasteful duty to their husbands, and to bring forth children, as the
Bible says, in pain; affected, if necessary, but certainly underscored in
hysterics. He dreaded the thought of having to deal with her; he'd been too
tired and depressed lately to be patient with her righteous ignorance.

Mrs. Knoss was not like that. Though she was well into her forties, she was
as excited about this baby as many young women are about their first. There
was no doubt in Ellison's mind that the child he would deliver tonight, as
well as all the Knosses' children, was the product of genuine, unself-
conscious love.

She'd first visited Ellison when her pregnancy was in its fifth month. She
and her husband, Luther, had moved to the Arkansas Ozarks from some
place in Kentucky, where they had briefly lived, having come there from
West Virginia. Merrilee had wanted only the most superficial care from
Ellison. She'd shown no interest in having an ultrasound image, or in
learning about PKU testing or any of the other modern medical assurances
that other expectant mothers usually required. The couple had been
peculiarly elusive in answering many of Ellison's questions during their
monthly visits. He knew they were poor: their clothes were dated and
shabby. He'd also gathered that they were virtually illiterate. And all they
would say about Luther's profession was that he was a "wildcrafter," selling
herbs and roots gathered in the woods at flea markets and county fairs, along
roadsides, or wherever he could set up a table.

Ellison shifted in his seat uncomfortably. Driving these winding gravel
roads always exhausted him. He was accustomed to wide, well-lit asphalt
streets and sidewalks. In the past few months, he had begun to regret his
decision to leave his profitable but relentless Chicago practice to become a
country doctor. Things had not been as idyllic as he had imagined. The air
was clean and the countryside beautiful, but the workload was no easier. In
fact, the work seemed more oppressive because there were no cultural
distractions, no nightlife, none of the urban things he was missing now,
things that he was certain only a couple of years ago that he would not miss.
And there were poverty and ignorance, two things he hadn't encountered
much in Lake Forest. He had felt genuine compassion for these people at
first, but now he found himself growing annoyed and resentful of having to
treat patients who believed that opossums mate through their noses, and
that urinating in a road will result in a sty in one's eye. Still, some of his
patients, like the Knosses, made it more bearable. He rather envied their
affection for each other and their apparent indifference to their poverty. He
smiled to himself, remembering Merrilee's enthusiastic optimism after her
last examination: "I know I'm going to do everything right. With you there
a-keepin' an eye on me, I know I'll do it right."

Ellison had been getting more involved with home births lately than he
really wanted to be. Yes, he believed that women should have an alternative

to the regimentation and assembly-line rapidity sometimes found in hospital deliveries, but he never dreamed the idea would catch on to this extent, and that he would be called upon to give up so much sleep. The Knosses didn't belong to the generation of new parents who had rediscovered home birth. They were from some sequestered, unchanging place in the Blue Ridge or Smokey Mountains, a place unaware of or unconcerned with national trends. Ellison doubted whether either of them had ever seen the inside of a hospital.

Ellison's head felt numb and he was finding it almost impossible to concentrate on his driving. He thought for a moment that he heard a new tapping or clicking noise coming from his engine. He shuddered at the thought of being stranded out here ten or eleven miles from the highway, and another eight from Staleyville. His mind drifted back to Mrs. Grasse—back to her first visit after he had set up his practice the year before last. She had been a long-standing patient of Ellison's chief competitor in town, Dr. Castellano, who was notoriously brusque with historionic women. "He's an odd bird," Mrs. Grasse had confided, "all that money and he married an Oriental!"

Ellison started. For a moment he wasn't sure where he was. He had made a trip out to the Knosses' cottage only once before, in daylight. He rubbed his eyes and stared into the dark woods. Off to the right, down in a small hollow, he spotted a dim yellow light. A porchlight. He remembered now. A few feet farther there should be a drive.

As soon as Ellison turned his car into the nearly washed-out gravel drive, a light came on in the front room of the cottage. The front door opened and Ellison could see Luther peering out anxiously toward him.

"Jest pull 'er up here anywheres, Doctor," Luther called, scurrying out to pull open the car door almost before Ellison had stopped the car. Ellison groped for his bag with his right hand as Luther tugged at his left arm, trying, it seemed, to lift him off the car seat. Ellison had forgotton how tall Luther was. Tall and amazingly thin, with a whiskerless face whose age was impossible to guess. Ellison intended to say something about nearly getting lost, but Luther, guiding him anxiously toward the house, was talking nonstop.

"Her water broke at ten minutes to two. The pains is down to six minutes. The kids is so excited. I thaink I got evethaing ready for ye . . ."

The inside of the cottage was as dreary as Ellison had remembered. It had apparently been abandoned for ten or twelve years before the Knosses had moved in, and they had done little to restore it, except for having the electricity turned back on. There were boxes of dusty jars on the floor as well as various automobile engine parts. Most of the original wallpaper had long ago been pulled from the walls, or had fallen from the weight of the slowly crumbling structure behind it. In its place, dirty sheets of corrugated cardboard had been nailed up to contain the dust of disintegrating plaster. A clothesline had been tacked across the corner of the west and north walls in the front room, and several articles of Merrilee and Luther's clothing hung from it. Conspicuously absent were any children's clothes, and Ellison wondered for a moment if the children might be self-sufficient enough to wash their own laundry. Alongside the front door stood the aquarium that had puzzled Ellison on his first visit. It seemed absurd to him that people as impoverished as these would keep pet fish. The ten-gallon tank was so green with algae that nothing distinct was visible within. The dark, nondescript shapes which were suspended motionlessly in the water could have been weeds and mosses, though some of the mass looked like thick, wide clumps of dirty cotton. Vaguely disgusted, Ellison assumed that the contents of the aquarium filter had been dumped into the water. The children must have done it. Did Luther and Merrilee let their kids run wild, and were they not expected to clean up the results of their vandalism? Surely they had noticed the mess. Ellison was certain that there was nothing left alive in the tank except the algae and perhaps a few hopelessly overworked snails.

Something else about the house seemed familiar and in place. From out in the nearby woods—or perhaps it was the small strip of yard bordering the drive—came the mewing of a cat. The sound never became the scream or meow of an older cat, but was the mewing of a kitten, though the resonance and volume of the sound suggested an adult animal. Ellison remembered reading somewhere, *Natural History*, probably, that tiger cubs at a certain stage in their development must be taught to kill with one bite by their mothers. A cub that does not learn this never matures emotionally. Perhaps the same is true of domesticated cats, he thought.

Luther led Ellison into the bedroom where Merrilee sat naked in their sagging double bed, propped up by pillows and partially covered with a sheet. She looked old in the harsh light of a bare light bulb which dangled tentatively from the ceiling. The room was filled with the smell of stale sweat. It was an odor which always accompanied her on her visits to the office. She smiled broadly as they approached her.

"Sorry ta call ye out in the middle of the night like this, Dr. Ellison," she said in a voice cracking with weariness.

"Don't worry about that. How are you doing?"

"I'm fine. I don't thaink I'll keep ye a-waitin' fer long."

Luther sat beside her on the bed and began to dab at her face with a cloth he had dampened in a bowl of water on the floor. Ellison placed his bag on a trunk which stood against the east wall, and, snapping it open, he removed his stethoscope.

"Let's see how he's doing," he said in a tone which was intended to sound soothing, but instead seemed to him overrehearsed and mechanical. He fixed the stethoscope earpieces in place and listened to Merrilee's stomach.

"It's good and strong, as usual. Now . . . if he's in position . . ." He slid his hands over the smooth orb of her belly. As in previous examinations, he could not tell in what position the child lay inside her. He sighed heavily to himself.

"Is somethin' wrong?" Luther asked nervously.

"This is a tricky little guy in here," Ellison smiled wearily, dreading the possibility of a breech birth. "In four months I haven't been able to plot his position. I ought to check your dilation . . ."

"Not jest yet," Merrilee winced as another contraction began. "I don't want to be touched jest yet."

Ellison nodded his assent. He knew better than to press the point with her.

"Three minutes apart now," Luther noted as he looked at his pocket watch.

"It shouldn't be too much longer," Ellison said, suppressing a yawn. "Are your other kids going to witness the birth?"

"Oh, yes," Merrilee gasped.

"Are they in bed? I'd think with all the excitement . . ."

"No, they're awake," Luther interrupted. "They're as excited as we are."

"Where are they?"

"They're around."

Ellison was annoyed—and a little insulted—by Luther's elusiveness. Surely they felt close enough to him by now to show him the courtesy of answering his questions. Why were they so secretive? He felt like telling them that he had only been making conversation, that he really didn't give a *damn* about where the kids were. He had assumed when he asked the question that they were peeking out at him from behind their door, having been told to keep out of the way until their mother could cope with their presence during the delivery. He felt himself getting a headache.

The contractions continued to come at three-minute intervals for the next hour and a half. Ellison sat on the trunk against the wall and his eyes felt as if hot blasts of air were hitting them. The harsh light in the room was making his headache worse. He craved a cup of coffee, but if Luther had offered one, he would have refused it. He'd have rather fallen asleep during the delivery than consume anything prepared in the Knoss home.

If he were still in the city, he would have spent the evening at the Schubert with a late dinner at Benihana's. He thought of Piper's Alley and Old Town, of the jazz bands at Rick's, and the sight of the moon on Lake Michigan from atop the Hancock Building. He rubbed the back of his neck. His nerves were fraying slowly and he knew it. Over the past few weeks he had begun to notice it more and more. The less sleep he got and the greater his workload, the more difficult it was for him to face his daily responsibilities. Two weeks ago he had started taking lithium to stabilize his moods. If only he could take one now . . .

The cat could be heard mewing at the rear of the house just beyond a window behind the bed. As he stood to retrieve his bag, Elison glanced toward the front room. He hadn't noticed it before, but nearly the entire inside of the house was visible from his vantage point. There was the front room with its doorless, empty closet, the kitchen-dining area and the bedroom in which he stood, with the bathroom adjoining it. He saw no other doors. There were no children's rooms. Suddenly and inexplicably, Ellison felt a stab of fear in his stomach. For a reason he couldn't pinpoint, he found himself compelled to act as if he hadn't noticed anything. The four Knoss children for whom he had imaged names and personalities were abruptly and brutally wiped out in his mind. Almost against his will, his eyes darted around the house again. If the children *were* hiding, there was no place for them to conceal themselves. They *must* be outside. But it was no warmer than forty-five degrees outside, and Ellison had been there nearly two hours. It wasn't possible. They must be in the house *somewhere*.

Merrilee and Luther hadn't noticed the momentary shift in Ellison's attention. He knew his exhaustion was distorting everything. "These are simple, good people," he found the thought repeating itself in his mind, though they were beginning to seem filthy and malevolent. The problem of the children dogged him; maybe they had never existed, or maybe they had died. They might even have been killed. These ignorant, inbred mountain families, isolated from society and immune to the law, could be capable of anything. Ellison breathed in and out deeply in an attempt to regain control of his thoughts. After a moment, his mind cleared and he smiled to himself. "I've got to start getting more sleep," he thought. "I'm getting as hysterical as Edna Grasse."

He pulled the sheet that covered Merrilee back to her knees and for a second he was sick at the thought of giving her a pelvic examination. He removed a roll of thin plastic gloves from his bag, tore one off and slipped it over his right hand.

"I've got to check your dilation now."

This time Merrilee nodded obligingly as Luther continued to dab at her flushed cheeks. Ellison probed gently for the cervix. One, two, three centimeters. She would have to be nine or ten centimeters to give birth to a normal-sized child. She would be entering the transitional phase just before birth soon. Why wasn't she dilated? He felt further. He should have been able to feel the child's head, unless it were to be a breech birth. He felt nothing recognizable.

The cat's mewing had continued nonstop for many minutes. Ellison found the sound was distracting him.

"You're not dilated," he said in an abrupt, almost accusatory tone.

"I'll be all right," she cooed softly. "I know I'm going to do everything right."

Ellison found himself annoyed with her placidity. *He* was the doctor. *He* was the best judge of whether or not she was going to be all right. The throbbing in his head intensified.

"You're going to have the baby in the next ten minutes or so, and there isn't enough room for it to come out."

"We really thaink she's a-goin' ta be all right this time," Luther interjected. "We're proud of our other kids, but this one's a-goin' ta be the best."

Ellison suddenly wondered if these people were mocking him. Their expressions, their vocal inflections, no longer seemed genuine. Perhaps Merrilee wasn't in labor at all. He realized he hadn't felt her stomach during a contraction yet this evening. She couldn't fake the feel of a contraction. If she were faking, he'd know. Perhaps they intended to isolate him out here for some sinister reason. "This is preposterous," he thought. "If ever a woman looked like she was in labor, Merrilee does. I've got to get a hold on myself. I can't believe I'm thinking these things." Ellison breathed deeply again until he felt himself calming. "This is great. She's having a baby and I'm the one who has to do the breathing exercises!" He was certain the Knosses had noticed that he was acting peculiarly. He felt the need to say something offhanded and chatty.

"Those kids of yours must be hiding from me." He felt immediately that this was not the chatty thing he wanted to say. Whatever was going on here between these people and their children, he didn't want to know.

"They ain't hidin'," Luther said.

"Oh . . . well, all I meant was . . ."

"Only three lives with us; that's Lester, Lonny, and Virgil. Walter's at college."

Ellison grew angry now. They'd been toying with him, lying to him for no reason. The thought of a Knoss child in an academic setting was ridiculous, and somehow offensive.

"*You've* got a son going to college?"

"He ain't a-goin' there, he's there!"

"How'd you pay for it? By selling roots and weeds on the roadside?"

"We don't pay for it," Luther looked puzzled. "They pay us."

Ellison was so angry he couldn't think clearly for a moment.

"They pay you? They pay students to attend this college?"

"He ain't a student. He's there to be . . . studied."

The mewing from the back of the house had reached a maddening crescendo. Ellison could think of nothing else. He stood and faced the window.

"Can't you shut that . . ." Ellison's voice failed him. The mewing thing that peered in at him from the darkness was a filmy-eyed glistening mass with three or four appendages dangling limply off the windowsill. Several black orifices punctured its nearly gelatinous body; these were partially veiled in shimmering mucous membranes. Ellison was transfixed. He felt the muscles in his back and shoulders freeze and tighten to the point of pain.

"There's Lonny now," Luther smiled, nodding toward the window. "And Lester's in there." He tapped the trunk which stood against the wall with his foot, and an animated scratching and gurgling sound arose from within. "And in there, in the 'quarium, that's Virgil."

Merrilee grasped Luther's hand tightly as another contraction began.

"This time," she said weakly, but in a voice tentative with joyous anticipation, "this time I'm going to get it *right*!"

CALIFORNIA

A Return to the Sabbath
by Robert Block

IT'S NOT the kind of story that the columnists like to print; it's not the yarn press-agents love to tell. When I was still in the Public Relations Department at the studio, they wouldn't let me break it. I knew better than to try, for no paper would print such a tale.

We publicity men must present Hollywood as a gay place; a world of glamor and stardust. We capture only the light, but underneath the light there must always be shadows. I've always known that—it's been my job to gloss over those shadows for years—but the events of which I speak form a disturbing pattern too strange to be withheld. The shadow of these incidents is not *human*.

It's been the cursed weight of the whole affair that has proved my own mental undoing. That's why I resigned from the studio post, I guess. I wanted to forget, if I could. And now I know that the only way to relieve my mind is to tell the story. I must break the yarn, come what may. Then perhaps I can forget Karl Jorla's eyes. . . .

The affair dates back to one September evening almost three years ago. Les Kincaid and I were slumming down on Main Street in Los Angeles that night. Les is an asssistant producer up at the studio, and there was some purpose in his visit; he was looking for authentic types to fill minor roles in a gangster film he was doing. Les was peculiar that way; he preferred the real article, rather than the Casting Bureau's ready-made imitations.

We'd been wandering around for some time as I recall, past the great stone Chows that guard the narrow alleys of Chinatown, over through the tourist-trap that is Olvera Street, and back along the flophouses of lower Main. We walked by the cheap burlesque houses, eyeing the insolent

Filipinos that sauntered past, and jostling our way through the usual Saturday night slumming parties.

We were both rather weary of it all. That's why, I suppose, the dingy little theatre appealed to us.

"Let's go in and sit down for awhile," Les suggested. "I'm tired."

Even a Main Street burlesque show has seats in it, and I felt ready for a nap. The callipygy of the stage-attraction did not appeal to me, but I acceded to the suggestion and purchased our tickets.

We entered, sat down, suffered through two striptease dances, an incredibly ancient black-out sketch, and a "Grand Finale." Then, as is the custom in such places, the stage darkened and the screen flickered into life.

We got ready for our doze, then. The pictures shown in these houses are usually ancient specimens of the "quickie" variety; fillers provided to clear the house. As the first blaring notes of the sound-track heralded the title of the opus, I closed my eyes, slouched lower in my seat, and mentally beckoned to Morpheus.

I was jerked back to reality by a sharp dig in the ribs. Les was nudging me and whispering.

"Look at this," he murmured, prodding my reluctant body into wakefulness. "Ever see anything like it?"

I glanced up at the screen. What I expected to find I do not know, but I saw—*horror*.

There was a country graveyard, shadowed by ancient trees through which flickered rays of mildewed moonlight. It was an old graveyard, with rotting headstones set in grotesque angles as they leered up at the midnight sky.

The camera cut down on one grave, a fresh one. The music on the sound-track grew louder, in cursed climax. But I forgot camera and film as I watched. That grave was reality—hideous reality.

The grave was *moving!*

The earth beside the headstone was heaving and churning, as though it were being dug out. Not from above, but from *below*. It quaked upward ever so slowly; terribly. Little clods fell. The sod pulsed out in a steady stream and little rills of earth kept falling in the moonlight as though there were something clawing the dirt away . . . something clawing from beneath.

That something—it would soon appear. And I began to be afraid. I—I didn't want to see what it was. The clawing from below was not natural; it held a purpose not altogether *human*.

Yet I had to look. I had to see him—it—emerge. The sod cascaded in a mound, and then I was staring at the edge of the grave, looking down at the black hole that gaped like a corpse-mouth in the moonlight. Something was coming out.

Something slithered through that fissure, fumbled at the side of the opening. It clutched the ground above the grave, and in the baleful beams of that demon's moon I knew it to be a human hand. A thin, white human hand that held but half its flesh. The hand of a lich, a skeleton claw . . .

A second talon gripped the other side of the excavation top. And now, slowly, insidiously, arms emerged. Naked, fleshless arms.

They crawled across the earth-sides like leprous white serpents. The arms of a cadaver, a rising cadaver. It was pulling itself up. And as *it* emerged, a cloud fell across the moon-path. The light faded to shadows as the bulky head and shoulders came into view. One could see nothing, and I was thankful.

But the cloud was falling away from the moon now. In a second the face would be revealed. The face of the thing from the grave, the resurrected visage of that which should be rotted in death—what would it be?

The shadows fell back. A figure rose out of the grave, and the face turned toward me. I looked and saw—

Well, you've been to "horror pictures." You know what one usually sees. The "ape-man," or the "maniac," or the "death's-head." The papier-mâché grotesquerie of the make-up artist. The "skull" of the dead.

I saw none of that. Instead, there was *horror*. It was the face of a child, I thought, at first; no, not a child, but a man with a child's soul. The face of a poet, perhaps, unwrinkled and calm. Long hair framed a high forehead; crescent eyebrows tilted over closed lids. The nose and mouth were thin and finely chiseled. Over the entire countenance was written an unearthly peace. It was as though the man were in a sleep of somnambulism or catalepsy. And then the face grew larger, the moonlight brighter, and I saw—more.

The sharper light disclosed tiny touches of evil. The thin lips were fretted, maggot-kissed. The nose had *crumbled* at the nostrils. The forehead was flaked with putrefaction, and the dark hair was dead, encrusted with slime. There were shadows in the bony ridges beneath the closed eyes. Even now, the skeletal arms were up, and bony fingers brushed at those dead pits as the rotted lids fluttered apart. The eyes opened.

They were wide, staring, flaming—and in them was the grave. They were eyes that had closed in death and opened in the coffin under earth. They were eyes that had seen the body rot and the soul depart to mingle in worm-ravened darkness below. They were eyes that held an alien life, a life so dreadful as to animate the cadaver's body and force it to claw its way back to outer earth. They were *hungry* eyes—triumphant, now, as they gazed in graveyard moonlight on a world they had never known before. They hungered for the world as only Death can hunger for Life. And they blazed out of the corpse-pallid face in icy joy.

Then the cadaver began to walk. It lurched between the graves, lumbered before ancient tombs. It shambled through the forest night until it reached a road. Then it turned up that road slowly . . . slowly.

And the hunger in those eyes flamed again as the lights of a city flared below. Death was preparing to mingle with men.

II

I sat through all this entranced. Only a few minutes had elapsed, but I felt as though uncounted ages had passed unheeded. The film went on. Les and I didn't exchange a word, but we watched.

The plot was rather routine after that. The dead man was a scientist whose wife had been stolen from him by a young doctor. The doctor had tended him in his last illness and unwittingly administered a powerful narcotic with cataleptic effects.

The dialog was foreign and I could not place it. All of the actors were unfamiliar to me, and the setting and photography were quite unusual; unorthodox treatment as in *The Cabinet of Dr. Caligari* and other psychological films.

There was one scene where the living-dead man became enthroned as arch-priest as a Black Mass ceremonial, and there was a little child. . . . His eyes as he plunged the knife. . .

He kept—*decaying* throughout the film . . . the Black Mass worshippers knew him as an emissary of Satan, and they kidnapped the wife as sacrifice for his own resurrection . . . the scene with the hysterical woman when she saw and recognized her husband for the first time, and the deep, evil whispering voice in which he revealed his secret to her . . . the final pursuit of the devil-worshippers to the great altar-stone in the mountains . . . the death of the resurrected one.

Almost a skeleton in fact now, riddled by bullets and shot from the weapons of the doctor and his neighbors, the dead one crumbled and fell from his seat on the altar-stone. And as those eyes glazed in second death the deep voice boomed out in a prayer to Sathanas. The lich crawled across the ground to the ritual fire, drew painfully erect, and tottered into the flames. And as it stood weaving for a moment in the blaze the lips moved again in infernal prayer, and the eyes implored not the skies, but the earth. The ground opened in a final flash of fire, and the charred corpse fell through. The Master claimed his own. . . .

It was grotesque, almost a fairy-tale in its triteness. When the film had flickered off and the orchestra blared the opening for the next "flesh-show" we rose in our seats, conscious once more of our surroundings. The rest of the mongrel audience seemed to be in a stupor almost equal to our own. Wide-eyed Japanese sat staring in the darkness; Filipinos muttered covertly to one another; even the drunken laborers seemed incapable of greeting the "Grand Opening" with their usual ribald hoots.

Trite and grotesque the plot of the film may have been, but the actor who played the lead had instilled it with ghastly reality. He *had* been dead; his eyes *knew*. And the voice was the voice of Lazarus awakened.

Les and I had no need to exchange words. We both felt it. I followed him silently as he went up the stairs to the manager's office.

Edward Relch was glowering over the desk. He showed no pleasure at seeing us barge in. When Les asked him where he had procured the film for this evening and what its name was, he opened his mouth and emitted a cascade of curses.

We learned that *Return to the Sabbath* had been sent over by a cheap agency from out Inglewood way, that a Western had been expected, and the "damned foreign junk" substituted by mistake. A hell of a picture this was, for a girl-show! Gave the audience the lousy creeps, and it wasn't even in English! Stinking imported films!

It was some time before we managed to extract the name of the agency from the manager's profane lips. But five minutes after that, Les Kincaid was on the phone speaking to the head of the agency; an hour later we were out at the office. The next morning Kincaid went in to see the big boss, and the following day I was told to announce for publication that Karl Jorla, the Austrian horror-star, had been signed by cable to our studio; and he was leaving at once for the United States.

III

I printed these items, gave all the build-up I could. But after the initial announcements I was stopped dead. Everything had happened too swiftly; we knew nothing about this man Jorla, really. Subsequent cables to Austrian and German studios failed to disclose any information about the fellow's private life. He had evidently never played in any film prior to *Return to the Sabbath*. He was utterly unknown. The film had never been shown widely abroad, and it was only by mistake that the Inglewood agency had obtained a copy and run it here in the United States. Audience reaction could not be learned, and the film was not scheduled for general release unless English titles could be dubbed in.

I was up a stump. Here we had the "find" of the year, and I couldn't get enough material out to make it known!

We expected Karl Jorla to arrive in two weeks, however. I was told to get to work on him as soon as he got in, then flood the news agencies with stories. Three of our best writers were working on a special production for him already; the Big Boss meant to handle it himself. It would be similar to the foreign film, for that "return from the dead" sequence must be included.

Jorla arrived on October seventh. He put up at a hotel; the studio sent down its usual welcoming committee, took him out to the lot for formal testing, then turned him over to me.

I met the man for the first time in the little dressing-room they had assigned him. I'll never forget that afternoon of our first meeting, or my first sight of him as I entered the door.

What I expected to see I don't know. But what I did see amazed me. For Karl Jorla was the dead-alive man of the screen *in life*.

The features were not fretted, of course. But he was tall, and almost as cadaverously thin as in his role; his face was pallid, and his eyes blue-circled. And the eyes were the dead eyes of the movie; the deep, *knowing* eyes!

The booming voice greeted me in hesitant English. Jorla smiled with his lips at my obvious discomfiture, but the expression of the eyes never varied in their alien strangeness.

Somewhat hesitantly I explained my office and my errand. "No pub-leecity," Jorla intoned. "I do not weesh to make known what is affairs of mine own doeeng."

I gave him the usual arguments. How much he understood I cannot say, but he was adamant. I learned only a little; that he had been born in Prague, lived in wealth until the upheavals of the European depression, and entered film work only to please a director friend of his. This director had made the picture in which Jorla played, for private showings only. By mischance a print had been released and copied for general circulation. It had all been a mistake. However, the American film offer had come opportunely, since Jorla wanted to leave Austria at once.

"After the feelm app-ear, I am in bad lights weeth my—friends," he explained, slowly. "They do not weesh it to be shown that cere-monee."

"The Black Mass?" I asked. "Your *friends*?"

"Yes. The wor-ship of Lucifer. It was real, you know."

Was he joking? No—I couldn't doubt the man's sincerity. There was no room for mirth in those alien eyes. And then I knew what he meant, what he so casually revealed. He had been a devil-worshipper himself—he and that director. They had made the film and meant it for private display in their own occult circles. No wonder he sought escape abroad!

It was incredible, save that I knew Europe, and the dark Northern mind. The worship of Evil continues today in Budapest, Prague, Berlin. And he, Karl Jorla the horror-actor, admitted to being one of them!

"What a story!" I thought. And then I realized that it could, of course, never be printed. A horror-star admitting belief in the parts he played? Absurd!

All the features about Boris Karloff played up the fact that he was a gentle man who found true peace in raising a garden. Lugosi was pictured as a sensitive neurotic, tortured by the roles he played in the films. Atwill was a socialite and a stage star. And Peter Lorre was always written up as being gentle as a lamb, a quiet student whose ambition was to play comedy parts.

No, it would never do to break the story of Jorla's devil-worship. And he was so damnably reticent about his private affairs!

I sought out Kincaid after the termination of our unsatisfactory interview. I told him what I had encountered and asked for advice. He gave it.

"The old line," he counseled. "Mystery man. We say nothing about him until the picture is released. After that I have a hunch things will work out for themselves. The fellow is a marvel. So don't bother about stories until the film is canned."

Consequently I abandoned publicity efforts in Karl Jorla's direction. Now I am very glad I did so, for there is no one to remember his name, or suspect the horror that was soon to follow.

IV

The script was finished. The front office approved. Stage Four was under construction; the casting director got busy. Jorla was at the studio every day; Kincaid himself was teaching him English. The part was one in which very few words were needed, and Jorla proved a brilliant pupil, according to Les.

But Les was not as pleased as he should have been about it all. He came to me one day about a week before production and unburdened himself. He strove to speak lightly about the affair, but I could tell that he felt worried.

The gist of his story was very simple. Jorla was behaving strangely. He had had trouble with the front office; he refused to give the studio his living address, and it was known that he had checked out from his hotel several days after first arriving in Hollywood.

Nor was that all. He wouldn't talk about his part, or volunteer any information about interpretation. He seemed to be quite uninterested— admitting frankly to Kincaid that his only reason for signing a contract was to leave Europe.

He told Kincaid what he had told me—about the devil-worshippers. And he hinted at more. He spoke of being followed, muttered about "avengers" and "hunters who waited." He seemed to feel that the witch-cult was angry at him for the violation of secrets, and held him responsible for the release of *Return to the Sabbath*. That, he explained, was why he would not give his address, nor speak of his past life for publication. That is why he must use very heavy make-up in his film debut here. He felt at times as though he were being watched, or followed. There were many foreigners here . . . too many.

"What the devil can I do with a man like that?" Kincaid exploded, after he had explained this to me. "He's insane, or a fool. And I confess that he's too much like his screen character to please me. The damned casual way in which he professes to have dabbled in devil-worship and sorcery! He believes all this, and—well, I'll tell you the truth I came here today because of the last thing he spoke of to me this morning.

"He came down to the office, and at first when he walked in I didn't know him. The dark glasses and muffler helped, of course, but he himself had changed. He was trembling, and walked with a stoop. And when he spoke his voice was like a groan. He showed me—this."

Kincaid handed me the clipping. It was from the London *Times*, through European press dispatches. A short paragraph, giving an account of the death of Fritz Ohmmen, the Austrian film director. He had been found strangled in a Paris garret, and his body had been frightfully mutilated; it mentioned an inverted cross branded on his stomach above the ripped entrails. Police were seeking the murderer . . .

I handed the clipping back in silence. "So what?" I asked. But I had already guessed his answer.

"Fritz Ohmmen," Kincaid said, slowly, "was the director of the picture in which Karl Jorla played; the director, who with Jorla, knew the devil-worshippers. Jorla says that he fled to Paris, and that *they* sought him out."

I was silent.

"Mess," grunted Kincaid. "I've offered Jorla police protection, and he's refused. I can't coerce him under the terms of our contract. As long as he plays the part, he's secure with us. But he has the jitters. And I'm getting them."

He stormed out. I couldn't help him. I sat thinking of Karl Jorla, who believed in devil-gods; worshipped, and betrayed them. And I could have smiled at the absurdity of it all if I hadn't seen the man on the screen and watched his evil eyes. He *knew*! It was then that I began to feel thankful we had not given Jorla any publicity. I had a hunch.

During the next few days I saw Jorla but seldom. The rumors, however, began to trickle in. There had been an influx of foreign "sight-seers" at the studio gates. Someone had attempted to crash through the barriers in a racing-car. An extra in a mob scene over on Lot Six had been found carrying an automatic beneath his vest; when apprehended he had been lurking under the executive office windows. They had taken him down to headquarters, and so far the man had refused to talk. He was a German . . .

Jorla came to the studios every day in a shuttered car. He was bundled up to the eyes. He trembled constantly. His English lessons went badly. He spoke to no one. He had hired two men to ride with him in his car. They were armed.

A few days later news came that the German extra had talked. He was evidently a pathological case . . . he babbled wildly of a "Black Cult of Lucifer" known to some of the foreigners around town. It was a secret society purporting to worship the Devil, with vague connections in the mother countries. He had been "chosen" to avenge a wrong. More than that he dared not say, but he did give an address where the police might find cult headquarters. The place, a dingy house in Glendale, was quite deserted, of course. It was a queer old house with a secret cellar beneath the basement, but everything seemed to have been abandoned. The man was being held for examination by an alienist.

I heard this report with deep misgivings. I knew something of Los Angeles' and Hollywood's heterogeneous foreign population; God knows, Southern California has attracted mystics and occultists from all over the world. I've even heard rumors about stars being mixed up in unsavory secret societies, things one would never dare to admit in print. And Jorla was afraid.

That afternoon I tried to trail his black car as it left the studio for his mysterious home, but I lost the track in the winding reaches of Topanga Canyon. It had disappeared into the secret twilight of the purple hills, and I knew then that there was nothing I could do. Jorla had his own defenses, and if they failed, we at the studio could not help.

That was the evening he disappeared. At least he did not show up the next morning at the studio, and production was to start in two days. We heard about it. The boss and Kincaid were frantic. The police were called in, and I did my best to hush things up. When Jorla did not appear the following morning I went to Kincaid and told him about my following the car to Topanga Canyon. The police went to work. Next morning was production.

We spent a sleepless night of fruitless vigil. There was no word. Morning came, and there was unspoken dread in Kincaid's eyes as he faced me across the office table. Eight o'clock. We got up and walked silently across the lot to the studio cafeteria. Black coffee was badly needed; we hadn't had a police report for hours. We passed Stage Four, where the Jorla crew was at work. The noise of hammers was mockery. Jorla, we felt, would never face a camera today, if ever.

Bleskind, the director of the untitled horror opus, came out of the Stage office as we passed.

His paunchy body quivered as he grasped Kincaid's lapels and piped, "Any news?"

Kincaid shook his head slowly. Bleskind thrust a cigar into his tense mouth.

"We're shooting ahead," he snapped. "We'll shoot around Jorla. If he doesn't show up when we finish the scenes in which he won't appear, we'll get another actor. But we can't wait." The squat director bustled back to the Stage.

Moved by a sudden impulse, Kincaid grasped my arm and propelled me after Bleskind's waddling form.

"Let's see the opening shots," he suggested. "I want to see what kind of a story they've given him."

We entered Stage Four.

A Gothic Castle, the ancestral home of Baron Ulmo. A dark, gloomy stone crypt of spidery horror. Cobwebbed, dust-shrouded, deserted by men and given over to the rats by day and the unearthly horrors that crept by night. An altar stood by the crypt, an altar of evil, the great black stone on which the ancient Baron Ulmo and his devil-cult had held their sacrifices. Now, in the pit beneath the altar, the Baron lay buried. Such was the legend.

According to the first shot scheduled, Sylvia Channing, the heroine, was exploring the castle. She had inherited the place and taken it over with her young husband. In this scene she was to see the altar for the first time, read the inscription on its base. This inscription was to prove an unwitting invocation, opening up the crypt beneath the altar and awakening Jorla, as Baron Ulmo, from the dead. He was to rise from the crypt then, and walk. It was at this point that the scene would terminate, due to Jorla's strange absence.

The setting was magnificently handled. Kincaid and I took our places beside Director Bleskind as the shot opened. Sylvia Channing walked out on the set; the signals were given, lights flashed, and the action began.

It was pantomimic. Sylvia walked across the cobwebbed floor, noticed the altar, examined it. She stooped to read the inscription, then whispered it aloud. There was a drone, as the opening of the altar-crypt was mechanically begun. The altar swung aside, and the black gaping pit was revealed. The upper cameras swung to Sylvia's face. She was to stare at the crypt in horror, and she did it most magnificently. In the picture she would be watching Jorla emerge.

Bleskind prepared to give the signal to cut action. Then—

Something emerged from the crypt!

It was dead, that thing—that horror with a mask of faceless flesh. Its lean body was clothed in rotting rags, and on its chest was a bloody crucifix, inverted—carved out of dead flesh. The eyes blazed loathsomely. It was Baron Ulmo, rising from the dead. *And it was Karl Jorla!"*

The make-up was perfect. His eyes were dead, just as in the other film. The lips seemed shredded again, the mouth even more ghastly in its slitted blackness. And the touch of the bloody crucifix was immense.

Bleskind nearly swallowed his cigar when Jorla appeared. Quickly he controlled himself, silently signaled the men to proceed with the shooting. We strained forward, watching every move, but Les Kincaid's eyes held a wonder akin to my own.

Jorla was acting as never before. He moved slowly, as a corpse must move. As he raised himself from the crypt, each tiny effort seemed to cause him utter agony. The scene was soundless; Sylvia had fainted. But Jorla's lips moved, and we heard a faint whispering murmur which heightened the horror. Now the grisly cadaver was almost half out of the crypt. It strained upward, still murmuring. The bloody crucifix of flesh gleamed redly on the chest . . . I thought of the one found on the body of the murdered foreign director, Fritz Ohmmen, and realized where Jorla had gotten the idea.

The corpse strained up . . . it was to rise now . . . up . . . and then, with a sudden rictus, the body stiffened and slid back into the crypt.

Who screamed first I do not know. But the screaming continued after the prop-boys had rushed to the crypt and looked down at what lay within.

When I reached the brink of the pit I screamed, too.

For it was utterly empty.

V

I wish there were nothing more to tell. The papers never knew. The police hushed things up. The studio is silent, and the production was dropped immediately. But matters did not stop there. There was a sequel to that horror on Stage Four.

Kincaid and I cornered Bleskind. There was no need of any explanation; how could what we have just seen be explained in any sane way?

Jorla had disappeared; no one had let him into the studio; no make-up man had given him his attention. Nobody had seen him enter the crypt. He had appeared in the scene, then disappeared. The crypt was empty.

These were the facts. Kincaid told Bleskind what to do. The film was developed immediately, though two of the technicians fainted. We three sat in the projection booth and watched the morning's rushes flicker across the screen. The sound-track was specially dubbed in.

That scene—Sylvia walking and reading the incantation—the pit opening—and God, when *nothing* emerged!

Nothing but that great red scar suspended in midair—that great inverted crucifix cut in bleeding flesh; no Jorla visible at all! That bleeding cross in the air, and then the mumbling . . .

Jorla—the thing—whatever it was—had mumbled a few syllables on emerging from the crypt. The sound-track had picked them up. And we couldn't see anything but that scar; yet we heard Jorla's voice now coming from nothingness. We heard what he kept repeating, as he fell back into the crypt.

It was an address in Topanga Canyon.

The lights flickered on, and it was good to see them. Kincaid phoned the police and directed them to the address given on the sound-track.

We waited, the three of us, in Kincaid's office, waited for the police call. We drank, but did not speak. Each of us was thinking of Karl Jorla the devil-worshipper who had betrayed his faith; of his fear of vengeance. We thought of the director's death, and the bloody crucifix on his chest; remembered Jorla's disappearance. And then that ghastly ghost-thing on the screen, the bloody thing that hung in midair as Jorla's voice groaned the address . . .

The phone rang.

I picked it up. It was the police department. They gave their report. I fainted.

It was several minutes before I came to. It was several more minutes before I opened my mouth and spoke.

"They've found Karl Jorla's body at the address given on the screen," I whispered. "He was lying dead in an old shack up in the hills. He had been—murdered. There was a bloody cross, inverted on his chest. They think it was the work of some fanatics, because the place was filled with books on sorcery and Black Magic. They say—"

I paused. Kincaid's eyes commanded. "Go on."

"They say," I murmured, "that Jorla had been dead for at least three days."

COLORADO

The Autopsy
by Michael Shea

DR. WINTERS stepped out of the tiny Greyhound station and into the midnight street that smelt of pines and the river, though the street was in the heart of the town. But then it was a town of only five main streets in breadth, and these extended scarcely a mile and a half along the rim of the gorge. Deep in that gorge though the river ran, its blurred roar flowed, perfectly distinct, between the banks of dark shop windows. The station's window showed the only light, save for a luminous clock face several doors down and a little neon beer logo two blocks farther on. When he had walked a short distance, Dr. Winters set his suitcase down, pocketed his hands, and looked at the stars—thick as cobblestones in the black gulf.

"A mountain hamlet—a mining town," he said. "Stars. No moon. We are in Bailey."

He was talking to his cancer. It was in his stomach. Since learning of it, he had developed this habit of wry communion with it. He meant to show courtesy to this uninvited guest. Death. It would not find him churlish, for that would make its victory absolute. Except, of course, that its victory would *be* absolute, with or without his ironies.

He picked up his suitcase and walked on. The starlight made faint mirrors of the windows' blackness and showed him the man who passed: lizard-lean, white-haired (at fifty-seven), a man traveling on death's business, carrying his own death in him, and even bearing death's wardrobe in his suitcase. For this was filled—aside from his medical kit and some scant necessities—with mortuary bags. The sheriff had told him on the phone of the improvisations that presently enveloped the corpses, and so the doctor had packed these, laying them in his case with bitter amusement, checking the last one's

65

breadth against his chest before the mirror, as a woman will gauge a dress before donning it, and telling his cancer:

"Oh, yes, that's plenty roomy enough for both of us!"

The case was heavy and he stopped frequently to rest and scan the sky. What a night's work to do, probing soulless filth, eyes earthward, beneath such a ceiling of stars! It had taken five days to dig them out. The autumnal equinox had passed, but the weather here had been uniformly hot. And warmer still, no doubt, so deep in the earth.

He entered the courthouse by a side door. His heels knocked on the linoleum corridor. A door at the end of it, on which was lettered NATE CRAVEN, COUNTY SHERIFF, opened well before he reached it, and his friend stepped out to meet him.

"Damnit, Carl, you're *still* so thin they could use you for a whip. Gimme that. You're in too good a shape already. You don't need the exercise."

The case hung weightless from his hand, imparting no tilt at all to his bull shoulders. Despite his implied self-derogation, he was only moderately paunched for a man his age and size. He had a rough-hewn face and the bulk of brow, nose, and jaw made his greenish eyes look small until one engaged them and felt the snap and penetration of their intelligence. He half-filled two cups from a coffee urn and topped both off with bourbon from a bottle in his desk. When they had finished these, they had finished trading news of mutual friends. The sheriff mixed another round, and sipped from his, in a silence clearly prefatory to the work at hand.

"They talk about rough justice," he said. "I've sure seen it now. One of those . . . patients of yours that you'll be working on? He was a killer. 'Killer' don't even half say it, really. You could say that *he* got justly executed in that blast. That much was justice for damn sure. But rough as hell on those other nine. And the rough don't just stop with their being dead either. That kiss-ass boss of yours! He's breaking his god-damned back touching his toes for Fordham Mutual. How much of the picture did he give you?"

"You refer, I take it, to the estimable Coroner Waddleton of Fordham County." Dr. Winters paused to sip his drink. With a delicate flaring of his nostrils he communicated all the disgust, contempt and amusement he had felt in his four years as Pathologist in Waddleton's office. The sheriff laughed.

"Clear pictures seldom emerge from anything the coroner says," the doctor continued. "He took your name in vain. Vigorously and repeatedly. These expressions formed his opening remarks. He then developed the theme of our office's strict responsibility to the letter of the law, and of the workmen's compensation law in particular. Death benefits accrue only to the dependents of decedents whose deaths arise *out of the course* of their employment, not merely *in* the course of it. Victims of a maniacal assault, though they die on the job, are by no means necessarily compensable under the law. We then contemplated the tragic injustice of an insurance company—*any* insurance company—having to pay benefits to unentitled persons, solely through the laxity and incompetence of investigating officers. Your name came up again.''

Craven uttered a bark of mirth and fury. "The impartial public servant! Ha! The impartial brown-nose, flim-flam and bullshit man is what he *is*. Ten to one, Fordham Mutual will slip out of it *without* his help, and those men's families won't see a goddamn nickel." Words were an insufficient vent; the sheriff turned and spat into his wastebasket. He drained his cup, and sighed. "I beg your pardon, Carl. We've been five days digging those men out and the last two days sifting half that mountain for explosive traces, with those insurance investigators hanging on our elbows, and the most they could say was that there was 'strong presumptive evidence' of a bomb. Well, I don't budge for that because I don't have to. Waddleton can shove his 'extraordinary circumstances.' If you don't find anything in those bodies, then that's all the autopsy there is to it, and they get buried right here where their families want 'em."

The doctor was smiling at his friend. He finished his cup and spoke with his previous wry detachment, as if the sheriff had not interrupted.

"The honorable coroner then spoke with remarkable volubility on the subject of Autopsy Consent forms and the malicious subversion of private citizens by vested officers of the law. He had, as it happened, a sheaf of such forms on his desk, all signed, all with a rider clause typed in above the signatures. A cogent paragraph. It had, among its other qualities, the property of turning the coroner's face purple when he read it aloud. He read it aloud to me three times. It appeared that the survivors' consent was contingent on two conditions: that the autopsy be performed *in locem mortis*, that is to say in Bailey, and that only if the coroner's pathologist found concrete evidence of homicide should the decedents be subject either to removal from Bailey or to futher necropsy. It was well written. I remember wondering who wrote it."

The sheriff nodded musingly. He took Dr. Winters' empty cup, set it by his own, filled both two-thirds with bourbon, and added a splash of coffee to the doctor's. The two friends exchanged a level stare, rather like poker players in the clinch. The sheriff regarded his cup, sipped from it.

"*In locem mortis*. What-all does that mean exactly?"

"'In the place of death.'"

"Oh. Freshen that up for you?"

"I've just started it, thank you."

Both men laughed, paused, and laughed again, some might have said immoderately.

"He all but told me that I *had* to find something to compel a second autopsy," the doctor said at length. "He would have sold his soul—or taken out a second mortgage on it—for a mobile x-ray unit. He's right of course. If those bodies have trapped any bomb fragments, that would be the surest and quickest way of finding them. It still amazes me your Dr. Parsons could let his x-ray go unfixed for so long."

"He sets bones, stitches wounds, writes prescriptions, and sends anything tricky down the mountain. Just barely manages that. Drunks don't get much done."

"He's gotten that bad?"

"He hangs on and no more. Waddleton was right there, not deputizing him pathologist. I doubt he could find a cannonball in a dead rat. I wouldn't say it where it could hurt him, as long as he's still managing, but everyone here knows it. His patients sort of look after *him* half the time. But Waddleton would have sent you, no matter who was here. Nothing but his best for party contributors like Fordham Mutual."

The doctor looked at his hands and shrugged. "So. There's a killer in the batch. *Was* there a bomb?"

Slowly, the sheriff planted his elbows on the desk and pressed his hands against his temples, as if the question had raised a turbulence of memories. For the first time the doctor—half harkening throughout to the never-quite-muted stirrings of the death within him—saw his friend's exhaustion: the tremor of hand, the bruised look under the eyes.

"I'm going to give you what I have, Carl. I told you I don't think you'll find a damn thing in those bodies. You're probably going to end up assuming what I do about it, but assuming is as far as anyone's going to get with this one. It is truly one of those Nightmare Specials that the good Lord tortures lawmen with and then hides the answers to forever.

"All right then. About two months ago, we had a man disappear—Ronald Hanley. Mine worker, rock-steady, family man. He didn't come home one night, and we never found a trace of him. OK, that happens sometimes. About a week later, the lady that ran the laundromat, Sharon Starker, *she* disappeared, no trace. We got edgy then. I made an announcement on the local radio about a possible weirdo at large, spelled out special precautions everybody should take. We put both our squadcars on the night beat, and by day we set to work knocking on every door in town collecting alibis for the two times of disappearance.

"No good. Maybe you're fooled by this uniform and think I'm a law officer, protector of the people, and all that? A natural mistake. A lot of people were fooled. In less than seven weeks, six people vanished, just like that. Me and my deputies might as well have stayed in bed round the clock, for all the good we did." The sheriff drained his cup.

"Anyway, at last we got lucky. Don't get me wrong now. We didn't go all hog-wild and actually prevent a crime or anything. But we *did* find a body—except it wasn't the body of any of the seven people that had disappeared. We'd took to combing the woods nearest town, with temporary deputies from the miners to help. Well, one of those boys was out there with us last week. It was hot—like it's been for a while now—and it was real quiet. He heard this buzzing noise and looked around for it, and he saw a bee-swarm up in the crotch of a tree. Except he was smart enough to know that that's not usual around here—bee hives. So it wasn't bees. It was bluebottle flies, a god-damned big cloud of them, all over a bundle that was wrapped in a tarp."

The sheriff studied his knuckles. He had, in his eventful life, occasionally met men literate enough to understand his last name and rash enough to be openly amused by it, and the knuckles—scarred knobs—were eloquent of his reactions. He looked back into his old friend's eyes.

"We got that thing down and unwrapped it. Billy Lee Davis, one of my deputies, he was in Viet Nam, been near some bad, bad things and held on. Billy Lee blew his lunch all over the ground when we unwrapped that thing. It was a man. Some of a man. We knew he'd stood six-two because all the bones were there, and he'd probably weighed between two fifteen and two twenty-five, but he folded up no bigger than a big-size laundry package. Still had his face, both shoulders, and the left arm, but all the rest was clean. It wasn't animals work. It was knife work, all the edges neat as butcher cuts. Except butchered meat, even when you drain it all you can, will bleed a good deal afterwards, and there wasn't one god-damned drop of blood on the tarp, nor in that meat. It was just as pale as fish meat."

Deep in his body's center, the doctor's cancer touched him. Not a ravening attack—it sank one fang of pain, questioningly, into new, untasted flesh, probing the scope for its appetite there. He disguised his tremor with a shake of the head.

"A cache, then."

The sheriff nodded. "Like you might keep a pot roast in the icebox for making lunches. I took some pictures of his face, then we put him back and erased our traces. Two of the miners I'd deputized did a lot of hunting, were woods-smart. So I left them on the first watch. We worked out positions and cover for them, and drove back.

"We got right on tracing him, sent out descriptions to every town within a hundred miles. He was no one I'd ever seen in Bailey, nor anyone else either, it began to look like, after we'd combed the town all day with the photos. Then, out of the blue, Billy Lee Davis smacks himself on the forehead and says, 'Sheriff, *I* seen this man somewhere in town, and not long ago!'

"He'd been shook all day since throwing up, and then all of a sudden he just snapped to. Was dead sure. Except he couldn't remember where or when. We went over and over it and he tried and tried. It got to where I wanted to grab him by the ankles and hang him upside down and shake him till it dropped out of him. But it was no damn use. Just after dark we went back to that tree—we'd worked out a place to hide the cars and a route to it through the woods. When we were close we walkie-talkied the men we'd left for an all-clear to come up. No answer at all. And when we got there, all that was left of our trap was the tree. No body, no tarp, no Special Assistant Deputies. Nothing."

This time Dr. Winters poured the coffee and bourbon. "Too much coffee," the sheriff muttered, but drank anyway. " Part of me wanted to chew nails and break necks. And part of me was scared shitless. When we got back I got on the radio station again and made an emergency broadcast and then had the man at the station rebroadcast it every hour. Told everyone to do everything in groups of three, to stay together at night in threes at least, to go out little as possible, keep armed and keep checking up on each other. It had such a damn-fool sound to it, but just pairing-up was no protection if half of one of those pairs was the killer. I deputized more men and put them on the streets to beef up the night patrol.

"It was next morning that things broke. The sheriff of Rakehell called— he's over in the next county. He said our corpse sounded a lot like a man named Abel Dougherty, a millhand with Con Wood over there. I left Billy Lee in charge and drove right out.

"This Dougherty had a cripple older sister he always checked back to by phone whenever he left town for long, a habit no one knew about, probably embarrassed him. Sheriff Peck there only found out about it when the woman called him, said her brother'd been four days gone for vacation and not rung her once. Without that Peck might not've thought of Dougherty just from our description, though the photo I showed him clinched it, and one would've reached him by mail soon enough. Well, he'd hardly set it down again when a call came through for me. It was Billy Lee. He'd remembered.

"When he'd seen Dougherty was the Sunday night three days before we found him. Where he'd seen him was the Trucker's Tavern outside the north end of town. The man had made a stir by being jolly drunk and latching onto a miner who was drinking there, man named Joe Allen, who'd started at the mine about two months back. Dougherty kept telling him that he wasn't Joe Allen, but Dougherty's old buddy named Sykes that had worked with him at Con Wood for a coon's age, and what the hell kind of joke was this, come have a beer old buddy and tell me why you took off so sudden and what the hell you been doing with yourself.

"Allen took it laughing. Dougherty'd clap him on the shoulder, Allen'd clap him right back and make every kind of joke about it, say 'Give this man another beer, I'm standing in for a long-lost friend of his.' Dougherty was so big and loud and stubborn, Billy Lee was worried about a fight starting, and he wasn't the only one worried. But this Joe Allen was a natural good ol' boy, handled it perfect. We'd checked him out weeks back along with everyone else, and he was real popular with the other miners. Finally Dougherty swore he was going to take him on to another bar to help celebrate the vacation Dougherty was starting out on. Joe Allen got up grinning, said god damn it, he couldn't accommodate Dougherty by being this fellow Sykes, but he could sure as hell have a glass with any serious drinking man that was treating. He went out with him, and gave everyone a wink as he left, to the general satisfaction of the audience."

Craven paused. Dr. Winters met his eyes and knew his thought, two images: the jolly wink that roused the room to laughter, and the thing in the tarp aboil with bright blue flies.

"It was plain enough for me," the sheriff said. "I told Billy Lee to search Allen's room at the Skettles' boarding house and then go straight to the mine and take him. We could fine-polish things once we had him. Since I was already in Rakehell, I saw to some of the loose ends before I started back. I went with Sheriff Peck down to Con Wood and we found a picture of Eddie Sykes in the personnel files. I'd seen Joe Allen often enough, and it was his picture in that file.

"We found out Sykes lived alone, was an on-again, off-again worker, private in his comings and goings, and hadn't been around for a while. But one of the sawyers there could be pretty sure of when Skyes left Rakehell because he'd gone to Sykes' cabin the morning after a big meteor shower they had out there about nine weeks back, since some thought the shower might have reached the ground, and not far from Sykes' side of the mountain. He wasn't in that morning, and the sawyer hadn't seen him since.

"It looked sewed up. It *was* sewed up. After all those weeks. I was less than a mile out of Bailey, had the pedal floored. Full of rage and revenge. I felt . . . like a *bullet*, like I was one big thirty-caliber slug that was going to go right through that blood-sucking cannibal, tear the whole truth right out of his heart, enough to hang him a hundred times. That was the closest I got. So close that I *heard* it when it all blew to shit.

"I sound squirrelly. I know I do. Maybe all this gave me something I'll never shake off. We had to put together what happened. Billy Lee didn't have my other deputy with him. Travis was out with some men on the mountain dragnetting around that tree for clues. By luck, he was back at the car when Billy Lee was trying to raise him. He said he'd just been through Allen's room and had got something we could maybe hold him on. It was a sphere, half again big as a basketball, heavy, made of something that wasn't metal or glass but was a little like both. He could half-see into it and it looked to be full of some kind of circuitry and components. If someone tried to spring Allen, we could make a theft rap out of this thing, or say we suspected it was a bomb. Jesus! Anyway, he said it was the only strange thing he found, but it was plenty strange. He told Travis to get up to the mine for back-up. He'd be there first and should already have Allen by the time Travis arrived.

"Tierney, the shift boss up there, had an assistant that told us the rest. Billy Lee parked behind the offices where the men in the yard wouldn't see the car. He went upstairs to arrange the arrest with Tierney. They got half a dozen men together. Just as they came out of the building, they saw Allen take off running from the squadcar with the sphere under his arm.

"The whole compound's fenced in and Tierney'd already phoned to have all the gates shut. Allen zigged and zagged some but caught on quick to the trap. The sphere slowed him, but he still had a good lead. He hesitated a minute and then ran straight for the main shaft. A cage was just going down with a crew, and he risked every bone in him jumping down after it, but he got safe on top. By the time they got to the switches, the cage was down to the second level, and Allen and the crew had got out. Tierney got it back up.

Billy Lee ordered the rest back to get weapons and follow, and him and Tierney rode the cage right back down. And about two minutes later half the god-damned mine blew up."

The sheriff stopped as if cut off, his lips parted to say more, his eyes registering for perhaps the hundredth time his amazement that there was no more, that the weeks of death and mystification ended here, with this split-second recapitulation: more death, more answerless dark, sealing all.

"Nate."

"What."

"Wrap it up and go to bed. I don't need your help. You're dead on your feet."

"I'm not on my feet. And I'm coming along."

"Give me a picture of the victims' position relative to the blast. I'm going to work and you're going to bed."

The sheriff shook his head absently. "They're mining in shrinkage stopes. The adits—levels—branch off lateral from the vertical shaft. From one level they hollow out overhand up to the one above. Scoop out big chambers and let most of the broken rock stay inside so they can stand on the heaps to cut the ceilings higher. They leave sections of support wall between stopes, and those men were buried several stopes in from the shaft. The cave-in killed *them*. The mountain just folded them up in their own hill of tailings. No kind of fragments reached them. I'm dead sure. The only ones they *found* were of some standard charges that the main blast set off, and those didn't even get close. The big one blew out where the adit joined the shaft, right where, and right when Billy Lee and Tierney got out of the cage. And there is *nothing* left there, Carl. No sphere, no cage, no Tierney, no Billy Lee Davis. Just rock blown fine as flour."

Dr. Winters nodded and, after a moment, stood up.

"Come on, Nate. I've got to get started. I'll be lucky to have even a few of them done before morning. Drop me off and go to sleep, till then at least. You'll still be there to witness most of the work."

The sheriff rose, took up the doctor's suitcase, and led him out of the office without a word, concession in his silence.

The patrol car was behind the building. The doctor saw a crueller beauty in the stars than he had an hour before. They got in, and Craven swung them out onto the empty street. The doctor opened the window and harkened, but the motor's surge drowned out the river sound. Before the thrust of their headlights, ranks of old-fashioned parking meters sprouted shadows tall across the sidewalks, shadows which shrank and were cut down by the lights' passage. The sheriff said:

"All those extra dead. For nothing! Not even to . . . *feed* him! If it *was* a bomb, and he made it, he'd know how powerful it was. He wouldn't try some stupid escape stunt with it. And how did he even know the thing was there? We worked it out that Allen was just ending a shift, but he wasn't even up out of the ground before Billy Lee'd parked out of sight."

"Let it rest, Nate. I want to hear more, but after you've slept. I know you. All the photos will be there, and the report complete, all the evidence neatly boxed and carefully described. When I've looked things over I'll know exactly how to proceed by myself."

Bailey had neither hospital nor morgue, and the bodies were in a defunct ice-plant on the edge of town. A generator had been brought down from the mine, lighting improvised, and the refrigeration system reactivated. Dr. Parsons' office, and the tiny examining room that served the sheriff's station in place of a morgue, had furnished this makeshift with all the equipment that Dr. Winters would need beyond what he carried with him. A quarter-mile outside the main body of the town, they drew up to it. Tree-flanked, unneighbored by any other structure, it was a double building; the smaller half—the office—was illuminated. The bodies would be in the big, windowless refrigerator segment. Craven pulled up beside a second squadcar parked near the office door. A short, rake-thin man wearing a large white stetson got out of the car and came over. Craven rolled down his window.

"Trav. This here's Dr. Winters."

"Lo, Nate. Dr. Winters. Everything's shipshape inside. Felt more comfortable out here. Last of those newshounds left two hours ago."

"They sure do hang on. You take off now, Trav. Get some sleep and be back at sunup. What temperature we getting?"

The pale stetson, far clearer in the starlight than the shadow face beneath it, wagged dubiously. "Thirty-six. She won't get lower—some kind of leak."

"That should be cold enough," the doctor said.

Travis drove off and the sheriff unlocked the padlock on the office door. Waiting behind him, Dr. Winters heard the river again—a cold balm, a whisper of freedom—and overlying this, the stutter and soft snarl of the generator behind the building, a gnawing, remorseless sound that somehow fed the obscure anguish which the other soothed. They went in.

The preparations had been thoughtful and complete. "You can wheel 'em out of the fridge on this and do the examining in here," the sheriff said, indicating a table and a gurney. "You should find all the gear you need on this big table here, and you can write up your reports on that desk. The phone's not hooked up—there's a pay phone at that last gas station if you have to call me."

The doctor nodded, checking over the material on the larger table: scalpels, post-mortem and cartilage knives, intestine scissors, rib shears, forceps, probes, mallet and chisels, a blade saw and electric bone saw, scale, jars for specimens, needles and suture, sterilizer, gloves. . . . Beside this array were a few boxes and envelopes with descriptive sheets attached, containing the photographs and such evidentiary objects as had been found associated with the bodies.

"Excellent," he muttered.

"The overhead light's fluorescent, full spectrum or whatever they call it. Better for colors. There's a pint of decent bourbon in that top desk drawer.

"Ready to look at 'em?"

"Yes."

The sheriff unbarred and slid back the big metal door to the refrigeration chamber. Icy, tainted air boiled out of the doorway. The light within was dimmer than that provided in the office—a yellow gloom wherein ten oblong heaps lay on trestles.

The two stood silent for a time, their stillness a kind of unpremeditated homage paid the eternal mystery at its threshold. As if the cold room were in fact a shrine, the doctor found a peculiar awe in the row of veiled forms. The awful unison of their dying, the titan's grave that had been made for them, conferred on them a stern authority, Death's chosen Ones. His stomach hurt, and he found he had his hand pressed to his abdomen. He glanced at Craven and was relieved to see that his friend, staring wearily at the bodies, had missed the gesture.

"Nate. Help me uncover them."

Starting at opposite ends of the row, they stripped the tarps off and piled them in a corner. Both were brusque now, not pausing over the revelation of the swelled, pulpy faces—most three-lipped with the gaseous burgeoning of their tongues—and the fat, livid hands sprouting from the filthy sleeves. But at one of the bodies Craven stopped. The doctor saw him look, and his mouth twist. Then he flung the tarp on the heap and moved to the next trestle.

When they came out Dr. Winters took out the bottle and glasses Craven had put in the desk, and they had a drink together. The sheriff made as if he would speak, but shook his head and sighed.

"I *will* get some sleep, Carl. I'm getting crazy thoughts with this thing." The doctor wanted to ask those thoughts. Instead he laid a hand on his friend's shoulder.

"Go home, Sheriff Craven. Take off the badge and lie down. The dead won't run off on you. We'll all still be here in the morning."

When the sound of the patrol car faded, the doctor stood listening to the generator's growl and the silence of the dead, resurgent now. Both the sound and the silence seemed to mock him. The after-echo of his last words made him uneasy. He said to his cancer:

"What about it, dear colleague? We *will* still be here tomorrow? All of us?"

He smiled, but felt an odd discomfort, as if he had ventured a jest in company and roused a hostile silence. He went to the refrigerator door, rolled it back, and viewed the corpses in their ordered rank, with their strange tribunal air. "What, sirs?" he murmured. "Do you judge me? Just who is to examine whom tonight, if I may ask?"

He went back into the office, where his first step was to examine the photographs made by the sheriff, in order to see how the dead had lain at their uncovering. The earth had seized them with terrible suddenness. Some crouched, some partly stood, others sprawled in crazy, free-fall postures. Each successive photo showed more of the jumble as the shovels continued their work between shots. The doctor studied them closely, noting the identifications inked on the bodies as they came completely into view.

One man, Robert Willet, had died some yards from the main cluster. It appeared he had just straggled into the stope from the adit at the moment of the explosion. He should thus have received, more directly than any of the others, the shockwaves of the blast. If bomb fragments were to be found in any of the corpses, Mr. Willet's seemed likeliest to contain them. Dr. Winters pulled on a pair of surgical gloves.

He lay at one end of the line of trestles. He wore a thermal shirt and overalls that were strikingly new beneath the filth of burial. Their tough fabrics jarred with that of his flesh—blue, swollen, seeming easily torn or burst, like ripe fruit. In life Willet had grease-combed his hair. Now it was a sculpture of dust, spikes and whorls shaped by the head's last grindings against the mountain that clenched it.

Rigor had come and gone—Willet rolled laxly onto the gurney. As the doctor wheeled him past the others, he felt a slight self-consciousness. The sense of some judgment flowing from the dead assembly—unlike most such vagrant emotional embellishments of experience—had an odd tenacity in him. This stubborn unease began to irritate him with himself, and he moved more briskly.

He put Willet on the examining table and cut the clothes off him with shears, storing the pieces in an evidence box. The overalls were soiled with agonal waste expulsions. The doctor stared a moment with unwilling pity at his naked subject.

"You won't ride down to Fordham in any case," he said to the corpse. "Not unless I find something pretty damned obvious." He pulled his gloves tighter and arranged his implements.

Waddleton had said more to him than he had reported to the sheriff. The doctor was to find, and forcefully to record that he had found, strong "indications" absolutely requiring the decedents' removal to Fordham for x-ray and an exhaustive second post-mortem. The doctor's continued employment with the Coroner's Office depended entirely on his compliance in this. He had received this stipulation with a silence Waddleton had not thought it necessary to break. His present resolution was all but made at that moment. Let the obvious be taken as such. If the others showed as plainly as Willet did the external signs of death by asphyxiation, they would receive no more than a thorough external exam. Willet he would examine internally as well, merely to establish in depth for this one what should appear obvious in all. Otherwise, only when the external exam revealed a clearly anomalous feature—and clear and suggestive it must be—would he look deeper.

He rinsed the caked hair in a basin, poured the sediment into a flask and labeled it. Starting with the scalp, he began a minute scrutiny of the body's surfaces, recording his observations as he went.

The characteristic signs of asphyxial death were evident, despite the complicating effects of autolysis and putrefaction. The eyeballs' bulge and the tongue's protrusion were by now at least partly due to gas pressure as well as the mode of death, but the latter organ was clamped between locked teeth, leaving little doubt as to that mode. The coloration of degenerative change—a greenish-yellow tint, a darkening and mapping-out of superficial veins—was marked, but not sufficient to obscure the blue of cyanosis on the face and neck, nor the pinpoint hemorrhages freckling neck, chest, and shoulders. From the mouth and nose the doctor scraped matter he was confident was the blood-tinged mucous typically ejected in the airless agony.

He began to find a kind of comedy in his work. What a buffoon death made of man! A blue, pop-eyed, three-lipped thing. And there was himself, his curious, solicitous intimacy with this clownish carrion. Excuse me, Mr. Willet, while I probe this laceration. How does it feel when I do this? Nothing? Nothing at all? Fine, now what about these nails. Split them clawing at the earth, did you? Yes. A nice bloodblister under this thumbnail I see—got it on the job a few days before your accident no doubt? Remarkable calluses here, still quite tough. . . .

The doctor looked for an unanalytic moment at the hands—puffed, dark paws, gestureless, having renounced all touch and grasp. He felt the wastage of the man concentrated in the hands. The painful futility of the body's fine articulation when it is seen in death—this poignancy he had long learned not to acknowledge when he worked. But now he let it move him a little. This Roger Willet, plodding to his work one afternoon, had suddenly been scrapped, crushed to a nonfunctional heap of perishable materials. It simply happened that his life had chanced to move too close to the passage of a more powerful life, one of those inexorable and hungry lives that leave human wreckage—known or undiscovered—in their wakes. Bad luck, Mr. Willet. Naturally, we feel very sorry about this. But this Joe Allen, your co-worker. Apparently he was some sort of . . . cannibal. It's complicated. We don't understand it all. But the fact is we have to dismantle you now to a certain extent. There's really no hope of your using these parts of yourself again, I'm afraid. Ready now?

The doctor proceeded to the internal exam with a vague eagerness for Willet's fragmentation, for the disarticulation of that sadness in his natural form. He grasped Willet by the jaw and took up the post-mortem knife. He sank its point beneath the chin and began the long, gently sawing incision that opened Willet from throat to groin.

In the painstaking separation of the body's laminae Dr. Winters found absorption and pleasure. And yet throughout he felt, marginal but insistent, the movement of a stream of irrelevant images. These were of the building that contained him, and of the night containing it. As from outside, he saw the plant—bleached planks, iron roofing—and the trees crowding it, all in starlight, a ghost-town image. And he saw the refrigerator vault beyond the wall as from within, feeling the stillness of murdered men in a cold, yellow light. And at length a question formed itself, darting in and out of the weave of his concentration as the images did: Why did he still feel, like some stir of the air, that sense of mute vigilance surrounding his action, furtively touching his nerves with its inquiry as he worked? He shrugged, overtly angry now. Who else was attending but Death? Wasn't he Death's hireling, and this Death's place? Then let the master look on.

Peeling back Willet's cover of hemorrhage-stippled skin, Dr. Winters read the corpse with an increasing dispassion, a mortuary text. He confined his inspection to the lungs and mediastinum and found there unequivocal testimony to Willet's asphyxial death. The pleurae of the lungs exhibited the expected ecchymoses—bruised spots in the glassy, enveloping membrane. Beneath, the polyhedral surface lobules of the lungs themselves were bubbled and blistered—the expected interstitial emphysema. The lungs, on section, were intensely and bloodily congested. The left half of the heart he found contracted and empty, while the right was over-distended and engorged with dark blood, as were the large veins of the upper mediastinum. It was a classic picture of death by suffocation, and at length the doctor, with needle and suture, closed up the text again.

He returned the corpse to the gurney and draped one of his mortuary bags over it in the manner of a shroud. When he had help in the morning, he would weigh the bodies on a platform scale the office contained and afterwards bag them properly. He came to the refrigerator door, and hesitated. He stared at the door, not moving, not understanding why.

Run. Get out, now.

The thought was his own, but it came to him so urgently he turned around as if someone behind him had spoken. Across the room a thin man in smock and gloves, his eyes shadows, glared at the doctor from the black windows. Behind the man was a shrouded cart, behind that, a wide metal door.

Quietly, wonderingly, the doctor asked, "Run from what?" The eyeless man in the glass was still half-crouched, afraid.

Then, a moment later, the man straightened, threw back his head and laughed. The doctor walked to the desk and sat down shoulder to shoulder with him. He pulled out the bottle and they had a drink together, regarding each other with identical bemused smiles. Then the doctor said, "Let me pour you another. You need it, old fellow. It makes a man himself again."

Nevertheless his re-entry of the vault was difficult, toilsome, each step seeming to require a new summoning of the will to move. In the freezing half-light all movement felt like defiance. His body lagged behind his craving to be quick, to be done with this molestation of the gathered dead. He returned Willet to his pallet and took his neighbor. The name on the tag wired to his boot was Ed Moses. Dr. Winters wheeled him back to the office and closed the big door behind him.

With Moses his work gained momentum. He expected to perform no further internal necropsies. He thought of his employer, rejoicing now in his seeming submission to Waddleton's ultimatum. The impact would be dire.

He pictured the coroner in shock, a sheaf of Pathologist's Reports in one hand, and smiled.

Waddleton could probably make a plausible case for incomplete examination. Still, a pathologist's discretionary powers were not well-defined. Many good ones would approve the adequacy of the doctor's method, given his working conditions. The inevitable litigation with a coalition of compensation claimants would be strenuous and protracted. Win or lose, Waddleton's venal devotion to the insurance company's interest would be abundantly displayed. Further, immediately on his dismissal the doctor would formally disclose its occult cause to the press. A libel action would ensue which he would have as little cause to fear as he had to fear his firing. Both his savings and the lawsuit would long outlast his life.

Externally, Ed Moses exhibited a condition as typically asphyxial as Willet's had been, with no slightest mark of fragment entry. The doctor finished his report and returned Moses to the vault, his movements brisk and precise. His unease was all but gone. That queasy stirring of the air—had he really felt it? It had been, perhaps, some new reverberation of the death at work in him, a psychic shudder of response to the cancer's stealthy probing for his life. He brought out the body next to Moses in the line.

Walter Lou Jackson was big, 6' 2" from heel to crown, and would surely weigh out at more than two hundred pounds. He had writhed mightily against his million-ton coffin with an agonal strength that had torn his face and hands. Death had mauled him like a lion. The doctor set to work.

His hands were fully themselves now—fleet, exact, intricately testing the corpse's character as other fingers might explore a keyboard for its latent melodies. And the doctor watched them with an old pleasure, one of the few that had never failed him, his mind at one remove from their busy intelligence. All the hard deaths! A worldful of them, time without end. Lives wrenched kicking from their snug meat-frames. Walter Lou Jackson had died very hard. Joe Allen brought this on you, Mr. Jackson. We think it was part of his attempt to escape the law.

But what a botched flight! The unreason of it—more than baffling—was eerie in its colossal futility. Beyond question, Allen had been cunning. A ghoul with a psychopath's social finesse. A good old boy who could make a tavernful of men laugh with delight while he cut his victim from their midst, make them applaud his exit with the prey, who stepped jovially into the darkness with murder at his side clapping him on the shoulder. Intelligent, certainly, with a strange technical sophistication as well, suggested by the sphere. Then what of the lunacy yet more strongly suggested by the same object? In the sphere was concentrated all the lethal mystery of Bailey's long nightmare.

Why the explosion? Its location implied an ambush for Allen's pursuers, a purposeful detonation. Had he aimed at a limited cave-in from which he schemed some inconceivable escape? Folly enough in this—far more if, as seemed sure, Allen had made the bomb himself, for then he would have to know its power was grossly inordinate to the need.

But if it was not a bomb, had a different function and only incidentally an explosive potential, Allen might underestimate the blast. It appeared the object was somehow remotely monitored by him, for the timing of events showed he had gone straight for it the instant he emerged from the shaft—shunned the bus waiting to take his shift back to town and made a beeline across the compound for a patrol car that was hidden from his view by the office building. This suggested something more complex than a mere explosive device, something, perhaps, whose destruction was itself more Allen's aim than the explosion produced thereby.

The fact that he risked the sphere's retrieval at all pointed to this interpretation. For the moment he sensed its presence at the mine, he must have guessed that the murder investigation had led to its discovery and removal from his room. But then, knowing himself already liable to the extreme penalty, why should Allen go to such lengths to recapture evidence incriminatory of a lesser offense, possession of an explosive device?

Then grant that the sphere was something more, something instrumental to his murders that could guarantee a conviction he might otherwise evade. Still, his gambit made no sense. Since the sphere—and thus the lawmen he could assume to have taken it—were already at the mine office, he must expect the compound to be sealed at any moment. Meanwhile, the gate was open, escape into the mountains a strong possibility for a man capable of stalking and destroying two experienced and well-armed woodsmen lying in ambush for him. Why had he all but insured his capture to weaken a case against himself that his escape would have rendered irrelevant? Dr. Winters saw his fingers, like a hunting pack round a covert, converge on a small puncture wound below Walter Lou Jackson's xiphoid process, between the eighth ribs.

His left hand touched its borders, the fingers' inquiry quick and tender. The right hand introduced a probe, and both together eased it into the wound. It inched unobstructed deep into the body, curving upwards through the diphragm towards the heart. The doctor's own heart accelerated. He watched his hands move to record the observation, watched them pause, watched them return to their survey of his corpse, leaving pen and page untouched.

Inspection revealed no further anomaly. All else he observed the doctor recorded faithfully, wondering throughout at the distress he felt. When he had finished, he understood it. Its cause was not the discovery of an entry wound that might bolster Waddleton's case. For the find had, within moments, revealed to him that, should he encounter anything he thought to be a mark of fragment penetration, he was going to ignore it. The damage Joe Allen had done was going to end here, with this last grand slaughter, and would not extend to the impoverishment of his victims' survivors. No more internals. The externals will-they nill-they, would from now on explicitly contraindicate the need for them.

The problem was that he did not believe the puncture in Jackson's thorax *was* a mark of fragment entry. Why? And, finding no answer to this question, why was he, once again, afraid? Slowly, he signed the report on Jackson, set it aside, and took up the post-mortem knife.

First the long, sawing slice, unzippering the mortal overcoat. Next, two great, square flaps of flesh reflected, scrolled laterally to the armpits' line, disrobing the chest: one hand grasping the flap's skirt, the other sweeping beneath it with the knife, flensing through the glassy tissue that joined it to the chest-wall, and shaving all muscles from their anchorages to bone and cartilage beneath. Then the dismantling of the strong-box within. Rib-shears—so frank and forward a tool, like a gardener's. The steel beak bit through each rib's gristle anchor to the sternum's centerplate. At the sternum's crownpiece the collarbones' ends were knifed, pried, and sprung free from their sockets. The coffer unhasped, unhinged, a knife teased beneath the lid and levered it off.

Some minutes later the doctor straightened up and stepped back from his subject. He moved almost drunkenly, and his age seemed scored more deeply in his face. With loathing haste he stripped his gloves off. He went to the desk, sat down, and poured another drink. If there was something like horror in his face, there was also a hardening in his mouth's line, and the muscles of his jaw. He spoke to his glass: "So be it, your Excellency. Something new for your humble servant. Testing my nerve?"

Jackson's pericardium, the shapely capsule containing his heart, should have been all but hidden between the big, blood-fat loaves of his lungs. The doctor had found it fully exposed, the lungs flanking it wrinkled lumps less than a third their natural bulk. Not only they, but the left heart and the superior mediastinal veins—all the regions that should have been grossly engorged with blood—were utterly drained of it.

The doctor swallowed his drink and got out the photographs again. He found that Jackson had died on his stomach across the body of another worker, with the upper part of a third trapped between them. Neither these two subjacent corpses nor the surrounding earth showed any stain of a blood loss that must have amounted to two liters.

Possibly the pictures, by some trick of shadow, had failed to pick it up. He turned to the Investigator's Report, where Craven would surely have mentioned any significant amounts of bloody earth uncovered during the disinterment. The sheriff recorded nothing of the kind. Dr. Winters returned to the pictures.

Ronald Pollock, Jackson's most intimate associate in the grave, had died on his back, beneath and slightly askew of Jackson, placing most of their torsos in contact, save where the head and shoulder of the third interposed. It seemed inconceivable Pollock's clothing should lack any trace of such massive drainage from a dead mate thus embraced.

The doctor rose abruptly, pulled on fresh gloves, and returned to Jackson. His hands showed a more brutal speed now, closing the great incision temporarily with a few widely spaced sutures. He replaced him in the vault and brought out Pollock, striding, heaving hard at the dead shapes in the shifting of them, thrusting always—so it seemed to him—just a step ahead of urgent thoughts he did not want to have, deformities that whispered at his back, emitting faint, chill gusts of putrid breath. He shook his head—denying, delaying—and pushed the new corpse onto the worktable. The scissors undressed Pollock in greedy bites.

But at length, when he had scanned each scrap of fabric and found nothing like the stain of blood, he came to rest again, relinquishing that simplest, desired resolution he had made such haste to reach. He stood at the instrument table, not seeing it, submitting to the approach of the half-formed things at his mind's periphery.

The revelation of Jackson's shriveled lungs had been more than a shock. He felt a stab of panic too, in fact that same curiously explicit terror of this place that had urged him to flee earlier. He acknowledged now that the germ of that quickly suppressed terror had been a premonition of this failure to find any trace of the missing blood. Whence the premonition? It had to do with a problem he had steadfastly refused to consider: the mechanics of so complete a drainage of the lungs' densely reticulated vascular structure. Could the earth's crude pressure by itself work so thoroughly, given only a single vent both slender and strangely curved? And then the photograph he had studied. It frightened him now to recall the image—some covert meaning stirred within it, struggling to be seen. Dr. Winters picked the probe up from the table and turned again to the corpse. As surely and exactly as if he had already ascertained the wound's presence, he leaned forward and touched it: a small, neat puncture, just beneath the xiphoid process. He introduced the probe. The wound received it deeply, in a familiar direction.

The doctor went to the desk, and took up the photograph again. Pollock's and Jackson's wounded areas were not in contact. The third man's head was sandwiched between their bodies at just that point. He searched out another picture, in which this third man was more central, and found his name inked in below his image: Joe Allen.

Dreamingly, Dr. Winters went to the wide metal door, shoved it aside, entered the vault. He did not search, but went straight to the trestle where his friend had paused some hours before, and found the same name on its tag.

The body, beneath decay's spurious obesity, was trim and well-muscled. The face was square-cut, shelf-browed, with a vulpine nose skewed by an old fracture. The swollen tongue lay behind the teeth, and the bulge of decomposition did not obscure what the man's initial impact must have been—handsome and open, his now-waxen black eyes sly and convivial. Say, good buddy, got a minute? I see you comin' on the swing shift every day, don't I? Yeah, Joe Allen. Look, I know it's late, you want to get home, tell the wife you ain't been in there drinkin' since you got off, right? Oh, yeah, I heard that. But this damn disappearance thing's got me so edgy, and I'd swear to God just as I was coming here I seen someone moving around back of that frame house up the street. See how the trees thin out a little back of the yard, where the moonlight gets in? That's right. Well, I got me this little popper here. Oh, yeah, that's a beauty, we'll have it covered between us. I knew I could spot a man ready for some trouble—couldn't find a patrol car anywhere on the street. Yeah, just down in here now, to that clump of pine. Step careful, you can barely see. That's right. . . .

The doctor's face ran with sweat. He turned on his heel and walked out of the vault, heaving the door shut behind him. In the office's greater warmth he felt the perspiration soaking his shirt under the smock. His stomach rasped with steady oscillations of pain, but he scarcely attended it. He went to Pollock and seized up the post-mortem knife.

The work was done with surreal speed, the laminae of flesh and bone recoiling smoothly beneath his desperate but unerring hands, until the thoracic cavity lay exposed, and in it, the vampire-stricken lungs, two gnarled lumps of grey tissue.

He searched no deeper, knowing what the heart and veins would show. He returned to sit at the desk, weakly drooping, the knife, forgotten, still in his left hand. He looked at the window, and it seemed his thoughts originated with that fainter, more tenuous Dr. Winters hanging like a ghost outside.

What was this world he lived in? Surely, in a lifetime, he had not begun to guess. To feed in such a way! There was horror enough in this alone. But to feed thus *in his own grave*. How had he accomplished it—leaving aside how he had fought suffocation long enough to do anything at all? How was it to be comprehended, a greed that raged so hotly it would glut itself at the very threshold of its own destruction? That last feast was surely in his stomach still.

Dr. Winters looked at the photograph, at Allen's head snugged into the others' middles like a hungry suckling nuzzling to the sow. Then he looked at the knife in his hand. The hand felt empty of all technique. Its one impulse was to slash, cleave, obliterate the remains of this gluttonous thing, this Joe Allen. He must do this, or flee it utterly. There was no course between. He did not move.

"I *will* examine him," said the ghost in the glass, and did not move. Inside the refrigerator vault, there was a slight noise.

No. It had been some hitch in the generator's murmur. Nothing in there could move. There was another noise, a brief friction against the vault's inner wall. The two old men shook their heads at one another. A catch clicked and the metal door slid open. Behind the staring mage of his own amazement, the doctor saw that a filthy shape stood in the doorway and raised its arms towards him in a gesture of supplication. The doctor turned in his chair. From the shape came a whistling groan, the decayed fragment of a human voice.

Pleadingly, Joe Allen worked his jaw and spread his purple hands. As if speech were a maggot struggling to emerge from his mouth, the blue, tumescent face toiled, the huge tongue wallowed helplessly between the viscid lips.

The doctor reached for the telephone, lifted the receiver. Its deadness to his ear meant nothing—he could not have spoken. The thing confronting him, with each least movement that it made, destroyed the very frame of sanity in which words might have meaning, reduced the world itself around him to a waste of dark and silence, a starlit ruin where already, everywhere, the alien and unimaginable was awakening to its new dominion. The corpse raised and reached out one hand as if to stay him—turned, and walked towards the instrument table. Its legs were leaden, it rocked its shoulders like a swimmer, fighting to make its passage through gravity's dense medium. It reached the table and grasped it exhaustedly. The doctor found himself on his feet, crouched slightly, weightlessly still. The knife in his hand was the only part of himself he clearly felt, and it was like a tongue of fire, a crematory flame. Joe Allen's corpse thrust one hand among the instruments. The thick fingers, with a queer, simian ineptitude, brought up a scalpel. Both hands clasped the little handle and plunged the blade between the lips, as a thirsty child might a popsicle, then jerked it out again, slashing the tongue. Turbid fluid splashed down to the floor. The jaw worked stiffly, the mouth brought out words in a wet, ragged hiss:

"Please. Help me. Trapped in *this*." One dead hand struck the dead chest. "Starving."

"What are you?"

"Traveler. Not of earth."

"An eater of human flesh. A drinker of human blood."

"No. No. Hiding only. Am small. Shape hideous to you. Feared death."

"You brought death." The doctor spoke with the calm of perfect disbelief, himself as incredible to him as the thing he spoke with. It shook its head, the dull, popped eyes glaring with an agony of thwarted expression.

"Killed none. Hid in this. Hid in this not to be killed. Five days now. Drowning in decay. Free me. Please."

"No. You have come to feed on us, you are not hiding in fear. We are your food, your meat and drink. You fed on those two men within your grave. *Their* grave. For you, a delay. In fact, a diversion that has ended the hunt for you."

"No! No! Used men already dead. For me, five days, starvation. Even less. Fed only from necessity. Horrible necessity!"

The spoiled vocal instrument made a mangled gasp of the last word—an inhuman, snakepit noise the doctor felt as a cold flicker of ophidian tongues within his ears—while the dead arms moved in a sodden approximation of the body language that swears truth.

"No," the doctor said. "You killed them all. Including your . . . tool—this man. *What are you?*" Panic erupted in the question which he tried to bury by answering himself instantly. "Resolute, yes. That surely. You used death for an escape route. You need no oxygen perhaps."

"Extracted more than my need from gasses of decay. A lesser component of our metabolism."

The voice was gaining distinctness, developing makeshifts for tones lost in

the agonal rupturing of the valves and stops of speech, more effectively
wrestling vowel and consonant from the putrid tongue and lips. At the same
time the body's crudity of movement did not quite obscure a subtle,
incessant experimentation. Fingers flexed and stirred, testing the give of
tendons, groping the palm for the old points of purchase and counter-press-
ure there. The knees, with cautious repetitions, assessed the new limits of
their articulation.

"What was the sphere?"

"My ship. Its destruction our first duty facing discovery." (Fear touched
the doctor, like a slug climbing his neck; he had seen, as it spoke, a sharp,
spastic activity of the tongue, a pleating and shrinkage of its bulk as at the tug
of some inward adjustment.) "No chance to re-enter. Leaving this take far
too long. Not even time to set for destruct—must extrude a cilium, chemical
key to broach hull shield. In shaft my only chance to halt host."

The right arm tested the wrist, and the scalpel the hand still held cut white
sparks from the air, while the word "host" seemed itself a little knife-prick, a
teasing abandonment of fiction—though the dead mask showed no irony—
preliminary to attack.

But he found that fear had gone from him. The impossibility with which he
conversed, and was about to struggle, was working in him an overwhelming
amplification of his life's long helpless rage at death. He found his parochial
pity for earth alone stretched to the trans-stellar scope this traveler
commanded, to the whole cosmic trashyard with its bulldozed multitudes of
corpses; galactic wheels of carnage—stars, planets with their most majestic
generations—all trash, cracked bones and foul rags that pooled, settled,
reconcatenated in futile symmetries gravid with new multitudes of briefly
animate trash.

And this, standing before him now, was the death it was given him
particularly to deal—his mite was being called in by the universal Treasury
of death, and Dr. Winters found himself, an old healer, on fire to pay. His
own, more lethal blade, tugged at his hand with its own sharp appetite. He
felt entirely the Examiner once more, knew the precise cuts he would make,
swiftly and without error. *Very soon now*, he thought and cooly probed for
some further insight before its onslaught:

"Why must your ship be destroyed, even at the cost of your host's life?"

"We must not be understood."

"The livestock must not understand what is devouring them."

"Yes, doctor. Not all at once. But one by one. You will understand what is
devouring you. That is essential to my feast."

The doctor shook his head. "You are in your grave already, Traveler.
That body will be your coffin. You will be buried in it a second time, for all
time."

The thing came one step nearer and opened its mouth. The flabby throat
wrestled as with speech, but what sprang out was a slender white filament,
more than whip-fast. Dr. Winters saw only the first flicker of its eruption,

and then his brain nova-ed, thinning out at light-speed to a white nullity.

When the doctor came to himself, it was in fact to a part of himself only. Before he had opened his eyes he found that his wakened mind had repossessed proprioceptively only a bizarre truncation of his body. His head, neck, left shoulder, arm and hand declared themselves—the rest was silence.

When he opened his eyes, he found that he lay supine on the gurney, and naked. Something propped his head. A strap bound his left elbow to the gurney's edge, a strap he could feel. His chest was also anchored by a strap, and this he could not feel. Indeed, save for its active remnant, his entire body might have been bound in a block of ice, so numb was it, and so powerless was he to compel the slightest movement from the least part of it.

The room was empty, but from the open door of the vault there came slight sounds: the creak and soft frictions of heavy tarpaulin shifted to accommodate some business involving small clicking and kissing noises.

Tears of fury filled the doctor's eyes. Clenching his one fist at the starry engine of creation that he could not see, he ground his teeth and whispered in the hot breath of strangled weeping:

"Take it back, this dirty little shred of life! I throw it off gladly like the filth it is." The slow knock of bootsoles loudened from within the vault, and he turned his head. From the vault door Joe Allen's corpse approached him.

It moved with new energy, though its gait was grotesque, a ducking, hitching progress, jerky with circumventions of decayed muscle, while above this galvanized, struggling frame, the bruise-colored face hung inanimate, an image of detachment. With terrible clarity it revealed the thing for what it was—a damaged hand-puppet vigorously worked from within. And when that frozen face was brought to hang above the doctor, the reeking hands, with the light, solicitous touch of friends at sickbeds, rested on his naked thigh.

The absence of sensation made the touch more dreadful than if felt. It showed him that the nightmare he still desperately denied at heart had annexed his body while he—holding head and arm free—had already more than half-drowned in its mortal paralysis. There lay his nightmare part, a nothingness freely possessed by an unspeakability. The corpse said:

"Rotten blood. Thin nourishment. Only one hour alone before you came. Fed from neighbor to my left—barely had strength to extend siphon. Fed from the right while you worked. Tricky going—you are alert. Expected Dr. Parsons. Energy needs of animating this"—one hand left the doctor's thigh and smote the dusty overalls—"and of host-transfer, very high. Once I have you synapsed, will be near starvation again."

A sequence of unbearable images unfolded in the doctor's mind, even as the robot carrion turned from the gurney and walked to the instrument table: the sheriff's arrival just after dawn, alone of course, since Craven always took thought for his deputies' rest and because on this errand he would want privacy to consider any indiscretion on behalf of the miners' survivors that the situation might call for; his finding his old friend, supine and alarmingly weak; his hurrying over, his leaning near. Then, somewhat later, a police car containing a rack of still wet bones might plunge off the highway above some deep spot in the gorge.

The corpse took an evidence box from the table and put the scalpel in it. Then it turned and retrieved the mortuary knife from the floor and put that in as well, saying as it did so, without turning, "The sheriff will come in the morning. You spoke like close friends. He will probably come alone."

The coincidence with his thoughts had to be an accident, but the intent to terrify and appall him was clear. The tone and timing of that patched-up voice were unmistakably deliberate—sly probes that sought his anguish specifically, sought his mind's personal center. He watched the corpse—back at the table—dipping an apish but accurate hand and plucking up rib shears, scissors, clamps, adding all to the box. He stared, momentarily emptied by shock of all but the will to know finally the full extent of the horror that had appropriated his life. Joe Allen's body carried the box to the worktable beside the gurney, and the expressionless eyes met the doctor's. "I have gambled. A grave gamble. But now I have won. At risk of personal discovery we are obliged to disconnect, contract, hide as well as possible in host body. Suicide in effect. I disregarded situational imperatives, despite starvation before disinterment and subsequent autopsy all but certain. I caught up with crew, tackled Pollock and Jackson microseconds before blast. Computed five days' survival from this cache, could disconnect at limit of strength to do so, but otherwise would chance an autopsy, knowing doctor was alcoholic incompetent. And now see my gain. You are a prize host, can feed with near impunity even when killing too dangerous. Safe meals delivered to you still warm."

The corpse had painstakingly aligned the gurney parallel to the worktable but offset, the table's foot extending past the gurney's, and separated from it by a distance somewhat less than the reach of Joe Allen's right arm. Now the dead hands distributed the implements along the right edge of the table, save for the scissors and the box. These the corpse took to the table's foot, where it set down the box and slid the scissors' jaws round one strap of its overalls. It began to speak again, and as it did, the scissors dismembered its cerements in unhesitating strokes.

"The cut must be medical, forensically right, though a smaller one easier. Must be careful of the pectoral muscles or arms will not convey me. I am no larva anymore—over fifteen hundred grams."

To ease the nightmare's suffocating pressure, to thrust out some flicker of his own will against its engulfment, the doctor flung a question, his voice more cracked than the other's now was:

"Why is my arm free?"

"The last, fine neural splicing needs a sensory-motor standard, to perfect my brain's fit to yours. Lacking this eye-hand coordinating check, much coarser motor control of host. This done, I flush out the paralytic, unbind us, and we are free together."

The grave-clothes had fallen in a puzzle of fragments, and the cadaver stood naked, its dark, gas-rounded contours making it seem some sleek marine creature, ruddered with the black-veined, gas-distended sex. Again the voice had teased for his fear, had uttered the last word with a savoring protraction, and now the doctor's cup of anguish brimmed over; horror and outrage wrenched his spirit in brutal alternation as if trying to tear it naked from its captive frame. He rolled his head in this deadlock, his mouth beginning to split with the slow birth of a mind-emptying outcry.

The corpse watched this, giving a single nod that might have been approbation. Then it mounted the worktable and, with the concentrated caution of some practiced convalescent reentering his bed, lay on its back. The dead eyes again sought the living and found the doctor staring back, grinning insanely.

"Clever corpse!" the doctor cried. "Clever, carnivorous corpse! Able alien! Please don't think I'm criticizing. Who am I to criticize? A mere arm and shoulder, a talking head, just a small piece of a pathologist. But I'm confused." He paused, savoring the monster's attentive silence and his own buoyancy in the hysterical levity that had unexpectedly liberated him. "You're going to use your puppet there to pluck you out of itself and put you on me. But once he's pulled you from your driver's seat, won't he go dead, so to speak, and drop you? You could get a nasty knock. Why not set a plank between the tables—the puppet opens the door, and you scuttle, ooze, lurch, flop, slither, as the case may be, across the bridge. No messy spills. And in any case, isn't this an odd, rather clumsy way to get around among your cattle?" Shouldn't you at least carry your own scalpels when you travel? There's always the risk you'll run across that one host in a million that isn't carrying one with him."

He knew his gibes would be answered to his own despair. He exulted, but solely in the momentary bafflement of the predator—in having, for just a moment, mocked its gloating assurance to silence and marred its feast.

Its right hand picked up the post-mortem knife beside it, and the left wedged a roll of gauze beneath Allen's neck, lifting the throat to a more prominent arch. The mouth told the ceiling:

"We retain larval form till entry of the host. As larvae we have locomotor structures, and sense-buds usable outside our ships' sensory amplifiers. I waited coiled round Ed Sykes' bed leg till night, entered by his mouth as he slept." Allen's hand lifted the knife, held it high above the dull, quick eyes, turning it in the light. "Once lodged, we have three instars to adult form," the voice continued absently—the knife might have been a mirror from which the corpse read its features. "Larvally we have only a sketch of our full neural tap. Our metamorphosis is cued and determined by the host's

endosomatic ecology. I matured in three days." Allen's wrist flexed, tipping
the knife's point downmost. "Most supreme adaptations are purchased at
the cost of inessential capacities." The elbow pronated and slowly flexed,
hooking the knife body-wards. "Our hosts are all sentients, eco-dominants,
are already carrying the baggage of coping structures for the planetary
environment. Limbs, sensory portals"—the fist planted the fang of its tool
under the chin, tilted it and rode it smoothly down the throat, the voice
proceeding unmarred from under the furrow that the steel ploughed—
"somatic envelopes, instrumentalities"—down the sternum, diaphragm,
abdomen the stainless blade painted its stripe of gaping, muddy tissue—
"with a host's brain we inherit all these, the mastery of any planet, netted in
its dominant's cerebral nexus. Thus our genetic codings are now all but
disencumbered of such provision."

So swiftly the doctor flinched, Joe Allen's hand slashed four lateral cuts
from the great wound's axis. The seeming butchery left two flawlessly drawn
thoracic flaps cleanly outlined. The left hand raised the left flap's hem, and
the right coaxed the knife into the aperture, deepening it with small stabs
and slices. The posture was a man's who searches a breast pocket, with the
dead eyes studying the slow recoil of flesh. The voice, when it resumed, had
geared up to an intenser pitch:

"Galactically, the chordate nerve/brain paradigm abounds, and the
neural labyrinth is our dominion. Are we to make plank bridges and worm
across them to our food? Are cockroaches greater than we for having legs to
run up walls and antennae to grope their way! All the quaint, hinged
crutches that life sports! The stilts, fins, fans, springs, stalks, flippers and
feathers, all in turn so variously terminating in hooks, clamps, suckers,
scissors, forks or little cages of digits! And besides all the gadgets it concocts
for wrestling through its worlds, it is all knobbed, whiskered, crested,
plumed, vented, spiked or measleed over with perceptual gear for combing
pittances of noise or color from the environing plentitude."

Invincibly calm and sure, the hands traded tool and tasks. The right flap
eased back, revealing ropes of ingeniously spared muscle while promising a
genuine appearance once sutured back in place. Helplessly the doctor felt
his delirious defiance bleed away and a bleak fascination rebind him.

"We are the taps and relays that share the host's aggregate of afferent
nerve-impulse precisely at its nodes of integration. We are the brains that
peruse these integrations, integrate them with our existing banks of
host-specific data, and, lastly, let their consequences flow down the motor
pathway—either the consequences they seek spontaneously, or those we
wish to graft upon them. We are besides a streamlined alimentary/circula-
tory system and a reproductive apparatus. And more than this we need not
be."

The corpse had spread its bloody vest, and the feculent hands now took up
the rib shears. The voice's sinister coloration of pitch and stress grew yet
more marked—the phrases slid from the tongue with a cobra's seeking sway,

winding their liquid rhythms round the doctor till a gap in his resistance should let them pour through to slaughter the little courage left him.

"For in this form we have inhabited the densest brainweb of three hundred races, lain intricately snug within them like thriving vine on trelliswork. We've looked out from too many variously windowed masks to regret our own vestigial senses. None read their worlds definitely. Far better then, our nomad's range and choice, than an unvarying tenancy of one poor set of structures. Far better to slip on as we do whole living beings and wear at once all of their limbs and organs, memories and powers—wear all as tightly congruent to our wills as a glove is to the hand that fills it."

The shears clipped through the gristle, stolid, bloody jaws monotonously feeding, stopping short of the sterno-clavicular joint in the manubrium where the muscles of the pectoral girdle have an important anchorage.

"No consciousness of the chordate type that we have found has been impermeable to our finesse—no dendritic pattern so elaborate we could not read its stitchwork and thread ourselves to match, precisely map its each synaptic seam till we could loosen it and retailor all to suit ourselves. We have strutted costumed in the bodies of planetary autarchs, venerable manikins of moral fashion, but cut of the universal cloth: the weave of fleet electric filaments of experience which we easily re-shuttled to the warp of our wishes. Whereafter—newly hemmed and gathered—their living fabric hung obedient to our bias, investing us with honor and influence unlimited."

The tricky verbal melody, through the corpse's deft, unfaltering self-dismemberment—the sheer neuromuscular orchestration of the compound activity—struck Dr. Winters with the detached enthrallment great keyboard performers could bring him. He glimpsed the alien's perspective—a Gulliver waiting in a brobdingnagian grave, then marshalling a dead giant against a living, like a dwarf in a huge mechanical crane, feverishly programming combat on a battery of levers and pedals, waiting for the robot arms' enactments, the remote, titanic impact of the foes—and he marveled, filled with a bleak wonder at life's infinite strategy and plasticity. Joe Allen's hands reached into his half-opened abdominal cavity, reached deep below the uncut anterior muscle that was exposed by the shallow, spurious incision of the epidermis, till by external measure they were extended far enough to be touching his thighs. The voice was still as the forearms advertised a delicate rummaging with the buried fingers. The shoulders drew back. As the steady withdrawal brought the wrists into view, the dead legs tremored and quaked with diffuse spasms.

"You called your kind our food and drink, doctor. If you were merely that, an elementary usurpation of your motor tracts alone would satisfy us, give us perfect cattle-control—for what rarest word or subtlest behavior is more than a flurry of varied muscles? That trifling skill was ours long ago. It is not mere blood that feeds this lust I feel now to tenant you, this craving for an intimacy that years will not stale. My truest feast lies in compelling you to feed in that way and in the utter deformation of your will this will involve.

Had gross nourishment been my prime need, then my gravemates—Pollock and Jackson—could have eked out two weeks of life for me or more. But I scorned a cowardly parsimony in the face of death. I reinvested more than half the energy that their blood gave me in fabricating chemicals to keep their brains alive, and fluid-bathed with oxygenated nutriment."

Out of the chasmed midriff the smeared hands dragged two long tresses of silvery filament that writhed and sparkled with a million simultaneous coilings and contractions. The legs jittered with faint, chaotic pulses throughout their musculature, until the bright, vermiculate tresses had gathered into two spheric masses which the hands laid carefully within the incision. Then the legs lay still as death.

"I had accessory neural taps only to spare, but I could access much memory, and all of their cognitive responses, and having in my banks all the organ of Corti's electrochemical conversions of English words, I could whisper anything to them directly into the eighth cranial nerve. Those are our true feast, doctor, such bodiless electric storms of impotent cognitiation as I tickled up in those two little bone globes. I was forced to drain them yesterday, just before disinterment. They lived till then and understood everything—*everything* I did to them."

When the voice paused, the dead and living eyes were locked together. They remained so a moment, and then the dead face smiled.

It recapitulated all the horror of Allen's first resurrection—this waking of expressive soul from those grave-mound contours. And it was a demon-soul the doctor saw awaken: the smile was barbed with fine, sharp hooks of cruelty at the corners of the mouth, while the barbed eyes beamed fond, langorous anticipation of his pain. Remotely, Dr. Winters heard the flat sound of his own voice asking:

"And Eddie Sykes?"

"Oh, yes, doctor. He is with us now, has been throughout. I grieve to abandon so rare a host! He is a true hermit-philosopher, well-read in four languages. He is writing a translation of Marcus Aurelius—he was, I mean, in his free time. . . ."

Long minutes succeeded of the voice accompanying the surreal self-autopsy, but the doctor lay stilled, emptied of reactive power. Still, the full understanding of his fate reverberated in his mind—an empty room through which the voice, not heard exactly but somehow implanted directly as in the subterranean torture it had just described, sent aftershocks of realization, amplifications of the Unspeakable.

The parasite had traced and tapped the complex interface between cortical integration of input and the consequent neural output shaping response. It had interposed its brain between, sharing consciousness while solely commanding the pathways of reaction. The host, the bottled personality, was mute and limbless for any least expression of its own will, while hellishly articulate and agile in the service of the parasite's. It was the host's own hands that bound and wrenched the life half out of his prey, his own loins that experienced the repeated orgasms crowning his other despoliations of their bodies. And when they lay, bound and shrieking still, ready for the consummation, it was his own strength that hauled the smoking entrails from them, and his own intimate tongue and guzzling mouth he plunged into the rank, palpitating feast.

And the doctor had glimpses of the history behind this predation, that of a race so far advanced in the essentializing, the inexorable abstraction of their own mental fabric that through scientific commitment and genetic self-cultivation they had come to embody their own model of perfected consciousness, streamlined to permit the entry of other beings and the direct acquisition of their experiential worlds. All strictest scholarship at first, until there matured in the disembodied scholars their long-germinal and now blazing, jealous hatred for all "lesser" minds rooted and clothed in the soil and sunlight of solid, particular worlds. The parasite spoke of the "cerebral music," the "symphonies of agonized paradox" that were its invasion's chief plunder. The doctor felt the truth behind this grandiloquence: its actual harvest from the systematic violation of encoffined personalities was the experience of a barren supremacy of means over lives more primitive, perhaps, but vastly wealthier in the vividness and passionate concern with which life for them was imbued.

Joe Allen's hands had scooped up the bunched skeins of alien nerve, with the wrinkled brain-node couched amidst them, and for some time had waited the slow retraction of a last major trunkline which seemingly had followed the spine's axis. At last, when only a slender subfiber of this remained implanted, the corpse, smiling once more, held up for him to view its reconcatenated master. The doctor looked into its eyes then and spoke—not to their controller, but to the captive who shared them with it, and who now, the doctor knew, neared his final death.

"Goodbye, Joe Allen. Eddie Sykes. You are guiltless. Peace be with you at last."

The demon smile remained fixed, the right hand reached its viscid cargo across the gap and over the doctor's groin. He watched the hand set the glittering medusa's head—his new self—upon his flesh, return to the table, take up the scalpel, and reach back to cut in his groin a four-inch incision—all in eerie absence of tactile stimulus. The line that had remained plunged into the corpse suddenly whipped free of the mediastinal crevice, retracted across the gap and shortened to a taut stub on the seething organism atop the doctor.

Joe Allen's body collapsed, emptied, all slack. He was a corpse again entirely, but with one anomalous feature to his posture. His right arm had not dropped to the nearly vertical hang that would have been natural. At the instant of the alien's unplugging, the shoulder had given a fierce shrug and wrenching of its angle, flinging the arm upward as it died so that it now lay in the orientation of an arm that reaches up for a ladder's next rung. The slightest tremor would unfix the joints and dump the arm back into the gravitational bias; it would also serve to dump the scalpel from the proferred, upturned palm that implement still precariously occupied.

The man had repossessed himself one microsecond before his end. The doctor's heart stirred, woke, and sang within him, for he saw that the scalpel was just in reach of his fingers at his forearm's fullest stretch from the bound elbow. The horror crouched on him and, even now slowly feeding its trunkline into his groin incision, at first stopped the doctor's hand with a pang of terror. Then he reminded himself that, until implanted, the enemy was a senseless mass, bristling with plugs, with input jacks for senses, but, until installed in the physical amplifiers of eyes and ears, an utterly deaf, blind monad that waited in a perfect solipsism between two captive sensory envelopes.

He saw his straining fingers above the bright tool of freedom, thought with an insane smile of God and Adam on the Sistine ceiling, and then, with a lifespan of surgeon's fine control, plucked up the scalpel. The arm fell and hung.

"Sleep," the doctor said. "Sleep revenged."

But he found his retaliation harshly reined-in by the alien's careful provisions. His elbow had been fixed with his upper arm almost at right angles to his body's long axis; his forearm could reach his hand inward and present it closely to the face, suiting the parasite's need of an eye-hand coordinative check, but could not, even with the scalpel's added reach, bring its point within four inches of his groin. Steadily the parasite fed in its tapline. It would usurp motor control in three or four minutes at most, to judge by the time its extrication from Allen had taken.

Frantically the doctor bent his wrist inwards to its limit, trying to pick through the strap where it crossed his inner elbow. Sufficient pressure was impossible, and the hold so awkward that even feeble attempts threatened the loss of the scalpel. Smoothly the root of alien control sank into him. It was a defenseless thing of jelly against which he lay lethally armed, and he was still doomed—a preview of all his thrall's impotence-to-be.

But of course there was a way. Not to survive. But to escape, and to have vengeance. For a moment he stared at his captor, hardening his mettle in the blaze of hate it lit in him. Then, swiftly, he determined the order of his moves, and began.

He reached the scalpel to his neck and opened his superior thyroid vein—his inkwell. He laid the scalpel by his ear, dipped his finger in his blood, and began to write on the metal surface of the gurney, beginning by his thigh and moving towards his armpit. Oddly, the incision of his neck, though this was muscularly awake, had been painless, which gave him hopes that raised his courage for what remained to do. His neat, sparing strokes scribed with ghastly legibility.

When he had done the message read:

MIND PARASITE
FM ALLEN IN ME
CUT *all* TILL FIND
1500 GM MASS
NERVE FIBRE

He wanted to write goodbye to his friend, but the alien had begun to pay out smaller, auxiliary filaments collaterally with the main one, and all now lay in speed.

He took up the scalpel, rolled his head to the left, and plunged the blade deep in his ear.

Miracle! Last, accidental mercy! It was painless. Some procedural, highly specific anesthetic was in effect. With careful plunges, he obliterated the right inner ear and then thrust silence, with equal thoroughness, into the left. The slashing of the vocal chords followed, then the tendons in the back of the neck that holds it erect. He wished he were free to unstring knees and elbow too, but it could not be. But blinded, with centers of balance lost, with only rough motor control—all these conditions should fetter the alien's escape, should it in the first place manage the reanimation of a bloodless corpse in which it had not yet achieved a fine-tuned interweave. Before he extinguished his eyes, he paused, the scalpel poised above his face, and blinked them to clear his aim of tears. The right, then the left, both retinas meticulously carved away, the yolk of vision quite scooped out of them. The scalpel's last task, once it had tilted the head sideways to guide the bloodflow absolutely clear of possible effacement of the message, was to slash the external carotid artery.

When this was done the old man sighed with relief and laid his scalpel down. Even as he did so, he felt the deep, inward prickle of an alien energy—something that flared, crackled, flared, *groped for* but did not quite find its purchase. And inwardly, as the doctor sank towards sleep—cerebrally, as a voiceless man must speak—he spoke to the parasite these carefully chosen words:

"Welcome to your new house. I'm afraid there's been some vandalism—the lights don't work, and the plumbing has a very bad leak. There are some other things wrong as well—the neighborhood is perhaps a little *too* quiet, and you may find it hard to get around very easily. But it's been a lovely home to me for fifty-seven years, and somehow I think you'll stay. . . ."

The face, turned towards the body of Joe Allen, seemed to weep scarlet tears, but its last movement before death was to smile.

CONNECTICUT

The Believers
by Robert Arthur

"THIS IS IT," Nick Deene said with enthusiasm, after he had stared down at the old Carriday house for a couple of minutes. "This is what I had in mind. Right down to the last rusty hinge and creaking floorboard."

Danny Lomax heaved a sigh of relief.

"Praise be to Allah!" he intoned. "We've wasted almost a week finding a joint that suited you just right, and that dosn't leave us much time to start beating the drum. Although I'll admit"—Danny squinted down at the brooding old pile of stone and lumber that still retained some traces of a one-time dignity—"I'll admit you've really turned up a honey at last. If that ain't a haunted house, it'll do until one comes along."

Nick Deene stood for a moment longer, appraising the Carriday mansion, on whose arched entrance the carved figure 1784 still defied the corroding elements. The building was a long, L-shaped Colonial type house, with stone foundations and hand-sawed clapboard upper structure. It had been painted some dark color once, but the color had gone with the years, leaving the structure a scabrous, mottled hue that had, to the eye of one who stared too long at it in the uncertain light of dusk, an unpleasant appearance of slow, sinuous movement.

The building was two-storied, with attics, and seemed to contain a number of rooms. Woods, once cut back, had crept up almost to the walls, and though it was only second growth stuff, pine and cedar, they gave the place a cramped, crowded feeling. A weed-grown dirt carriage drive connecting with a half-impassable county road that seemed never to be used any more, and the tumbled ruins of a couple of outbuildings finished off the scene.

"It has everything, Danny!" Nick Deene went on, with animation. "Absolutely everything but a ghost."

"Which is just fine and dandy with me," the technical assistant alloted him by his radio hour sponsors—*So-Pure Soaps present "Dare Danger with Deene!"*—asserted. "Of course, I don't believe in ghosts, as the hill-billy said about the hippopotamus, but that's all the more reason I don't want to go meeting one. I'm too old to go around revising my beliefs just to please a spook."

"That's just it," Nick Deene told him. "A resident ha'nt that somebody or other had seen, or thought he'd seen, and described, would cramp my style. Of course, nobody comes out here, and it's spooky enough to make any casual passerby take another road, but there's no definite legend attached to it, and what I've been looking for—that, plus a proper background. And this has the proper background. Three generations of Carridays died here— malaria, probably; look at the swamp back there. The last Carriday ran away to sea and died in Java. The place's been empty fifteen years now, except for a tramp found in it one winter, dead of pneumonia. Nobody's going to buy it, not away out here in a swampy section of woods, and for a couple thousand dollars the estate agent will be glad enough to let us have the key and do anything we want to it, including furnishing it with a nice, brand new ghost. Which is just what I'm going to do. And, believe me, it'll be a lulu."

"Nicholas Deene, Hand-Tailored Spooks, Ghost Maker to the Nobility," Danny Lomax grunted. "You know, I used to read your books, and believe 'em. That chapter where you told about the doomed virgin dancing girl in the old temple at Anghor Vat, and how you saved her just before the priest came for her, gave me a big kick once. I was sap enough to think it had really happened!"

"Well, there *is* a temple at Anghor Vat," Nick Deene grinned. "And dancing girls too. For all I know, one of them may be a virgin. So if you enjoyed the story, why complain? You believed it when you read it, didn't you?"

"Yeah," Danny Lomax agreed, stamping out a cigarette. "I believed it."

"Then you got your money's worth," the tall, bronzed man—sun lamp treatments every evening, carefully timed by his valet, Walters, kept that bronze in good repair—asserted. "And a million people still believe it. Just as five million people are going to believe in the Carriday Curse."

"Okay, okay," the small, wiry man assented. "I'm not here to argue. Let's scram. Even if the Carriday Curse is strictly a Nick Deene phony, I don't like this dump in these shadows. If I had a lot of baby spooks I wanted to raise to be nice, big ha'nts, I'd bring 'em here and plant 'em. The atmosphere is so unhealthy!"

Nick Deene grinned again, the flashing-toothed smile that had won him indulgence all around the globe, had been photographed against the columns of the Athenaeum, halfway up Mount Everest, atop an elephant going over the Alps, and too many other places to list. He brushed back the jet black hair that lay so smoothly against his skull, and started back toward the road from the little knoll they'd climbed to get a view of the house. Danny Lomax followed, making plans out loud.

"We can have 'em run a rebroadcast unit on a truck up to the road, here," he decided. "You'll have a portable sender on your back, and the truck will pick it up and retransmit to Hartford. Hartford will pipe it into New York and out through the networks. We'll give the equipment a thorough check, and there's not much chance of anything going wrong. Your Crosley rating has been falling off lately, but this'll hypo the box office up to the top again. Most of your listeners have already read the stuff you've been dramatizing on the ether, you know. This one, a direct broadcast from a haunted house at night on Friday the 13th, will pull 'em in. You're a phony, Deene, but you got some good ideas, and this is one of the better ones. *If.*"

"If what?" Nick demanded challengingly, as they reached the road and prepared to clamber into the gleaming roadster that had gotten them there.

"If you put it over." Danny Lomax took the right hand seat and slammed the door. "A lot of newspaper guys don't like you any too well, and if there's any stink to this thing they'll horse-laugh it to death. There's gotta be a ghost, and your audience's got to believe in it. Don't make any mistake about that."

"There'll be a ghost," Nick Deene shrugged, putting the roadster into motion. "And they'll believe in it. I'll be right in the room with 'em. I'm working on the script now. I'm going to ask them to turn out the light when they listen, and imagine they're with me, waiting in the dark for the Thing that for a hundred years has been the Curse of the Carridays to appear. I'll be armed only with a flashlight, a bible, and—"

"And a contract," Danny interrupted. "Sorry. Don't mind my cynical ways. I was dropped from the Social Register on my head while still a babe."

"And a crucifix," Deene continued, a little nettled by now. "They'll hear boards creaking, and a death-watch beetle ticking in the wall. And plenty of other details. I'll make them up as I go along. Spontaneity always gives the most convincing effect, I've found. And they'll be convinced. Aren't they always?"

"Yeah," the little advertising man agreed reluctantly. "When you turn on the heat, old ladies swoon with excitement and little kids scream all night in their cribs. There was one heart-failure—an old maid in Dubuque—after last month's show, the one in which you were fighting an octopus forty feet beneath the surface, down in the Malay pearling waters."

"There'll be half a dozen this time," Nick Deene prophesied complacently. "When I start into the Carriday house to meet the Thing with a face like an oyster—"

"A face like an oyster, huh?" Danny Lomax repeated, and swallowed hard. "That's what it's going to look like?"

Nick Deene chuckled and nodded.

"If there's anything deader looking than a watery blue oyster that's been open too long," he said, "I don't know what it is. Where was I? Oh, yes. Well, when I start into that house to wait for the approach of the Thing with an oyster face, I'm going to scare the living livers out of five million people, if you guys do your jobs right."

"We will, we will," Danny promised. "We'll ship out photos of the house, I'll plant the story the locals should repeat to a couple of fellows in the village, we'll ballyhoo you all the way down the line. The only thing we won't do is try to fix the weatherman to make it a stormy night. You'll have to take your chances on that."

"It's generally foggy down here in the swamps at night," Deene replied, quite seriously. "Fog is as good as a storm any time."

"Yeah," Danny Lomax acquiesced, twisting around to look down at the house in the hollow below—the road having taken them up a slope behind it. Fog was already forming in tenuous gray wisps, as the disappearance of the sun brought cool air currents rolling down into the swampy dell. They made a little dancing approach toward the empty, silent building that was quite unappetizing to any one with a good imagination. "Fog's good enough for me, any time. You know, Deene, maybe it's a good thing you don't believe in spooks yourself."

"Maybe it is, at that," Nick Deene grinned as they topped a rise and the Carriday house disappeared from view. "Maybe it is, at that."

It was not a foggy night. Yet there were mists about the Carriday house as Danny Lomax, Nicholas Deene, and two newspapermen—Ken Blake and Larry Miller—prepared to enter it.

Sitting as it did in the very bottom of a little glen, so that any cool, mist-producing air currents there might be would flow toward it, it was wrapped in pale vapor that danced and shifted in slow, stately movements. A quarter moon thrust a weak finger of radiance down into the woods. It was eleven o'clock, and time for *Dare Danger With Deene* to hit the ether with its special broadcast.

Danny Lomax had earphones clamped to his ears, tentacles of wire trailing back from them to the broadcast truck pulled up beside the road, on the little rise that overlooked the house. The house was four hundred yards away, and Danny Lomax was conscious of a vague regret it wasn't four million as he snatched off the earphones and dropped his hand.

Nick Deene caught the signal, which meant that the theme song was finished, as well as the lengthy announcement outlining the circumstances of the broadcast, from the New York studio. His deep, expressive voice took up the tale without a hitch.

"This is Nicholas Deene speaking," he said easily into the mike attached to his chest, and connected to the pack broadcaster slung over his shoulder. "The old Carriday mansion lies in a depression below me, some four hundred yards away. Wan moonlight illuminates it. Veils of fog wrap around it as if to hide it from man's gaze. For fifteen years no human being has spent a night beneath its roof—alive."

His voice paused significantly, to let his unseen audience experience its first prickle of pleasurable terror.

"But tonight I am going to brave the curse of the Carridays. I am going to enter the house, and in the great master bedroom where three generations of Carridays died, I am going to wait for the unknown Thing that legends tell of to appear.

"I am going toward the house now, with two reputable newspaper men at my side. One of them has a pair of handcuffs, the other the key. They are going to cuff me to the sturdy bedposts of the ancient four-poster that can be seen through the window, dust-covered, in the master bedroom. That is to insure that I shall not leave before midnight strikes—before this ill-omened Friday the thirteenth passes away into the limbo of the vanished days."

Nick Deene's voice went on, rising and falling in carefully cadenced rolls, doing little tricks to the emotions of listeners a mile, a thousand miles, three thousand miles away. He and Danny Lomax and the two reporters trudged on downhill toward the house.

This was a last-minute inspiration of Nick Deene's, this handcuff business. The press had taken a somewhat scoffing note toward the stunt broadcast. But Nick Deene's showman instinct had risen to the occasion. There was a compellingness to the idea of a man being chained in a deserted house, haunted or not—being unable to leave—which had impressed the radio-column writers.

Deene kept on talking as they approached the old mansion, flashlight beams dancing ahead of them. He described the woods, the night sounds, the dancing mist, the appearance of the empty, silent mansion ahead of them, and did a good job. Not that it was necessary for the three men with him. Even before they reached the house, the carefully cultivated skepticism which Blake and Miller had sported was gone from their faces. Cynical though they were, Danny Lomax thought he could catch traces of uneasiness on their countenances. The place had that kind of an atmosphere about it.

"We are standing on the rotten, creaking porch now," Deene was telling his audience. "One reporter is unlocking the door with the key given us reluctantly by the white-haired agent for the property, a man whose expression tells us that he knows many things about this house his closed lips will not reveal.

"The door creaks open. Our lights probe the black throat of the hall. Dust is everywhere, seeming inches thick. It rises and swirls about us as we enter—"

They went in, and Nick Deene's tread was the firmest of the four as they strode the length of a narrow hall and reached the stairs. Their lights showed side rooms, filled with old furniture whose dust covers had not been removed in almost two decades. The stairs were winding, and creaked. The air was as musty as it always is in houses long closed.

They reached the upstairs, and a finger of moonlight intruded through an end window. Their flashlights reflected off a dusty mirror, and Larry Miller jumped uneasily. Nick Deene chuckled into the microphone, and a million listeners nodded in quick approval of his courage.

"My friends are nervous," Nick Deene was telling them. "They feel the atmosphere that hangs so heavy in these silent rooms trod only by creatures of the unseen. I do not blame them. I would feel nervous too, if I did not have a complete belief in the inability of any spiritual creature to harm a living man. Their existence I do not deny. I do, instead, affirm it resolutely. But their harmlessness I am convinced of.

"We are now in the bedroom where I shall wait—"

The bedroom was big. The door leading into it, though, was low, and narrow, and the windows were small. A broken shutter hanging outside creaked ever so slightly in an unseen air current.

There was a bureau, two old chairs, a cedar chest, a rag rug—and the four poster bedstead. A coverlet, gray with dust, lay over the mattress. Nick Deene grimaced as he saw it, but his voice did not falter.

Danny Lomax snatched the coverlet off the bed and shook it. Dust filled the air, and he coughed as he put the coverlet back into place. He slid a chair up beside the bed, and Nick Deene, without disturbing the broadcast, slid off his pack transmitter and placed it on the chair.

He lay down on the bed, and Larry Miller, with a pair of handcuffs from his pocket, linked one ankle to the left bedpost. Danny Lomax adjusted the mike so that Nick Deene could speak into it without having to hold it, and Deene waved his hand in a signal of preparedness.

"My friends are preparing to depart," he told his audience, and his words leaped from the room to the waiting truck, from there to Hartford, twenty miles away, and thence to New York, then to the world, or whatever part of it might be listening. "In a moment I will be alone. I have a flashlight, but to conserve the batteries. I am going to turn it out.

"May I make a suggestion? Why do not you, who listen, turn out your lights too, and we will wait together in darkness for the approach of the creature known as the Curse of the Carridays—a creature which I hope, before the next hour is over, to describe to you.

"What it is or what it looks like, I do not know. The one man who could tell—the agent for the property, faithful to his trust though the last Carriday died long since in far off Java—will not speak. Yet, if the portents are favorable, we, you and I, may see it tonight."

Clever, Danny Lomax thought, his trick of identifying the audience with himself, making them feel as if they were on the spot, too. One of the big secrets of his success.

"Now," Nick Deene was saying, "I take my leave of my companions—"

Then Danny and the two reporters were leaving. Nick Deene kicked his leg, the chain of the handcuff rattled, and Larry Miller jumped. Nick waved a sardonic hand after them.

They went downstairs, not dawdling, and no one spoke until they were outside. Then Blake drew a deep breath.

"He's a phony," he said, with a reluctant admiration. "And you know as well as I do that if he sees anything tonight, it'll be strictly the product of his imagination—or of that bottle in his coat pocket. But just the same, I wouldn't spend an hour in that joint, handcuffed to the furniture for a month's pay."

Without hesitating, they set off for the waiting truck, and the small knot of men—technicians, reporters, and advertising agency men—clustered around it. And as they hurried—in Boston, in Sioux Falls, Kalmazoo, Santa Barbara and a thousand other towns, lights went out in a house here, another there, as some of Nick Deene's farflung audience obeyed his melodramatic suggestion to listen to him in the darkness. And two hundred thousand families settled themselves to wait with him, hanging on his every word, their acceptance of everything he said complete, their belief utter.

When the three of them reached the rebroadcast truck again, the little group of half a dozen men there were clustered about the rear, where a half-circle of light burned through the darkness and a loudspeaker repeated Nick Deene's every word.

Deene was building atmosphere still. His resonant voice was picturing the house, the shadows, the dust, the darkness that seemed to crouch within the hallways, and as he spoke, not a man there but could see the pictures he evoked rising up before their eyes.

"Listen," Nick Deene was saying, and Danny Lomax could visualize the big bronze man grinning sardonically as he spoke, "and here with me the small night sounds that infest this ancient, spirit-ridden dwelling. Somewhere a board is creaking—perhaps for no tangible cause. I cannot tell. But it comes to me clearly—"

Listening, they could hear it, too. The eerie, chill-provoking creak of a floor board or stairway, in midnight silence. Nick Deene had two bits of wood in his pocket that he rubbed together to get that effect, but only Danny Lomax knew that. And even knowing, he did not like the sound.

"I hear the creaking—" Nick Deene's voice was low, suspense-filled now—"I hear the creaking, and something else. A monotonous tick-tick-tick that seems to become louder and louder as I listen to it, the frightening beat of the death-watch beetle within the walls of this room—"

They could hear it too, as Nick Deene's voice died out. Hear it, and their own breathing became diminuendo as if they too were in that room, listening with a man bound to the great four-poster there.

And in Atlanta, in Rochester, in Cincinnati, in Memphis, Mobile, Reno, Cheyenne, and a thousand other cities, a thousand other towns, a thousand other villages, in two hundred thousand homes Nick Deene's listeners heard it too in the hushed silence with which they listened, and swallowed a little harder, looked about them a little uneasily, and smiled—smiles that were palpably artificial. And they believed—

Danny Lomax would have believed, too, if he hadn't known of the small metal contrivance by which Nick Deene managed the "death-watch beetle" noises. Even knowing, he admitted to himself that it was an impressive performance. When Nick Deene had boasted that he would make five million people believe in the "curse of the Carridays" he had exaggerated—but not about their believing. His audience probably didn't number more that a million. But he had that million by now in a complete state of acceptance for anything he might want to say next. Danny glanced at his watch, turning his wrist so that the timepiece caught the light. Thirty-five minutes gone. Twenty-five to go. Time now for Deene to start turning on the heat. Time for the sock punch to start developing. He'd built up his background and sold his audience. Now he ought to begin to deliver.

He did. A moment later, Nick Deene's voice paused abruptly. The sudden silence held more suspense than any words he could have spoken. It held for ten seconds, twenty, thirty. Then he broke it only with a half-whispered announcement.

"I think I can hear something moving outside the house—"

Around the sound truck, there was utter silence, save for the whine of the generator that was pumping the broadcast over the hills and woods to Hartford.

"Whatever it is—" Nick Deene's voice was still low, still that of a man who whispers an aside even while intent upon something else—"whatever it is, it's coming closer. It seems to be moving slowly up from the small patch of swamp just south of the house."

Absently, Danny Lomax reached for a cigarette. Nick was sticking to the general script they'd outlined. Almost at the last minute, they'd decided against a spiritual manifestation, a ghost, pure and simple.

Instead, with his usual instinct for getting the right note, Nick Deene had switched to a *Thing*. Something nameless, something formless, something unclassifiable. Something out of the night and the swamp and the unknown. Something that might be alive and might not be alive. But something that, when Nick Deene got through describing it, would be very, very real——

"Whatever it is, it's coming closer," Nick Deene reported then. "I hear a dragging, dull sound, as of something heavy moving through dead brush and over rough ground. It may be just an animal, perhaps even a stray cow, or a horse, or a wild pig escaped from a pen somewhere on an adjacent farm—"

A million listeners held their breath a moment, then prepared to let it go. Of course, just a starving horse, or a cow. Something warm, something familiar, something harmless. Then—

"It's pulling at the boards which cover the cellar windows!" Nick Deene exclaimed. "It's trying to get into the house!"

Danny Lomax held his cigarette unlighted, until the flaring match burned his fingers. In spite of their determined skepticism, there was an intentness to the faces of the reporters and technicians gathered around the end of the sound truck. They knew or guessed this was a phony. Yet the sudden jolt, after Deene had given their nerves a moment in which to relax, got them all. Just as it was getting the whole great, unseen audience.

Danny Lomax, from years of listening to radio programs behind the scenes, had developed a sixth sense of his own. He could tell almost to a degree just how a program was going over—whether it was smashing home or laying an egg. He could feel the audience that listened reacting, and he could sense what their reactions were.

Now something was pulling at him—something strained and tense and uneasy. A million people or more were listening, were believing, were living through the scene with Nicholas Deene, and crouched there in the chilly night beside the broadcast truck, Danny Lomax could feel the waves of their belief sweeping past him, impalpable but very real.

Nick Deene's voice had quickened. He was reporting now the sound of nails shrieking as they pulled free, as boards gave way. He described a heavy, squashy body forcing its way through the tiny window. He made his listeners hear the soft, squashy sounds of something large and flabby moving through the darkness of the cellar of the house, finding the stairs, going up them slowly, slowly, slowly—

"Now it's in the hall." The big man's words were short, sharp, electric. "It's coming toward the door. I hear boards creaking beneath its weight. It senses that I'm here. It's searching for me. I confess I'm frightened. No sane man could fail to be. However, I am convinced it can't hurt me. If it's a psychic manifestation, it's harmless, however horrifying its appearance may be. So I am keeping a firm grip on my nerves. Only if they betray me can I be endangered. They will not betray me.

"Whatever it is, it's just outside the doorway now. I can sense it looking in at me. The room is in darkness. The moon has set. I have my flashlight, though, and I am going to turn it full on the thing in the doorway.

"I can smell a musty, damp odor, as of swamps and wet places. It is very strong. Almost overpowering. But now I'm going to turn on the light—"

Nick Deene's voice ceased. Danny Lomax's wristwatch ticked as loudly as an alarm clock. The seconds passed. Ten. Twenty. Thirty. Forty. Someone shifted position. Someone's breath was rasping like that of a choking sleeper.

Then—"It's going!" Nick Deene's voice was a whisper. "It looked at me, and would have entered. I could sense what it wished. It wished—*me*. But I have the bible and crucifix I brought tightly in my hand, the light has been shining full into its—its face, if I can call it that. I did not lower my gaze, and now it's going. I can no longer see it. The light of my flash falls on the black, empty frame of the doorway. *It* is slithering back down the hall, toward the steps. It is returning to the swamp from which it came when it sensed my presence here.

"I can hardly describe it. I don't know what it was. It stood as high as a man, yet its legs were only stumps of grayness without feet of any kind. Its body was long and bulbous, like a misshapen turnip, its flesh grayish and uneven. It shone a little, as if with slime, and I saw droplets of water on it catch the light of my torch.

"It had a head, a great round head that was as hairless as the rest of it. And a face—I cannot make you see it as I saw it. Staring into it, I could only think of an oyster. A monstrous, wet, blue-gray oyster, with two darker spots that must have been eyes.

"It had arms. At least, two masses of matter attached to either side of its body reached out a little toward me. There were no hands on the end of them. Just strings of—corruption.

"That was all I could see. Then it turned. Now it has gone. It has reached the bottom steps, going down with a shuffling, bumping noise. It is moving toward the cellar stairs, the floor creaking beneath it, back to the cellar window through which it forced itself, back to the depths of the swamp from which it emerged. Yet the sense of it still hangs in this room, and I know that if my will should slacken, it could feel it, and return. But it must not. I will not let it. It *must* return to the bottomless muck from which it came—"

Danny Lomax touched his dry lips with his tongue. This was it. This was the high spot. This was where Nick Deene got over, or fell flat on his face. Danny knew that whichever it was, he'd be able to sense it.

And he did. Not failure. Success! The unseen currents that eddied around him were belief. The belief of a million people, wrapped in a skein spun of words. The belief of a million listeners seeing in their minds something that had never existed, but which Nick Deene had created and put there.

Tomorrow they might laugh. They might belittle and ridicule the very fact they had listened. But they'd never be able to forget how they had felt. And now, for the moment at least, they believed.

Danny let out a breath, and looked at his watch. Almost midnight. Nick Deene was speaking again.

"It's gone, now. It's outside again, seeking the swamp from which it came. This is Nicholas Deene speaking. I'm going to sign off now. I've been through quite a nerve strain. Thanks for listening, everybody. I'm glad that you weren't disappointed, that something happened tonight to make this broadcast worth your listening. Good night, all. This is Nicholas Deene saying good night."

Danny Lomax saw the chief of the rebroadcast crew throw a switch, and nod to him. He leaned forward, toward a secondary mike in the truck, slipping on a pair of headphones.

"All right, Nick," he said. "You're off the air. We're coming down to unlock you now."

"Okay," Nick Deene's voice came back, a little ragged. "Hurry, will you? I'm getting sick of it here. The last couple of minutes, I could swear I *have* heard noises outside. Maybe I'm too good. I'm believing myself. How'd it go?"

"Went fine," Danny told him. "They ate it up. A million people are sitting in their parlors this minute, getting the stiffness out of their muscles, and trying to pretend they didn't believe you."

"I told you they would." Deene's voice was momentarily complacent. Then it became edged again. "Listen, hurry, will you? Damn it, there *is* something moving around outside this house— You say they ate it up?"

"Straight," Danny Lomax told him. "I could feel it. They're all still seeing that Thing you described, with the oyster face, crawling in through the cellar window, slithering up the stairs, standing in your doorway—"

"Cut it!" Deene ordered abruptly. "And come down here. I'm—*There's something coming in the cellar window where we loosened the boards for the reporters to find!*"

Lomax turned.

"Oh, Joe," he called to the driver. "Take the truck down in front of the house, will you? Save walking. . . . What did you say then, Nick? I missed it."

"I said there's something coming in the cellar window!" Nick Deene's voice was almost shrill. "It's knocking around in the cellar. It's coming toward the stairs!"

"Steady, Nick, steady," Danny Lomax cautioned. "Don't let your nerves go now. You and I know it's just a gag. Don't go and—"

"Mother of Heaven!" Deene's breath was coming in gasps. Danny could hear it whistle into the mike at the other end of the two-way hook-up. "*There's something coming up the stairs!* Come and get me out of here!"

Danny looked up, a frown between his eyes.

"Joe, get going, will you?" he snapped, and the driver looked around in annoyed surprise.

"Right away," he grunted, and the truck jerked forward. "This fast enough to suit you?"

Danny Lomax didn't answer.

"Nick, you all right?" he demanded of the mike, and Deene's voice, almost unrecognizable, came back.

"Danny, Danny," it gobbled, "there's something coming up the stairs with a sort of thump-thump. I can smell marsh gas and ammonia. There's something making a slithery sound. *I tell you something has got into this house from the swamp and is after me!*"

The truck was jolting in second down the long unused road. The reporters had swung on. They were staring at Danny, sensing something, they didn't know what, going wrong. Danny, the earphones tight, hung over the mike.

"Take it easy, take it easy," he soothed. "Just had one drink too many, Nick. We wrote all that down. It's just on the paper. You just said it. A million people believed it, but you and I don't have to, Nick. We—"

"Christ!" Nick's cry was a prayer, not a curse. "There's something in the hall. Something that scrapes and thumps. The floorboards are creaking. Danny, don't you know I'm chained here and it's coming after me. It is! It is!" Nick Deene's voice was hysterical. "It's at the doorway. It's—"

The voice was drowned out by a scraping of gravel as the truck's brakes went on abruptly. Wheels fought for traction, lost it. A muddy spot underfoot had slewed the broadcast truck to one side. The long untended road gave no hold. The rear wheels slid toward the ditch beside the road, and in. The truck jolted, toppled, was caught as the hubs dug into a clay bank. The newspapermen were jolted off. Danny Lomax was bounced away from the mike, his earphones torn off his head.

He scrambled back toward the mike, pulling himself up against the slant of the body. The earphones were cracked. He threw a switch cutting in the speaker.

"Nick!" he cried. "Nick!"

"—*in the doorway now*!" came the terror-shrill wail from the speaker. "Coming in! Oyster-face—great, blank, watery oyster-face—Danny, Danny, put me back on the air, tell 'em all it's just a joke, tell 'em it isn't so, tell 'em not to believe, not to believe. Danny, do you hear, tell 'em not to believe!

"It's coming in! It wants me! It smells, and it's all wet and watery and its face—its *face*! Danny, tell 'em not to believe! It's cause they believe. It didn't exist. I thought it up. But they all believed me. You said they did! A million people, all believing at the same time! Believing strong enough for you to feel! They've made it, Danny, they've brought it to life! It's doing just what I said it did, and it looks just like I—I like I—*Danny! Help me! HELP ME!*"

The speaker screamed, vibrated shrilly at the overload and was silent. And in the sudden hush, an echo came from the night. No, not an echo, but the scream itself they had been hearing. Faint, and dreadful, it reached them, and Danny Lomax was quite unable to move for an instant that stretched on and on as he listened.

Then he galvanized into life, and as he darted into the darkness, the others followed. With horrifying abruptness, Nick Deene's faint screams had ceased. He could see the Carriday house ahead, dark, silent, tomb-like. It was three hundred yards away, and the curve of the road—they couldn't go through the brush in black night—hid it momentarily.

The three hundred yards took almost a minute. Then Danny, gasping, turned into the old carriage drive, Nick Deene's words still screamed in his mind.

"They've made it, Danny! They've brought it to life! A million people, all believing at the same time—"

Could—Could— His mind wouldn't ask itself the question, or answer it. But he had felt the currents of belief. In two hundred thousand homes a million people had sat, and listened, and believed. Believed, and in the concentrated power of their believing, had they stirred some spark of force into life, had they jelled into the form of their belief a creature that—

Fleet pounded behind him. Someone had a flashlight. The beam of it, thrown out ahead, stabbed the night. It played over the house, and for a moment darted into the darkness beyond and to one side.

And Danny Lomax caught a glimpse of movement.

A vague, gray-white glimmer of motion, a half-seen shape that moved with speed through the dense vegetation toward the half-acre swamp south of the house and for an instant shone faintly, as if with slime and wetness.

If there was any sound of movement, Danny Lomax did not hear it, because the scuffle of running feet and the hoarse breathing of running men behind drowned it out. But as he listened intently, he thought he heard a single scream, muffled and cut abruptly short, as though a man had tried to cry out with his mouth almost covered by something wet and soft and pulpy—

Danny Lomax pulled up and stood quite still, as the newspapermen and technicians came up with him and ran past. He scarcely heard them, was scarcely aware of them, for his whole body was cold, something was squeezing his insides with a giant hand, and he knew that in just an instant he was going to be deathly sick.

And he knew already that the bedroom upstairs was empty. That the searchers would find only half a handcuff hanging from the footboard of the bed, its chain twisted in two, some marks in the dust, and a few drops of slimy water to tell where Nick Deene had gone.

Only those and an odor hanging pungent and acrid in the halls——

DELAWARE

A Teacher's Rewards
by Robert Phillips

"WHAT'D YOU say your name was?" the old lady asked through the screen door. He stood on the dark porch somewhere in rural Delaware.

"Raybe. Raybe Simpson. You taught me in the third grade, remember?"

"Simpson . . . Simpson. Yes, I suppose so," she said. Her hand remained on the latch.

"Of course you do. I was the boy with white hair. 'Old Whitehead,' my grandfather used to call me, though you wouldn't know that. I sat in the front row. You used to rap my knuckles with your ruler, remember?"

"Oh, I rapped a lot of knuckles in my time. Boys will be boys. Still, the white hair, the front row. . . ." Her voice trailed off as she made an almost audible effort to engage the ancient machinery of her memory.

"Sure you remember," he said. "'Miss Scofield never forgets a name.' That's what all the older kids told us. That's what all the other teachers said. 'Miss Scofield never forgets a name.'"

"Of course she doesn't. I never forgot a pupil's name in forty-eight years of teaching. Come right in." She unlatched the screen door and swung it wide. The spring creaked.

"I can't stay long. I was in town for the day and thought I'd look you up. You were such a good teacher. I've never forgotten what you did for me."

"Well, now, I consider that right kindly of you." She looked him up and down through wire-rimmed spectacles. "Just when was it I taught you?"

"Nineteen thirty-eight. Out to the old school."

"Ah, yes. The old school. A pity about that fire."

"I heard something about it burning down. But I've been away. When was that fire?"

"Oh, years ago. A year or two before I retired. After that I couldn't teach in the new brick schoolhouse they built. Something about the place. Too cold, too bright. And the classroom was so long. A body couldn't hardly see from the one end of it to the other. . . ." She made a helpless gesture with her hand. He watched the hand in its motion: tiny, fragile, transparent, a network of blue veins running clearly beneath the surface; the skin hung in wrinkles like wet crepe paper. Denison paper, it had been called, when he was in school.

"That's rough. But you must have been about ready to retire anyhow, weren't you?"

Her watery blue eyes snapped. "I should say not! All my life I've had a real calling for teaching. A real calling. I always said I would teach until I dropped in my tracks. It's such a rewarding field. A teacher gets her reward in something other than money. . . . It was just that new red-brick schoolhouse! The lights were too bright, new-fangled fluorescent lights, bright yellow. And the room was too long. . . ." Her gaze dared him to contradict her.

"I don't think much of these modern buildings, either."

"Boxes," she said firmly.

"Come again?"

"Boxes, boxes, nothing but boxes, that's all they are. I don't know what we're coming to, I declare. Well, now Mister—"

"Simpson. Mister Simpson. But you can call me Raybe, like you always did."

"Yes. Raybe. That's a nice name. Somehow it has an *honest* sound. Really, the things people name their children *these* days! There's one family named their children Cindy, Heidi, and Dawn. They sound like creatures out of Walt Disney. The last year I taught, I had a student named Crystal. A little girl named Crystal! Why not name her Silverware, or China? And a boy named Jet. That was his first name, Jet. Or was it Astronaut? I don't know. Whatever it was, it was terrible."

"You once called me Baby-Raybe, and it caught on. That's what all the kids called me after that."

"Did I? Oh, dear. Well, you must have done something babyish at the time."

A shaft of silence fell between them. At last she smiled, as if to herself, and said cheerily, "I was just fixing to have some tea before you happened by. Would you like some nice hot tea?"

"Well, I wasn't fixing to stay long, like I said." He shuffled his feet.

"It'll only take a second. The kettle's been on all this time." She seemed to have her heart set, and he was not one to disappoint. "Okay, if you're having some."

"Good. Do you take lemon or cream?"

"Neither. Actually I don't drink much tea. I'll just try it plain. With sugar. I've got a sweet tooth."

"A sweet tooth! Let me see. Is that one of the things I remember about you? Raybe Simpson, a sweet tooth? No, I don't think so. One of the boys always used to eat Baby Ruth candy bars right in class. The minute my back was turned he'd sneak another Baby Ruth out of his desk. But that wasn't you, was it?"

"No."

"I didn't think it was you," she said quickly. "I called it the blackboard. Did you know, in that new school building, it was green?"

"What was green?"

"The blackboard was *green*. And the chalk was *yellow*. Something about it being easier on the children's eyes. And they had the nerve to call them blackboards, too, mind you. How do you expect children to learn if you call what's green, black?"

"Hmmm."

She was getting down two dainty cups with pink roses painted on them. She put them on a tin tray and placed a sugar bowl between them. The bowl was cracked down the middle and had been taped with Scotch tape, which had yellowed. When the tea finally was ready, they adjourned to the living room. The parlor, she called it.

"Well, how've you been, Miss Scofield?" he asked.

"Can't complain, except for a little arthritis in my hands. Can't complain."

"Good." He studied her hands, then glanced around. "Nice little place you got here." He took a sip of the tea, found it strong and bitter, added two more heaping spoons of sugar.

"Well, it's small, of course, but it serves me. It serves me." She settled back in her rocker.

"You still Miss Scofield?"

"How's that?" She leaned forward on her chair, as if to position her ear closer to the source.

"I asked you, your name is still Miss Scofield? You never got married?"

"Mercy no. I've always been an unclaimed blessing. That's what I've always called myself. "An unclaimed blessing." She smiled sweetly.

"You still live alone, I take it."

"Yes indeed. I did once have a cat. A greedy old alley cat named Tom. But he died. Overeating did it, I think. Ate me out of house and home, pretty near."

"You don't say."

"Oh, yes indeed. He'd eat anything. Belly got big as a basketball, nearabout. He was good company, though. Sometimes I miss that old Tom."

"I should think so."

An old-fashioned clock chimed overhead.

"What business did you say you were in, Mr. Simp . . . Raybe?"

"Didn't say."

"That's right, you didn't say. Well, just what is it?"

"Right now I'm unemployed."

She set her teacup upon a lace doily on the table top and made a little face of disapproval. "Unemployed. I see. Then how do you get along?"

"Oh, I manage, one way or the other. I've been pretty well taken care of these last ten years. I been away."

"You're living with your folks? Is that it?" Encouragement bloomed on her cheeks.

"My folks are dead. They were dead when I was your student, if you'll remember. Grandfather died too. I lived with an aunt. She's dead now."

"Oh, I'm sorry. I don't think I realized at the time—"

"No, I don't think you did. . . . That's all right, Miss Scofield. You had a lot of students to look after."

"Yes, but still and all, it's unlike me not to have remembered or known that one of my boys was an *orphan*. You don't mind if I use that word, do you, Mr. . . . Raybe? Lots of people are sensitive about words."

"I don't mind. I'm not sensitive."

"No, I should think not. You're certainly a big boy, now. And what happened to all that hair. Why, you're bald as a baby." Looking at his head, she laughed a laugh as scattered as buckshot. "My, you must be hot in that jacket. Why don't you take it off? It looks very heavy."

"I'll keep it on, if you don't mind."

"Don't mind a bit, so long's you're comfortable." What did he have in that jacket, she wondered. He was carrying something in there.

"I'm just fine," he said, patting the jacket.

She began to rock in her chair and looked around the meager room to check its presentability to unexpected company. Maybe he had his dinner in there, in a paper poke, and was too embarrassed to show it.

"Well, now, what do you remember about our year together that I may have forgotten? Were you in Jay McMaster's class. Jay was a *lovely* boy. So polite. You can always tell good breeding—"

"He was a year or two ahead of me. You're getting close, though."

"Well of course I am. How about Nathan Pillsbury? The dentist's son. He was in your class, wasn't he?"

"That's right."

"See!" She exclaimed triumphantly. "Another lovely boy. His parents had a swimming pool. One Christmas Nathan brought me an enormous poinsettia plant. It filled the room, nearly."

"He was in my class, all right. He was the teacher's pet, you might say." Raybe observed her over the rim of his bitter cup. He looked at her knuckles.

"Nathan, my pet? Nathan Pillsbury? I don't remember any such thing. Besides, I never played favorites. That's a bad practice." She worked her lips to and fro.

"So's rapping people's knuckles," he laughed, putting his half-full cup on the floor.

She laughed her scattered little laugh again. "Oh, come now, Raybe. Surely it was deserved, if indeed I ever *did* rap your knuckles."

"You rapped them, all right," he said soberly.

"Did I? Did I really? Yes, I suppose I did. What was it for, do you remember? Passing notes? Gawking out the window?"

"Wasn't for any one thing. You did it lots of times. *Dozens* of time." He cleared his throat.

"Did I? Mercy me. It doesn't seem to me that I did. I only rapped knuckles upon extreme provocation, you know. *Extreme* provocation." She took a healthy swallow of tea. What was it she especially remembered about this boy? Something. It nagged at her. She couldn't remember what it was. Some trait of personality.

"You did it lots of times," he continued. "In front of the whole class. They laughed at me."

"I did? Goodness, what a memory! Well, it doesn't seem to have done you any harm. A little discipline never hurt anybody. . . . What was it you said you've been doing professionally?"

"I been in prison," he said with a pale smile. He watched her mouth draw downward.

"Prison? You've been in *prison*? Oh, I see, it's a joke." She tried to laugh again, but this time the little outburst wouldn't scatter.

"*You* try staying behind those walls for ten years and see if you think it's a joke." He fumbled in his pocket for a pack of cigarettes, withdrew a smoke and slowly lit it. He blew a smoke ring across the table.

"Well, I must say! You're certainly the only boy I ever had that . . . that ended up in prison! But I'm sure there were . . . *circumstances* . . . leading up to that. I'm sure you're a fine lad, through it all." She worked her lips faster now. Her gaze traveled to the window that looked out upon the night.

"Yeah, there were *circumstances*, as you call it. Very special circumstances." He blew an enormous smoke ring her way. The old woman began to cough. "It's the smoke. I'm not used to people smoking around me. Do you mind refraining?"

"Yeah, I do mind," he said roughly. "I'm going to finish this cigarette, no matter what."

"Well, if you must, you must," she said nervously, half rising. "But let me just open that window a little—"

"SIT BACK DOWN IN THAT CHAIR!"

She fell back into the rocker.

"Now, you listen to me, you old bitch," he began.

"Don't call me names. Don't you dare! How *dare* you? No wonder you were behind bars. A common jailbird. A degenerate. No respect for your elders."

"Shut up, Grandma." He tossed the cigarette butt to the floor and ground it out on what looked like an oriental rug. Her eyes bulged.

"I remember you very clearly, now," she exclaimed, her hands to her brow. "I remember you! You were no good to start with. No motivation. No follow-through. I knew just where you'd end up. You've run true to form" Her gaze was defiant.

"Shut your mouth, bitch," he said quietly, beginning at last to unzip his leather jacket.

"I will *not*, I'll have my say. You were a trouble-maker, too. I remember the day you wrote nasty, nasty words on the wall in the supply closet. Horrible words. And then when I went back to get papers to distribute, I saw those words. I had to read them, and I knew who wrote them, all right."

"I didn't write them."

"Oh, you wrote them, all right. And I whacked your knuckles good with a ruler, if I remember right."

"You whacked my knuckles good, but I didn't write those words."

"*Did!*"

"*Didn't.*" They sounded like a pair of schoolchildren. He squirmed out of the jacket.

"I never made mistakes of that kind," she said softly, watching him shed the jacket. "I knew just who needed strict discipline in my class."

He stood before her now, holding the heavy jacket in his hand. Underneath he wore only a tee shirt of some rough grey linsey-woolsey material. She saw that his arms were heavily muscled, and he saw that she saw. She was positive she could smell the odor of the prison upon him, though the closest she had come to a prison was reading Dickens.

"I never made mistakes," she repeated feebly. "And now, you'd better put that coat right back on and leave. Go back to wherever you came from."

"Can't do that just yet, bitch. I got a score to settle."

"Score? To settle?" She placed her hands upon the rocker arms for support.

"Yeah. I had a long time to figure it all out. Ten years to figure it out. Lots of nights I'd lie there on that board of a bed in that puke-hole and I'd try to piece it all together. How I come to be *there*. Was it my aunt? Naw, she did the best she could without any money. Was it the fellas I took up with in high school? Naw, something happened before that, or I'd never have taken up with the likes of them in the first place, that rocky crowd. And then one night it came to me. *You* were the one."

"Me? The one? The one for what?" Her lips worked furiously now, in and out like a bellows. Her hands tightly gripped the rocker's spindle arms.

"The one who sent me there. Because you *picked* on me all the time. Made me out worse than I was. You never gave me the chance the others had. The other kids left me out of things, because you were always saying I was bad. And you always told me I was dirty. Just because my aunt couldn't keep me in clean shirts like some of the others. You punished me for everything that happened. But the worst was the day of the words on the wall. You hit me so hard my knuckles bled. My hands were sore as boils for weeks."

"*That*'s an exaggeration."

"No it isn't. They're *my* hands, I ought to know. And do you know who wrote those words on the closet wall? *Do you know?*" he screamed, putting his face right down next to hers.

"No, who?" she whispered, breathless with fright.

"*Nathan Pillsbury*, that's who!" he shouted, clenching his teeth and shaking her frail body within his grasp. "*Nathan Pillsbury, Nathan Pillsbury*!"

"Let me go," she whimpered. "Let me go."

"I'll let you go after my score is settled."

The old woman's eyes rolled toward the black, unseeing windows. "What are you going to do to me?" she rasped.

"Just settle, lady," he said, taking the hammer from his jacket. "Now, put your hands on the table top."

"My hands? On the table top?" she whispered.

"On the table top," he repeated pedantically, a teacher. "Like this." He made two fists and placed them squarely on the surface.

She refused.

"LIKE THIS!" he yelled, wrenching her quivering hands and forcing them to the table top. Then with his free hand he raised the hammer.

It remained suspended in the air for seconds. He was sweating profusely. The old woman rolled her eyes from the hammer to him. Then after a time she raised one hand, reached into his soul, and took the hammer away. Slowly, firmly, like a teacher.

"You never *could* finish anything you started, Raybe Simpson," she said with satisfaction. The man fell to his knees and began to cry.

DISTRICT OF COLUMBIA

Chico Lafleur Talks Funny
by Suzette Haden Elgin

IT WAS the third brutal beating in just under three weeks; nobody had been able to pull the officer away quickly enough this time either.

"Oh, shit," said the reporters on the scene, shivering not only from the damp and the cold but from the stomach-twisting contrast between the mess at their feet and the gold-and-silver Christmas garlands rattling in the wind above their heads. They didn't care much for the little balls attached to the garlands in clusters on the lampposts, either. "You can't tell people about some kid's eyes . . . like that," they muttered, trying not to look. "You can't go telling people about . . ." Their voices trailed off, because they couldn't tell each *other*, for that matter; they couldn't say any of it out loud. Later, when they'd had a couple of beers and a chance to get used to it, they'd be able to talk about it, but they couldn't talk about it while they were still looking at it.

They shook their heads while the medics covered the kid decently and took him away to be cared for. It was going to take one hell of a plastic surgeon to turn him back into a reasonable facsimile of a normal kid again. And they stared down at the grimy pavement when a different set of medics, the rubber room mechanics, came and scooped up the cop in their net and took *him* away too for the obligatory three days of psychiatric observations at St. Elizabeth's.

Jesus . . . what could make a grown man go berserk like that? Make him go after a kid in that way? Sure, it was a punk kid. A gang kid, probably running his smart mouth full bore. Some of the other officers had said it wasn't the first time this kid had had an unpleasant conversation with the same cop;

117

probably he'd been worrying away at the man's patience for a long time, could be he'd been throwing eggs and garbage and worse . . . but *shit*! It was still only a kid, for all that it looked more like mutilated meat right now. And any cop working Washington D.C.'s southwest ghetto and expecting mannerly talk from the kids was one crazy cop. . . . Whatever it was the kid was saying and doing, the cop should have been able to handle it.

They stuck their hands in their pockets, and they avoided each other's eyes, and they went away without saying anything more, trying to figure out how much they would have to tell and how much they could try to bury deep in their heads where it wouldn't leak out into their nightmares.

At the precinct station, Shawn Gilbert talked to his men. He knew there'd be no point talking to the man they'd taken off to St. Elizabeth's, not for a while. "What happened out there?" he asked them.

"Blake went over and talked to the kid, Captain."

"What for?"

"Well . . . the kid was acting funny. You know? He was making people uncomfortable."

Gilbert chewed on his upper lip and prayed for patience.

"Was he doing anything *wrong*?" he asked. Please God, let the kid have been doing something wrong this time. "Was he breaking any *laws*?"

"No," said the officer, and Gilbert sagged in his chair. "But Blake wasn't arresting the kid, Captain. He just went over, like we told you, and he talked to him. Just to check it out—maybe the kid was on something, maybe he was freaked out. You know . . . he's that kind of kid, Captain. Blake wasn't accusing him of anything."

"Did any of the rest of you talk to the kid?"

They shook their heads. "Just Blake," they said.

"And then?"

They shrugged and looked at their shoes.

"Then Blake just went crazy, Captain."

"Right away?"

"Naah. He talked awhile. The kid talked awhile. They talked back and forth. And then Blake just went clean crazy. Clear off his head. He started—doing stuff."

"The kid didn't push Blake? Didn't throw anything at him? Flash a knife, maybe?"

"No, sir, Captain. They were just talking."

There was a silence, with the captain glaring; and one of the men said hesitantly, "You know, Captain . . . they talk funny."

"Well, sweet suffering *Christ*, Kresge, since when is that a crime? You don't talk so great yourself!" the captain shouted at him.

He smashed one fist into the palm of his other hand, and turned his back on them, going over to stare out of the window, while the men filed silently out of the office. What do you *do* if you're a precinct captain with a good record and all of a sudden you've got yourself three officers out on charges of attempted murder and aggravated assault, in less than one month? They sure as hell didn't know the answer to that question. They could understand why the captain didn't have anything more to say to them.

The last of the men was just reaching to push the button that would seal the door behind them, when the captain spoke one more time.

"Sergeant Dougherty?" he said. "You still there?"

"Yeah, Captain."

"You call Memorial, Dougherty. And you tell them."

"Tell them what, Captain Gilbert?"

"You tell them to send out the linguists."

Dougherty started to say something, and then he changed his mind. This was no time for arguing; the captain had enough on his plate.

"Yes, sir," he said instead. "Sure." And pushed the button by the door. Whatever, he thought. Linguists, snake charmers, fortune tellers, witch doctors . . . whatever. The captain had to do *some*thing, he could see that. If he wanted the linguists, Dougherty would by God get him the linguists.

Marvin Crike was not as calm about all this as Officer Dougherty had been. He didn't like the idea of taking a linguist team down into the swarming neighborhood in southwest Washington where the gang hung out. He didn't like being assigned to go talk to the members of the Channel Rats. He wouldn't have liked it even if he'd had a dozen armed police along to back them up. But being told he had to go with nobody but himself and Annie Lee Shofer and Tony Nahum was downright horrifying. One hospital staff linguist, one linguist from Social Services, and one flaming academic. On their own. He wasn't about to do that off the top of his head the way they were trying to get him to do it. No way.

"Data," he told Tim Bakerdon, the hospital's chief administrator. "Dr. Bakerdon, I need *lots* of data. Before I set even one of my timid little pampered feet down on those cold mean sidewalks."

Tim Bakerdon sighed, wishing not for the first time that it was police he was chief of instead of hospital personnel; it must be nice to simply give an order and know that it would be obeyed without argument, or else. He didn't have anything much in the way of an or-else option, especially with his staff linguist. Getting an equally competent replacement who'd come work here in the middle of the city, for the salary Memorial could pay, would not be easy. He'd only gotten Crike because Crike was a fanatic for challenge and Memorial was *all* challenge; Blakerdon knew that very well.

"Marvin," he said carefully, "this is an emergency."

"I know that."

"There isn't time for you to do one of your everlasting 'preliminary studies,' man, or spend six weeks in the library, or whatever it was you had in mind." He smiled at his crotchety subordinate, doing his hypocritical best to hide the way he really felt about the bastard's arrogance. "There've been three brutal—fiendishly brutal—beatings in Washington in the past three weeks, all committed by ordinary members of our own police force on the persons of young males from the Channel Rats. This city can't afford to go on losing one Channel Rat a week to berserker cops while you and your colleagues pile up the data."

Marvin raised his eyebrows. "You want *me* in the psych ward charged with aggravated assault?"

"You're not law enforcement. You don't go around beating up the public."

"Neither do our cops."

"Now, Marvin. . . . Police brutality is ugly, but it's a standard problem in any big city, any area with youth gangs. This is just an inflated and unusually nasty version of that standard problem. *Linguist* brutality, so far as I know, does not exist."

Marvin shrugged. "I don't care," he said. "I'll go talk to the Rats. I'll take a team in there. Okay. But we don't go till I know what I'm doing."

"How long?"

"Mmmm. That depends."

"On what?"

"On what's already available and what I have to go dig up for myself."

"Okay." Bakerdon shoved the pile of stuff in front of him toward the linguist. "Here's what we've got. Copy of the complete police file on this gang—they've only been around about a year and a half, so it's a skinny file. Neighborhood complaints, most of it—people despise these kids. Psych profiles on the three officers who went bonkers, and reports on half a dozen others involved in earlier, less serious, incidents. Apparently there's been very real trouble between the Channel Rats and the police ever since that young punk—what's his name? Chico Lafleur? That's not his real name, that's not *any*body's real name—ever since he took over the gang, anyway. Maybe the past seven or eight months."

"They should have called and asked for linguists sooner—any fool could surely see that this was a communications problem."

"That'll be the day," Bakerdon snorted. "Not until they are backs and asses to the wall and it's glowing red hot, will they ask for you eggheads. You know that."

"What else have you got?"

"There's a sociologist's preliminary report here—it doesn't look useful to me, but then I'm trained in medicine, what do I know? There's a list . . . names of the members, their ages, their addresses, known offenses, that sort of information. Some photographs from the scene of the three attacks—those I wish I hadn't seen, and as soon as I realized what they were I stopped looking at them, Marvin. Miscellaneous stuff. News reports, clippings. You know. You want data, this is data. I don't see what else you could need."

Marvin tapped the stack. "Anything alive in there?"

"What do you mean, alive?"

"I mean tapes. Recordings. Videotapes. Films."

"You need those?"

"I need those," said the linguist patiently. "I need to hear their speech. I need to watch them talking, see their body-parl."

"You can do that when you take the team down to Fourth Street, Crike."

"No, I can't. *First* I see a tape. And I analyze it. Thoroughly. *Then* I take the team in."

Bakerdon threw up his hands, knowing it was no use to argue with Marvin Crike. "There's nothing like that available," he objected. He cleared his throat elaborately and leaned back in his chair to stare at the other man. "I knew you'd ask for it," he said, "so I told them we needed it. And we asked around. We asked Georgetown University, we asked Howard University, we asked the libraries, we asked the news stations. Nobody's got anything. The Channel Rats are too new. Hell's Angels, I can get you. Dominos. Green Fiends. Sons of Satan. And so on. But nobody's recorded or filmed the Rats yet."

"Well, then," said Marvin, "that's probably the only other background material I need. Let's get it."

"How do you propose to do that?"

"The victims—the three youngsters that were attacked by the cops—they're all here in Memorial, right? Okay, you call police gang liaison. You have them call in some of the kids' friends to cheer them up. Hell, it's only a couple of weeks till Christmas—nobody's going to question the need for *cheer*, for God's sakes! And you make me a tape."

"That's illegal, Crike. We'd never get permission."

"Have you tried?"

"Marvin, for God's sake—"

"Get a court order. Give them a guarantee—once I've analyzed the video I'll destroy it. Tell *them* it's an emergency! And put cameras in those rooms."

"I don't know, Marvin," said Bakerdon dubiously.

"Do it," Marvin told him. "Or we can wait until a chance to film the kids falls into our laps. It's up to you."

"You're a pain in the butt, Marvin, you know that?"

Marvin shoved the chair back and gathered up the pile of materials. "I'm a scientist, Dr. Bakerdon," he said grimly. "That's why you hired me. I know what has to be done, and I know how to do it. And unlike you med-Sammys, flying by the seat of your pants while the patients drop like flies all around you, I don't do it any other way."

It took them only two days to get through the formalities, get the boys in, get the videos done. When they were finished, they had approximately an hour of usable tape that actually showed Channel Rats talking. They had lots and lots of backs of heads, and backs of backs, and long silences broken only by tinny Christmas carols playing through the speakers out in the halls.

"It's all right," Marvin told them. "I can manage."

"You're sure? It wouldn't be easy to get more. Even if we could get them to come back, nobody will talk to them more than a few seconds."

"I can manage, I said."

"What happens now?"

"I watch the tapes. I set them up for freeze-frames, so I can look long and hard at things that catch my eye. I run the tapes at all kinds of speeds. I run them forward, I run them backward. I analyze what I see and what I hear."

"Looking for *what*?"

Marvin shrugged. "How do I know? If I'd had a good working hypothesis, I wouldn't have needed the tapes. I'm looking for abnormal language behavior—that's all I can tell you."

"How long?"

"Maybe a week. Maybe a little more."

"*Shit!*"

"Sorry. It takes time."

"There's been another beating, Marvin."

"I'm sorry."

"This time the youngster was damn near dead on arrival. He was thirteen years old."

"*I cannot do it any faster than I do it.*"

"You could hurry, damn it," said Bakerdon furiously. "*We* hurried!"

"Linguists," Marvin Crike told him for what had to be the five hundredth time, "do not hurry."

"Make an exception just this once! In the spirit of the season! What's it going to cost you?"

"Sorry, Bakerdon. Can't be done."

The administrator put his head in his hands. "All right," he said wearily. "All right. Just go on and get started then, Crike. Whatever it is you do, go on and get started doing it. Before another kid gets mangled."

Four days later, when he had finished with the videos, Marvin sat in his cubbyhole of an office and thought it over. He was badly shaken; he didn't like this. It was both too simple and too hard, at the same time—and too scary. He was even less eager to go down to Fourth Street now than he had been before doing the analysis. Furthermore, he was pretty sure there was no *need* to go down there, after what he'd seen on the tapes. But how much of the certainty he felt was real, and how much was just his passionate desire not to go?

Marvin didn't know the answer to that. And so he called in the team and he told them what he thought he'd found; he ran the tapes for them, and he gave them hard copies of his analysis. And then he asked *them* if it was really necessary to go.

"You could be completely wrong, Marvin," stated Professor Tony Nahum, shaking his head. "You talk about improbable—you talk about un*like*ly! You could be clear off base."

"Sure," said Marvin. "And I could also be right, Tony."

Nahum pursed his lips and rubbed his chin with one finger, all pondering scholar, and said. "You've got to realize that what we're seeing here may be nothing but artifact. You've got gang kids here, Marvin. In a big hospital, at the request of the police, right before Christmas. Looking at the godawful mess those same police have made of their young friends. You can't base any conclusions on that kind of data. It could just be atypical behavior resulting from shock. From strain."

"I don't think so."

"Nobody here in the hospital laid a hand on the kids, Marvin."

"Nobody here in the hospital had time to talk to them more than half a minute at most, Tony! That's not long enough to set it off."

"You're really stretching for it," Nahum scoffed.

"I know I'm right," said Marvin stubbornly. "There's no question about it. You're just too pigheaded to admit it."

The other man flushed, and jabbed a finger at him like an aimed pistol. "Well, all right, hotshot, you want to explain to me how you *could* be right? I see what you mean, sure; but these kids are 100 percent worthless ignorant illiterate toughs with over-used sawdust for brains. How the *hell* would they learn to pull off the stuff you're proposing?"

"Marvin," Annie Lee broke in, "you can't even begin to guess what their speech or body-parl would be like under normal circumstances. You know better than that. These circumstances are *bizarre*—anybody's behavior would be off."

"What makes you think it'll be any better if we go down to Fourth Street?" Marvin demanded. "That's still artificial. It's still a bunch of outsiders poking around on their turf. We won't get normal speech that way, either, Annie Lee."

Annie Lee smiled at him, not fooled; she had known Marvin a very long time. "We can do a lot better than those tapes, Crike, so cut it out. At least the boys will be on familiar ground. And they won't be looking at other kids with their eyeballs gouged out and their ears torn off and all the rest of it."

"You both think we have to go?"

"I know we do," Tony answered. "So does Annie Lee. So do you."

"I don't want to."

"So what? It's the job we do, Marvin."

Marvin could have pointed out that it was damn rarely the job that Tony Nahum did. Ordinarily Tony was an old-fashioned linguist; he sat safe and serene and cozy in a classroom at Georgetown and told graduate students about Athabaskan verb prefixes. But he had come along willingly enough when Marvin had called him—he let it pass. And of course they were right. He'd known that before he asked them. He had just been hoping that they'd be better at inventing excuses than he was.

"Okay," he sighed. "Break out the street stuff. Stow away the lab coats. Into the valley of death. And so on."

"When do you want to go?"

"Never, but let's try for nine o'clock tomorrow morning. Maybe that's a reasonably safe time of day on Fourth Street."

They left, and Marvin sat down to run the tapes one more time. all the necessary reference materials right at hand, hoping he'd have a different reaction. But it was the same. Ten minutes into it, and he was sweating. None of the kids was talking to him directly, none of them was saying anything more than ordinary smartass kid stuff, but he was doing a slow burn. They were talking to the nurses, talking to the housekeeping staff, talking to doctors . . . not talking to him. And he still wanted to jump them. Wanted to hit them. He wasn't into kinky stuff yet, but he was headed that direction, and he was *not* a violent man. He was a man who cried in *Lassie* remakes. And the cops, Jesus, they'd been talking to those kids one on one, face to face, half an hour at a time. With the kids being snots at least, and probably worse than snots. Marvin was repulsed by his own reactions, but he could almost begin to understand what the cops had done.

If he was right. Could he be wrong, and the deviant behavior on the tape nothing more than the result of the tension the kids felt there in the hospital? Could be. He remembered visiting a friend dying of leukemia, in great pain, nothing anybody could do . . . if somebody had videotaped Marvin Louie Crike, Ph.D., that afternoon, they'd have gotten some damn strange-looking stuff. Could be. And so they were going to have to go take a look and a listen.

Slowly, viciously, Marvin kept his promise and destroyed the tapes. It wasn't as satisfactory as punching one of those snotnose kids would have been, but it was better than nothing.

The team of linguists went into the neighborhood at five minutes before nine. They weren't trained for undercover work, and they wouldn't have had time to set up a cover anyway. They tried for a decent compromise. They wore bluejeans and parkas, which marked them as old folks. And they carried nothing in their hands or on their persons. No notebooks, no recorders, no money, no plastic. Just their eyes and ears. Which marked them as *harmless* old folks.

And they came right straight back out forty minutes later, sick at their stomachs and twitching.

"If I'd been a cop," Marvin began. "If I had—"

"Don't, Marvin," said Annie Lee. "We were all there. We don't have to have you crossing the *t*'s for us. Please don't."

If he'd been a cop, if he had had a weapon, if he'd been trained for street fighting—or any kind of fighting—he would have attacked those kids. He was almost sure of it. He was almost sure that the only thing stopping him had been his fear. Which was no doubt the same thing that made the ordinary people on Fourth Street swallow hard and do nothing but call the precinct with vague complaints about the Rats having dirty mouths.

And he'd been right. There was that. It was a certain amount of personal satisfaction to know that, and to point it out to Tony and Annie Lee.

They told him to shut up.

The meeting was held that afternoon. With Bakerdon representing the hospital, and Gilbert there for the precinct, and an assortment of other bureaucrats from around the city. The purpose of the meeting was to explain what was going on, and what had to be done, and how to do it; looking at the hostile faces around the table, Marvin wished he had not torn up those tapes. It would have helped if he could have shown them to these men, especially if he had used the freeze-frame. But he hadn't thought of it, and now he was going to have to manage without them.

"What this gang is doing, gentlemen," he said hesitantly, testing the waters, "is something we've never seen done before. Not like this. Not deliberately, systematically, like this."

"Yeah?" The fellow from Family Court raised his eyebrows. "So what is it?"

"They're using language—deliberately, systematically—to provoke rage and violence."

"Ah, *shit*," declared Captain Gilbert with elaborate sarcasm, "now there's *new*! *Damn*, I wish I had a Ph.D. and could figure out good stuff like that!"

"No, it's not new," Marvin admitted. "Any time you give a cop the finger and go 'piggy-piggy-piggy' at him, that's what you're trying to do. But that's baby stuff, Captain, and you didn't let me finish. Police officers are trained to ignore that kind of behavior. It doesn't work on competent officers, even when it's a lot more subtle than my example. But these kids are way beyond that—these kids *know how to do it*."

Tim Bakerdon glared at him and Metcalf from Family Court made a rude noise and tipped his chair back and clasped his hands beside his head, and somebody at the far end told Marvin to quit beating around the bush for crissakes.

"These kids," Marvin said, "know how to use language to make even good cops . . . and good linguists . . . go into blind frenzies of rage they can't control. And they are getting a real kick out of what they're doing, too. It's a real power trip for them, a bunch of kids like that, making the police force of this city look like mindless maniacs."

"Worth getting beaten up for? Mutilated for? *Killed for*? It's that much fun?"

"I don't think that's supposed to happen," Marvin told them. "The idea is for the kid to keep pushing the cop right to the edge, over and over, without ever actually pushing him *off*. The idea is to see how close you can come. I think we're only getting these . . . incidents . . . when one of the younger ones cuts it too close. And you've got to remember . . . these are street kids. Boxing's never been a gentle pastime, but that hasn't kept kids like these from wanting the power and the status that go with that kind of abuse."

He grinned at them. "Think about it," he said. "Here's this big powerful cop, with his badge and his gun and his honcho image, and you're just a little kid, and you can pull his strings and make him dance. Sure, they'll take some risks for that! That's status. That's *points*. And these kids aren't used to tender loving care anyway."

"You said they can make good *linguists* go into blind rages," said a man with a Press badge and a good nose. "Does that mean you attacked them, too, Dr. Crike?"

Mervin saw Tim Bakerdon wince, with the reflex pain the Doctor of Medicine feels when the Doctor of Anything Else is granted the courtesy of the title, and he grinned again. A reciprocal reflex. "No," he answered, "we didn't touch them. But only because we were scared to. The police aren't scared of them—they don't have fear as a constraint on their reactions. We would have liked very much to attack them, believe me."

"But why? They're just kids!"

"Uhuh. They're just kids, but they're like kids with a big truck full of high explosives to play with. They've learned an extremely dangerous skill, and they're having dangerous fun with it, sir. They've learned to use their language—their spoken words and their body-parl, to cause rage—and that's very dangerous indeed."

"What, *exactly*, are they doing?" That was Captain Gilbert, sticking to the subject, both his arms folded on the table in front of him, and his jaw set tight.

"I've got a list here," Marvin said uneasily.

"Well? What's on it? Voodoo?"

Marvin stared at his notes, and he thought about it. The kids were systematically shifting the normal stresses in their speech one word forward; that was one item. They were using presuppositions to hide away the ugliest damn assertions inside the most innocent-sounding sentences. That was another item. They were using, over and over again, gestures representing the essentic forms that both expressed rage and hatred and evoked those two emotions in their listeners. That was yet another item. And he couldn't explain any of it without a set of preliminary lectures that would take a couple of forty-hour weeks and the willing cooperation of all these impatient alpha males.

"There's a lot of stuff on it," he told them, stalling, trying to think what he could give them that would be enough. Slowly, he said, "Basically, they're doing one big thing and throwing in all the rest of it as backup. And they're doing it with remarkable skill—none of it's easy."

"If they weren't so young," Annie Lee Sofer put in, "they probably couldn't do it. Except for the Lafleur fellow . . . he must be twenty-two, twenty-three . . . they're all of them young enough to still have a lot of their language acquisition skills intact." She shivered, then. "We'd rather not think about the really little kids, still at the peak of those skills, that have been following these boys around and looking up to them as role models."

The audience was restless, and more restless listening to a woman; Marvin looked thanks at Annie Lee out of the corner of one eye and hoisted the bale again. Tony, as always, was no help; he just sat and glowered and thought Significant Thoughts.

"Gentlemen," he said, "bear with us, please. This isn't easy to explain. Let's start with the one big thing I mentioned. It's more than enough."

"Go ahead," Bakerdon snapped. "*If* you'd be so kind."

"The primary tactic the Channel Rats are using is disruption of interactional synchrony." They all jerked, and he hurried to soothe them. "Now, wait! That's all the jargon you have to hear. Just give me a minute to explain, will you? When you talk, you use body language, and that body language is synchronized tidily with your speech. You'd expect that. But that's only half of it. When people *listen* to someone, they use body language too, whether they're saying any words aloud or not. And here's what is important—the listener's body language is *also* synchronized with the speaker's. That match, gentlemen, that shared rhythm, is called *interactional synchrony*, and it's a primary characteristic of all normal human speech. When you don't see it, you're usually seeing speech pathology. In this case, however, the Channel Rats aren't language impaired. On the contrary . . . they're pretty awesomely skilled."

Captain Gilbert made a rude noise and shoved his chair back through the shag. "Look here, Dr. Crike," he said, making no effort to conceal his disgust, "you can't expect us to take this seriously. You can't expect us to believe that what you're describing could possibly be enough to cause my men to—go apeshit the way they've been doing."

"Captain," Marvin said, "the Channel Rats are using those incredible skills to disrupt normal body-synch when they talk to people. And that—plus some other frills I'll put into a memo for you to read later, instead of burdening you with it now—is enough."

"I don't believe it," said the captain flatly. "I'm sorry I called you in. I must have been out of *my* mind. I do *not* believe it!"

"Believe it," Tony Nahum announced. And retired immediately back into his lofty silence, having done what he saw as his part.

"They have two techniques for this," Marvin said doggedly. He had known it would be bad, but this was worse than he had expected. He hadn't expected a flat declaration that he was either a liar or an idiot. Maybe he'd give up the hospital post and go back into the ivory tower himself. "One way is to delay their own body language just a fraction. Normal delay between a speaker's body language and the listener's is no more than twenty milliseconds—these kids are delaying a full half second. That puts them *always* out of synch just that much. And it's maddening for the person talking to them. The longer it goes on, the more maddening it gets. It takes tremendous control, tremendous concentration. It's a quantum jump from saying 'piggy, piggy.'"

He waited to be interrupted, but they were just sitting there looking at him, so he went on. "The other technique isn't as obviously a disruption, but it's just as abnormal. Normal listeners move when the speaker moves, sure. But they don't make the *same* moves the speaker makes. It's the rate and frequency of movement, of change of position, that's synchronized. But these kids are matching the speaker's body language *exactly*. Oh, they're smart—they'll leave out a grossly obvious gesture that might tip the speaker off—but except for that, they match it flawlessly. Every facial expression, every gesture, every shift in posture."

"Jesus," said the man from Family Court.

Did that mean he'd finally begun to get through to them?

"At *least*," Marvin said. "Maybe Joseph and Mary, too. You know how furious you can get when somebody mocks you? Remember when you were a kid and somebody did that, how it made you want to kill? Well, this is the same thing, except that it's Super-Mockery. And you wouldn't even know *why* you were getting so furious, you see—you'd have no reason to suspect what was going on."

"They switch back and forth," Annie Lee added, giving Marvin a break. "They'll do one for a while, then the other. Or they'll split it up—one kid will do the delay thing, and another kid will do the mirror trick. And although we didn't see it done, gentlemen, I am willing to bet that there are times when they do both at the same time. Which would be enough to drive an unsuspecting person *stark raving mad*."

The silence was thick and resentful, and Marvin wondered if he ought to bring up the other stuff. Should he try to tell them about essentic forms, the algorithms in the brain that associated one wave form with each of a set of basic emotions? Or try to explain normal English stress, and what its displacement could accomplish?

Nope; looking at their faces, he knew better. He would have needed at least a week of their time. It was going to be hard enough to get them to read about it in his memo.

"Are there any questions?" he asked. Carefully, he asked. Not pushing.

"Yeah," said the cop, gripping the table with both hands. "Yeah! You say this tactic made you linguists furious, too?"

"Damn straight it did, Captain Gilbert! Even watching the tapes, where the kids weren't talking directly to us, made us steam."

"That's hard to believe, Dr. Crike."

"I know it is," said Marvin. And saw an opening he could not resist. "Those kids," he said in his most casual voice, "have been taking shameless advantage of the ignorance of your officers."

Gilbert flinched, and gripped the table even harder. He would not have missed the reference to the Police Department's steadfast refusal, year after year, to add courses in linguistics to the curriculum at the Police Academy.

Bakerdon's function in life was to spread oil on troubled waters that might flow down his corridors. He spoke up before Marvin could create any more hard feelings. "Well, well, well," he said. His smile was pure yellow butter, fresh-melted. "Let's say we accept this, for the time being. I don't say I'm convinced, Marvin, but let's say we accept this as a kind of working diagnosis. If this *is* the problem, what can be done about it?"

"Shoot every last damn one of them," said one of the more impulsive officials present, and the others chuckled sympathetically.

"It's not any really big deal," Marvin told them. "You don't have to shoot them. Just send linguists to train the police to do their tricks back at them. Your officers will be too old to learn to do it really well, maybe, but they can get good enough at it to make it clear that that's what they're doing, and spoil all the fun. And those that genuinely cannot master the techniques can learn to *expect* the disruption of synchrony, and to recognize it, and to ignore it the same way they've learned to ignore obscenities in similar situations. And they can all learn things—we can teach them things—that will make it a lot harder for the Rats to do what they're doing."

"Will that—"

"Wait. I'm not through. Then you've got to go public with this," he said. "You've got to put out plenty of information, over all the news sources. You want the public to know what the tricks are, too, so that they won't get caught by their lack of linguistic sophistication the way the police have gotten caught."

"And then?" demanded Bakerdon. "Then what happens?"

"And then the Rats will quit doing what they're dong."

"It's that simple?"

"It's that simple. If what they're doing doesn't work, if it doesn't get them attention any longer, they'll quit doing it. Believe me, it's one hell of a lot too much work for them to do if it doesn't accomplish anything for them."

It was late when Marvin got back to his office. He'd had to sit through the obligatory closing ceremonies where the speeches were made about it being necessary to look into all of this very closely, and to get some additional opinions, and about how of *course* everybody had the utmost respect for linguists and appreciated the work they did and was *so* glad they'd been added to their staffs, but it wouldn't be proper not to at least consider other possibilities, no offense intended, blah blah blah.

He closed the door behind him, and took out of his desk drawer the manila envelope he'd had to pull in a few favors at M.I.T. to get his hands on and had had no chance to do more than glance at before the meeting. He didn't know what that bunch of idiots was going to do. Maybe they'd take the good advice given them and let the linguists teach them how to handle the effing little bastards and their cute tricks, and maybe they wouldn't. That wasn't his problem. His job, and his team's job, had been to tell them what had to be done and how to do it, and that was over. He had something else to think about now.

The men in that meeting hadn't even *asked* the most obvious question: where had these kids, these little 100-percent remedial and illiterate kids, learned *how* to do those fancy linguistic tricks? Shoot, the kids were only *talk*ing, right? They could *all* talk. They hadn't been impressed. Marvin saw it very differently.

From the very beginning, he'd had an idea—had formulated the only credible hypothesis. The behavior that had triggered the disturbed responses in the police had begun when Chico Lafleur took over as leader of the Channel Rats; therefore, they had learned all their tricks from Lafleur. And there was only one place that Lafleur could have learned them. Which had meant two tasks for Marvin: first, find out what the young man's real name was; second, get a copy of his college transcript. Because unless something preposterous was going on, there *would be* a college transcript, and the set of universities it could have come from was a small one and quickly investigated.

To Marvin's surprise, the man's name really *was* Lafleur. John Lafleur, not Chico, but Lafleur all the same, out of southern Louisiana. The transcript was not a surprise in any way. It had just what he'd expected it to have: neat rows of A's, one for each of the linguistics classes listed; neat rows of F's, one for each of the other classes he'd wandered into. It would have jarred Marvin if the A's had been in chemistry or English literature. And then the rubber-stamped note that Lafleur had dropped out. . . . Marvin knew how that happened. Professors who'd petrified long ago, and a case of terminal fedupness in the kid. He'd seen a lot of that before he got off the Ivory Tower Circuit.

He was a patient man, and he wanted what Lafleur had, badly. He'd wait for it. He'd spend the time it took. It would mean making a lot of phone calls; it would mean hassling the precinct's Gang Liaison people again, it would mean pulling some strings. But eventually he'd have John Lafleur on the other end of a telephone line. Maybe he'd get lucky and be able to offer Lafleur something he hadn't expected for Christmas.

He knew how he was going to approach the man. "John Lafleur?" he'd say. "Listen, this is Marvin Crike, Staff Linguist over at Memorial. Listen, I want you to come on down here and talk to me, Mr. Lafleur. I've got a lot of work for you to do. I've got work you'd *pay* for the chance to do, Lafleur, but I've got a surprise for you—you don't have to. No way. In fact, it's the other way around. I've got money to pay *you* for doing it, a whole lot of money. Lafleur, we need you down here. We need you to do some real linguistics, no more mickeymouse, and we can afford you. Come on down, Lafleur, and let me make you a rich and happy man!"

Marvin intended to lay it on so thick that even somebody as streetwise as this man would stop by, just to see if he was as outrageous as he sounded. Because he wanted to know everything Lafleur knew; he wanted to pick Lafleur's brains clean the way you pick the last fragment of pale meat out of a walnut. He positively lusted after the brains of John Lafleur, whose professors had obviously been pompous old farts far gone in punctuation worship.

He sat there smiling to himself, thinking about what he was going to do with the things Lafleur could teach him, and the things he and Lafleur could move on to do, working together. It was going to be a long and a satisfying association.

"Silent night, holy night," sang Marvin Crike, under his breath. Wishing himself a Merry Christmas and a spectacular New Year, while the five o'clock dark plunged down over Washington, and the lights came on outside, one by one.

FLORIDA

The Legend of Joe Lee
by John D. MacDonald

"TONIGHT," Sergeant Lazeer said, "we get him for sure."

We were in a dank office in the Afaloosa County Courthouse in the flat wetlands of south central Florida. I had come over from Lauderdale on the half chance of a human interest story that would tie in with the series we were doing on the teenage war against the square world of the adult.

He called me over to the table where he had the county map spread out. The two other troopers moved in beside me.

"It's a full moon night and he'll be out for sure," Lazeer said, "and what we're fixing to do is bottle him on just the right stretch, where he got no way off it, no old back country roads he knows like the shape of his own fist. And here we got it." He put brackets at either end of a string-straight road.

Trooper McCollum said softly, "That there, Mister, is a eighteen mile straight, and we cruised it slow, and you turn on off it you're in the deep ditch and the black mud and the 'gator water."

Lazeer said, "We stake out both ends, hide back good with lights out. We got radio contact, so when he comes whistling in either end, we got him bottled."

He looked up at me as though expecting an opinion, and I said, "I don't know a thing about road blocks, Sergeant, but it looks as if you could trap him."

"You ride with me, Mister, and we'll get you a story."

"There's one thing you haven't explained, Sergeant. You said you know who the boy is. Why don't you just pick him up at home?"

The other trooper Frank Gaiders said, "Because that fool kid ain't been home since he started this crazy business five-six months ago. His name is

133

Joe Lee Cuddard, from over to Lasco City. His folks don't know where he is, and don't much care, him and that Farris girl he was running with, so we figure the pair of them is off in the piney woods someplace, holed up in some abandoned shack, coming out at night for kicks, making fools of us."

"Up till now, boy," Lazeer said. "Up till tonight. Tonight is the end."

"But when you've met up with him on the highway," I asked, "you haven't been able to catch him?"

The three big, weathered men looked at each other with slow, sad amusement, and McCollum sighed, "I come the closest. The way these cars are beefed up as interceptors, they can do a dead honest hundred and twenty. I saw him across the flats, booming to where the two road forks come together up ahead, so I floored it and I was flat out when the roads joined, and not over fifty yards behind him. In two minutes he had me by a mile, and in four minutes it was near two, and then he was gone. That comes to a hundred and fifty, my guess."

I showed my astonishment. "What the hell does he drive?"

Lazeer opened the table drawer and fumbled around in it and pulled out a tattered copy of a hot-rodder magazine. He opened it to a page where readers had sent in pictures of their cars. It didn't look like anything I had ever seen. Most of it seemed to be bare frame, with a big chromed engine. There was a teardrop shaped passenger compartment mounted between the big rear wheels, bigger than the front wheels, and there was a tail-fin arrangement that swept up and out and then curved back so that the high rear ends of the fins almost met.

"That engine," Frank Gaiders said, "it's a '61 Pontiac, the big one he bought wrecked and fixed up, with blowers and special cams and every damn thing. Put the rest of it together himself. You can see in the letter there, he calls it a C.M. Special. C.M. is for Clarissa May, that Farris girl he took off with. I saw that thing just one time, oh, seven, eight months ago, right after he got it all finished. We got this magazine from his daddy. I saw it at the Amoco gas in Lasco City. You could near give it a ticket standing still. Strawberry flake paint it says in the letter. Damnedest thing, bright strawberry with little like gold flakes in it, then covered with maybe seventeen coats of lacquer all rubbed down so you look down into that paint like it was six inches deep. Headlights all the hell over the front of it and big taillights all over the back, and shiny pipes sticking out. Near two years he worked on it. Big racing flats like the drag strip kids use over to the airport."

I looked at the coarse screen picture of the boy standing beside the car, hands on his hips, looking very young, very ordinary, slightly self-conscious.

"It wouldn'd spoil anything for you, would it," I asked, "if I went and talked to his people, just for background?"

"'Long as you say nothing about what we're fixing to do," Lazeer said. "Just be back by eight thirty this evening."

Lasco City was a big brave name for a hamlet of about five hundred. They told me at the sundries store to take the west road and the Cuddard place was a half mile on the left, name on the mailbox. It was a shacky place, chickens in the dusty yard, fence sagging. Leo Cuddard was home from work and I found him out in back, unloading cinder block from an ancient pickup. He was stripped to the waist, a lean, sallow man who looked undernourished and exhausted. But the muscles in his spare back writhed and knotted when he lifted the blocks. He had pale hair and pale eyes and a narrow mouth. He would not look directly at me. He grunted and kept on working as I introduced myself and stated my business.

Finally he straightened and wiped his forehead with his narrow arm. When those pale eyes stared at me, for some reason it made me remember the grisly reputation Florida troops acquired in the Civil War. Tireless, deadly, merciless.

"That boy warn't no help to me, Mister, but he warn't no trouble neither. The onliest thing on his mind was that car. I didn't hold with it, but I didn't put down no foot. He fixed up that old shed there to work in, and he needed something, he went out and earned up the money to buy it. They was a crowd of them around most times, helpin' him, boys workin' and gals watchin'. Them tight-pants girls. Have radios on batteries set around so as they could twisty dance while them boys hammered that metal out. When I worked around and overheard 'em, I swear I couldn't make out more'n one word from seven. What he done was take that car to some national show, for prizes and such. But one day he just took off, like they do nowadays."

"Do you hear from him at all?"

He grinned. "I don't hear *from* him, but I sure God hear *about* him."

"How about brothers and sisters?"

"They's just one sister, older, up to Waycross, Georgia, married to an electrician, and me and his stepmother."

As if on cue, a girl came out onto the small back porch. She couldn't have been more than eighteen. Advanced pregnancy bulged the front of her cotton dress. Her voice was a shrill, penetrating whine. "Leo? Leo, honey, that can opener thing just now busted clean off the wall."

"Mind if I take a look at that shed?"

"You help yourself, Mister."

The shed was astonishingly neat. The boy had rigged up droplights. There was a pale blue pegboard wall hung with shining tools. On closer inspection I could see that rust was beginning to fleck the tools. On the workbench were technical journals and hot-rodder magazines. I looked at the improvised engine hoist, at the neat shelves of paint and lubricant.

The Farris place was nearer the center of the village. Some of them were having their evening meal. There were six adults as near as I could judge, and perhaps a dozen children from toddlers on up to tall, lanky boys. Clarissa May's mother came out onto the front porch to talk to me explaining that her husband drove an interstate truck from the cooperative and he was away from the next few days. Mrs. Farris was grossly fat, but with delicate features, an indication of the beauty she must have once had. The rocking chair creaked under her weight and she fanned herself with a newspaper.

"I can tell you, it like to broke our hearts the way Clarissa May done us. If'n I told LeRoy once, I told him a thousand times, no good would ever come of her messin' with that Cuddard boy. His daddy is trashy. Ever so often they take him in for drunk and put him on the county road gang sixty or ninety days, and that Stubbins child he married, she's next door to feeble-witted. But children get to a certain size and know everything and turn their backs on you like an enemy. You write this up nice and in it put the message her momma and daddy want her home bad, and maybe she'll see it and come on in. You know what the Good Book says about sharper'n a serpent's tooth. I pray to the good Lord they had the sense to drive that fool car up to Georgia and get married up at least. Him nineteen and her seventeen. The young ones are going clean out of hand these times. One night racing through this county the way they do, showing off, that Cuddard boy is going to kill hisself and my child too."

"Was she hard to control in other ways, Mrs. Farris?"

"No, sir, she was neat and good and pretty and quiet, and she had the good marks. It was just about Joe Lee Cuddard she turned mulish. I think I would have let LeRoy whale that out of her if it hadn't been for her trouble.

"You're easier on a young one when there's no way of knowing how long she could be with you. Doc Mathis, he had us taking her over to the Miami clinic. Sometimes they kept her and sometimes they didn't, and she'd get behind in her school and then catch up fast. Many times we taken her over there. She's got the sick blood and it takes her poorly. She should be right here, where's help to care for her in the bad spells. It was October last year, we were over to the church bingo, LeRoy and me, and Clarissa May been resting up in her bed a few days, and that wild boy come in and taking her off in that snorty car, the little ones couldn't stop him. When I think of her out there . . . poorly and all. . . ."

At a little after nine we were in position. I was with Sergeant Lazeer at the west end of that eighteen mile stretch of State Road 21. The patrol car was backed into a narrow dirt road, lights out. Gaiders and McCollum were similarly situated at the east end of the trap. We were smeared with insect repellent, and we had used spray on the backs of each other's shirts where the mosquitoes were biting through the thin fabric.

Lazeer had repeated his instructions over the radio, and we composed ourselves to wait. "Not much travel on this road this time of year," Lazeer said. "But some tourists come through at the wrong time, they could mess this up. We just got to hope that don't happen."

"Can you block the road with just one car at each end?"

"If he comes through from the other end, I move up quick and put it crosswise where he can't get past, and Frank has a place like that at the other end. Crosswise with the lights and the dome blinker on, but we both are going to stand clear because maybe he can stop it and maybe he can't. But whichever way he comes, we got to have the free car run close herd so he can't get time to turn around when he sees he's bottled."

Lazeer turned out to be a lot more talkative than I had anticipated. He had been in law enforcement for twenty years and had some violent stories. I sensed he was feeding them to me, waiting for me to suggest I write a book about him. From time to time we would get out of the car and move around a little.

"Sergeant, you're pretty sure you've picked the right time and place?"

"He runs on the nights the moon is big. Three or four nights out of the month. He doesn't run the main highways, just these back country roads—the long straight paved stretches where he can really wind that thing up. Lord God, he goes through towns like a rocket. From reports we got, he runs the whole night through, and this is one way he comes, one way or the other, maybe two, three times before moonset. We got to get him. He's got folks laughing at us."

I sat in the car half listening to Lazeer tell a tale of blood and horror. I could hear choruses of swamp toads mingling with the whine of insects close to my ears, looking for a biting place. A couple of times I had heard the bass throb of a 'gator.

Suddenly Lazeer stopped and I sensed his tenseness. He leaned forward, head cocked. And then, mingled with the wet country shrilling, and then overriding it, I heard the oncoming high-pitched snarl of high combustion.

"Hear it once and you don't forget it," Lazeer said, and unhooked the mike from the dash and got through to McCollum and Gaiders. "He's coming through this end, boys. Get yourself set."

He hung up and in the next instant the C.M. Special went by. It was a resonant howl that stirred echoes inside the inner ear. It was a tearing, bursting rush of wind that rattled fronds and turned leaves over. It was a dark shape in the moonlight, slamming by, the howl diminishing as the wind of passage died.

Lazeer plunged the patrol car out onto the road in a screeching turn, and as we straightened out, gathering speed, he yelled to me, "Damn fool runs without lights when the moon is bright enough."

As had been planned, we ran without lights too, to keep Joe Lee from smelling the trap until it was too late. I tightened my seat belt and peered at the moonlit road. Lazeer had estimated we could make it to the far end in ten minutes or a little less. The world was like a photographic negative—white world and black trees and brush, and no shades of grey. As we came quickly up to speed, the heavy sedan began to feel strangely light. It toe-danced, tender and capricious, the wind roar louder than the engine sound. I kept wondering what would happen if Joe Lee stopped dead up there in darkness. I kept staring ahead for the murderous bulk of his vehicle.

Soon I could see the distant red wink of the other sedan, and then the bright cone where the headlights shone off the shoulder into the heavy brush. When my eyes adjusted to that brightness, I could no longer see the road. We came down on them with dreadful speed. Lazeer suddenly snapped our lights on, touched the siren. We were going to see Joe Lee trying to back and turn around on the narrow paved road, and we were going to block him and end the night games.

We saw nothing. Lazeer pumped the brakes. He cursed. We came to a stop ten feet from the side of the other patrol car. McCollum and Gaiders came out of the shadows. Lazeer and I undid our seat belts and got out of the car.

"We didn't see nothing and we didn't hear a thing," Frank Gaiders said.

Lazeer summed it up. "OK, then. I was running without lights too. Maybe the first glimpse he got of your flasher, he cramps it over onto the left shoulder, tucks it over as far as he dares. I could go by without seeing him. He backs around and goes back the way he came, laughing hisself sick. There's the second chance he tried that and took it too far, and he's wedged in a ditch. Then there's the third chance he lost it. He could have dropped a wheel off onto the shoulder and tripped hisself and gone flying three hundred feet into the swamp. So what we do, we go back there slow. I'll go first and keep my spotlight on the right, and you keep yours on the left. Look for that car and for places where he could have busted through."

At the speed Lazeer drove it took over a half hour to traverse the eighteen mile stretch. He pulled off at the road where we had waited. He seemed very depressed, yet at the same time amused.

They talked, then he drove me to the courthouse where my car was parked. He said. "We'll work out something tighter and I'll give you a call. You might as well be in at the end."

I drove sedately back to Lauderdale.

Several days later, just before noon on a bright Sunday, Lazeer phoned me at my apartment and said, "You want to be in on the finish of this thing, you better do some hustling and leave right now."

"You've got him?"

"In a manner of speaking." He sounded sad and wry. "He dumped that machine into a canal off Route 27 about twelve miles south of Okeelanta. The wrecker'll be winching it out anytime now. The diver says he and the gal are still in it. It's been on the radio news. Diver read the tag, and it's his. Last year's. He didn't trouble hisself getting a new one."

I wasted no time driving to the scene. I certainly had no trouble identifying it. There were at least a hundred cars pulled off on both sides of the highway. A traffic control officer tried to wave me on by, but when I showed him my press card and told him Lazeer had phoned me, he had me turn in the park beside a patrol car near the center of activity.

I spotted Lazeer on the canal bank and went over to him. A big man in face mask, swim fins and air tank was preparing to go down with the wrecker hook.

Lazeer greeted me and said, "It pulled loose the first time, so he's going to try to get it around the rear axle this time. It's in twenty feet of water, right side up, in the black mud."

"Did he lose control?"

"Hard to say. What happened early this morning a fellow was goofing around in a little airplane, flying low, parallel to the canal, the water like a mirror, and he seen something down in there so he came around and looked again, then he found a way to mark the spot, opposite those three trees away over there, so he came into his home field and phoned it in, and we had that diver down by nine this morning. I got here about ten."

"I guess this isn't the way you wanted it to end, Sergeant."

"It sure God isn't. It was a contest between him and me, and I wanted to get him my own way. But I guess it's a good thing he's off the night roads."

I looked around. The red and white wrecker was positioned and braced. Ambulance attendants were leaning against their vehicle, smoking and chatting. Sunday traffic slowed and was waved on by.

"I guess you could say his team showed up," Lazeer said.

Only then did I realize the strangeness of most of the waiting vehicles. The cars were from a half-dozen counties, according to the tag numbers. There were many big, gaudy, curious monsters not unlike the C.M. Special in basic layout, but quite different in design. They seemed like a visitation of Martian beasts. There were dirty fenderless sedans from the thirties with modern power plants under the hoods, and big rude racing numbers painted on the side doors. There were other cars which looked normal at first glance, but then seemed to squat oddly low, lines clean and sleek where the Detroit chrome had been taken off, the holes leaded up.

The cars and the kids were of another race. Groups of them formed, broke up and re-formed. Radios brought in a dozen stations. They drank Cokes and perched in dense flocks on open convertibles. They wandered from car to car. It had a strange carnival flavor, yet more ceremonial. From time to time somebody would start one of the car engines, rev it up to a bursting roar, and let it die away.

All the girls had long burnished hair and tidy blouses or sun tops and a stillness in their faces, a curious confidence of total acceptance which seemed at odds with the frivolous and provocative tightness of their short shorts, stretch pants, jeans. All the boys were lean, their hairdos carefully ornate, their shoulders high and square, and they moved with the lazy grace of young jungle cats. Some of the couples danced indolently, staring into each other's eyes with a frozen and formal intensity, never touching, bright hair swinging, girls' hips pumping in the stylized ceremonial twist.

Along the line I found a larger group. A boy was strumming slow chords on a guitar, a girl making sharp and erratic fill-in rhythm on a set of bongos.

Another boy, in nasal and whining voice, seemed to improvise lyrics as he sang them. "C.M. Special, let it get out and *go*./C.M. Special, let it way out and *go*./Iron runs fast and the moon runs slow."

The circle watched and listened with a contained intensity.

Then I heard the winch whining. It seemed to grow louder as, one by one, the other sounds stopped. The kids began moving toward the wrecker. They formed a big silent semicircle. The taut woven cable, coming in very slowly, stretched down at an angle through the sun glitter on the black-brown water.

The snore of a passing truck covered the winch noise for a moment.

"Coming good now," a man said.

First you could see an underwater band of silver, close to the drop-off near the bank. Then the first edges of the big sweeping fins broke the surface then the broad rear bumper, then the rich curves of the strawberry paint. Where it wasn't clotted with wet weed or stained with mud, the paint glowed rich and new and brilliant. There was a slow sound from the kids, a sigh, a murmur, a shifting.

As it came up further, the dark water began to spurt from it, and as the water level inside dropped, I saw, through a smeared window, the two huddled masses, the slumped boy and girl, side by side, still belted in.

I wanted to see no more. Lazeer was busy, and I got into my car and backed out and went home and mixed a drink.

I started work on it at about three thirty that afternoon. It would be a feature for the following Sunday. I worked right on through until two in the morning. It was only two thousand words, but it was very tricky and I wanted to get it just right. I had to serve two masters. I had to give lip service to the editorial bias that this sort of thing was wrong, yet at the same time I wanted to capture, for my own sake, the flavor of legend. These kids were making a special world we could not share. They were putting all their skills and dreams and energies to work composing the artifacts of a subculture, power, beauty, speed, skill and rebellion. Our culture was giving them damned little, so they were fighting for a world of their own, with its own customs, legends and feats of valor, its own music, its own ethics and morality.

I took it in Monday morning and left it on Si Walther's desk, with the hope that if it were published intact, it might become a classic. I called it "The Little War of Joe Lee Cuddard."

I didn't hear from Si until just before noon. He came out and dropped it on my desk. "Sorry," he said.

"What's the matter with it?"

"Hell, it's a very nice bit. But we don't publish fiction. You should have checked it out better, Marty, like you usually do. The examiner says those kids have been in the bottom of that canal for maybe eight months. I had Sam check her out through the clinic. She was damn near terminal eight months ago. What probably happened, the boy went to see her and found her so bad off he got scared and decided to rush her to Miami. She was still in her pajamas, with a sweater over them. That way it's a human interest bit. I had Helen do it. It's page one this afternoon, boxed."

I took my worthless story, tore it in half and dropped it into the wastebasket. Sergeant Lazeer's bad guess about the identity of his moonlight road runner had made me look like an incompetent jackass. I vowed to check all facts, get all names right, and never again indulge in glowing, strawberry flake prose.

Three weeks later I got a phone call from Sergeant Lazeer.

He said, "I guess you figured out we got some boy coming in from out of county to fun us these moonlight nights."

"Yes, I did."

"I'm right sorry about you wasting that time and effort when we were thinking we were after Joe Lee Cuddard. We're having some bright moonlight about now, and it'll run full tomorrow night. You want to come over, we can show you some fun, because I got a plan that's dead sure. We tried it last night, but there was just one flaw, and he got away through a road we didn't know about. Tomorrow he won't get that chance to melt away."

I remembered the snarl of that engine, the glimpse of a dark shape, the great wind of passage. Suddenly the backs of my hands prickled. I remembered the emptiness of that stretch of road when we searched it. Could there have been that much pride and passion, labor and love and hope, that Clarissa May and Joe Lee could forever ride the night roads of their home county, balling through the silver moonlight? And what curious message had assembled all those kids from six counties so quickly?

"You there? You still there?"

"Sorry, I was trying to remember my schedule. I don't think I can make it."

"Well, we'll get him for sure this time."

"Best of luck. Sergeant."

"Six cars this time. Barricades. And a spotter plane. He hasn't got a chance if he comes into the net."

I guess I should have gone. Maybe hearing it again, glimpsing the dark shape, feeling the stir of the night wind, would have convinced me of its reality. They didn't get him, of course. But they came so close, so very close. But they left just enough room between a heavy barricade and a live oak tree, an almost impossibly narrow place to slam through. But thread it he did, and rocket back onto the hard top and plunge off, leaving the fading, dying contralto drone.

Sergeant Lazeer is grimly readying next month's trap. He says it is the final one. Thus far, all he has captured are the two little marks, a streak of paint on the rough edge of a timber sawhorse, another nudge of paint on the trunk of the oak. Strawberry red. Flecked with gold.

GEORGIA

Seventh Sister
by Mary Elizabeth Counselman

THE NIGHT Seven Sisters was born, a squinch-owl hollered outside the cabin from sundown until the moment of her birth. Then it stopped its quavering cry. Everything stopped—the whippoorwills in the loblollies; the katydids in the fig tree beside the well; even the tree-frogs, burring their promise of rain as "sheet lightning" flickered across the black sky.

The row of slave cabins behind the Old Place looked ramshackle and deserted; had been deserted, for a fact, ever since Grant took Richmond. Daylight or a moon would have shown their shingle roofs fallen in and their sagging porches overgrown with jimson weed and honeysuckle. Only one cabin was livable now and inhabited. Dody, grandson of a Saunders slave, had wandered back to the Old Place, with a wife and a flock of emaciated little pickaninnies.

They had not thrived on odd-job fare in the city. So Dody had come home, the first year of the Depression, serenely certain of his welcome. He knew Cap'm Jim and Miss Addie would give them a cabin with a truck garden, in return for whatever sporadic labor was needed on the old rundown plantation smack on the Alabama–Georgia line.

That was in '29, six years ago. Miss Addie was dead now and buried in the family cemetery on the south hill. Most of the land had been sold to meet taxes. Miss Addie's grandson, Cap'm Jim, alone was left. Cap'm Jim was a baby doctor in Chattanooga. He kept the Old Place closed up except for weekend trips down with his wife and two young sons.

The red clay fields lay fallow and uncultivated. The rail fences had fallen, and even the white-columned Place itself was leaky and in some need of paint. Whenever Dody or Mattie Sue thought of it, they had one of the young-uns sweep the leaves and chicken-sign from the bare sanded clay of the front yard. But aside from that weekly chore, they had the deserted plantation all to themselves, and lived accordingly. The children grew fat and sassy on yams and chitterlings. Dody drank more homebrew and slept all day in the barrel-slat hammock. And Mattie cooked, quarreled and bore another pickaninny every year. . . .

That is, until Seven Sisters was born.

That night a squinch-owl hollered. And somewhere beyond the state highway, a dog howled three times. More than that, one of the martins, nesting in the gourd-pole in front of the cabin, got into the house and beat its brains out against the walls before anyone could set it free.

Three Signs! Small wonder that at sundown Mattie Sue was writhing in agony of premature childbirth. Not even the two greased axes, which Ressie and Clarabelle—her oldest unmarried daughters; aged fifteen and seventeen—had placed under her bed to cut the pain, did any good.

"Oh, Lawsy—Mammy done took bad!" Ressie whimpered.

She hovered over the fat groaning black woman on the bed, eyewhites large and frightened in her pretty Negro face. Ressie had seen many of her brothers and sisters come into the world. But always before, Mattie Sue had borne as easily and naturally as a cat.

"Do, my Savior!" Clarabelle whispered. "We got to git somebody to midwife her! Aunt Fan. . . . Go 'long and fotch her, quick! Oh Lawsy. . . ." she wailed, holding high the kerosene lamp and peering down at the woman in pain. "I . . . I'se sho skeered. . . . What you waitin' on fool? Run! . . . Oh, Lawsy, mammy . . . mammy?"

Ressie plunged out into the night. The *slap-slap* of her bare feet trailed into silence.

The cabin's front room was very still. Save for the regular moaning of Dody's wife—and an occasional snore from Dody himself, drunk and asleep on the kitchen floor—there was no sound within. The other children were clustered in one corner, silent as young foxes. Only the whites of their eyes were visible against the dark. Clarabelle tiptoed about in her mail-order print dress, her chemically straightened hair rolled up on curlers for the church social tomorrow.

Light from the sooty lamp threw stunted shadows. The reek of its kerosene and the smell of Negro bodies blended with the pungent odor of peaches hung in a string to dry beside the window. Hot summer scents drifted in: sun-baked earth, guano from the garden, the cloying perfume of a clematis vine running along the porch rafters.

It was all so familiar—the smells, the night-sounds. The broken and mended furniture, discarded by four generations of Saunderses. The pictures tacked on the plank walls—of a snow-scene, of a Spanish dancer, of the president—torn from old magazines Cap'm Jim and Miss Ruth had cast aside. The last year's feedstore calendar, dated January 1934. The gilded wreath, saved from Miss Addie's funeral, now decorating the mantel with its purple and gilt ribbon rain-marred to read: ABID WI H MF.

Even the childbirth scene was familiar to all of Mattie's children except the youngest. And yet. . . .

There was an eerie quality about the night, throwing the familiar out of focus. The young-uns felt it, huddled, supperless, in the corner while Clarabelle fluttered ineffectually about the bed and its burden. It was so hot and oppressive, with a curious air of waiting. Even a rumble of thunder along the horizon sounded hushed and furtive.

And the screech-owl's cry drifted nearer.

The woman on the bed writhed and moaned again. Clarabelle twisted her black hands together, bright with pink nail polish—relic of the winters spent in Chattanooga as nurse for Cap'm Jim's youngest. She went to the open door for a fourth time, listening for the sound of approaching footsteps.

Aunt Fan had a cabin down the road about a half a mile, and had washed for the Andrews as far back as anyone remembered. She was a church woman; in fact, one of her three husbands had been a preacher before he knifed a man and got sent away to prison. If anyone could help Mattie Sue in her extremity, it would be Aunt Fan. . . .

The squinch-owl wailed again. Clarabelle drew a quick circle on the cabin floor and spat in it. But the moaning of her mother went on and on, incoherent, rising and falling as though in imitation of the owl's ill-omened call.

Clarabelle stiffened, listening. The hurried *crunch-crunch* of shod feet came to her ears at last. With a gasp of relief she ran out to meet the pair—Ressie, returning, and a tiny wizened old Negress with a wen in the center of her forehead, jutting out like a blunt horn.

"Aunt Fan, what I tell you? Listen yonder!" Ressie whimpered. "Dat ole squinch-owl been holl'in' fit to be tied ever since sundown!"

The old midwife poised on the porch step, head cocked. She grunted, and with a slow, precise gesture took off her apron, to don it again wrong-side out.

"Dah. Dat oughta fix 'im. What-at Mattie Sue? My land o' Goshen, dat young-un don't b'long to get borned for two month yet! She been workin' in de garden?"

"Well'm. . . ." Clarabelle started to lie, then nodded, contrite. "Seem like she did do a little weedin' yestiddy. . . ."

"Uh-huh! So dat's hit! I done tole her! Dat low-down triflin' Dody. . . ." Aunt Fan, with a snort that included all men, switched into the cabin.

Outside, the screech-owl chuckled mockingly, as though it possessed a deeper knowledge of the mystery of birth and death.

Ressie and Clarabelle hunched together on the front stoop. Through the door they could hear Aunt Fan's sharp voice ordering the pickaninnies out of her way into the kitchen. Mattie Sue's regular moaning had risen in timbre to a shrill cry. Clarabelle, squatting on the log step of the porch, whispered under her breath.

"Huh!" Ressie muttered. "Ain't no use prayin' wid dat ole squinch-owl holl'in' his fool head off! Oh, Lawsy, Clary, you reckon Aunt Fan can . . .?"

The older girl shivered but did not reply. Her eyes, wide and shining from the window's glow, swept across the flat terrain. Fireflies twinkled in the scrub pines beyond the cornfield. A muffled roar from above caught her ear once. She raised her head. Wing lights on a transport plane, racing the storm from Birmingham to Atlanta, winked down at her, then vanished in the clouds.

"'Leb'm-thirty," she murmured. "Less hit's late tonight. . . . Daggone! If'n dat ole fool don't shet up his screechin'. . . ." She hushed herself, sheepishly fearful of her own blasphemy.

Of course there was nothing to all that stuff her mammy and Aunt Fan had passed down to them, huddling before the fire on rainy nights. Signs! Omens! Juju . . . Cap'm Jim had laughed and told them, often enough, that. . . .

The girl started violently. From the cabin a scream shattered the night. High-pitched. Final.

Then everything was still. The tree-frogs. The quarreling katydids. The whippoorwills. The muttering thunder. A trick of wind even carried away the sound of the transport plane.

And the screech-owl stopped hollering, like an evil spirit swallowed up by the darkness.

A few minutes later Aunt Fan came to the door, a tiny bundle in her arms swaddled in an old dress of Mattie's. The girls leaped to their feet, wordless, eager.

But the old Negress in the doorway did not speak. She was murmuring something under her breath that sounded like a prayer—or an incantation. There was a sinister poise to her tiny form framed in the lighted doorway, silent, staring out into the night.

Suddenly she spoke.

"Clary honey . . . Ressie. You' Mammy done daid. Wan't nothin' I could do. But . . . my soul to Glory! Hit's somep'm funny about dis gal-baby! She white as cotton! I reckon yo' mammy musta had a sin on she soul, how come de Lawd taken her. . . ."

Clarabelle gasped a warning. A broad hulk had blotted out the lamplight behind Aunt Fan—Dody, awake, still drunk, and mean. A tall sepia Negro, wearing only his overalls, he swayed against the door for support, glowering down at the bundle in Aunt Fan's arms.

"Woods-colt!" Dody growled. "I ain't gwine feed no woods-colt. . . . Git hit on out'n my cabin! I got eight young-uns o' my own to feed, workin' myself down to a frazzle. . . . Git hit on out, I done tole you!" he snarled, aiming a side swipe at Aunt Fan that would have knocked her sprawling if it had landed.

But the old Negress ducked nimbly, hopped out onto the porch, and glared back at Dody. Her tiny black eyes glittered with anger and outrage, more for herself than for the squirming handful of life in her embrace.

"You Dody Saunders!" Aunt Fan shrilled. "You big low-down triflin' piece o' trash! I gwine tell Cap'm Jim on you! Jes' wait and see don't I tell 'im! Th'owin' Mattie's own baby out'n de house like she want nothin' but a mess o' corn shucks! And Mattie layin' daid in yonder. . . ."

Dody swayed, bleary eyes trying to separate the speaker from her alcoholic image.

"Daid? M-mattie Sue . . . my Mattie Sue done daid? Oh, Lawsy—why'n you tell me . . . ?"

His blunt, brutal features crumpled all at once, childlike in grief. He whirled back into the cabin toward the quilt-covered bed. "Mattie?" the three on the porch heard his voice. "Mattie honey? Hit's your Dody—say somep'm, honey. . . . Don't sull up like dat and be mad at Dody! What I done now? . . . Mattie . . . ?"

Clarabelle and Ressie clung together, weeping.

Only Aunt Fan was dry-eyed, practical. In the dark she looked down at the mewling newborn baby. And slowly her eyes widened.

With a gesture almost of repugnance the old woman held the infant at arm's length, peering at it in the pale glow from the open cabin door.

"My Lawd a-mercy!" she whispered. "No wonder Mattie Sue died a-birthin' dis-heah one! Makes no diff'rence if'n hit's a woods-colt or not, dis heah chile. . . ."

She stopped, staring now at Clarabelle and Ressie. They paused in their grieving, caught by Aunt Fan's queer tone. The old woman was mumbling under her breath, counting on her black fingers; nodding.

"Dat ole squinch-owl!" Ressie sobbed. "I knowed it! If'n hit hadn't a-hollered, mammy wouldn't. . . ."

"Squinch-owl don't mean nothin' tonight," Aunt Fan cut in with an odd intensity. "Eh, Lawd, hit's jes' stomp-down nachel dat a squinch-owl'd come around to holler at dis-heah birthin'. Nor neither hit wouldn't do no good to put no axes under Mattie's bed, nor do no prayin'. You know why? Dis-heah young-un got six sisters, ain't she? Dat makes she a seb'm-sister! *She gwine have de Power!*"

Like a solemn period to her words, a clap of thunder boomed in the west, scattering ten-pin echoes all over the sky.

"Yessirree, a seb'm-sister," Aunt Fan repeated, rubbing the wen on her wrinkled forehead for good luck. "Y'all gwine have trouble wid dis chile! Hit's a pyore pity she didn't die alongside she mammy."

Ressie and Clarabelle, saucer-eyed, peered at their motherless newborn sister, at her tiny puckered face that resembled nothing so much as a small monkey. But she was *white*, abnormally white! Paler than any "high yaller" pickaninny they had ever seen; paler even than a white baby. Her little eyes were a translucent watery pink. Her faint fuzz of hair was like cotton.

"De Lawd he'p us to git right!" Clarabelle whispered in awe. "What us gwine do wid her? Pappy won't leave her stay here—not no woods-colt, and *sho* not no seb'm-sister! Will you keep care of her, Aunt Fan? Anyways, till after de funeral?"

The old Negress shook her head. With flat emphasis she thrust the wailing bundle into Ressie's arms, and stumped down the porch step.

"Nawsuh, honey! Not me! Hit say in de Good Book not to have no truck wid no conjure 'oman. And dat little seb'm-sister of yourn gwine be a plain-out, hard down conjure 'oman, sho as you born! . . . Jes' keep her out in de corncrib; Dody won't take no notice of her. Feed her on goat's milk. . . . Mm-mmm!" Aunt Fan shook her head in wonder. "She sho is a funny color!"

It was a month after Mattie's funeral before Cap'm Jim came down to the Old Place again with the boys and Miss Ruth. When he heard, by neighborhood grapevine, that Dody's new baby was being hidden out in the corncrib like an infant Moses, he stormed down to the cabin with proper indignation.

He took one startled look at the baby, white as a slug that has spent its life in darkness under a rock. Pink eyes blinked up at him painfully. The little thing seemed to be thriving very well on goat's milk, but the corncrib was draughty and full of rats. Cap'm Jim attacked Dody with the good-natured tyranny of all Deep-Southerners toward the darkies who trust and depend upon them.

"I'm ashamed of you, boy!"—Dody was over ten years older than Dr. Saunders. "Making your own baby sleep out in a corncrib, just for some damn-fool notion that she's a hoodoo! And of course she is your own baby. She's just an albino; that's why she's so white."

Dody bobbed and scratched his head. "Yassuh, cap'm? Sho nuff?"

"Yes. It's a lack of pigment in the skin . . . er. . . ." Dr. Saunders floundered, faced by the childlike bewilderment in the big Negro's face. "I mean, she's black, but her skin is white. She . . . Oh, the devil! You take that child into your cabin and treat her right, or I'll turn you out so quick it'll make your head swim!"

"Yassuh . . ." Dody grinned and bobbed again, turning his frayed straw hat around and around by the brim. "Yassuh, cap'm . . . You ain't got a quarter you don't need, is you? Seem like we's plumb out o' salt and stuff. Ain't got no nails, neither, to mend de chicken house. . . ."

Dr. Saunders grunted and handed him fifty cents. "Here. But if you spend it on bay rum and get drunk this weekend, I'll tan your hide!"

"Nawsuh!" Dody beamed, and guffawed his admiration of the bossman's unerring shot. "I ain't gwine do dat, cap'm! Does you want me for anything, jes' ring de bell. I'll send Clarabelle on up to look after de boys."

Dody shambled off, grinning. Cap'm Jim let out a baffled sigh. He strode back toward the Place, well aware that Dody would be drunk on dime-store bay rum by nightfall, and that the big rusty plantation bell in the yard would clang in vain if he wanted any chores performed. But he had laid the law down about the new baby, and that order at least would be obeyed.

"A pure albino!" he told his wife later, at supper. "Poor little mite; it's amazing how healthy she is on that treatment! They won't even give her a name. They just call her Seven Sisters . . . and cross their fool fingers every time she looks at 'em! I'll have to say, myself, she is weird-looking with that paper-white hair and skin. Oh, well—they'll get used to her. . . ."

Cap'm Jim laughed, shrugged and helped himself to some more watermelon pickle.

Dody, with his fifty cents, rode mule-back to the nearest town five miles away. In a fatherly moment, while buying his bay rum at the five-and-ten, he bought a nickel's worth of peppermints for the young-uns. He bought salt, soda, and some nails.

Plodding back home up the highway, he passed Aunt Fan's cabin and hailed her with due solemnity.

"Us sho got a seb'm-sister, all right," he called over the sagging wire gate, after a moment of chitchat. "Cap'm Jim say she ain't no woods-colt. He say she black, but she got pigmies in de skin, what make her look so bright-colored. Do, my Savior! I bet she got de blue-gum! I sho ain't gwine let her chaw on my fingers like them other young-uns when she teethin'! I ain't fixin' to git pizened!"

"Praise de Lawd!" Aunt Fan answered noncommitally, rocking and fanning herself on the front stoop. "Reckon what-all she gwine be up to when she old enough to be noticin'? Whoo-ee! Make my blood run cold to study 'bout it!"

Dody shivered, clutching his store-purchases as though their prosaic touch could protect him from his own thoughts. If there was any way to get rid of the baby, without violence. . . . But Cap'm Jim had said his say, and there was nothing for him to do but raise her along with the others.

It was a fearful cross to bear. For, Seven Sisters began to show signs of "the Power" at an early age. She could touch warts and they would disappear; if not at once, at least within a few weeks. She would cry, and almost every time, a bullbat would fly out of the dusk, to go circling and screeching about the cabin's fieldstone chimney.

Then there was the time when she was three, playing quietly in the cabin's shade, her dead-white skin and hair in freakish contrast with those of her black brothers and sisters. The other pickaninnies were nearby—but not too near; keeping the eye on her demanded by Clarabelle without actually playing with her.

Willie T., five, was playing train with a row of bricks tied on a string. Booger and Gaynelle, twins of eight, were fishing for jackworms—poling a blade of grass down each hole, and jerking up the tiny dragonlike insects. Lula and Willene and Buzz, aged twelve, nine and thirteen, were engaged in a game of squat tag under the fig trees. They were not paying much attention to their queer-colored sister, though from time to time she glanced at them wistfully.

Willie T. it was who happened to look up and see the bird clumsily winging along overhead in the clear June sky. He pointed, not greatly interested.

"Look at dat ole shypoke!" Snatching up a stick, he aimed it at the flapping target, closed one eye and shouted: "*Bang! Bang! Babloom!*" in imitation of Cap'm Jim's rifle. The bird flew on.

The other children glanced up idly. Only the little albino, lonesome and longing for attention, feigned an interest in this byplay. Squinting eagerly up at the distant bird, she pointed the old chicken foot with which she was playing, and trebled in mimicry of her brother: "*Bang, bang! Boom!*"

And a weird, incredible thing happened.

The shypoke, flapping along, wavered suddenly, one wing drooping. With a lurching, fluttering motion it veered—then fell like a plummet, striking the ground not three yards from where the little girl sat.

Willie T. stared. The bird was dead. There was blood on its feathers.

In a stunned, silent, wide-eyed group, Mattie's other children backed away from their ghostly sister. She blinked at them, her pinkish eyes squinting painfully in the sunlight.

"*Bang-bang . . . ?*" Seven Sisters repeated in a hopeful undertone.

There was a shuffle of running feet. Her lower lip quivered when she saw that she had been left alone.

She was always alone after that, partly because the other children shunned her, and partly because she could not see well enough to run after them. She had developed a peculiar squint, holding her tow-head to one side, slit-eyed, upper lip drawn back to show her oddly pointed little teeth. For a "seven-sister" she tripped over things and hurt herself twice as often as her brothers and sisters who were not gifted with supernatural powers.

Cap'm Jim, on a flying visit to the plantation one Sunday, had noticed the way the child kept always to the shadowy places.

"Weak eyes," he pronounced. "Typical of albinos. Have to get her some special glasses. . . ." He sighed, mentally adding up his vanishing bank account. "Oh, well—time enough when she starts to school. Though, Lord help the little thing at recess!"

That preference for shadow was given another connotation by dark-skinned observers.

"Dah! Ain't I done tole you?" Aunt Fan was triumphant. "See jes' like a cat in de dark, but can't see hardly nothin' in de daytime. Yessirree—she a plain-out, hard-down conjure 'oman, and I knowed hit de first time I sot eyes on her!"

By this time, the lone screech-owl which had attracted Seven Sister's birth had become seven screech-owls, hovering in a ring around the cabin to demand Mattie's soul in return for the new baby's "Power."

This "Power" mystified Seven Sisters, though she did not doubt that she had it. Clarabelle and Dody had told her so, ever since she could understand words. Now a thin, too-quiet child of six, she accepted the fact as simply and sadly as one might accept having been born with an interesting club-foot. But, because it was the only way in which she could attract attention—half fear, half respect—the little albino drew on her imagination, and did not herself know where fact ended and fancy began

The other children jeered at her but were frankly envious. The elders laughed and remarked that nobody but "ig'nant country niggers" believed in conjures any more.

Secretly they came to her by night, and hissed at her window, and proffered silver in return for her magic. Seven Sisters never saw any of the money, however, as the business was always transacted through Clarabelle or Dody.

Some of the things they wanted were incomprehensible to her at first. Mojoes—tiny bags of cloth that might contain anything at all, plus the one thing only she possessed: "the Power." In Atlanta, in Birmingham, and Memphis, especially in Harlem, a good one might sell for as much as ten dollars. These, according to whatever words the conjurer mumbled over them, were able to perform all sorts of miracles for the wearer— from restoring the affection of a bored mate to insuring luck in the numbers game.

Seven Sisters, with the precocity of all outcasts, caught the idea early. Like the little girls who started the witch-scare in Salem, she felt pains and saw apparitions for the bug-eyed approval of kin and neighbors. She made up words and mumbled them on every occasion, squinting weirdly and impressively. She hummed tuneless little chants, in the eerie rhythm of all darkies. She memorized the better-known household "conjures"; such as, burying three hairs from the end of a hound's tail under the front steps to keep him from straying. With a ready wit she invented new ones, then forgot them and supplied others on call.

True, most of these tricks had, at one time or another, been subtly suggested by Aunt Fan or Clarabelle as the proper procedure for a "seven-sister." But the little albino, pleased and excited by any substitute for affection, threw herself into the part—a pale wistful Shirley Temple in the role of Cybele.

She wanted to be admired, however. She did not want to be feared.

But even Clarabelle, who loved her in a skittish way one might grow to love a pet snake, gave her a wide berth after the incident of the stomachache.

It happened one sultry August day when Dody came stumbling into the cabin, drunker than usual and in a nasty mood.

"Whah dah low-down triflin' Seb'm-Sister?" he bellowed. "Whah she at? I gwine wear de hide off'n her back—takin' dat four-bit piece from Ole Man Wilson for a huntin' mojo. Hidin' it fum her po' ole pappy what feed her! Whah she at? . . . Young-un, you come out fum under dat table! I sees you!"

The other children, gnawing pork chop bones beside the fireplace— thanks to the sale of a "health mojo" purported to contain the infallible John the Conqueror root—stirred uneasily. In this mood Dody was apt to throw things at anyone within range. But it appeared that Seven Sisters, quaking under the table, was the main object of his wrath tonight.

"Come on out, you heah me?" Dody snarled, grabbing up a stick of lightwood from the hearth and advancing toward the culprit. "I'm gwine whup you good! Stealin' my four-bits. . . ."

"I . . . done lost it, pappy. . . ." Seven Sisters's childish treble was drowned out by his bellow of rage. "Don't whup me! I drapped it in de field. I couldn't see whereat I drapped it— I'll go git it. . . ."

"Now you's lyin' to me!" Dody roared, waving his club. "Come on out! I'll learn you. . . ."

The other pickaninnies, fascinated, stopped gnawing their chop bones for an instant to watch, their greasy black faces gleaming in the firelight. Dody jerked the table aside. Seven Sisters cringed. Then:

"Don't you hit me wid no stick!" the frightened child shrilled. "I'll put a hoodoo on you! I'll . . ."

Dody lunged, and fell over the table. His stick whistled dangerously close to the child's tow-head.

The next moment Dody was groaning with pain, doubled over, hugging his stomach. Sweat stood out on his black face. He stared at his weirdly white daughter: backed away, thick lips trembling. Seven Sisters made a dive through the open door and out into the friendly night.

Cap'm Jim happened to be at the Place that day; it was a Sunday. He rushed Dody to the nearest city in his car. Appendicitis, Cap'm Jim called it, to the man at the hospital. He and Miss Ruth had a good laugh over Dody's version of the attack.

But after that, Clarabelle stopped giving her little albino sister a playful spank when she was naughty. No one would touch her, even in fun.

"I done tole you!" Aunt Fan intoned. "Do, Moses! Puttin' a hoodoo on she own pappy! Dat ole Seb'm-Sister, she jes' born to trouble! She *bad*!"

For more than a week thereafter, Seven Sisters hid in the woods, creeping out only to sneak food from the kitchen. She was deeply frightened. So frightened that when Cap'm Jim came to bring Dody back from the hospital, she ran from him like a wild creature. If she had not tripped over a log and knocked the breath from her slight body, he would never have caught her.

Dr. Saunders helped her up and held her gently by the shoulders, marveling anew at her Negroid features and cotton-white hair and skin. Her single garment, a faded dress which had not been changed for eight days, hung half-off one shoulder, torn and filthy. She was trembling all over, squinting up at him with white-lashed pinkish eyes dilated by terror.

"Now, now, child," the tall bossman was saying, in a tone as gentle as the grip of his hands. "What have those fools been telling you? That it's your fault about Dody's appendix? Well Heaven help us!" He threw back his head, laughing, but stopped when he saw how it frightened his smal!

captive. "Why, don't be scared. Cap'm Jim won't hurt you. Look here—I've got a present for you! Don't let the other young-uns get hold of it, you hear? Just hide it and play with it all by yourself, because it's yours."

The little albino stopped trembling. Gingerly she took the proffered box and gaped at the treasure inside. A doll-baby a foot high! With real hair, red hair, and eyes that opened and shut. When she turned it over, it gave a thin cry: "*Mama!*" Seven Sisters giggled.

The Cap'm chuckled. "Oh, I don't reckon you want this old doll-baby," he made a pretense of taking it back, eyes twinkling. The child clutched at it. "You do? Well, then, what do you say?"

Seven Sisters ducked her head shyly. "I don' care," she whispered—polite rural South for "Thank you!"

Dr. Saunders chuckled again. "That's a good girl." He stood up; gave her a careless pat. Then he strode off toward the Place, frowning over his own problems—not the least of which was mother-in-law trouble.

He and Ruth and their two boys had been so happy in their touch-and-go way. Then his wife's mother, a forthright lady from Oklahoma, had descended upon them and decided to run their lives with a new efficiency. With her customary dispatch she had found a buyer for the old Saunders plantation, and was now raging at her slipshod son's reluctance to sell.

Even Cap'm Jim had to admit that the price was half again as much as the property was worth. Besides, his practice in Chattanooga had been dwindling of late. A mother-in-law could point out such matters so vividly . . . . !

Seven Sisters blinked after his retreating back. Keeping to the shade of the pine coppice, she followed the tall white man a little way, the doll squeezed tightly against her soiled blue-gingham dress. Cap'm Jim waved at someone, who met him in the orchard—a pretty redheaded woman. They went on to the house together, arms about each other's waists. Seven Sisters watched them until they were out of sight.

Thereafter she listened attentively whenever Dody or Clary spoke of cap'm. She grew to love anyone that he loved, and to hate anyone that he hated, with a doglike loyalty. In her child's mind, Good became personified as Dr. Saunders, and Evil as the sheriff or Old Miz Beecher.

It was common knowledge about the mother-in-law trouble. Clarabelle, who cooked all year round for the Saunderses now, had passed along every word of the quarrel.

"Us'll git turnt out like white-trash if'n de cap'm sell de Place," Dody mourned. "Dat old Miz Beecher! Do, Lawd! Dat old 'oman mean as a cottonmouth! She don't care what happen to us niggers, nor nobody. Miss Ruth sho don't take after her none. I wisht she'd fall down de steps and bus' her brains out, so she wouldn't plague de cap'm no more! If'n he don' sell come Thursday, Thanksgivin', she gwine jes' make his life mis'able!"

Seven Sisters listened, huddled apart from her black kin in a shadowy corner of the cabin. Her little heart began to beat rapidly as a mad idea crept into her tow-head. Without a sound, she slipped out into the frosty night of mid-November.

There was a thing Aunt Fan had hinted to her one day—or rather, to Clarabelle within her hearing, since no one ever spoke directly to a seven-sister in idle conversation. Something about a . . . a *graven image*. There was even, Aunt Fan said, a passage about it in the Good Book, warning all Christians to steer clear of the matter.

But Seven Sisters was not a Christian. She had never been baptized in the creek like the rest of Dody's brood. Nothing hindered the plan. And . . . it sounded remarkably simple.

". . . whatever you does to de image, you does to de one you names it!" Aunt Fan's solemn words came back to her clearly. "Jes' wrop somep'm around it what dey wears next to dey skin—don't make no never-mind what hit is. And dat's de conjure! Eh, Lawd, I seed a conjure man do dat when I was married up wid my first husband. And de 'oman he conjure drap daid as a doornail dat same winter. . . . And dey do say as how hit were a big black cat got in de room whah dey was settin' up wid de corp. Hit jump up on de bed and go to yowlin' like ole Satan hisself! Yessirree, dat's de Lawd's truth like I'm tellin' you!"

Seven Sisters, picking her way easily through the dark, slipped into the pine coppice. After a moment, heart pounding, she dug up something from under a pile of leaves. A faint sound issued from it, causing her to start violently—"*Mama!*"

Like a small white ghost, the child then ran through the peach orchard. The Place, dark now since Cap'm Jim had gone back to Chattanooga, loomed just ahead. Seven Sisters found what she was looking for, under the steps of the isolated kitchen—an old piece of silk nightgown that she had seen Miss Ruth's mother herself give Clarabelle as a polishing rag for the flat silver. The older girl had used it and flung it under the kitchen steps. Seven Sisters retrieved it now furtively, and padded swiftly back through the orchard.

Deep in the pine coppice, illumined only by the filtered light of a quarter moon, she sat down cross-legged. For a long time she stared at the lovely thing Cap'm Jim had given her, the only thing that had ever been truly her own. The hair was so soft, the glass eyes so friendly. But now the doll had taken on a new personality, a hated one. Seven Sisters glared at it, shivering a little.

Then, deftly, she tied the silk rag about its china neck, and stood up.

"Ole Miz Beecher—you's ole Miz Beecher!" she hissed with careful emphasis; then clarified against all mistake, to whatever dark pointed ears might be listening: "Miss Ruth's mama. Cap'm Jim's wife's mama. Dat's who you is, doll; you heah me? Ole Miz Beecher . . . !"

With a fierce motion she banged the poppet hard against a tree trunk. The china head broke off and rolled at her bare feet.

"*Mama!*" wailed the headless body, accusingly.

Seven Sisters dropped it as though it were red-hot. She backed away, rubbing her hands on her dress like an infant Lady Macbeth, and shuddering in the Indian summer chill. Panting, shaken, she turned and ran back to the cabin.

But she paused in the half-open door.

Excited activity was going on inside. Aunt Fan was there, puffing with importance and fumbling for her box of snuff. Dody was shouting questions, wringing his big hands. Clarabelle, Ressie and the others were milling about like a flock of chickens, clucking and squawking in chorus.

". . . and de phome call say for you to clean up de fambly plot on de south hill," Aunt Fan made herself heard shrilly. "She gwine be buried fum de Place like Miss Addie. . . ."

"Oh, Lawsy! Ain't it awful?" This from Ressie.

"Sho is, honey," Aunt Fan agreed complacently. "I don't reckon the cap'm'll ever be de same, hit was so awful. I don't reckon he care what become of de Place, nor nothin', he so cut up about hit."

"Lawd he'p us!" Dody shouted for a fifth time. "When it happen? How come?"

"I done tole you," Aunt Fan repeated, relishing the drama of her words. "Truck run slap into 'em. She was plumb flang out'n de car. Cap'm want even scratched up. But it broke her pore neck. . . ."

The child in the doorway caught her breath sharply. The conjure had worked! So soon? A little knot of nausea gathered in her stomach, in memory of the china head rolling against her bare foot. Then an angry thought came.

"Aunt Fan—cap'm ain't gwine bury that old 'oman in de fambly plot, is he?" Seven Sisters piped above the chatter. "Not dat ole Miz Beecher . . . !"

The excited group barely glanced at her, impatient of the interruption.

"Miz Beecher?" Aunt Fan grunted. "Lawd, chile, hit ain't ole Miz Beecher what got killt. Hit was Miss Ruth. . . ." The aged Negress went on with her narrative, dwelling on the details with relish. "And de man tole Marse Joe Andrews over de phome. . . . Eh, Lawd; he say de cap'm jes' set dah by she bed and hold she hand. Don't cry nor nothin'. Jes' set dah and stare, like he daid, too. . . ."

Seven Sisters heard no more. A sound like falling timber roared in her ears. Through it, dimly, she thought she heard a screech-owl's quavering cry— eerie, mocking, malicious.

She turned and ran. Ran, blindly sobbing. Cap'm Jim's Miss Ruth! She had forgotten Miss Ruth's hair was red, exactly like the doll's. And . . . that soiled bit of nightgown might not have been ole Miz Beecher's at all, but Miss Ruth's. Cap'm Jim's Miss Ruth. . . .

Beyond the cornfield the black woods opened up to receive the small ghostly figure, running like an animal in pain; running nowhere, anywhere, into the chill autumn night.

Sawbriars tore dark scratches in her dead-white skin, but Seven Sisters did not feel them. She ran, careening into tree trunks and fighting through scuppernong vines, until the salt taste of blood came into her mouth. Twice she fell and lay in the damp leaves for a long time, her thin shoulders racked with sobs.

"Oh, cap'm! Cap'm Jim . . . I . . . I didn't go to do it!" she whimpered aloud once. "I didn't mean to! I didn'—hones' I didn'. . . ."

At that moment she heard the dogs baying.

Tense as a fox, she sat up and listened. Was it only Old Man Wilson, hunting with his pack along the north ridge? Or was it . . . the Law? A posse, with guns, following the deputy sheriff and his two flop-eared bloodhounds through the canebrake. Following a trail of small bare feet. *Her* feet. . . .

The little albino sprang up, her features contorted with panic. Harrowing yarns crowded her memory. Of the time Aunt Fan's preacher husband had hid in the canebrake for eight days, with the dogs baying closer and closer. And Aunt Fan's husband had only cut a man with his razor, while *she*. . . .

Just then she heard the screech-owl, right over her head.

Seven Sisters was running again, goaded now by the spurs of terror. But now the very woods seemed hostile. Gnarled branches snatched at her cottony hair and tore a jagged flap in her gingham dress. Old spider webs clung to her face. The dogs sounded nearer. Once more she tripped and fell, panting, but sprang up again with a scream as something slithered out from beneath her arm.

The screech-owl tittered again, from somewhere above her. It seemed to be trailing the ghostly little fugitive, so white against the ground.

Seven Sisters ran on, blindly, staggering with exhaustion. Once she cried out in her terror—oddly, the very name of the one she was running from:

"*Cap'm . . . ! Cap'm Jim. . . .*"

Of a sudden the ground dropped from beneath her feet. She pitched forward, and felt herself falling into space. Dark icy water rushed up out of nowhere to meet and engulf her. . . .

Mist rose from the cornfield in front of Dody's cabin. Dry leaves rattled. The gourds of the martin pole swung in the wind.

Somewhere a screech-owl quavered again, far away, in the direction of the creek—whose muddy waters had washed away the sins of many a baptized little darky.

HAWAII

The Isle of Voices
by Robert Louis Stevenson

KEOLA WAS married with Lehua, daughter of Kalamake, the wise man of Molokai, and he kept his dwelling with the father of his wife. There was no man more cunning than that prophet; he read the stars, he could divine by the bodies of the dead, and by the means of evil creatures: he could go alone into the highest parts of the mountain, into the region of the hobgoblins, and there he would lay snares to entrap the spirits of the ancients.

For this reason no man was more consulted in all the kingdom of Hawaii. Prudent people bought, and sold, and married, and laid out their lives by his counsels, and the king had him twice to Kona to seek the treasures of Kamehameha. Neither was any man more feared: of his enemies, some had dwindled in sickness by the virtue of his incantations, and some had been spirited away, the life and the clay both, so that folk looked in vain for so much as a bone of their bodies. It was rumored that he had the art or the gift of the old heroes. Men had seen him at night upon the mountains, stepping from one cliff to the next; they had seen him walking in the high forest, and his head and shoulders were above the trees.

This Kalamake was a strange man to see. He was come of the best blood in Molokai and Maui, of a pure descent; and yet he was more white to look upon than any foreigner; his hair the color of dry grass, and his eyes red and very blind, so that "Blind as Kalamake that can see across tomorrow," was a byword in the islands.

Of all these doings of his father-in-law, Keola knew a little by the common repute, a little more he suspected, and the rest he ignored. But there was one thing troubled him. Kalamake was a man that spared for nothing, whether to eat or to drink, or to wear, and for all he paid in bright new dollars. "Bright

157

as Kalamake's dollars," was another saying in the Eight Isles. Yet he neither sold, nor planted, nor took hire—only now and then from his sorceries—and there was no source conceivable for so much silver.

It chanced one day Keola's wife was gone upon a visit to Kaunakai on the lee side of the island, and the men were forth at the sea-fishing. But Keola was an idle dog, and he lay in the verandah and watched the surf beat on the shore and the birds fly about the cliff. It was a chief thought with him always—the thought of the bright dollars. When he lay down to bed he would be wondering why they were so many, and when he woke at morn he would be wondering why they were all new; and the thing was never absent from his mind. But this day of all days he made sure in his heart of some discovery. For it seems he had observed the place where Kalamake kept his treasure, which was a lock-fast desk against the parlor wall, under the print of Kamehameha the fifth, and a photograph of Queen Victoria with her crown; and it seems again that, no later than the night before, he found occasion to look in, and behold! the bag lay there empty. And this was the day of the steamer; he could see her smoke off Kalaupapa; and she must soon arrive with a month's goods, tinned salmon and gin, and all manner of rare luxuries for Kalamake.

"Now if he can pay for his goods today," Keola thought, "I shall know for certain that the man is a warlock, and the dollars come out of the devil's pocket."

While he was so thinking, there was his father-in-law behind him, looking vexed.

"Is that the steamer?" he asked.

"Yes," said Keola. "She has but to call at Pelekunu, and then she will be here."

"There is no help for it them," returned Kalamake, "and I must take you in my confidence, Keola, for the lack of anyone better. Come here within the house."

So they stepped together into the parlor, which was a very fine room, papered and hung with prints, and furnished with a rocking-chair, and a table and a sofa in the European style. There was a shelf of books besides, and a family Bible in the midst of the table, and the lock-fast writing-desk against the wall; so that anyone could see it was the house of a man of substance.

Kalamake made Keola close the shutters of the windows, while he himself locked all the doors and set open the lid of the desk. From this he brought forth a pair of necklaces hung with charms and shells, a bundle of dried herbs, and the dried leaves of trees, and a green branch of palm.

"What I am about," said he, "is a thing beyond wonder. The men of old were wise; they wrought marvels, and this among the rest: but that was at night, in the dark, under the fit stars and in the desert. The same will I do here in my own house, and under the plain eye of day." So saying, he put the Bible under the cushion of the sofa so that it was all covered, brought out from the same place a mat of a wonderfully fine texture, and heaped the herbs and leaves on sand in a tin pan. And then he and Keola put on the necklaces and took their stand upon the opposite corners of the mat.

"The time comes," said the warlock, "be not afraid."

With that he set flame to the herbs, and began to mutter and wave the branch of palm. At first the light was dim because of the closed shutters, but the herbs caught strongly afire, and the flames beat upon Keola, and the room glowed with the burning; and next the smoke rose and made his head swim and his eyes darken, and the sound of Kalamake muttering ran in his ears. And suddenly, to the mat on which they were standing came a snatch or twitch, that seemed to be more swift than lightning. In the same wink the room was gone, and the house, the breath all beaten from Keola's body. Volumes of sun rolled upon his eyes and head, and he found himself transported to a beach of the sea, under a strong sun, with a great surf roaring: he and the warlock standing there on the same mat, speechless, gasping and grasping at one another, and passing their hands before their eyes.

"What was this?" cried Keola, who came to himself the first, because he was the younger. "The pang of it was like death."

"It matters not," panted Kalamake. "It is now done."

"And, in the name of God, where are we?" cried Keola.

"That is not the question," replied the sorcerer. "Being here, we have matter in our hands, and that we must attend to. Go while I recover my breath, into the borders of the wood, and bring me the leaves of such and such an herb, and such and such a tree, which you will find to grow there plentifully—three handfuls of each. And be speedy. We must be home again before the steamer comes; it would seem strange if we had disappeared." And he sat on the sand and panted.

Keola went up the beach, which was of shining sand and coral, strewn with singular shells; and he thought in his heart:

"How do I not know this beach? I will come here again and gather shells."

In front of him was a line of palms against the sky; not like the palms of the Eight Islands, but tall and fresh and beautiful and hanging out withered fans like gold among the green, and he thought in his heart:

"It is strange I should not have found this grove. I will come here again, when it is warm, to sleep." And he thought, "How warm it has grown suddenly!" For it was winter in Hawaii, and the day had been chill. And he thought also, "Where are the gray mountains? And where is the high cliff with the hanging forests and the wheeling birds?" And the more he considered, the less he might conceive in what quarter of the islands he was fallen.

In the border of the grove, where it met the beach, the herb was growing, but the tree farther back. Now, as Keola went towards the tree, he was aware of a young woman who had nothing on her body but a belt of leaves.

"Well!" thought Keola, "they are not very particular about their dress in this part of the country." And he paused, supposing she would observe him and escape; and seeing that she still looked before her, he stood and hummed aloud. Up she leaped at the sound. Her face was ashen; she looked this way and that, and her mouth gaped with the terror of her soul. But it was a strange thing that her eyes did not rest upon Keola.

"Good day," said he. "You need not be so frightened, I will not eat you." And he had scarce opened his mouth before the young woman fled into the bush.

"These are strange manners," thought Keola, and, not thinking what he did, ran after her.

As she ran, the girl kept crying in some speech that was not practiced in Hawaii, yet some of the words were the same, and he knew she kept calling and warning others. And presently he saw more people running—men, women and children, one with another, all running and crying like people at a fire. And with that he began to grow afraid himself, and returned to Kalamake bringing the leaves. Him he told just what he had seen.

"You must pay no heed," said Kalamake. "All this is like a dream and shadows. All will disappear and be forgotten."

"It seemed none saw me," said Keola.

"And none did," replied the sorcerer. "We walk here in the broad sun invisible by reason of these charms. Yet they hear us; and therefore it is well to speak softly, as I do."

With that he made a circle round the mat with stones, and in the midst he set the leaves.

"It will be your part," he said, "to keep the leaves alight, and feed the fire slowly. While they blaze (which is but for a little moment) I must do my errand; and before the ashes blacken, the same power that brought us carries us away. Be ready now with the match; and do you call me in good time lest the flames burn out and I be left."

As soon as the leaves caught, the sorcerer leaped like a deer out of the circle, and began to race along the beach like a hound that has been bathing. As he ran, he kept stooping to snatch shells; and it seemed to Keola that they glittered as he took them. The leaves blazed with a clear flame that consumed them swiftly; and presently Keola had but a handful left, and the sorcerer was far off, running and stopping.

"Back!" cried Keola. "Back! The leaves are near done."

At that Kalamake turned, and if he had run before, now he flew. But fast as he ran, the leaves burned faster. The flame was ready to expire when, with a great leap, he bounded on the mat. The wind of his leaping blew it out; and with that the beach was gone, and the sun and the sea; and they stood once more in the dimness of the shuttered parlor, and were once more shaken and blinded; and on the mat betwixt them lay a pile of shining dollars. Keola ran to the shutters; and there was the steamer tossing in the swell close in.

The same night Kalamake took his son-in-law apart, and gave him five dollars in his hand.

"Keola," said he; "if you are a wise man (which I am doubtful of) you will think you slept this afternoon on the verandah, and dreamed as you were sleeping. I am a man of few words, and I have for my helpers people of short memories."

Never a word more said Kalamake, nor referred again to that affair. But it ran all the while in Keola's head—if he were lazy before, he would now do nothing.

"Why should I work," thought he, "when I have a father-in-law who makes dollars of seashells?"

Presently his share was spent. He spent it all upon fine clothes. And then he was sorry:

"For," thought he, "I had done better to have bought a concertina, with which I might have entertained myself all day long." And then he began to grow vexed with Kalamake.

"This man has the soul of a dog," thought he. "He can gather dollars when he pleases on the beach, and he leaves me to pine for a concertina! Let him beware: I am no child, I am as cunning as he, and hold his secret." With that he spoke to his wife Lehua, and complained of her father's manners.

"I would let my father be," said Lehua. "He is a dangerous man to cross."

"I care that for him!" cried Keola; and snapped his fingers. "I have him by the nose. I can make him do what I please." And he told Lehua the story. But she shook her head.

"You may do what you like," said she; "but as sure as you thwart my father, you will be no more heard of. Think of this person, and that person; think of Hua, who was a noble of the House of Representatives, and went to Honolulu every year: and not a bone or a hair of him was found. Remember Kamau, and how he wasted to a thread, so that his wife lifted him with one hand. Keola, you are a baby in my father's hands; he will take you with his thumb and finger and eat you like a shrimp."

Now Keola was truly afraid of Kalamake, but he was vain too; and these words of his wife's incensed him.

"Very well," said he, "if that is what you think of me, I will show how much you are deceived." And he went straight to his father-in-law.

"Kalamake," said he, "I want a concertina."

"Do you, indeed?" said Kalamake.

"Yes," said he, "and I may as well tell you plainly, I mean to have it. A man who picks up dollars on the beach can certainly afford a concertina."

"I had no idea you had so much spirit," replied the sorcerer. "I thought you were a timid, useless lad, and I cannot describe how much pleased I am to find I was mistaken. Now I begin to think I may have found an assistant and successor in my difficult business. A concertina? You shall have the best in Honolulu. And tonight, as soon as it is dark, you and I will go and find the money."

"Shall we return to the beach?" asked Keola.

"No, no!" replied Kalamake; "you must begin to learn more of my secrets. Last time I taught you to pick shells; this time I shall teach you to catch fish. Are you strong enough to launch Pili's boat?"

"I think I am," returned Keola. "But why should we not take your own?"

"I have a reason which you will understand thoroughly before tomorrow," said Kalamake. "Pili's boat is the better suited for my purpose. So, if you please, let us meet there as soon as it is dark; and in the meanwhile, let us keep our own counsel, for there is no cause to let the family into our business."

Honey is not more sweet than was the voice of Kalamake, and Keola could scarce contain his satisfaction.

"I might have had my concertina weeks ago," thought he, "and there is nothing needed in this world but a little courage." Presently after he spied Lehua weeping, and was half in a mind to tell her all was well.

"But no," thinks he; "I shall wait till I can show her the concertina; we shall see that the chit will do then. Perhaps she will understand in the future that her husband is a man of some intelligence."

As soon as it was dark father and son-in-law launched Pili's boat and set the sail. There was a great sea, and it blew strong from the leeward; but the boat was swift and light and dry, and skimmed the waves. The wizard had a lantern, which he lit and held with his finger through the ring, and the two sat in the stern and smoked cigars, of which Kalamake had always a provision, and spoke like friends of magic and the great sums of money which they could make by its exercise, and what they should buy first, and what second; and Kalamake talked like a father.

Presently he looked all about, and above him at the stars, and back at the island, which was already three parts sunk under the sea, and he seemed to consider ripely his position.

"Look!" says he, "there is Molokai already far behind us, and Maui like a cloud; and by the bearing of these three stars I know I am come to where I desire. This part of the sea is called the Sea of the Dead. It is in this place extraordinarily deep, and the floor is all covered with the bones of men, and in the holes of this part gods and goblins keep their habitation. The flow of the sea is to the north, stronger than a shark can swim, and any man who shall here be thrown out of a ship it bears away like a wild horse into the uttermost ocean. Presently he is spent and goes down, and his bones are scattered with the rest, and the gods devour his spirit."

Fear came on Keola at the words, and he looked, and by the light of the stars and the lantern, the warlock seemed to change.

"What ails you?" cried Keola, quick and sharp.

"It is not I who am ailing," said the wizard; "but there is one here sick."

With that he changed his grasp upon the lantern, and, behold—as he drew his finger from the ring, the finger stuck and the ring was burst, and his hand was grown to be the bigness of three.

At that sight Keola screamed and covered his face.

But Kalamake held up the lantern. "Look rather at my face!" said he—and his head was huge as a barrel; and still he grew and grew as a cloud grows on a mountain, and Keola sat before him screaming, and the boat raced on the great seas.

"And now," said the wizard, "what do you think about that concertina? and are you sure you would not rather have a flute? No?" says he; "that is well, for I do not like my family to be changeable of purpose. But I begin to think I had better get out of this paltry boat, for my bulk swells to a very unusual degree, and if we are not the more careful, she will presently be swamped."

With that he threw his legs over the side. Even as he did so, the greatness of the man grew thirty-fold and forty-fold as swift as sight or thinking, so that he stood in the deep sea to the armpits, and his head and shoulders rose like the high isle, and the swell beat and burst upon his bosom, as it beats and breaks against a cliff. The boat ran still to the north, but he reached out his hand, and took the gunwale by the finger and thumb, and broke the side like a biscuit, and Keola was spilled into the sea. And the pieces of the boat the sorcerer crushed in the hollow of his hand and flung miles away into the night.

"Excuse me taking the lantern," said he; "for I have a long wade before me, and the land is far, and the bottom of the sea uneven, and I feel the bones under my toes."

And he turned and went off walking with great strides; and as soon as Keola sank in the trough he could see him no longer; but as often as he was heaved upon the crest, there he was striding and dwindling, and he held the lamp high over his head, and the waves broke white about him.

Since first the islands were fished out of the sea, there was never a man so terrified as this Keola. He swam indeed, but he swam as puppies swim when they are cast in to drown, and knew not wherefore. He could but think of the hugeness of the swelling of the warlock, of that face which was great as a mountain, of those shoulders that were broad as an isle, and of the seas that beat on them in vain. He thought, too, of the concertina, and shame took hold upon him; and of the dead men's bones, and fear shook him.

Of a sudden he was aware of something dark against the stars that tossed, and a light below, and a brightness of the cloven sea; and he heard speech of men. He cried out aloud and a voice answered; and in a twinkling the bows of a ship hung above him on a wave like a thing balanced, and swooped down. He caught with his two hands in the chains of her, and the next moment was buried in the rushing seas, and the next hauled on board by seamen.

They gave him gin and biscuit and dry clothes, and asked him how he came where they found him, and whether the light which they had seen was the lighthouse, Lae o Ka Laau. But Keola knew white men are like children and only believe their own stories; so about himself he told them what he pleased, and as for the light (which was Kalamake's lantern) he vowed he had seen none.

This ship was a schooner bound for Honolulu, and then to trade in the low islands; and by a very good chance for Keola she had lost a man off the bowsprit in a squall. It was no use talking. Keola durst not stay in the Eight Islands. Word goes so quickly, and all men are so fond to talk and carry news, that if he hid in the north end of Kauai or in the south end of Kaü, the wizard would have wind of it before a month, and he must perish. So he did what seemed the most prudent, and shipped sailor in the place of the man who had been drowned.

In some ways the ship was a good place. The food was extraordinarily rich and plenty, with biscuits and salt beef every day, and pea soup and puddings made of flour and suet twice a week, so that Keola grew fat. The captain also was a good man, and the crew no worse than other whites. The trouble was the mate, who was the most difficult man to please Keola had ever met with, and beat and cursed him daily, both for what he did and what he did not. The blows that he dealt were very sure, for he was strong; and the words he used were very unpalatable, for Keola was come of a good family and accustomed to respect. And what was the worst of all, whenever Keola found a chance to sleep, there was the mate awake and stirring him up with a rope's end. Keola saw it would never do; and he made up his mind to run away.

They were about a month out from Honolulu when they made the land. It was a fine starry night, the sea was smooth as well as the sky fair; it blew a steady trade; and there was the island on their weather bow, a ribbon of palm trees lying flat along the sea. The captain and the mate looked at it with the night glass, and named the name of it, and talked of it, beside the wheel where Keola was steering. It seemed it was an isle where no traders came. By the captain's way, it was an isle besides where no man dwelt; but the mate thought otherwise.

"I don't give a cent for the directory," said he. "I've been past here one night in the Schooner *Eugenie*: it was just such a night as this; they were fishing with torches, and the beach was thick with lights like a town."

"Well, well," says the captain, "it's steep-to, that's the great point; and there ain't any outlying dangers by the chart, so we'll just hug the lee side of it. Keep her ramping full, don't I tell you!" he cried to Keola, who was listening so hard that he forgot to steer.

And the mate cursed him, and swore that Kanaka was for no use in the world, and if he got started after him with a belaying-pin, it would be a cold day for Keola. And so the captain and mate lay down on the house together, and Keola was left to himself.

"This island will do very well for me," he thought, "if no traders deal there, the mate will never come. And as for Kalamake, it is not possible he can ever get as far as this."

With that he kept edging the schooner nearer in. He had to do this quietly, for it was the trouble with these white men, and above all with the mate, that you could never be sure of them; they would all be sleeping sound, or else pretending, and if a sail shook, they would jump to their feet and fall on you with a rope's end. So Keola edged her up little by little, and kept all drawing. And presently the land was close on board.

With that, the mate sat up suddenly upon the house.

"What are you doing?" he roars. "You'll have the ship ashore!"

And he made one bound for Keola, and Keola made another clear over the rail and plump into the starry sea. When he came up again, the schooner had payed off on her true course and the mate stood by the wheel himself, and Keola heard him cursing. The sea was smooth under the lee of the island, it was warm besides, and Keola had his sailor's knife, so he had no fear of sharks. A little way before him the trees stopped; there was a break in the line of the land like the mouth of a harbor; and the tide, which was then flowing, took him up and carried him through. One minute he was without, and the next within, had floated there in a wide shallow water, bright with ten thousand stars, and all about him was the ring of the land with its string of palm trees.

The time of Keola in that place was in two periods—the period when he was alone, and the period when he was there with the tribe. At first he sought everywhere and found no man; only some houses standing in a hamlet, and the marks of fires. But the ashes of the fires were cold and the rains had washed them away; and the winds had blown, and some of the huts were overthrown. It was here he took his dwelling; and he made a fire drill, and a shell hook, and fished and cooked his fish, and climbed after green cocoanuts, the juice of which he drank, for in all the isle there was no water. The days were long for him, and the nights terrifying. He made a lamp of cocoa-shell, and drew the oil off the ripe nuts, and made a wick of fiber; and when evening came he closed up his hut, and lit his lamp, and lay and trembled till morning. Many a time he thought in his heart he would have been better in the bottom of the sea, his bones rolling there with the others.

All this while he kept by the inside of the island, for the huts were on the shore of the lagoon, and it was there the palms grew best, and the lagoon itself abounded with good fish. And to the outer side he went once only, and he looked but once at the beach of the ocean, and came away shaking. For the look of it, with its bright sand, and strewn shells, and strong sun and surf, went sore against his inclination.

"It cannot be," he thought, "and yet it is very like. And how do I know? These white men, although they pretend to know where they are sailing, must take their chances like other people. So that after all we have sailed in a circle, and I may be quite near to Molokai, and this may be the very beach where my father-in-law gathers his dollars."

It was perhaps a month later, when the people of the place arrived—the fill of six great boats. They were a fine race of men, and spoke a tongue that sounded very different from the tongue of Hawaii, but so many of the words were the same that it was not difficult to understand. The men besides were very courteous, and the women very towardly; and they made Keola welcome, and built him a house, and gave him a wife; and what surprised him the most, he was never sent to work with the young men.

And now Keola had three periods. First he had a period of being very sad, and then he had a period when he was pretty merry. Last of all, came the third, when he was the most terrified man in the four oceans.

The cause of the first period was the girl he had to wife. He was in doubt about the island, and he might have been in doubt about the speech, of which he had heard so little when he came there with the wizard on the mat. But about his wife there was no mistake conceivable, for she was the same girl that ran from him crying in the wood. So he had sailed all this way, and might as well have stayed in Molokai; and had left home and wife and all his friends for no other cause but to escape his enemy, and the place he had come to was that wizard's hunting ground, and the place where he walked invisible. It was at this period when he kept the most close to the lagoon side, and as far as he dared, abode in the cover of his hut.

The cause of the second period was talk he had heard from his wife and the chief islanders. Keola himself said little. He was never so sure of his new friends, for he judged they were too civil to be wholesome, and since he had grown better acquainted with his father-in-law the man had grown more cautious. So he told them nothing of himself, but only his name and descent, and that he came from the Eight Islands, and what fine islands they were; and about the king's palace in Honolulu, and how he was a chief friend of the king and the missionaries. But he put many questions and learned much. The island where he was was called the Isle of Voices; it belonged to the tribe, but they made their home upon another, three hours' sail to the southward. There they lived and had their permanent houses, and it was a rich island, where were eggs and chickens and pigs, and ships came trading with rum and tobacco. It was there the schooner had gone after Keola deserted; there, too, the mate had died, like the fool of a white man he was. It seems, when the ship came, it was the beginning of the sickly season in that isle, when the fish of the lagoon are poisonous, and all who eat of them swell up and die. The mate was told of it; he saw the boats preparing, because in that season the people leave that island and sail to the Isle of Voices; but he was a fool of a white man, who would believe no stories but his own, and he caught one of these fish, cooked it and ate it, and swelled up and died, which was good news to Keola. As for the Isle of Voices, it lay solitary the most of the year, only now and then a boat's crew came for copra, and in the bad season, when the fish at the main isle were poisonous, the tribe dwelt there in a body. It had its name from a marvel, for it seemed the seaside of it was beset with invisible devils; day and night you heard them talking with one another in strange tongues; day and night little fires blazed up and were extinguished on the beach; and what was the cause of these doings no man might conceive. Keola asked them if it were the same in their own island where they stayed, and they told him no, not there; nor yet in any other of some hundred isles that lay all about them in that sea; but it was a thing peculiar to the Isle of Voices. They told him also that these fires and voices were ever on the seaside and in the seaward fringes of the wood, and a man might dwell by the lagoon two thousand years (if he could live so long) and never be any way troubled; and even on the seaside the devils did no harm if let alone. Only once a chief had cast a spear at one of the voices, and the same night he fell out of a cocoanut palm and was killed.

Keola thought a good bit with himself. He saw he would be all right when the tribe returned to the main island, and right enough where he was, if he kept by the lagoon, yet he had a mind to make things righter if he could. So he told the high chief he had once been in an isle that was pestered the same way, and the folk had found a means to cure that trouble.

"There was a tree growing in the bush there," says he, "and it seems these devils came to get the leaves of it. So the people of the isle cut down the tree wherever it was found, and the devils came no more."

They asked what kind of a tree this was, and he showed them the tree of which Kalamake burned the leaves. They found it hard to believe, yet the idea tickled them. Night after night the old men debated it in their councils, but the high chief (though he was a brave man) was afraid of the matter, and reminded them daily of the chief who cast a spear against the voices and was killed, and the thought of that brought all to a stand again.

Though he could not yet bring about the destruction of the trees, Keola was well enough pleased, and began to look about him and take pleasure in his days; and, among other things, he was the kinder to his wife, so that the girl began to love him greatly. One day he came to the hut, and she lay on the ground lamenting.

"Why," said Keola, "what is wrong with you now?"

She declared it was nothing.

The same night she woke him, and he saw by her face she was in sorrow.

"Keola," she said, "put your ear to my mouth that I may whisper, for no one must hear us. Two days before the boats begin to be got ready, go you to the seaside of the isle and lie in a thicket. We shall choose that place beforehand, you and I; and hide food; and every night I shall come near by there singing. So when a night comes and you do not hear me, you may know we are clean gone out of the island, and you may come forth again."

The soul of Keola died within him.

"What is this?" he cried. "I cannot live among devils. I will not be left behind upon this isle. I am dying to leave it."

"You will never leave it alive, my poor Keola," said the girl; "for to tell you the truth, my people are eaters of men; but this they keep secret. And the reason they will kill you before we leave is because in our island ships come, and Donat–Kimaran comes and talks for the French, and there is a white trader there in a house with a verandah, and a catechist. Oh, that is a fine place indeed! The trader has barrels filled with flour; and a French warship once came in the lagoon and gave everybody wine and biscuit. Ah, my poor Keola, I wish I could take you there, for great is my love to you, and it is the finest place in the seas except Papeete."

So now Keola was the most terrified man in the four oceans. He had heard tell of eaters of men in the south islands, and the thing had always been a fear to him; and here it was knocking at his door. He had heard besides, by travelers, of their practices, and how when they are in a mind to eat a man, they cherish and fondle him like a mother with a favorite baby. And he saw this must be his own case; and that was why he had been housed, and fed, and wived, and liberated from all work; and why the old men and the chiefs discoursed with him like a person of weight. So he lay on his bed and railed upon his destiny; and the flesh curdled on his bones.

The next day the people of the tribe were very civil, as their way was. They were elegant speakers, and they made beautiful poetry, and jested at meals, so that a missionary must have died laughing. It was little enough Keola cared for their fine ways: all he saw was the white teeth shining in their mouths, and his gorge rose at the sight; and when they were done eating, he went and lay in the bush like a dead man.

The next day it was the same, and then his wife followed him.

"Keola," she said, "if you do not eat, I tell you plainly you will be killed and cooked tomorrow. Some of the old chiefs are murmuring already. They think you are fallen sick and must lose flesh."

With that Keola got to his feet, and anger burned in him.

"It is little I care one way or the other," said he. "I am between the devil and the deep sea. Since die I must, let me die the quickest way; and since I must be eaten at the best of it, let me rather be eaten by hobgoblins than by men. Farewell," said he, and walked to the seaside of that island.

It was all bare in the strong sun; there was no sign of man, only the beach was trodden, and all about him as he went, the voices talked and whispered, and the little fires sprang up and burned down. All tongues of the earth were spoken there: the French, the Dutch, the Russian, the Tamil, the Chinese. Whatever land knew sorcery, there were some of its people whispering in Keola's ear. That beach was thick as a cried fair, yet no man seen; and as he walked he saw the shells vanish before him, and no man to pick them up. I think the devil would have been afraid to be alone in such a company; but Keola was past fear and courted death. When the fires sprang up, he charged for them like a bull. Bodiless voices called to and fro; unseen hands poured sand upon the flames; and they were gone from the beach before he reached them.

"It is plain Kalamake is not here," he thought, "as I must have been killed long since."

With that he sat him down in the margin of the wood, for he was tired, and put his chin upon his hands. The business before his eyes continued; the beach babbled with voices, and the fires sprang up and sank, and the shells vanished and were renewed again even while he looked.

"It was a by-day when I was here before," he thought, "for it was nothing to this."

And his head was dizzy with the thought of these millions and millions of dollars, and all these hundreds and hundreds of persons culling them upon the beach, and flying in the air higher and swifter than eagles.

"And to think how they have fooled me with their talk of mints," says he, "and that money was made there, when it is clear that all the new coin in all the world is gathered on these sands! But I will know better the next time!" said he. And at last, he knew not very well how or when, sleep fell on Keola, and he forgot the island and all his sorrows.

Early the next day, before the sun was yet up, a bustle woke him. He awoke in fear, for he thought the tribe had caught him napping; but it was no such matter. Only, on the beach in front of him, the bodiless voices called and shouted one upon another, and it seemed they all passed and swept beside him up the coast of the island.

"What is afoot now?" thinks Keola. And it was plain to him it was something beyond ordinary, for the fires were not lighted nor the shells taken, but the bodiless voices kept posting up the beach, and hailing and dying away; and by the sound of them these wizards should be angry.

"It is not me they are angry at," thought Keola, "for they pass me close."

As when hounds go by, or horses in a race, or city folk coursing to a fire, and all men join and follow after, so it was now with Keola; and he knew not what he did, nor why he did it, but there, lo and behold! he was running with the voices.

So he turned one point of the island, and this brought him in view of a second; and there he remembered the wizard trees to have been growing by the score together in a wood. From this point there went up a hubbub of men crying not to be described; and by the sound of them, those that he ran with shaped their course for the same quarter. A little nearer, and there began to mingle with the outcry the crash of many axes. And at this a thought came at last into his mind that the high chief had consented; that the men of the tribe had set to cutting down these trees; that word had gone about the isle from sorcerer to sorcerer, and these were all now assembling to defend their trees. Desire of strange things swept him on. He posted with the voices, crossed the beach, and came into the borders of the wood, and stood astonished. One tree had fallen, others were part hewed away. There was the tribe clustered. They were back to back, and bodies lay, and blood flowed among their feet. The hue of fear was on all their faces; their voices went up to heaven shrill as a weasel's cry.

Have you seen a child when he is all alone and has a wooden sword, and fights, leaping and hewing with the empty air? Even so the man-eaters huddled back to back and heaved up their axes and laid on, and screamed as they laid on, and behold! no man to contend with them! only here and there

Keola saw an axe swinging over against them without hands; and time and again a man of the tribe would fall before it, clove in twain or burst asunder, and his soul sped howling.

For a while Keola looked upon this prodigy like one that dreams, and then fear took him by the midst as sharp as death, that he should behold such doings. Even in that same flash the high chief of the clan espied him standing, and pointed and called out his name. Thereat the whole tribe saw him also, and their eyes flashed, and their teeth clashed.

"I am too long here," thought Keola, and ran farther out of the wood and down the beach, not caring whither.

"Keola!" said a voice close by upon the empty sand.

"Lehua! is that you!" he cried, and gasped, and looked in vain for her, but by the eyesight he was stark alone.

"I saw you pass before," the voice answered, "but you would not hear me. Quick! get the leaves and the herbs, and let us flee."

"You are there with the mat?" he asked.

"Here, at your side," said she. And felt her arms about him. "Quick! the leaves and the herbs, before my father can get back!"

So Keola ran for his life, and fetched the wizard fuel; and Lehua guided him back, and set his feet upon the mat, and made the fire. All the time of its burning, the sound of the battle towered out of the wood; the wizards and the man-eaters hard at fight; the wizards, the viewless ones, roaring out aloud like bulls upon a mountain, and the men of the tribe replying shrill and savage out of the terror of their souls. And all the time of the burning, Keola stood there and listened, and shook, and watched how the unseen hands of Lehua poured the leaves. She poured them fast, and the flame burned high, and scorched Keola's hands, and she speeded and blew the burning with her breath. The last leaf was eaten, the flame fell, and the shock followed, and there were Keola and Lehua in the room at home.

Now, when Keola could see his wife at last he was mighty pleased, and he was mighty pleased to be home again in Molokai and sit down beside a bowl of poi—for they made no poi on board ships, and there was none in the Isle of Voices—and he was out of the body with pleasure to be clean escaped out of the hands of the eaters of men. But there was another matter not so clear, and Lehua and Keola talked of it all night and were troubled. There was Kalamake left upon the isle. If, by the blessing of God, he could but stick there, all were well: but should he escape and return to Molokai, it would be an ill day for his daughter and her husband. They spoke of his gift of swelling and whether he could wade that distance in the seas. But Keola knew by this time where that island was—and that is to say, in the Low or Dangerous Archipelago. So they fetched the atlas and looked upon the distance in the map, and by what they could make of it, it seemed a far way for an old gentleman to walk. Still, it would not do to make too sure of a warlock like Kalamake, and they determined at last to take counsel of a white missionary.

So the first one that came by Keola told him everything. And the missionary was very sharp on him for taking the second wife in the low island; but for all the rest, he vowed he could make neither head nor tail of it.

"However," says he, "if you think this money of your father's ill-gotten, my advice to you would be to give some of it to the lepers and some to the missionary fund. And as for this extraordinary rigmarole, you cannot do better than keep it to yourselves." But he warned the police at Honolulu that, by all he could make out, Kalamake and Keola had been coining false money, and it would not be amiss to watch them.

Keola and Lehua took his advice, and gave many dollars to the lepers and the fund. And no doubt the advice must have been good, for from that day to this, Kalamake has never more been heard of. But whether he was slain in the battle by the trees, or whether he is still kicking his heels upon the Isle of Voices, who shall say?

IDAHO

One Man's Harp
by Babette Rosmond

HARRY JORDAN put down his magazine and listened politely to the man in the next chair who'd been talking to him on and off for the last hour. The man seemed to be aware of one subject only: skiing. Harry Jordan knew what a ski was, he knew where Sun Valley was—his neighbor's destination —and he knew he hated snow. Outside of that, he knew nothing and cared less. He was bored; it was time to be getting to work on this tanned, tall and patently ingenuous stranger.

"These trains certainly are slow," sighed his neighbor. He yawned extensively. "Wish there was something exciting to do."

"Well," suggested Jordan carefully, "I don't know how much excitement I can promise you with my brand of card playing—never touch the stuff except when I'm driven to it—but how about a friendly little game?"

"Well! That sounds fine," said his neighbor with enthusiasm. "My name's Taft, by the way. Gene Taft. Olympics. Skiing team."

"Oh, yes." said Jordan. "I'm Harry Jordan. Pleased to meet you." His hands were beginning to itch. "Gin rummy O.K.?" he asked. "It's about the only game I know. Two cents a point suit you?"

Taft nodded and showed fine white teeth in a big smile.

"Boy, this is going to be a cinch," he said. "Hate to take your money."

Jordan grinned and rang for the porter, who returned with two new decks. Jordan slid the cards out on the table that the porter rigged up between their seats and picked the jokers out of the decks. Then he shuffled the cards clumsily. They cut for deal, and the high card fell to Jordan. He dealt ten cards to each, picked up his own and expertly separated two aces from the others. As he placed them at one end of his hand he lightly ran his fingernail

173

over a corner of each, cutting a ridge perceptible only to his trained fingertips. He stifled a yawn and settled down to the game. It was such routine stuff that his air of disinterest was completely real.

They played for a half hour. Taft was winning. When he was thirty-five dollars ahead, Jordan had marked the deck to his own satisfaction and good-naturedly proposed that they raise the stakes to five cents a point. In another hour the stakes were raised to twenty-five cents a point. Languidly, Jordan came in for the kill. Taft found himself unable to fill a single sequence. Every card he dropped was picked up by Jordan. The score rose higher and higher and all the scoring was on Jordan's side of the sheet. Finally Jordan added up an astounding column of figures.

"My, my," he said, with a look of amazement that would have registered as pure corn with anyone else but Taft. "I seem to be winning. Imagine. That's forty-seven hundred you owe me."

Taft looked a little pale under his magnificent tan, but his tone was quiet. "That happens to be just four hundred dollars more than I have or could raise." He reached into his pocket and drew out a bank book. "There's forty-three hundred dollars in this account, and it was supposed to keep me until the end of the year. Which means I owe you four hundred I don't have, and that I'm short another four hundred for this"—and here his voice broke a little—"for this skiing trip."

He raised his eyes to Jordan. "Tell you what. I'll cut you for eight hundred dollars, high card takes all. If I win, you'll give me back the four hundred I need and we'll be even on what I owe you. If I lose—"

"Yes," interrupted Jordan, smiling benignly. "If you lose?"

"If I lose," said Taft, evenly, I'll transfer you—my share of Paradise!"

Jordan stared at Taft. "Out of all the suckers on this train, I have to pick this whack," he thought. "Paradise he wants to give me. Could I get a liquor license in Paradise, could I get a floor show going there, could I fix deals with The Boys there? Well, I'll be off this train in about ten minutes. I might as well take what I can get. At least the cops won't ever nail me with it."

"Ha, ha," he said aloud, showing very bad, jagged, little, dirty teeth. "Eight hundred dollars. Against your share of Paradise."

Taft extended his hand toward the stack of cards. He hesitated for a fraction of a second and then pulled out a card. It was the ten of diamonds. He flipped it face up on the table and watched Jordan's hand move toward the deck. Jordan cut the cards. The card facing Taft was the jack of hearts.

Taft looked solemn.

"That's it," he said. "O.K. With all due respects to Those who arrange such affairs, I hereby confer upon you my share of Paradise as of this moment. All the good that was to befall me is now yours."

He had just about finished his sentence when there was a nerve-chilling screech of steel against steel. Jordan rushed to the window. Headed toward them, at a miraculous, terrifying and inevitable speed, was the blinding headlight of another engine. How the tracks had branched Jordan never had time to figure out. In another moment the trains had thundered together and Jordan was smashed with sickening force against the floor of the Pullman car.

Jordan picked himself up from the snow-covered ground and brushed some flakes off his right leg. He felt cold, and more important, he felt lonely—unutterably lonely. He was not at all reassured to find that at the end of his right leg there was a ski. Beyond the ski, his leg seemed to be clothed with a close-fitting silky green trouser tucked into a woolen sock. His foot was covered by a bulky shoe which, in turn, was thrust into the metal and leather strips which bound it to the ski.

He looked around him. He was alone on a vast snow-covered mountain. Stretching down at a thirty-degree angle from where he stood was an icy slope studded with tree stumps and scattered boulders. He tried to find tracks on the thick snow, but couldn't. He realized he must have arrived somewhat unconventionally.

He removed his skis, with difficulty, and trudged up the hill, slipping frequently. Several hundred feet higher he found the trail of skis, which disappeared and then reappeared at the very spot where he had been a few moments before. He saw in his mind the picture of an intrepid skier, hurtling down the mountain—like in the movies—coming to earth on the rim of disaster on a tiny shelf overhanging the valley. A bitter wind chilled him to the core, as he started to climb the hill; then, suddenly he stopped. There was no one else about. It was he who had been standing on the landing marks of the skis.

That intrepid skier, that defier of death, had been himself.

Shivering with fright and cold, he continued his climb. In about half an hour he saw a curl of smoke. His feet, by then, felt as if he had left them off that morning; his ski boots were saturated with icy water. Through the tattered folds of his pants his blue knees poked, lacerated and bleeding from frequent contact with the sharp snow crust.

The smoke was coming from the chimney of a long, low house. Jordan swung open the door without knocking. His heart leaped at the beautiful sight before him. A great fire was crackling in a massive fireplace. Several assorted ski suits, with people in them, were sitting around the fire, drinking hot rum. Jordan staggered to a fine, big leather couch and collapsed.

A servant in a white jacket unlaced Jordan's boots and drew them from his feet, which had returned but were not yet really feet: just clumps of ice. He thrust a mug into Jordan's hand and waited until Jordan had drained it before he spoke:

"My, you're late. We expected you at least an hour ago."

Jordan looked at him. "How did you know I was coming? I'm sure *I* didn't."

The servant looked scornful.

"Now, now, stop with the Here-Comes-Mr.-Jordan stuff. We're all very tired of being whimsied up in the movies. However, you are most welcome here. Everyone respects and admires Gene Taft."

"Taft, Taft?" Jordan rubbed his head. "Where is this? Sun Valley?"

"No, sir. This is Paradise."

And then, of course, Jordan remembered. This was Gene Taft's share of Paradise. This was what he had won in a gin-rummy game.

Jordan looked around him. No one seemed particularly ethereal. Everyone wore old shirts, worn slippers, slacks, jackets and other things which he had known about, dimly, but had never worn. The women were husky but beautiful. Six of them were staring at him, invitingly. Jordan felt better.

One of the women sat next to him. As she bounced reassuringly against him he noticed a trace of perfume. He felt lots better. This was familiar stuff.

"That's nice perfume, sister," he said in his best Humphrey Bogart manner.

The woman smiled and moved closer to him.

"I'm glad you like it," she said. "I've been waiting for you. I've admired you for years. I remember you in the Olympics. My name is Sally Ransome."

Jordan would have liked to continue the conversation, but he felt unreasonably tired. Murmuring excuses, he allowed himself to be led upstairs by the servant. He sank into a bed, and knew nothing until, hours later, a hand tapped his shoulder.

He opened his eyes. He was conscious of pain. Every muscle ached. His face felt like stretched leather; his lips were cracked and bleeding.

The white-coated servant was standing at his bedside. Beyond him, the open window looked out upon the valley. The first rays of light were rising from a sun which had not yet come up.

"It's five thirty, sir," whispered the servant. "I let you sleep longer this morning."

Then the servant pulled him from his bed and led him across the cold floor to a bathroom. Half asleep, he felt himself being stripped of his pajamas and placed under a shower. Then the icicles hit him. Sharp and frigid, they drove into his back and face and limbs. He leaped into the air in agony as the cold, cold deluge met his blistered legs. He was almost unconscious by the time the servant started rubbing him with a rough towel. Jordan broke away and ran back into bed.

"Say, look, bub," he said to the servant. "I don't know who told you to call me, but don't. Don't wake me at five, don't wake me at six. And don't wake me at eleven unless I tell you that I want to get up very, very early in the morning."

"And I don't bathe in the morning. I bathe at night. I do not bathe in ice; I bathe in warm water. If there is anything that I do not like, that is cold water. Now go away. I am a sick man. I am a cold and sick man."

The servant stood there, smiling.

"Oh, you skiers. You will have your little joke. Why, Mr. Taft, you know as well as I do that you'll be getting up every morning at five and taking your nice cold shower. You'll do it all the time, if you'll pardon a colloquialism. Time really means eternity, you know. And now your massage, sir."

There followed an unspeakable half hour of torture, during which Jordan felt as though he were a professional demonstrator of Iron Marys.

Finally, somehow, Jordan dressed. He went down into the dining room, where only Sally Ransome was left.

She smiled a welcome. "I thought you were never coming. I'd have been out an hour ago but I didn't want you to eat alone. Isn't this a honey of a day?"

"I," said Jordan, "have known better."

"Yes," she went on, "it's glorious here. Every day is colder than the one before it. After you're here ten years or so, you'll find that it will seem like fifty degrees below zero! Imagine how grand the snow is then."

Jordan frowned at Sally, and ordered some orange juice. The servant brought it in a pint-sized glass, and asked if he would have oatmeal or farina, and did he prefer ham or sausages with his eggs?

"I will have one cup of black coffee," said Jordan. "Black."

The servant tittered.

"You're a one, sir. First joking about your shower and now— Why, first thing we know you'll be asking for a cigar!"

Sally giggled.

"You are funny, Mr. Taft. Why, the oatmeal is wonderful this morning. I had two bowls. Lots of brown sugar and I think the cook has mixed in some raw eggs. Jensen, bring Mr. Taft the works!"

She laughed again. Beautiful as she was, Jordan felt slightly revolted at that laughter. Then Jensen brought breakfast. The oatmeal looked as if it were prepared for a hungry family of twelve; the hot milk had skin floating on it.

Jordan swallowed his nausea and said quickly: "You'll think this is foolish, I know, but isn't there something else we could do today besides ski?"

"Silly boy! As if we could do anything here *but* ski! Just try to do anything else, and you'll see what happens. Why, you could *not* ski if you wanted to—which you don't, of course!"

"You know," Sally chattered on and on as he ate, "the funniest thing happened the other day. I was out with Mr. James and we stopped for lunch. It was really hot—only ten below—so we took off our jackets to cool off and found some nice lumps of ice to curl up on. Well, by the time we'd finished, I looked around and our jackets just weren't there any more. Then I realized we'd been sitting on a glacier and it had just moved us along with it. Well, Mr. James had to carry me up because the snow was too deep to walk—and he was *puffing* when we got there. Imagine a man not able to carry me up a hill for a couple of miles on skis without puffing? I only weigh a hundred and forty. Do you think that's too light for cross-country runs?"

"Er, you say we don't come back for lunch?" asked Jordan.

"Oh, no. The lodge simply isn't here in the daytime. It disappears. Comes back about five o'clock. Oh, do hurry! I want you to show me so many things today."

"I suppose," said Jordan, cleverly, "this being Paradise, no one ever gets in, well, any skiing accidents?"

"Oh, you!" Sally laughed. And now Jordan hated her and wished she and her laugh were inside a glacier with oatmeal and brown sugar. "Of course we can't die. But if any of us are stupid enough to blunder in the snow, we get hurt. Not that many of us do, but occasionally some fool breaks his leg and has to wait weeks before another one grows. But we're all professionals here, so there's not much danger—even though there's a punishment for those who try to take it easy."

"Punishment," mumbled Jordan. Then he looked around. He was sitting in the snow.

"See," laughed Sally. "I told you the lodge disappeared during the day. Come on, let's ski!"

"Excuse me just a moment," said Jordan. "Got to see a man. Be right back."

He dashed behind a tree stump out of Sally's sight and sat down, panting. What manner of game was this, what doom had he bargained for? Was this icy mess Paradise? Was this the land of milk and honey? No, this was the land of oatmeal and ice—and he would have none of it. Better hell than this. Better nice warm hell fires than fifty below zero. This might be heaven for Gene Taft, wherever he was now—probably enjoying himself in some celestial burlesque house, smoking cigars and drinking gin—but for him it was—

Why not? The thought hit him full in the stomach, or at least in the cold region where a stomach had once functioned. Perhaps he could arrange something with—well, call him Satan. People did it. They made bargains. And Jordan knew that whatever happened to him now, he'd be getting the best of the bargain. But how did one summon Satan?

Remembering dimly something he had once read, he drew a crude circle in the snow. The he started mumbling to himself, "Please, Satan, honey, come up here just a minute, please, Satan, just this once, be a good guy, you don't know what I'd do to leave this heaven-hole, honey, please."

The man standing before him was tall and slim and dressed in a snappy white linen suit.

"I'm delighted to see you, sir," said Jordan sincerely.

"Well, what's this?" asked Satan. "Want to trade heaven for hell, do you? Crazy. But that's your affair."

"Pardon me," said Jordan, beginning to feel like a new man, "but aren't you supposed to wear black? Or red?"

"Quit reading dime magazines," said Satan. "Don't you wear white suits in the summer? Well, it's plenty hot where I live. So I wear them."

"That reminds me," said Jordan. "If I come to you . . . if I trade this no-good heaven for a nice, personal hell—I'd like to have you promise me that it won't get too hot. Say, nothing over ninety degrees."

"Done," said Satan. "You won't find it too hot. It'll be a nice, personal hell, that's all. After all, Jordan, I've had my eye on you for years. You crossed me up in that gin-rummy game, all right. I thought sure I'd get you for some of the things you've done. Hiring killers, driving people to suicide on account of gambling debts. Oh, you certainly fooled me with that Taft switch. But I'm a good sport. I don't hold grudges. Come on, let's get out of here. You'll get your own hell—at your own request."

Jordan's head began to ache. He grew dizzy. The snow melted around him and swirled in pretty patterns over his head. Then there was a period of blackness. Then a great light. Then—

Jordan picked himself up from the snow-covered ground. He looked around him. He was quite alone on a vast snow-covered mountain. He looked down. There was a ski at the end of his leg. He began to sob.

ILLINOIS

Cannibalism in the Cars
by Mark Twain

I VISITED St. Louis lately, and on my way West, after changing cars at Terre Haute, Indiana, a mild, benevolent-looking gentleman of about forty-five, or maybe fifty, came in at one of the way stations and sat down beside me. We talked together pleasantly on various subjects for an hour, perhaps, and I found him exceedingly intelligent and entertaining. When he learned that I was from Washington, he immediately began to ask questions about various public men, and about congressional affairs; and I saw very shortly that I was conversing with a man who was perfectly familiar with the ins and outs of political life at the capital, even to the ways and manners, and customs of procedure of senators and representatives in the chambers of the national legislature. Presently two men halted near us for a single moment, and one said to the other: "Harris, if you'll do that for me, I'll never forget you, my boy."

My new comrade's eye lighted pleasantly. The words had touched upon a happy memory, I thought. Then his face settled into thoughtfulness—almost into gloom. He turned to me and said, "Let me tell you a story; let me give you a secret chapter of my life—a chapter that has never been referred to by me since its events transpired. Listen patiently, and promise that you will not interrupt me."

I said I would not, and he related the following strange adventure, speaking sometimes with animation, sometimes with melancholy, but always with feeling and earnestness.

On the nineteenth of December, 1853, I started from St. Louis on the evening train bound for Chicago. There were only twenty-four passengers, all told. There were no ladies and no children. We were in excellent spirits, and pleasant acquaintanceships were soon formed. The journey bade fair to be a happy one; and no individual in the party, I think, had even the vaguest presentiment of the horrors we were soon to undergo.

At 11:00 P.M. it began to snow hard. Shortly after leaving the small village of Welden, we entered upon that tremendous prairie solitude that stretches its leagues on leagues of houseless dreariness far away toward the Jubilee Settlements. The winds, unobstructed by trees or hills, or even vagrant rocks, whistled fiercely across the level desert, driving the falling snow before it like spray from the crested waves of a stormy sea. The snow was deepening fast; and we knew, by the diminished speed of the train, that the engine was plowing through it with steadily increasing difficulty. Indeed, it almost came to a dead halt sometimes, in the midst of great drifts that piled themselves like colossal graves across the track. Conversation began to flag. Cheerfulness gave place to grave concern. The possibility of being imprisoned in the snow, on the bleak prairie, fifty miles from any house, presented itself to every mind, and extended its depressing influence over every spirit.

At two o'clock in the morning I was aroused out of an uneasy slumber by the ceasing of all motion about me. The appalling truth flashed upon me instantly—we were captives in a snowdrift! "All hands to the rescue!" Every man sprang to obey. Out into the wild night, the pitchy darkness, the billowy snow, the driving storm, every soul leaped, with the consciousness that a moment lost now might bring destruction to us all. Shovels, hands, boards—anything, everything that could displace snow, was brought into instant requisition. It was a weird picture, that small company of frantic men fighting the banking snows, half in the blackest shadow and half in the angry light of the locomotive's reflector.

One short hour sufficed to prove the utter uselessness of our efforts. The storm barricaded the track with a dozen drifts while we dug one away. And worse than this, it was discovered that the last grand charge the engine had made upon the enemy had broken the fore-and-aft shaft of the driving wheel! With a free track before us we should still have been helpless. We entered the car wearied with labor, and very sorrowful. We gathered about the stoves, and gravely canvassed our situation. We had no provisions whatever—in this lay our chief distress. We could not freeze, for there was a good supply of wood in the tender. This was our only comfort. The discussion ended at last in accepting the disheartening decision of the conductor, viz., that it would be death for any man to attempt to travel fifty miles on foot through snow like that. We could not send for help, and even if we could it would not come. We must submit, and await, as patiently as we might, succor or starvation! I think the stoutest heart there felt a momentary chill when those words were uttered.

Within the hour conversation subsided to a low murmur here and there about the car, caught fitfully between the rising and falling of the blast; the lamps grew dim; and the majority of the castaways settled themselves among the flickering shadows to think—to forget the present, if they could—to sleep, if they might.

The eternal night—it surely seemed eternal to us—wore its lagging hours away at last, and the cold gray dawn broke in the east. As the light grew stronger the passengers began to stir and give signs of life, one after another, and each in turn pushed his slouched hat up from his forehead, stretched his stiffened limbs and glanced out of the windows upon the cheerless prospect. It was cheerless, indeed!—not a living thing visible anywhere, not a human habitation; nothing but a vast white desert; uplifted sheets of snow drifting hither and thither before the wind—a world of eddying flakes shutting out the firmament above.

All day we moped about the cars, saying little, thinking much. Another lingering dreary night—and hunger.

Another dawning—another day of silence, sadness, wasting hunger, hopeless watching for succor that could not come. A night of restless slumber, filled with dreams of feasting—wakings distressed with the gnawings of hunger.

The fourth day came and went—and the fifth! Five days of dreadful imprisonment! A savage hunger looked out at every eye. There was in it a sign of awful import—the foreshadowing of a something that was vaguely shaping itself in every heart—a something which no tongue dared yet to frame into words.

The sixth day passed—the seventh dawned upon as gaunt and haggard and hopeless a company of men as ever stood in the shadow of death. It must out now! That thing which had been growing up in every heart was ready to leap from every lip at last! Nature had been taxed to the utmost—she must yield. Richard H. Gaston of Minnesota, tall, cadaverous, and pale, rose up. All knew what was coming. All prepared—every emotion, every semblance of excitement was smothered—only a calm, thoughtful seriousness appeared in the eyes that were lately so wild.

"Gentlemen: It cannot be delayed longer! The time is at hand! We must determine which of us shall die to furnish food for the rest!"

MR. JOHN J. WILLIAMS of Illinois rose and said: "Gentlemen—I nominate the Reverend James Sawyer of Tennessee."

MR. WM. R. ADAMS of Indiana said: "I nominate Mr. Daniel Slote of New York."

MR. CHARLES J. LANGDON: "I nominate Mr. Samuel A. Bowen of St. Louis."

MR. SLOTE: "Gentlemen—I desire to decline in favor of Mr. John A. Van Nostrand, Jr., of New Jersey."

MR. GASTON: "If there be no objection, the gentleman's desire will be acceded to."

Mr. Van Nostrand objecting, the resignation of Mr. Slote was rejected. The resignations of Messrs. Sawyer and Bowen were also offered, and refused upon the same grounds.

MR. A. L. BASCOM of Ohio: "I move that the nominations now close, and that the House proceed to an election by ballot."

Mr. SAWYER: "Gentlemen—I protest earnestly against these proceed-ings. They are, in every way, irregular and unbecoming. I must beg to move that they be dropped at once, and that we elect a chairman of the meeting and proper officers to assist him, and then we can go on with the business before us understandingly."

Mr. BELL of Iowa: "Gentlemen—I object. This is no time to stand upon forms and ceremonious observances. For more than seven days we have been without food. Every moment we lose in idle discussion increases our distress. I am satisfied with the nominations that have been made—every gentleman present is, I believe—and I, for one, do not see why we should not proceed at once to elect one or more of them. I wish to offer a resolution—"

Mr. GASTON: "It would be objected to, and have to lie over one day under the rules, thus bringing about the very delay you wish to avoid. The gentleman from New Jersey—"

Mr. VAN NOSTRAND: "Gentlemen—I am a stranger among you; I have not sought the distinction that has been conferred upon me, and I feel a delicacy—"

Mr. MORGAN of Alabama (interrupting): "I move the previous question."

The motion was carried, and further debate shut off, of course. The motion to elect officers was passed, and under it Mr. Gaston was chosen chairman, Mr. Blake, sectetary, Messrs. Holcomb, Dyer and Baldwin a committee on nominations, and Mr. R. M. Howland, purveyor, to assist the committee in making selections.

A recess of half an hour was then taken, and some little caucusing followed. At the sound of the gavel the meeting reassembled, and the committee reported in favor of Messrs. George Ferguson of Kentucky, Lucien Herrman of Louisiana and W. Messick of Colorado as candidates. The report was accepted.

Mr. ROGERS of Missouri: "Mr. President—The report being properly before the House now, I move to amend it by substituting for the name of Mr. Herrman that of Mr. Lucius Harris of St. Louis, who is well and honorably known to us all. I do not wish to be understood as casting the least reflection upon the high character and standing of the gentleman from Louisiana—far from it. I respect and esteem him as much as any gentleman here present possibly can; but none of us can be blind to the fact that he had lost more flesh during the week that we have lain here than any among us—none of us can be blind to the fact that the committee has been derelict in its duty, either through negligence or a graver fault, in thus offering for our suffrages a gentleman who, however pure his own motives may be, has really less nutriment in him—"

THE CHAIR: "The gentleman from Missouri will take his seat. The Chair cannot allow the integrity of the committee to be questioned save by the regular course, under the rules. What action will the House take upon the gentleman's motion?"

MR. HALLIDAY of Virginia: "I move to further amend the report by substituting Mr. Harvey Davis of Oregon for Mr. Messick. It may be urged by gentlemen that the hardships and privations of a frontier life have rendered Mr. Davis tough; but, gentlemen, is this a time to cavil at toughness? Is this a time to be fastidious concerning trifles? Is this a time to dispute about matters of paltry significance? No, gentlemen, bulk is what we desire—substance, weight, bulk—these are the supreme requisites now—not talent, not genius, not education. I insist upon my motion."

MR. MORGAN (excitedly): "Mr Chairman—I do most strenuously object to this amendment. The gentleman from Oregon is old, and furthermore is bulky only in bone—not in flesh. I ask the gentleman from Virginia if it is soup we want instead of solid sustenance? if he would delude us with shadows? if he would mock our suffering with an Oregonian specter? I ask him if he can look upon the anxious faces around him, if he can gaze into our sad eyes, if he can listen to the beating of our expectant hearts, and still thrust this famine-stricken fraud upon us? I ask him if he can think of our desolate state, of our past sorrows, of our dark future, and still unpityingly foist upon us this wreck, this ruin, this tottering swindle, this gnarled and blighted and sapless vagabond from Oregon's inhospitable shores? Never!" [Applause.]

The amendment was put to vote, after a fiery debate, and lost. Mr. Harris was substituted on the first amendment. The balloting then began. Five ballots were held without a choice. On the sixth, Mr. Harris was elected, all voting for him but himself. It was then moved that his election should be ratified by acclamation, which was lost, in consequence of his again voting against himself.

Mr. Radway moved that the House now take up the remaining candidates, and go into an election for breakfast. This was carried.

On the first ballot there was a tie, half the members favoring one candidate on account of his youth, and half favoring the other on account of his superior size. The president gave the casting vote for the latter, Mr. Messick. This decision created considerable dissatisfaction among the friends of Mr. Ferguson, the defeated candidate, and there was some talk of demanding a new ballot; but in the midst of it a motion to adjourn was carried, and the meeting broke up at once.

The preparations for supper diverted the attention of the Ferguson faction from the discussion of their grievance for a long time, and then, when they would have taken it up again, the happy announcement that Mr. Harris was ready drove all thought of it to the winds.

We improvised tables by propping up the backs of car seats, and sat down with hearts full of gratitude to the finest supper that had blessed our vision for seven torturing days. How changed we were from what we had been a few short hours before! Hopeless, sad-eyed misery, hunger, feverish anxiety, desperation, then; thankfulness, serenity, joy too deep for utterance now. That I know was the cheeriest hour of my eventful life. The winds howled, and blew the snow wildly about our prison house, but they were powerless to distress us anymore. I liked Harris. He might have been better done, perhaps, but I am free to say that no man ever agreed with me better than Harris, or afforded me so large a degree of satisfaction. Messick was very well, though rather high-flavored, but for genuine nutritiousness and delicacy of fiber, give me Harris. Messick had his good points—I will not attempt to deny it, nor do I wish to do it—but he was no more fitted for breakfast than a mummy would be, sir—not a bit. Lean?—why, bless me!— and tough? Ah, he was very tough! You could not imagine it—you could never imagine anything like it.

"Do you mean to tell me that—"

"Do not interrupt me, please. After breakfast we elected a man by the name of Walker, from Detroit, for supper. He was very good. I wrote his wife so afterward. He was worthy of all praise. I shall always remember Walker. He was a little rare, but very good. And then the next morning we had Morgan of Alabama for breakfast. He was one of the finest men I ever sat down to—handsome, educated, refined, spoke several languages fluently—a perfect gentleman—he was a perfect gentleman, and singularly juicy. For supper we had that Oregon patriarch, and he *was* a fraud, there is no question about it—old, scraggy, tough, nobody can picture the reality. I finally said, 'Gentlemen, you can do as you like, but *I* will wait for another election.' And Grimes of Illinois said, 'Gentlemen, *I* will wait also. When you elect a man that has *something* to recommend him, I shall be glad to join you again.' It soon became evident that there was general dissatisfaction with Davis of Oregon, and so, to preserve the good will that had prevailed so pleasantly since we had had Harris, an election was called, and the result of it was that Baker of Georgia was chosen. He was splendid! Well, well—after that we had Doolittle, and Hawkins, and McElroy (there was some complaint about McElroy, because he was uncommonly short and thin), and Penrod, and two Smiths, and Bailey (Bailey had a wooden leg, which was clear loss, but he was otherwise good), and an Indian boy, and an organ-grinder and a gentleman by the name of Buckminster—a poor stick of a vagabond that wasn't any good for company and no account for breakfast. We were glad we got him elected before relief came."

"And so the blessed relief *did* come at last?"

"Yes, it came one bright, sunny morning, just after election. John Murphy was the choice, and there never was a better, I am willing to testify; but John Murphy came home with us, in the train that came to succor us, and lived to marry the widow Harris—"

"Relict of—"

"Relict of our first choice. He married her, and is happy and respected and prosperous yet. Ah, it was like a novel, sir—it was like a romance. This is my stopping-place, sir; I must bid you goodbye. Any time that you can make it convenient to tarry a day or two with me, I shall be glad to have you. I like you, sir; I have conceived an affection for you. I could like you as well as I liked Harris himself, sir. Good day, sir, and a pleasant journey."

He was gone. I never felt so stunned, so distressed, so bewildered in my life. But in my soul I was glad he was gone. With all his gentleness of manner and his soft voice, I shuddered whenever he turned his hungry eye upon me; and when I heard that I had achieved his perilous affection, and that I stood almost with the late Harris in his esteem, my heart fairly stood still!

I was bewildered beyond description. I did not doubt his word; I could not question a single item in a statement so stamped with the earnestness of truth as his; but its dreadful details overpowered me, and threw my thoughts into hopeless confusion. I saw the conductor looking at me. I said, "Who is that man?"

"He was a member of congress once, and a good one. But he got caught in a snowdrift in the cars, and like to have been starved to death. He got so frostbitten and frozen up generally, and used up for want of something to eat, that he was sick and out of his head two or three months afterward. He is all right now, only he is a monomaniac, and when he gets on that old subject he never stops till he has eat up that whole carload of people he talks about. He would have finished the crowd by this time, only he had to get out here. He has got their names as pat as *ABC*. When he gets them all eat up but himself, he always says: "Then the hour for the unusual election for breakfast having arrived, and there being no opposition, I was duly elected, after which, there being no objections offered, I resigned. Thus I am here.""

I felt inexpressibly relieved to know that I had only been listening to the harmless vagaries of a madman instead of the genuine experiences of a bloodthirsty cannibal.

INDIANA

The Smell of Cherries
by Jeffrey Goddin

TAYLOR HAD never been in the army. Too young for Korea, he'd pulled a high number during the Vietnamese shindig. But he liked guns, and he liked excitement of the low-key variety. This might explain why he still found security work mildly interesting, even though he'd almost had his car shot up on an industrial espionage job, and had had to wrestle a coked-out robber to the floor on a pawnshop beat.

The problem with Taylor was, he was a romantic, and more or less incapable of taking orders from anyone on an eight-hour basis. This was probably the reason that what he'd regarded as merely a stopgap job on the way to better things was heading into its second year.

Now, near midnight, driving down a narrow river road on the Indiana side of the Ohio across from Louisville, he was humming softly to himself. He looked forward to a night of sipping spiced coffee and watching the perimeter of a small trucking company for intruders.

This was a holiday job. Happy Thanksgiving. He'd never done the Coleman trucking shift before. All he knew about Coleman was that they had trouble keeping guards on it. The guards got spooked, for some reason. This, too, made the shift mildly attractive.

The lights of Jeffersonville were fading in the distance. Night closed in around the inverted cones of his headlights. Skeletal November trees lined the road, with now and again a car parked by the roadside, interior lights on, kids smoking dope or drinking with the radio throbbing.

Nice, calm, dark road. But Taylor had a slight uneasiness this night, a new feeling, as if in some way he were going into battle. And a part of him liked the feeling.

He passed a stretch of river, distant lights, then the road ran back inland. Now on the left a series of large buildings came up, set well away from the road. A few, but only a few, of the buildings showed light.

Taylor remembered that Coleman's lay along the edge of a large World War II military base, now mostly empty barracks space, a seldom-used proving ground with a skeleton administrative staff.

Almost there. He saw the red eyes of the reflectors marking the entrance to the wide staging lot, a dozen or so trailers ranged around the perimeter waiting for drivers. At the rear of the lot he recognized the El Camino of the day guard.

On a whim, he killed his lights. He accelerated a little, then let the car coast up beside the El Camino, which was facing to the rear.

It was one of those minor precognitions, like when he'd known that the next guy to walk into the pawnshop was the one he'd have to deal with. He'd also known in some strange fashion that the duty guard in the El Camino would be sleeping, and he was right.

The driver's head was thrown back, a cap pulled across his eyes. Taylor rolled down his window, smelled the cool country air, a scent of dead leaves and earth. He was tempted to blow his horn to wake the shift cop, but he didn't.

Funny, the man was talking to himself in his sleep. In the half-light, half-shadow of the interior, his face was contorted. He was talking quickly, then suddenly he screamed.

The man's eyes shot open. Immediately he saw Taylor, and his hand was halfway to the gun on the seat when he recognized him.

"Snuck up on me, you bastard!"

"Any kid could have. It's a wonder you still have tires. Must have been some dream you were having!"

Brewster laughed. "Hope I don't have any more like it. Dreamed I was sitting right here in my Hillbilly Cadillac and some fucking monsters were creeping up on me out of the woods over there."

Inadvertently, Taylor looked over to the darkly wooded perimeter. A full moon made the nearer trees stand out starkly, dark shadows beneath. He could almost see things moving in there.

"'Course, *you're* the one they're waitin' for."

Taylor shook his head. "Your sense of humor hasn't improved since the G.E. job, leaving that dead cat by the first keystop . . ."

"Hey, it gets better." Brewster consulted his watch. "Shit, past midnight, gotta haul, my momma's waitin'."

"One thing," said Taylor, reaching for the walkie-talkie that Brewster handed him through the window, "I hear you have trouble keeping people on this shift, why?"

"Tales gettin' to ya? Hell if I know. As far as action goes, don't think anybody ever tried to hit this place. Nice and quiet and dead dull, out in the sticks like this. Maybe that's it. City boys get lonesome. See ya."

Brewster slammed the Camino into low, shot gravel across the lot as he took off. Taylor watched the red tail lights wink at the turn and disappear up the road toward Jeffersonville.

The beginning of a twelve-hour shift. A good time, as far as Taylor was concerned. He climbed out of the car, stretched, pulled out his shotgun, and walked across the loose gravel to the perimeter at the back of the lot.

To the left, the woods; to his rear, the road. Ahead was an empty field of autumn weeds, with a few desultory crickets chiming under the full moon and, very far away it seemed, the nearest of the abandoned barracks.

The night was quiet, so still. He took a deep breath of cool air, turned around.

He could see his old Chevy quite clearly in the moonlight. Someone was standing beside it.

Taylor's nerves froze. He was an experienced guard. He had a twelve-gauge automatic shotgun with deer slugs under his arm. Yet there was something about the tall, apparently male figure beside his car that made him dizzy with fear. And there was only one thing to do about it.

He began to walk slowly back across the lot, the shotgun in his hands. It seemed to take a very long time. With each step, the figure was slightly clearer. It was a man, bareheaded, wearing a loose overcoat, facing away from Taylor, peering into the car.

Taylor suddenly remembered that, like an idiot, he'd left the keys in the ignition. All this dude had to do was climb in and drive away. He began to run, holding the shotgun across his chest.

He was quite close. The man must hear him, but he didn't move. Fifteen, ten yards. Taylor slowed to a walk, brought the gun up in one hand, his flashlight in the other.

"You, don't move!" he yelled.

The figure didn't move. Five yards, four, three. He could see the fellow clearly now, hands in his pockets, shoulders hunched into the old khaki raincoat, a bald spot on the top of his head.

"Take your hands out of your pockets, real slow, and turn around."

Slowly the figure took his hands out of his pockets. The bare fingers that protruded from the ends of the overcoat seemed very slender, very pale.

It turned around, and Taylor shone his flashlight in its face.

He didn't scream, but he wanted to.

There was no face.

Taylor stood frozen, motionless.

The man was gone. There was only a faint sweetish smell in the air.

"Base calling 2101. Base calling 2101."

Taylor jerked open the door and collapsed in the front seat. He fumbled at the walkie-talkie.

"2101 receiving."

"Everything 10-2 down on the ranch?"

"Got a spook here, otherwise 10-2."

"Copy?"

"Spook. S-P-O-O-K. But harmless. Everything 10-2."

"Lay off the funny cigarettes, 2101."

But the switchboard girl giggled.

"10-4. 2101 over and out."

Taylor put down the walkie-talkie. What the hell *had* he seen? He'd never seen anything like it before, even when he'd dropped acid a few times. Was his psyche gunning for him? He put the thought out of his mind.

It was a nice night. He turned on the radio low, and had a first sip of the sweet, scalding coffee. The moon was just touching the tops of the slender black trees, the paired lights of a car passed in the distance. It *would* be a good night, now that his unconscious had had its little fling.

Taylor had a game he played with himself on long security shifts. He'd either mentally write the novel he'd promised himself he owed the world one day, or he'd reminisce about old girl friends.

The girl friends generally came a bit more toward the early morning hours. He decided to pick up on the novel.

The last time, he'd had his protagonist traveling across Ohio in a drunken haze. Now he would stop in a small Pennsylvania town, and meet a lonely woman who ran a rooming house. She would be in her early thirties, pale, divorced, and pretty. She would invite him to dinner one night. Outside the rain would be falling softly. Inside the candlelight danced across her face, softening its lines . . .

Taylor heard a sound.

His preconscious heard the sound and registered it before his conscious mind. His conscious mind didn't want anything to do with it.

Distant, but not too distant, the sound of a woman crying in pain.

He scanned the lot. The moon rode high, the small floods illuminating the terminal building. The sound seemed to be coming from the far right rear of the perimeter, where a few trailers were parked.

This is weird, but it is not as weird as it seems.

Taylor climbed out of the car, taking shotgun and flashlight. He walked quickly across the lot, the sound of boots crunching gravel loud in the night.

It came again, the cry, louder, a catch of horrible pain in the woman's voice. Taylor began to run.

It was coming from directly behind the line of four trailers. Instead of running between them into the darkness, he slowed and went around them to the left.

The moonlight was bright. It seemed as if that icy white moon were chilling the air. There were narrow black shadows behind the trailers, but the cries hadn't come from there. Taylor paused to catch his breath.

The cry came again, piercing, agonized. A young woman's voice. It sounded as if she were dying, horribly.

Beyond the edge of the lot there was a stand of dry cattails, perhaps ten yards deep, indicating swampy ground. Taylor walked cautiously toward them. A scent hit his nose, not of the swamp: a faint, sweetish scent.

He almost did not go on, for it was the same scent that he'd smelled when he saw the man by his car.

But that was insane. The cry had subsided to a horrible gasping sob. Carefully placing his feet in the soggy ground, Taylor flipped on his flashlight and pressed through the cattails.

There was a small clearing in the center of the cattails. Here he saw a pool of water a few yards across, and lying half in the greenish pool was . . .

The corpse of a young woman. A pale, mottled, decayed thing whose long fair hair was entangled in the weeds, and whose hands still clutched something long and dull and metal that it had plunged into its chest.

Taylor shuddered, the light shaking in his hands, the odd, sweet smell very strong.

This thing could have made no sound.

Even as he watched, it slowly straightened, and the eyes rolled open and flashed moonlight into his.

Taylor heard his own scream. The shotgun roared in his hand, and he fell back, stumbled to his feet, crashed through the cattails back to the parking lot, wiping frantically at bits of moist . . . something . . . that the blast had scattered across his face and clothes.

He stood in the open, panting, looked back, terrified that the thing would follow. The smoke of the shotgun blast hung low over the little patch of cattails. There was no sound. He forced himself to turn and walk slowly back to the car.

The walkie-talkie was calling. Taylor answered, grateful for the human voice.

"See any more spooks, 2101?"

Silence.

"2101, copy?"

"No, Base, no more spooks. Everything 10-2."

"You kinda sound like one, 2101. Base out."

"10-4, 2101 out."

Taylor turned his car so that he faced the terminal, and had the swamp to his left, the entrance to his right. His back was to the woods, but at the moment he was not worried about anything that might come out of the woods.

His hands were shaking. He poured himself half a cup of coffee and filled it with bourbon from the pint he kept under the seat. For emergencies. This was an emergency.

The bourbon felt good going down. Slowly he began to relax.

He tried to consider the . . . things . . . he'd seen in a calm, rational manner. There were really only three alternatives: the most likely was that someone was playing tricks on him. Elaborate tricks, to be sure, but it was possible.

The second possibility was that his own mind was playing tricks on him. But why now? Tonight? Why not at the LSD parties of the old days, when he'd sat cool, calm, and collected while everybody else was freaking their heads off? No, that was out. He was *not* an unstable person.

The third alternative was that there were spooks out there. No, and no, and no. Taylor was a romantic, but he did not believe in spooks in any way, shape, or form.

He raised the doctored coffee to his lips, savoring the old bourbon. Suddenly it came to him. It was so simple!

They'd had trouble keeping guards out here before. A few had told crazy stories, but management would have put that down to boozing on the job.

Someone was going to a lot of trouble to scare the guards off. He knew there were "hot loads"—booze or electronics—here occasionally. It was one thing to tackle an armed guard, but if you could just scare him off with some Dark Shadows routine, the rest would be a piece of cake!

Tricky. Well, he'd show them a trick or two! Taylor finished the coffee and decided to take another walk back to the perimeter.

Bright light filled the car. Someone was turning in off the river road.

The big Ford passed him, heading for the side door of the terminal. Taylor was halfway across the lot when a tall man in a suede jacket and western hat climbed out.

"Don't shoot," he said, "I gotta piss like a racehorse."

"Sorry, this place is—"

"It's okay. My name's Stahl, day dispatch here. Yours is Taylor, right?"

He produced a ring of keys from his pocket and proceeded to open the door.

"Why don't you come in for a minute? Just don't drop that cannon. Browning auto, isn't it? Good deer gun, close up."

Taylor followed the big man into a narrow panelled room with a half-window like a doctor's office, where truckers picked up their lading bills and logged in. Stahl took off his jacket and put a tin pot on an old two-burner hotplate for coffee, then plugged in the large electric heater by the desk.

Taylor sat close to the heater. It felt good. He hadn't realized he was shivering.

Stahl disappeared behind a door marked *Private* and returned a few minutes later, zipping up his trousers. In the light of a couple of bare bulbs, he looked older. Taylor placed his age at about sixty, a healthy sixty.

"So you're the new replacement guard," said Stahl, half to himself.

"Nope, I've got a regular beat over across the river, pawnshops and trucking, but they needed someone for the holidays."

Stahl shifted a pile of papers on his desk, spooned instant coffee into a couple of cups, poured the steaming water, and handed one to Taylor.

"Well, hope you enjoy yourself out here. They kind of have a hard time keeping guards here."

Taylor had a brief suspicion that Stahl might know something about the "tricks" someone was playing. But looking into the brown, lined face, he thought not.

"Spooks, probably," said Taylor. "This is kind of a weird spot, what with the old barracks and all. Wouldn't be surprised if somebody might try a few tricks to scare a guard off."

Stahl's eyes narrowed, his nose twitching above his close-trimmed gray moustache, as if he might sneeze.

"You seen something?"

Taylor smiled, "Thought I *did* see somebody around earlier, but it turned out I was wrong."

Stahl sipped his coffee, watching Taylor closely.

"You haven't heard the history of this place, have you?"

"Only that it was once part of the military base."

Stahl smiled almost mischievously.

"Well, there's a bit more to it than that. This was a real active base, on around World War II. Had two, three thousand men in training at a time. They'd work 'em up, outfit 'em, and send 'em on down to Fort Knot, Kentucky, to fly out for parts unknown.

"I've lived around the Valley all my life. Soldiers used to come into town on weekends, raise holy hell. But we liked 'em."

Stahl paused, eyes distant.

"But part of the history of this place is a little darker. Between World War II and Korea, they brought in some scientists, chemists. Top secret, hush-hush kind of thing. We'd see 'em around town sometimes, but they were a pretty close-mouthed bunch, wouldn't say what they were up to.

"They had a little factory, looked like, maybe fifty people workin' there, sat right where this terminal is now, but nobody, I mean nobody, knew what they were makin' in there. Most of us in town thought they were making' some kind of new rocket, missile, somesuch.

"Well, one morning early, County Sheriff, old Thompson, has been out checkin' on a burglary. He's driving by here, and somebody almost walks in front of his car. He yells at the guy, thinks he's some damned drunk. Then he takes a good look at him, the blood on his clothes.

"He looks over at the factory, and sees maybe a dozen people, some of 'em lying on the ground, some of 'em just stumbling around, blood all over 'em. And he smells a smell, a funny sweet smell, real strong, that kind of makes him dizzy just to breathe it.

"Thompson's no fool. He doesn't even get out of the car. He heads down the road, burns rubber up to the guard post, and has 'em wake up the Adjutant.

"The Adjutant turns a dead shade of pale when he hears the Sheriff's story, but tells him not to worry, that they're keeping a few mental patients down by the factory, and that he'll handle it.

"Well, I've known Thompson a long time. He's like me, he can smell something fishy about a mile off. He goes back to town, wakes up his deputies, calls up the National Guard, and has a small army together when he heads back.

"By this time there's almost no way of keeping it under wraps. The Adjutant, looking like he just wants to be somewhere else, drafts Thompson's men and the guard to help clean up the mess.

"That factory," Stahl paused, "was makin' nerve gas."

"Jeeze!"

"Yeah, Jesus and Mary, too. They had a whole batch set up to ship off God knows where, when there was a little fire and one of the big canisters blew. They had masks, sure, but the stuff spread so fast that most of 'em didn't have time to get 'em on.

"Well, like I was sayin', the Adjutant got his men and us—I was there, 'cause I was in the Guard—together. We had to wear full gas suits. One thing he told us. If we smelled cherries, to get the hell out of there."

"Cherries?" Something, a recent memory, came to the back of Taylor's mind, did not quite surface.

"Cherries. The gas was scented with cherries so they could tell if it leaked. Lot of good it did 'em.

"When we went in," Stahl's voice had gone dry, "when we went in, it was . . . like a horror movie, or one of those pictures of hell. Some of 'em were still alive, all with blood all over 'em, theirs or somebody else's. They looked weird, some of 'em in those white lab suits. A couple of 'em attacked us, with knives, glass, their teeth, and a few people got hurt. But there weren't too many left.

"I mean, the people working in that factory had gone plain nuts, went at each other with chairs, nails, teeth. We found one guy disemboweled with a protractor."

Stahl shook his head at the memory and grinned.

"Anyway, that's the sweet story of this place. They buried a few of 'em over in that little woods across the lot, behind where you're parked. County hassled the State until they made the Army take that factory out, and the building had one of those mysterious fires not so long after, burned it to the ground. The lot was vacant for a long time, Army sold off some land, and Coleman put in the depot here."

Taylor's coffee was cold. He sipped it anyway to give his hand something to do.

"Surprised you hadn't heard that story."

"No," said Taylor, "but it's one of the damnedest tales I've ever heard."

The story left him with an uneasy feeling, something more than just the horror of it, something he couldn't pin down. He stood up and stretched, bumping the table with his knee. Automatically he checked his watch.

"Thanks for the coffee and the yarn, gotta get back to the dispatcher. They'll be wondering what's happened to me."

"Sure thing. You be careful out there, you hear?"

Taylor laughed and closed the door.

The cold hit him like a wave, but it was stimulating. It also helped clear his mind of the thing that had been bugging him for some time.

The nerve gas had smelled like cherries. And the goddamned sweet smell that had gone along with the two bizarre incidents he'd had this morning had been, yes, the smell of cherries.

But, he told himself, there was no connection. There *could be no* logical connection. He'd probably imagined the smell, due to some odd mental association. It was the kind of thing that could weigh on a person's mind—if you let it. Taylor would not be fool enough to let it.

Before he went back to his car, Taylor walked behind the trailers to the rear of the lot and on into the small stand of cattails. Outside of a few broken stems from the shotgun blast, there were no traces of the thing he'd seen. Of course there weren't. On his way back he checked each of the trailers, but all were completely empty, or closed, with their small aluminum seals intact.

He walked through the pale moonlight, back to the old Chevy. He started the car and ran the engine for a while to get the heater up, then called in and took a mild chewing-out from the dispatcher. He let the engine run until the car was good and hot, then settled back to watch the lot.

A half hour, the moon rose a little higher in the sky, a funny moon, near full, looking as if someone had just cut a thin sliver off the edge. He saw Stahl leave the terminal and drive away, and fought down the sudden sense of loneliness.

An hour. He checked in. Everything 10-2, 10-4.

Soon it was early morning. A faint trace of frost, unpleasantly like a face, etched across the window. Taylor started the engine, turned on the defroster, melted it away.

He felt fairly confident that the trickster, whoever, had gone home for the night. Taylor slipped into a half-doze, the images of old girl friends, each with their unique, ah, qualities, coming, as inevitably they did at this hour of the morning. He heard a train pass, and perhaps did fall into a doze momentarily.

Suddenly he was wide awake. The wind had come up, the moon a shade lower. He saw something white. Something large, winged, grotesque, shuffling across the parking lot toward his car.

This was too much. He could only watch it. Suddenly it rushed forward, leaped into the air . . .

Taylor found himself clutching the seat, looking at the open newspaper plastered across the windshield.

The newspaper blew away. One thing about it he had not noticed. The date on the paper had been 1949. November 22, 1949, thirty-two years to the day.

Taylor sighed, reached for the whiskey under the seat. This shift *had* gotten on his nerves a bit, but it would only be a couple of hours until dawn.

*   *   *

Then he heard the footsteps. Running. From behind him, the direction of the woods, coming quickly.

And suddenly he just wanted to be out of there. His hands were shaking, but he did manage to start the car.

The footsteps came up on the passenger side.

In the moonlight he saw . . .

He almost collapsed with relief. The face pressed to the window was that of a young girl. A pretty young girl, smiling and shivering and pointing at the lock on the door.

He unlocked the door and pushed it open.

She tumbled into the seat with a shy laugh, bouncing up and down. She was young, perhaps nineteen, with tousled black hair and bright dark eyes. Her cloth coat, loafers, and white knee socks seemed kind of dated, but somehow this only added to her charm.

"Brrrrr! Am I glad to see you! I never thought I'd find a way back to town!"

"Well," said Taylor, "I can't take you right back, because I'm the security cop here tonight. But I *can* call in and have the dispatcher call you a cab. How would that be?"

"Grrrrreat!"

"What happened, car run out of gas?"

She nodded, frowning.

"I think so. Must have bumped my head or something when it stopped."

She rubbed her forehead briskly. "Ouch! Yep, there's a bruise all right, funny . . ."

Slowly she turned toward Taylor, a look of almost theatrical surprise on her face.

"Yes! I kinda remember . . ."

Her voice went flat on "remember," but he hardly noticed. This girl was pretty indeed! Maybe he could put off calling a cab for a while, say, an hour or two. It wasn't long to dawn. She might like a little breakfast.

She was quiet, watching him with an almost embarrassing intensity. Nervously she pulled up those funny knee socks. He was not, he knew, entirely unattractive, as far as that went. Then for the first time he consciously noticed her perfume, a very faint, sweet scent. Fruity.

Cherries.

Her face contorted, maniacal, teeth bared like a beast.

Long pointed nails streaking for his face.

Cherries.

Taylor screamed and lashed out. The impact of the blow flung her across the seat, against the half-latched passenger door as he jammed the car into gear, still screaming.

The Chevy spun in a full circle in the loose gravel as he fought to straighten it out, not realizing that he had the accelerator all the way to the floor. He was vaguely aware of the passenger door swinging open and slamming shut again as it crashed against a post going through the entrance.

Taylor did not slow until a State trooper racing beside him fired a shot across the hood. By that time, he was halfway through Kentucky.

Slowly he rolled down the window. Somewhere deep inside a touch of rationality surfaced, reminding him of the size of the fine he could well wind up paying. Loss of money is always good for restoring sanity. The voice told him, gathering confidence, that he'd had one hell of a nightmare, a stupid, vivid nightmare, and that now he'd make a total ass of himself as a result.

The trooper flashed his light around the front seat.

"What's the gun doing there?"

"I'm a security cop."

"I'd hate to have you watching *my* place."

He flashed his light back to Taylor's face.

"Shoulda been a race driver, buddy. If you're not sober, your ass is fried." The cop peered closer. "Say what's that on your face? Jesus Christ! You been makin' out with a wildcat, or what?"

But Taylor, whose hand had lightly traced the dried blood from the five deep scratches in his cheek, had fainted.

IOWA

Away
by Barry N. Malzberg

MY NAME is Josiah Bushnell Grinnell. In 1853, responding to the invocation of the famous Horace Greeley, publisher of the New York Tribune, I take myself to the new state of Iowa and thereupon establish both a town and a college. "Go west young man, go west and grow with the country," Greeley has said, and solemn young fellow that I am, I take him seriously. What a surprise, what a disappointment to learn only after I am established where the tall corn grows that Greeley stole this from an obscure Indiana newspaperman named Soule and has appropriated the statement as his own. If I had known this, I might have gone to Indiana.

Instead, here I am in Iowa. What an unusually solemn man I am! I have always taken the invocations of my elders seriously, which is why the college I establish, the town to be named after me, the entire state itself takes on a somewhat sectarian whiff. A century later it is impossible for citizens to enter upon our interstates without murmuring prayers. In 1857, Sioux Indians massacre men, women, and children at Spirit Lake, the last massacre by Indians in the midwest and the released souls, the violated spirits add their pain and terror to the general chatter. On a hot May afternoon, the dead sun sprawling low in the panels of sky, the sounds of the cattle rising toward the dusk, it is possible to imagine oneself if one were a small man lying in a field, gazing, that one had entered upon the outer regions of the landscape painted by the honorable John Calvin. It is a difficult state, a difficult time.

I, Josiah Bushnell Grinnell, know this; know of all the interstices and difficulties of the sovereign state of Iowa. Cleaved from the Wisconsin territory, admitted to statehood on December 28, 1846, Iowa sprawls, flatland, on the way to the west. There are ways around it—there are ways around everything, the good Lord knows—but once on the interstate, it is hard to find the way.

Here it is. It is 1954. I have been deceased for many decades, however, my spirit—no less than those massacred at Spirit Lake—lives on. Iowa is the possessor of its inhabitants, no one who has ever lived in this state has known true release. We hang around. This may seem an unlikely statement, a remarkable condition, but wait your turn, enjoy the common passage before you act in judgment. Here in 1954 the senior senator from this great state, the honorable, if that is quite the term I am seeking, Bourke B. Hickenlooper is inveighing against the Communists at a Fourth of July picnic. Hickenlooper, with McCarthy, with Jenner, is the pride of what may be called the conservative wing. To Hickenlooper it is an insult when the first Negro set the first Negro foot on the Negro shores of the first Negro city in this country, uttering incoherent Negro chants. It is not that Hickenlooper is a racist, you understand. It is merely that he is still linked to Spirit Lake by ancestry and blood, still sees the frame of the assassin arched against the moonlight. "We must expel the Communists from our shores," Hicken-looper says. He is on a podium, at some remove from the crowd, screaming without benefit of microphone. Fourth of July picnics are still important in the Iowa of this time. Politicians are expected to make speeches, to invoke Americana. Hickenlooper is merely doing his duty. Of his true thoughts of the matter we know not. He may or may not have an interior. Most politicians do not. "McCarran Act!" Hickenlooper screams. "Joseph McCarthy! Millard Tydings! Eighty-seven hundred card-carrying Commun-ists!" And so on. The crowd reacts stiffly. It is very hot. A band plays in the distance, raucous parade ground arias of the kind soon enough to be popularized by Meredith Wilson (born in Mason City) in *The Music Man*. "Who promoted Peress?" Hickenlooper asks. The crowd mutters. Their mood is not hostile but they are tired.

My name is Josiah Bushnell Grinnell. It is hard to explain exactly what I am doing at this picnic or what I expect to come of it. We Iowans (or transplanted Iowans) as I have said, our spirits live on. Even after death. Relegated to some limbo we come in and out, reincarnates or observers, bound to some flatland of the spirit, replicating our history, moving in and out of time. Screams of the settlers at Spirit Lake. Bullshit of Greeley. Moving ever west. From this limbo I emerge at odd times, strange moments, find myself at Iowa State Events. Such seems to be the case now. I am jammed in with this crowd, listening to Bourke B. Hickenlooper. To my left and right are Iowans of various sexes and ages, most of them young, in a burst of color, standing at parade rest, listening to the rantings of the honorable senator. Now and then a baby yowls or a young woman faints, her parasol preceding her on a graceless slide to the ground. Men leap to the rescue of the women, the babies are pacified in other ways. The huge bowl of the sky presses. It is indecently hot, even for a spirit, even for the gullible sectarian spirit of a man who would listen to Horace Greeley (at least I never knew of Horatio Alger; it is impossible to say to what state he might have sent me.) "Hickenlooper!" I shout. "Hey, Hickenlooper!"

The crowd stares at me. Sometimes I can be heard and sometimes not; sometimes I am visible and at other times invisible. Reincarnation, like life itself, is a chancy business. At this time it would appear that I can be seen. Yards downrange the senator stares at me, his stride momentarily broken. "Hey, Senator!" I shout. Hickenlooper removes his enormous hat, peers at me. I stride forward, closing the ground between us.

"You're all wrong, don't you know that?" I say. "Listen to me!" I say, turning around, gesturing at the farmers, their wives, the beaus and beauxettes in their holiday undress who look at me incuriously. "This man is not telling the truth. We lived to open frontiers, he is closing them!"

I am stared at incomprehendingly. One could, after all, envision no other possibility. Politics may be entertainment but metaphysics is unendurable in the Hawkeye State. "He speaketh with forked tongue!" I point out.

There are a forest of shrugs around me. I turn back toward the podium, find Hickenlooper in brisk conference with several aides who have jumped to the sides of the platform. He cups an ear, listens intently. They gesture at me. "Answer the charge!" I yell. "Don't hide behind the others, explain yourself. Tell why you are breeding fear, why you are seeking to close off that which will be opened."

Hickenlooper points at me. The hand is commanding, enormous. At my side, suddenly, are two earnest, honest Iowa state police; they seize me by the elbows. "If you will, sir," one says, "if you'll just come along."

"Don't arrest me" I say, struggling in their grasp, "arrest that man. That man is the assassin. I am Josiah Bushnell Grinnell, the founder of Grinnell College. I am a man of substance—"

"*Card-carrying!*" I hear Hickenlooper shout and then, this is the truth, I hear no more; speedily, forcibly, forcefully, I am carried from the grounds. Beaus and beauxettes, farmers and their daughters, little towheaded children and Iowa cattle, they all look at me mournfully. The troopers are insistent. "Don't you understand?" I say to them. "This isn't the end, this is just the passage, it's going to happen again, again and *again*—"

Stay calm, sir, one says, "everything will be all right. Just don't struggle, understand the situation—"

I close my eyes. Again and again and it is too late. In the sudden, cool rushing darkness ninety-seven years are taken from me as if by death itself and I am at Spirit Lake once more, oh God, I am at Spirit Lake and in the sudden, clinging, rushing, tumultuous darkness, I hear the sound of the Sioux closing in around us; one high wail coming then, concentrating them, poised—

I scream then, try once more to give the alarm. But I cannot; my throat is dry, my lungs are cut out, my fate is darkness; in the night, eleven years after union, three years before the Civil War, they are coming, they are coming and the stain will leach outward, ever outward—

Go west young man, go west—

I listened, I came, I propagated, and I could not save them. And in the face of the Hickenloopers, through to dissolution itself, I never, never will. Until by something that is, at last, beyond me, I too will be cut off.

KANSAS

Twilla
by Tom Reamy

TWILLA GILBREATH blew into Miss Mahan's life like a pink butterfly wing that same day in early December the blue norther dropped the temperature forty degrees in two hours. Mr. Choate, the principal, ushered Twilla and her parents into Miss Mahan's ninth grade home room shortly after the tardy bell rang. She had just checked the roll: all seventeen ninth graders were present except for Sammy Stocker who was in the Liberal hospital having his appendix removed. She was telling the class how nice it would be if they sent a get-well card when the door opened.

"Goooood morning, Miss Mahan," Mr. Choate smiled cheerfully. He always smiled cheerfully first thing in the morning, but soured as the day wore on. You could practically tell time by Mr. Choate's mouth. "We have a new ninth grader for you this morning, Miss Mahan. This is Mr. and Mrs. Gilbreath and their daughter, Twilla."

Several things happened at once. Miss Mahan shook hands with the parents; she threw a severe glance at the class when she heard a snigger—but it was only Alice May Turner, who would probably giggle if she were being devoured by a bear; and she had to forcibly keep her eyebrows from rising when she got a good look at Twilla. Good Lord, she thought, and felt her smile falter.

Miss Mahan had never in her life, even when it was fasionable for a child to look like that, seen anyone so perfectly . . . pink and . . . doll-like. She wasn't sure why she got such an impression of pinkness, because the child was dressed in yellow, and had golden hair (*that's* the color they mean when they say golden hair, she thought with wonder) done in, of all things, drop

205

curls, with a big yellow bow in back. Twilla looked up at her with a sweet, radiant, sunny smile and clear periwinkle-blue eyes.

Miss Mahan detested her on sight.

She thought she saw, when Alice May giggled, the smile freeze and the lovely eyes dart toward the class, but she wasn't sure. It all happened in an instant, and then Mr. Choate continued his Cheerful Charlie routine.

"Mr. Gilbreath has bought the old Peacock place."

"Really?" she said, tearing her eyes from Twilla. "I didn't know it was for sale."

Mr. Gilbreath chuckled. "Not the entire farm, of course. I'm no farmer. Only the house and grounds. Such a charming old place. The owner lives in Wichita and had no use for them."

"I would think the house is pretty run down," Miss Mahan said, glancing at Twilla still radiating at the world. "No one's lived in it since Wash and Grace Elizabeth died ten years ago."

"It is a little," Mrs. Gilbreath said pleasantly.

"But structurally sound," interjected Mr. Gilbreath pleasantly.

"We'll enjoy fixing it up," Mrs. Gilbreath continued pleasantly.

"Miss Mahan teaches English to the four upper grades," said Mr. Choate, bringing them back to the subject, "as well as speech and drama. Miss Mahan has been with the Hawley school system for thirty-one years."

The Gilbreaths smiled pleasantly. "My . . . ah . . . Twilla seems very young to be in the ninth grade." That get-up made her look about eleven, Miss Mahan thought.

The Gilbreaths beamed at their daughter. "Twilla is only thirteen," Mrs. Gilbreath crooned, pride swelling her like yeast. "She's such an intelligent child. She was able to skip the second grade."

"I see. From where have you moved?"

"Boston," replied Mr. Gilbreath.

"Boston. I hope . . . ah . . . Twilla doesn't find it difficult to adjust to a small town school. I'm sure Hawley, Kansas, is quite unlike Boston."

Mr. Gilbreath touched Twilla lovingly on the shoulder. "I'm sure she'll have no trouble."

"Well," Mr. Choate rubbed his palms together. "Twilla is in good hands. Shall I show you around the rest of the school?"

"Of course," smiled Mrs. Gilbreath.

They departed with fond murmurings and goodbyes, leaving Twilla like a buttercup stranded in a cabbage patch. Miss Mahan mentally shook her head. She hadn't seen a family like that since Dick and Jane and Spot and Puff were sent the way of *McGuffey's Reader*. Mr. and Mrs. Gilbreath were in their middle thirties, good looking without being glamorous, their clothes nice though as oddly wrong as Twilla's. They seemed cut with some out-dated Ideal Family template. Surely, there must be an older brother, a dog, and a cat somewhere.

"Well . . . ah, Twilla," Miss Mahan said, trying to reinforce the normal routine, "if you will take a seat; that one there behind Alice May Turner. Alice May, will you wave a flag or something so Twilla will know which one? Alice May giggled. "Thank you, dear." Twilla moved gracefully toward the empty desk. Miss Mahan felt as if she should say something to the child. "I hope you will . . . ah . . . enjoy going to school in Hawley, dear."

Twilla sat primly and glowed at her. "I'm sure I shall, Miss Mahan," she said, speaking for the first time. Her voice was like the tinkle of fairy bells—just as Miss Mahan was afraid it would be.

"Good," she said and went back to the subject of a get-well card for Sammy Stocker. She had done this so often—there had been a great many sick children in thirty-one years—it had become almost a ritual needing only a small portion of her attention. The rest she devoted to the covert observation of Twilla Gilbreath.

Twilla sat at her desk, displaying excellent posture, with her hands folded neatly before her, seemingly paying attention to the Great Greeting Card Debate, but actually giving the rest of the class careful scrutiny. Miss Mahan marveled at the surreptitious calculation in the girl's face. She realizes she's something of a green monkey, Miss Mahan thought, and I'll bet my pension she doesn't let the situation stand.

And the class surveyed Twilla, in their superior position of established territorial rights, with open curiosity—and with the posture of so many sacks of corn meal. Some of them looked at her, Miss Mahan was afraid, with rude amusement—especially the girls, and especially Wanda O' Dell who had bloomed suddenly last summer like a plump rose. Oh, yes, Wanda was going to be a problem. Just like her five older sisters. Thank goodness, she sighed, Wanda was the last of them.

Children, Miss Mahan sighed again, but fondly.

Children?

They were children when she started teaching and certainly were when she was fifteen, but, now, she wasn't sure. Fifteen is such an awkward, indefinite age. Take Ronnie Dwyer: he looks like a prepubescent thirteen at most. And Carter Redwine, actually a couple of months younger than Ronnie, could pass for seventeen easily and was anything but prepubescent. Poor Carter, a child in a man's body. To make matters worse, he was the best looking boy in town; and to make matters even worse yet, he was well aware of it.

And, she noticed, so was Twilla. Forget it, Little Pink Princess. Carter already has more than he can handle, Miss Mahan chuckled to herself. Can't you see those dark circles under his eyes? They didn't get there from studying. And then she blushed inwardly.

Oh, the poor children. They think they have so many secrets. If they only knew. Between the tattle-tales and the teachers' gossip, she doubted if the whole student body had three secrets among them.

Miss Mahan admonished herself for having such untidy thoughts. She didn't use to think about things like that, but then, fifteen-year-olds didn't

lead such overtly sexual lives back then. She remembered reading somewhere that only thirty-five per cent of the children in America were still
virgins at fifteen. But those sounded like Big City statistics, not applicable to
Hawley.

Then she sighed. It was all beyond her. The bell rang just as the get-well
card situation was settled. The children rose reluctantly to go to their first
class: algebra with Mr. Whittaker. She noticed that Twilla had cozied up to
Alice May, though she still kept her eye on Carter Redwine. Carter was not
unaware and, with deliberate, lordly indifference, sauntered from the room
with his hand on Wanda O' Dell's shoulder. Miss Mahan thought the glint
she observed in Twilla's eyes might lead to an interesting turn of events.

Children.

She cleared her mind of random speculation and geared it to *Macbeth* as
the senior class filed in with everything on their minds but Shakespeare.
Raynelle Franklin, Mr. Choate's secretary, lurked nervously among them,
looking like a chicken who suddenly finds herself with a pack of coyotes. She
edged her middle-aged body to Miss Mahan's desk, accepted the absentee
report, and scuttled out. Miss Mahan looked forward to Raynelle's
performance every morning.

During lunch period, Miss Mahan walked to the dime store for a get-well
card which the ninth grade class would sign that afternoon when they
returned for English. She glanced at the sky and unconsciously pulled her
gray tweed coat tighter about her. The sky had turned a cobalt blue in the
north. It wouldn't be long now. Though the temperature must be down to
thirty-five already, it seemed colder. She guessed her blood was getting thin,
she knew her flesh was. Old age, she thought, old age. Thin blood, thin flesh,
and brittle bones. She sometimes felt as if she were turning into a bird.

She almost bumped into Twilla's parents emerging from the dry goods
store, their arms loaded with packages. Their pleasant smiles turned on.
Click, click. They chatted trivialities for a moment, adding new dimensions
to Twilla's already flawless character. Miss Mahan had certainly seen her
share of blindly doting parents, but this was unbelievable. She had seen the
cold calculation with which Twilla had studied the class, and that was hardly
the attribute of an angel. Something didn't jibe somewhere. She speculated
on the contents of the packages, but thought she knew. Then she couldn't
resist; she asked if Twilla were an only child. She was. Well, there went that.

She looked at the clock on the high tower of the white rococo courthouse,
and, subtracting fourteen minutes, decided she'd better hurry if she wanted
to eat lunch and have a rest before her one o' clock class.

The teacher's lounge was a reasonably comfortable room where students
were forbidden to enter on pain of death—though it seemed to be a
continuing game on their part to try. Miss Mahan hung her coat on a hanger
and shivered. "Has anyone heard a weather forecast?" she asked the room
in general.

Mrs. Latham (home economics) looked up from her needlepoint and shook her head vaguely. Poor old dear, thought Miss Mahan. Due to retire this year, I think. Seems like she's been here since Creation. She taught me when I was in school. Leo Whittaker (math) was reading a copy of *Playboy*. Probably took it from one of the children. "Supposed to be below twenty by five," he said, then grinned and held up the magazine. "Ronnie Dwyer."

Miss Mahan raised her eyebrows. Loretta McBride (history/civics) tsked, shook her head, and went back to her book. Miss Mahan retrieved her carton of orange juice from the small refrigerator and drank it with her fried egg sandwich. She put part of the sandwich back in the Baggie. She hardly had any appetite at all anymore. Guess what they say is true: the older you get . . .

She began to crochet on her interminable afghan. The little squares were swiftly becoming a pain in the neck, and she regretted ever starting it. She looked at Mrs. Latham and her needlepoint. She sighed, I guess it's expected of us old ladies. Anyway, it gave her something to hide behind when she didn't feel like joining the conversation. But today she felt like talking, though it didn't seem as if anyone else did.

She finished a square and snipped the yarn. "What do you think of the Shirley Temple doll who joined our merry group this morning?"

Mrs. Latham looked up and smiled. "Charming child."

"Yes," said Loretta, putting away her book, "absolutely charming. And smart as a whip. Really knows her American History. Joined in the discussion as if she'd been in the class all semester." Miss McBride was one of the few outsiders teaching in Hawley who gave every indication of remaining. Usually they came and went as soon as greener pastures opened up. Most were like Miss Mahan, Mrs. Latham, and Leo Whittaker, living their entire lives there.

It was practically incestuous, she thought. Mrs. Latham had taught her, she had taught Leo, and he was undoubtedly teaching part of the next crop. Miss Mahan had to admit that Leo had been something of a surprise. He was only twenty-five and had given no indication in high school that he was destined for anything better than a hanging. She wondered how long it would be before Leo connected his students' inability to keep secrets from the teachers with his own disreputable youth.

Now here he was. Two years in the army, four years in college, his second year of teaching, married to Lana Redwine (Carter's cousin and one of the nicest girls in town) with a baby due in a couple of months. You never can tell. You just never can tell.

"Well, Leo," Miss Mahan asked bemused, "what did you think of Twilla Gilbreath?"

"Oh, I don't know. She seems very intelligent—at least in algebra. Quiet and well-behaved—unlike a few others. Dresses kinda funny. Seems to have set her sights on my cousin-in-law." He grinned. "Fat chance!" Miss Mahan wouldn't say Leo was handsome—not in the way Carter Redwine was—but that grin was the reason half the girls in school had a crush on him.

"Oh? You noticed that too? I imagine she may have a few surprises up her sleeve. I don't think our Twilla is the fairy tale princess she's made out to be." She began another square.

"You must be mistaken, Miss Mahan," Loretta said wide-eyed. "The child is an absolute darling. And the very idea: a baby like that running after Carter Redwine. I never heard of such a thing!"

"Really?" Miss Mahan smiled to herself and completed a shell stitch. "We shall see what we shall see."

The norther hit during the ninth grade English class, bringing a merciful, if only temporary, halt to the sufferings of Silas Marner. The glass in the windows rattled and pinged. The wind played on the downspouts like a mad flautist. Sand ticked against the windows and the guard lights came on in the school yard. Outside had become a murky indigo, as if the world were under water. Miss Mahan switched on the lights, making the windows seem even darker. Garbage cans rolled down the street, but you could hardly hear them above the howl of the wind. And the downtown Christmas decorations were whipping loose, as they always did at least once every year.

The sand was only temporary; a cloud of it blown along before the storm, but the wind could last all night or all week. Miss Mahan remembered when she was a girl during the great drought of the thirties, when the sand wasn't temporary, when it came like a mile-high, solid tidal wave of blown away farmland, when you couldn't tell noon from midnight, when houses were half buried when the wind finally died down. She shuddered.

"All right, children. Settle down. You've all seen northers before."

Leo and Loretta were right about one thing: Twilla was intelligent. She was also perceptive, imaginative . . . and adaptable. She had already dropped the Little Mary Sunshine routine, though Miss Mahan couldn't imagine why she had used it in the first place. It must have been a pose—as if the child had somehow confused the present and 1905.

The temperature had dropped to eighteen by the time school was out. The wind hit Miss Mahan like icy needles. Her gray tweed coat did about as much good as tissue paper. She grabbed at her scarf as it threatened to leave her head and almost lost her briefcase. She walked as fast as her aging legs would go and made it to her six-year-old Plymouth. The car started like a top, billowing a cloud of steam from the exhaust pipe to be whipped away by the wind.

She sat a moment, getting her breath back, letting the car warm up. She saw Twilla, huddled against the wind, dash to a new black Chrysler and get in with her parents. The car backed out and moved away. Miss Mahan wasn't the least surprised that little Miss Gilbreath wasn't riding the school bus. The old Peacock place was a mile off the highway at Miller's Corners, a once-upon-a-time town eight miles east of Hawley.

Well, I guess I'm not much better, she thought. I only live four blocks away—but I'll be darned if I'll walk today. She always did walk except when the weather was bad, and, oddly enough, the older she got, the worse the weather seemed to get.

She pulled into the old carriage house that served equally well with automobiles, and walked hurriedly across the yard into the big, rather ancient house that had belonged to her grandfather. She knew it was silly to live all alone in such a great pile—she had shut off the upstairs and hadn't been up in months—but it was equally silly not to live there. It was paid for and her grandfather had set up a trust fund to pay the taxes. It was a very nice house, really; cool in the summer, but (she turned up the fire) a drafty old barn in the winter.

She turned on the television of see if there were any weather bulletins. While it warmed up, she closed off all the downstairs rooms except the kitchen, her bedroom, and the parlor, putting rolled up towels along the bottoms of the doors to keep the cold air out. She returned to the parlor to see the television screen covered with snow and horizontal streaks of lightning.

She knew it. The aerial had blown down again. She turned off the set and put on a kettle of tea.

The wind had laid somewhat by the time Miss Mahon reached school the next morning, but still blew in fitful gusts. The air was the color of ice and so cold she expected to hear it crackle as she moved through it. The windows in her room were steamed over and she was busily wiping them when Twilla arrived. Although Miss Mahan had expected something like this, she stared nevertheless.

Twilla's hair was still the color of spun elfin gold but the drop curls were missing. Instead it fell in soft folds to below her shoulders in a style much too adult for a thirteen-year-old. But, then, this morning Twilla looked as much like thirteen as Miss Latham. All the physical things were there: the hair, just the right amount of makeup, a short, stylish skirt, a pale green jersey that displayed her small but adequate breasts, a lovely antique pendant on a gold chain nestling between them.

But it wasn't only the physical things—any thirteen-year-old would have appeared more mature with a similar overhaul—it was something in the face, in her bearing: an attitude of casual sophistication, a confidence usually attainable only by those secure in their power. Twilla smiled. Shirley Temple and Mary Pickford were gone; this was the smile of a conqueror.

Miss Mahan realized her face was hanging out, but before she was forced to say anything, several students, after a prelude of clanging locker doors, barged in. Twilla turned to look at them and the moment was electric. Their inane chatter stopped as if someone had thrown a switch. They gaped. Twilla gave them time for the full effect, then strolled to them and began chatting as if nothing were new.

Miss Mahan sat at her desk feeling a little weak in the knees. She waited for Carter Redwine to arrive as, obviously, was Twilla. When he did, it was almost anticlimactic. His recently acquired worldliness and sexual sophistication melted away in one callow gawk. But he recovered quickly and his feelers popped up, testing the situation. Twilla moved to her desk, giving him a satisfied smile. Wanda O' Dell looked as if she'd eaten a bug.

Miss Mahan had to admit the obvious. Twilla was a stunning beauty. But the whole thing was . . . curious . . . to say the least.

The conversation in the teachers' lounge was devoted almost exclusively to the transformation of Twilla Gilbreath. Mrs. Latham had noted it vaguely. Loretta McBride ceded reluctantly to Miss Mahan's observations of the previous day. Leo Whittaker expressed a masculine appreciation of the new Twilla, earning a fishy look from Loretta. "I never saw Carter act so goofy," he said grinning.

But neither they nor any of the others noted the obvious strangeness of it all. At least, Miss Mahan thought, it seems obvious to me.

That day Miss Mahan set out on a campaign of Twilla-watching. She even went upstairs to her grandfather's study and purloined one of the black journals from the bottom drawer of his desk. She curled up in the big chair, after building a fire in the parlor fireplace—the first one this year—and opened the journal to the first page ruled with pale blue lines. She wrote *Twilla*, after rejecting *The Twilla Gilbreath Affair*, *The Peculiar Case of Twilla Gilbreath*, and others in a similar vein.

She felt silly and conspiratorial and almost put the journal away, but, instead, wrote further down the page: *Is my life so empty that I must fill it by spying on a student?*

She thought about what she had written and decided it was either unfair to Twilla or unfair to herself, but let it remain. She turned to the second page and wrote *Tuesday, the 5th* at the top. She filled that page and the next with her impressions of Twilla's first day. She headed the fourth page *Wednesday, the 6th* and noted the events of the day just ending.

On rereading, she thought perhaps she might have over emphasized the oddities, the incongruities, and the anachronisms, but, after all, that was what it was about, wasn't it?

It began snowing during the night. Miss Mahan drove to school through a fantasy landscape. The wind was still blowing and the steely flakes came down almost horizontally. She loved snow, always had, but she preferred the Christmas card variety when the big fluffy flakes floated down through still, crisp air like so many pillow fights.

She knew there had been developments as soon as Carter Redwine entered the room. His handsome face was glum and sullen and looked as if he hadn't slept. He sat at his desk with his head hunched between his shoulders and didn't look up until Twilla came in. Miss Mahan darted her eyes from one to the other. Carter looked away again, his neck and ears glowing red. Twilla ignored him; more than that—she consigned him to total nonexistence.

Miss Mahan was dumbfounded. What on earth. . . ? Had Carter made advances and been rebuffed? That wouldn't explain it. Surely he had been turned down before. Hadn't he? Of course, she knew he had. Leo, who viewed his cousin-in-law's adventures with bemused affection, had been laughing about it in the teachers' lounge one day. "He'll settle down," Leo had said, "he just has a new toy." Which made her blush after she'd thought about it a while.

Surely he hadn't tried to take Twilla . . . by force? She couldn't believe that. Despite everything, Carter was a very decent boy. He had just developed too early, was too handsome, and knew too many willing girls. What then? Was it the first pangs of love? That look on his face wasn't love-sickness. It was red, roaring mortification. Then she knew what must have happened. Carter had not been rebuffed, maybe even encouraged. But, whatever she had expected, he had been inadequate.

Twilla had made another error. She had failed to realize Carter, despite the way he looked, was only fifteen. Then the ugly enormity of it struck her. My God, she thought, Twilla is only thirteen. What had she wanted from Carter that he was too inexperienced or naïve to give her?

Friday, the 8th

Billy Jermyn came in this morning with a black eye. It's all over the school that Carter gave it to him in Gym yesterday when Billy teased him about Twilla. What did she do to humiliate him so? I've never known Carter to fight. I guess that's one secret that'll never penetrate the teachers' lounge.

Twilla is taking over the class. I've seen it coming since Wednesday. It's subtle but pretty obvious when you know what to look for. The others defer to her in lots of little ways. Twilla is being very gracious about it. Butter wouldn't melt in her mouth. (Wonder where that little saying came from?—doesn't make much sense when you analyze it.)

I also wonder who Twilla's got her amorous sights on, now that Carter failed to make the grade. She hasn't shown an interest in anyone in particular that I've noticed. And there's been no gossip in the lounge. The flap created by Carter has probably shown her the wisdom of keeping her romances to herself. She's adaptable.

Sonny Bowen offered to put my TV aerial back up for me. I knew one of them would. Bless their conniving little hearts.

TGIF!

Miss Mahan closed the journal and sat watching a log in the fireplace that was about to fall. The whole Twilla affair was curious, but no more curious than her own attitude. She should have been scandalized (you didn't see too many thirteen-year-old combinations of Madame Bovary and the Dragon Lady—even these days), but she only felt fascination. Somehow it didn't seem quite real; more as if she were watching a movie. She smiled slightly.

Wonder if it would be rated R or X, she thought. R, I guess. Haven't seen anyone with their clothes off yet.

The log fell, making her jump. She laughed in embarrassment, banked the fire, and went to bed.

The snow was still falling Monday morning, though the fierceness of the storm had passed. There was little wind and the temperature had risen somewhat. That's more like it, Miss Mahan said to herself, watching the big soft flakes float down in random zig-zags.

The bell rang and she turned away from the windows to watch the ninth grade home room clatter out. The Gilbreaths must have been out of town over the weekend, she observed. Twilla didn't get that outfit in Hawley. But she was still wearing that lovely, rather barbaric pendant around her neck. She sighed. Two days away from Twilla had made her wonder if she weren't getting senile; if she weren't making a mystery out of a molehill; if she weren't imagining the whole thing. Twilla was certainly a picture of normalcy this morning.

Raynelle Franklin came for the absentee report looking more like a frightened chicken than ever. She followed an evasive course to Miss Mahan's desk and took the report as if she were afraid of being struck. There were only two names on the report: Sammy Stocker and Yvonne Wilkins.

Raynelle glanced at the names and paled. "Haven't you *heard*?" she whispered.

"Heard what?"

Raynelle looked warily at the senior class shuffling in and backed away, motioning for Miss Mahan to follow. Miss Mahan groaned and followed her into the hall. Students were milling about everywhere, chattering and banging locker doors. Raynelle grimaced in distress.

"Raynelle, will you stand still and tell me!" Miss Mahan commanded in exasperation.

"Someone will hear," she pleaded.

"Hear *what*?"

Raynelle fluttered her hands and blew air through her teeth. She looked quickly around and then huddled against Miss Mahan. "Yvonne Wilkins," she hissed.

"Well?"

"She's . . . she's . . . *dead*!"

Miss Mahan thought Raynelle was going to faint. She grabbed her arm. "How?" she asked in her no-nonsense voice.

"I don't know," Raynelle gasped. "No one will tell me."

Miss Mahan thought for a moment. "Go on with what you were doing." She released Raynelle and marched into Mr. Choate's office.

Mr. Choate looked up with a start. He was already wearing his three o' clock face. "I see you've heard." He was resigned.

"Yes. What is going on? Raynelle was having a conniption fit." Miss

Mahan looked at him over her glasses the same way she would a recalcitrant student.

"Miss Mahan," he sighed, "Sheriff Walker thought it best if the whole thing were kept quiet."

"Quiet? Why?"

"He didn't want a panic."

"Panic? What did she die of, bubonic plague?"

"No." He looked at her as if he wished she would vanish. "I guess I might as well tell you. It'll be all over town by ten o'clock anyway. Yvonne was murdered." He said the last word as if he'd never heard it before.

Miss Mahan felt her knees giving way and quickly sat down. "This is unbelievable," she said weakly. Mr. Choate nodded. "Why does Robin Walker want to keep it quiet? What happened?"

"Miss Mahan, I've told you all I can tell you."

"Surely Robin knows secrecy will only make it worse? Making a mystery out of it is guaranteed to create a panic."

Mr. Choate shrugged. "I have my instructions. You're late for your class."

Miss Mahan went back to her room in a daze, her imagination ringing up possibilities like a cash register. She couldn't keep her mind on *Macbeth* and the class was restless. They obviously didn't know yet, but their radar had picked up something they couldn't explain.

When the class was over she went into the hall and saw the news moving through like a shock wave. She accomplished absolutely nothing the rest of the morning. The children were fidgety and kept whispering among themselves. She was as disturbed as they and made only half-hearted attempts to restore order.

At lunch time, she bundled up and trounced through the snow to the courthouse. It was too hot inside and the heat only accentuated the courthouse smell. She didn't know what it was, but they all smelled the same. Maybe it was the state-issue disinfectant. The Hawley courthouse hadn't changed since she could remember. The same wooden benches lined the hall; the same ceiling fans encircled the round lights. No, she corrected herself, there was a change: the brass spittoons had been removed some twelve years ago. It seemed subtly wrong without the spittoons.

She was removing her coat when Rose Newcastle emerged in a huff from the sheriff's office, her heels popping on the marble floor, sending echoes ringing down the hall. Rose was the last of the three Willet girls, the daughters of old Judge Willet. People still called them the Willet girls, although Rose was considerably older than Miss Mahan. She was a widow now, her husband having finally died of insignificance.

"Hello, Rose," she said, feeling trapped. Rose puffed to a halt like a plump locomotive.

"Oh, Miss Mahan, isn't it *awful!*" she wailed. "And Robin Walker absolutely refuses to do anything! We could all be murdered in our beds!"

"I'm sure he's doing everything he can, Rose. What did he tell you?"

"*Nothing*! Absolutely nothing! If my father were still alive, I'd have that man's job. I told him he'd better watch his step come next election. I told him, as a civic leader in this town, I had a right to know what's going on. I told him I had a good mind to organize a Citizens Committee to investigate the whole affair."

"Give him a chance. Robin is a very conscientious man."

"He's a child."

"Come on, Rose. He's at least thirty. I taught him for four years and I have complete confidence in him. You'll have to excuse me. I'm here to see him myself."

"He won't tell you anything." Rose said, sounding slightly mollified.

"Perhaps," Miss Mahan said. Rose echoed off down the hall. "He might have if you haven't put his tail over the dashboard," she muttered and pushed open the door.

Loreen Whittaker, Leo's aunt by marriage, looked up and smiled. "Hello, Miss Mahan. What can I do for you?"

"Hello, Loreen. I'd like to see Robin, if I may."

Loreen chuckled. "He gave me strict orders to let no one in but the governor—right after Mrs. Newcastle left."

Miss Mahan grimaced. "I met her in the hall. Would you ask him? It's important."

Loreen arose from her desk and went into the sheriff's private office. Miss Mahan felt that she and Robin were good friends. She had not only taught him, but his sister, Mary Ellen, and his little brother, Curtis, was a senior this year. She liked all of them and thought they liked her. Robin's son was in the second grade and a little doll. She was looking forward to teaching him, too.

Loreen came out of his office, grinning. "He said you could come in but I was to frisk you first." Her smile wavered. "Try to cheer him up, Miss Mahan. It's the first . . . murder we've had since he's been in office, and it's getting to him."

Miss Mahan nodded and went in. The sheriff sat hunched over his desk. His hair was mussed where he had been running his hand through it. There was a harried look on his face but he dredged up a thin smile for her.

"You aren't gonna give me trouble, too, are you?" he asked warily.

"I ran into Rose in the hall," she smiled back at him.

He motioned her to a chair. "What's the penalty for punching a civic leader in the nose?"

"You should know that better than I."

He grunted. "Yeah." He leaned back in the chair and stretched his long legs. "I can't discuss Yvonne Wilkins, if that's what you're here for."

"That's why I'm here. Don't you think this secrecy is worse than the facts? People will be imagining all sorts of horrible things."

"I doubt if anything they could imagine would be worse than the actual facts, Miss Mahan. You'll have to trust me. I have to do it this way." He ran his fingers through his hair again. "I'm afraid I may be in over my head on this. There's just me and five deputies for the whole county. And we haven't anything to work on. Nothing."

"Where did they find her?"

"Okay," he sighed. "I'll tell you this much. Yvonne went out yesterday afternoon in her father's car to visit Linda Murray. When she didn't come home last night, Mr. Wilkins called the Murrays and they said Yvonne left about six-thirty. He was afraid she'd had an accident in the snow, so he called me. We found her about three this morning out on the dirt road nearly to the old Weatherly place. She was in the car . . . dead. It's been snowing for five days. There wasn't a track of any kind and no fingerprints that didn't belong. And that's all you're gonna worm out of me."

Miss Mahan had an idea. "Had she been . . . molested?"

Robin looked at her as if he'd been betrayed. "Yes," he said simply.

"But," she protested, "why the big mystery? I know it's horrible, but it's not likely to cause a . . . a panic."

He got up and paced around the office. "Miss Mahan, I can't tell you any more."

"Is there more? Is there more than rape and murder?" She felt something like panic rising in her.

Robin squatted in front of her, taking her hands in his. "If there's anyone in town I'd tell, it would be you. You know that. I've loved you ever since I was fourteen years old. If you keep after me, I'll tell you, so have a little pity on a friend and stop pushing."

She felt her eyes burning and motioned for him to get up. "Robin, you're not playing fair." She stood up and he held her coat for her. "You always were able to get around me. Okay, you win."

"Thank you, Miss Mahan," he said genuinely relieved and kissed her on the forehead. She stopped in the hall and dabbed at her eyes.

But I haven't given up yet, she thought as she huddled in her coat on the way to Paul Sullivan's office. The bell tinkled on the door and the nurse materialized from somewhere.

"Miss Mahan. What are you doing out in this weather?"

"I'd like to see the doctor, Elaine." She hung her coat on the rack.

"He's with the little Archer girl now. She slipped on the snow and twisted her ankle."

"I'll wait." She sat and picked up a magazine without looking at it. Elaine Holliday had been one of her students. Who in town hadn't, she wondered. Elaine wanted to talk about the murder as did Louise Archer when she emerged with her limping daughter, but Miss Mahan wasn't in the mood for gossip and speculation. She marched into Dr. Sullivan's sanctorium.

"Hello, Paul," she said before he could open his mouth. "I've just been to see Robin. He told me Yvonne had been raped but he wouldn't tell me what the big mystery is. I know you're what passes for the County Medical Examiner, so you know as much as he does. I've known you for fifty years and even thought at one time you might propose to me, but you didn't. So

don't give me any kind of runaround. Tell me what happened to Yvonne."
She plopped into a chair and glared at him.

He shook his head in dismay. "I thought I might propose to you at one
time too, but right now is a good example of why I didn't. You were so
independent and bull-headed, you scared me to death."

"Don't change the subject."

"You won't like it."

"I don't expect to."

"There's no way I can 'put it delicately,' as they say."

"You don't know high school kids. I doubt if you *know* anything indelicate
that I haven't heard from them."

"Even if I tell you everything I know about it, it'll still be a mystery. It is to
me."

"Quit stalling."

"Okay, you asked for it. And if you repeat this to anyone, I'll wring your
scrawny old neck."

"I won't."

"All right. Yvonne was . . . how can I say it? . . . she was sexually
mutilated. She was split open. Not cut—torn, ripped. As if someone had
forced a two by four into her—probably something larger than that."

"Had they?" Miss Mahan felt her throat beginning to burn from the bile
rising in it.

"No. At least there was no evidence of it. No splinters, no soil, no foreign
matter of any kind."

"My Lord," she moaned. "How she must have suffered."

"Yes," he said softly, "but only for a few seconds. She must have lost
consciousness almost immediately. And she was dead long before they
finished with her."

"They? What makes you think there was more than one?"

"Are you sure you want to hear the rest of it?"

"Yes," she said, but she didn't.

"I said we found no foreign matter, but we found semen."

"Wasn't that to be expected?"

"Yes, I suppose. But not in such an amount."

"What do you mean?"

"We found nearly a hundred and fifty cc's. There was probably even
more. A lot of it had drained out onto the car seat." His voice was dull.

She shook her head in confusion. "A hundred and fifty cc's?"

"About a cup full."

She felt nauseous. "How much . . . how much. . . ?"

"The average male produces about two or three cc's. Maybe four."

"Does that mean she was . . . what? . . . fifty times?"

"And fifty different men."

"That's impossible."

"Yes. I know. One of the deputies took it to Wichita to be analyzed. To see if it's human."

"Human?"

"Yes. We thought someone might . . ."

She held up her hand. "You don't need to go . . . go any further." They sat for a while, not saying anything.

After a bit he said, "You can see why Robin wanted to keep it quiet?"

"Yes." She shivered, wishing she had her coat even though the office was warm. "Is there any more?"

He shook his head and slumped morosely deep in the chair. "No. Only that Robin is pretty sure she was . . . killed somewhere else and then taken out on the old road, because there was almost no blood in or around the car. How they ever drove so far out on that road in the snow is another mystery, although a minor one. The deputy was about to give up and turn around, and he had on snow chains."

Miss Mahan was late for her one o'clock class. The children hadn't become unruly as they usually did, but were subdued and talking in hushed voices. A discussion of *Silas Marner* proved futile, so she told them to sit quietly and read. She didn't feel anymore like classwork than they did. She noticed that Twilla's eyes were bright with suppressed excitement. Well, she thought, I guess you can't expect her to react like the others. She hardly knew Yvonne.

It had stopped snowing by the time Mr. Choate circulated a memo that school would be closed Wednesday for the funeral. Apparently Robin had managed to keep a lid on knowledge of the rape. There was speculation on the subject, but she could tell it was only speculation.

When she got home, she saw the Twilla journal lying beside the big chair in front of the cold fireplace. Strange, Twilla had hardly crossed her mind all day. She guessed it only proved how silly and stupid her Twilla-watching really was. She put the journal away in the library table drawer and decided that was enough of that nonsense.

> *Tuesday, the 12th*
> This morning I saw Twilla jab Alice May Turner in the thigh
> with a large darning needle.

Miss Mahan stopped in the middle of a sentence and stared in disbelief. She walked slowly to Twilla's desk, feeling every eye in the class following her. "What's going on here?" she asked in a deathly quiet voice. Twilla looked up at her with such total incomprehension she wondered if she had imagined the whole thing. But she looked at Alice May and saw her mouth tight and trembling and the tears being held in her eyes only by surface tension.

"What do you mean, Miss Mahan?" Twilla asked in a bewildered voice.

"Why did you stick Alice May with a needle?"

"Miss Mahan, I didn't!"

"I saw you."

"But I didn't!" Twilla's eyes were becoming damp as if she were about to cry in injured innocence.

"Don't bother to cry," Miss Mahan said calmly. "I'm not impressed." Twilla's mouth tightened for the briefest instant. Miss Mahan turned to Alice May. "Did she jab you with a needle?"

Alice May blinked and a tear rolled down each cheek. "No, ma'am," she answered in a strained voice.

"Then why are you crying?" Miss Mahan demanded.

"I'm not crying," Alice May insisted, wiping her face.

"I think both of you had better come with me to Mr. Choate's office."

Mr. Choate wouldn't or, I guess, couldn't do anything. They both lied their heads off, insisting that nothing happened. Twilla even had the gall to accuse me of spying on her and persecuting her. I think Mr. Choate believed me. He could hardly help it when Alice May began rubbing her thigh in the midst of her denials.

Miss Mahan sent Twilla back to the room and kept Alice May in the hall. Alice May began to snuffle and wouldn't look at her. "Alice May, dear," she said patiently. "I saw what Twilla did. Why are you fibbing to me?"

"I'm not!" she wailed softly.

"Alice May, I don't want any more of this nonsense!" Why on earth did Twilla do it, she wondered. Alice May was such a silly, harmless girl. Why would anyone want to hurt her?

"Miss Mahan, I can't tell you," she sobbed.

"Here." Miss Mahan gave her a handkerchief. Alice May took it and rubbed at her red eyes. "Why can't you tell me? What's going on between you and Twilla?"

"Nothing," she sniffed.

"Alice May. I promise to drop the whole subject if you'll just tell me the truth."

Alice May finally looked at her. "Will you?"

"Yes," she groaned in exasperation.

"Well, my . . . my giggling gets on her nerves."

"What?"

"She told me if I didn't stop, I'd be sorry."

"Why didn't you pick up something and brain her with it?"

Alice May's eyes widened in disbelief. "Miss Mahan, I couldn't do that!"

"She didn't mind hurting you, did she?"

"I'm . . . I'm afraid of her. Everybody is."

"Why? What has she done?"

"I don't know. Nothing. I'm just afraid. You promise not to let her know I told you?"

"I promise. Now, go to the restroom and wash your face."

Twilla kept watching me the rest of the period. I imagine she suspects Alice May spilled the beans. The other children were very quiet and expectant as if they thought Twilla and I would go at each other tooth and claw. I wonder who they would root for if we did.

I'll have to admit to a great deal of perverse pleasure in tarnishing Twilla's reputation in the teacher's lounge. I was a little surprised to find a few of the others had become somewhat disenchanted with her also. They didn't have such a concrete example of viciousness as I had, but she was making them uncomfortable.

I also discovered who Twilla's romantic (if you can call it that) interest is since Carter flunked out.

Leo Whittaker!

I was never so shocked and disappointed in my life. An affair between a teacher and student is bad enough but—Leo! No wonder she was being quiet about it. I thought he acted a bit peculiar when we discussed Twilla, so I said bold as brass: "I wonder who she's sleeping with?" He turned red and left the room, looking guilty as sin.

I don't know what to do about it. I've got to do something. But what? what? what? I can't do anything to hurt Leo, because it'll also hurt poor Lana.

How could Leo be so stupid?

Dark clouds hung oppressively low the morning of the funeral. They scudded across the sky so rapidly Miss Mahan got dizzy looking at them. She stood with the large group huddled against the cold outside the First Christian Church of Hawley, waiting for the formation of the procession to the County Line Cemetery. The services had drawn a capacity crowd, mostly from curiosity, she was afraid. The entire ninth grade was there, with the exception of Sammy Stocker, of course, and Twilla. Only two teachers were missing: Mrs. Bryson (first grade) who had the flu, and Leo Whittaker. Leo's absence was peculiar because Lana was there, looking pale and beautifully pregnant. She was with Carter Redwine and his parents. Carter seems to be recovering nicely from his little misadventure, she thought.

She spotted Paul Sullivan and crunched through the snow to his side. He saw her coming and frowned. "Hello, Paul. Did you get the report from Wichita?"

"Do you think this is the place to discuss it?"

"Why not? No one will overhear. Did you?"

He sighed. "Yes."

"Well?"

"It was human—although there were certain peculiarities."

"What peculiarities?"

He cocked his eyes at her. "If I told you, would it mean anything?"

She shrugged. "What else?"

"Well, it all came from the same person—as far as they could tell. At least, there was nothing to indicate that it didn't. Also all the sperm was the same age."

"What does that mean?"

"The thought occurred to us that someone might be trying to create a grisly hoax. That someone might have . . . well . . . saved it up until they had that much."

"I get the picture," she grimaced. She thought a moment. "Can't they . . . ah . . . freeze it? Haven't I read something about that?"

"You can't do it in your Frigidaire. If the person who did it had the knowledge and the laboratory equipment to do that . . . well . . . it's as improbable as the other theories."

"Robin hasn't learned anything yet?"

"I don't know. Some of us aren't as nosy as others"

She smiled at him as she spotted Lana Whittaker moving toward the Redwine car. She began edging away. "Will you keep me posted?"

"No."

"Thank you, Paul." She caught up with Lana. "Hello, dear."

Lana started and turned, then smiled thinly. "Hello, Miss Mahan."

She exchanged greetings with Mr. and Mrs. Redwine and Carter as they entered their car. "Should you be out in this weather, Lana?"

Lana shrugged. She looked a little haggard and her eyes were puffy. "I'll be all right."

Miss Mahan took her arm. "Come on. My car is right here. Get in out of the cold and talk to me. We'll have plenty of time before they get this mess untangled." Lana went unprotesting and sat in the car staring straight ahead. Miss Mahan started the car and switched on the heater although it was still fairly warm. She turned and looked at Lana.

"When you were in school," she said quietly, "you came to me with all your problems. It made me feel a little like I had a daughter of my own."

Lana turned and looked at her with love and pain in her eyes. "I'm not a little girl anymore, Miss Mahan. I'm a married lady with a baby on the way. I should be able to handle my own problems."

"Where's Leo?"

Lana leaned back against the seat and put her fingers on the sides of her nose. "I don't know," she said simply as if her tears had been used up. "He went out last night and I haven't seen him since. I told my aunt and uncle he went to Liberal to buy some things for the baby."

"Did you call Robin? Maybe he had an accident."

"No. There was no accident. I thought so the first time."

"When was that?"

"Last Friday night. He didn't come in until after midnight. The same thing Saturday. He didn't show up until dawn Monday and Tuesday. This time he didn't come back at all."

"What did he say?"

"Nothing. He wouldn't say anything. Miss Mahan, I know he still loves me; I can tell. He seems genuinely sorry and ashamed of what he's doing, but he keeps . . . keeps doing it. I've tried to think who she might be, but I can't imagine anyone. He's so tired and worn out when he comes home, it would be funny if it . . . if it were happening to someone else."

"Do you still love him?"

Lana smiled. "Oh yes," she said softly. "More than anything. I love him so much it . . ." she blushed, " . . . it gives me goosebumps. I was crazy about Leo even when we were in high school, but he was so wild he scared me to death. I thought . . . I thought he had changed."

"I think he has." Miss Mahan took Lana's hand as she saw Robin get in his car and pull out with the pall bearers and the hearse directly behind him. "They're starting. You'd better go back to your car. I'm glad you told me. I'll do all I can to help."

Lana opened the car door. "I appreciate it, Miss Mahan, but I really don't see what you can do."

"We shall see what we shall see."

Miss Mahan managed to hang back until she was last in the funeral procession. The highway had been cleared of snow and she hoped it wouldn't start again before they all got back to town. But she didn't know. The sky looked terrible. She turned off the highway at Miller's Corners, down the dirt road to the old Peacock place. There was nothing left of Miller's Corners now except a few scattered farm houses. The cafe had been moved into Hawley eight years ago and the Gulf station had closed when George Cuttsanger died last fall. The Gulf people had even taken down the signs.

If the Gilbreaths were fixing up the old Peacock farm, they must have started on the inside. It was still as gray and weary looking as it was ten years ago, if not more so. The black Chrysler was in the old carriage house and smoke drifted this way and that from one of the chimneys, caught by small erratic gusts of air.

She parked and sat looking at the house a moment before getting out. The snow was clean and undisturbed on the front walk. She guessed they must use the back door; it was closer to the carriage house.

No one answered her knock, but she knew they were home. She waited and knocked again. Still no response. She took a deep breath and pushed open the door. "Mrs Gilbreath?" she called. She listened carefully but there was not a sound. She could hear the melting snow dripping from the eaves and the little ticking sounds an old house makes. She went in and closed the door behind her. "Mrs. Gilbreath?" she called again, hearing nothing but a faint echo. The house was warm but even more dilapidated than the last time she was in it.

She stepped into the parlor and saw them both sitting there. "Oh!" she gasped, startled, and then laughed in embarrassment. "I didn't mean to barge in, but no one answered my knock." Mr. and Mrs. Gilbreath sat in highback easy chairs facing away from her. She could only see the tops of their heads. They didn't move.

"Mrs. Gilbreath?" she said, beginning to feel queasy. She walked slowly around them, her eyes fixed so intently on the chairs she momentarily experienced an optical illusion that the chairs were turning slowly to face her. She blinked and took an involuntary step backward. They sat in the chairs dressed to go out, their eyes focussed on nothing. Neither of them moved, not even the slight movements of breathing, nor did their eyes blink. She stared at them in astonishment, fearing they were dead.

Miss Mahan approached them cautiously and touched Mrs. Gilbreath on the arm. The flesh was warm and soft. She quickly drew her hand back with a gasp. Then she reached again and shook the woman's shoulder. "Mrs. Gilbreath?" she whispered.

"She won't answer you." Miss Mahan gave a little shriek and looked up with a jerk. Twilla was strolling down the stairs, tying the sash of a rather barbaric looking floor-length fur robe. The antique pendant she always wore was around her neck. She stopped at the foot of the stairs and leaned against the newell post. She smiled. "They're only simulacra, you know."

"What?" Miss Mahan was bewildered. She hadn't expected Twilla to be here. She thought she would be with Leo.

Twilla indicated her parents. "Watch." Miss Mahan jerked her head back toward the people in the chairs. Suddenly, their heads twisted on their necks until the blank faces looked at each other. Then they grimaced and stuck out their tongues. The faces became expressionless again, and the heads swiveled back to stare at nothing.

Twilla's laugh trilled through the house. Miss Mahan jerked her eyes back to the beautiful child, feeling like a puppet herself. "They're rather clever, don't you think?" she cooed as she walked toward Miss Mahan, the fur robe making a soft sound against the floor. "I'm glad you came, Miss Mahan. It saves me the trouble of going to you."

"What?" Miss Mahan felt out of control. Her heart was beating like a hammer and she clutched the back of Mrs. Gilbreath's chair to keep from falling.

Twilla smiled at her panic. "I haven't been unaware of your interest in me, you know. I had decided it was time to get you out of the way before you became a problem."

"Get me out of the way?"

"Of course."

"What are you?" She felt her voice rising to a screech but she couldn't stop it. "What are these things pretending to be your parents?"

Twilla laughed. "A thirteen-year-old is quite limited in this society. I had to have parents to do the things I couldn't do myself." She shrugged. "There are other ways but this is the least bothersome."

"I won't let you get me out of the way." Miss Mahan hissed, dismissing the things she didn't understand and concentrating on that single threat, trying to pull her reeling senses together.

"Don't be difficult, Miss Mahan. There's nothing you can do to stop me." Twilla's face had become petulant and then she smiled slyly. "Come with me. I want to show you something." Miss Mahan didn't budge. Twilla took a few steps and then turned back. "Come along, now. Don't you want all your questions answered?"

She started up the stairs. Miss Mahan followed her. Her legs felt mechanical. Half way up she turned and looked back at the two figures sitting in the chairs like department store dummies. Twilla called to her and she continued to the top.

A hallway ran the length of the house upstairs with bedroom doors on either side. Twilla opened one of them and motioned Miss Mahan in. The house wasn't as old as her own but it still had the fourteen foot ceilings. But the ceilings, as well as the walls, had been removed. This side of the hall was one big area, opening into the attic, the roof at least twenty feet overhead with what appeared to be some sort of trap door recently built into it. The area was empty except for a large gray mass hunched in one corner like a partially collapsed tent.

"He's asleep," Twilla said and whistled. The mass stirred. The tent unfolded slowly, rustling like canvas sliding on canvas. Bony ribs spread gracefully, stretching the canvas-like flesh into vast bat wings which lifted out and up to bump against the roof. The wings trembled slightly as they stretched lazily and then settled, folding neatly behind the thing sitting on the floor.

It was a man, or almost a man. He would have been about sixteen feet tall had he been standing. His body was massively muscled and covered with purplish gray scales that shimmered metallically even in the dim light. His chest, shoulders, and back bulged with wing-controlling muscles. He stretched his arms and yawned, then rubbed at his eyes with horny fists. His head was hairless and scaled; his ears rose to points reaching above the crown of his skull. The face was angelically beautiful but the large liquid eyes were dull and the mouth was slack like an idiot's. He scratched his hip with two-inch talons, making the sound of a rasp on metal. He was completely naked and emphatically male. His massive sex lay along his heavy thigh like a great purple-headed snake.

"This is Dazreel," Twilla said pleasantly. The creature perked up at the sound of his name and looked toward them. "He's a djinn," Twilla continued. He turned his empty gaze away and began idly fondling himself. Twilla sighed. "I'm afraid Dazreel's pleasures are rather limited."

Miss Mahan ran.

She clattered down the stairs, clutching frantically at the bannister to keep her balance. She lost her right shoe and stumbled on the bottom step, hitting her knees painfully on the floor. She reeled to her feet, unaware of her shins shining through her torn stockings. Twilla's crystal laughter pealing down the stairs hardly penetrated the shimmering white layer of panic blanketing her mind.

She bruised her hands on the front door, clawing at it, trying to open it the wrong way. She careened across the porch, into the snow, not feeling the cold on her stockinged right foot. But her lopsided gait caused her to fall, sprawling on her face, burying her arms to the elbows in the snow. She crawled a few feet before gaining enough momentum to regain her feet. Her whole front was frosted with white but she didn't notice.

She locked the car doors, praying it would start. But she released the clutch too quickly, and it bucked and stalled. She ground the starter and turned her head to see Twilla standing on the porch, her arms hugging a pillar, her cheek caressing it, her smile mocking. The motor caught. Miss Mahan turned the car in a tight circle. The rear wheels lost traction and the car fishtailed.

Take it easy, she screamed to herself. You've made it. You've gotten away. Don't end up in the far ditch.

She was halfway to Miller's Corners when the loose snow began whipping in a cloud around her. She half heard the dull boom of air being compressed by vast wings. A shadow fell over her and Dazreel landed astraddle the hood of her car. The metal collapsed with a hollow *whump* as the djinn leaned down to peer curiously at her through the windshield. She began screaming, tearing her throat with short, hysterical, mindless shrieks that seemed to come from a great distance.

Her screams ended suddenly with a grunt as the front wheels struck the ditch, bringing the car to an abrupt halt. Dazreel lost his balance and flopped over backwards with a glitter of purplish gray and a tangle of canvas-flesh into the snow drifts. Miss Mahan watched in paralyzed shock as he got to his feet, grinning an idiot grin, shaking the snow from his wings, and walked around the car. His wings kept opening and closing slightly to give him balance. Her head turned in quick jerks like a wooden doll, following his movements. He leaned over the car from behind and the glass of both side windows crumbled with a gravelly sound as his huge fingers poked through to grasp the tops of the doors.

The dim light became even dimmer as his wings spread in a mantle over the car. The snow swirled into the air and she could see the tips of each wing as it made a downward stroke. The car shifted and groaned and rose from the ground.

She fainted.

A smiling angel face floated out of a golden mist. Soft, pink lips moved solicitously but no sound emerged. Miss Mahan felt a glass of water at her mouth and she drank greedily, soothing her raw throat. Sound returned.

"Are you feeling better, Miss Mahan? We don't want you to have a heart attack just yet, do we?" Twilla's eyes glittered with excitement.

Miss Mahan sucked oxygen, fighting the fog in her brain. Then, raw, red fingers of anger tore away the silvery panic. She looked at the beautiful monstrous child kneeling before her, the extravagant robe parted enough at the top to reveal a small, perfect bare breast. The nipple looked as if it had been rouged. "I'm feeling quite myself again, thank you."

Twilla rose and moved to a facing chair. They were in the parlor. Miss

Mahan looked around, but the djinn was absent. Only the parent dolls were there in the same positions.

"Dazreel is back upstairs," Twilla assured her, watching her speculatively. "You have nothing to fear." She smiled slightly. "He will have only virgins."

Miss Mahan felt the blood draining from her face and she weaved in the chair, feeling the panic creeping back. Twilla threw her head back and her crystal laugh was harsh and strident, like a chandelier tumbling down marble stairs.

"Miss Mahan, you never cease to amaze me," she gasped. "Imagine! And at your age, too."

The anger returned in full control. "It's none of your business," she stated unequivocally.

"I'm ever so glad you decided to pay me a visit, Miss Mahan. It's, what do you say? Killing two birds with one stone?"

"What do you mean?"

"Dazreel has, as I said, limited, but strong appetites. If they aren't satisfied, he becomes quite unmanageable. And don't think he will reject you because you're a scrawny old crow. He has no taste at all, and only one criterion: virginity." Twilla was almost fidgety with anticipation.

"What possible difference could it make to that monster?" I must be losing my mind, Miss Mahan thought, I'm sitting here having a calm conversation with this wretched child who is going to kill me!

Twilla was thoughtful. "I really don't know. I never thought about it. That's just the way it's always been. It could be a personal idiosyncracy, or perhaps it's religious." She shrugged. "Something like *kosher*, do you think? Anyway, you can't fool him."

"I don't understand any of this," Miss Mahan said in confusion. "Did you say he was a . . . a djinn?"

"Surely you've heard of them. King Solomon banished the entire race, if you remember." She smiled, pleased. "But I saved Dazreel."

"How old are you?" Miss Mahan breathed.

Twilla chuckled. "You wouldn't believe me if I told you. Don't let the body mislead you. It's relatively new. Dazreel has great power if you can control him. But he's crafty and very literal. One wrong move and . . ." She ran her forefinger across her throat.

"But . . ." Miss Mahan was completely confused. "If this is all true, why are you going to school in Hawley, Kansas, for heaven's sake?"

Twilla sighed. "Boredom is the curse of the immortal, Miss Mahan. I thought it might offer some diversion."

"If you're so bored with life, why don't you die?"

"Don't be absurd!"

"How could you be so inhuman? What you did to Yvonne . . . does life mean nothing to you?"

Twilla shifted in irritation. "Don't be tiresome. How could your brief, insignificant lives concern me?"

There was a restless sound from above. Twilla glanced at the stairs. "Dazreel is becoming impatient." She turned back to Miss Mahan with a smirk. "Are you ready to meet your lover, Miss Mahan?"

Miss Mahan sat frozen, the blood roaring in her eyes. "You might as well go," Twilla continued. "It's inevitable. Think of your dignity, Miss Mahan. Do you really want to go kicking and screaming? Or perhaps you'd like another run in the snow?"

Miss Mahan stood up suddenly. "I won't give you the satisfaction," she said calmly. She walked to the stairs, bobbing up and down with one shoe off. Twilla rose and ran after her, circling her in glee.

Twilla leaned against the newell post, blocking the stairs. She smiled wistfully. "I rather envy you, Miss Mahan. I've often wished . . . Dazreel knows the ancient Oriental arts, and sex *was* an art." She grimaced. "Now it's like two goats in heat!" Her smile returned. "I've often wished I had the capacity."

Miss Mahan ignored her and marched slowly up the stairs with lopsided dignity. Twilla clapped her hands and backed up ahead of her, taunting her, encouraging her, plucking at her gray tweed coat. Twilla danced around, swirling the fur robe with graceful turns. Miss Mahan looked straight ahead, one hand on the bannister for balance.

Then, at the third step from the top, she stumbled. She fell against the railing and then to her knees. She shifted and sat on the step, rubbing her shins.

"Don't lose heart now, Miss Mahan," Twilla sang. "We're almost there." Twilla tugged at her coat sleeve. Miss Mahan clutched Twilla's wrist as if she needed help in getting up. Then she heaved with all her might. Twilla's laughter became a gasp and then a shriek as she plummeted down the stairs with a series of very satisfying thumps and crashes. Miss Mahan hurried after her but the fall had done the job.

Twilla lay on her back a few feet from the bottom step, her body twisted at the wrong angle. She was absolutely motionless except for her face. It contorted in fury and her eyes were metallic with hate. Her rose petal lips writhed and spewed the most vile obscenities Miss Mahan had ever imagined, some of them in languages she'd never heard.

"Dazreel!" Twilla keened. "Dazreel! Dazreel!" over and over. A howl reverberated through the house. It shook. Plaster crashed and wood splintered. Dazreel appeared at the top of the stairs, barely able to squeeze through the opening.

Twilla continued her call. Miss Mahan took a trembling step backward. Dazreel started down the steps. Miraculously they didn't collapse. Only the bannister splintered and swayed outward.

Miss Mahan commanded herself to think. What did she know about djinns? Very little, practically nothing. Wasn't there supposed to be a controlling device of some sort? A lamp? A bottle? A magic ring? A talisman? Something. She looked at Twilla and then at the djinn. She almost fainted. Dazreel approached the bottom of the stairs with an enormous erection.

She looked frantically at Twilla. She's not wearing rings. Then something caught her eye.

The pendant! Was it the pendant? It had slipped up and over her shoulder and beneath her neck. Miss Mahan scrambled for it. She pushed Twilla's head aside. The child screamed in horrible agony. She grasped the pendant and pulled. The chain cut into the soft flesh of Twilla's neck and then snapped, leaving a red line that oozed blood.

She looked at Dazreel. He had stopped and was looking at her tentatively. It *was* the pendant! "Give it back," Twilla groaned. "Give it back. Please. Please, give it back. It won't do you any good. You don't know how to use it."

Miss Mahan threw the pendant at him. Twilla screamed and the hair on the back of Miss Mahan's neck bristled. It was not a scream of pain or rage, but of the damned. Dazreel's huge hand darted out and caught the pendant. He held his fist to his face and opened his fingers, gazing at what he held. He looked at Miss Mahan and smiled an angelic smile. Then he rippled, like heat waves on the desert, and . . . vanished.

Miss Mahan sat on the bottom step, weak with relief, gulping air. She looked at Twilla, as motionless as the parent dolls in the chairs. Only her face moved, twisting in sobs of self-pity. Miss Mahan almost felt sorry for her . . . but not quite.

She stood up and walked through the kitchen and out the back door. She thought she knew where it would be. Everyone kept it there. She went to the shed behind the carriage house, floundering through the snow drift. She scooped away the snow to get the door open. She stepped in and looked around. There was almost no light. The scudding clouds seemed even lower and darker and the single window in the shed was completely grimed over.

She spotted it behind some shovels, misted over with cob-webs. She pushed the shovels aside, grasped the handle and lifted the gasoline can. It was heavy. She shook it. There was a satisfying slosh. She smiled grimly and started back to the house, walking more lopsided than ever.

Then she stopped and gaped when she saw Leo Whittaker's car parked out of sight behind the house. She hurried on, letting the heavy can bounce against the ground with every other step. She opened the kitchen door and shrieked.

Mrs. Gilbreath stood in the doorway, smiling pleasantly at her, and holding a butcher knife. Without reasoning, without even thinking, Miss Mahan took the handle of the heavy gasoline can in both hands and swung it as hard as she could.

The sharp rim around the bottom caught Mrs. Gilbreath across the face, destroying one eye, shearing away her nose, and opening one cheek. Her expression didn't change. Blood flowed over her pleasant smile as she staggered drunkenly backward.

Miss Mahan lost her balance completely. The momentum of the gasoline can swung her around and she sat in the snow, flat on her skinny bottom. The can slipped from her fingers and bounced across the ground with a descending scale of clangs. She lurched to her feet and looked in the kitchen door. Mrs. Gilbreath had slammed against the wall and was sitting on the floor, still smiling her gory smile, her right arm twitching like a metronome.

Miss Mahan scrambled after the gasoline can and hid it in the pantry. She ducked up the kitchen stairs when she heard footsteps.

Mr. Gilbreath walked through the kitchen, ignoring Mrs. Gilbreath, and went out the back door. Miss Mahan hurried up the stairs. Oh Lord, she thought, I'll be so sore, I can't move for a week.

She entered the upstairs hall from the opposite end. She stepped carefully over the debris from the wall shattered by the djinn. She looked in the bedrooms on the other side. The first one was empty with a layer of dust, but the second . . . She stared. It looked like a set from a Maria Montez movie. A fire burned in the fireplace and Leo Whittaker lay stark-naked on the fur-covered bed.

"Leo Whittaker!" she bellowed. "Get up from there and put your clothes on this instant!" But he didn't move. He was alive; his chest moved gently as he breathed. She went to him, trying to keep from looking at his nakedness. Then she thought, what the dickens? There's no point in being a prude at this stage. Her eyes widened in admiration. Then she ceded him a few additional points for being able to satisfy Twilla. Why couldn't she have found a beautiful man like that when she was twenty-three, she wondered. She sighed. It wouldn't have made any difference, she guessed. It would have all turned out the same.

She put her hand on his shoulder and shook him. He moaned softly and shifted on the bed. "Leo! Wake up! What's the matter with you?" She shook him again. He acted drugged or something. She saw a long golden hair on his stomach and plucked it off, throwing it on the floor. She took a deep breath and slapped him in the face. He grunted. His head lifted slightly and then fell back. "Leo!" she shouted and slapped him again. His body jerked and his eyes clicked open but didn't focus.

"Leo!" Slap!

"Owww," he said and looked at her. "Miss Mahan?"

"Leo, are you awake?"

"Miss Mahan? What are you doing here? Is Lana all right?" He sat up in the bed and saw the room. He grunted in bewilderment.

"Leo. Get up and get dressed. Hurry!" she commanded. She heard the starter of a car grinding. Leo looked at himself, turned red, and tried to move in every direction at once. Miss Mahan grinned and went to the window. She could hear Leo thumping and bumping as he tried to put his clothes on. The car motor caught and steam billowed from the carriage house. "Hurry, Leo!" The black Chrysler began slowly backing out, Mr. Gilbreath at the wheel. Then the motor stalled and died.

He's trying to get away, she thought. No, he's only a puppet. He's planning to take Twilla away! She turned back to Leo. He was dressed, sitting on the edge of the bed, putting on his shoes. He looked at her shame-faced, like a little boy.

"Leo," she said in her sternest, most no-nonsense, unruly child voice. The car motor started again. "Don't ask any questions. Go down the kitchen stairs, and to your car. Hurry as fast as you can. Don't let Mr. Gilbreath see you. Bring your car around to the front and to the end of the lane. Block the lane so Mr. Gilbreath can't get out. Keep yourself locked in your car because he's dangerous. Do you understand?"

"No," he said, shaking his head.

"Never mind. Will you do what I said?"

He nodded.

"All right, then. Hurry!" They left the bedroom. Leo gave it one last bewildered glance. They ran down the kitchen stairs as fast as they could, Leo keeping her steady. She propelled him out the back door before he could see Mrs. Gilbreath still smiling and twitching. The black Chrysler was just pulling around to the front of the house.

She ran to the pantry, retrieved the gasoline can, and staggered into the entry hall. She could see Mr. Gilbreath getting out of the car. She locked the door and hobbled into the parlor. Twilla had been moved to the divan and covered with a quilt. He shouldn't have moved her, Miss Mahan thought, with an injury like that it could have killed her.

Twilla saw her enter and began screeching curses at her. Miss Mahan shook her head. She put the gasoline can down by the divan and tried to unscrew the cap on the spout. It wouldn't budge. It was rusted solid. Miss Mahan growled in frustration. The front door began to rattle and clatter.

Twilla's curses stopped suddenly and Miss Mahan looked at her. Twilla was staring at her in round-eyed horror. Miss Mahan went to the fireplace and got the poker. Twilla's eyes followed her. She drew the poker back and swung it as hard as she could at the gasoline can. It made a very satisfactory hole. She swung the poker several more times and tossed it away. She picked up the can as Twilla began to scream and plead. She rested it on the back of the divan and stripped away the blanket. She tipped it over and pale pink streams of gasoline fell on Twilla.

Glass shattered in the front door. Miss Mahan left the can resting on the back of the divan, still gurgling out its contents, and went to the fireplace again. She picked up the box of matches as Mr. Gilbreath walked in. His expression didn't change as he hurried toward her. She took a handful of wooden matches. She struck them all on the side of the box and tossed them on Twilla.

Twilla's screams and the flames ballooned upward together. Mr. Gilbreath shifted directions and waded into the flames, reaching for Twilla. Miss Mahan ran out of the house as fast as she could.

She was past the black Chrysler, its motor still running, when the gasoline can exploded. Leo had parked his car where she told him. Now he jumped out and ran to her. They looked at the old Peacock house.

It was old and dry as dust. The flames engulfed it completely. The snow was melting in a widening circle around it. They had to back all the way to Leo's car because of the heat.

They heard a siren and turned to see Sheriff Walker's car hurrying down the lane, followed by some of the funeral procession on its way back to Hawley. The ones who hadn't turned down the road were stopped on the highway, looking.

"Leo, dear," she said. "Do you know what you're doing here?"

He rubbed his hand across his face, his eyes still a little bleary. "Yes, I think so. It all seems like a dream. Twilla . . . Miss Mahan," he said in pain. "I don't know why I did it."

"I do," she said soothingly and put her arm around him. "And it wasn't your fault. You have to believe that. Don't tell Lana or anyone. Forget it ever happened. Do you understand?"

He nodded as Robin Walker got out of his car and ran toward them. He looks very handsome in his uniform, she thought. My, my, I've suddenly become very conscious of good-looking men. Too bad it's thirty years too late.

"Miss Mahan? Leo? What's going on here?" Robin asked in bewilderment. "Is anyone still in there?" He looked at her feet. "Miss Mahan, why are you running around in the snow with only one shoe on?"

She followed his gaze. "I'll declare," she said in astonishment. "I didn't know I'd lost it. Leo, Robin, let's get in your car. I have a lot to tell you both."

Miss Mahan sat before the fireplace in her comfortable old house, tearing the pages from her Twilla journal and feeding them one at a time to the fire. Paul Sullivan had doctored her cuts and bruises and she felt wonderful—stiff and sore, to be sure—but wonderful. Tomorrow the news would be all over town that, with brilliant detective work, Robin Walker, aided by Leo Whittaker, had discovered that Twilla Gilbreath's father was Yvonne's killer. In an attempt to arrest him, the house had burned and all three had perished.

She had told Robin and Leo everything that happened—well, almost everything. She had left out her own near encounter with Dazreel and a few other related items. She had also given the impression—sort of—that the house had burned by accident. Poor, sweet Robin hadn't believed a word of it. But, after hearing Leo's account, taking a look at her demolished car, and seeing the footprints in the snow, he finally, grudgingly, agreed to go along with it. And it did explain all the mysteries of Yvonne's death.

She knew the *public* story was full of holes and loose ends, but she also knew the people in Hawley. They wanted to hear that an outsider had done it, and they wanted to hear that he had been discovered. Their own imaginations would fill in the gaps.

Lana Whittaker didn't really believe that Leo was working with Robin all those nights he was away, but they loved each other enough. They'd be all right.

She fed the last pages to the fire and looked around her parlor. She decided to put up a tree this year. She hadn't bothered with one in years. And a party. She'd have a party. There hadn't been more than three people in the house at one time in ages.

She hobbled creakily up the stairs, humming "Deck the Hall with Boughs of Holly," considerably off key, heading for the attic to search for the box of Christmas tree ornaments.

KENTUCKY

His Name Was Not Forgotten
by Joel Townsley Rogers

THE OLD sorrel horse had come to the end of another furrow, down at the far corner of the cleared land. The gaunt man in deerskin leggings and bearskin moccasins heeled his bar-spear plow with an easy grip on the smooth-worn handles, as the old horse plodded around.

"Ho!" he said.

The flash of something streaked black and white, like a woodpecker, had caught the hinder edge of his vision for an instant flitting between trees of the young woods beside him. He turned his mild wrinkled gaze as the old horse stopped, though too late to see what it had been.

For the moment he paused, relaxing, stretching his backbone, scratching his naked ribs, savoring all the good smells of the virgin soil turned up black by his moldboard, and of the May woods and the south wind blowing.

Only one more furrow to plow, up along the thin woods' edge, and then back to his new-built cabin in the field's far corner. He would have time to finish setting in the puncheon floor this afternoon or perhaps to do a little fishing before returning at sundown to Bersheba and the young ones, at the station a mile away.

He had stripped off his linsey shirt a while back, and left it draped on the old oak stump which stood over toward the middle of the plowed land, with his ax resting against it. His flat-chested torso, pale as buttermilk after the long winter of store-tending and crowded indoor living at the little backwoods station, was oiled with a pleasant sweat beneath the noon sun. The life-giving rays tingled through his skin. He felt the light wind stirring the roots of his gray-streaked hair and beard.

Pink and yellow flowering shrubs spotted the woods beside him. Through the sapling trunks and dappled undergrowth he could glimpse the sparkling waters of Long Run, where it went between its grassy banks a hundred yards away. Birds sang and twittered, flitting about, building their nests. The gaunt man fumbled his lips, stirred with an impulse to try imitating their exultant notes. But he was of an inarticulate nature, and even though there was no one to hear him, his lips felt dry and his throat constricted.

Purty, he thought. *Durned purty*.

He was forty-two years old, and his life had been meager and toilsome. He had never learned to express himself in any way. Even as a boy, there had never been any time for him of carefree joy. The weight of poverty and responsibility had always lain heavily on him. A hewer of wood for other men, a plower of others' fields, a wandering trapper and a landless squatter, a small storekeeper at impoverished backwoods settlements doling out needles and pins, with no great love for business, and the shillings few, and losing repeatedly, through bad judgment and lack of trading sharpness, what small gains he made, the barren years stretched back of him. Hunger and want, and defeat and grief—all the things which a man has learned to know when his eyes have become wrinkles and there is gray in his beard—had been his in full measure. Yet for the moment now he felt all the ecstasy of the spring as much as the singing birds.

Like them, he had his own nest this spring—the new cabin which he and his two big boys, Mort and Josh, had built during the past winter, on the Government land grant for his war service which had come through for him at last. He liked to pause down here at the end of the field to admire it in perspective, where it stood at the upper corner of the plowed land, catercorner across the deep furrows from him, at the edge of the pine woods, close to the entrance of the trail that came down from the station.

It was no mere half-face hunter's shelter, built of felled sapling trunks and beaver skins, with only a hearth of piled stones at the open end to huddle over against the winter's cold, such as he and his strong-limbed, competent Mary had known during those hard years of his young manhood when Mort and Josh had been small, and the little girl who had died. No floorless, unchinked field hand's shack, either, too poor even to quarter black slaves in any more, like the one which he had had to take his young Anne to, in that time of youth and brief first love, back in Virginia so long ago. It was a complete four-wall cabin, solidly laid, of spacious dimensions, fourteen by eighteen feet, with a stone fireplace at one end, with a split-slab roof tightly weather-lapped, and with a puncheon floor soon to be installed—a home such as any man might be proud to own.

This was an end to the meager years, the homeless years, the years of insecurity and grief. Mary Shipley lay dead somewhere beside the yellow Ohio, in an unmarked grave, and his young love Anne back across the mountains, in a land that he would never see again. There were times when he almost forgot her.

He had not done too well by either of them. He had not done too well by

Bersheba, either, poor young thing, in the six years they had been married. Crowded quarters behind a calico curtain in shared cabins, with the dogs and crying children underfoot, and the drunken quarreling and laughter, and the snoring and the steaming of snow-wet bodies, and no privacy and dignity to it all. Why, at Hughes Station this past winter there had been nineteen families in the eight cabins, a total of more than a hundred souls, including the nine babies which had been born, and not counting the itinerant trappers and Indian traders who might be bunking for a week or two at a time in the blockhouses. That was too crowded living for anyone who liked to breathe. A man couldn't feel that he belonged to himself. And a woman like Bersheba, with her poetry reading and her dainty airs and her feckless dreaming—always areading books and adreaming, when she should be putting the dinner in the pot and getting the washing done—must find it even harder than he did, though she had never complained.

Nothing like that anymore. His own land and his own cabin. A faint curl of smoke rose from the chimney, from the banked wood coals on the hearth keeping warm his dinner of johnnycake and beans. His rifle leaned beside the door. The pelt of the bobcat which he had shot last week was pegged upon the slabs. A seven-foot length of split log, thirty inches wide, lay on the ground near the door, needing only auger holes to be bored in its round underside for legs to make a dining table. With a few last items completed and with a crop in, he would soon be able to move the family out, and they would all live here in freedom and security on the good earth for the rest of their days, his two big boys, Mort and Josh, and Bersheba with her baby girls and little Tom.

It was almost as if his life were just beginning, with all the happiness of untasted springs stored up for him, to be enjoyed from this time forth. He was not an old man yet. He was just at the beginning of his prime. Already, with a dream in his faded eyes, he saw the bare earth green and yellow with tall standing corn. Already he saw the windows of clear glass set in the blank cabin walls. Already a barn for cows and horses, and more fields and meadows cleared away, down to the edge of Long Run and beyond, where the deep woods stood on the other side. Already apple trees white in the spring, and chickens pecking in the dooryard, and himself standing in his doorway in a plum coat with brass buttons on Sundays, looking out over his rich acres. Perhaps someday he would even be elected to the territorial legislature and they would call him squire.

The house that he had built, on the land that God had given him. With his hands upon the handles of his bar-spear plow, the gaunt man lifted up his face.

He was an inarticulate man. He had never been able to stand up to give testimony in meeting. He had never prayed aloud, even to himself alone. Yet there was such a pressure of almost unendurable happiness about his heart that he must give utterance to it, as the birds were doing. His bearded lips fumbled and he swallowed.

"I thank Thee, Lord," he said.

And suddenly the locked gates seemed to open. The flood of words came surging forth. He was blessed with the gift of tongues.

"I thank Thee, Lord," he said, his face upturned, while the patient horse waited. "I thank Thee for this here rich land of Kaintucky which Thou has given to Thy people. I thank Thee that Thou tookest me, a poor man, and led me over the mountains with Dan'el Boone beneath the shadder of Thy wing. I thank Thee for the worldly riches which Thou has showered upon me; for my good old sorrel hoss, Brandywine, here, worth eight pounds; for my bar-spear plow and tackling, worth two pounds, five shillings; for my brindle cow and calf back at the station, worth four pounds ten; for my dozen pewter plates, worth a pound and a shilling; for my ax, worth nine shillings; for my three weeding hoes, worth seven pounds; for my Dutch oven and cule, worth fifteen shillings at a shilling to the pound weight; for my handsaw and my bucksaw, my adze and auger, my drawing knife and currying knife, my three bedsteads with turkey feathers, my two good rifle guns, worth fifty-five shillings and three pounds ten, and my old smooth bore, worth ten shillings, all a total of nigh on seventy pounds.

"I thank Thee for the increasing riches and civilization which Thou has caused in Thy bounty to be brought upon this here land, for the newspaper that they are atalking of starting up next year in Lexington, and for the academy that they are agoing to have in Louisville, to learn reading and writing to the young ones, and ciphering through the rule of three. I thank Thee for the tailor and the dancing master that are already there. I thank Thee for the good five hundred acres I have here beside Long Run, seven of them already cleared, and for the fine substantial cabin which Thou hast helped me to build.

"I thank Thee for my two able boys, Mordecai and Josiah, that Mary Shipley bore me sixteen and fourteen year ago, that will be a prop and support to me in my old age, and a credit to me after I am gone. I thank Thee for my good wife, Bersheba, who, although kind of dreamy and not very up and gitting, is still a good woman and strives to walk well in Thy sight. I thank Thee for my two purty gals, Mary and Nancy, that she bore me last year and the year before, that will grow up to be fine women and the mothers of men and the solaces of their helpmeets, because of Mary Shipley that they were named after and Anne Boone, my first wife, that Thou gavest me, that I laid away beneath the sod in old Virginny so long ago, with her yaller curls and the blue ribbon in her hair, and her little baby in her arms, when she was no more'n sixteen. I thank Thee also for my little Tom, that Bersheba bore me five year ago; though he is a dreamer like her and will never amount to much in the world, like Mort and Josh.

"I thank Thee for the United States of America and for its divine freedom, which Thou hast given it, and I ask that Thy peace may be upon it from this time forth. I thank Thee for all the blessings which Thou has bestowed upon me, a poor and humble man, and for the tribulations too. I ask Thee, Lord, to watch over my little Tom in the hard life that he must lead, and be kind to him also, as Thou has been kind to me. And, O Lord, I don't ask nothing more, only that I may stay upon this land here for the rest of the days which it shall please Thee in They wisdom to bestow upon me, and that my name shall be honorable in this great country after I am gone. For Thy Son's sake, amen."

It seemed to him that a hand was laid upon his shoulder in that moment; that he heard a voice speak in his ear while all the world was still. *Thy seed shall be a star in the heavens. Thy name shall be known to the generations.*

He stood there with face uplifted while a shiver ran through him. It was only the soft wind blowing. It was only the quiet rippling of Long Run beyond the trees. It was only the glorious sun shining down on him, tingling all his blood with its strength of life immortal.

He wiped his forearm across his face. He pulled out a brown tobacco leaf from the waistband of his leggings and tore off a fragment of it, methodically folding it and inserting it into his cheek, with a half grin at himself, a little ashamed of his outburst of emotion, and glad that there was no one to know about it. He gripped the handles of his plow again, setting his blade to rip up the last furrow. And in that moment he realized that all the world was still.

The waters of Long Run still sparkled beyond the dappled trees with that rippling over stones. The south wind still blew, lazy and warm. But in the woods the birds no longer sang. And suddenly, in that instant, the gaunt man felt cold. There seemed a shadow on the bright day. The marrow of his bones felt cold.

From the corner of his eye he had glimpsed again within the woods a flash of black and white, like a woodpecker. Behind a sloping sycamore bole it had been, a hundred or a hundred and twenty feet within the woods, darting into sight and out again, at about the height of a man's head from the ground.

He did not turn to look this time. He spoke to his old sorrel horse easily. "Giddy-ap, Brandywine!" But his eyes slanted in their sockets, measuring the distance catercornered across the plowed gound to his cabin, where his rifle leaned beside the door, and to the entrance of the dark trail nearby. And he felt the long sinews of his thighs and calves flex and tighten, and his throat, as he chewed his tobacco leaf, was tight.

Again, from the edges of his eyes, he caught another black-and-white flash in the woods farther up, closer to the field's edge than the big sycamore. And there was still no song of thrush or oriole. But there was a catbird's cry. The catbird's cry. It had been years since he had heard it, but he knew it. There was the flash of a third black-and-white-painted face with a feathered topknot.

In a time of peace like this. In the bright spring day. Wabashes, from up north of the Ohio. A whole war party of them. He had thought all that was done. A civilized country, schools and newspapers. Great towns of hundreds and thousands of people, like Louisville and Lexington. It was all a freezing nightmare. It was all unreal. But now, now! Creeping on him from Long Run's deep banks, through the woods, with their painted faces and shaved heads, adorned for death and war.

He did not turn his head. He moved a step still onward, and another step, behind the plodding sorrel. But his hands were light upon the handles of his plow, and he eased his knees to spring and run. Not for nothing had he run with Dan'el Boone. Not for nothing had they called him Deerlegs and Long Slim up on the Ohio fifteen and twenty years ago. He was forty-two years old, and maybe he was a mite less spry than he had been once, and the rheumatism of wet clothes and bitter winters had got into his bones, but he was still about as fast as any in Kaintucky.

For his life. For his life within the instant he must run, as in those days with Mary up on the Ohio. Within a time of twenty seconds the speed within his legs must save his desperate life or lose it. Across the plowed land, in long leaps, flying like the wind. He should be half across the field before they could break from the woods and unleash their whanging arrows. Zigzagging, dodging, with speed he could reach his rifle or the packed-earth trail back to the station before the whooping hostiles could overtake him, before the whanging arrows caught him and brought him down.

He balanced on the balls of his feet, with lean leg sinews flexing, estimating the distances in a glance, noting each furrow that he must leap, and where to dodge and turn. He seeped a soft breath in his flattened lungs. His old sorrel, feeling the plow drag light, had stopped. Now—

He saw, within that split second as he started to break, a flash of white emerging from the entrance of the forest trail near his cabin across the field, five hundred feet away. He heard the carefree young voices. O God, Mordecai and Josiah had come down from the station. O God, that white was little Tommy's shirt. They had brought little Tommy with them, five years old.

"Hi, pappy!" shouted Mordecai. "Sheba took over the store for us'ns! Come to help you finish that table and set the floor! Brung you the auger that you forgot!"

He swallowed in his tight throat. Just for a moment still he had the terrible impulse instantly to run, shouting to them to turn around themselves and fly. With their head start, the two big boys, though not so long-limbed as he, could get away, with him pounding on their heels, back up the hard-packed path toward the station. Mary's boys, his two big fine stalwart boys, the pride of his manhood, the hope of his posterity. The two of them and he. Within this instant, if he started now. But, O God, there was little Tom.

He eased down flat-footed on his heels again, with his hands still on the plow.

"Take Tom into the cabin out of the sun, Mort, and give him a drink out of the hard-cider jug!" he called without a quaver... "Josh, you trot back to the station and fetch my gold watch for me! I done forgot the time!"

They stood staring at him across the sunlit field from the edge of the forest shadows, the two big boys, with golden-haired Tommy between them. Their faces were wan. They stood like wooden toys. For endless seconds they seemed motionless, while in the thin woods beside him the catbird screamed and the painted faces came flitting on.

They knew that he had no gold watch. They knew that he had no jug of cider in the cabin, and if he had, that it would not be for little Tommy to drink. He was afraid that they might shout back and ask him what the joke was.

But they understood. Oh thank God, they understood. Suddenly, little Tom begun to cry. Big Mordecai had him by the hand, and was dragging him, whimpering and wailing with an unknown fear, toward the cabin door. Josiah had turned and vanished back up the trail, running.

A matter of ten seconds lost. Or twenty. Those flitting shapes within the woods were so near now, they were so near he dared not look to see. Yet if he could only start off now toward the cabin at an easy pace, with apparent unconcern, they might wait for Josh to return with the gold watch. They might—at least, for a few seconds more—hesitate and delay. If he could only gain half the field or at least a quarter—

But Josh's gesture of flight had been too spasmodic and abrupt, or the little fellow's frightened wails too revealing. He had taken one long easy step away from his plow, and a second, and a third. There was the whooping scream behind him.

He broke and ran, bent from the waist. He leaped aside, with long legs sprawling, his knuckles touching earth, as the whanging arrows shot above. He was on his feet again instantly, with a lunging stagger. He ran with sprawling headlong strides, leaping the cloddy furrows with a sobbing breath, feeling his twisted ankle shot with fire and buckling underneath him, while those howling whoops came at his heels like a dozen wildcats' screams.

Mordecai, across the field, had snatched the rifle at the cabin door. He had got little Tom inside. But for himself, he was a man with a leaden leg, and those seconds of lost time while he shouted to the boys and stood waiting for them to move had let those painted faces get too near.

He was still a leap from the stump in middle field when the whanging, flint-tipped shaft got him between the shoulders. He staggered forward with a great sobbing groan. He fell upon his knees, reaching for his ax where it leaned against the stump, sprawling half around. Up the field's edge his old horse was running, dragging the bumping plowshare, with an arrow in its flank. But he had it between the shoulder blades, close to his heart, and all the world was dim.

Two of the whooping black-and-white-painted faces were rushing at him with lifted tomahawks. From his knees, from the ground, he swung the heavy ax. It went crashing into the side of one of those devil shapes beneath a lifted arm, and the savage screamed. He tried to get to his feet from his sagging knees, to swing again. But the strength of him was like spilled water, and the sun had faded.

He lay upon his face. He heard the quiet waters of the Rappahasnock in old Virginia, and in the twilight he was lying on its honeysuckle banks again with his young love, with the ribbon in her yellow hair.

"Anne," he whispered. But in another world than this.

From the door of the cabin a hundred yeards away a puff of smoke rose, and the painted savage who was bending over with scalping knife threw up his arms with a yell.

The rifle cracked again. The painted shapes with their catbird screams were dodging among the furrows. The gaunt man lay on his face by the stump in middle field. Close by him lay two of the painted shapes, and another back toward the thin woods' edge.

Behind the cabin door the boy Mordecai loaded the long rifle coolly again, with dead black eyes. The little boy Tom whimpered and sobbed in a corner against the wall, with sniffling nose and dirt-streaked face.

"Shut up, you little sniveler!" said Mordecai. "You're worse of a woman nor your ma Sheba. They hain't agoing to get his scalp. What are you crying fur?"

He thrust his rifle forth and fired again, with a catamountain screech.

Up the trail through the pine woods the boy Josiah ran. He heard the whooping screams, the rifle cracks. He ran with sobbing breath. Still there was a tingling excitement in him, mingled with his fright. It was like the times which he had heard his father tell of before he could well remember, of days with Simon Kenton and Dan'el Boone. He had been afraid that such exciting days would never come again with the country all so civilized.

"Injuns!" he shouted. "Injuns! The Injuns are out!"

The alarm bell at the station was ringing before he got there, and men with rifles were running down the trail toward him. He turned and ran back with them to the cabin, from which Mordecai's rifle still coolly cracked. On the field's far side, in the thin woods by Long Run's edge and in the deep woods beyond the stream, the painted shapes fled and the catbird screaming died away.

The men with rifles gathered about that gaunt figure with the gray-streaked hair, lying beside the stump in middle field.

"Poor feller," said one of them. "One of the old-timers. Come over the mountains with Dan'el Boone, I've often heard him say. What was his name? Old Ike, old Abe, or so'thing like that. Been trading with him all winter from my place to the crik, and never could remember his name from one time to the next. Well, it don't make no difference what it was, I don't reckon. They ain't going to name no counties after him. He left a widdy, didn't he? Somebody had better go ahead and tell her we're bringing him."

It was night, and the woman Bersheba sat at the little writing table in the cabin at the station.

The women had been kind. They had taken care of her boy and the baby girls for her, giving them their supper and putting them to bed. One of them had lent her a black cashmere shawl to throw over her butternut gown for widow's weeds. They had given her their condolences, and now, in greater kindness, for a little while they had left her alone.

Her dark hair was parted in the middle and smoothly brushed. In the pine-knot firelight her delicate face had an elfin quality. An intaglio brooch with a gold rope band which her Grandmother Reed had brought over from Scotland was pinned beneath the white collar at her throat. The women sometimes commented behind her back, she was half aware, over the time she spent in the brushing of her long hair and over the little touches which she gave her dress, as if she thought she was too fine for them and could not forget that her people had been gentry back in Carolina. Yet she could not help that. All her life she had lived half in a dream of beautiful splendid things, of gracious worlds beyond this world, of what she did not know.

She had laid upon the little writing table the big Bible, printed in London, which had come from Philadelphia and over the mountains from Virginia. A horn of elderberry ink stood on the table, and a goose-quill pen. She opened the ponderous book to the pages in the center, of glossy heavy paper, with their border adornments of cupids and broken marble columns for the recording of marriages and of births and deaths.

A sadness too deep for tears lay in her. He had been such a kind man, and life had given him so little. A poor man in a hard young land, and himself not quite assertive and shrewd enough to make his way in it. He also had had his little dreams, she knew. Little dreams of being respected and esteemed, a man of some importance, a man to stand out. Yet he had lacked the forcefulness or luck. Humble and obscure, he had gone through life without significance; and now the end of it must be written in the book, and hereafter it would be as though he had never been.

He was the only man who had ever been in her life or who would ever be. She had been an old maid, twenty-six years old, when he had married her. No other man or boy had ever courted her. She was not strong and robustly built, she was inept with her hands, and all the details of practical living did not have sufficient reality for her. A boy or man choosing a helpmeet didn't want to be burdened with a wife who couldn't milk, make soap, render lard, help harvest a crop or even keep a fire going beneath a pot without getting lost in a far-off dream. She didn't know why he had married her, except that there had been such a dearth of other women, and he had needed one to mother his two boys.

He had not been the dashing cavalier that she had dreamed of, but she had learned that life is never like the dreams. He had been kind to her, and she had come to love him dearly. She had tried to do the best she could. Still she had given him so little. Only a shadow in his life. His eyes, though gentle, had always passed her by. His thoughts had always been with his competent Mary Shipley, his young manhood's mate. His heart and secret dream had always been with his first love, in the springtime of his life so long ago.

She had given him so little. Her boy had meant nothing to him beside Mary Shipley's boys. He had not even wanted the boy named after him, when she had suggested it; saying it was a kind of comical name, he guessed, and why inflict it on the little fellow. The little girls had meant something more to him, she thought, because of Mary Shipley's little girl, who had died in infancy, and Anne Boone's, who had been buried with her child mother. But that was all she had given him—two baby girls to name after his dead loves.

The boy, only a few minutes ago, had been quietly sobbing to himself where he had been put to bed behind the curtain, but the baby girls had gone at once to sleep. They would have no memory of this day and night, no memory of the gaunt man, laborious and humble and obscure, who had been their father. They would go on into life and marry, and their children would not know where their grandfather had been born, nor where he had died and been buried, not even perhaps his name. Her little Tom would remember longer. Yet even to him it would be no more than a dark dream.

Next door to the cabin, in the adjacent corner blockhouse, there were the sounds of sawing and hammering as they made the pine coffin. Mordecai and Josiah were helping with it. The two boys had been up and down the little station street all afternoon and evening, bursting with excitement and a feeling of triumphant manhood, telling the story over and over to fresh groups of incoming settlers of how Mort had held those tarnation varmints off, and how Josh had run for help. It was like the old exciting days. Once their mother, their own real mother, not Sheba, had held off a whole swarm of them danged Wabashes in the camp on the Ohio. They had been only little fellows then, but Mort remembered him and Josh hiding in a hollow log as quiet as chipmunks, and Josh hadn't been more than a year old, but he hadn't let out a squeak. Not like that danged howling little Tom. If Mort had only been able to move toward the rifle at the cabin a mite faster, without having to drag Tom along, or if the old man had been able to start running a quarter minute sooner, without having to wait to see that little Tom was safe—

She felt a pang of futile but agonizing responsibility. It had been at her suggestion that they had taken little Tom along. She had given him nothing. She had even robbed him of his last desperate chance of life.

She had found the page of births and deaths in the Bible where his name was entered, beneath his father John's: "Born in Redstone, Pennsylvania, August 17, 1744." She dipped the goose-quill pen. By the red firelight she wrote the final word: "Died Hughes Station, Jefferson County, Territory of Kaintucky, May 13, 1786."

And that was all. An obscure and humble man he had lived and died, and his name would be soon forgotten by those few who had ever known it.

There was a knock upon the door. She put down the pen. She arose and stood against the fireplace.

"Come in," she said.

A young man in a white buckskin jacket of rare and elegant design, jackboots and doeskin riding breeches which fitted his strong thighs like gloves, came in the door. He doffed his three-cornered hat, which had a military cockade on it. He was a stocky young man, with blue eyes and yellow hair that came down on his shoulders.

"The Widdy Linkern?" he said.

"Yes," she said. She was a widow now.

He came toward her with his bold buccaneering eyes fixed on her in male admiration, though she was not aware of it. She made a picture by the fireplace, with her smooth dark hair and crimson mouth, and her great eyes in her pale face.

"Captain George Pomeroy, of General George Rogers Clark's command, from Louisville," he said. "I just rode in. I'm sorry to hear about your trouble, ma'am. He was a good man, I hear."

"Yes," she said. "He was a good man."

"I'm sorry to bother you in your time of grief," he said. "Yet it is a business about which you would not want me to wait. General Clark has been organizing an army, ma'am, to go against the Wabash nation. They have been doing this same thing up north of the Ohio, and it has got to stop. I have been detailed to make up a subscription list for the equipping and provisioning of the expedition, from the various towns and stations. I would like to put you down on the list for what in the way of guns or provender you are able to contribute."

"He had two rifle guns," she said, "and one old smoothbore. You are welcome to them, sir."

He drew a sheet of paper from the bosom of his buckskin jacket, with his hat pressed beneath his arm.

"I'll set the two rifle guns down, ma'am, if you have pen and ink handy," he said with satisfaction. "On the table with your Bible here, I see. They'll be appraised at a fair price, and compensation made if not returned. I reckon those two big boys of yours will be wanting to come along to use them. I was talking to them in the blockhouse. They aim to get a scalp or two. A pair of fine boys, of whom any mother should be proud."

"I am, indeed," she said.

She bit her trembling lip. She was, of course, proud of them. Yet it was always Mary Shipley's boys. Mary Shipley's boys to bury and avenge him. Even if her little Tom were old enough, perhaps he would be afraid. He had her helpless blood in him, and she had spoiled him too much, in her yearning for something to which to cling. "Is there anything else you would want?" she said.

"No," said the young captain. "The guns will be enough for your fair share, I reckon. Don't want to strip you, ma'am, I'll put it down, two rifle guns from the Widdy Linkern."

"That's not the way to spell it," she said.

Her lip was still trembling. He had been a poor man, he had been an obscure and unimportant man. None of his ancestors had ever attained to any fame. There would be no towns named after him, like Colonel Boone.

He would not even have a tombstone. The place where he should be buried would be forgotten. Yet he might as well have his name spelled right. He had always been a mite particular about it.

"There," she said. "Like that."

She pointed to the Bible on the table, where the ink was not yet dry on the last entry which she had made.

Abraham Lincoln, born Redstone, Pennsylvania, August 17, 1744 Died Hughes Station, Jefferson County, Territory of Kaintucky, May 13, 1786.

And that was all. The record of his life. But she wanted the name spelled right.

"Lincoln," she said. "Like that."

The young captain copied the name on his list dutifully. "The Widdy Lincoln, two rifle guns," he said. "Don't worry, ma'am; I've got it right."

Perhaps he was amused that she should bother with the precise spelling of the name of an obscure man like that. Did she think it was a name to go down in history, like Jefferson or Washington?

Bersheba Lincoln stirred from a dream. She went across the room. Her little Tommy had got out of bed. In his long nightgown sweeping the rough planked floor, he was stumbling toward her from behind the curtain, sobbing.

"Oh, mammy, I had a dream!" he sobbed. "He was lying dead and the whole world was crying!"

Bersheba picked up the weeping boy in her arms. She held him tight against her breast. So close was he to her, blood of her blood and spirit of her spirit, that she could see the vision which he saw of that gaunt, humble man lying dead beneath the assassin's stroke. She stood rocking the boy with her eyes rapt. And for the moment there was the sound of martial music playing in her ears, with muffled drums, and there were draped flags and the cry of a nation mourning.

"Perhaps someday you will have a son, my little Tom," she said, "and name him Abraham."

LOUISIANA

Désirée's Baby
by Kate Chopin

As THE day was pleasant, Madame Valmondé drove over to L'Abri to see Désirée and the baby.

It made her laugh to think of Désirée with a baby. Why, it seemed but yesterday that Désirée was little more than a baby herself; when Monsieur, in riding through the gateway of Valmondé, had found her lying asleep in the shadow of the big stone pillar.

The little one awoke in his arms and began to cry for "Dada." That was as much as she could do or say. Some people thought she might have strayed there of her own accord, for she was of the toddling age. The prevailing belief was that she had been purposely left by a party of Texans, whose canvas-covered wagon, late in the day, had crossed the ferry that Coton Maïs kept, just below the plantation. In time Madame Valmondé abandoned every speculation but the one that Désirée had been sent to her by a beneficent Providence to be the child of her affection, seeing that she was without child of the flesh. For the girl grew to be beautiful and gentle, affectionate and sincere—the idol of Valmondé.

It was no wonder, when she stood one day against the stone pillar in whose shadow she had lain asleep, eighteen years before, that Armand Aubigny riding by and seeing her there, had fallen in love with her. That was the way all the Aubignys fell in love, as if struck by a pistol shot. The wonder was that he had not loved her before; for he had known her since his father brought him home from Paris, a boy of eight, after his mother died there. The passion that awoke in him that day, when he saw her at the gate, swept along like an avalanche, or like a prairie fire, or like anything that drives headlong over all obstacles.

Monsieur Valmondé grew practical and wanted things well-considered: that is, the girl's obscure origin. Armand looked into her eyes and did not care. He was reminded that she was nameless. What did it matter about a name when he could give her one of the oldest and proudest in Louisiana? He ordered the *corbeille* from Paris, and contained himself with what patience he could until it arrived; then they were married.

Madame Valmondé had not seen Désirée and the baby for four weeks. When she reached L'Abri she shuddered at the first sight of it, as she always did. It was a sad looking place, which for many years had not known the gentle presence of a mistress, old Monsieur Aubigny having married and buried his wife in France, and she having loved her own land too well to ever leave it. The roof came down steep and black like a cowl, reaching out beyond the wide galleries that encircled the yellow stuccoed house. Big, solemn oaks grew close to it, and their thick-leaved, far-reaching branches shadowed it like a pall. Young Aubigny's rule was a strict one, too, and under it his negroes had forgotten how to be gay, as they had been during the old master's easy-going and indulgent lifetime.

The young mother was recovering slowly, and lay full length, in her soft white muslins and laces, upon a couch. The baby was beside her, upon her arm, where he had fallen asleep, at her breast. The yellow nurse woman sat beside a window fanning herself.

Madame Valmondé bent her portly figure over Désirée and kissed her, holding her an instant tenderly in her arms. Then she turned to the child.

"This is not the baby!" she exclaimed, in startled tones. French was the language spoken at Valmondé in those days.

"I knew you would be astonished," laughed Désirée, "at the way he has grown. The little *cochon de lait*! Look at his legs, mamma, and his hands and fingernails—real fingernails. Zandrine had to cut them this morning. Isn't it true, Zandrine?"

The woman bowed her turbaned head majestically, "Mais si, Madame."

"And the way he cries," went on Désirée, "is deafening. Armand heard him the other day as far away as La Blanche's cabin."

Madame Valmondé had never removed her eyes from the child. She lifted it and walked with it over to the window that was the lightest. She scanned the baby narrowly, then looked as searchingly at Zandrine, whose face was turned to gaze across the fields.

"Yes, the child has grown, has changed," said Madame Valmondé, slowly, as she replaced it beside its mother. "What does Armand say?"

Désirée's face became suffused with a glow that was happiness itself.

"Oh, Armand is the proudest father in the parish, I believe, chiefly because it is a boy, to bear his name; though he says not—that he would have loved a girl as well. But I know it isn't true. I know he says that to please me. And mamma," she added, drawing Madame Valmondé's head down to her, and speaking in a whisper, "he hasn't punished one of them—not one of them—since baby is born. Even Négrillon, who pretended to have burnt his leg that he might rest from work—he only laughed, and said Négrillon was a great scamp. Oh, mamma, I'm so happy; it frightens me."

What Désirée said was true. Marriage, and later the birth of his son, had softened Armand Aubigny's imperious and exacting nature greatly. This was what made the gentle Désirée so happy, for she loved him desperately. When he frowned she trembled, but loved him. When he smiled, she asked no greater blessing of God. But Armand's dark, handsome face had not often been disfigured by frowns since the day he fell in love with her.

When the baby was about three months old, Désirée awoke one day to the conviction that there was something in the air menacing her peace. It was at first too subtle to grasp. It had only been a disquieting suggestion; an air of mystery among the blacks; unexpected visits from far-off neighbors who could hardly account for their coming. Then a strange, an awful change in her husband's manner, which she dared not ask him to explain. When he spoke to her, it was with averted eyes, from which the old love-light seemed to have gone out. He absented himself from home; and when there, avoided her presence and that of her child, without excuse. And the very spirit of Satan seemed suddenly to take hold of him in his dealings with the slaves. Désirée was miserable enough to die.

She sat in her room, one hot afternoon, in her *peignoir*, listlessly drawing through her fingers the strands of her long, silky brown hair that hung about her shoulders. The baby, half naked, lay asleep upon her own great mahogany bed, that was like a sumptuous throne, with its satin-lined half-canopy. One of La Blanche's little quadroon boys—half naked too—stood fanning the child slowly with a fan of peacock feathers. Désirée's eyes had been fixed absently and sadly upon the baby, while she was striving to penetrate the threatening mist that she felt closing about her. She looked from her child to the boy who stood beside him, and back again; over and over. "Ah!" It was a cry that she could not help; which she was not conscious of having uttered. The blood turned like ice in her veins, and a clammy moisture gathered upon her face.

She tried to speak to the little quadroon boy; but no sound would come, at first. When he heard his name uttered, he looked up, and his mistress was pointing to the door. He laid aside the great, soft fan, and obediently stole away, over the polished floor, on his bare tiptoes.

She stayed motionless, with gaze riveted upon her child, and her face the picture of fright.

Presently her husband entered the room, and without noticing her, went to a table and began to search among some papers which covered it.

"Armand," she called to him, in a voice which must have stabbed him, if he was human. But he did not notice. "Armand," she said again. Then she rose and tottered toward him. "Armand," she panted once more, clutching his arm, "look at our child. What does it mean? Tell me."

He coldly but gently loosened her fingers from about his arm and thrust the hand away from him. "Tell me what it means!" she cried despairingly.

"It means," he answered lightly, "that the child is not white; it means that you are not white."

A quick conception of all that this accusation meant for her nerved her with unwonted courage to deny it. "It is a lie; it is not true, I am white! Look at my hair, it is brown; and my eyes are gray, Armand, you know they are gray. And my skin is fair," seizing his wrist. "Look at my hand; whiter than yours, Armand," she laughed hystericaly.

"As white as La Blanche's," he returned cruelly; and went away leaving her alone with their child.

When she could hold a pen in her hand, she sent a despairing letter to Madame Valmondé.

"My mother, they tell me I am not white. Armand has told me I am not white. For God's sake tell them it is not true. You must know it is not true. I shall die. I must die. I cannot be so unhappy, and live."

The answer that came was as brief:

"My own Désirée: Come home to Valmondé; back to your mother who loves you. Come with your child."

When the letter reached Désirée she went with it to her husband's study, and laid it open upon the desk before which he sat. She was like a stone image: silent, white, motionless after she had placed it there.

In silence he ran his cold eyes over the written words. He said nothing. "Shall I go, Armand?" she asked in tones sharp with agonized suspense.

"Yes, go."

"Do you want me to go?"

"Yes, I want you to go."

He thought Almighty God had dealt cruelly and unjustly with him; and felt, somehow, that he was paying Him back in kind when he stabbed thus into his wife's soul. Moreover he no longer loved her, because of the unconscious injury she had brought upon his home and his name.

She turned away like one stunned by a blow, and walked slowly toward the door, hoping he would call her back.

"Goodby, Armand," she moaned.

He did not answer her. That was his last blow at fate.

Désirée went in search of her child. Zandrine was pacing the somber gallery with it. She took the little one from the nurse's arms with no word of explanation, and descending the steps, walked away, under the live-oak branches.

It was an October afternoon; the sun was just sinking. Out in the still fields the negroes were picking cotton.

Désirée had not changed the thin white garment nor the slippers which she wore. Her hair was uncovered and the sun's rays brought a golden gleam from its brown meshes. She did not take the broad, beaten road which led to the far-off plantation of Valmondé. She walked across a deserted field, where the stubble bruised her tender feet, so delicately shod, and tore her thin gown to shreds.

She disappeared among the reeds and willows that grew thick along the banks of the deep, sluggish bayou; and she did not come back again.

Some weeks later there was a curious scene enacted at L'Abri. In the center of the smoothly swept back yard was a great bonfire. Armand Aubigny sat in the wide hallway that commanded a view of the spectacle: and it was he who dealt out to a half dozen negroes the material which kept this fire ablaze.

A graceful cradle of willow, with all its dainty furbishings, was laid upon the pyre, which had already been fed with the richness of a priceless *layette*. There there were silk gowns, and velvet and satin ones added to these; laces, too, and embroideries; bonnets and gloves; for the *corbeille* had been of rare quality.

The last thing to go was a tiny bundle of letters; innocent little scribblings that Désirée had sent to him during the days of their espousal. There was the remnant of one back in the drawer from which he took them. But it was not Désirée's; it was part of an old letter from his mother to his father. He read it. She was thanking God for the blessing of her husband's love:

"But, above all," she wrote, "night and day, I thank the good God for having so arranged our lives that our dear Armand will never know that his mother, who adores him, belongs to the race that is cursed with the brand of slavery."

MAINE

The Children of Noah
by Richard Matheson

IT WAS just past three a.m. when Mr. Ketchum drove past the sign that read *Zachry: pop. 67*. He groaned. Another in an endless string of Maine seaside towns. He closed his eyes hard a second, then opened them again and pressed down on the accelerator. The Ford surged forward under him. Maybe, with luck, he'd reach a decent motel soon. It certainly wasn't likely there'd be one in Zachry: pop. 67.

Mr. Ketchum shifted his heavy frame on the seat and stretched his legs. It had been a sour vacation. Motoring through New England's historic beauty, communing with nature and nostalgia was what he'd planned. Instead, he'd found only boredom, exhaustion and over-expense.

Mr. Ketchum was not pleased.

The town seemed fast asleep as he drove along its Main Street. The only sound was that of the car's engine, the only sight that of his raised headbeams splaying out ahead, lighting up another sign. *Speed 15 Limit*.

"Sure, sure," he muttered digustedly pressing down on the gas pedal. Three o' clock in the morning and the town fathers expected him to creep through their lousy hamlet. Mr. Ketchum watched the dark buildings rush past his window. Good-by Zachry, he thought. Farewell, pop. 67.

Then the other car appeared in the rear-view mirror. About half a block behind, a sedan with a turning red spotlight on its roof. He knew what kind of car it was. His foot curled off the accelerator and he felt his heartbeat quicken. Was it possible they hadn't noticed how fast he was going?

The question was answered as the dark car pulled up to the Ford and a man in a big hat leaned out of the front window. "Pull over!" he barked.

Swallowing dryly, Mr. Ketchum eased his car over to the curb. He drew

253

up the emergency brake, turned the ignition key and the car was still. The police car nosed in toward the curb and stopped. The right front door opened.

The glare of Mr. Ketchum's headlights outlined the dark figure approaching. He felt around quickly with his left foot and stamped down on the knob, dimming the lights. He swallowed again. Damned nuisance this. Three a.m. in the middle of nowhere and a hick policeman picks him up for speeding. Mr. Ketchum gritted his teeth and waited.

The man in the dark uniform and wide-brimmed hat leaned over into the window. "License."

Mr. Ketchum slid a shaking hand into his inside pocket and drew out his billfold. He felt around for his license. He handed it over, noticed how expressionless the face of the policeman was. He sat there quietly while the policeman held a flashlight beam on the license.

"From New Jersey."

"Yes, that . . . that's right," said Mr. Ketchum.

The policeman kept staring at the license. Mr. Ketchum stirred restlessly on the seat and pressed his lips together. "It hasn't expired," he finally said.

He saw the dark head of the policeman lift. Then, he gasped as the narrow circle of flashlight blinded him. He twisted his head away.

The light was gone. Mr. Ketchum blinked his watering eyes.

"Don't they read traffic signs in New Jersey?" the policeman asked.

"Why, I . . . You mean the sign that said p-population sixty-seven?"

"No, I don't mean that sign," said the policeman.

"Oh." Mr. Ketchum cleared his throat. "Well, that's the only sign I saw," he said.

"You're a bad driver then."

"Well, I'm—"

"The sign said the speed limit is fifteen miles an hour. You were doing fifty."

"Oh. I . . . I'm afraid I didn't see it."

"The speed limit is fifteen miles an hour whether you see it or not."

"Well . . . at—at *this* hour of the morning?"

"Did you see a timetable on the sign?" the policeman asked.

"No, of course not. I mean, I didn't see the sign at all."

"*Didn't* you?"

Mr. Ketchum felt hair prickling along the nape of his neck. "Now, now see here," he began faintly, then stopped and stared at the policeman. "May I have my license back?" he finally asked when the policeman didn't speak.

The policeman said nothing. He stood on the street, motionless.

"May I—?" Mr. Ketchum started.

"Follow our car," said the officer abruptly and strode away.

Mr. Ketchum stared at him, dumbfounded. *Hey wait!* he almost yelled. The officer hadn't even given him back his license. Mr. Ketchum felt a sudden coldness in his stomach.

"What *is* this?" he muttered as he watched the policeman getting back into his car. The police car pulled away from the curb, its roof light spinning again.

Mr. Ketchum followed.

"This is ridiculous," he said aloud. They had no right to do this. Was this the Middle Ages? His thick lips pressed into a jaded mouth line as he followed the polic car along Main Street.

Two blocks up, the polic car turned. Mr. Ketchum saw his headlights splash across a glass store front. *Hand's Groceries* read the weather-worn letters.

There were no lamps on the street. It was like driving along an inky passage. Ahead were only the three red eyes of the police car's rear lights and spotlight; behind only impenetrable blackness. The end of a perfect day, thought Mr. Ketchum; picked up for speeding in Zachry, Maine. He shook his head and groaned. Why hadn't he just spent his vacation in Newark; slept late, gone to shows, eaten, watched television?

The police car turned right at the next corner, then, a block up, turned left again and stopped. Mr. Ketchum pulled up behind it as its lights went out. There was no sense in this. This was only cheap melodrama. They could just as easily have fined him on Main Street. It was the rustic mind. Debasing someone from a big city gave them a sense of vengeful eminence.

Mr. Ketchum waited. Well, he wasn't going to haggle. He'd pay his fine without a word and depart. He jerked up the hand brake. Suddenly he frowned, realizing that they could fine him anything they wanted. They could charge him $500 if they chose! The heavy man had heard stories about small town police, about the absolute authority they wielded. He cleared his throat viscidly. Well, this is absurd, he thought. What foolish imagination.

The policeman opened the door.

"Get out," he said.

There was no light in the street or in any building. Mr. Ketchum swallowed. All he could really see was the black figure of the policeman.

"Is this the—station?" he asked.

"Turn out your lights and come on," said the policeman.

Mr. Ketchum pushed in the chrome knob and got out. The policeman slammed the door. It made a loud, echoing noise; as if they were inside an unlighted warehouse instead of on a street. Mr. Ketchum glanced upward. The illusion was complete. There were neither stars nor moon. Sky and earth ran together blackly.

The policeman's hard fingers clamped on his arm. Mr. Ketchum lost balance a moment, then caught himself and fell into a quick stride beside the tall figure of the policeman.

"Dark here," he heard himself saying in a voice not entirely familiar.

The policeman said nothing. The other policeman fell into step on the other side of him. Mr. Ketchum told himself: These damned hick-town nazis were doing their best to intimidate him. Well, they wouldn't succeed.

Mr. Ketchum sucked in a breath of the damp, sea-smelling air and let it shudder out. A crumby town of 67 and they have two policemen patrolling the streets at three in the morning. Ridiculous.

He almost tripped over the step when they reached it. The policeman on his left side caught him under the elbow.

"Thank you," Mr. Ketchum muttered automatically. The policeman didn't reply. Mr. Ketchum licked his lips. Cordial oaf, he thought and managed a fleeting smile to himself. There, that was better. No point in letting this get to him.

He blinked as the door was pulled open and, despite himself, felt a sigh of relief filtering through him. It was a police station all right. There was the podiumed desk, there a bulletin board, there a black, pot-bellied stove unlit, there a scarred bench against the wall, there a door, there the floor covered with a cracked and grimy linoleum that had once been green.

"Sit down and wait," said the first policeman.

Mr. Ketchum looked at his lean, angled face, his swarthy skin. There was no division in his eyes between iris and pupil. It was all one darkness. He wore a dark uniform that fitted him loosely.

Mr. Ketchum didn't get to see the other policeman because both of them went into the next room. He stood watching the closed door a moment. Should he leave, drive away? No, they'd have his address on the license. Then again, they might actually want him to attempt to leave. You never knew what sort of warped minds these small-town police had. They might even—shoot him down if he tried to leave.

Mr. Ketchum sat heavily on the bench. No, he was letting imagination run amuck. This was merely a small town on the Maine seacoast and they were merely going to fine him for—

Well, why didn't they fine him then? What was all this play-acting? The heavy man pressed his lips together. Very well, let them play it the way they chose. This was better than driving anyway. He closed his eyes. I'll just rest them, he thought.

After a few moments he opened them again. It was damned quiet. He looked around the dimly lit room. The walls were dirty and bare except for a clock and one picture that hung behind the desk. It was a painting—more likely a reproduction—of a bearded man. The hat he wore was a seaman's hat. Probably one of Zachry's ancient mariners. No; probably not even that. Probably a Sears Roebuck print: *Bearded Seaman*.

Mr. Ketchum grunted to himself. Why a police station should have such a print was beyond him. Except, of course, that Zachry was on the Atlantic. Probably its main source of income was from fishing. Anyway, what did it matter? Mr. Ketchum lowered his gaze.

In the next room he could hear the muffled voices of the two policemen. He tried to hear what they were saying but he couldn't. He glared at the closed door. Come *on*, will you? he thought. He looked at the clock again. Three twenty-two. He checked it with his wrist watch. About right. The door opened and the two policemen came out.

One of them left. The remaining one—the one who had taken Mr. Ketchum's license—went over to the raised desk and switched on the gooseneck lamp over it, drew a big ledger out of the top drawer and started writing in it. *At last*, thought Mr. Ketchum.

A minute passed.

"I—" Mr. Ketchum cleared his throat. "I beg your—"

His voice broke off as the cold gaze of the policeman raised from the ledger and fixed on him.

"Are you . . . That is, am I to be—fined now?"

The policeman looked back at the ledger. "Wait," he said.

"But it's past three in the mor—" Mr. Ketchum caught himself. He tried to look coldly belligerent. "Very well," he said curtly. "Would you kindly tell me how long it will be?"

The policeman kept writing in the ledger. Mr. Ketchum sat there stiffly, looking at him. *Insufferable*, he thought. This was the last damned time he'd ever go within a hundred miles of this damned New England.

The policeman looked up. "Married?" he asked.

Mr. Ketchum stared at him.

"Are you married?"

"No, I—it's on the license," Mr. Ketchum blurted. He felt a tremor of pleasure at his retort and, at the same time, an impaling of strange dread at talking back to the man.

"Family in Jersey?" asked the policeman.

"Yes. I mean no. Just a sister in Wiscons—"

Mr. Ketchum didn't finish. He watched the policeman write it down. He wished he could rid himself of this queasy distress.

"Employed?" asked the policeman.

Mr. Ketchum swallowed. "Well," he said, "I—I have no one particular em—"

"Unemployed," said the policeman.

"Not at all; not at *all*," said Mr. Ketchum stiffly. "I'm a—a free-lance salesman. I purchase stocks and lots from . . ." His voice faded as the policeman looked at him. Mr. Ketchum swallowed three times before the lump stayed down. He realized that he was sitting on the very edge of the bench as if poised to spring to the defense of his life. He forced himself to settle back. He drew in a deep breath. Relax, he told himself. Deliberately, he closed his eyes. There. He'd catch a few winks. May as well make the best of this, he thought.

The room was still except for the tinny, resonant ticking of the clock. Mr. Ketchum felt his heart pulsing with slow, dragging beats. He shifted his heavy frame uncomfortably on the hard bench. *Ridiculous*, he thought.

Mr. Ketchum opened his eyes and frowned. That damned picture. You could almost imagine that bearded seaman was looking at you.

"*Uh!*"

Mr. Ketchum's mouth snapped shut, his eyes jerked open, irises flaring.

He started forward on the bench, then shrank back.

A swarthy-faced man was bent over him, hand on Mr. Ketchum's shoulder.

"Yes?" Mr. Ketchum asked, heart jolting.

The man smiled.

"Chief Shipley," he said. "Would you come into my office?"

"Oh," said Mr. Ketchum. "Yes. Yes."

He straightened up, grimacing at the stiffness in his back muscles. The man stepped back and Mr. Ketchum pushed up with a grunt, his eyes moving automatically to the wall clock. It was a few minutes past four.

"Look," he said, not yet awake enough to feel intimidated. "Why can't I pay my fine and leave?"

Shipley's smile was without warmth.

"We run things a little different here in Zachry," he said.

They entered a small, musty-smelling office.

"Sit down," said the chief, walking around the desk while Mr. Ketchum settled into a straight-backed chair that creaked.

"I don't understand why I can't pay my fine and leave."

"In due course," said Shipley.

"But—" Mr. Ketchum didn't finish. Shipley's smile gave the impression of being no more than a diplomatically veiled warning. Gritting his teeth, the heavy man cleared his throat and waited while the chief looked down at a sheet of paper on his desk. He noticed how poorly Shipley's suit fitted. Yokels, the heavy man thought, don't even know how to dress.

"I see you're not married," Shipley said.

Mr. Ketchum said nothing. Give them a taste of their own no-talk medicine he decided.

"Have you friends in Maine?" Shipley asked.

"Why?"

"Just routine questions, Mr. Ketchum," said the chief. "Your only family is a sister in Wisconsin?"

Mr. Ketchum looked at him without speaking. What had all this to do with a traffic violation?

"Sir?" asked Shipley.

"I already told you; that is, I told the officer. I don't see—"

"Here on business?"

Mr. Ketchum's mouth opened soundlessly.

"Why are you asking me all these questions?" he asked. *Stop shaking!* he ordered himself furiously.

"Routine. Are you here on business?"

"I'm on my vacation. And I don't see this at all! I've been patient up to now but, *blast it*, I demand to be fined and released!"

"I'm afraid that's impossible," said the chief.

Mr. Ketchum's mouth fell open. It was like waking up from a nightmare and discovering that the dream was still going on. "I—I don't understand," he said.

"You'll have to appear before the judge."

"But that's ridiculous."

"Is it?"

"Yes, it is. I'm a citizen of the United States. I demand my rights."

Chief Shipley's smile faded.

"You limited those rights when you broke our law," he said. "Now you have to pay for it as we declare."

Mr. Ketchum stared blankly at the man. He realized that he was completely in their hands. They could fine him anything they pleased or put him in jail indefinitely. All these questions he'd been asked; he didn't know why they'd asked them but he knew that his answers revealed him as almost rootless, with no one who cared if he lived or—

The room seemed to totter. Sweat broke out on his body.

"You can't *do* this," he said; but it was not an argument.

"You'll have to spend the night in jail," said the chief. "In the morning you'll see the judge."

"But this is ridiculous!" Mr. Ketchum burst out. "*Ridiculous!*"

He caught himself. "I'm entitled to one phone call," he said quickly. "I can make a telephone call. It's my legal right."

"It would be," said Shipley, "if there was any telephone service in Zachry."

When they took him to his cell, Mr. Ketchum saw a painting in the hall. It was of the same bearded seaman. Mr. Ketchum didn't notice if the eyes followed him or not.

Mr. Ketchum stirred. A look of confusion lined his sleep-numbed face. There was a clanking sound behind him; he reared up on his elbow.

A policeman came into the cell and set down a covered tray.

"Breakfast," he said. He was older than the other policemen, even older than Shipley. His hair was iron-gray, his cleanly shaved face seamed around the mouth and eyes. His uniform fitted him badly.

As the policeman started relocking the door, Mr. Ketchum asked, "When do I see the judge?"

The policeman looked at him a moment. "Don't know," he said and turned away.

"Wait!" Mr. Ketchum called out.

The receding footsteps of the policeman sounded hollowly on the cement floor. Mr. Ketchum kept staring at the spot where the policeman had been. Veils of sleep peeled from his mind.

He sat up, rubbed deadened fingers over his eyes and held up his wrist. Seven minutes past nine. The heavy man grimaced. By God, they were going to hear about this! His nostrils twitched. He sniffed, started to reach for the tray; then pulled back his hand.

"No," he muttered. He wouldn't eat their damned food. He sat there stiffly, doubled at the waist, glaring at his sock-covered feet.

His stomach grumbled uncooperatively.

"Well," he muttered after a minute. Swallowing, he reached over and lifted off the tray cover.

He couldn't check the *oh* of surprise that passed his lips.

The three eggs were fried in butter, bright yellow eyes focused straight on the ceiling, ringed about with long, crisp lengths of meaty, corrugated bacon. Next to them was a platter of four book-thick slices of toast spread with creamy butter swirls, a paper cup of jelly leaning on them. There was a tall glass of frothy orange juice, a dish of strawberries bleeding in alabaster cream. Finally, a tall pot from which wavered the pungent and unmistakable fragrance of freshly brewed coffee.

Mr. Ketchum picked up the glass of orange juice. He took a few drops in his mouth and rolled them experimentally over his tongue. The citric acid tingled deliciously on his warm tongue. He swallowed. If it was poisoned it was by a master's hand. Saliva tided in his mouth. He suddenly remembered that, just before he was picked up, he'd been meaning to stop at a *café* for food.

While he ate, warily but decidedly, Mr. Ketchum tried to figure out the motivation behind this magnificent breakfast.

It was the rural mind again. They regretted their blunder. It seemed a flimsy notion, but there it was. The food was superb. One thing you had to say for these New Englanders; they could cook like a son-of-a-gun. Breakfast for Mr. Ketchum was usually a sweet roll, heated, and coffee. Since he was a boy in his father's house he hadn't eaten a breakfast like this.

He was just putting down his third cup of well-creamed coffee when footsteps sounded in the hall. Mr. Ketchum smiled. Good timing, he thought. He stood.

Chief Shipley stopped outside the cell. "Had your breakfast?"

Mr. Ketchum nodded. If the chief expected thanks he was in for a bad surprise. Mr. Ketchum picked up his coat.

The chief didn't move.

"*Well . . . ?*" said Mr. Ketchum after a few minutes. He tried to put it coldly and authoritatively. It came out somewhat less.

Chief Shipley looked at him expressionlessly. Mr. Ketchum felt his breath faltering.

"May I inquire—?" He began.

"Judge isn't in yet," said Shipley.

"But . . ." Mr. Ketchum didn't know what to say.

"Just came in to tell you," said Shipley. He turned and was gone.

Mr. Ketchum was furious. He looked down at the remains of his breakfast as if they contained the answer to this situation. He drummed a fist against his thigh. *Insufferable!* What were they trying to do—intimidate him? Well, by God—

—they were succeeding.

Mr. Ketchum walked over to the bars. He looked up and down the empty hallway. There was a cold knot inside him. The food seemed to have turned to dry lead in his stomach. He banged the heel of his right hand once against the cold bar. By God! *By God!*

It was two o'clock in the afternoon when Chief Shipley and the old policeman came to the cell door. Wordlessly the policeman opened it. Mr. Ketchum stepped into the hallway and waited again, putting on his coat while the door was relocked.

He walked in short, inflexible strides between the two men, not even glancing at the picture on the wall. "Where are we going?" he asked.

"Judge is sick," said Shipley. "We're taking you out to his house to pay your fine."

Mr. Ketchum sucked in his breath. He wouldn't argue with them; he just wouldn't. "All right," he said. "If that's the way you have to do it."

"Only way to do it," said the chief, looking ahead, his face an expressionless mask.

Mr. Ketchum pressed down the corners of a slim smile. This was better. It was almost over now. He'd pay his fine and clear out.

It was foggy outside. Sea mist rolled across the street like driven smoke. Mr. Ketchum pulled on his hat and shuddered. The damp air seemed to filter through his flesh and dew itself around his bones. Nasty day, he thought. He moved down the steps, eyes searching for his Ford.

The old policeman opened the back door of the police car and Shipley gestured toward the inside.

"What about *my* car?" Mr. Ketchum asked.

"We'll come back here after you see the judge," said Shipley.

"Oh. I . . ."

Mr. Ketchum hesitated. Then he bent over and squeezed into the car, dropping down on the back seat. He shivered as the cold of the leather pierced trouser wool. He edged over as the chief got in.

The policeman slammed the door shut. Again that hollow sound, like the slamming of a coffin lid in a crypt. Mr. Ketchum grimaced as the simile occurred to him.

The policeman got into the car and Mr. Ketchum heard the motor cough into liquid life. He sat there breathing slowly and deeply while the policeman out-choked warmth into the engine. He looked out the window at his left.

The fog was *just* like smoke. They might have been parked in a burning garage. except for that bone-gripping dampness. Mr. Ketchum cleared his throat. He heard the chief shift on the seat beside him.

"Cold," Mr. Ketchum said, automatically.

The chief said nothing.

Mr. Ketchum pressed back as the car pulled away from the curb, V-turned and started slowly down the fog-veiled street. He listened to the crisp sibilance of tires on wet paving, the rhythmic swish of the wipers as they cleared off circle segments on the misted windshield.

After a moment he looked at his watch. Almost three. Half a day shot in this blasted Zachry.

He looked out through the window again as the town ghosted past. He thought he saw brick buildings along the curb but he wasn't sure. He looked down at his white hands, then glanced over at Shipley. The chief was sitting stiffly upright on the seat, staring straight ahead. Mr. Ketchum swallowed. The air seemed stagnant in his lungs.

On Main Street the fog seemed thinner. Probably the sea breezes, Mr. Ketchum thought. He looked up and down the street. All the stores and offices looked closed. He glanced at the other side of the street. Same thing.

"Where is everybody?" he asked.

"What?"

"I said where *is* everybody?"

"Home," the chief said.

"But it's Wednesday," said Mr. Ketchum. "Aren't your—stores open?"

"Bad day," said Shipley. "Not worth it."

Mr. Ketchum glanced at the sallow-faced chief, then withdrew his look hastily. He felt cold premonition spidering in his stomach again. What in God's name *is* this? he asked asked himself. It had been bad enough in the cell. Here, tracking through this sea of mist, it was altogether worse.

"That's right," he heard his nerve-sparked voice saying. "There are only sixty-seven people, aren't there?"

The chief said nothing.

"How . . . h-how old is Zachry?"

In the silence he heard the chief's finger joints crackle dryly.

"Hundred fifty years," said Shipley.

"That old," said Mr. Ketchum. He swallowed with effort. His throat hurt a little. Come *on*, he told himself, *Relax*.

"How come it's named Zachry?" The words spilled out, uncontrolled.

"Noah Zachry founded it," said the chief.

"Oh. Oh. I see. I guess that picture in the station . . . ?"

"That's right," said Shipley.

Mr. Ketchum blinked. So that was Noah Zachry, founder of this town they were driving through—

—*block after block after block*. There was a cold, heavy sinking in Mr. Ketchum's stomach as the idea came to him.

In a town so big why were there only 67 people?

He opened his mouth to ask it, then couldn't. The answer might be wrong.

"Why are there only—?" The words came out anyway before he could stop them. His body jolted at the shock of hearing them.

"What?"

"Nothing, nothing. That is—" Mr. Ketchum drew in a shaking breath. No help for it. He had to know.

"How come there are only sixty-seven?"

"They go away," said Shipley.

Mr. Ketchum blinked. The answer came as such an anticlimax. His brow furrowed. Well, what else? he asked himself defensively. Remote, anti-quated, Zachry would have little attraction for its younger generations. Mass gravitation to more interesting places would be inevitable.

The heavy man settled back against the seat. Of course. Think how much *I* want to leave the dump, he thought, and I don't even live here.

His gaze slid forward through the windshield, caught by something. A banner hanging across the street. BARBECUE TONIGHT. Celebration, he thought. They probably went berserk every fortnight and had themselves a rip-roaring taffy pull or fishnet-mending orgy.

"Who was Zachry anyway?" he asked. The silence was getting to him again.

"Sea captain," said the chief.

"Oh?"

"Whaled in the South Seas," said Shipley.

Abruptly, Main Street ended. The police car veered left onto a dirt road. Out the window Mr. Ketchum watched shadowy bushes glide by. There was only the sound of the engine laboring in second and of gravelly dirt spitting out from under the tires. Where does the judge live, on a mountain top? He shifted his weight and grunted.

The fog began thinning now. Mr. Ketchum could see grass and trees, all with a grayish cast to them. The car turned and faced the ocean. Mr. Ketchum looked down at the opaque carpet of fog below. The car kept turning. It faced the crest of the hill again.

Mr. Ketchum coughed softly. "Is . . . uh, that the judge's house up there?" he asked.

"Yes," the chief answered.

"High," said Mr. Ketchum.

The car kept turning on the narrow, dirt road, now facing the ocean, now Zachry, now the bleak, hill-topping house. It was a grayish-white house, three stories high, at each end of it the crag of an attic tower. It looked as old as Zachry itself, thought Mr. Ketchum. The car turned. He was facing the fog-crusted ocean again.

Mr. Ketchum looked down at his hands. Was it a deception of the light or were they really shaking? He tried to swallow but there was no moisture in his throat and he coughed instead, rattlingly. This is so *stupid*, he thought; there's no reason in the world for this. He saw his hands clench together.

The car was moving up the final rise toward the house now. Mr. Ketchum felt his breaths shortening. *I don't want to go*, he heard someone saying in his mind. He felt a sudden urge to shove out the door and run. Muscles tensed emphatically.

He closed his eyes. For God's sake, *stop* it! he yelled at himself. There was nothing wrong about this but his distorted interpretation of it. These were modern times. Things had explanations and people had reasons. Zachry's people had a reason too; a narrow distrust of city dwellers. This was their socially acceptable revenge. That made sense. After all—

The car stopped. The chief pushed open the door on his side and got out.

The policeman reached back and opened the other door for Mr. Ketchum. The heavy man found one of his legs and foot to be numb. He had to clutch at the top of the door for support. He stamped the foot on the ground.

"Went to sleep," he said.

Neither of the men answered. Mr. Ketchum glanced at the house; he squinted. Had he seen a dark green drape slip back into place? He winced and made a startled noise as his arm was touched and the chief gestured toward the house. The three men started toward it.

"I, uh . . . don't have much cash on me, I'm afraid," he said, "I hope a traveler's check will be all right."

"Yes," said the chief.

They went up the porch steps, stopped in front of the door. The policeman turned a big, brass key-head and Mr. Ketchum heard a bell ring tinnily inside. He stood looking through the door curtains. Inside, he could make out the skeletal form of a hat rack. He shifted weight and the boards creaked under him. The policeman rang the bell again.

"Maybe he's—too sick," Mr. Ketchum suggested faintly.

Neither of the men looked at him. Mr. Ketchum felt his muscles tensing. He glanced back over his shoulder. Could they catch him if he ran for it?

He looked back disgustedly. You pay your fine and you leave, he explained patiently to himself. That's all; you pay your fine and you leave.

Inside the house there was dark movement. Mr. Ketchum looked up, startled in spite of himself. A tall woman was approaching the door.

The door opened. The woman was thin, wearing an ankle-length black dress with a white oval pin at her throat. Her face was swarthy, seamed with threadlike lines. Mr. Ketchum slipped off his hat automatically.

"Come in," said the woman.

Mr. Ketchum stepped into the hall.

"You can leave your hat there," said the woman, pointing toward the hat rack that looked like a tree ravaged by flame. Mr. Ketchum dropped his hat over one of the dark pegs. As he did, his eye was caught by a large painting near the foot of the staircase. He started to speak but the woman said, "This way."

They started down the hall. Mr. Ketchum stared at the painting as they passed it.

"Who's that woman," he asked, "standing next to Zachry?"

"His wife," said the chief.

"But she—"

Mr. Ketchum's voice broke off suddenly as he heard a whimper rising in his throat. Shocked, he drowned it out with a sudden clearing of the throat. He felt ashamed of himself. Still . . . Zachry's wife?

The woman opened a door. "Wait in here," she said.

The heavy man walked in. He turned to say something to the chief. Just in time to see the door shut.

"Say, uh . . . ." He walked to the door and put his hand on the knob. It didn't turn.

He frowned. He ignored the pile-driver beats of his heart. "Hey, what's going on?" Cheerily bluff, his voice echoed off the walls. Mr. Ketchum turned and looked around. The room was empty. It was a square, empty room.

He turned back to the door, lips moving as he sought the proper words. "Okay," he said, abruptly, "it's very—" He twisted the knob sharply. "Okay, it's a very funny joke." By God, he was mad. "I've taken all I'm—"

He whirled at the sound, teeth bared.

There was nothing. The room was still empty. He looked around dizzily. What was that sound? A dull sound, like water rushing.

"Hey," he said automatically. He turned to the door. "Hey!" he yelled, "cut it out! Who do you think you are anyway?"

He turned on weakening legs. The sound was louder. Mr. Ketchum ran a hand over his brow. It was covered with sweat. It was warm in there.

"Okay, okay," he said, "it's a fine joke but—"

Before he could go on, his voice had corkscrewed into an awful wracking sob. Mr. Ketchum staggered a little. He stared at the room. He whirled and fell back against the door. His outflung hand touched the wall and jerked away.

It was hot.

"*Huh?*" he asked incredulously.

This was impossible. This was a joke. This was their deranged idea of a little joke. It was a game they played. Scare the City Slicker was the name of the game.

"Okay!" he yelled. "*Okay!* It's funny, it's very funny! Now let me out of here or there's going to be trouble!"

He pounded at the door. Suddenly he kicked it. The room was getting hotter. It was almost as hot as an—

Mr. Ketchum was petrified. His mouth sagged open.

The questions they'd asked him. The loose way the clothes fit everyone he'd met. The rich food they'd given him to eat. The empty streets. The savagelike swarthy coloring of the men, of the woman. They way they'd all looked at him. And the woman in the painting, Noah Zachry's wife—*a native woman with her teeth filed to a point*.

BARBECUE TONIGHT.

Mr. Ketchum screamed. He kicked and pounded on the door. He threw his heavy body against it. He shrieked at the people outside.

"Let me out! *Let me out!* LET . . . ME . . . OUT!"

The worst part about it was he just couldn't believe it was really happening.

MARYLAND

The Man Who Collected Poe
by Robert Bloch

DURING THE whole of a dull, dark, and soundless day in the autumn of the year, when the clouds hung oppressively low in the heavens, I had been passing alone, by automobile, through a singularly dreary tract of country, and at length found myself, as the shades of the evening drew on, within view of my destination.

I looked upon the scene before me—upon the mere house, and the simple landscape features of the domain—upon the bleak walls—upon the vacant eye-like windows—upon a few rank sedges—and upon a few white trunks of decayed trees—with a feeling of utter confusion commingled with dismay. For it seemed to me as though I had visited this scene once before, or read of it, perhaps, in some frequently re-scanned tale. And yet assuredly it could not be, for only three days had passed since I had made the acquaintance of Launcelot Canning and received an invitation to visit him at his Maryland residence.

The circumstances under which I met Canning were simple; I happened to attend a bibliophilic meeting in Washington and was introduced to him by a mutual friend. Casual conversation gave place to absorbed and interested discussion when he discovered my preoccupation with works of fantasy. Upon learning that I was traveling upon a vacation with no set itinerary, Canning urged me to become his guest for a day and to examine, at my leisure, his unusual display of memorabilia.

"I feel, from our conversation, that we have much in common," he told me. "For you see, sir, in my love of fantasy I bow to no man. It is a taste I have perhaps inherited from my father and from his father before him, together with their considerable acquisitions in the genre. No doubt you

267

would be gratified with what I am prepared to show you, for in all due modesty, I beg to style myself the world's leading collector of the works of Edgar Allan Poe."

I confess that his invitation as such did not enthrall me, for I hold no brief for the literary hero-worshipper or the scholarly collector as a type. I own to a more than passing interest in the tales of Poe, but my interest does not extend to the point of ferreting out the exact date upon which Mr. Poe first decided to raise a mustache, nor would I be unduly intrigued by the opportunity to examine several hairs preserved from that hirsute appendage.

So it was rather the person and personality of Launcelot Canning himself which caused me to accept his proffered hospitality. For the man who proposed to become my host might have himself stepped from the pages of a Poe tale. His speech, as I have endeavored to indicate, was characterized by a courtly rodomontade so often exemplified in Poe's heroes—and beyond certainty, his appearance bore out the resemblance.

Launcelot Canning had the cadaverousness of complexion, the large, liquid, luminous eye, the thin, curved lips, the delicately modeled nose, finely molded chin, and dark, web-like hair of a typical Poe protagonist.

It was this phenomenon which prompted my acceptance and led me to journey to his Maryland estate which, as I now perceived, in itself manifested a Poe-esque quality of its own, intrinsic in the images of the gray sedge, the ghastly tree-stems, and the vacant and eye-like windows of the mansion of gloom. All that was lacking was a tarn and a moat—and as I prepared to enter the dwelling I half-expected to encounter therein the carved ceiling, the somber tapestries, the ebon floors, and the phantasmagoric armorial trophies so vividly described by the author of *Tales of the Grotesque and Arabesque*.

Nor, upon entering Launcelot Canning's home was I too greatly disappointed in my expectation. True to both the atmospheric quality of the decrepit mansion and to my own fanciful presentiments, the door was opened in response to my knock by a valet who conducted me, in silence, through dark and intricate passages to the study of his master.

The room in which I found myself was very large and lofty. The windows were long, narrow, and pointed, and at so vast a distance from the black oaken floor as to be altogether inaccessible from within. Feeble gleams of encrimsoned light made their way through the trellised panes, and served to render sufficiently distinct the more prominent objects around; the eye, however, struggled in vain to reach the remoter angles of the chamber or the recesses of the vaulted and fretted ceiling. Dark draperies hung upon the walls. The general furniture was profuse, comfortless, antique, and tattered. Many books and musical instruments lay scattered about, but failed to give any vitality to the scene.

Instead they rendered more distinct that peculiar quality of quasi-recollection; it was as though I found myself once again, after a protracted absence, in a familiar setting. I had read, I had imagined, I had dreamed, or I had actually beheld this setting before.

Upon my entrance, Launcelot Canning arose from a sofa on which he had been lying at full length, and greeted me with a vicacious warmth which had much in it, I at first thought, of an overdone cordiality.

Yet his tone, as he spoke of the object of my visit, of his earnest desire to see me, and of the solace he expected me to afford him in a mutual discussion of our interests, soon alleviated my initial misapprehension.

Launcelot Canning welcomed me with the rapt enthusiasm of the born collector—and I came to realize that he was indeed just that. For the Poe collection he shortly proposed to unveil before me was actually his birthright.

Initially, he disclosed, the nucleus of the present accumulation had begun with his grandfather, Christopher Canning, a respected merchant of Baltimore. Almost eighty years ago he had been one of the leading patrons of the arts in his community and as such was partially instrumental in arranging for the removal of Poe's body to the southeastern corner of the Presbyterian Cemetery at Fayette and Green Streets, where a suitable monument might be erected. This event occurred in the year 1875, and it was a few years prior to that time that Canning laid the foundation of the Poe collection.

"Thanks to his zeal," his grandson informed me, "I am today the fortunate possessor of a copy of virtually every existing specimen of Poe's published works. If you will step over here"—and he led me to a remote corner of the vaulted study, past the dark draperies, to a bookshelf which rose remotely to the shadowy ceiling—"I shall be pleased to corroborate that claim. Here is a copy of *Al Aaraaf, Tamerlane, and Minor Poems* in the eighteen twenty-nine edition, and here is the still earlier *Tamerlane and Other Poems* of eighteen twenty-seven. The Boston edition, which, as you doubtless know, is valued today at fifteen thousand dollars. I can assure you that Grandfather Canning parted with no such sum in order to gain possession of this rarity."

He displayed the volumes with an air of commingled pride and cupidity which is oft-times characteristic of the collector and is by no means to be confused with either literary snobbery or ordinary greed. Realizing this, I remained patient as he exhibited further treasures—copies of the *Philadelphia Saturday Courier* containing early tales, bound volumes of *Southern Literary Messenger* during the period of Poe's editorship, *Graham's Magazine*, editions of the *New York Sun* and the *New York Mirror* boasting, respectively of *The Balloon Hoax* and *The Raven*, and files of *Burton's Gentleman's Magazine*. Ascending a short library ladder, he handed down to me the Lea and Blanchard edition of *Tales of the Grotesque and Arabesque*, and *Conchologist's First Book*, the Putnam *Eureka*, and, finally, the little paper booklet, published in 1843 and sold for 12½¢, entitled *The Prose Romances of Edgar A. Poe*; an insignificant trifle containing two tales which is valued by present-day collectors at $50,000.

Canning informed me of this last fact, and, indeed, kept up a running commentary upon each item he presented. There was no doubt but that he was a Poe scholar as well as a Poe collector, and his words informed tattered specimens of the *Broadway Journal* and *Godey's Lady's Book* with a singular fascination not necessarily inherent in the flimsy sheets or their contents.

"I owe a great debt to Grandfather Canning's obsession," he observed, descending the ladder and joining me before the bookshelves. "It is not altogether a breach of confidence to admit that his interest in Poe did reach the point of an obsession, and perhaps eventually of an absolute mania. The knowledge, alas, is public property, I fear.

"In the early seventies he built this house, and I am quite sure that you have been observant enough to note that it in itself is almost a replica of a typical Poe-esque mansion. This was his study, and it was here that he was wont to pore over the books, the letters, and the numerous mementoes of Poe's life.

"What prompted a retired merchant to devote himself so fanatically to the pursuit of a hobby, I cannot say. Let it suffice that he virtually withdrew from the world and from all other normal interests. He conducted a voluminous and lengthy correspondence with aging men and women who had known Poe in their lifetime—made pilgrimages to Fordham, sent his agents to West Point, to England and Scotland, to virtually every locale in which Poe had set foot during his lifetime. He acquired letters and souvenirs as gifts, he bought them, and—I fear—stole them, if no other means of acquisition proved feasible."

Launcelot Canning smiled and nodded. "Does all this sound strange to you? I confess that once I, too, found it almost incredible, a fragment of romance. Now, after years spent here, I have lost my own objectivity."

"Yes, it is strange," I replied. "But are you quite sure that there was not some obscure personal reason for your grandfather's interest? Had he met Poe as a boy, or been closely associated with one of his friends? Was there, perhaps, a distant, undisclosed relationship?"

At the mention of the last word, Canning started visibly, and a tremor of agitation overspread his countenance.

"Ah!" he exclaimed. "There you voice my own inmost conviction. A relationship—assuredly there must have been one—I am morally, instinctively certain that Grandfather Canning felt or knew himself to be linked to Edgar Poe by ties of blood. Nothing else could account for his strong initial interest, his continuing defense of Poe in the literary controversies of the day, and his final melancholy lapse into a world of delusion and illusion.

"Yet he never voiced a statement or put an allegation upon paper—and I have searched the collection of letters in vain for the slightest clue.

"It is curious that you so promptly divine a suspicion held not only by myself but by my father. He was only a child at the time of my Grandfather

Canning's death, but the attendant circumstances left a profound impression upon his sensitive nature. Although he was immediately removed from this house to the home of his mother's people in Baltimore, he lost no time in returning upon assuming his inheritance in early manhood.

"Fortunately being in possession of a considerable income, he was able to devote his entire lifetime to further research. The name of Arthur Canning is still well known in the world of literary criticism, but for some reason he preferred to pursue his scholarly examination of Poe's career in privacy. I believe this preference was dictated by an inner sensibility; that he was endeavoring to unearth some information which would prove his father's, his, and for that matter, my own, kinship to Edgar Poe."

"You say your father was also a collector?" I prompted.

"A statement I am prepared to substantiate," replied my host, as he led me to yet another corner of the shadow-shrouded study. "But first, if you would accept a glass of wine?"

He filled, not glasses, but veritable beakers from a large carafe, and we toasted one another in silent appreciation. It is perhaps unnecessary for me to observe that the wine was a fine old Amontillado.

"Now, then," said Launcelot Canning. "My father's special province in Poe research consisted of the accumulation and study of letters."

Opening a series of large trays or drawers beneath the bookshelves, he drew out file after file of glassined folios, and for the space of the next half hour I examined Edgar Poe's correspondence—letters to Henry Herring, to Doctor Snodgrass, Sarah Shelton, James P. Moss, Elizabeth Poe—missives to Mrs. Rockwood, Helen Whitman, Anne Lynch, John Pendleton Kennedy—notes to Mrs. Richmond, to John Allan, to Annie, to his brother, Henry—a profusion of documents, a veritable epistolary cornucopia.

During the course of my perusal my host took occasion to refill our beakers with wine, and the heady draught began to take effect—for we had not eaten, and I own I gave no thought to food, so absorbed was I in the yellowed pages illumining Poe's past.

Here was wit, erudition, literary criticism; here were the muddled, maudlin outpourings of a mind gone in drink and despair; here was the draft of a projected story, the fragments of a poem; here were a pitiful cry for deliverance and a paean to living beauty; here were a dignified response to a dunning letter and an editorial pronunciamento to an admirer; here were love, hate, pride, anger, celestial serenity, abject penitence, authority, wonder, resolution, indecision, joy, and soul-sickening melancholia.

Here were the gifted elocutionist, the stammering drunkard, the adoring husband, the frantic lover, the proud editor, the indigent pauper, the grandiose dreamer, the shabby realist, the scientific inquirer, the gullible metaphysician, the dependent stepson, the free and untrammeled spirit, the hack, the poet, the enigma that was Edgar Allan Poe.

Again the beakers were filled and emptied.

I drank deeply with my lips, and with my eyes more deeply still.

For the first time the true enthusiasm of Launcelot Canning was communicated to my own sensibilities—I divined the eternal fascination found in a consideration of Poe the writer and Poe the man; he who wrote Tragedy, lived Tragedy, was Tragedy; he who penned Mystery, lived and died in Mystery, and who today looms on the literary scene as Mystery incarnate.

And Mystery Poe remained, despite Arthur Canning's careful study of the letters. "My father learned nothing," my host confided, "even though he assembled, as you see here, a collection to delight the heart of a Mabbott or a Quinn. So his search ranged further. By this time I was old enough to share both his interest and his inquiries. Come," and he led me to an ornate chest which rested beneath the windows against the west wall of the study.

Kneeling, he unlocked the repository, and then drew forth, in rapid and marvelous succession, a series of objects each of which boasted of intimate connection with Poe's life.

There were souvenirs of his youth and his schooling abroad—a book he had used during his sojourn at West Point—mementoes of his days as a theatrical critic in the form of play-bills, a pen used during his editorial period, a fan once owned by his girl-wife, Virginia, a brooch of Mrs. Clemm's; a profusion of objects including such diverse articles as a cravat-stock and—curiously enough—Poe's battered and tarnished flute.

Again we drank, and I own the wine was potent. Canning's countenance remained cadaverously wan—but, moreover, there was a species of mad hilarity in his eye—an evident restrained hysteria in his whole demeanor. At length, from the scattered heap of curiosa, I happened to draw forth and examine a little box of no remarkable character, whereupon I was constrained to inquire its history and what part it had played in the life of Poe.

"In the *life* of Poe?" A visible tremor convulsed the features of my host, then rapidly passed in transformation to a grimace, a rictus of amusement. "This little box—and you will not how, by some fateful design of contrived coincidence it bears a resemblance to the box he himself conceived and described in his tale *Berenice*—this little box is concerned with his death, rather than his life. It is, in fact, the selfsame box my Grandfather Christopher Canning clutched to his bosom when they found him down there."

Again the tremor, again the grimace. "But say, I have not yet told you of the details. Perhaps you would be interested in seeing the spot where Christopher Canning was stricken; I have already told you of his madness, but I did not more than hint at the character of his delusions. You have been patient with me, and more than patient. Your understanding shall be rewarded, for I perceive you can be fully entrusted with the facts."

What further revelations Canning was prepared to make I could not say, but his manner was such as to inspire a vague disquiet and trepidation in my breast.

Upon perceiving my unease he laughed shortly and laid a hand upon my shoulder. "Come, this should interest you as an *aficionado* of fantasy," he said. "But first, another drink to speed our journey."

He poured, we drank, and then he led the way from that vaulted chamber, down the silent halls, down the staircase, and into the lowest recesses of the building until we reached what resembled a donjon-keep, its floor and the interior of a long archway carefully sheathed in copper. We paused before a door of massive iron. Again I felt in the aspect of this scene an element evocative of recognition or recollection.

Canning's intoxication was such that he misinterpreted, or chose to misinterpret, my reaction.

"You need not be afraid," he assured me. "Nothing has happened down here since that day, almost seventy years ago, when his servants discovered him stretched out before this door, the little box clutched to his bosom; collapsed, and in a state of delirium from which he never emerged. For six months he lingered, a hopeless maniac—raving as wildly from the very moment of his discovery as at the moment he died—babbling his visions of the giant horse, the fissured house collapsing into the tarn, the black cat, the pit, the pendulum, the raven on the pallid bust, the beating heart, the pearly teeth, and the nearly liquid mass of loathsome—of detestable putridity from which a voice emanated.

"Nor was that all he babbled," Canning confided, and here his voice sank to a whisper that reverberated through the copper-sheathed hall and against the iron door. "He hinted other things far worse than fantasy; of a ghastly reality surpassing all of the phantasms of Poe.

"For the first time my father and the servants learned the purpose of the room he had built beyond this iron door, and learned what Christopher Canning had done to establish his title as the world's foremost collector of Poe.

"For he babbled again of Poe's death, thirty years earlier, in eighteen forty-nine—of the burial in the Presbyterian Cemetery—and of the removal of the coffin in eighteen seventy-four to the corner where the monument was raised. As I told you, and as was known then, my grandfather had played a public part in instigating that removal. But now we learned of the private part—learned that there was a monument and a grave, but no coffin in the earth beneath Poe's alleged resting place. The coffin now rested in the secret room at the end of this passage. That is why the room, the house itself, had been built.

"I tell you, he had stolen the body of Edgar Allan Poe—and as he shrieked aloud in his final madness, did not this indeed make him the greatest collector of Poe?

"His ultimate intent was never divined, but my father made one significant discovery—the little box clutched to Christopher Canning's bosom contained a portion of the crumbled bones, the veritable dust that was all that remained of Poe's corpse."

My host shuddered and turned away. He led me back along that hall of horror, up the stairs, into the study. Silently, he filled our beakers and I drank as hastily, as deeply, as desperately as he.

"What could my father do? To own the truth was to create a public scandal. He chose instead to keep silence; to devote his own life to study in retirement.

"Naturally the shock affected him profoundly; to my knowledge he never entered the room beyond the iron door and, indeed, I did not know of the room or its contents until the hour of his death—and it was not until some years later that I myself found the key among his effects.

"But find the key I did, and the story was immediately and completely corroborated. Today I am the greatest collector of Poe—for he lies in the keep below, my eternal trophy!"

This time I poured the wine. As I did so, I noted for the first time the imminence of a storm; the impetuous fury of its gusts shaking the casements, and the echoes of its thunder rolling and rumbling down the time-corroded corridors of the old house.

The wild, overstrained vivacity with which my host hearkened, or apparently hearkened, to these sounds did nothing to reassure me—for his recent revelation led me to suspect his sanity.

That the body of Edgar Allan Poe had been stolen—that this mansion had been built to house it—that it was indeed enshrined in a crypt below—that grandsire, son, and grandson had dwelt here alone, apart, enslaved to a sepulchral secret—was beyond sane belief.

And yet, surrounded now by the night and the storm, in a setting torn from Poe's own frenzied fancies, I could not be sure. Here the past was still alive, the very spirit of Poe's tales breathed forth its corruption upon the scene.

As thunder boomed, Launcelot Canning took up Poe's flute, and, whether in defiance of the storm without or as a mocking accompaniment, he played; blowing upon it with drunken persistence, with eery atonality, with nerve-shattering shrillness. To the shrieking of that infernal instrument the thunder added a braying counterpoint.

Uneasy, uncertain, and unnerved, I retreated into the shadows of the bookshelves at the farther end of the room, and idly scanned the titles of a row of ancient tomes. Here was the *Chiromancy* of Robert Flud, the *Directorium Inquisitorum*, a rare and curious book in quarto Gothic that was the manual of a forgotten church; and betwixt and between the volumes of pseudo-scientific inquiry, theological speculation, and sundry incunabula I found titles that arrested and appalled me. *De Vermis Mysteriis* and the *Liber Eibon*, treatises on demonology, on witchcraft, on sorcery mouldered in crumbling binding. The books were old, but the books were not dusty. They had been read—

"Read them?" It was as though Canning divined my inmost thoughts. He had put aside his flute and now approached me, tittering as though in continued drunken defiance of the storm. Odd echoes and boomings now sounded through the long halls of the house, and curious grating sounds threatened to drown out his words and laughter.

"Read them?" said Canning. "I study them. Yes, I have gone beyond grandfather and father, too. It was I who procured the books that held the key, and it was I who found the key. A key more difficult to discover, and more important, than the key to the vaults below. I often wonder if Poe himself had access to these selfsame tomes, knew the selfsame secrets. The secrets of the grave and what lies beyond, and what can be summoned forth if one but holds the key."

He stumbled away and returned with wine. "Drink," he said. "Drink to the night and the storm."

I brushed the proffered glass aside. "Enough," I said. "I must be on my way."

Was it fancy or did I find fear frozen on his features? Canning clutched my arm and cried, "No, stay with me! This is no night on which to be alone; I swear I cannot abide the thought of being alone, I can bear to be alone no more!"

His incoherent babble mingled with the thunder and the echoes; I drew back and confronted him. "Control yourself," I counseled. "Confess that this is a hoax, an elaborate imposture arranged to please your fancy."

"Hoax? Imposture? Stay, and I shall prove to you beyond all doubt"—and so saying, Launcelot Canning stooped and opened a small drawer set in the wall beneath and beside the bookshelves. "This should repay you for your interest in my story, and in Poe," he murmured. "Know that you are the first, other person than myself, to glimpse these treasures."

He handed me a sheaf of manuscripts on plain white paper; documents written in ink curiously similar to that I had noted while perusing Poe's letters. Pages were clipped together in groups, and for a moment I scanned titles alone.

"*The Worm of Midnight, by Edgar Poe,*" I read, aloud, "*The Crypt,*" I breathed. And here, "*The Further Adventures of Arthur Gordon Pym*"— and in my agitation I came close to dropping the precious pages. "Are these what they appear to be—the unpublished tales of Poe?"

My host bowed.

"Unpublished, undiscovered, unknown, save to me—and to you."

"But this cannot be," I protested. "Surely there would have been a mention of them somewhere, in Poe's own letters or those of his contemporaries. There would have been a clue, an indication, somewhere, someplace, somehow."

Thunder mingled with my words, and thunder echoed in Canning's shouted reply.

"You dare to presume an imposture? Then compare!" He stooped again and brought out a glassined folio of letters. "Here—is this not the veritable script of Edgar Poe? Look at the calligraphy of the letter, then at the manuscripts. Can you say they are not penned by the selfsame hand?"

I looked at the handwriting, wondered at the possibilities of a monomaniac's forgery. "Could Launcelot Canning, a victim of mental disorder, thus painstakingly simulate Poe's hand?"

"Read, then!" Canning screamed through the thunder. "Read, and dare to say that these tales were written by any other than Edgar Poe, whose genius defies the corruption of Time and the Conqueror Worm!"

I read but a line or two, holding the topmost manuscript close to eyes that strained beneath wavering candlelight; but even in the flickering illumination I noted that which told me the only, the incontestable truth. For the paper, the curiously *unyellowed* paper, bore a visible watermark; the name of a firm of well-known modern stationers, and the date—1949.

Putting the sheaf aside, I endeavored to compose myself as I moved away from Launcelot Canning. For now I knew the truth; knew that, one hundred years after Poe's death a semblance of his spirit still lived in the distorted and disordered soul of Canning. Incarnation, reincarnation, call it what you will; Canning was, in his own irrational mind, Edgar Allan Poe.

Stifled and dull echoes of thunder from a remote portion of the mansion now commingled with the soundless seething of my own inner turmoil, as I turned and rashly addressed my host.

"Confess!" I cried. "Is it not true that you have written these tales, fancying yourself the embodiment of Poe? Is it not true that you suffer from a singular delusion born of solitude and everlasting brooding upon the past; that you have reached a stage characterized by the conviction that Poe still lives on in your own person?"

A strong shudder came over him and a sickly smile quivered about his lips as he replied. "Fool! I say to you that I have spoken the truth. Can you doubt the evidence of you senses? This house is real, the Poe collection exists, and the stories exist—they exist, I swear, as truly as the body lying in the crypt below!"

I took up the little box from the table and removed the lid. "Not so," I answered. "You said your grandfather was found with this box clutched to his breast, before the door of the vault, and that it contained Poe's dust. Yet you cannot escape the fact that the box is empty." I faced him furiously. "Admit it, the story is a fabrication, a romance. Poe's body does not lie beneath this house, nor are these his unpublished works, written during his lifetime and concealed."

"True enough." Canning's smile was ghastly beyond belief. "The dust is gone because I took it and used it—because in the works of wizardry I found the formulae, the arcana whereby I could raise the flesh, re-create the body from the essential salts of the grave. Poe does not *lie* beneath this house—he *lives!* And the tales are *his posthumous works!*"

Accented by thunder, his words crashed against my consciousness.

"That was the end-all and the be-all of my planning, of my studies, of my work, of my life! To raise, by sorcery, the veritable spirit of Edgar Poe from the grave—reclothed and animate in flesh—set him to dwell and dream and do his work again in the private chambers I built in the vaults below—and this I have done! To steal a corpse is but a ghoulish prank; mine is the achievement of true genius!"

The distinct, hollow, metallic, and clangorous, yet apparently muffled reverberation accompanying his words caused him to turn in his seat and face the door of the study, so that I could not see the workings of his countenance—nor could he read my own reaction to his ravings.

His words came but faintly to my ears through the thunder that now shook the house in a relentless grip; the wind rattling the casements and flickering the candle-flame from the great silver candelabra sent a soaring sighing in an anguished accompaniment to his speech.

"I would show him to you, but I dare not; for he hates me as he hates life. I have locked him in the vault, alone, for the resurrected have no need of food nor drink. And he sits there, pen moving over paper, endlessly moving, endlessly pouring out the evil essence of all he guessed and hinted at in life and which he learned in death.

"Do you not see the tragic pity of my plight? I sought to raise his spirit from the dead, to give the world anew of his genius—and yet these tales, these works, are filled and fraught with a terror not to be endured. They cannot be shown to the world, he cannot be shown to the world; in bringing back the dead I have brought back the fruits of death!"

Echoes sounded anew as I moved towards the door—moved, I confess, to flee this accursed house and its accursed owner.

Canning clutched my hand, my arm, my shoulder. "You cannot go!" he shouted above the storm. "I spoke of his escaping, but did you not guess? Did you not hear it through the thunder—the grating of the door?"

I pushed him aside and he blundered backwards upsetting the candelabra, so that flames licked now across the carpeting.

"Wait!" he cried. "Have you not heard his footstep on the stair? *Madman, I tell you that he now stands without the door!*"

A rush of wind, a roar of flame, a shroud of smoke rose all about us. Throwing open the huge, antique panels to which Canning pointed, I staggered into the hall.

I speak of wind, of flame, of smoke—enough to obscure all vision. I speak of Canning's screams, and of thunder loud enough to drown all sound. I speak of terror born of loathing and of desperation enough to shatter all my sanity.

Despite these things, I can never erase from my consciousness that which I beheld as I fled past the doorway and down the hall.

There without the doors there *did* stand a lofty and enshrouded figure; a figure all too familiar, with pallid features, high, domed forehead, mustache set above a mouth. My glimpse lasted but an instant, an instant during which the man—the corpse—the apparition—the hallucination, call it what you will—moved forward into the chamber and clasped Canning to his breast in an unbreakable embrace. Together, the two figures tottered toward the flames, which now rose to blot out vision forever more.

From that chamber, and from that mansion, I fled aghast. The storm was still abroad in all is wrath, and now fire came to claim the house of Canning for its own.

Suddenly there shot along the path before me a wild light, and I turned to see whence a gleam so unusual could have issued—but it was only the flames, rising in supernatural splendor to consume the mansion, and the secrets, of the man who collected Poe.

MASSACHUSETTS

Pickman's Model
by H. P. Lovecraft

You NEEDN'T think I'm crazy, Eliot—plenty of others have queerer prejudices than this. Why don't you laugh at Oliver's grandfather, who won't ride in a motor? If I don't like that damned subway, it's my own business; and we got here more quickly anyhow in the taxi. We'd have had to walk up the hill from Park Street if we'd taken the car.

I know I'm more nervous than I was when you saw me last year, but you don't need to hold a clinic over it. There's plenty of reason, God knows, and I fancy I'm lucky to be sane at all. Why the third degree? You didn't use to be so inquisitive.

Well, if you must hear it, I don't know why you shouldn't. Maybe you ought to, anyhow, for you kept writing me like a grieved parent when you heard I'd begun to cut the Art Club and keep away from Pickman. Now that he's disappeared I go around to the club once in a while, but my nerves aren't what they were.

No, I don't know what's become of Pickman, and I don't like to guess. You might have surmised I had some inside information when I dropped him—and that's why I don't want to think where he's gone. Let the police find what they can—it won't be much, judging from the fact that that they don't know yet of the old North End place he hired under the name of Peters. I'm not sure that I could find it again myself—not that I'd ever try, even in broad daylight! Yes, I do know, or am afraid I know, why he maintained it. I'm coming to that. And I think you'll understand before I'm through why I don't tell the police. They would ask me to guide them, but I couldn't go back there even if I knew the way. There was something there—and now I can't use the subway or (and you may as well have your laugh at this, too) go down into cellars any more.

I should think you'd have known I didn't drop Pickman for the same silly reasons that fussy old women like Dr. Reid or Joe Minot or Rosworth did. Morbid art doesn't shock me, and when a man has the genius Pickman had I feel it an honor to know him, no matter what direction his work takes. Boston never had a greater painter than Richard Upton Pickman. I said it at first and I say it still, and I never swerved an inch, either, when he showed that "Ghoul Feeding." That, you remember, was when Minot cut him.

You know, it takes profound art and profound insight into Nature to turn out stuff like Pickman's. Any magazine-cover hack can splash paint around wildly and call it a nightmare or a Witches' Sabbath or a portrait of the devil, but only a great painter can make such a thing really scare or ring true. That's because only a real artist knows the actual anatomy of the terrible or the physiology of fear—the exact sort of lines and proportions that connect up with latent instincts or hereditary memories of fright, and the proper color contrasts and lighting effects to stir the dormant sense of strangeness. I don't have to tell you why a Fuseli really brings a shiver while a cheap ghost-story frontispiece merely makes us laugh. There's something those fellows catch—beyond life—that they're able to make us catch for a second. Doré had it. Sime has it. Angarola of Chicago has it. And Pickman had it as no man ever had it before or—I hope to heaven—ever will again.

Don't ask me what it is they see. You know, in ordinary art, there's all the difference in the world between the vital, breathing things drawn from Nature or models and the artificial truck that commercial small fry reel off in a bare studio by rule. Well, I should say that the really weird artist has a kind of vision which makes models, or summons up what amounts to actual scenes from the spectral world he lives in. Anyhow, he manages to turn out results that differ from the pretender's mince-pie dreams in just about the same way that the life painter's results differ from the concoctions of a correspondence-school cartoonist. If I had ever seen what Pickman saw—but no! Here, let's have a drink before we get any deeper. Gad, I wouldn't be alive if I'd ever seen what that man—if he was a man—saw!

You recall that Pickman's forte was faces. I don't believe anybody since Goya could put so much of sheer hell into a set of features or a twist of expression. And before Goya you have to go back to the medieval chaps who did the gargoyles and chimeras on Notre Dame and Mont Saint-Michel. They believed all sorts of things—and maybe they saw all sorts of things, too, for the Middle Ages had some curious phases. I remember your asking Pickman yourself once, the year before you went away, wherever in thunder he got such ideas and visions. Wasn't that a nasty laugh he gave you? It was partly because of that laugh that Reid dropped him. Reid, you know, had just taken up comparative pathology, and was full of pompous "inside stuff" about the biological or evolutionary significance of this or that mental or physical symptom. He said Pickman repelled him more and more every day, and almost frightened him toward the last—that the fellow's features and expression were slowly developing in a way he didn't like; in a way that wasn't human. He had a lot of talk about diet, and said Pickman must be abnormal and eccentric to the last degree. I suppose you told Reid, if you and he had any correspondence over it, that he'd let Pickman's paintings get on his nerves or harrow up his imagination. I know I told him that myself—then.

But keep in mind that I didn't drop Pickman for anything like this. On the contrary, my admiration for him kept growing; for that "Ghoul Feeding" was a tremendous achievement. As you know, the club wouldn't exhibit it, and the Museum of Fine Arts wouldn't accept it as a gift; and I can add that nobody would buy it, so Pickman had it right in his house till he went. Now his father has it in Salem—you know Pickman comes of old Salem stock, and had a witch ancestor hanged in 1692.

I got into the habit of calling on Pickman quite often, especially after I began making notes for a monograph on weird art. Probably it was his work which put the idea into my head, and anyhow, I found him a mine of data and suggestions when I came to develop it. He showed me all the paintings and drawings he had about; including some pen-and-ink sketches that would, I verily believe, have got him kicked out of the club if many of the members had seen them. Before long I was pretty nearly a devotee, and would listen for hours like a schoolboy to art theories and philosophic speculations wild enough to qualify him for the Danvers asylum. My hero worship, coupled with the fact that people generally were commencing to have less and less to do with him made him get very confidential with me; and one evening he hinted that if I were fairly close-mouthed and none too squeamish, he might show me something rather unusual—something a bit stronger than anything he had in the house.

"You know," he said, "there are things that won't do for Newbury Street—things that are out of place here, and that can't be conceived here, anyhow. It's my business to catch the overtones of the soul, and you won't find those in a parvenu set of artificial streets on made land. Back Bay isn't Boston—it isn't anything yet, because it's had no time to pick up memories and attract local spirits. If there are any ghosts here, they're the tame ghosts of a salt marsh and a shallow cove; and I want human ghosts—the ghosts of beings highly organized enough to have looked on hell and known the meaning of what they saw.

"The place for an artist to live is the North End. If any aesthete were sincere, he'd put up with the slums for the sake of the massed traditions. God, man! Don't you realize that places like that weren't merely *made*, but actually *grew*? Generation after generation lived and felt and died there, and in days when people weren't afraid to live and feel and die. Don't you know there was a mill on Copp's Hill in 1632, and that half the present streets were laid out by 1650? I can show you houses that have stood two centuries and a half and more; houses that have witnessed what would make a modern house crumble into powder. What do moderns know of life and the forces behind it? You call the Salem witchcraft a delusion, but I'll wager my four-times-great-grandmother could have told you things. They hanged her on Gallows Hill, with Cotton Mather looking sanctimoniously on. Mather, damn him, was afraid somebody might succeed in kicking free of this accursed cage of monotony—I wish someone had laid a spell on him or sucked his blood in the night!

"I can show you a house he lived in, and I can show you another one he was afraid to enter in spite of all his fine bold talk. He knew things he didn't dare put into that stupid *Magnalia* or that puerile *Wonders of the Invisible World*. Look here, do you know the whole North End once had a set of tunnels that kept certain people in touch with each other's houses, and the burying ground, and the sea? Let them prosecute and persecute above ground—things went on every day that they couldn't reach, and voices laughed at night that they couldn't place!

"Why, man, out of ten surviving houses built before 1700 and not moved since I'll wager that in eight I can show you something queer in the cellar. There's hardly a month that you don't read of workmen finding bricked-up arches and wells leading nowhere in this or that old place as it comes down—you could see one near Henchman Street from the elevated last year. There were witches and what their spells summoned; pirates and what they brought in from the sea; smugglers; privateers—and I tell you, people knew how to live, and how to enlarge the bounds of life, in the old time! This wasn't the only world a bold and wise man could know—faugh! And to think of today in contrast, with such pale pink brains that even a club of supposed artists get shudders and convulsions if a picture goes beyond the feelings of a Beacon Street tea table!

"The only saving grace of the present is that it's too damned stupid to question the past very closely. What do maps and records and guidebooks really tell of the North End? Bah! At a guess I'll guarantee to lead you to thirty or forty alleys and networks of alleys north of Prince Street that aren't suspected by ten living beings outside of the foreigners that swarm them. And what do those dagoes know of their meaning? No, Thurber, these ancient places are dreaming gorgeously and overflowing with wonder and terror and escapes from the commonplace, and yet there's only one living soul to understand or profit by them. Or rather, there's only one living soul—for I haven't been digging around in the past for nothing!

"See here, you're interested in this sort of thing. What if I told you that I've got another studio up there, where I can catch the night spirit of antique horror and paint things that I couldn't even think of in Newbury Street? Naturally I don't tell those cursed old maids at the club—with Reid, damn him, whispering even as it is that I'm a sort of monster bound down the toboggan of reverse evolution. Yes, Thurber, I decided long ago that one must paint terror as well as beauty from life, so I did some exploring in places where I had reason to know terror lives.

"I've got a place that I don't believe three living Nordic men besides myself have ever seen. It isn't so very far from the elevated as distance goes, but it's centuries away as the soul goes. I took it because of the queer old brick well in the cellar—one of the sort I told you about. The shack's almost tumbling down, so that nobody else would live there, and I'd hate to tell you now little I pay for it. The windows are boarded up, but I like that all the better, since I don't want daylight for what I do. I paint in the cellar, where the inspiration is thickest, but I've other rooms furnished on the ground floor. A Sicilian owns it, and I've hired it under the name of Peters.

"Now if you're game, I'll take you there tonight. I think you'd enjoy the pictures, for as I said, I've let myself go a bit there. It's no vast tour—I sometimes do it on foot, for I don't want to attract attention with a taxi in such a place. We can take the shuttle at the South Station for Battery Street, and after that the walk isn't much."

Well, Elliot, there wasn't much for me to do after that harangue but to keep myself from running instead of walking for the first vacant cab we could sight. We changed to the elevated at the South Station, and at about twelve o' clock had climbed down the steps at Battery Street and struck along the old waterfront past Constitution Wharf. I didn't keep track of the cross streets, and can't tell you yet which it was we turned up, but I know it wasn't Greenough Lane.

When we did turn, it was to climb through the deserted length of the oldest and dirtiest alley I ever saw in my life, with crumbling-looking gables, broken small-paned windows, and archaic chimneys that stood out half-disintegrated against the moonlit sky. I don't believe there were three houses in sight that hadn't been standing in Cotton Mather's time—certainly I glimpsed at least two with an overhang, and once I thought I saw a peaked roof line of the almost forgotten pregambrel type, though antiquarians tell us there are none left in Boston.

From that alley, which had a dim light, we turned to the left into an equally silent and still narrower alley with no light at all: and in a minute made what I think was an obtuse-angled bend toward the right in the dark. Not long after this Pickman produced a flashlight and revealed an antediluvian ten-paneled door that looked damnably worm-eaten. Unlocking it, he ushered me into a barren hallway with what was once splendid dark oak paneling—simple, of course, but thrillingly suggestive of the time of Andros and Phipps and the Witchcraft. Then he took me through a door on the left, lighted an oil lamp, and told me to make myself at home.

Now, Eliot, I'm what the man in the street would call fairly "hard-boiled," but I'll confess that what I saw on the walls of that room gave me a bad turn. They were his pictures, you know—the ones he couldn't paint or even show in Newbury Street—and he was right when he said he had "let himself go." Here—have another drink—I need one anyhow!

There's no use in trying to tell you what they were like, because the awful, the blasphemous horror, and the unbelievable loathsomeness and moral foetor came from simple touches quite beyond the power of words to classify. There was none of the exotic technique you see in Sidney Sime, none of the trans-Saturnian landscapes and lunar fungi that Clark Ashton Smith uses to freeze the blood. The backgrounds were mostly old churchyards, deep woods, cliffs by the sea, brick tunnels, ancient paneled rooms, or simple vaults of masonry. Copp's Hill Burying Ground, which could not be many blocks away from this very house, was a favorite scene.

The madness and monstrosity lay in the figures in the foreground—for Pickman's morbid art was preeminently one of demoniac portraiture. These figures were seldom completely human, but often approached humanity in varying degree. Most of the bodies, while roughly bipedal, had a forward slumping, and a vaguely canine cast. The texture of the majority was a kind of unpleasant rubberiness. Ugh! I can see them now! Their occupations— well, don't ask me to be too precise. They were usually feeding—I won't say on what. They were sometimes shown in groups in cemeteries or underground passages, and often appeared to be in battle over their prey—or rather, their treasure trove. And what damnable expressiveness Pickman sometimes gave the sightless faces of this charnel booty! Occasionally the things were shown leaping through open windows at night, or squatting on the chests of sleepers, worrying at their throats. One canvas showed a ring of them baying about a hanged witch on Gallows Hill, whose dead face held a close kinship to theirs.

But don't get the idea that it was all this hideous business of theme and setting which struck me faint. I'm not a three-year-old kid, and I'd seen much like this before. It was the *faces*, Eliot, those accursed *faces*, that leered and slavered out of the canvas with the very breath of life! By God, man, I verily believe they *were* alive! That nauseous wizard had waked the fires of hell in pigment, and his brush had been a nightmare-spawning wand. Give me that decanter, Eliot!

There was one thing called "The Lesson"—heaven pity me, that I ever saw it! Listen—can you fancy a squatting circle of nameless dog-like things in a churchyard teaching a small child how to feed like themselves? The price of a changeling, I suppose—you know the old myth about how the weird people leave their own spawn in cradles in exchange for the human babes they steal. Pickman was showing what happens to those stolen babes—how they grow up—and then I began to see a hideous relationship in the faces of the human and nonhuman figures. He was, in all his gradations of morbidity between the frankly nonhuman and the degradedly human, establishing a sardonic linkage and evolution. The dog-things were developed from mortals!

And no sooner had I wondered what he made of their own young as left with mankind in the form of changelings, then my eye caught a picture embodying that very thought. It was that of an ancient Puritan interior—a heavily beamed room with lattice windows, a settle, and clumsy seventeenth-century furniture, with the family sitting about while father read from the Scriptures. Every face but one showed nobility and reverence, but that one reflected the mockery of the pit. It was that of a young man in years, and no doubt belonged to a supposed son of that pious father, but in essence it was the kin of the unclean things. It was their changeling—and in a spirit of supreme irony Pickman had given the features a very perceptible resemblance to his own.

By this time Pickman had lighted a lamp in an adjoining room and was politely holding open the door for me; asking me if I would care to see his "modern studies." I hadn't been able to give him much of my opinions—I was too speechless with fright and loathing—but I think he fully understood and felt highly complimented. And now I want to assure you again, Eliot, that I'm no mollycoddle to scream at anything which shows a bit of departure from the usual. I'm middle-aged and decently sophisticated, and I guess you saw enough of me in France to know I'm not easily knocked out. Remember, too, that I'd just about recovered my wind and gotten used to those frightful pictures which turned colonial New England into a kind of annex of hell. Well, in spite of all this, that next room forced a real scream out of me, and I had to clutch at the doorway to keep from keeling over. The other chamber had shown a pack of ghouls and witches overrunning the world of our forefathers, but this one brought the horror right into our own daily life.

Gad, how that man could paint! There was a study called "Subway Accident," in which a flock of the vile things were clambering up from some unknown catacomb through a crack in the floor of the Boylston Street subway and attacking a crowd of people on the platform. Another showed a dance on Copp's Hill among the tombs with the background of today. Then there were any number of cellar views, with monsters creeping in through holes and rifts in the masonry and grinning as they squatted behind barrels or furnaces and waited for their first victim to descend the stairs.

One disgusting canvas seemed to depict a vast cross-section of Beacon Hill, with antlike armies of the mephitic monsters squeezing themselves through burrows that honeycombed the ground. Dances in the modern cemeteries were freely pictured, and another conception somehow shocked me more than all the rest—a scene in an unknown vault, where scores of beasts crowded about one who held a well-known Boston guidebook and was evidently reading aloud. All were pointing to a certain passage, and every face seemed so distorted with epileptic and reverberant laughter that I almost thought I heard the fiendish echoes. The title of the picture was, "Holmes, Lowell, and Longfellow Lie Buried in Mount Auburn."

As I gradually steadied myself and got readjusted to this second room of deviltry and morbidity, I began to analyze some of the points in my sickening loathing. In the first place, I said to myself, these things repelled because of the utter inhumanity and callous cruelty they showed in Pickman. The fellow must be a relentless enemy of all mankind to take such glee in the torture of brain and flesh and the degradation of the mortal tenement. In the second place, they terrified because of their very greatness. Their art was the art that convinced—when we saw the pictures we saw the demons themselves and were afraid of them. And the queer part was, that Pickman got none of his power from the use of selectiveness or bizarrerie. Nothing was blurred, distorted, or conventionalized; outlines were sharp and lifelike, and details were almost painfully defined. And the faces!

It was not any mere artist's interpretation that we saw; it was pandemonium itself, crystal clear in stark objectivity. That was it, by heaven! The man was not a fantaisiste or romanticist at all—he did not even try to give us the churning, prismatic ephemera of dreams, but coldly and sardonically reflected some stable, mechanistic, and well-established horror-world which he saw fully, brilliantly, squarely and unfalteringly. God knows what that world can have been, or where he ever glimpsed the blasphemous shapes that loped and trotted and crawled through it; but whatever the baffling source of his images, one thing was plain. Pickman was in every sense—in conception and in execution—a thorough, painstaking and almost scientific *realist*.

My host was now leading the way down cellar to his actual studio and I braced myself for some hellish effects among the unfinished canvases. As we reached the bottom of the damp stairs he turned his flashlight to a corner of the large open space at hand, revealing the circular brick curb of what was evidently a great well in the earthen floor. We walked nearer, and I saw that it must be five feet across, with walls a good foot thick and some six inches above the ground level—solid work of the seventeenth century, or I was much mistaken. That, Pickman said, was the kind of thing he had been talking about—an aperture of the network of tunnels that used to undermine the hill. I noticed idly that it did not seem to be bricked up, and that a heavy disc of wood formed the apparent cover. Thinking of the things this well must have been connected with if Pickman's wild hints had not been mere rhetoric, I shivered slightly; then turned to follow up a step and through a narrow door into a room of fair size, provided with a wooden floor and furnished as a studio. An acetylene gas outfit gave the light necessary for work.

The unfinished pictures on easels or propped against the walls were as ghastly as the finished ones upstairs, and showed the painstaking methods of the artist. Scenes were blocked out with extreme care, and penciled guide lines told of the minute exactitude which Pickman used in getting the right perspective and proportions. The man was great—I say it even now, knowing as much as I do. A large camera on a table excited my notice, and Pickman told me that he used it in taking scenes for backgrounds, so that he might paint them from photographs in the studio instead of carting his outfit around the town for this or that view. He thought a photograph quite as good as an actual scene or model for sustained work, and declared he employed them regularly.

There was something very disturbing about the nauseous sketches and half-finished monstrosities that leered around from every side of the room, and when Pickman suddenly unveiled a huge canvas on the side away from the light I could not for my life keep back a loud scream—the second I had emitted that night. It echoed and echoed through the dim vaultings of that ancient and nitrous cellar, and I had to choke back a flood of reaction that threatened to burst out as hysterical laughter. Merciful Creator! Eliot, but I don't know how much was real and how much was feverish fancy. It doesn't seem to me that earth can hold a dream like that!

It was a colossal and nameless blasphemy with glaring red eyes, and it held in bony claws a thing that had been a man, gnawing at the head as a child nibbles at a stick of candy. Its position was a kind of crouch, as as one looked one felt that at any moment it might drop its present prey and seek a juicier morsel. But damn it all, it wasn't even the fiendish subject that made it such an immortal fountainhead of all panic—not that, nor the face with its pointed ears, bloodshot eyes, flat nose and drooling lips. It wasn't the scaly claws nor the mould-caked body nor the half-hooved feet—none of these, though any one of them might well have driven an excitable man to madness.

It was the technique, Eliot—the cursed, the impious, the unnatural technique! As I am a living being, I never elsewhere saw the actual breath of life so fused into a canvas. The monster was there—it glared and gnawed and gnawed and glared—and I knew that only a suspension of Nature's laws could ever let a man paint a thing like that without a model—without some glimpse of the netherworld which no mortal unsold to the Fiend has ever had.

Pinned with a thumbtack to a vacant part of the canvas was a piece of paper now badly curled up—probably, I thought, a photograph from which Pickman meant to paint a background as hideous as the nightmare it was to enhance. I reached out to uncurl and look at it, when suddenly I saw Pickman start as if shot. He had been listening with peculiar intensity ever since my shocked scream had waked unaccustomed echoes in the dark cellar, and now he seemed struck with a fright which, though not comparable to my own, had in it more of the physical than of the spiritual. He drew a revolver and motioned me to silence, then stepped out into the main cellar and closed the door behind him.

I think I was paralyzed for an instant. Imitating Pickman's listening, I fancied I heard a faint scurrying sound somewhere, and a series of squeals or beats in a direction I couldn't determine. I thought of huge rats and shuddered. There there came a subdued sort of clatter which somehow set me all in gooseflesh—a furtive, groping kind of clatter, though I can't attempt to convey what I mean in words. It was like heavy wood falling on stone or brick—wood on brick—what did that make me think of?

It came again, and louder. There was a vibration as if the wood had fallen farther than it had fallen before. After that followed a sharp grating noise, a shouted gibberish from Pickman, and the deafening discharge of all six chambers of a revolver, fired spectacularly as a lion tamer might fire in the air for effect. A muffled squeak or squawk, and a thud. Then more wood and brick grating, a pause, and the opening of the door—at which I'll confess I started violently. Pickman reappeared with his smoking weapon, cursing the bloated rats that infested the ancient wall.

"The deuce knows what they eat, Thurber," he grinned, "for those archaic tunnels touched graveyard and witch-den and seacoast. But whatever it is, they must have run short, for they were devilish anxious to get out. Your yelling stirred them up, I fancy. Better be cautious in these old places—our rodent friends are the one drawback, though I sometimes think they're a positive asset by way of atmosphere and color."

Well, Eliot, that was the end of the night's adventure. Pickman had promised to show me the place, and heaven knows he had done it. He led me out of the tangle of alleys in another direction, it seems, for when we sighted a lamp post we were in a half-familiar street with monotonous rows of mingled tenement blocks and old houses. Charter Street, it turned out to be, but I was too flustered to notice just wherre we hit it. We were too late for the elevated, and walked back downtown through Hanover Street. I remember that walk. We switched from Tremont up Beacon, and Pickman left me at the corner of Joy, where I turned off. I never spoke to him again.

Why did I drop him? Don't be impatient. Wait till I ring for coffee. We've had enough of the other stuff, but I for one need something. No—it wasn't the paintings I saw in that place; though I'll swear they were enough to get him ostracized in nine-tenths of the homes and clubs of Boston, and I guess you won't wonder now why I have to steer clear of subways and cellars. It was—something I found in my coat the next morning. You know, the curled-up paper tacked to that frightful canvas in the cellar; the thing I thought was a photograph of some scene he meant to use as a background for that monster. That last scare had come while I was reaching to uncurl it, and it seems I had vacantly crumpled it into my pocket. But here's the coffee—take it black, Eliot, if you're wise.

Yes, that paper was the reason I dropped Pickman; Richard Upton Pickman, the greatest artist I have ever known—and the foulest being that ever leaped the bounds of life into the pits of myth and madness. Eliot—old Reid was right. He wasn't strictly human. Either he was born in strange shadow, or he'd found a way to unlock the forbidden gate. It's all the same now, for he's gone—back into the fabulous darkness he loved to haunt. Here, let's have the chandelier going.

Don't ask me to explain or even conjecture about what I burned. Don't ask me, either, what lay behind the molelike scrambling Pickman was so keen to pass off as rats. There are secrets, you know, which might have come down from old Salem times, and Cotton Mather tells even stranger things. You know how damned lifelike Pickman's paintings were—how we all wondered where he got those faces.

Well—that paper wasn't a photograph of any background, after all. What it showed was simply the monstrous being he was painting on that awful canvas. It was the model he was using—and its background was merely the wall of the cellar studio in minute detail. But by God, Eliot, *it was a photograph from life.*

MICHIGAN

The Screwfly Solution
by James Tiptree, Jr.

THE YOUNG man sitting at 2°N, 75°W sent a casually venomous glance up at the nonfunctional shoofly *ventilador* and went on reading his letter. He was sweating heavily, stripped to his shorts in the hotbox of what passed for a hotel room in Cuyapán.

> How do other wives *do* it? I stay busy-busy with the Ann Arbor grant review programs and the seminar, saying brightly, 'Oh yes, Alan is in Colombia setting up a biological pest control program, isn't it wonderful?' But inside I imagine you being surrounded by nineteen-year-old raven-haired cooing beauties, every one panting with social dedication and filthy rich. And forty inches of bosom busting out of her delicate lingerie. I even figured it in centimeters, that's 101.6 centimeters of busting. Oh, darling, darling, do what you want only *come home safe*.

Alan grinned fondly, briefly imagining the only body he longed for. His girl, his magic Anne. Then he got up to open the window another cautious notch. A long pale mournful face looked in—a goat. The room opened on the goatpen, the stench was vile. Air, anyway. He picked up the letter.

> Everything is just about as you left it, except that the Peedsville horror seems to be getting worse. They're calling it the Sons of Adam cult now. Why can't they *do* something, even if it is a religion? The Red Cross has set up a refugee camp in Ashton,

289

Georgia. Imagine, refugees in the U.S.A. I heard two little girls
were carried out all slashed up. Oh, Alan.

Which reminds me, Barney came over with a wad of clippings
he wants me to send you. I'm putting them in a separate envelope;
I know what happens to very fat letters in foreign POs. He says, in
case you don't get them, what do the following have in common?
Peedsville, São Paulo, Phoenix, San Diego, Shanghai, New
Delhi, Tripoli, Brisbane, Johannesburg and Lubbock, Texas. He
says the hint is, remember where the Intertropical Convergence
Zone is now. That makes no sense to me, maybe it will to your
superior ecological brain. All I could see about the clippings was
that they were fairly horrible accounts of murders or massacres of
women. The worst was the New Delhi one, about "rafts of female
corpses" in the river. The funniest (!) was the Texas Army Officer
who shot his wife, three daughters and his aunt, because God told
him to clean the place up.

Barney's such an old dear, he's coming over Sunday to help me
take off the downspout and see what's blocking it. He's dancing
on air right now; since you left his spruce bud-worm-moth anti-
pheronome program finally paid off. You know he tested over
2,000 compounds? Well, it seems that good old 2,097 *really*
works. When I asked him what it does he just giggles, you know
how shy he is with women. Anyway, it seems that a one-shot spray
program will save the forests, without harming a single other
thing. Birds and people can eat it all day, he says.

Well sweetheart, that's all the news except Amy goes back to
Chicago to school on Sunday. The place will be a tomb, I'll miss
her frightfully in spite of her being at the stage where I'm her
worst enemy. The sullen sexy subteens, Angie says. Amy sends
love to her Daddy. I send you my whole heart, all that words can't
say.

Your Anne

Alan put the letter safely in his notefile and glanced over the rest of the thin
packet of mail, refusing to let himself dream of home and Anne. Barney's "fat
envelope" wasn't there. He threw himself on the rumpled bed, yanking off
the lightcord a minute before the town generator went off for the night. In the
darkness the list of places Barney had mentioned spread themselves around a
misty globe that turned, troublingly, briefly in his mind. Something . . .

But then the memory of the hideously parasitized children he had worked
with at the clinic that day took possession of his thoughts. He set himself to
considering the data he must collect. *Look for the vulnerable link in the
behavioral chain*—how often Barney—Dr. Barnhard Braithwaite—had
pounded it into his skull. Where was it, where? In the morning he would start
work on bigger canefly cages . . .

At that moment, five thousand miles North, Anne was writing:

Oh, darling, darling, your first three letters are here, they all came together. I *knew* you were writing. Forget what I said about swarthy heiresses, that was all a joke. My darling I know, I know . . . us. Those dreadful canefly larvae, those poor little kids. If you weren't my husband I'd think you were a saint or something. (I do anyway.)

I have your letters pinned up all over the house, makes it a lot less lonely. No real news here except things feel kind of quiet and spooky. Barney and I got the downspout out, it was full of a big rotted hoard of squirrel-nuts. They must have been dropping them down the top. I'll put a wire over it. (Don't worry, I'll use a ladder this time.)

Barney's in an odd, grim mood. He's taking this Sons of Adam thing very seriously, it seems he's going to be on the investigation committee if that ever gets off the ground. The weird part is that nobody seems to be doing anything, as if it's just too big. Selina Peters has been printing some acid comments, like When one man kills his wife you call it murder, but when enough do it we call it a lifestyle. I think it's spreading, but nobody knows because the media have been asked to down-play it. Barney says it's being viewed as a form of contagious hysteria. He insisted I send you this ghastly interview, printed on thin paper. It's *not* going to be published, of course. The quietness is worse, though, it's like something terrible was going on just out of sight. After reading Barney's thing I called up Pauline in San Diego to make sure she was all right. She sounded funny, as if she wasn't saying everything . . . my own sister. Just after she said things were great she suddenly asked if she could come and stay here awhile next month. I said come right away, but she wants to sell her house first. I wish she'd hurry.

Oh, the diesel car is okay now, it just needed its filter changed. I had to go out to Springfield to get one but Eddie installed it for only $2.50. He's going to bankrupt his garage.

In case you didn't guess, those places of Barney's are all about latitude 30°N or S—the horse latitudes. When I said not exactly, he said remember the equatorial convergence zone shifts in winter, and to add in Libya, Osaka, and a place I forget—wait, Alice Springs, Australia. What has this to do with anything? I asked. He said, "Nothing—I hope." I leave it to you, great brains like Barney can be weird.

Oh my dearest, here's all of me to all of you. Your letters make life possible. But don't feel you *have* to, I can tell how tired you must be. Just know we're together, always everywhere.

Your Anne

Oh PS I had to open this to put Barney's thing in, it wasn't the secret police. Here it is. All love again. A.

In the goat-infested room where Alan read this, rain was drumming on the roof. He put the letter to his nose to catch the faint perfume once more, and folded it away. Then he pulled out the yellow flimsy Barney had sent and began to read, frowning.

PEEDSVILLE CULT/SONS OF ADAM SPECIAL. Statement by driver Sgt. Willard Mews, Globe Fork, Ark. We hit the roadblock about 80 miles west of Jacksonville. Major John Heinz of Ashton was expecting us, he gave us an escort of two riot vehicles headed by Capt. T. Parr. Major Heinz appeared shocked to see that the NIH medical team included two women doctors. He warned us in the strongest terms of the danger. So Dr. Patsy Putnam (Urbana, Ill.), the psychologist, decided to stay behind at the Army cordon. But Dr. Elaine Fay (Clinton, N.J.) insisted on going with us, saying she was the epi-something (epidemiologist).

We drove behind one of the riot cars at 30 mph for about an hour without seeing anything unusual. There were two big signs saying "SONS OF ADAM—LIBERATED ZONE." We passed some small pecan packing plants and a citrus processing plant. The men there looked at us but did not do anything unusual. I didn't see any children or women of course. Just outside Peedsville we stopped at a big barrier made of oil drums in front of a large citrus warehouse. This area is old, sort of a shantytown and trailer park. The new part of town with the shopping center and developments is about a mile further on. A warehouse worker with a shotgun came out and told us to wait for the Mayor. I don't think he saw Dr. Elaine Fay then, she was sitting sort of bent down in back.

Mayor Blount drove up in a police cruiser and our chief, Dr. Premack, explained our mission from the Surgeon General. Dr. Premack was very careful not to make any remarks insulting to the Mayor's religion. Mayor Blount agreed to let the party go on into Peedsville to take samples of the soil and water and so on and talk to the doctor who lives there. The mayor was about 6'2", weight maybe 230 or 240, tanned, with grayish hair. He was smiling and chuckling in a friendly manner.

Then he looked inside the car and saw Dr. Elaine Fay and he blew up. He started yelling we had to all get the hell back. But Dr. Premack managed to talk to him and cool him down and finally the Mayor said Dr. Fay should go into the warehouse office and stay there with the door closed. I had to stay there too and see she didn't come out, and one of the Mayor's men would drive the party.

So the medical people and the Mayor and one of the riot vehicles went on into Peedsville and I took Dr. Fay back into the warehouse office and sat down. It was real hot and stuffy. Dr. Fay opened a window, but when I heard her trying to talk to an old man outside I told her she couldn't do that and closed the window. The old man went away. Then she wanted to talk to me but I told her I did not feel like conversing. I felt it was real wrong, her being there.

So then she started looking through the office files and reading papers there. I told her that was a bad idea, she shouldn't do that. She said the government expected her to investigate. She showed me a booklet or magazine they had there, it was called *Man Listens to God* by Reverend McIllhenny. They had a carton full in the office. I started reading it and Dr. Fay said she wanted to wash her hands. So I took her back along a kind of enclosed hallway beside the conveyor to where the toilet was. There were no doors or windows so I went back. After awhile she called out that there was a cot back there, she was going to lie down. I figured that was all right because of the no windows, also I was glad to be rid of her company.

When I got to reading the book it was very intriguing. It was very deep thinking about how man is now on trial with God and if we fulfill our duty God will bless us with a real new life on Earth. The signs and portents show it. It wasn't like, you know, Sunday school stuff. It was deep.

After awhile I heard some music and saw the soldiers from the other riot car were across the street by the gas tanks, sitting in the shade of some trees and kidding with the workers from the plant. One of them was playing a guitar, not electric, just plain. It looked so peaceful.

Then Mayor Blount drove up alone in the cruiser and came in. When he saw I was reading the book he smiled at me sort of fatherly, but he looked tense. He asked me where Dr. Fay was and I told him she was lying down in back. He said that was okay. Then he kind of sighed and went back down the hall, closing the door behind him. I sat and listened to the guitar man, trying to hear what he was singing. I felt really hungry, my lunch was in Dr. Premack's car.

After awhile the door opened and Mayor Blount came back in. He looked terrible, his clothes were messed up and he had bloody scrape marks on his face. He didn't say anything, he just looked at me hard and fierce, like he might have been disoriented. I saw his zipper was open and there was blood on his clothing and also on his (private parts).

I didn't feel frightened, I felt something important had happened. I tried to get him to sit down. But he motioned me to follow him back down the hall, to where Dr. Fay was. "You must see," he said. He went into the toilet and I went into a kind of little room there, where the cot was. The light was fairly good, reflected off the tin roof from where the walls stopped. I saw Dr. Fay lying on the cot in a peaceful appearance. She was lying straight, her clothing was to some extent different but her legs were together. I was glad to see that. Her blouse was pulled up and I saw there was a cut or incision on her abdomen. The blood was coming out there, or it had been coming out there, like a mouth. It wasn't moving at this time. Also her throat was cut open.

I returned to the office. Mayor Blount was sitting down, looking very tired. He had cleaned himself off. He said, "I did it for you. Do you understand?"

He seemed like my father. I can't say it better than that. I realized he was under a terrible strain, he had taken a lot on himself for me. He went on to explain how Dr. Fay was very dangerous, she was what they call a cripto-female (crypto?), the most dangerous kind. He had exposed her and purified the situation. He was very straightforward, I didn't feel confused at all, I knew he had done what was right.

We discussed the book, how man must purify himself and show God a clean world. He said some people raise the question of how can man reproduce without women but such people miss the point. The point is that as long as man depends on the old filthy animal way God won't help him. When man gets rid of his animal part which is woman, this is the signal God is awaiting. Then God will reveal the new true clean way, maybe angels will come bringing new souls, or maybe we will live forever, but it is not our place to speculate, only to obey. He said some men here had seen an Angel of the Lord. This was very deep, it seemed like it echoed inside me, I felt it was an inspiration.

Then the medical party drove up and I told Dr. Premack that Dr. Fay had been taken care of and sent away, and I got in the car to drive them out of the Liberated Zone. However four of the six soldiers from the roadblock refused to leave. Capt. Parr tried to argue them out of it but finally agreed they could stay to guard the oil-drum barrier.

I would have liked to stay too the place was so peaceful but they needed me to drive the car. If I had known there would be all this hassle I never would have done them the favor. I am not crazy and I have not done anything wrong and my lawyer will get me out. That is all I have to say.

In Cuyapán the hot afternoon rain had temporarily ceased. As Alan's fingers let go of Sgt. Willard Mews's wretched document he caught sight of pencil-scrawled words in the margin. Barney's spider hand. He squinted.

Man's religion and metaphysics are the voices of his glands.
Schönweiser, 1878.

Who the devil Schönweiser was Alan didn't know, but he knew what Barney was conveying. This murderous crackpot religion of McWhosis was a symptom, not a cause. Barney believed something was physically affecting the Peedsville men, generating psychosis, and a local religious demagogue had sprung up to "explain" it.

Well, maybe. But cause or effect, Alan thought only of one thing: eight hundred miles from Peedsville to Ann Arbor. Anne should be safe. She *had* to be.

He threw himself on the lumpy cot, his mind going back exultantly to his work. At the cost of a million bites and cane-cuts he was pretty sure he'd found the weak link in the canefly cycle. The male mass-mating behavior, the comparative scarcity of ovulant females. It would be the screwfly solution all over again with the sexes reversed. Concentrate the pheromone, release sterilized females. Luckily the breeding populations were comparatively isolated. In a couple of seasons they ought to have it. Have to let them go on spraying poison meanwhile, of course; damn pity, it was slaughtering everything and getting in the water, and the caneflies had evolved to immunity anyway. But in a couple of seasons, maybe three, they could drop the canefly populations below reproductive viability. No more tormented human bodies with those stinking larvae in the nasal passages and brain. . . . He drifted off for a nap, grinning.

Up north, Anne was biting her lip in shame and pain.

Sweetheart, I shouldn't admit it but your wife is scared a bit jittery. Just female nerves or something, nothing to worry about. Everything is normal up here. It's so eerily normal, nothing in the papers, nothing anywhere except what I hear through Barney and Lillian. But Pauline's phone won't answer out in San Diego; the fifth day some strange man yelled at me and banged the phone down. Maybe she's sold her house—but why wouldn't she call?

Lillian's on some kind of Save-the-Women committee, like we were an endangered species, ha-ha—you know Lillian. It seems the Red Cross has started setting up camps. But she says, after the first rush, only a trickle are coming out of what they call "the affected areas". Not many children, either, even little boys. And they have some air-photos around Lubbock showing what look like mass graves. Oh, Alan . . . so far it seems to be mostly spreading west, but something's happening in St. Louis, they're cut off. So many places seem to have just vanished from the news, I had a nightmare that there isn't a woman left alive down there. And nobody's *doing* anything. They talked about spraying with tranquillizers for awhile and then that died out. What could it do? Somebody at the U.N. has proposed a convention on—you won't believe this—*femicide*. It sounds like a deodorant spray.

Excuse me, honey, I seem to be a little hysterical. George Searles came back from Georgia talking about God's will— Searles the life-long atheist. Alan, something crazy is happening.

But there are no facts. Nothing. The Surgeon General issued a report on the bodies of the Rahway Rip-Breast Team—I guess I didn't tell you about that. Anyway, they could find no pathology. Milton Baines wrote a letter saying in the present state of the art we can't distinguish the brain of a saint from a psychopathic killer, so how could they expect to find what they don't know how to look for?

Well, enough of these jitters. It'll be all over by the time you get back, just history. Everything's fine here, I fixed the car's muffler again. And Amy's coming home for the vacations, *that'll* get my mind off faraway problems.

Oh, something amusing to end with—Angie told me what Barney's enzyme does to the spruce bud-worm. It seems it blocks the male from turning around after he connects with the female, so he mates with her *head* instead. Like clockwork with a cog missing. There're going to be some pretty puzzled female spruceworms. Now why couldn't Barney tell me that? He really is such a sweet shy old dear. He's given me some stuff to put in, as usual. I didn't read it.

Now don't worry my darling everything's fine.

I love you, I love you so.

                                        Always, all ways your Anne

Two weeks later in Cuyapán when Barney's enclosures slid out of the envelope, Alan didn't read them either. He stuffed them into the packet of his bush-jacket with a shaking hand and started bundling his notes together on the rickety table, with a scrawled note to Sister Dominique on top. *Anne, Anne my darling*. The hell with the canefly, the hell with everything except that tremor in his fearless girl's firm handwriting. The hell with being five thousand miles away from his woman, his child, while some deadly madness raged. He crammed his meager belongings into his duffel. If he hurried he could catch the bus through to Bogotá and maybe make the Miami flight.

In Miami he found the planes north jammed. He failed a quick standby; six hours to wait. Time to call Anne. When the call got through some difficulty he was unprepared for, the rush of joy and relief that burst along the wires.

"Thank God—I can't believe it—Oh, Alan, my darling, are you really—I can't believe—"

He found he was repeating too, and all mixed up with the canefly data. They were both laughing hysterically when he finally hung up.

Six hours. He settled in a frayed plastic chair opposite *Aerolineas Argentinas*, his mind half back at the clinic, half on the throngs moving by him. Something was oddly different here, he perceived presently. Where was the decorative fauna he usually enjoyed in Miami, the parade of young girls in crotch-tight pastel jeans? The flounces, boots, wild hats and hairdos and startling expanses of newly-tanned skin, the brilliant fabrics barely confining the bob of breasts and buttocks? Not here—but wait; looking closely, he glimpsed two young faces hidden under unbecoming parkas, their bodies draped in bulky nondescript skirts. In fact, all down the long vista he could see the same thing: hooded ponchos, heaped-on clothes and baggy pants, dull colors. A new style? No, he thought not. It seemed to him their movements suggested furtiveness, timidity. And they moved in groups. He watched a lone girl struggle to catch up with others ahead of her, apparently strangers. They accepted her wordlessly.

They're frightened, he thought. Afraid of attracting notice. Even that gray-haired matron in a pantsuit resolutely leading a flock of kids was glancing around nervously.

And at the Argentine desk opposite he saw another odd thing: two lines had a big sign over them, *Mujeres*. Women. They were crowded with the shapeless forms and very quiet.

The men seemd to be behaving normally; hurrying, lounging, griping and joking in the lines as they kicked their luggage along. But Alan felt an undercurrent of tension, like an irritant in the air. Outside the line of storefronts behind him a few isolated men seemed to be handing out tracts. An airport attendant spoke to the nearest man; he merely shrugged and moved a few doors down.

To distract himself Alan picked up a *Miami Herald* from the next seat. It was surprisingly thin. The international news occupied him for awhile; he had seen none for weeks. It too had a strange empty quality, even the bad news seemed to have dried up. The African war which had been going on seemed to be over, or went unreported. A trade summit-meeting was haggling over grain and steel prices. He found himself at the obituary pages, columns of close-set type dominated by the photo of an unknown defunct ex-senator. Then his eye fell on two announcements at the bottom of the page. One was too flowery for quick comprehension, but the other stated in bold plain type:

THE FORSETTE FUNERAL HOME REGRETFULLY ANNOUNCES
IT WILL NO LONGER ACCEPT FEMALE CADAVERS

Slowly he folded the paper, staring at it numbly. On the back was an item headed *Navigational Hazard Warning*, in the shipping news. Without really taking it in, he read:

AP/Nassau: The excursion liner *Carib Swallow* reached port under tow today after striking an obstruction in the Gulf Stream off Cape Hatteras. The obstruction was identified as part of a commercial trawler's seine floated by female corpses. This confirms reports from Florida and the Gulf of the use of such seines, some of them over a mile in length. Similar reports coming from the Pacific coast and as far away as Japan indicate a growing hazard to coastwise shipping.

Alan flung the thing into the trash receptacle and sat rubbing his forehead and eyes. Thank God he had followed his impulse to come home. He felt totally disoriented, as though he had landed by error on another planet. Four and a half hours more to wait. . . . At length he recalled the stuff from Barney he had thrust in his pocket, and pulled it out and smoothed it.

The top item, however, seemed to be from Anne, or at least the Ann Arbor News. Dr. Lillian Dash, together with several hundred other members of her organization, had been arrested for demonstrating without a permit in front of the White House. They seemed to have started a fire in an oil drum, which was considered particularly heinous. A number of women's groups had participated, the total struck Alan as more like thousands than hundreds. Extraordinary security precautions were being taken, despite the fact that the President was out of town at the time.

The next item had to be Barney's, if Alan could recognize the old man's acerbic humor.

UP/Vatican City   19 June. Pope John IV today intimated that he does not plan to comment officially on the so-called Pauline Purification cults advocating the elimination of women as a means of justifying man to God. A spokesman emphasized that the Church takes no position on these cults but repudiates any doctrine involving a "challenge" to or from God to reveal His further plans for man.

Cardinal Fazzoli, spokesman for the European Pauline movement, reaffirmed his view that the Scriptures define woman as merely a temporary companion and instrument of Man. Women, he states, are nowhere defined as human, but merely as a transitional expedient or state. "The time of transition to full humanity is at hand," he concluded.

The next item appeared to be a thin-paper Xerox from a recent issue of *Science*:

SUMMARY REPORT OF THE AD HOC EMERGENCY COMMITTEE
ON FEMICIDE
The recent world-wide though localized outbreaks of femicide appear to represent a recurrence of similar outbreaks by some

group or sect which are not uncommon in world history in times of psychic stress. In this case the root cause is undoubtedly the speed of social and technological change, augmented by population pressure, and the spread and scope are aggravated by instantaneous world communications, thus exposing more susceptible persons. It is not viewed as a medical or epidemiological problem; no physical pathology has been found. Rather it is more akin to the various manias which swept Europe in the 17th century, e.g., the Dancing Manias, and like them, should run its course and disappear. The chiliastic cults which have sprung up around the affected areas appear to be unrelated, having in common only the idea that a new means of human reproduction will be revealed as a result of the "purifying" elimination of women.

We recommend that (1) inflammatory and sensational reporting be suspended; (2) refugee centers be set up and maintained for women escapees from the focal areas; (3) containment of affected areas by military cordon be continued and enforced; and (4) after a cooling-down period and the subsidence of the mania, qualified mental health teams and appropriate professional personnel to go in to undertake rehabilitation.

SUMMARY OF THE MINORITY REPORT OF THE AD HOC COMMITTEE

The nine members signing this report agree that there is no evidence for epidemiological contagion of femicide in the strict sense. *However*, the geographical relation of the focal areas of outbreak strongly suggest that they cannot be dismissed as purely psychosocial phenomena. The initial outbreaks have occurred around the globe near the 30th parallel, the area of principal atmospheric downflow of upper winds coming from the Intertropical Convergence Zone. An agent or condition in the upper equatorial atmosphere would thus be expected to reach ground level along the 30th parallel, with certain seasonal variations. One principal variation is that the downflow moves north over the East Asian continent during the late winter months, and these areas south of it (Arabia, Western India, parts of North Africa) have in fact been free of outbreaks until recently, when the downflow zone has moved south. A similar downflow occurs in the Southern Hemisphere, and outbreaks have been reported along the 30th parallel running through Pretoria and Alice Springs, Australia. (Information from Argentina is currently unavailable.)

This geographical correlation cannot be dismissed, and it is therefore urged that an intensified search for a physical cause be instituted. It is also urgently recommended that the rate of

spread from known focal points be correlated with wind conditions. A watch for similar outbreaks along the secondary
down-welling zones at 60° north and south should be kept.

(signed for the minority)
Barnhard Braithwaite

Alan grinned reminiscently at his old friend's name, which seemed to
restore normalcy and stability to the world. It looked as if Barney was onto
something, too, despite the prevalence of horses' asses. He frowned,
puzzling it out.

Then his face slowly changed as he thought how it would be, going home
to Anne. In a few short hours his arms would be around her, the tall, secretly
beautiful body that had come to obsess him. Theirs had been a late-bloom-
ing love. They'd married, he supposed now, out of friendship, even out of
friends' pressure. Everyone said they were made for each other, he big and
chunky and blond, she willowy brunette; both shy, highly controlled,
cerebral types. For the first few years the friendship had held, but sex hadn't
been all that much. Conventional necessity. Politely reassuring each other,
privately—he could say it now—disappointing.

But then, when Amy was a toddler, something had happened. A
miraculous inner portal of sensuality had slowly opened to them, a liberation
into their own secret unsuspected heaven of fully physical bliss. . . . Jesus,
but it had been a wrench when the Colombia thing had come up. Only their
absolute sureness of each other had made him take it. And now, to be about
to have her again, trebly desirable from the spice of separation—feeling-
seeing-hearing-smelling-grasping. He shifted in his seat to conceal his body's
excitement, half mesmerized by fantasy.

And Amy would be there, too; he grinned at the memory of that
prepubescent little body plastered against him. She was going to be a
handful, all right. His manhood understood Amy a lot better than her
mother did; no cerebral phase for Amy. . . . But Anne, his exquisite shy one,
with whom he'd found the way into the almost unendurable transports of the
flesh. . . . First the conventional greeting, he thought; the news, the
unspoken, savored, mounting excitement behind their eyes; the light
touches; then the seeking of their own room, the falling clothes, the
caresses, gentle at first—the flesh, the *nakedness*— the delicate teasing, the
grasp, the first thrust—

—A terrible alarm-bell went off in his head. Exploded from his dream, he
stared around, then finally down at his hands. *What was he doing with his
open clasp-knife in his fist?*

Stunned, he felt for the last shreds of his fantasy, and realized that the
tactile images had not been of caresses, but of a frail neck strangling in his
fist, the thrust had been the Plunge of a blade seeking vitals. In his arms,
legs, phantasms of striking and trampling bones cracking. And Amy—

Oh God, Oh God—

Not sex, bloodlust.

That was what he had been dreaming. The sex was there, but it was driving some engine of death.

Numbly he put the knife away, thinking only over and over, it's got me. It's got me. Whatever it is, it's got me. *I can't go home.*

After an unknown time he got up and made his way to the United counter to turn in his ticket. The line was long. As he waited, his mind cleared a little. What could he do, here in Miami? Wouldn't it be better to get back to Ann Arbor and turn himself in to Barney? Barney could help him, if anyone could. Yes, that was best. But first he had to warn Anne.

The connection took even longer this time. When Anne finally answered he found himself blurting unintelligibly, it took awhile to make her understand he wasn't talking about a plane delay.

"I tell you, I've caught it. Listen, Anne, for God's sake. If I should come to the house don't let me come near you. I mean it. I mean it. I'm going to the lab, but I might lose control and try to get to you. Is Barney there?"

"Yes, but darling—"

"Listen. Maybe he can fix me, maybe this'll wear off. But I'm not safe, Anne, Anne, I'd kill you, can you understand? Get a—get a weapon. I'll try not to come to the house. But if I do, don't let me get near you. Or Amy. It's a sickness, it's real. Treat me—treat me like a fucking wild animal. Anne, say you understand, say you'll do it."

They were both crying when he hung up.

He went shaking back to sit and wait. After a time his head seemed to clear a little more. *Doctor, try to think.* The first thing he thought of was to take the loathesome knife and throw it down a trash-slot. As he did so he realized there was one more piece of Barney's material in his pocket. He uncrumpled it; it seemed to be a clipping from *Nature.*

At the top was Barney's scrawl: "Only guy making sense. U.K. infected now, Oslo, Copenhagen out of communication. Damfools still won't listen. Stay put."

COMMUNICATION FROM PROFESSOR IAN MACINTYRE,
GLASGOW UNIV.

A potential difficulty for our species has always been implicit in the close linkage between the behavioural expression of aggression/predation and sexual reproduction in the male. This close linkage involves (a) many of the same neuromuscular pathways which are utilized both in predatory and sexual pursuit, grasping, mounting, etc., and (b) similar states of adrenergic arousal which are activated in both. The same linkage is seen in the males of many other species; in some, the expression of aggression and copulation alternate or even coexist, an all-too-familiar example being the common house cat. Males of many species bite, claw, bruise, tread or otherwise assault receptive females during the act of intercourse; indeed, in some species the male attack is necessary for female ovulation to occur.

In many if not all species it is the aggressive behaviour which appears first, and then changes to copulatory behaviour when the appropriate signal is presented (*e.g.* the three-tined stickleback and the European robin). Lacking the inhibiting signal, the male's fighting response continues and the female is attacked or driven off.

It seems therefore appropriate to speculate that the present crisis might be caused by some substance, perhaps at the viral, or enzymatic level, which effects a failure of the switching or triggering function in the higher primates. (Note: Zoo gorillas and chimpanzees have recently been observed to attack or destroy their mates; rhesus not.) Such a dysfunction could be expressed by the failure of mating behaviour to modify or supervene over the aggressive/predatory response; *i.e.*, sexual stimulation would produce attack only, the stimulation discharging itself through the destruction of the stimulating object.

In this connection it might be noted that exactly this condition is a commonplace of male functional pathology, in those cases where murder occurs as a response to and apparent completion of, sexual desire.

It should be emphasized that the aggression/copulation linkage discussed here in specific to the male; the female response (*e.g.*, lordotic reflex) being of a different nature.

Alan sat holding the crumpled sheet a long time; the dry, stilted Scottish phrases seemed to help clear his head, despite the sense of brooding tension all around him. Well, if pollution or whatever had produced some substance, it could presumably be countered, filtered, neutralized. Very very carefully, he let himself consider his life with Anne, his sexuality. Yes; much of their loveplay could be viewed as genitalized, sexually-gentled savagery. Play-predation. . . . He turned his mind quickly away. Some writer's phrase occurred to him: "The panic element in all sex." Who? Fritz Leiber? The violation of social distance, maybe; another threatening element. Whatever, it's our weak link, he thought. Our vulnerability. . . . The dreadful feeling of *rightness* he had experienced when he found himself knife in hand, fantasizing violence, came back to him. As though it was the right, the only way. Was that what Barney's budworms felt when they met with their females wrong-end-to?

At long length, he became aware of body need and sought a toilet. The place was empty, except for what he took to be a heap of clothes blocking the door of the far stall. Then he saw the red-brown pool in which it lay, and the bluish mounds of bare, thin buttocks. He backed out, not breathing, and fled into the nearest crowd, knowing he was not the first to have done so.

Of course. Any sexual drive. Boys, men, too.

At the next washroom he watched to see men enter and leave normally before he ventured in.

Afterward he returned to sit, waiting, repeating over and over to himself: *Go to the lab.* Don't go home. Go straight to the lab. Three more hours; he sat numbly at 26° N, 81° W, breathing, breathing . . .

Dear diary, Big scene tonite, Daddy came home!!! Only he acted so funny, he had the taxi wait and just held onto the doorway, he wouldn't touch me or let us come near him. (I mean funny weird, not funny Ha-ha). He said, I have something to tell you, this is getting worse not better. I'm going to sleep in the lab but I want you to get out, Anne, Anne, I can't trust myself any more. First thing in the morning you both get on the plane for Martha's and stay there. So I thought he had to be joking. I mean with the dance next week and Aunt Martha lives in Whitehorse where there's nothing nothing nothing. So I was yelling and Mother was yelling and Daddy was groaning. Go now! And then he started crying. Crying!!! So I realized, wow, this is serious, and I started to go over to him but Mother yanked me back and then I saw she had this big KNIFE!!! And she shoved me in back of her and started crying too Oh Alan, Oh Alan, like she was insane. So I said, Daddy, I'll never leave you, it felt like the perfect thing to say. And it was thrilling, he looked at me real sad and deep like I was a grown-up while Mother was treating me like I was a mere infant as usual. But Mother ruined it raving Alan the child is mad, darling go. So he ran out the door yelling Be gone, Take the car, Get out before I come back.

Oh I forgot to say I was wearing what but my gooby green with my curltites still on, wouldn't you know of all the shitty luck, how could I have known such a beautiful scene was ahead we never know life's cruel whimsy. And Mother is dragging out suitcases yelling Pack your things hurry! So she's going I guess but I am not repeat not going to spend the fall sitting in Aunt Martha's grain silo and lose the dance and all my summer credits. And Daddy was trying to communicate with us, right? I think their relationship is obsolete. So when she goes upstairs I am splitting. I am going to go over to the lab and see Daddy.

Oh PS Diane tore my yellow jeans she promised me I could use her pink ones Ha-ha that'll be the day.

I ripped that page out of Amy's diary when I heard the squad car coming. I never opened her diary before but when I found she'd gone I looked . . . Oh, my darling little girl. She went to him, my little girl, my poor little fool child. Maybe if I'd taken time to explain, maybe—

Excuse me, Barney. The stuff is wearing off, the shots they gave me. I didn't feel anything. I mean, I knew somebody's daughter went to see her father and he killed her. And cut his throat. But it didn't mean anything.

Alan's note, they gave me that but then they took it away. Why did they have to do that? His last handwriting, the last words he wrote before his hand picked up the, before he—

I remember it. "*Sudden and light as that, the bonds gave And we learned of finalities besides the grave. The bonds of our humanity have given, we are finished, I love—*"

I'm all right, Barney, really. Who wrote that, Robert Frost? *The bonds gave.* . . . Oh, he said, tell Barney: *The terrible rightness.* What does that mean?

You can't answer that, Barney dear. I'm just writing this to stay sane, I'll put it in your hidey-hole. Thank you, thank you Barney dear. Even as blurry as I was, I knew it was you. All the time you were cutting off my hair and rubbing dirt on my face, I knew it was right because it was you. Barney I never thought of you as those horrible words you said. You were always Dear Barney.

By the time the stuff wore off I had done everything you said, the gas, the groceries. Now I'm here in your cabin. With those clothes you made me put on I guess I do look like a boy, the gas man called me "Mister."

I still can't really realize, I have to stop myself from rushing back. But you saved my life, I know that. The first trip in I got a paper, I saw where they bombed the Apostle Islands refuge. And it had about those three women stealing the Air Force plane and bombing Dallas, too. Of course they shot them down, over the Gulf. Isn't it strange how we do nothing? Just get killed by ones and twos. Or more, now they've started on the refuges. . . . Like hypnotized rabbits. We're a toothless race.

Do you know I never said "we" meaning women before? "We" was always me and Alan, and Amy of course. Being killed selectively encourages group identification. . . . You see how sane-headed I am.

But I still can't really realize.

My first trip in was for salt and kerosene. I went to that little Red Deer store and got my stuff from the old man in the back, as you told me—you see, I remembered! He called me "Boy," but I think maybe he suspects. He knows I'm staying at your cabin.

Anyway, some men and boys came in the front. They were all so *normal*, laughing and kidding. I just couldn't believe, Barney. In fact I started to go out past them when I heard one of them say "Heinz saw an angel." An *angel*. So I stopped and listened. They said it was big and sparkly. Coming to see if man is carrying out

God's will, one of them said. And he said, Moosenee is now a Liberated Zone, and all up by Hudson Bay. I turned and got out the back, fast. The old man had heard them too. He said to me quietly, I'll miss the kids.

Hudson Bay, Barney, that means it's coming from the north too, doesn't it? That must be about 60°.

But I have to go back once again, to get some fishhooks. I can't live on bread. Last week I found a deer some poacher had killed, just the head and legs. I made a stew. It was a doe. Her eyes; I wonder if mine look like that now.

I went to get the fishhooks today. It was bad, I can't ever go back. There were some men in front again, but they were different. Mean and tense. No boys. And there was a new sign out in front, I couldn't see it; maybe it says Liberated Zone too.

The old man gave me the hooks quick and whispered to me, "Boy, them woods'll be full of hunters next week." I almost ran out.

About a mile down the road a blue pickup started to chase me. I guess he wasn't from around there, I ran the VW into a logging draw and he roared on by. After a long while I drove out and came on back, but I left the car about a mile from here and hiked in. It's surprising how hard it is to pile enough brush to hide a yellow VW.

Barney, I can't stay here. I'm eating perch raw so nobody will see my smoke, but those hunters will be coming through. I'm going to move my sleeping bag out to the swamp by that big rock, I don't think many people go there.

Since the last lines I moved out. It feels safer. Oh, Barney, how did this *happen*?

Fast, that's how. Six months ago I was Dr. Anne Alstein. Now I'm a widow and bereaved mother, dirty and hungry, squatting in a swamp in mortal fear. Funny if I'm the last woman left alive on Earth. I guess the last one around here, anyway. Maybe some holed out in the Himalayas, or sneaking through the wreck of New York City. How can we last?

We can't.

And I can't survive the winter here, Barney. It gets to 40° below. I'd have to have a fire, they'd see the smoke. Even if I worked my way south, the woods end in a couple hundred miles. I'd be potted like a duck. No. No use. Maybe somebody is trying something somewhere, but it won't reach here in time . . . and what do I have to live for?

No. I'll just make a good end, say up on that rock where I can see the stars. After I go back and leave this for you. I'll wait to see the beautiful color in the trees one last time.

I know what I'll scratch for an epitaph.

HERE LIES THE SECOND MEANEST PRIMATE ON EARTH

Good-bye, dearest dearest Barney.

I guess nobody will ever read this, unless I get the nerve and energy to take it to Barney's. Probably I won't. Leave it in a Baggie, I have one here; maybe Barney will come and look. I'm up on the big rock now. The moon is going to rise soon, I'll do it then. Mosquitoes, be patient. You'll have all you want.

The thing I have to write down is that I saw an angel too. This morning. It was big and sparkly, like the man said; like a Christmas tree without the tree. But I knew it was real because the frogs stopped croaking and two bluejays gave alarm calls. That's important; it was *really there*.

I watched it, sitting under my rock. It didn't move much. It sort of bent over and picked up something, leaves or twigs, I couldn't see. Then it did something with them around its middle, like putting them into an invisible sample-pocket.

Let me repeat—it was *there*. Barney, if you're reading this, THERE ARE THINGS HERE. And I think they've done whatever it is to us. Made us kill ourselves off.

Why? Well, it's a nice place, if it wasn't for people. How do you get rid of people? Bombs, death-rays—all very primitive. Leave a big mess. Destroy everything, craters, radioactivity, ruin the place.

This way there's no muss, no fuss. Just like what we did to the screwfly. Pinpoint the weak link, wait a bit while we do it for them. Only a few bones around; make good fertilizer.

Barney dear, good-bye. I saw it. It was there.

But it wasn't an angel.

I think I saw a real-estate agent.

MINNESOTA

The Unpleasantness at Carver House
by Carl Jacobi

AT THE junction of Highway 7 and County Road 16 the motor coughed and died and the car coasted to a halt. For several minutes I ground on the starter, vainly fiddled with the ignition key. But it was evident that the crash had caused more damage to the motor than I had supposed. I said to my sister,

"I'll carry you the rest of the way. I can have the car picked up in the morning."

I lifted her in my arms, climbed a wire fence with some difficulty and set off across the fields, walking briskly over the uneven ground, gradually slowing down as her dead weight made itself felt. In the full moonlight the summer countryside stretched beyond me like a smoke-edged quilt. Rolling hills and lush farmland made a blue patchwork of light and darker shadow. Even with the numbing pain at the back of my head, the intermittent dizziness, and the dull hypnosis of shock from the accident, I couldn't help but be aware of the beauty of the night.

"You'll feel better," I said, "when you're in your bed and had a cup of strong tea."

A quarter of an hour later I topped a last hill in the treeless meadow and came within view of Carver House. It stood there below me, a white box-like rectangle with tall windows refracting the moonlight, a crumbling brick wall enclosing the grounds dotted with life-size statuary. Carver House, the only home I had known for thirty years.

I carried my sister up to her room, second floor back, helped her onto the bed and put a blanket over her, for although the month was August, the night air carried a perceptible chill. I bathed her face with warm water and left a carafe and a glass on the night table.

"If you want anything, call me," I told her, "I'll brew some tea later."

Then I went into the bathroom and looked at my face in the mirror. It was a study in horror, the flesh ashen grey, streaked with dirt and caked with blood. I couldn't see the wound at the back of my head but touching it sent a sharp pain through my skull and a feeling of nausea in the pit of my stomach. I applied a mild disinfectant and bandaged it as well as I could and then, somewhat unsteadily, went down stairs to the study. Five minutes later steps sounded outside and someone knocked at the door.

It was Sheriff Barson, an insufferable busybody who, since his election, I barely tolerated. Barson was a small stubby man whose mild appearing features belied his physical strength and endurance. He was smoking a cigar.

"A bit late for you, isn't it?" I said. "I hope this isn't a duty call."

"Yes, it is," he said in his nasal voice, dropping unasked into a chair. "How come you left the scene of an accident without reporting it?"

"Because it wasn't an accident. Not in the exact sense of the word anyway. I ran into the side of a train, not into another car. No one was hurt, and the only damage was to my machine."

"You don't look it," Sheriff Barson said, glancing at my head bandages.

"Oh, I did get a little rap on the head. It's nothing."

"The engineer reported seeing a woman in your car . . ."

"My sister. Her injuries are superficial, too."

The sheriff relit his cigar, carefully dropped the burnt match in an ash tray. His watery eyes roved the room, returned meditatively to me. "About insurance . . ."

"There won't be enough damage to put in a claim," I said irritably. In my present mood I was anxious to be alone.

Barson nodded and got to his feet. "Just the same I think I'll tell Doc Evans to stop by. You never can tell about these car accidents."

"You'll do nothing of the sort!" I snapped. "If I need a doctor, I'm still able to use a telephone."

He shrugged, went out the door and got into his station wagon. I watched him drive away, then went back upstairs to my sister.

"The sheriff was here. I told the old butinsky we didn't want a doctor."

She lay there, a slight figure, prematurely grey for her forty years, with prominent cheek bones and wide set eyes. The shock of the accident was still upon her and, never a garrulous person anyway, she lacked the strength to reply.

In the morning I called the garage in Victoria and made arrangements to have my car picked up and repaired. After such a brilliant night, it was a somber melancholy day. Wind-driven rain pelted the windows and the wrought iron gate of Oak Ridge Cemetery directly across the road was barely discernible through the mist. But at intervals the rain would let up, and then I could see the scant few tombstones and beyond them, diminishing to the vanishing point, the tracks of the M. N. and S. railroad, tracks which had caused such a controversy in recent weeks. For it was the cemetery's close proximity to trackage that had made it suddenly industrially desirable, whereas other adjacent land in either direction was fit for plant erection only at considerable expense. A group of men in Chaska, the county seat, wanted to sell the land to a tax-reduction-seeking concern in Minneapolis. I was definitely against such a sale. In the first place I didn't want a factory that close to my house. Some of the burial plots dated back almost a hundred years and of these reburial in new grounds would be of course impossible.

Standing before the window, I realized that I had come to like the view of that rusting gate and the irregular rows of monuments. There was something homely macabre about it that was in harmony with Carver House and grounds. Carver House had been built before the turn of the century, a faithful example of Americanized Victorian architecture with gingerbread scrollwork and railings and a box-like facade. The last owner before I had taken over had been a stonecutter by trade, and he had left examples of his work scattered about the grounds. There was a large fountain (with no water connection) the basin of which was supported by three stone cupids, one of them so crudely carved the face seemed to be of an old man. Similar grotesque images flanked either side of the land that led from the road to the house. A statue of a Civil War soldier stood in silent contemplation at each corner of the property. And there were several stone benches scattered about. In the past there had been times when I had looked upon these carvings with an acute depression of spirit, but now I couldn't understand how I ever had such a feeling. Even with the numbing pain at the back of my head I felt strangely at ease with the world.

Shortly after noon I took a book of poems from the study up to my sister's room and read to her for an hour. Though she didn't say so, I think she preferred *Thanatopsis* to the other verses. Then I was called downstairs by the garage man, returning my car. I paid him and drove him as far as the highway where he could pick up a bus back to Victoria.

On the way back to Carver House I saw that there was another new grave in the cemetery. That made three in the last month, more than there had been in the last ten years. With the gloom of the day I thought of Grey's *Elegy*, with the wind sighing through the wet cedars in lieu of "the lowing of cattle." Overhead a hundred sheen-black starlings perched motionless on the telegraph wires. As I turned up the lane, it occurred to me that if I could return my sister to the scene of the accident and demonstrate to her how simple carelessness on my part had been responsible for the crash some of the shock which still clung to her would be dissipated. When the proposal was made she hesitated, then somewhat doubtfully consented. Accordingly I helped her into a lightweight coat and out to the car. "The best way to end a feeling like yours," I told her, "is to nip it in the bud. Lou Gregory over in Eureka didn't drive for a month after he had his accident, and now he's mortally afraid to get into a car. Even if you don't drive, I don't want that to happen to you."

Though I had said nothing about it, the wound at the back of my head was giving me some concern. A pulse was noticeable in it and the surrounding area was hot and feverish. Moreover, for some time my eyes had been affected. There was a strangeness about the look of everything now. Somehow I got the impression I was seeing through a cube of mirrors.

We reached the crossing, and it was a site of commonplace reality in the daylight. I stopped the car and went into a detailed explanation of how the crash had occurred: how this was a secondary road and therefore no automatic signal was necessary; how the long curve of trackage was treelined and partially hidden from sight; how no trains normally were expected at that hour; how this had been a "fast special" thundering past the crossing almost before I was aware it. My words seemed to quiet her and I felt with satisfaction that the trip had been well worthwhile.

I swung into the Victoria cut-off and headed back for Carver House, cruising along slowly so that no touch of nervousness would return to my sister. On either side the wind rippled the grain fields like waves of water and overhead ragged clouds raced across the sky, at intervals casting great shadows like a giant camera shutter. The black-top road, marked at intervals by dripping red cedars, seemed unfamiliar, and gradually I sensed something was wrong. This wasn't Victoria cut-off! In some way I must have taken the wrong turn; and yet I knew these roads like the palm of my hand. In exasperation I stopped the car abreast of a small boy who was tripping down the shoulder and called out to him:

"Does this road go to . . . ?"

The boy advanced to the door of the car and peered in at me. Before I could finish my query his mouth went slack, his eyes widened and a look of terror entered his eyes. For perhaps a minute he stood there staring, his knuckles white as he gripped the car door. A step at a time he backed away toward the shoulder, then with a little cry he turned and ran. I watched him until he disappeared at a bend of the road, then with a sigh I started the car again.

"Stupid kid! What do you suppose ailed him?"

The road Y'd into two lanes and with some hesitation I swung into the left fork. Presently I was on familiar ground again. But I had gone twenty miles out of the way.

The rain had stopped by the time we reached Carver House. As we passed Oak Ridge Cemetery I thought I saw three men standing, talking, amid the tombstones. The Chaska men or perhaps the men from the industrial plant in Minneapolis came to make a last survey before converting it into a factory site. Anger rose within me. How could they justify selling the grounds when they were still being used for burial? The flower-strewn mounds of the three new graves were visible through the trees. Something about them aroused in me a feeling of possession as if I were the owner of the property and not a mere close-by resident.

That night I again read to my sister, this time exerpts from Lodge's *Raymond*, but the book seemed dull and it was evident that she was little

interested. In the study the titles of no other book attracted me. Around ten
o'clock I glanced out the window and I saw a light, apparently an electric
lantern, bobbing in and out among the trees of the cemetery. Curious, I
watched it. Several times it winked out, only to reappear with an uncertain
source like St. Elmo's fire. Yet I never doubted but that it was a lantern,
diffused by the wetness. On impulse I put on my hat and coat and headed
down the lane. But the light had disappeared when I pushed open the
lockless gate and there was only the glow of the night sky. Nevertheless I
continued to move through the long grass between the neglected markers.
There was no sign of anyone, however, and I stopped before one of the
graves—so new that one of the digger's loam-encrusted spades lay beside it.
As I stood there, the cloying sweetness of the dying flowers heaped on the
mound rose and entered my nostrils like perfumed smoke. Simultaneously
the dizziness, which had been affecting me at intervals since the accident,
suddenly came again, leaving me to sway off balance. Blackness entered my
vision and I felt myself falling. . . .

Over breakfast next morning I welcomed the three men and told them
Carver House was at their disposal. For the life of me I couldn't remember
recovering from my fainting spell and inviting them to spend the night at my
home. But they were here; that was all that was important. The three were
neatly dressed in dark suits, white shirts and conservative ties.

"Have another cup of tea, gentlemen," I said. My sister sat at one end of
the table, I at the other. From the music room there drifted a record-player
orchestration of the overture to *Semiramide*, one of my favorite selections.
"You're welcome to stay here as long as you like. When you're through, I'll
take you out and show you the grounds."

To get necessary supplies I drove that afternoon the twenty miles to
Chaska. I had no qualms about leaving my sister alone with the three
strangers; she was capable of taking care of herself, and besides the men
appeared to be perfect gentlemen. However I was none too sure they were
representatives of the Minneapolis factory. Something about them discounted that. It may have been their almost studied correctness. Today
there's a dash, a certain casualness about the business man on location that
these men somehow lacked.

In Chaska I purchased groceries, pipe tobacco, some aluminum-bound
weather stripping, and in the drug store I asked for a bottle of formaldehyde.

"Sorry, we don't stock it," the druggist said. "What're you going to use it
for?"

"I'm experimenting with a new kind of plastic."

"Well, I can order you some. Have it here in a couple of days."

"Do that," I said, "I'll drop by Thursday and pick it up."

Arriving back home I saw that the three men were in their room and
apparently had given no thought to leaving. In a way this both irritated and
pleased me. Irritated, because the fact remained that they still were

strangers and thus were imposing on their welcome; pleased, because they provided an interlude in the loneliness that had been mine during my later years at Carver House. Of course my sister had shared that loneliness, but she was a reserved person, able to keep her emotions inside. Sometimes days would pass on end without our speaking a word to each other.

I got a hammer and some brads and proceeded to weather-strip the doors of the rooms on the second floor. It was none too soon. We were getting into autumn and cold weather would be upon us any day now.

Just before dusk the sheriff's car drove up the road but did not turn in my lane. Instead he stopped before the cemetery gate and he and two men got out and stood there talking. One of the men turned and pointed toward Carver House. Then they moved into the graveyard. As I watched them through the bay window I recognized the two as Barson's deputies.

"There's been more activity in that cemetery in the past week than there has been in the last ten years," I said to myself. "I wonder what's up?"

I turned from the window. If the wound at the back of my head didn't improve I would be forced to see a physician whether I wanted to or not. Spells of dizziness were with me now almost constantly, becoming progressively more severe as the night hours approached. The simplest every-day scene from time to time took on a quality of strangeness as if viewed through a series of lenses that were out of alignment.

But my faulty vision did not prevent me from reading aloud to my sister. For almost twenty years I have followed this nightly custom. Tonight I selected *The Dark Elements of Survival*, a book that was macabre in subject, dealing with eighteenth-century sorcery in some of its ugliest forms. I found it absorbing. My sister, however, made no comment and it was not difficult to see that it was not her cup of tea.

About ten o'clock Sheriff Barson knocked on the door. He made no mention of his visit to the cemetery earlier in the evening but entered my study carelessly, smoking a strong, odorous cigar.

"How's your sister?" he asked, gazing at me through wreaths of smoke.

"She's much better, thank you," I said. "But she's still suffering a little from shock."

"You really should call in a doctor. Shock can be dangerous."

"My experience with doctors has been that you're better off without them," I said slowly. "Not that I'm a fanatic, you understand. But I know my sister's nervous temperament and her aversion to medical men. She'll be all right in a day or so."

Barson began to walk idly about the room, stopping at intervals to scrutinize the water colors and etchings on the walls. These pictures represented some of my youthful ambitions of twenty years ago; when I was sure I was going to be an artist. The remorseless enemy of all ambition— time—had stolen so much of my energy. Before one of the etchings Barson halted.

"Some of these are good," he said. "I may be only a country sheriff but my daughter has been studying art and . . . well, some of it is bound to wash off. This is a newer one, isn't it?"

That etching was now one of my favorites. It showed the wrought-iron gate of Oak Ridge Cemetery as viewed across the road from the grounds of Carver House. I prided myself that I had caught the atmosphere of the scene with the high grass turned to weeds and the neglected monuments in the background.

"Yes," I said. "The others are years old, but that one I did only a day or so ago."

Barson passed on to another picture and then headed for the door.

"Tell me," he said, "have you seen two or three men about the cemetery lately?"

"Yes," I said, "I have. Probably the men from the Minneapolis factory."

He looked at me curiously. "Factory? What factory?"

"Why the one they want to build on the cemetery property. You must have heard all the talk and argument . . ."

He licked the side of his cigar, the wrapper of which was beginning to loosen. "I've been out of town for three weeks. Why would anyone want to build a factory way out here?"

"To be close to railroad trackage and escape high taxes," I said. Barson was a shrewd one all right. Pretending ignorance of the entire controversy was no doubt his method of gaining my vote in the forthcoming election. About to leave, he suddenly stepped past me and returned to the etching of the cemetery gate.

"How long did it take you to do this?" he said.

"Not long. The better part of a day I suppose. Why?"

He shrugged and this time prepared to leave. "You should install air conditioning," he said thoughtfully. "These old houses always smell moldy in wet weather."

I watched him as he walked across the gravel driveway and climbed into his station wagon. A moment later, gunning the motor needlessly, he drove off.

I slept restlessly that night. About two in the morning I got up, put on slippers and a robe, and moved across to the window. The storm clouds had left. Full moonlight spread a dusky radiance over the countryside. The rolling hills stretched beyond the Carver House grounds, diffused into an uncertain horizon. The old stone fountain and, farther on, the image of the Civil War soldier were a study in black and grey. All was silent save for the occasional far-off whistle of a night train. Trains did not often go by Carver House; trackage there was a spur line, connecting with Victoria, the main line running two or three miles to the north. As usual I turned my gaze from my own property to the cemetery across the road. But a moment later, looking directly down again, an alertness seized me.

The door to the house was opened and four shadowy figures emerged. Three of them gave me little concern; if the three stangers were inclined to go on another nocturnal stroll it was little business of mine. But what was my sister doing in that strange company? Watching, I saw her link arms with two of the three men and then they moved out into the moonlit grounds with the lightness of ballet dancers. To the eastern end of the property they walked, their faces marked in shadow, their arms swinging in rhythm. Reaching the garden wall, they turned like automatons and retraced their steps to the western wall. And this was the horror of it—their movements were without motivation like the aimlessness of four congenital idiots. Back and forth they paced; suddenly they swung and moved the length of the lane, across the road to the cemetery gate. There they paused motionless.

At that moment it struck me what an effective picture the scene would make. Even though I was greatly disturbed by the unexplained presence of my sister, I turned from the window and, fumbling in the table drawer, got out my 35MM Orlando camera and telescopic lens and its table-top tripod. It was loaded with a fairly fast film. Working with haste, I set up the camera and focused it while the four figures remained where they were like models waiting for me. Then I took picture after picture until they disappeared from sight, moving behind a copse of trees in the cemetery. They did not reappear, and quitting my watchpost, I went downstairs with some concern and let myself out into the grounds.

But there was no sign of my sister or the men; in a highly disturbed state I returned to the house again. There, opening her bedroom door, I saw to my relief that she was sleeping peacefully; in the guest room, also asleep, were the three strangers. Apparently all had returned unobserved while I was still in the grounds.

Next day, having completed the *Survival* book, I was prompted to ransack my library in search of similar volumes. Many of the books had been handed down from one owner of Carver House to another. There were several treatises on stone carving by my predecessor. There were a number of books on witchcraft which I couldn't see how I had overlooked and a number of works which had been banned and thus were very rare. These included an expurgated edition of Richard Verstegan's *Restitution of Decayed Intelligence*. By far the two that interested me the most, however, were a chemical handbook on preservatives, which would be of value to my experiments with plastics and the treatise on transposition of life and survival.

As I have explained, although retired for some years from day by day employment I have a number of interests that occupy my time, some of them financially profitable. There was my work in plastics, my translations from Latin and German of medical papers, and more recently the growing of mushrooms and vegetable seedlings in the expansive rooms beneath Carver House.

It was to inspect and care for my mushrooms that I went down to the south cellar. Presently I was bent over one of the aluminum frames, carefully breaking clods of dirt. The feeling of the cool earth soothed me and I thought it pleasant and restful in the half darkness. The south cellar had been used as a storeroom by the former owner of Carver House; pieces of his unfinished carvings littered an area of perhaps ten feet wide along the far wall. The man had been a desultory worker, starting one image, urn or ornament before he had completed another. Mallets and chisels, the tools of his trade, lay entangled in cobwebs on a table by the staircase door.

Suddenly I looked up, startled to see that I wasn't alone. A figure had descended the stairs and now was moving in the deep shadows away from the small cones of daylight that filtered through the ceiling-high window slits. Like a figure on an Egyptian frieze it edged sideways, head and shoulders pressed against the wall, face turned at right angles from me. For a fleeting second I thought it was my sister.

"Is there something wrong?" I said. "Did you want me?"

But it wasn't my sister. In the gloom I caught a gleam of what I thought was one of the heavy chisels and for an instant it seemed it was about to be thrown as a weapon. Then outside clouds momentarily parted, permitting rays of sunlight to probe downward. The light showed me how strained my nerves had become the last few days. For there was no one there, merely the crude carving of a winged angel, a cemetery monument, standing on a wooden box and thus life size several feet above the other discarded carvings.

This trick of my vision or of my fancy disturbed me considerably and, a hypochondriac at best, I fell to worrying about my health. To calm myself, to get a grip on my nerves I gave a small dinner party that night—in the music room which was more convenient than the dining room on the main floor. The three guests were in good spirits as they sat about the table. Earlier, acting as a group, they had proposed lengthening their stay at Carver House and had offered me a tidy sum for the privilege. The payment of course I refused. Also they had revealed their identity; as I had suspected, they had nothing to do with the Minneapolis factory, but were three salesmen from the East who had met, become acquainted, and accompanied one of their number to the cemetery where he had visited the grave of a relative.

For the first time I learned their names: Caldwell, Hokanson, and Eilers. Though I had never met them previously, I seemed to recall seeing their names in print somewhere. They liked Carver House, they said, they liked the rolling farm land, and they liked the grounds about the house and what they called "the artistic statuary" there. Yet my suspicions were not entirely abated. Salesmen from the East they might be, but their speech was pure Midwest.

Of the three, Caldwell, the oldest, had an incisive face that was a colorless grey and his lips were continually parted, revealing bad teeth. The other two were comparatively young, in their early forties. They too were not outdoorsmen; that is to say they lacked the flush of the wind on their cheeks and the sparkle of health in their eyes. I asked about their residence in the East. But they were chary of the subject or perhaps not interested, and conversation about the table lapsed into silence.

The next day being Thursday I drove to Chaska to pick up the formaldehyde I had ordered, though the chemical was no longer needed, the new plastic upon which I had been working having "jellied" without it. On the way home I stopped at the furniture store to exchange a few words with Lehman Krupp, who doubled as one of the town's two morticians. Krupp was a stoic who would do little more than answer my questions. Yes he knew a family named Caldwell. They lived on a farm over toward Waconia. Hi Caldwell had had a launch on Clear Water Lake. But if I were interested in the boat I wouldn't be able to get it for some time.

"His estate has to go through probate first," Krupp said.

Of the other two names I mentioned, he suggested I see his competitor.

I drove home in a blue mood, dissatisfied with my retirement and envious of the man I had just visited. He had a well-patronized store, he was respected in the town, and he had a nice secondary business which he took care of in a room back of the store. I had wanted to see that back room but Krupp was too unfriendly for me to broach the subject.

For the past eight hours the pain in my head had been completely absent, but now as I headed home on 41, it suddenly returned, increased in intensity, impairing my vision. I got the impression that I was not driving my station wagon but a team of plumed black horses. It was an odd fancy, partially remembered from my childhood. Also, when I looked at the grain fields on either side of the road they seemed to be staggered, one over another, like broad tilted steps.

A sense of anxiety accompanied my troubled vision and I returned to Carver House, tense and ill-at-ease. No longer was it a sanctuary of rest and quiet; instead it seemed to be a place toward which black events, as yet unknown, were moving. Seeking companionship, I went upstairs to the room of my sister, but she was sleeping and I closed the door again without awakening her. I went into the music room and put on the record-player the scherzo from *Midsummer Night's Dream*. The music only increased the nervousness within me. I went downstairs to the study and sought to calm myself with a book. But the printed lines staggered before my eyes. Nevertheless I did manage to reread several sections—one could hardly call them chapters—of the *Survival* book. One passage I went over several times:

> And Falon went forth from the land of milk and honey until he came to a vast battlefield where all were dead or dying. And birds of carrion soared and circled overhead and a moldering stench took sweep with the yellow wind and poisoned the air. Their armor rusted with blood, their eyes glazed. Time, the invincible, the relentless, moved among them, already counting them dust of the past.
>
> But Falon was strong and not to be defeated. He went among the fallen of his regiment and drew from the charnal piles those

who had been his friends and companions. He drew the three interlocking triangles in the earth and within each triangle placed the number seven and gathered about the whole circle. Then he intoned *Invicta! . . . Invicta!* and other magic syllables and behold! his friends and companions breathed again and Falon had won an interlude and for the nonce was content.

I understood this well enough and sought to put the procedure into practice. But the feeling of impending doom became more intense and I could feel my heart accelerate and my hands begin to tremble. What a strange creature man is, I thought, to create terrors and set them upon himself. I got a piece of chalk and removed the spread from the Chippendale table, exposing its dull unpolished surface. Then I turned to the engraved diagrams of the survival book. The diagrams were not complete and I added to them from the text of *Restitution of Decayed Intelligence*. But information there was not complete either, and I rushed through the yellowed pages with frantic haste, a great fear that I would find what I wanted sweeping over me.

Evening came with my task still unfinished. The main floor of the house grew hot and sultry and through the window dark evil-looking clouds became visible, building up in the southwest. At intervals lightning flared across the sky.

In the music room the three men from the East still sat about the table. I had given each a very fine imported Rose Trofero cigar. They were discussing various aspects of psychic phenomena, and one of them, Caldwell, appeared to have considerably more than a layman's information on the subject. But he was embarrassed by my presence and spoke so softly his voice was almost inaudible. I returned to the main floor. And then to my utter disgust Sheriff Barson chose that time to pay another call.

He came in stern-faced and apparently disturbed and at once began asking foolish questions about the Oak Ridge Cemetery. Again he wanted to know whether I had seen anyone loitering there.

"No, I haven't," I said somewhat testily. "I've other things to attend to."

"How's your sister?" he said then. "Is she able to be up and about?"

"Of course she is? Necroya has completely recovered."

He looked up. "I thought her name was Helen."

"It is," I said. "But I call her Necroya on occasion. It's a nickname."

He sat there, smoking, looking down at the chalked symbols on the table-top. Damned butinsky, I thought. What did he want anyway?

Suddenly he rose to his feet. "You won't have any objection if I take a look." Turning he strode across the room and almost ran up the stairs. I was up in a flash, seeking to stop him. "Wait!" I yelled. "Wait!"

But he outran me. At the top of the stairs I saw him pace down the corridor and enter my sister's room. He was in there perhaps a minute. When he reappeared his face was ashen and his mouth open, hanging slack.

He blundered across the corridor and whipped open the door to the music room. Almost immediately he came out again, clutching a handkerchief to his nostrils.

"How could you," he said. "Good God, how could you?"

He went past me down the stairs, and I heard him pick up the phone. "This is Barson, I'm at Carver House," he said moments later. "Send the car . . . no, send two cars. There are four of them here. Yes, that's right, four."

He hung up and turned to me as I entered the study. "You need a doctor, not these," he said closing handcuffs about my wrists. "But, by heaven, I'm taking no chances!"

MISSISSIPPI

Mute Milton
by Harry Harrison

WITH PONDEROUS smoothness the big Greyhound bus braked to a stop at the platform, and the door swung open. "Springville," the driver called out, "Last stop!" The passengers stirred in the aisle and climbed down the steps into the glare of the sun. Sam Morrison sat patiently, alone, on the wide rear seat, waiting until the last passengers were at the door before he put the cigar box under his arm, rose and followed them. The glare of sunlight blinded him after the tinted glass dimness of the bus, and the moist air held the breathless heat of Mississippi summer. Sam went carefully down the steps, one at a time, watching his feet, and wasn't aware of the man waiting there until something hard pushed at his stomach.

"What business yuh got in Springville, boy?"

Sam blinked through his steel-rimmed glasses at the big man in the grey uniform who stood before him, prodding him with a short, thick nightstick. He was fat as well as big, and the smooth melon of his stomach bulged out over his belt worn low about his hips.

"Just passing through, sir," Sam Morrison said and took his hat off with his free hand disclosing his cut-short grizzled hair. He let his glance slide across the flushed reddened face and the gold badge on the shirt before him, then lowered his eyes.

"An' just where yuh going to, boy? Don' keep no secrets from me . . . ," the voice rasped again.

"Carteret, sir, my bus leaves in an hour."

The only answer was an uncommunicative grunt. The lead weighted stick tapped on the cigar box under Sam's arm. "What yuh got in there—a gun?"

"No, sir, I wouldn't carry a gun." Sam opened the cigar box and held it

319

out: it contained a lump of metal, a number of small electronic components and a two-inch speaker, all neatly wired and soldered together. "It's a . . . a radio, sir."

"Turn it on."

Sam threw a switch and made one or two careful adjustments. The little speaker rattled, and there was the squeak of tinny music barely audible above the rumble of bus motors. The red-faced man laughed.

"Now that's what ah call a real nigger radio . . . piece uh trash." His voice hardened again. "See that you're on that bus, okay?"

"Yes, sir," Sam said to the retreating, sweat-stained back of the shirt, then carefully closed the box. He started towards the colored waiting room, but when he passed the window and looked in, he saw that it was empty. And there were no dark faces visible anywhere on the street. Without changing pace Sam passed the waiting room and threaded his way between the buses in the cinder parking lot and out of the rear gate. He had lived all of his sixty-seven years in the State of Mississippi; so he knew at once that there was trouble in the air—and the only thing to do about trouble was to stay away from it. The streets became narrower and dirtier, and he trod their familiar sidewalks until he saw a field worker in patched overalls turn into a doorway ahead under the weathered BAR sign. Sam went in after him; he would wait here until a few minutes before the bus was due.

"Bottle of Jax, please." He spread his coins on the damp, scratched bar and picked up the cold bottle. There was no glass. The bartender said nothing. After ringing up the sale he retired to a chair at the far end of the bar with his head next to the murmuring radio and remained there, dark and impenetrable. The only light came from the street outside, and the high-backed booths in the rear looked cool and inviting. There were only a few other customers here, each of them sitting separately with a bottle of beer on the table before him. Sam threaded his way through the close-spaced tables and had already started to slide into the booth near the rear door when he noticed that someone was already there, seated on the other side of the table.

"I'm sorry, I didn't see you," he said and started to get up, but the man waved him back onto the bench and took an airline bag with TWA on it from the table and put it down beside him.

"Plenty of room for both," he said and raised his own bottle of beer. "Here's looking at you." Sam took a sip from his own bottle, but the other man kept drinking until he had drained half of his before he lowered it with a relaxed sigh. "That's what I call foul beer," he said.

"You seem to be enjoying it," Sam told him, but his slight smile took the edge from his words.

"Just because it's cold and wet—but I'd trade a case of it for a bottle of Bud or a Ballantine."

"Then you're from the North, I imagine?" Sam had thought so from the way he talked, sharp and clipped. Now that his eyes were getting used to the dimness, he could see that the other was a young man in his twenties with medium-dark skin, wearing a white shirt with rolled up sleeves. His face was taut and the frown wrinkles on his forehead seemed etched there.

"You are damned right. I'm from the North and I'm going back . . ." He broke off suddenly and took another swig of beer. When he spoke again his voice was cautious.

"Are you from these parts?"

"I was born not far from here, but right now I live in Carteret, just stopping off here between buses."

"Carteret—that's where the college is, isn't it?"

"That is correct. I teach there."

The younger man smiled for the first time. "That sort of puts us in the same boat; I go to NYU, majoring in economics." He put his hand out. "Charles Wright. Everyone but my mother calls me Charlie."

"Very pleased to meet you," Sam said in his slow, old-fashioned way. "I am Sam Morrison, and it is Sam on my birth certificate too."

"I'm interested in your college; I meant to step in there but . . ." He broke off suddenly at the sound of a car's engine in the street outside and leaned forward so that he could see out the front door, remaining there until the car ground into gear and moved away. When he dropped back onto the seat, Sam could see that there were fine beads of sweat in the lines of his forehead. He took a quick drink from his bottle.

"When you were at the bus station, you didn't happen to see a big cop with a big gut, red face all the time?"

"Yes, I met him; he talked to me when I got off the bus."

"The bastard!"

"Don't get worked up, Charles; he is just a policeman doing his job."

"Just a . . . !" The young man spat a short, filthy word. "That's Brinkley; you must have heard of him, toughest man south of Bombingham. He's going to be elected sheriff next fall, and he's already grand knight of the Klan, a real pillar of the community."

"Talking like that's not going to do you any good," Sam said mildly.

"That's what Uncle Tom said—and as I remember he was still a slave when he died. Someone has got to speak up; you can't remain quiet forever."

"You talk like one of those freedom riders." Sam tried to look stern, but he was never very good at it.

"Well, I am, if you want to know the truth of it, but the ride ends right here. I'm going home. I'm scared and I'm not afraid to admit it. You people live in a jungle down here; I never realized how bad it could be until I came down. I've been working on the voter's committee, and Brinkley got word of it and swore he was going to kill me or put me in jail for life. And you know what—I believe it. I'm leaving today, just waiting for the car to pick me up. I'm going back North where I belong."

"I understand you have your problems up there too . . ."

"Problems!" Charlie finished his beer and stood up. "I wouldn't even call them problems after what I've seen down here. It's no paradise in New York—but you stand a chance of living a bit longer. Where I grew up in South Jamaica we had it rough, but we had our own house in a good neighborhood and—you take another beer?"

"No, one is enough for me, thank you."

Charlie came back with a fresh beer and picked up where he had left off. "Maybe we're second-class citizens in the North—but at least we're citizens of some kind and can get some measure of happiness and fulfillment. Down here a man is a beast of burden, and that's all he is ever going to be—if he has the wrong color skin."

"I wouldn't say that; things get better all the time. My father was a field hand, a son of a slave—and I'm a college teacher. That's progress of a sort."

"What sort?" Charlie pounded the table yet kept his voice in an angry whisper. "So one hundredth of one percent of the Negroes get a little education and pass it on at some backwater college. Look, I'm not running you down; I know you do your best. But for every man like you there must be a thousand who are born and live and die in filthy poverty, year after year, without hope. Millions of people. Is that progress? And even yourself—are you sure you wouldn't be doing better if you were teaching in a decent university?"

"Not me," Sam laughed. "I'm just an ordinary teacher and I have enough trouble getting geometry and algebra across to my students without trying to explain topology or Boolean algebra or anything like that."

"What on earth is that Bool . . . thing? I never heard of it."

"It's, well, an uninterpreted logical calculus, a special discipline. I warned you; I'm not very good at explaining these things, though I can work them out well enough on paper. That is my hobby, really, what some people call higher mathematics, and I know that if I were working at a big school I would have no time to devote to it."

"How do you know? Maybe they would have one of those big computers—wouldn't that help you?"

"Perhaps, of course, but I've worked out ways of getting around the need for one. It just takes a little more time, that's all."

"And how much time do you have left?" Charlie asked quietly, then was instantly sorry he had said it when he saw the older man lower his head without answering. "I take that back. I've got a big mouth. I'm sorry, but I get so angry. How do you know what you might have done if you had the training, the facilities . . . ?" He shut up, realizing he was getting in deeper every second.

There was only the murmur of distant traffic in the hot, dark silence, the faint sound of music from the radio behind the bar. The bartender stood, switched the radio off and opened the trap behind the bar to bring up another case of beer. From nearby the sound of the music continued like a remembered echo. Charlie realized that it was coming from the cigar box on the table before them.

"Do you have a radio in that?" he asked, happy to change the subject.

"Yes—well, really no, though there is an RF stage."

"If you think you're making sense—you're not. I told you, I'm majoring in economics."

Sam smiled and opened the box, pointing to the precisely wired circuits inside. "My nephew made this; he has a little I-fix-it shop, but he learned a lot about electronics in the Air Force. I brought him the equations, and we worked out the circuit together."

Charlie thought about a man with electronic training who was forced to run a handyman's shop, but he had the sense not to mention it. "Just what is it supposed to do?"

"It's not really supposed to do anything. I just built it to see if my equations would work out in practice. I suppose you don't know much about Einstein's unified field theory . . . ?" Charlie smiled ruefully and raised his hands in surrender. "It's difficult to talk about. Putting it the simplest way, there is supposed to be a relation between all phenomena, all forms of energy and matter. You are acquainted with the simpler interchanges, heat energy to mechanical energy as in an engine, electrical energy to light . . ."

"The light bulb!"

"Correct. To go further, the postulation has been made that time is related to light energy, as is gravity to electrical energy. That is the field I have been exploring. I have made certain suppositions that there is an interchange of energy within a gravitic field, a measurable interchange, such as the lines of force that are revealed about a magnetic field by iron particles—no, that's not a good simile—perhaps the ability of a wire to carry a current endlessly under the chilled condition of super conductivity—"

"Professor, you have lost me. I'm not ashamed to admit it. Could you maybe give me an example—like what is happening in this little radio here?"

Sam made a careful adjustment, and the music gained the tiniest amount of volume. "It's not the radio part that is interesting—that stage really just demonstrates that I have detected the leakage—no, we should call it the differential between the earth's gravitic field and that of the lead there in the corner of the box."

"Where is the battery?"

Sam smiled proudly. "*That* is the point—there is no battery. The input current is derived . . ."

"Do you mean you are running the radio off *gravity*? Getting electricity for nothing?"

"Yes . . . really, I should say no. It is not like that . . ."

"It sure looks like that?" Charlie was excited now, crouching half across the table so he could look into the cigar box. "I may not know anything about electronics, but in economics we learn a lot about power sources. Couldn't this gadget of yours be developed to generate electricity at little or no cost?"

"No, not at once. This is just a first attempt . . ."

"But it *could* eventually and that means—"

Sam thought that the young man had suddenly become sick. His face, just inches away, became shades lighter as the blood drained from it. His eyes were staring in horror as he slowly dropped back and down into his seat. Before Sam could ask him what was the matter a grating voice bellowed through the room.

"Anyone here seen a boy by the name of Charlie Wright? C'mon now, speak up. Ain't no one gonna get hurt for tellin' me the truth."

"Holy Jesus . . ." Charlie whispered, sinking deeper in the seat. Brinkley stamped into the bar, hand resting on his gun butt, squinting around in the darkness. No one answered him.

"Anybody try to hide him gonna be in trouble!" he shouted angrily. "I'm gonna find that black granny dodger!"

He started toward the rear of the room, and Charlie, with his airline bag in one hand, vaulted the back of the booth and crashed against the rear door.

"Come back here, you son of a bitch!"

The table rocked when Charlie's flying heel caught it and the cigar box slid to the floor. Heavy boots thundered. The door squealed open and Charlie pushed out through it. Sam bent over to retrieve the box.

"I'll kill yuh, so help me!"

The circuit hadn't been damaged. Sam sighed in relief and stood, the tinny music between his fingers.

He may have heard the first shot, but he could not have heard the second because the .38 slug caught him in the back of the head and killed him instantly. He crumpled to the floor.

Patrolman Marger ran in from the patrol car outside, his gun ready, and saw Brinkley come back into the room through the door in the rear.

"He got away, damn it, got clear away."

"What happened here?" Marger asked, slipping his gun back into the holster and looking down at the slight, crumpled body at his feet.

"I dunno. He must have jumped up in the way when I let fly at the other one what was running away. Must be another one of them commonists anyway; he was sittin' at the same table."

"There's gonna be trouble about this . . ."

"Why trouble?" Brinkley asked indignantly. "It's just anutha ol' dead nigger . . ."

One of his boots was on the cigar box, and it crumpled and fractured when he turned away.

MISSOURI

Dumb Supper
by Henderson Starke

("WHY SHUCKS, everybody *knows* black is the color of death. If you see something black coming at you in your dreams, you may just as well give up, 'cause you ain't long for *this* world.")

Rosalynn twisted in her chair and picked at a bit of lint on her wool skirt as she looked at the speaker.

("You should have seen the dress Nellie bought over in Joplin; the *cutest* thing.")

Rosalynn extended her legs and looked down at them.

("They sat it cost fifty dollars. My!")

Rosalynn hooked her toe under the rocker of the chair before her and set it in motion.

"Oh! Don't do that, dear," Marsha said. "A chair that's empty rocked, its owner will with ills be stocked."

Rosalynn looked up. "I'm sorry," she said.

("Of course it may be a little too low for her, you know. She doesn't have the *figure*.")

Jean Towers came over and sat down by Rosalynn. "Don't mind Marsha. She's just superstitious."

"I didn't mind," Rosalynn said.

"I guess you think we're unfriendly?"

"No," said Rosalynn.

("And they say they're gonna get married next month. And about time, too, if you ask me.")

"I don't think you're unfriendly. I'll just need a little time to get to know you, and then I'll be all right."

("Well, I certainly wish Jude would hurry up and ask me.")

"Amy told me your family just moved in last week."

"Yes," Rosalynn said. "From California. Fresno."

"What do you think of Carthage?"

"Oh," Rosalynn said, "it's—I mean, I think I'll like it. I mean, I'm *sure* I'll like it."

"Sure you will."

"It's just that now—at first, I mean—everybody is talking about people I don't know and places I—"

("And me too!" someone said, and it sent some of the girls off into peals of laughter.)

Jean Towers smiled sympathetically. "You'll get caught up in the swing of things."

"Uh-huh. Ah—could you tell me—" But Jean Towers had left her side.

("And I said to him, 'If you think for a minute that—'")

Rosalynn picked at the lint again. This was a new town and this was her first party and she wanted—oh, so very bad—to make a good impression: or they maybe wouldn't ask her again. And it was really her place, she knew, to be friendly.

("You girls better have a dumb supper.")

"What would you think of a dumb supper, Rosalynn?" Jean Towers asked.

Rosalynn said, "A dumb supper? Why—I guess, I mean—sure: if you girls want to. I think I'd like something like that."

"Do you have dumb suppers, ever, where you come from?" Amy asked. Rosalynn said, "It's a game, isn't it?"

"Not exactly—well, I guess you might say it was a game, too: sort of."

"Then I guess we have something like it back in Fresno," Rosalynn said and laughed. For the first time she was included in the general conversation and she was happy. "Why don't you tell me just what it is and then I'll tell you if we had anything like it."

"Well," Jean Towers said, "it's a kind of a legend. Nobody believes in it any more. Except some of the peckerwood people back in the hills. And maybe one or two of the old timers, like Uncle Alvin down on the river bottom." She made a deprecating little gesture. "'Course there *are* stories . . . ."

"Maybe you ought to tell her the one Grandma Wilson's always telling."

"I don't know—well— Would you like to listen to it, Rosalynn?"

Rosalynn said, "Yes."

"It all happened in the Rush family. (They're—the Rushes, that is—they're all over this section now; there's a lot of them around Pierce City, and the Roberts of Webb City are first cousins—but this was a long time ago, maybe a hundred years, when they'd just moved in from Kentucky.) There was a girl in the family, young, name of Sarah. A pretty little thing, friendly, the way Grandma Wilson tells it."

Rosalynn stared down at her shoe tops, wishing she were pretty, trying to believe what her mother told her, 'It's not what you look like, honey, that's important; it's the kind of a person you are,' and remembering, too, how she looked to herself in the mirror, wondering where she could find a husband for a face like that.

Jean Towers said: "One night at a party—a party like this, I imagine, when the old people were gone—somebody suggested that they have a dumb supper; just like you do suggest things, half joking, half serious: that way. Sarah thought it was a good idea (they used to do things like that back in Kentucky), and she wasn't afraid at all."

Sarah had been a friendly girl; Rosalynn wondered how people got to be that way; how they learned to say the right things and do the right things and make people like them.

"Of course, you understand, a dumb supper isn't really a *supper*. It's just a halfway supper. Nobody eats anything—and there isn't anything to eat, except two little pieces of corn bread."

Rosalynn wondered why she always was half frightened by people; why she had to screw her courage down tight even to come to a party like this. She really wanted to like people and have them like her. And after all, everyone here was friendly—and they'd wanted her to come: or Amy wouldn't have asked her. They were nice enough, too, a little different from the girls back home, but nice in their way, and she'd stop feeling like an outsider in a little while.

"Well, Sarah began to fix for the dumb supper. Now, fixing for a dumb supper has to be done in a special way."

At first Rosalynn thought they had resented her—maybe because her clothes were nicer than theirs, or maybe because her father had a better job than their fathers, or maybe because she lived in the big house out on South Main, or maybe because she didn't have an accent like they had and talked faster. But now, with them gathered around her, listening, she saw that they really didn't hate her and it had only been in her imagination all along.

"Everything has to be done *backwards*. Everything, like mixing the batter, striking the match, even walking. Everything opposite from usual."

Maybe she was afraid of people because she thought they all wanted to hurt her. (In her second year of high school: She could still remember burningly what she had heard her best friend say.) Her father had explained it all: "You see, people aren't really as bad as you think; they may be thoughtless, but they're very seldom cruel— Most people aren't like your friend Betty. They'd rather be friendly than unfriendly, if you'll only give them the chance."

"Sarah cooked her corn bread, doing everything backwards, the way it's supposed to be done. And then she set out the plates. Two of them. One for herself and one for her husband."

Rosalynn was going to be a different girl. She was going to make all kinds of new friends (like Jean and Amy and Marsha—the superstitious one). And she would have the best times talking to them, and parties at her big house—and maybe dates (for she wasn't *that* ugly: only she always seemed to scare the few boys off because she was so timid: but it would be different this time). Then maybe—

"You see, if you do everything just right, according to the story, at least, when you set down at your plate with the backward corn bread on it, your husband will come in (not *really*, I mean, but like a ghost) and set down at *his* plate so you can see his face and that way you get to find out who your husband is going to be."

"Oh," said Rosalynn, resolving to listen more carefully, for if she wanted to make friends, she must remember not to feel sorry for herself, but to be very polite and listen very closely whether or not she was interested.

"At each plate Sarah put down a knife. (They had funny knives in those days with bone handles: and the one she put at her husband's plate had a big, star-shaped chip knocked off of it.)

"By this time the wind was coming up in the North (as it always does at a dumb supper), and you could hear it moan in the trees. It was very quiet in the house, for you mustn't talk—not anyone—at a dumb supper.

"Sarah put a piece of corn bread on each plate and then she sat down, as calm as anything, to wait.

"Everybody was holding their breath, and you could hear the wind blowing louder and louder."

Rosalynn shivered; she really didn't want to hear the rest of the story.

"And then—bang!—the front door flew open and slammed back against the wall, hard, making the house shake. And the wind blew in and made the candles flicker. (This was long ago, before electricity.)

"And just as the candles went out, a figure all in white came rushing in to set down beside Sarah."

Jean Towers paused, and Rosalynn could hear her own heart beating in the stillness.

"When the candle was lit again, the figure was gone. And the knife that had lain by its plate was gone too."

"Is—is that all?" Rosalynn asked.

"No. No, that's just the first part. You see, she really got to see its face. (Or so she said.)"

"Well, sometime after that, maybe a year or two, a stranger came to town; name was Hall. Young man, handsome, good worker, although a quiet sort, not given to talking too much. When Sarah saw him, she knew that was the man who was going to be her husband, for his face was the face of the figure in white.

"She married him and they went to live in a little cabin on her father's property.

"Things went along fine for a year, for he was a good farmer and a sober, loving husband. But one day—

"Well, her father went down to see them, and when he got up to the top of the ridge (the cabin was down in a valley, like), he could see that there wasn't any sign of smoke in the chimney; which wasn't right, for it was a chilly autumn day. The cabin was still, as if there wasn't anyone around. (You know, sometimes you can tell when you see a house that there isn't anybody at home.) Well, he knew immediately that there was something wrong. So he hurried down.

"And what do you think he found in the cabin? . . . Sarah. Lying on the floor. She was lying there with her eyes closed and a knife sticking out between her breasts.

"She wasn't dead, though (but it was just a lucky thing that her father came along when he did or she would have been). And she didn't die, either. But it was quite a while before she could get up and around (the doctors didn't know as much in those days).

"Finally, she told everybody what had happened.

"That morning, when her father found her lying there in the cabin almost dead, she had told her husband (for the first time) about how she had seen his face there at the dumb supper.

"At first he didn't say anything at all—just sort of stared at her. Then he got up and went to a little box he always kept—he wore the key around his neck and wouldn't let anyone see what was in it—and opened it. He took out a knife that was there on a velvet cushion.

"And he turned back to Sarah."

"'So you're the witch that sent me through that night of hell!' he screamed, and then he plunged the knife into her.

"It was the knife with the star-shaped chip out of the bone handle."

"And she never saw her husband again."

Rosalynn swallowed. "That—that was—awful," she said.

Marsha laughed thinly.

"You mean that you actually still have dumb suppers?" Rosalynn asked.

"Well," Jean Towers said, "not very often. Oh, maybe once in a while. I mean there's nothing *in* it. Though some of the peckerwoods would say it was witchcraft. Just for a laugh, you know. We don't *believe* it. But it does give you a funny, creepy feeling."

"I think we ought to have one," Amy said. "Then Rosalynn can see—the kind of games we play."

"Yes, let's."

"Let's even let Rosalynn cook it."

"How about it, Rosalynn?"

Rosalynn said: "All right, I mean, if you want to. But let somebody else cook it, why not? I—I'm afraid I never learned how to cook—not even corn bread."

"If *that's* all. We can show you how that's done."

"Well," Rosalynn said slowly, "I'll do it if somebody will too." She turned to Marsha. "You?"

"I wouldn't do it for the *world*," Marsha said.

"Be still!" Jean told her. And then to Rosalynn: "She doesn't believe anything would happen of course. She—she just doesn't believe in taking chances. All of us here have cooked dumb suppers before."

"Yes," said Marsha. "We have."

"Well, how about you Amy?"

"Me? It's—more fun if only one person cooks the supper."

"Oh.... I mean, I guess, if you really *want* me to, of course...." Rosalynn realized vaguely that it was probably just an ordinary prank they were in on: trying to scare her. Maybe like an initiation stunt. And if she wanted them to be her friends she'd have to go through with it. And not show that she was scared.

"All right," she said, "I'll do it."

Before, it seemed a million times, Rosalynn had wished she wasn't so easy to frighten; even when she was little the parents had to stay in the room until she was asleep; and now and then, still, she would turn on the light at night (which took all her courage) just to be sure nothing was there.

She told herself something that usually worked; she told herself: 'They will all be laughing about it next week, and then I can tell them how scared I was and they won't mind at all.'

She looked at the wall clock.

There was no help there. Mr. and Mrs. Pierce, Amy's parents, wouldn't get back from Carthage until midnight.

The house was a farm house; four miles out of town. And Rosalynn had no way to leave, even if she wanted to, for she was depending on the Pierces to take her home when they came back.

"Come on," Jean said.

They went into the kitchen where Amy got the proper ingredients: there were three little cups of them, already set out; Rosalynn knew, then, that they had prepared for this.

"Flour," Amy said, pointing. "Corn meal. Baking powder." She drew a glass of water from the tap. "Mix the stuff all together and add the water until it's doughy."

"Salt?" Rosalynn asked.

"I thought you said you didn't know how to make corn bread."

"I—I don't: I just thought it ought to have salt in it—I mean, most things ought to have salt in them."

"Not *this* corn bread, Rosalynn. There isn't supposed to be any salt in *it*."

"Oh! I—see."

"Now. How would you mix these things together?"

"I'd—I'd put the baking powder and the corn meal in the flour and—shake them up, I guess. And then I'd add the water."

"Good. Now listen: Put the flour, the corn meal and the baking powder in the water. Then stir them up. Backwards, you see. And if you usually stir clockwise, be sure to stir counter clockwise this time. And walk backwards.

And strike the match for the oven away from you if you usually strike it towards you. Everything backwards."

"All right, I will, Amy. Don't worry."

Amy went on explaining all the details and Rosalynn listened, trying to remember, trying to play the game, so they would ask her to parties all the time.

It was only a silly superstition, and, contemplating the whole thing in the brightly lit kitchen of a farm house, she began to decide it was really nothing to be afraid of . . . Just a silly, childish prank, that's all.

"You're ready, then?"

"Yes, I guess so."

"All right, now. Remember this: no matter what happens: don't talk. None of us can talk. That's the *most* important thing of all. None of us can talk until it's all over."

"I won't say a word," Rosalynn said.

"Okay. Then you're ready?"

"Yes . . . Only first—I mean, I know it sounds silly, but look—You don't really believe anything's going to happen—I mean, my husband come, or anything like that?"

Amy looked levelly at her; she paused a moment before answering.

"No," she said.

"No more talking," Jean Towers said.

And there was silence.

Rosalynn did everything the way she had been told; everything, that is, but about striking the match. She always struck the match toward herself; and this time, in the spirit of a little girl crossing her fingers before telling one of the little fibs little girls tell, she struck the match in the usual way.

After the corn bread was in the oven, she walked backwards into the living room and sat down to wait for the ten minutes before it came time to set the table.

The other girls, silently as ghosts, had arranged themselves around the room; their eyes were upon her and she felt uncomfortable—like the first time she—well, she had felt everybody watching her then, too. It was something like that. As if they were waiting for something to give.

She thought Jean Towers' face was tense, and Marsha's eyes were—but she was letting her imagination run away with her.

Absolute silence. But for the clock.

She began to feel the vague, uneasy fingers of fear again.

The strangest thing was: None of the girls giggled. They were very still, waiting. They were—serious.

She heard the monotonous tick-tock, tick-tock of the clock.

There was the picture of the Indian, looking hopelessly into the chasm, there on the wall. Drooping spear.

(Tick-tock)

There were the goldfish, over in the corner. Slowly circling.

(Tick-tock)

There was—

Her heart leaped toward her throat.

The clock had stopped!

Rosalynn choked back a scream and her nails dug into her palms.

Slowly she relaxed. Only a clock had stopped, and clocks often stop: every minute, day and night, somewhere in the world, a clock stops.

Maybe the girls had arranged for that too; although it was a little difficult to imagine how they—

She looked at first one and then the other; and tension began to mount within her again. Their eyes were bright and they seemed to be leaned forward, tense, watching her.

Her father had said. 'People aren't really as bad as you think: they're very seldom cruel.' She tried to believe that.

It was time to begin setting the table. She had to fight with herself to stand; the eyes shifted upward with her.

Even if they hated her, she wasn't going to quit . . . to show she was afraid . . . not now.

(*But they would all laugh about it tomorrow.*)

She began to walk backward toward the kitchen. Hair along her neck bristled.

Silence.

She began the slow, awkward process of setting the table for herself and for a guest.

And then from far away! She tried to close her ears to it.

The second plate clattered loudly on the table.

She felt tears form, and her nose wrinkled and tingled. She could not scream.

She could only move toward the drawer, take two knives.

The expression on their faces: And she knew now. They *did* hate her: each of them. They were straining, listening, holding their breaths to hear it, and it grew louder!

They hated her: maybe because her father had a better job than their fathers, or maybe because she didn't have an accent and talked faster. *But they hated her*!

Rosalynn forgot about them. She was at the table again, and her movements were forced from her. She wanted to run and scream and cry.

She put the second knife before the second plate. (It had a good, stainless steel handle.)

Wind in winter! Wind from the North, moaning in the trees: wind in winter in Southern Missouri.

("It always comes up at a dumb supper," Jean Towers had said.)

. . . Mr. Pierce had said, that evening, that it was going to be a hard winter. But wind in winter? . . .

Marsha's eyes were glassy, and her breath came short.

Screaming wind, tearing at the house, gripping it, shaking it. In winter?

She took out the corn bread, using a pot holder to keep from burning her hands. She cut it into two pieces. The corn bread was soggy: she should have baked it longer.

She put the large piece on *his* plate.

She felt herself sitting down. There was nothing else she could do: she tried to fight but her muscles were caught in a clammy vice.

There was terror in her mind, overflowing it.

(The three goldfish, in the living room, were still circling slowly.)

The icy wind seemed all around her—caressing her, *kissing* her, muttering, muttering, like an obscene lover.

Weak. She was weak. Her skin crawled.

Something—from Outside.

Outside what?

Just Outside. That's all—Outside of—everything.

The girl-faces, now: blank, wide-eyed, drained. Waiting, waiting.

She tried to move her lips and the wind stopped them with a frozen kiss.

And the wind was everywhere; a laughing, insane fury; a cold, musty breath.

Frozen. Everything was frozen. Time stood still. Waiting for her husband to come.

He came.

She looked up from her plate and saw him.

A shadowy figure, unreal, tenuous, flowing into the room. Flowing toward her.

Her heart beat, beat, beat.

He was going to sit down beside her—her bridegroom!

Wind, evil wind.

The lights faded, growing weaker and weaker. And the white wrapped figure, settling into the chair prepared for it. It turned its head and stared full into Rosalynn's face.

She found that she could scream now; her voice was shrill, and it went on and on and on in the darkness. . . .

Finally the lights came back on.

The girls were circled tightly around her, their faces tense.

"What did he look like?" Marsha asked.

"He—he—it had no face; it wasn't my husband. It was—only—only blackness: awful black, blacker than the blackest night. . . ." She was sobbing.

"There, there, now," Jean Towers said, "you musn't cry. Take my handkerchief. It's nothing to cry about."

"No," said Marsha, "you musn't cry."

Suddenly the girls were bustling around her, wonderfully sweet and nice, drying her eyes, saying soft words to her, leaning over backwards to be helpful.

Rosalynn was shaking. "Let me alone," she begged. "*Please* let me alone. You *hate* me. I know you do."

"Shucks, no, we don't either," Marsha said.

For a long moment the words seemed to echo in her mind; and then they began to call up new echoes.

Slowly she came to remember it—an overheard scrap of conversation. She knew the meaning of black, and why they were being so nice to her. For Marsha had said, "Black is the color of Death."

And she knew, too, who was ultimately to be her only true Friend and bridegroom.

MONTANA

Lonely Train A' Comin'
by William F. Nolan

Lonely train a'comin'
I can hear its cry
Lonely train from nowhere
Takin' me to die
  —folk ballad fragment, circa 1881

AT BITTERROOT, Ventry waited.

Bone-cold, huddled on the narrow wooden bench against the paint-blistered wall of the depot, the collar of his fleece-lined coat turned up against the chill Montana winds blowing in from the Plains, he waited for the train. Beneath the wide brim of a work-blackened Stetson, sweat-stained along the headband, his eyes were intense, the gunmetal color of blued steel. Hard lines etched into the mahogany of his face spoke of deep-snow winters and glare-sun summers; his hands, inside heavy leather work gloves, were calloused and blunt-fingered from punishing decades of ranch work.

Autumn was dying, and the sky over Bitterroot was gray with the promise of winter. This would be the train's last run before snow closed down the route. Ventry had calculated it with consummate patience and precision. He prided himself on his stubborn practicality, and he had earned a reputation among his fellow ranchers as a hard-headed realist.

Paul Ventry was never an emotional man. Even at his wife's death he had remained stolid, rock-like in his grief. If it was Sarah's time to die, then so be it. He had loved her, but she was gone and he was alone and that was fact. Ventry accepted. Sarah had wanted children, but things hadn't worked out

335

that way. So they had each other, and the ranch, and the open Montana sky—and that had been enough.

Amy's death was not the same. Losing his sister had been wrong. He did *not* accept it. Which was why he was doing this, why he was here. In his view, he had no other choice.

He had been unable to pinpoint the train's exact arrival, but he was certain it would pass Bitterroot within a seven-day period. Thus, he had brought along enough food and water to last a week. His supplies were almost depleted now, but they could be stretched through two more days and nights if need be; Ventry was not worried.

The train *would* be here.

It was lonely at Bitterroot. The stationmaster's office was boarded over, and bars covered the windows. The route into Ross Fork had been dropped from the rail schedule six months ago, and main-line trains bound for Lewistown no longer made the stop. Now the only trains that rattled past were desolate freights, dragging their endless rusted flatcars.

Ventry shifted the holstered ax pressing against his thigh, and unzipping a side pocket on his coat, he took out the thumb-worn postcard. On the picture side, superimposed over a multicolored panoramic shot of a Plains sunset, was the standard Montana salutation: GREETINGS FROM THE BIG SKY COUNTRY! And on the reverse, Amy's last words. How many times had he read her hastily scrawled message, mailed from this depot almost a year ago to the day?

Dear Paulie, I'll write a long letter, I promise, when I get to Lewistown, but the train came early so I just have time, dear brother, to send you my love. And don't you worry about your little kid sister because life for me is going to be super with my new job! Luv and XXXXXXX, Amy

And she had added a quick P.S. at the bottom of the card:

You should see this beautiful old train! Didn't know they still ran steam locomotives like this one! Gotta rush—'cuz it's waiting for me!

Ventry's mouth tightened, and he slipped the card back into his coat, thinking about Amy's smiling eyes, about how much a part of his life she'd been. Hell, she was a better sheep rancher than half the valley men on Big Moccasin! But, once grown, she'd wanted city life, a city job, a chance to meet city men.

"Just you watch me, Paulie," she had told him, her face shining with excitement. "This li'l ole job in Lewistown is only the beginning. The firm has a branch in Helena, and I'm sure I can get transferred there within a year. You're gonna be real proud of your sis. I'll *make* you proud!"

She'd never had the chance. She'd never reached Lewistown. Amy had stepped aboard the train . . . and vanished.

Yet people don't vanish. It was a word Paul refused to accept. He had driven each bleak mile of the rail line from Bitterroot to Lewistown, combing every inch of terrain for a sign, a clue, a scrap of clothing. He'd spent two months along that route. And had found nothing.

Ventry posted a public reward for information leading to Amy's whereabouts. Which is when Tom Hallendorf contacted him.

Hallendorf was a game warden stationed at King's Hill Pass in the Lewis and Clark National Forest. He phoned Ventry, telling him about what he'd found near an abandoned spur track in the Little Belt range.

Bones. *Human* bones.

And a ripped, badly stained red leather purse.

The empty purse had belonged to Amy. Forensic evidence established the bones as part of her skeleton.

What had happened up there in those mountains?

The district sheriff, John Longbow, blamed it on a "weirdo." A roving tramp.

"Dirt-plain obvious, Mr. Ventry," the sheriff had said to him. "He killed her for what she had in the purse. You admit she was carryin' several hundred in cash. Which is, begging your pardon, a damn fool thing to do!"

But that didn't explain the picked bones.

"Lotta wild animals in the mountains," the lawman had declared. "After this weirdo done 'er in he just left her layin' there—and, well, probably a bear come onto 'er. It's happened before. We've found bones up in that area more than once. Lot of strange things in the Little Belt."

And the sheriff had grinned. "As a boy, with the tribe, I heard me stories that'd curl your hair. It's wild country."

The railroad authorities were adamant about the mystery train. "No steamers in these parts," they told him. "Nobody runs 'em anymore."

But Ventry was gut-certain that such a train existed, and that Amy had died on it. Someone had cold-bloodedly murdered his sister and dumped her body in the mountains.

He closed down the ranch, sold his stock, and devoted himself to finding out who that someone was.

He spent an entire month at the main library in Lewistown, poring through old newspaper files, copying names, dates, case details.

A pattern emerged. Ventry found that a sizable number of missing persons who had vanished in this area of the state over the past decade had been traveling by *rail*. And several of them had disappeared along the same basic route Amy had chosen.

Ventry confronted John Longbow with his research.

"An' just who is this killer?" the sheriff asked.

"Whoever owns the steamer. Some freak rail buff. Rich enough to run his own private train, and crazy enough to kill the passengers who get on board."

"Look, Mr. Ventry, how come nobody's *seen* this fancy steam train of yours?"

"Because the rail disappearances have happened at night, at remote stations off the main lines. He never runs the train by daylight. Probably keeps it up in the mountains. Maybe in one of the old mine shafts. Uses off-line spur tracks. Comes rolling into a small depot like Bitterroot *between* the regular passenger trains and picks up whoever's on the platform."

The sheriff had grunted at this, his eyes tight on Paul Ventry's face.

"And there's a definite *cycle* to these disappearances," Ventry continued. "According to what I've put together, the train makes its night runs at specific intervals. About a month apart, spring through fall. Then it's hidden away in the Little Belt each winter when the old spur tracks are snowed over. I've done a lot of calculation on this, and I'm certain that the train makes its final run during the first week of November—which means you've still got time to stop it."

The sheriff had studied Paul Ventry for a long, silent moment. Then he had sighed deeply. "That's an interesting theory, Mr. Ventry, *real* interesting. But . . . it's also about as wild and unproven as any I've heard—and I've heard me a few. Now, it's absolute natural that you're upset at your sister's death, but you've let things get way out of whack. I figger you'd best go on back to your ranch and try an' forget about poor little Amy. Put her out of your mind. She's gone. And there's nothing you can do about that."

"We'll see," Ventry had said, a cutting edge to his voice. "We'll see what I can do."

Ventry's plan was simple. Stop the train, board it, and kill the twisted son of a bitch who owned it. Put a .45 slug in his head. Blow his fucking brains out—and blow his train up with him!

I'll put an end to this if no one else will, Ventry promised himself. And I've got the tools to do it.

He slipped the carefully wrapped gun rig from his knapsack, unfolded its oiled covering, and withdrew his grandfather's long-barreled frontier Colt from its worn leather holster. The gun was a family treasure. Its bone handle was cracked and yellowed by the years, but the old Colt was still in perfect firing order. His granddaddy had worn this rig, had defended his mine on the Comstock against claim jumpers with this gun. It was fitting and proper that it be used on the man who'd killed Amy.

Night was settling over Bitterroot. The fiery orange disc of sun had dropped below the Little Belt Mountains, and the sky was gray slate along the horizon.

Time to strap on the gun. Time to get ready for the train.

It's coming tonight! Lord God, I can feel it out there in the gathering dark, thrumming the rails. I can feel it in my blood and bones.

Well, then, come ahead, god damn you, whoever you are.

I'm ready for you.

Ten P.M. Eleven. Midnight.

It came at midnight.

Rushing toward Bitterroot, clattering in fierce-wheeled thunder, its black bulk sliding over the track in the ash-dark Montana night like an immense, segmented snake—with a single yellow eye probing the terrain ahead.

Ventry heard it long before he saw it. The rails sang and vibrated around him as he stood tall and resolute in mid-track, a three-cell silver flashlight in his right hand, his heavy sheepskin coat buttoned over the gun at his belt.

Have to flag it down. With the depot closed it won't make a stop. No passengers. It's looking for live game, and it doesn't figure on finding any here at Bitterroot.

Surprise! I'm here. *I'm* alive. Like Amy. Like all the others. Man alone at night. Needs a ride. Climb aboard, pardner. Make yourself to home. Drink? Somethin' to eat? What's your pleasure?

My pleasure is your death—and the death of your freak train, mister! *That's* my pleasure.

It was in sight now, coming fast, slicing a bright round hole in the night—and its sweeping locomotive beam splashed Paul Ventry's body with a pale luminescence.

The rancher swung his flash up, then down, in a high arc. Again. And again.

Stop, you bastard! *Stop!*

The train began slowing.

Sparks showered from the massive driving wheels as the train reduced speed. Slowing . . . slower . . . steel shrieking against steel. An easing of primal force.

It was almost upon him.

Like a great shining insect, the locomotive towered high and black over Ventry, its tall stack shutting out the stars. The rusted tip of the train's thrusting metal cowcatcher gently nudged the toe of his right boot as the incredible night mammoth slid to a final grinding stop.

Now the train was utterly motionless, breathing its white steam into the cold dark, waiting for him as he had waited for it.

Ventry felt a surge of exultation fire his body. He'd been right! It was here—and he was prepared to destroy it, to avenge his sister. It was his destiny. He felt no fear, only a cool and certain confidence in his ability to kill.

A movement at the corner of his eye. Someone was waving from the far end of the train, from the last coach, the train's only source of light. All of the other passenger cars were dark and blind-windowed; only the last car glowed hazy yellow.

Ventry eased around the breathing locomotive, his boots crunching loudly in the cindered gravel as he moved over the roadbed.

He glanced up at the locomotive's high, double-windowed cabin, but the engineer was lost behind opaque, soot-colored glass. Ventry kept moving steadily forward, toward the distant figure, passing along the linked row of silent, lightless passenger cars. The train bore no markings; it was a uniform, unbroken black.

Ventry squinted at the beckoning figure. Was it the killer himself, surprised and delighted at finding another passenger at this deserted night station?

He slipped the flash into his shoulder knapsack, and eased a hand inside his coat, gripping the warm bone handle of the .45 at his waist. You've had one surprise tonight, mister. Get ready for another.

Then, abruptly, he stopped, heart pounding. Ventry recognized the beckoning figure. Impossible! An illusion. Just *couldn't* be. Yet there she was, smiling, waving to him.

"Amy!" Ventry rushed toward his sister in a stumbling run.

But she was no longer in sight when he reached the dimly illumined car. Anxiously, he peered into one of the smoke-yellowed windows. A figure moved hazily inside.

"Amy!" He shouted her name again, mounting the coach steps.

The moment Ventry's boot touched the car's upper platform the train jolted into life. Ventry was thrown to his knees as the coach lurched violently forward.

The locomotive's big driving wheels sparked against steel, gaining a solid grip on the rails as the train surged powerfully from Bitterroot Station.

As Paul Ventry entered the coach, the door snap-locked behind him. Remote-control device. To make sure I won't leave by the rear exit. No matter. He'd expected that. He could get out when he had to, when he was ready. He'd come prepared for whatever this madman had in mind.

But Ventry had *not* been prepared for the emotional shock of seeing Amy. Had he *really* seen her? *Was* it his sister?

No. Of course not. He'd been tricked by his subconscious mind. The fault was his. A lapse in concentration, in judgment.

But *someone* had waved to him—a young girl who looked, at first sight, amazingly like his dead sister.

Where was she now?

And just where was the human devil who ran this train?

Ventry was alone in the car. To either side of the aisle the rows of richly upholstered green velvet seats were empty. A pair of ornate, scrolled gas lamps, mounted above the arched doorway, cast flickering shadows over antique brass fittings and a handcarved wood ceiling. Green brocade draped the windows.

He didn't know much about trains, but Ventry knew this one *had* to be pre-1900. And probably restored by the rich freak who owned it. Plush was the word.

Well, it was making its last run; Ventry would see to that.

He pulled the flash from his shoulder pack, snapping on the bright beam as he moved warily forward.

The flashlight proved unnecessary. As Ventry entered the second car (door unlocked; guess he doesn't mind my going *forward*) the overhead gas lamps sputtered to life, spreading their pale yellow illumination over the length of the coach.

Again, the plush velvet seats were empty. Except for one. The last seat at the far end of the car. A woman was sitting there, stiff and motionless in the dim light, her back to Ventry.

As he moved toward her, she turned slowly to face him.

By Christ, it *was* Amy!

Paul Ventry rushed to her, sudden tears stinging his eyes. Fiercely, he embraced his sister; she was warm and solid in his arms. "Oh, Sis, I'm so glad you're *alive!*"

But there was no sound from her lips. No words. No emotion. She was rigid in his embrace.

Ventry stepped away from her. "What's wrong? I don't understand why you—"

His words were choked off. Amy had leaped from the seat, cat-quick, to fasten long pale fingers around his throat. Her thumbs dug like sharp spikes into the flesh of Ventry's neck.

He reeled back, gasping for breath, clawing at the incredibly strong hands. He couldn't break her grip.

Amy's face was changing. The flesh was falling away in gummy wet ribbons, revealing raw white bone! In the deep sockets of Amy's grinning skull her eyes were hot red points of fire.

Ventry's right hand found the butt of the Colt, and he dragged the gun free of its holster. Swinging the barrel toward Amy, he fired directly into the melting horror of her face.

His bullets drilled round, charred holes in the grinning skull, but Amy's fingers—now all raw bone and slick gristle—maintained their death grip at his throat.

Axe? Use the axe!

In a swimming red haze, Ventry snapped the short-handled woodsman's axe free of his belt. And swung it sharply downward, neatly removing Amy's head at shoulderlevel. The cleanly severed skull rolled into the aisle at his feet.

Yet, horribly, the bony fingers increased their deadly pressure.

Ventry's sight blurred; the coach wavered. As the last of his oxygen was cut off, he was on the verge of blacking out.

Desperately, he swung the blade again, missing the Amy-thing entirely. The axe buried itself in thick green velvet.

The train thrashed; its whistle shrieked wildly in the rushing night, a cry of pain—and the seat rippled in agony. Oily black liquid squirted from the sliced velvet.

At Ventry's throat, the bony fingers dropped away.

In numbed shock, he watched his sister's rotting corpse flow down into the seat, melting and mixing with the central train body, bubbling wetly. . . .

Oh, sweet Jesus! Everything's moving! The whole foul train is alive!

And Ventry accepted it. Sick with horror and revulsion, he accepted it. He was a realist, and this thing was real. No fantasy. No dream.

Real.

Which meant he had to kill it. Not the man who owned it, because such a man did not exist. Somehow, the train itself, ancient and rusting in the high mountains, had taken on a sentient life of its own. The molecular components of iron and wood and steel had, over a slow century, transformed themselves into living tissue—and this dark hell-thing had rolled out onto the Montana plains seeking food, seeking flesh to sustain it, sleeping, sated, through the frozen winters, hibernating, then stirring to hungry life again as the greening earth renewed itself.

Lot of strange things in the Little Belt.

Don't think about it, Ventry warned himself. Just do what you came to do: *kill it!* Kill the foul thing. Blow it out of existence!

He carried three explosive charges in his knapsack, each equipped with a timing device. All right, make your plan! Set one here at the end of the train, another in the middle coach, and plant the final charge in the forward car.

No good. If the thing had the power to animate its dead victims it also had the power to fling off his explosive devices, to rid itself of them as a dog shakes leaves from its coat.

I'll have to go after it the way you go after a snake; to kill a snake, you cut off its head.

So go for the brain.

Go for the engine.

The train had left the main rail system now, and was on a rusted spur track, climbing steeply into the Little Belt range.

It was taking Ventry into the high mountains. One last meal of warm flesh, then the long winter's sleep.

The train was going home.

Three cars to go.

Axe in hand, Ventry was moving steadily toward the engine, through vacant, gas-lit coaches, wondering how and when it would attack him again.

Did it know he meant to kill it? Possibly it had no fear of him. God knows it was strong. And no human had ever harmed it in the past. Does the snake fear the mouse?

Maybe it would leave him alone to do his work; maybe it didn't realize how lethal this mouse could be.

But Ventry was wrong.

Swaying in the clattering rush of the train, he was halfway down the aisle of the final coach when the tissue around him rippled into motion. Viscid black bubbles formed on the ceiling of the car, and in the seats. Growing. Quivering. Multiplying.

One by one, the loathsome globes swelled and burst—giving birth to a host of nightmare figures. Young and old. Man, woman, child. Eye red and angry.

They closed on Ventry in the clicking interior of the hell coach, moving toward him in a rotting tide.

He had seen photos of many of them in the Lewistown library. Vanished passengers, like Amy, devoured and absorbed and now regenerated as fetid ectoplasmic horrors—literal extensions of the train itself.

Ventry knew that he was powerless to stop them. The Amy-thing had proven that.

But he still had the axe, and a few vital seconds before the train-things reached him.

Ventry swung the razored blade left and right, slashing brutally at seat and floor, cutting deep with each swift blow. Fluid gushed from a dozen gaping wounds; a rubbery mass of coil-like innards, like spilled guts, erupted from the seat to Ventry's right, splashing him with gore.

The train screamed into the Montana night, howling like a wounded beast.

The passenger-things lost form, melting into the aisle.

Now Ventry was at the final door, leading to the coal car directly behind the engine.

It was locked against him.

The train had reached its destination at the top of the spur, was rolling down a side track leading to a deserted mine. Its home. Its cave. Its dark hiding place.

The train would feast now.

Paul Ventry used the last of his strength on the door. Hacking at it. Slashing wildly. Cutting his way through.

Free! In a freezing blast of night wind, Ventry scrambled across the coal tender toward the shining black locomotive.

And reached it.

A heavy, gelatinous membrane separated him from the control cabin. The membrane pulsed with veined life.

Got to get inside . . . reach the brain of the thing. . . .

Ventry drove the blade deep, splitting the veined skin. And burst through into the cabin.

Its interior was a shock to Ventry's senses; he was assailed by a stench so powerful that bile rushed into his throat. He fought back a rising nausea.

Brass and wood and iron had become throbbing flesh. Levers and controls and pressure gauges were coated with a thick, crawling slime. The roof and sides of the cabin were moving.

A huge, red, heart-like mass pulsed and shimmered wetly in the center of the cabin, its sickly crimson glow illuminating his face.

He did not hesitate.

Ventry reached into the knapsack, pulled out an explosive charge, and set the device for manual. All he needed to do was press a metal switch, toss the charge at the heart-thing, and jump from the cabin.

It was over. He'd won!

But before he could act, the entire chamber heaved up in a bubbled, convulsing pincer movement, trapping Ventry like a fly in a web.

He writhed in the jellied grip of the train-thing. The explosive device had been jarred from his grasp. The axe, too, was lost in the mass of crushing slime-tissue.

Ventry felt sharp pain fire along his back. *Teeth!* The thing had sprouted rows of needled teeth and was starting to eat him alive!

The knapsack; he was still wearing it!

Gasping, dizzy with pain, Ventry plunged his right hand into the sack, closing bloodied fingers around the second explosive device. Pulled it loose, set it ticking.

Sixty seconds.

If he could not fight free in that space of time he'd go up with the train. A far better way to die than being ripped apart and devoured. Death would be a welcome release.

Incredibly, the train-thing seemed to *know* that its life was in jeopardy. Its shocked tissues drew back, cringing away from the ticking explosive charge.

Ventry fell to his knees on the slimed floor.

Thirty seconds.

He saw the sudden gleam of rails to his right, just below him, and he launched himself in a plunging dive through the severed membrane.

Struck ground. Searing pain. Right shoulder, Broken bone.

Hell with it! *Move, damn you, move!*

Ventry rolled over on his stomach, pain lacing his body. Pushed himself up. Standing now.

Five seconds.

Ventry sprawled forward. *Legs won't support me!*

Then *crawl!*

Into heavy brush. Still crawling—dragging his lacerated, slime-smeared body toward a covering of rocks.

Faster! No more time. . . . Too late!

The night became sudden day.

The explosion picked up Ventry and tossed him into the rocks like a boneless doll.

The train-thing screamed in a whistling death-agony as the concussion sundered it, scattering its parts like wet confetti over the terrain.

Gobbets of bleeding tissue rained down on Ventry as he lay in the rocks. But through the pain and the stench and the nausea his lips were curved into a thin smile.

He was unconscious when the Montana sun rose that morning, but when Sheriff John Longbow arrived on the scene he found Paul Ventry alive.

Alive and triumphant.

NEBRASKA

Children of the Corn
by Stephen King

BURT TURNED the radio on too loud and didn't turn it down because they were on the verge of another argument and he didn't want it to happen. He was desperate for it not to happen.

Vicky said something.

"What?" he shouted.

"Turn it down! Do you want to break my eardrums?"

He bit down hard on what might have come through his mouth and turned it down.

Vicky was fanning herself with her scarf even though the T-Bird was air-conditioned. "Where are we, anyway?"

"Nebraska."

She gave him a cold, neutral look. "Yes, Burt. I know we're in Nebraska, Burt. But where the hell *are* we?"

"You've got the road atlas. Look it up. Or can't you read?"

"Such wit. This is why we got off the turnpike. So we could look at three hundred miles of corn. And enjoy the wit and wisdom of Burt Robeson."

He was gripping the steering wheel so hard his knuckles were white. He decided he was holding it that tightly because if he loosened up, why, one of those hands might just fly off and hit the ex-Prom Queen beside him right in the chops. We're saving our marriage, he told himself. Yes. We're doing it the same way us grunts went about saving villages in the war.

"Vicky," he said carefully. "I have driven fifteen hundred miles on turnpikes since we left Boston. I did that driving myself because you refused to drive. Then—"

"I did not refuse!" Vicky said hotly. "Just because I get migraines when I drive for a long time—"

"Then when I asked you if you'd navigate for me on some of the secondary roads, you said sure, Burt. Those were your exact words. Sure, Burt. Then—"

"Sometimes I wonder how I ever wound up married to you."

"By saying two little words."

She stared at him for a moment, white-lipped, and then picked up the road atlas. She turned the pages savagely.

It *had* been a mistake leaving the turnpike. Burt thought morosely. It was a shame, too, because up until then they had been doing pretty well, treating each other almost like human beings. It had sometimes seemed that this trip to the coast, ostensibly to see Vicky's brother and his wife but actually a last-ditch attempt to patch up their own marriage, was going to work.

But since they left the pike, it had been bad again. How bad? Well, terrible, actually.

"We left the turnpike at Hamburg, right?"

"Right."

"There's nothing more until Gatlin," she said. "Twenty miles. Wide place in the road. Do you suppose we could stop there and get something to eat. Or does your almighty schedule say we have to go until two o' clock like we did yesterday?"

He took his eyes off the road to look at her. "I've about had it, Vicky. As far as I'm concerned, we can turn around right here and go home and see that lawyer you wanted to talk to. Because this isn't working at—"

She had faced forward again, her expression stonily set. It suddenly turned to surprise and fear. "*Burt look out you're going to—*"

He turned his attention back to the road just in time to see something vanish under the T-Bird's bumper. A moment later, while he was only beginning to switch from gas to brake, he felt something thump sickeningly under the front and then the back wheels. They were thrown forward as the car braked along the centerline, decelerating from fifty to zero along black skidmarks.

"A dog," he said. "Tell me it was a dog, Vicky."

Her face was a pallid, cottage-cheese color. "A boy. A little boy. He just ran out of the corn and . . . congratulations, tiger."

She fumbled the car door open, leaned out, threw up.

Burt sat straight behind the T-Bird's wheel, hands still gripping it loosely. He was aware of nothing for a long time but the rich, dark smell of fertilizer.

Then he saw that Vicky was gone and when he looked in the outside mirror he saw her stumbling clumsily back toward a heaped bundle that looked like a pile of rags. She was ordinarily a graceful woman but now her grace was gone, robbed.

It's manslaughter. That's what they call it. I took my eyes off the road.

He turned the ignition off and got out. The wind rustled softly through the growing man-high corn, making a weird sound like respiration. Vicky was standing over the bundle of rags now, and he could hear her sobbing.

He was halfway between the car and where she stood and something caught his eye on the left, a gaudy splash of red amid all the green, as bright as barn paint.

He stopped, looking directly into the corn. He found himself thinking (anything to untrack from those rags that were not rags) that it must have been a fantastically growing season for corn. It grew close together, almost ready to bear. You could plunge into those neat, shaded rows and spend a day trying to find your way out again. But the neatness was broken here. Several tall cornstalks had been broken and leaned askew. And what was that farther back in the shadows?

"Burt!" Vicky screamed at him. "Don't you want to come see? So you can tell all your poker buddies what you bagged in Nebraska? Don't you—" But the rest was lost in fresh sobs. Her shadow was puddled starkly around her feet. It was almost noon.

Shade closed over him as he entered the corn. The red barn paint was blood. There was a low, somnolent buzz as flies lit, tasted, and buzzed off again . . . maybe to tell others. There was more blood on the leaves farther in. Surely it couldn't have splattered this far? And then he was standing over the object he had seen from the road. He picked it up.

The neatness of the rows was disturbed here. Several stalks were canted drunkenly, two of them had been broken clean off. The earth had been gouged. There was blood. The corn rustled. With a little shiver, he walked back to the road.

Vicky was having hysterics, screaming unintelligible words at him, crying, laughing. Who would have thought it could end in such a melodramatic way? He looked at her and saw he wasn't having an identity crisis or a difficult life transition or any of those trendy things. He hated her. He gave her a hard slap across the face.

She stopped short and put a hand against the reddening impression of his fingers. "You'll go to jail, Burt," she said solemnly.

"I don't think so," he said, and put the suitcase he had found in the corn at her feet.

"What—?"

"I don't know. I guess it belonged to him." He pointed to the sprawled, face-down body that lay in the road. No more than thirteen, from the look of him.

The suitcase was old. The brown leather was battered and scuffed. Two hanks of clotheslines had been wrapped around it and tied in large, clownish grannies. Vicky bent to undo one of them, saw the blood greased into the knot, and withdrew.

Burt knelt and turned the body over gently.

"I don't want to look," Vicky said, staring down helplessly anyway. And when the staring, sightless face flopped up to regard them, she screamed again. The boy's face was dirty, his expression a grimace of terror. His throat had been cut.

Burt got up and put his arms around Vicky as she began to sway. "Don't faint," he said very quietly. "Do you hear me, Vicky? Don't faint."

He repeated it over and over and at last she began to recover and held him tight. They might have been dancing, there on the noon-struck road with the boy's corpse at their feet.

"Vicky?"

"What?" Muffled against his shirt.

"Go back to the car and put the keys in your pocket. Get the blanket out of the back seat, and my rifle. Bring them here."

"The rifle?"

"Someone cut his throat. Maybe whoever is watching us."

Her head jerked up and her wide eyes considered the corn. It marched away as far as the eye could see, undulating up and down small dips and rises of land.

"I imagine he's gone, But why take chances? Go on. Do it."

She walked stiltedly back to the car, her shadow following, a dark mascot who stuck close at this hour of the day. When she leaned into the back seat, Burt squatted beside the boy. White male, no distinguishing marks. Run over, yes, but the T-Bird hadn't cut the kid's throat. It had been cut raggedly and inefficiently—no army sergeant had shown the killer the finer points of hand-to-hand assassination—but the final effect had been deadly. He had either run or been pushed through the last thirty feet of corn, dead or mortally wounded. And Burt Robeson had run him down. If the boy had still been alive when the car hit him, his life had been cut short by thirty seconds at most.

Vicky tapped him on the shoulder and he jumped.

She was standing with the brown army blanket over her left arm, the cased pump shotgun in her right hand, her face averted. He took the blanket and spread it on the road. He rolled the body onto it. Vicky uttered a desperate little moan.

"You okay?" He looked up at her. "Vicky?"

"Okay," she said in a strangled voice.

He flipped the sides of the blanket over the body and scooped it up, hating the thick, dead weight of it. It tried to make a U in his arms and slither through his grasp. He clutched it tighter and they walked back to the T-Bird.

"Open the trunk," he grunted.

The trunk was full of travel stuff, suitcases and souvenirs. Vicky shifted most of it into the back seat and Burt slipped the body into the made space and slammed the trunklid down. A sigh of relief escaped him.

Vicky was standing by the driver's side door, still holding the cased rifle.

"Just put it in the back and get in."

He looked at his watch and saw only fifteen minutes had passed. It seemed like hours.

"What about the suitcase?" she asked.

He trotted back down the road to where it stood on the white line, like the focal point in an Impressionist painting. He picked it up by its tattered handle and paused for a moment. He had a strong sensation of being watched. It was a feeling he had read about in books, mostly cheap fiction, and he had always doubted its reality. Now he didn't. It was as if there were people in the corn, maybe a lot of them, coldly estimating whether the woman could get the gun out of the case and use it before they could grab him, drag him into the shady rows, cut his throat—

Heart beating thickly, he ran back to the car, pulled the keys out of the trunk lock, and got in.

Vicky was crying again. Burt got them moving, and before a minute had passed, he could no longer pick out the spot where it had happened in the rearview mirror.

"What did you say the next town was?" he asked.

"Oh." She bent over the road atlas again. "Gatlin. We should be there in ten minutes."

"Does it look big enough to have a police station?"

"No. It's just a dot."

"Maybe there's a constable."

They drove in silence for a while. They passed a silo on the left. Nothing else but corn. Nothing passed them going the other way, not even a farm truck.

"Have we passed anything since we got off the turnpike, Vicky?"

She thought about it. "A car and a tractor. At that intersection."

"No, since we got on this road. Route 17."

"No. I don't think we have." Earlier this might have been the preface to some cutting remark. Now she only stared out of her half of the windshield at the unrolling road and the endless dotted line.

"Vicky? Could you open the suitcase?"

"Do you think it might matter?"

"Don't know. It might."

While she picked at the knots (her face was set in a peculiar way—expressionless but tight-mouthed—that Burt remembered his mother wearing when she pulled the innards out of the Sunday chicken), Burt turned on the radio again.

The pop station they had been listening to was almost obliterated in static and Burt switched, running the red marker slowly down the dial. Farm reports. Buck Owens. Tammy Wynette. All distant, nearly distorted into babble. Then, near the end of the dial, one single word blared out of the speaker, so loud and clear that the lips which uttered it might have been directly beneath the grill of the dashboard speaker.

"*ATONEMENT!*" this voice bellowed.

Burt made a surprised grunting sound. Vicky jumped.

"*ONLY BY THE BLOOD OF THE LAMB ARE WE SAVED!*" the

voice roared, and Burt hurriedly turned the sound down. This station was close, all right. So close that . . . yes, there it was. Poking out of the corn at the horizon, a spidery red tripod against the blue. The radio tower.

"Atonement is the word, brothers 'n' sisters," the voice told them, dropping to a more conversational pitch. In the background, offmike, voices murmured amen. "There's some that thinks it's okay to get out in the world, as if you could work and walk in the world without being smirched by the world. Now is that what the word of God teaches us?"

Offmike but still loud: "No!"

"*HOLY JESUS!*" the evangelist shouted, and now the words came in a powerful, pumping cadence, almost as compelling as a driving rock-and-roll beat: "When they gonna know that way is death? When they gonna know that the wages of the world are paid on the other side? Huh? Huh? The Lord has said there's many mansions in His house. But there's no room for the fornicator. No room for the covetor. No room for the defiler of the corn. No room for the hommasexshul. No room—"

Vicky snapped it off. "That drivel makes me sick."

"What did he say?" Burt asked her. "What did he say about corn?"

"I didn't hear it." She was picking at the second clothesline knot.

"He said something about corn. I know he did."

"I got it!" Vicky said, and the suitcase fell open in her lap. They were passing a sign that said: GATLIN 5 MI. DRIVE CAREFULLY PROTECT OUR CHILDREN. The sign had been put up by the Elks. There were .22 bullet holes in it.

"Socks," Vicky said. "Two pairs of pants . . . a shirt . . . a belt . . . a string tie with a—" She held it up, showing him the peeling gilt neck clasp. "Who's that?"

Burt glanced at it. "Hopalong Cassidy, I think."

"Oh." She put it back. She was crying again.

After a moment, Burt said: "Did anything strike you funny about that radio sermon?"

"No. I heard enough of that stuff as a kid to last me forever. I told you about it."

"Didn't you think he sounded kind of young? That preacher?"

She uttered a mirthless laugh. "A teen-ager, maybe, so what? That's what's so monstrous about that whole trip. They like to get hold of them when their minds are still rubber. They know how to put all the emotional checks and balances in. You should have been at some of the tent meetings my mother and father dragged me to . . . some of the ones I was 'saved' at.

"Let's see. There was Baby Hortense, the Singing Marvel. She was eight. She'd come on and sing 'Leaning on the Everlasting Arms' while her daddy passed the plate, telling everybody to 'dig deep, now, let's not let this little child of God down.' Then there was Norman Staunton. He used to preach hellfire and brimstone in this little Lord Fauntleroy suit with short pants. He was only seven."

She nodded at his look of unbelief.

"They weren't the only two, either. There were plenty of them on the circuit. They were good *draws*." She spat the word. "Ruby Stampnell. She was a ten-year-old faith healer. The Grace Sisters. They used to come out with little tin-foil haloes over their heads and—*oh!*"

"What is it?" He jerked around to look at her, and what she was holding in her hands. Vicky was staring at it raptly. Her slowly seining hands had snagged it on the bottom of the suitcase and had brought it up as she talked. Burt pulled over to take a better look. She gave it to him wordlessly.

It was crucifix that had been made from twists of corn husk, once green, now dry. Attached to this by woven cornsilk was a dwarf corncob. Most of the kernels had been carefully removed, probably dug out one at a time with a pocketknife. Those kernels remaining formed a crude cruciform figure in yellowish bas-relief. Corn-kernel eyes, each slit longways to suggest pupils. Outstretched kernel arms, the legs together, terminating in a rough indication of bare feet. Above, four letters also raised from the bone-white cob: I N R I.

"That's a fantastic piece of workmanship," he said.

"It's hideous," she said in a flat, strained voice. "Throw it out."

"Vicky, the police might want to see it."

"Why?"

"Well, I don't know why. Maybe—"

"Throw it out. Will you please do that for me? I don't want it in the car."

"I'll put it in back. And as soon as we see the cops, we'll get rid of it one way or the other. I promise. Okay?"

"Oh, do whatever you want with it!" she shouted at him. "You will anyway!"

Troubled, he threw the thing in back, where it landed on a pile of clothes. Its corn-kernel eyes stared raptly at the T-Bird's dome light. He pulled out again, gravel splurting from beneath the tires.

"We'll give the body and everything that was in the suitcase to the cops," he promised. "Then we'll be shut of it."

Vicky didn't answer. She was looking at her hands.

A mile farther on, the endless cornfields drew away from the road, showing farmhouses and outbuildings. In one yard they saw dirty chickens pecking listlessly at the soil. There were faded cola and chewing-tobacco ads on the roofs of barns. They passed a tall billboard that said: ONLY JESUS SAVES. They passed a café with a Conoco gas island, but Burt decided to go on into the center of town, if there was one. If not, they could come back to the café. It only occurred to him after they had passed it that the parking lot had been empty except for a dirty old pickup that had looked like it was sitting on two flat tires.

Vicky suddenly began to laugh, a high, giggling sound that struck Burt as being dangerously close to hysteria.

"What's so funny?"

"The signs," she said, gasping and hiccuping. "Haven't you been reading them? When they called this the Bible Belt, they sure weren't kidding. Oh, Lordy, there's another bunch." Another burst of hysterical laughter escaped her, and she clapped both hands over her mouth.

Each sign had only one word. They were leaning on whitewashed sticks that had been implanted in the sandy shoulder, long ago by the looks; the whitewash was flaked and faded. They were coming up at eighty-foot intervals and Burt read:

A . . . CLOUD . . . BY . . . DAY . . . A . . . PILLAR . . . OF . . . FIRE . . . BY . . . NIGHT

"They only forgot one thing," Vicky said, still giggling helplessly.

"What?" Burt asked, frowning.

"Burma Shave." She held a knuckled fist against her open mouth to keep in the laughter, but her semi-hysterical giggles flowed around it like effervescent ginger-ale bubbles.

"Vicky, are you all right?"

"I will be. Just as soon as we're a thousand miles away from here, in sunny sinful California with the Rockies between us and Nebraska."

Another group of signs came up and they read them silently.

TAKE . . . THIS . . . AND . . . EAT . . . SAITH . . . THE . . . LORD . . . GOD . . .

Now why, Burt thought, should I immediately associate that indefinite pronoun with corn? Isn't that what they say when they give you communion? It had been so long since he had been to church that he really couldn't remember. He wouldn't be surprised if they used cornbread for holy wafer around these parts. He opened his mouth to tell Vicky that, and then thought better of it.

They breasted a gentle rise and there was Gatlin below them, all three blocks of it, looking like a set from a movie about the Depression.

"There'll be a constable," Burt said, and wondered why the sight of that hick one-timetable town dozing in the sun should have brought a lump of dread into his throat.

They passed a speed sign proclaiming that no more than thirty was now in order, and another sign, rust-flecked, which said: YOU ARE NOW ENTERING GATLIN, NICEST LITTLE TOWN IN NEBRASKA—OR ANYWHERE ELSE! POP. 5431.

Dusty elms stood on both sides of the road, most of them diseased. They passed the Gatlin Lumberyard and a '76 gas station, where the price signs swung slowly in a hot noon breeze: REG 35.9 HI-TEST 38.9, and another which said: HI TRUCKERS DIESEL FUEL AROUND BACK.

They crossed Elm Street, then Birch Street, and came up on the town square. The houses lining the streets were plain wood with screened porches. Angular and functional. The lawns were yellow and dispirited. Up ahead a mongrel dog walked slowly out into the middle of Maple Street, stood looking at them for a moment, then lay down in the road with its nose on its paws.

"Stop," Vicky said. "Stop right here."

Burt pulled obediently to the curb.

"Turn around. Let's take the body to Grand Island. That's not too far, is it? Let's do that."

"Vicky, what's wrong?"

"What do you mean, what's wrong?" she asked, her voice rising thinly. "This town is empty, Burt. There's nobody here but us. Can't you feel that?"

He had felt something, and still felt it. But—

"It just seems that way," he said. "But it sure is a one-hydrant town. Probably all up in the square, having a bake sale or a bingo game."

"*There's no one here.*" She said the words with a queer, strained emphasis. "Didn't you see that '76 station back there?"

"Sure, by the lumberyard, so what?" His mind was elsewhere, listening to the dull buzz of a cicada burrowing into one of the nearby elms. He could smell corn, dusty roses, and fertilizer—of course. For the first time they were off the turnpike and in a town. A town in a state he had never been in before (although he had flown over it from time to time in United Airlines 747s) and somehow it felt all wrong but all right. Somewhere up ahead there would be a drugstore with a soda fountain, a movie house named the Bijou, a school named after JFK.

"Burt, the prices said thirty-five-nine for regular and thirty-eight-nine for high octane. Now how long has it been since anyone in this country paid those prices?"

"At least four years," he admitted. "But, Vicky—"

"We're right in town, Burt, and there's not a car! *Not one car!*"

"Grand Island is seventy miles away. It would look funny if we took him there."

"I don't care."

"Look, let's just drive up to the courthouse and—"

"*No!*"

There, damn it, there. Why our marriage is falling apart, in a nutshell. No I won't. No sir. And furthermore, I'll hold my breath till I turn blue if you don't let me have my way.

"Vicky," he said.

"I want to get out of here, Burt."

"Vicky, listen to me."

"Turn around. Let's go."

"Vicky, will you stop a minute?"

"I'll stop when we're driving the other way. Now let's go."

"*We have a dead child in the trunk of our car!*" he roared at her, and took a distinct pleasure at the way she flinched, the way her face crumbled. In a slightly lower voice he went on: "His throat was cut and he was shoved out into the road and I ran him over. Now I'm going to drive up to the courthouse or whatever they have here, and I'm going to report it. If you want to start walking back toward the pike, go to it. I'll pick you up. But don't you tell me to turn around and drive seventy miles to Grand Island like we had nothing in the trunk but a bag of garbage. He happens to be some mother's son, and I'm going to report it before whoever killed him gets over the hills and far away."

"You bastard," she said, crying. "What am I doing with you?"

"I don't know," he said. "I don't know anymore. But the situation can be remedied, Vicky."

He pulled away from the curb. The dog lifted its head at the brief squeal of tires and then lowered it to its paws again.

They drove the remaining block to the square. At the corner of Main and Pleasant, Main Street split in two. There actually was a town square, a grassy park with a bandstand in the middle. On the other end, where Main Street became one again, there were two official-looking buildings. Burt could make out the lettering on one: GATLIN MUNICIPAL CENTER.

"That's it," he said. Vicky said nothing.

Halfway up the square, Burt pulled over again. They were beside a lunch room, the Gatlin Bar and Grill.

"Where are you going?" Vicky asked with alarm as he opened his door.

"To find out where everyone is. Sign in the window there says 'open.'"

"You're not going to leave me here alone."

"So come. Who's stopping you?"

She unlocked her door and stepped out as he crossed in front of the car. He saw how pale her face was and felt an instant of pity. Hopeless pity.

"Do you hear it?" she asked as he joined her.

"Hear what?"

"The nothing. No cars. No people. No tractors. Nothing."

And then, from a block over, they heard the high and joyous laughter of children.

"I hear kids," he said, "Don't you?"

She looked at him, troubled.

He opened the lunchroom door and stepped into dry, antiseptic heat. The floor was dusty. The sheen on the chrome was dull. The wooden blades of the ceiling fans stood still. Empty tables. Empty counter stools. But the mirror behind the counter had been shattered and there was something else . . . in a moment he had it. All the beer taps had been broken off. They lay along the counter like bizarre party favors.

Vicky's voice was gay and near to breaking. "Sure, Ask anybody. Pardon me, sir, but could you tell me—"

"Oh, shut up." But his voice was dull and without force. They were standing in a bar of dusty sunlight that fell through the lunchroom's big plate-glass window and again he had that feeling of being watched and he thought of the boy they had in their trunk and of the high laughter of children. A phrase came to him for no reason, a legal-sounding phrase, and it began to repeat mystically in his mind: *Sight unseen. Sight unseen. Sight unseen.*

His eyes traveled over the age-yellowed cards thumbtacked up behind the counter: CHEESBURG 35¢ WORLD'S BEST JOE 10¢ STRAWBERRY RHUBARB PIE 25¢ TODAY'S SPECIAL HAM & RED EYE GRAVY W/MASHED POT 80¢.

How long since he had seen lunchroom prices like that?

Vicky had the answer. "Look at this," she said shrilly. She was pointing at the calendar on the wall. "They've been at that bean supper for twelve years, I guess." She uttered a grinding laugh.

He walked over. The picture showed two boys swimming in a pond while a cute little dog carried off their clothes. Below the picture was the legend: COMPLIMENTS OF GATLIN LUMBER & HARDWARE *You Breakum, We Fixum*. The month on view was August 1964.

"I don't understand," he faltered, "but I'm sure—"

"You're sure!" she cried hysterically. "Sure, you're sure! That's part of your trouble, Burt, you've spent your whole life being *sure!*"

He turned back to the door and she came after him.

"Where are you going?"

"To the Municipal Center."

"Burt, why do you have to be so stubborn? You know something's wrong here. Can't you just admit it?"

"I'm not being stubborn. I just want to get shut of what's in that trunk."

They stepped out onto the sidewalk, and Burt was struck afresh with the town's silence, and with the smell of fertilizer. Somehow you never thought of that smell when you buttered an ear and salted it and bit in. Compliments of sun, rain, all sorts of manmade phosphates, and a good healthy dose of cow shit. But somehow this smell was different from the one he had grown up with in rural upstate New York. You could say whatever you wanted to about organic fertilizer, but there was something almost fragrant about it when the spreader was laying it down in the fields. Not one of your great perfumes, God no, but when the late-afternoon spring breeze would pick up and waft it over the freshly turned fields, it *was* a smell with good associations. It meant winter was over for good. It meant that school doors were going to bang closed in six weeks or so and spill everyone out into summer. It was a smell tied irrevocably in his mind with other aromas that *were* perfume: timothy grass, clover, fresh earth, hollyhocks, dogwood.

But they must do something different out here, he thought. The smell was close but not the same. There was a sickish-sweet undertone. Almost a death smell. As a medical orderly in Vietnam, he had become well versed in that smell.

Vicky was sitting quietly in the car, holding the corn crucifix in her lap and staring at it in a rapt way Burt didn't like.

"Put that thing down," he said.

"No," she said without looking up. "You play your games and I'll play mine."

He put the car in gear and drove up to the corner. A dead stoplight hung overhead, swinging in a faint breeze. To the left was a neat white church. The grass was cut. Neatly kept flowers grew beside the flagged path up to the door. Burt pulled over.

"What are you doing?"

"I'm going to go in and take a look," Burt said. "It's the only place in town that looks as if there isn't ten years' dust on it. And look at the sermon board."

She looked. Neatly pegged white letters under glass read: THE POWER AND GRACE OF HE WHO WALKS BEHIND THE ROWS. The date was July 24, 1976—the Sunday before.

"He Who Walks Behind the Rows," Burt said, turning off the ignition. "One of nine thousand names of God only used in Nebraska, I guess. Coming?"

She didn't smile. "I'm not going in with you."

"Fine. Whatever you want."

"I haven't been in a church since I left home and I don't want to be in *this* church and I don't want to be in *this* town, Burt. I'm scared out of my mind, can't we just *go*?"

"I'll only be a minute."

"I've got my keys, Burt. If you're not back in five minutes, I'll just drive away and leave you here."

"Now just wait a minute, lady."

"That's what I'm going to do. Unless you want to assault me like a common mugger and take my keys. I suppose you could do that."

"But you don't think I will."

"No."

Her purse was on the seat between them, he snatched it up. She screamed and grabbed for the shoulder strap. He pulled it out of her reach. Not bothering to dig, he simply turned the bag upside down and let everything fall out. Her keyring glittered amid tissues, cosmetics, change, old shopping lists. She lunged for it but he beat her again and put the keys in his own pocket.

"You didn't have to do that," she said, crying. "Give them to me."

"No," he said, and gave her a hard, meaningless grin. "No way."

"*Please, Burt! I'm scared!*" She held her hand out, pleading now.

"You'd wait two minutes and decide that was long enough."

"I wouldn't—"

"And then you'd drive off laughing and saying to yourself, 'That'll teach Burt to cross me when I want something.' Hasn't that pretty much been your motto during our married life? That'll teach Burt to cross me?"

He got out of the car.

"Please, Burt!" she screamed, sliding across the seat. "Listen . . . I know . . . we'll drive out of town and call from a phone booth, okay? I've got all kinds of change. I just . . . we can . . . *don't leave me alone, Burt, don't leave me out here alone!*"

He slammed the door on her cry and then leaned against the side of the T-Bird for a moment, thumbs against his closed eyes. She was pounding on the driver's side window and calling his name. She was going to make a wonderful impression when he finally found someone in authority to take charge of the kid's body. Oh yes.

He turned and walked up the flagstone path to the church doors. Two or three minutes, just a look-around, and he would be back out. Probably the door wasn't even unlocked.

But it pushed in easily on silent, well-oiled hinges (reverently oiled, he thought, and that seemed funny for no really good reason) and he stepped into a vestibule so cool it was almost chilly. It took his eyes a moment to adjust to the dimness.

The first thing he noticed was a pile of wooden letters in the far corner, dusty and jumbled indifferently together. He went to them, curious. They looked as old and forgotten as the calendar in the bar and grill, unlike the rest of the vestibule, which was dustfree and tidy. The letters were about two feet high, obviously part of a set. He spread them out on the carpet—there were eighteen of them—and shifted them around like anagrams. *HURT BITE CRAG CHAP CS. Nope.* CRAP TARGET CHIBS HUC. That wasn't much good either. Except for the CH in CHIBS. He quickly assembled the word CHURCH and was left looking at RAPTAGET CIBS. Foolish. He was squatting here playing idiot games with a bunch of letters while Vicky was going nuts out in the car. He started to get up, and then saw it. He formed BAPTIST, leaving RAG EC—and by changing two letters he had GRACE. GRACE BAPTIST CHURCH. The letters must have been out front. They had taken them down and had thrown them indifferently in the corner, and the church had been painted since then so that you couldn't even see where the letters had been.

Why?

It wasn't the Grace Baptist Church anymore, that was why. So what kind of church was it? For some reason that question caused a trickle of fear and he stood up quickly, dusting his fingers. So they had taken down a bunch of letters, so what? Maybe they had changed the place into Flip Wilson's Church of What's Happening Now.

But what had happened then?

He shook it off impatiently and went through the inner doors. Now he was standing at the back of the church itself, and as he looked toward the nave, he felt fear close around his heart and squeeze tightly. His breath drew in, loud in the pregnant silence of this place.

The space behind the pulpit was dominated by a gigantic portrait of Christ, and Burt thought: If nothing else in this town gave Vicky the screaming meemies, this would.

The Christ was grinning, vulpine. His eyes were wide and staring, reminding Burt uneasily of Lon Chaney in *The Phantom of the Opera*. In each of the wide black pupils someone (a sinner, presumably) was drowning in a lake of fire. But the oddest thing was that this Christ had green hair . . . hair which on closer examination revealed itself to be a twining mass of early-summer corn. The picture was crudely done but effective. It looked like a comic-strip mural done by a gifted child—an Old Testament Christ, or a pagan Christ that might slaughter his sheep for sacrifice instead of leading them.

At the foot of the left-hand rank of pews was a pipe organ, and Burt could not at first tell what was wrong with it. He walked down the left-hand aisle and saw with slowly dawning horror that the keys had been ripped up, the stops had been pulled out . . . and the pipes themselves filled with dry cornhusks. Over the organ was a carefully lettered plaque which read: MAKE NO MUSIC EXCEPT WITH HUMAN TONGUE SAITH THE LORD GOD.

Vicky was right. Something was terribly wrong here. He debated going back to Vicky without exploring any further, just getting into the car and leaving town as quickly as possible, never mind the Municipal Building. But it grated on him. Tell the truth, he thought. You want to give her Ban 5000 a workout before going back and admitting she was right to start with.

He would go back out in a minute or so.

He walked toward the pulpit, thinking: People must go through Gatlin all the time. There must be people in the neighboring towns who have friends and relatives here. The Nebraska SP must cruise through from time to time. And what about the power company? The stoplight had been dead. Surely they'd know if the power had been off for twelve long years. Conclusion: What seemed to have happened in Gatlin was impossible.

Still, he had the creeps.

He climbed the four carpeted steps to the pulpit and looked out over the deserted pews, glimmering in the half-shadows. He seemed to feel the weight of those eldritch and decidedly unchristian eyes boring into his back.

There was a large Bible on the lectern, opened to the thirty-eighth chapter of Job. Burt glanced down at it and read: "Then the Lord answered Job out of the whirlwind, and said, 'Who is this that darkeneth counsel by words without knowledge? . . . Where wast thou when I laid the foundations of the earth? Declare, if thou hast understanding.' The Lord. He Who Walks Behind the Rows. Declare if thou hast understanding. And please pass the corn."

He fluttered the pages of the Bible, and they made a dry whispering sound in the quiet—the sound that ghosts might make if there really were such things. And in a place like this you could almost believe it. Sections of the Bible had been chopped out. Mostly from the New Testament, he saw. Someone had decided to take on the job of amending Good King James with a pair of scissors.

But the Old Testament was intact.

He was about to leave the pulpit when he saw another book on a lower shelf and took it out, thinking it might be a church record of weddings and confirmations and burials.

He grimaced at the words stamped on the cover, done inexpertly in gold leaf: THUS LET THE INIQUITOUS BE CUT DOWN SO THAT THE GROUND MAY BE FERTILE AGAIN SAITH THE LORD GOD OF HOSTS.

There seemed to be one train of thought around here, and Burt didn't care much for the track it seemed to ride on.

He opened the book to the first wide, lined sheet. A child had done the lettering, he saw immediately. In places an ink eraser had been carefully used, and while there were no misspellings, the letters were large and childishly made, drawn rather than written. The first column read:

Amos Deigan (Richard), b. Sept. 4, 1945   Sept. 4, 1964
Isaac Renfrew (William), b. Sept. 19, 1945   Sept. 19, 1964
Zepeniah Kirk (George), b. Oct. 14, 1945   Oct. 14, 1964
Mary Wells (Roberta), b. Nov. 12, 1945   Nov. 12, 1964
Yemen Hollis (Edward), b. Jan 5, 1946   Jan. 5, 1965

Frowning, Burt continued to turn through the pages. Three-quarters of the way through, the double columns ended abruptly:

Rachel Stigman (Donna), b. June 21, 1957   June 21, 1976
Moses Richardson (Henry), b. July 29, 1957
Malachi Boardman (Craig), b. August 15, 1957

The last entry in the book was for Ruth Clawson (Sandra), b. April 30, 1961. Burt looked at the shelf where he had found this book and came up with two more. The first had the same INIQUITOUS BE CUT DOWN logo, and it continued the same record, the single column tracing birth dates and names. In early September of 1964 he found Job Gilman (Clayton), b. September 6, and the next entry was Eve Tobin, b. June 16, 1965. No second name in parentheses.

The third book was blank.

Standing behind the pulpit, Burt thought about it.

Something had happened in 1964. Something to do with religion, and corn . . . and children.

Dear God we beg thy blessing on the crop. For Jesus' sake, amen.

And the knife raised high to sacrifice the lamb—but had it been a lamb? Perhaps a religious mania had swept them. Alone, all alone, cut off from the outside world by hundreds of square miles of the rustling secret corn. Alone under seventy million acres of blue sky. Alone under the watchful eye of God, now a strange green God, a God of corn, grown old and strange and hungry. He Who Walks Behind the Rows.

Burt felt a chill creep into his flesh.

Vicky, let me tell you a story. It's about Amos Deigan, who was born Richard Deigan on September 4, 1945. He took the name Amos in 1964, fine Old Testament name, Amos, one of the minor prophets. Well, Vicky, what happened—don't laugh—is that Dick Deigan and his friends—Billy Renfrew, George Kirk, Roberta Wells, and Eddie Hollis among others—they got religion and they killed off their parents. All of them. Isn't that a scream? Shot them in their beds, knifed them in their bathtubs, poisoned their suppers, hung them, or disemboweled them, for all I know.

Why? The corn. Maybe it was dying. Maybe they got the idea somehow that it was dying because there was too much sinning. Not enough sacrifice. They would have done it in the corn, in the rows.

And somehow, Vicky, I'm quite sure of this, somehow they decided that nineteen was as old as any of them could live. Richard "Amos" Deigan, the hero of our little story, had his nineteenth birthday on September 4, 1964—the date in the book. I think maybe they killed him. Sacrificed him in the corn. Isn't that a silly story?

But let's look at Rachel Stigman, who was Donna Stigman until 1964. She turned nineteen on June 21, just about a month ago. Moses Richardson was born on July 29—just three days from today he'll be nineteen. Any idea what's going to happen to ole Mose on the twenty-ninth?

I can guess.

Burt licked his lips, which felt dry.

One other thing, Vicky. Look at this. We have Job Gilman (Clayton) born on September 6, 1964. No other births until June 16, 1965. A gap of ten months. Know what I think? They killed all the parents, even the pregnant ones, that's what I think. And one of *them* got pregnant in October of 1964 and gave birth to Eve. Some sixteen- or seventeen-year-old girl. *Eve. The first woman.*

He thumbed back through the book feverishly and found the Eve Tobin entry. Below it: "Adam Greenlaw, b. July 11, 1965."

They'd be just eleven now, he thought, and his flesh began to crawl. And maybe they're out there. Someplace.

But how could such a thing be kept secret? How could it go on?

How unless the God in question approved?

"Oh Jesus," Burt said into the silence, and that was when the T-Bird's horn began to blare into the afternoon, one long continuous blast.

Burt jumped from the pulpit and ran down the center aisle. He threw open the outer vestibule door, letting in hot sunshine, dazzling. Vicky was bolt upright behind the steering wheel, both hands plastered on the horn ring, her head swiveling wildly. From all around the children were coming. Some of them were laughing gaily. They held knives, hatchets, pipes, rocks, hammers. One girl, maybe eight, with beautiful long blond hair, held a jackhandle. Rural weapons. Not a gun among them. Burt felt a wild urge to scream out: *Which of you is Adam and Eve? Who are the mothers? Who are the daughters? Fathers? Sons?*

Declare if thou hast understanding.

They came from the side streets, from the town green, through the gate in the chain-link fence around the school playground a block farther west.

Some of them glanced indifferently at Burt, standing frozen on the church steps, and some nudged each other and pointed and smiled . . . the sweet smiles of children.

The girls were dressed in long brown wool and faded sunbonnets. The boys, like Quaker parsons, were all in black and wore round-crowned flat-brimmed hats. They streamed across the town square toward the car, across the lawns, a few came across the front yard of what had been the Grace Baptist Church until 1964. One or two of them almost close enough to touch.

"The shotgun!" Burt yelled. "Vicky, get the shotgun!"

But she was frozen in her panic, he could see that from the steps. He doubted if she could even hear him through the closed windows.

They converged on the Thunderbird. The axes and hatchets and chunks of pipe began to rise and fall. My God, am I seeing this? he thought frozenly. An arrow of chrome fell off the side of the car. The hood ornament went flying, Knives scrawled spirals through the sidewalls of the tires and the car settled. The horn blared on and on. The windshield and side windows went opaque and cracked under the onslaught . . . and then the safety glass sprayed inward and he could see again. Vicky was crouched back, only one hand on the horn ring now, the other thrown up to protect her face. Eager young hands reached in, fumbling for the lock/unlock button. She beat them away wildly. The horn became intermittent and then stopped altogether.

The beaten and dented driver's side door was hauled open. They were trying to drag her out but her hands were wrapped around the steering wheel. Then one of them leaned in, knife in hand and—

His paralysis broke and he plunged down the steps, almost falling, and ran down the flagstone walk, toward them. One of them, a boy of about sixteen with long red hair spilling out from beneath his hat, turned toward him, almost casually, and something flicked through the air. Burt's left arm jerked backward, and for a moment he had the absurd thought that he had been punched at long distance. Then the pain came, so sharp and sudden that the world went gray.

He examined his arm with a stupid sort of wonder. A buck-and-a-half Pensy jackknife was growing out of it like a strange tumor. The sleeve of his J.C. Penney sport shirt was turning red. He looked at it for what seemed like forever, trying to understand how he could have grown a jackknife . . . was it possible?

When he looked up, the boy with the red hair was almost on top of him. He was grinning, confident.

"Hey, you bastard," Burt said. His voice was creaking, shocked.

"Remand your soul to God, for you will stand before His throne momentarily," the boy with the red hair said, and clawed for Burt's eyes.

Burt stepped back, pulled the Pensy out of his arm, and stuck it into the red-haired boy's throat. The gush of blood was immediate, gigantic. Burt was splashed with it. The red-haired boy began to gobble and walk in a large circle. He clawed at the knife, trying to pull it free, and was unable. Burt watched him, jaw hanging agape. None of this was happening. It was a dream. The red-haired boy gobbled and walked. Now his sound was the only one in the hot early afternoon. The others watched, stunned.

This part of it wasn't in the script, Burt thought numbly. Vicky and I, we were in the script. And the boy in the corn, who was trying to run away. But not one of their own. He stared at them savagely, wanting to scream, *How do you like it?*

The red-haired boy gave one last weak gobble, and sank to his knees. He stared up at Burt for a moment, and then his hands dropped away from the haft of the knife, and he fell forward.

A soft sighing sound from the children gathered around the Thunderbird. They stared at Burt. Burt stared back at them, fascinated . . . and that was when he noticed that Vicky was gone.

"Where is she?" he asked. "Where did you take her?"

One of the boys raised a blood-streaked hunting knife toward his throat and made a sawing motion there. He grinned. That was the only answer.

From somewhere in back, an older boy's voice, soft: "Get him."

The boys began to walk toward him. Burt backed up. They began to walk faster. Burt backed up faster. The shotgun, the goddamned shotgun! Out of reach. The sun cut their shadows darkly on the green church lawn . . . and then he was on the sidewalk. He turned and ran.

"*Kill him!*" someone roared, and they came after him.

He ran, but not quite blindly. He skirted the Municipal Building—no help there, they would corner him like a rat—and ran on up Main Street, which opened out and became the highway again two blocks farther up. He and Vicky would have been on that road now and away, if he had only listened.

His loafers slapped against the sidewalk. Ahead of him he could see a few more business buildings, including the Gatlin Ice Cream Shoppe and—sure enough—the Bijou Theater. The dust-clotted marquee letters read NOW HOWING L MITED EN AGEMEN ELI A TH TAYLOR CLEOPA RA. Beyond the next cross street was a gas station that marked the edge of town. And beyond that the corn, closing back in to the sides of the road. A green tide of corn.

Burt ran. He was already out of breath and the knife wound in his upper arm was beginning to hurt. And he was leaving a trail of blood. As he ran he yanked his handkerchief from his back pocket and stuck it inside his shirt.

He ran. His loafers pounded the cracked cement of the sidewalk, his breath rasped in his throat with more and more heat. His arm began to throb in earnest. Some mordant part of his brain tried to ask if he thought he could run all the way to the next town, if he could run twenty miles of two-lane blacktop.

He ran. Behind him he could hear them, fifteen years younger and faster than he was, gaining. Their feet slapped on the pavement. They whooped and shouted back and forth to each other. They're having more fun than a five-alarm fire, Burt thought disjointedly. They'll talk about it for years.

Burt ran.

He ran past the gas station marking the edge of town. His breath gasped and roared in his chest. The sidewalk ran out under his feet. And now there was only one thing to do, only one chance to beat them and escape with his life. The houses were gone, the town was gone. The corn had surged in a soft green wave back to the edges of the road. The green, swordlike leaves rustled softly. It would be deep in there, deep and cool, shady in the rows of man-high corn.

He ran past a sign that said: YOU ARE NOW LEAVING GATLIN, NICEST LITTLE TOWN IN NEBRASKA—OR ANYWHERE ELSE? DROP IN ANYTIME!

I'll be sure to do that, Burt thought dimly.

He ran past the sign like a sprinter closing on the tape and then swerved left, crossing the road, and kicked his loafers away. Then he was in the corn and it closed behind him and over him like the waves of a green sea, taking him in. Hiding him. He felt a sudden and wholly unexpected relief sweep him, and at the same moment ge hot his second wind. His lungs, which had been shallowing up, seemed to unlock and give him more breath.

He ran straight down the first row he had entered, head ducked, his broad shoulders swiping the leaves and making them tremble. Twenty yards in he turned right, parallel to the road again, and ran on, keeping low so they wouldn't see his dark head of hair bobbing amid the yellow corn tassels. He doubled back toward the road for a few moments, crossed more rows, and then put his back to the road and hopped randomly from row to row, always delving deeper and deeper into the corn.

At last, he collapsed onto his knees and put his forehead against the ground. He could only hear his own taxed breathing, and the thought that played over and over in his mind was: *Thank God I gave up smoking, thank God I gave up smoking, thank God—*

Then he could hear them, yelling back and forth to each other, in some cases bumping into each other ("Hey, this is my row!"), and the sound heartened him. They were well away to his left and they sounded very poorly organized.

He took his handkerchief out of his shirt, folded it, and stuck it back in after looking at the wound. The bleeding seemed to have stopped in spite of the workout he had given it.

He rested a moment longer, and was suddenly aware that he felt *good*, physically better than he had in years . . . excepting the throb of his arm. He felt well exercised, and suddenly grappling with a clearcut (no matter how insane) problem after two years of trying to cope with the incubotic gremlins that were sucking his marriage dry.

It wasn't right that he should feel this way, he told himself. He was in deadly peril of his life, and his wife had been carried off. She might be dead now. He tried to summon up Vicky's face and dispel some of the odd good feeling by doing so, but her face wouldn't come. What came was the red-haired boy with the knife in his throat.

He became aware of the corn fragrance in his nose now, all around him.

The wind through the tops of the plants made a sound like voices. Soothing. Whatever had been done in the name of this corn, it was now his protector.

But they were getting closer.

Running hunched over, he hurried up the row he was in, crossed over, doubled back, and crossed over more rows. He tried to keep the voices always on his left, but as the afternoon progressed, that became harder and harder to do. The voices had grown faint, and often the rustling sound of the corn obscured them altogether. He would run, listen, run again. The earth was hard-packed, and his stockinged feet left little or no trace.

When he stopped much later the sun was hanging over the fields to his right, red and inflamed, and when he looked at his watch he saw that it was quarter past seven. The sun had stained the corntops a reddish gold, but here the shadows were dark and deep. He cocked his head, listening. With the coming of sunset the wind had died entirely and the corn stood still, exhaling its aroma of growth into the warm air. If they were still in the corn they were either far away or just hunkered down and listening. But Burt didn't think a bunch of kids, even crazy ones, could be quiet for that long. He suspected they had done the most kidlike thing, regardless of the consequences for them: they had given up and gone home.

He turned toward the setting sun, which had sunk between the raftered clouds on the horizon, and began to walk. If he cut on a diagonal through the rows, always keeping the setting sun ahead of him, he would be bound to strike Route 17 sooner or later.

The ache in his arm had settled into a dull throb that was nearly pleasant. And the good feeling was still with him. He decided that as long as he was here, he would let the good feeling exist in him without guilt. The guilt would return when he had to face the authorities and account for what had happened in Gatlin. But that could wait.

He pressed through the corn, thinking he had never felt so keenly aware. Fifteen minutes later the sun was only a hemisphere poking over the horizon and he stopped again, his new awareness clicking into a pattern he didn't like. It was vaguely . . . well, vaguely frightening.

He cocked his head. The corn was rustling.

Burt had been aware of that for some time, but he had just put it together with something else. The wind was still. How could that be?

He looked around warily, half expecting to see the smiling boys in their Quaker coats creeping out of the corn, their knives clutched in their hands. Nothing of the sort. There was still that rustling noise. Off to the left.

He began to walk in that direction, not having to bull through the corn anymore. The row was taking him in the direction he wanted to go, naturally. The row ended up ahead. Ended? No, emptied out into some sort of clearing. The rustling was there.

He stopped, suddenly afraid.

The scent of the corn was strong enough to be cloying. The rows held onto the sun's heat and he became aware that he was plastered with sweat and chaff and thin spider strands of cornsilk. The bugs ought to be crawling all over him . . . but they weren't.

He stood still, staring toward that place where the corn opened out onto what looked like a large circle of bare earth.

There were no midges or mosquitoes in here, no blackflies or chiggers—what he and Vicky had called "drive-in-bugs" when they had been courting, he thought with sudden and unexpectedly sad nostalgia. And he hadn't seen a single crow. How was that for weird, a cornpatch with no crows?

In the last of the daylight he swept his eyes closely over the row of corn to his left. And saw that every leaf and stalk was perfect, which was just not possible. No yellow blight. No tattered leaves, no caterpillar eggs, no burrows, no—

His eyes widened.

My God, there aren't any weeds!

Not a single one. Every foot and a half the corn plants rose from the earth. There was no witchgrass, jimson, pikeweed, whore's hair, or poke salad. Nothing.

Burt stared up, eyes wide. The light in the west was fading. The raftered clouds had drawn back together. Below them the golden light had faded to pink and ocher. It would be dark soon enough.

It was time to go down to the clearing in the corn and see what was there—hadn't that been the plan all along? All the time he had thought he was cutting back to the highway, hadn't he been being led to this place?

Dread in his belly, he went on down to the row and stood at the edge of the clearing. There was enough light left for him to see what was here. He couldn't scream. There didn't seem to be enough air left in his lungs. He tottered in on legs like slats of splintery wood. His eyes bulged from his sweaty face.

"Vicky," he whispered. "Oh, Vicky, my God—"

She had been mounted on a crossbar like a hideous trophy, her arms held at the wrists and her legs at the ankles with twists of common barbed wire, seventy cents a yard at any hardware store in Nebraska. Her eyes had been ripped out. The sockets were filled with the moonflax of cornsilk. Her jaws were wrenched open in a silent scream, her mouth filled with cornhusks.

On her left was a skeleton in a moldering surplice. The nude jawbone grinned. The eye sockets seemed to stare at Burt jocularly, as if the onetime minister of the Grace Baptist Church was saying: *It's not so bad, being sacrificed by pagan devil-children in the corn is not so bad, having your eyes ripped out of your skull according to the Laws of Moses is not so bad—*

To the left of the skeleton in the surplice was a second skeleton, this one dressed in a rotting blue uniform. A hat hung over the skull, shading the eyes, and on the peak of the cap was a greenish-tinged badge reading POLICE CHIEF.

That was when Burt heard it coming: not the children but something much larger, moving through the corn and toward the clearing. Not the children, no. The children wouldn't venture into the corn at night. This was the holy place, the place of He Who Walks Behind the Rows.

Jerkily Burt turned to flee. The row he had entered the clearing by was gone. Closed up. All the rows had closed up. It was coming closer now and he could hear it, pushing through the corn. He could hear it breathing. An ecstasy of superstitious terror seized him. It was coming. The corn on the far side of the clearing had suddenly darkened, as if a gigantic shadow had blotted it out.

Coming.

He Who Walks Behind the Rows.

It began to come into the clearing. Burt saw something huge, bulking up to the sky . . . something green with terrible red eyes the size of footballs.

Something that smelled like dried cornhusks years in some dark barn.

He began to scream. But he did not scream long.

Some time later, a bloated orange harvest moon came up.

The children of the corn stood in the clearing at midday, looking at the two crucified skeletons and the two bodies . . . the bodies were not skeletons yet, but they would be. In time. And here, in the heartland of Nebraska, in the corn, there was nothing but time.

"Behold, a dream came to me in the night, and the Lord did shew all this to me."

They all turned to look at Isaac with dread and wonder, even Malachi. Isaac was only nine, but he had been the Seer since the corn had taken David a year ago. David had been nineteen and he had walked into the corn on his birthday, just as dusk had come drifting down the summer rows.

Now, small face grave under his round-crowned hat, Isaac continued:

"And in my dream, the Lord was a shadow that walked behind the rows, and he spoke to me in the words he used to our older brothers years ago. He is much displeased with this sacrifice."

They made a sighing, sobbing noise and looked at the surrounding walls of green.

"And the Lord did say: Have I not given you a place of killing, that you might make sacrifice there? And have I not shewn you favor? But this man has made a blasphemy within me, and I have completed this sacrifice myself. Like the Blue Man and the false minister who escaped many years ago."

"The Blue Man . . . the false minister," they whispered, and looked at each other uneasily.

"So now is the Age of Favor lowered from nineteen plantings and harvestings to eighteen," Isaac went on relentlessly. "Yet be fruitful and multiply as the corn multiplies, that my favor may be shewn you, and be upon you."

Isaac ceased.

The eyes turned to Malachi and Joseph, the only two among this party who were eighteen. There were others back in town, perhaps twenty in all.

They waited to hear what Malachi would say, Malachi who had led the hunt for Japheth, who evermore would be known as Ahaz, cursed of God. Malachi had cut the throat of Ahaz and had thrown his body out of the corn so the foul body would not pollute it or blight it.

"I obey the word of God," Malachi whispered.

The corn seemed to sigh its approval.

In the weeks to come the girls would make many corncob crucifixes to ward off further evil.

And that night all of those now above the Age of Favor walked silently into the corn and went to the clearing, to gain the continued favor of He Who Walks Behind the Rows.

"Goodbye, Malachi," Ruth called. She waved disconsolately. Her belly was big with Malachi's child and tears coursed silently down her cheeks. Malachi did not turn. His back was straight. The corn swallowed him.

Ruth turned away, still crying. She had conceived a secret hatred for the corn and sometimes dreamed of walking into it with a torch in each hand when dry September came and the stalks were dead and explosively combustile. But she also feared it. Out there, in the night, something walked, and it saw everything . . . even the secrets kept in human hearts.

Dusk deepened into night. Around Gatlin the corn rustled and whispered secretly. It was well pleased.

NEVADA

Legal Rites
by Isaac Asimov and Frederik Pohl

I

ALREADY THE stars were out, though the sun had just dipped under the horizon, and the sky of the west was a blood-stuck gold behind the Sierra Nevadas.

"Hey!" squawked Russell Harley. "Come back!"

But the one-lunged motor of the old Ford was making too much noise; the driver didn't hear him. Harley cursed as he watched the old car careen along the sandy ruts on its half-flat tires. Its taillight was saying a red *no* to him. *No, you can't get away tonight; no,* you'll have to stay here and fight it out.

Harley grunted and climbed back up the porch stairs of the old wooden house. It was well made, anyhow. The stairs, though half a century old, neither creaked beneath him nor showed cracks.

Harley picked up the bags he'd dropped when he experienced his abrupt change of mind—fake leather and worn out, they were—and carted them into the house. He dumped them on a dust-jacketed sofa and looked around.

It was stifling hot, and the smell of the desert outside had permeated the room. Harley sneezed.

"Water," he said out loud. "That's what I need."

He'd prowled through every room on the ground floor before he stopped still and smote his head. Plumbing—naturally there'd be no plumbing in this hole eight miles out on the desert! A well was the best he could hope for—

If that.

It was getting dark. No electric lights either, of course. He blundered irritatedly through the dusky rooms to the back of the house. The screen door shrieked metallically as he opened it. A bucket hung by the door. He picked it up, tipped it, shook the loose sand out of it. He looked over the "back yard"—about thirty thousand visible acres of hilly sand, rock and patches of sage and flame-tipped ocotillo.

No well.

The old fool got water from somewhere, he thought savagely. Obstinately he climbed down the back steps and wandered out into the desert. Overhead the stars were blinding, a million billion of them, but the sunset was over already and he could see only hazily. The silence was murderous. Only a faint whisper of breeze over the sand, and the slither of his shoes.

He caught a glimmer of starlight from the nearest clump of sage and walked to it. There was a pool of water, caught in the angle of two enormous boulders. He stared at it doubtfully, then shrugged. It was water. It was better than nothing. He dipped the bucket in the little pool. Knowing nothing of the procedure, he filled it with a quart of loose sand as he scooped it along the bottom. When he lifted it, brimful, to his lips, staggering under the weight of it, he spat out the first mouthful and swore vividly.

Then he used his head. He set the bucket down, waited a second for the sand grains to settle, cupped water in his hands, lifted it to his lips....

Pat. HISS. Pat. HISS. Pat. HISS—

"What the hell!" Harley stood up, looked around in abrupt puzzlement. It sounded like water dripping from somewhere, onto a red-hot stove, flashing into sizzling steam. He saw nothing, only the sand and the sage and the pool of tepid, sickly water.

Pat. HISS—

Then he saw it, and his eyes bulged. Out of nowhere it was dripping, a drop a second, a sticky, dark drop that was thicker than water, that fell to the ground lazily, in slow defiance of gravity. And when it struck each drop sizzled and skittered about, and vanished. It was perhaps eight feet from him, just visible in the starlight.

And then, "Get off my land!" said the voice from nowhere.

Harley got. By the time he got to Rebel Butte three hours later, he was barely managing to walk, wishing desperately that he'd delayed long enough for one more good drink of water, despite all the fiends of hell. But he'd run the first three miles. He'd had plenty of encouragement. He remembered with a shudder how the clear desert air had taken milky shape around the incredible trickle of dampness and had advanced on him threateningly.

And when he got to the first kerosene-lighted saloon of Rebel Butte, and staggered inside, the saloonkeeper's fascinated stare at the front of his shoddy coat showed him strong evidence that he hadn't been suddenly taken with insanity, or drunk on the unaccustomed sensation of fresh desert air. All down the front of him it was, and the harder he rubbed the harder it stayed, the stickier it got. Blood!

"Whiskey!" he said in a strangled voice, tottering to the bar. He pulled a threadbare dollar bill from his pocket flapped in onto the mahogany.

The blackjack game at the back of the room had stopped. Harley was acutely conscious of the eyes of the players, the bartender and the tall, lean man leaning on the bar. All were watching him.

The bartender broke the spell. He reached for a bottle behind him without looking at it, placed it on the counter before Harley. He poured a glass of water from a jug, set it down with a shot glass beside the bottle.

"I could of told you that would happen," he said casually. "Only you wouldn't of believed me. You had to meet Hank for yourself before you'd believe he was there."

Harley remembered his thirst and drained the glass of water, then poured himself a shot of the whiskey and swallowed it without waiting for the chaser to be refilled. The whiskey felt good going down, almost good enough to stop his internal shakes.

"What are you talking about?" he said finally. He twisted his body and leaned forward across the bar to partly hide the stains on his coat. The saloonkeeper laughed.

"Old Hank," he said. "I knowed who you was right away even before Tom came back and told me where he'd took you. I knowed you was Zeb Harley's no-good nephew, come to take Harley Hall an' sell it before he was cold in his grave."

The blackjack players were still watching him, Russell Harley saw. Only the lean man farther along the bar seemed to have dismissed him. He was pouring himself another drink quite occupied with his task.

Harley flushed. "Listen," he said, "I didn't come in here for advice. I wanted a drink. I'm paying for it. Keep your mouth out of this."

The saloonkeeper shrugged. He turned his back and walked away to the blackjack table. After a couple of seconds one of the players turned too, and threw a card down. The others followed suit.

Harley was just getting set to swallow his pride and talk to the saloonkeeper again—he seemed to know something about what Harley'd been through, and might be helpful—when the lean man tapped his shoulder. Harley whirled and almost dropped his glass. Absorbed and jumpy, he hadn't seen him come up.

"Young man," said the lean one, "my name's Nicholls. Come along with me, sir, and we'll talk this thing over. I think we may be of service to each other."

Even the twelve-cylinder car Nicholls drove jounced like a haywagon over the sandy ruts leading to the place old Zeb had—laughingly—named "Harley Hall."

Russell Harley twisted his neck and stared at the heap of paraphernalia in the open rumble seat. "I don't like it," he complained. "I never had anything to do with ghosts. How do I know this stuff'll work?"

Nicholls smiled. "You'll have to take my word for it. I've had dealings with ghosts before. You could say that I might qualify as a ghost exterminator, if I chose."

Harley growled. "I still don't like it."

Nicholls turned a sharp look on him. "You like the prospect of owning Harley Hall, don't you? And looking for all the money your late uncle is supposed to have hidden around somewhere?" Harley shrugged. "Certainly you do," said Nicholls, returning his eyes to the road. "And with good reason. The local reports put the figure pretty high, young man."

"That's where you come in, I guess," Harley said sullenly. "I find the money—that I own anyhow—and give some of it to you. How much?"

"We'll discuss that later," Nicholls said. He smiled absently as he looked ahead.

"We'll discuss it right now!"

The smile faded from Nicholls' face. "No," he said. "We won't. I'm doing you a favor, young Harley. Remember that. In return—you'll do as I say, all the way!"

Harley digested that carefully, and it was not a pleasant meal. He waited a couple of seconds before he changed the subject.

"I was out here once when the old man was alive," he said. "He didn't say nothing about any ghost."

"Perhaps he felt you might think him—well, peculiar," Nicholls said. "And perhaps you would have. When were you here?"

"Oh, a long time ago," Harley said evasively. "But I was here a whole day, and part of the night. The old man was crazy as a coot, but he didn't keep any ghosts in the attic."

"This ghost was a friend of his," Nicholls said. "The gentleman in charge of the bar told you that, surely. Your late uncle was something of a recluse. He lived in this house a dozen miles from nowhere, came into town hardly ever, wouldn't let anyone get friendly with him. But he wasn't exactly a hermit. He had Hank for company."

"Fine company."

Nicholls inclined his head seriously. "Oh, I don't know," he said. "From all accounts they got on well together. They played pinochle and chess—Hank's supposed to have been a great pinochle player. He was killed that way, according to the local reports. Caught somebody dealing from the bottom and shot it out with him. He lost. A bullet pierced his throat and he died quite bloodily." He turned the wheel, putting his weight into the effort, and succeeded in twisting the car out of the ruts of the "road," sent it jouncing across unmarked sand to the old frame house to which they were going.

"That," he finished as he pulled up before the porch, "accounts for the blood that accompanies his apparition."

Harley opened the door slowly and got out, looking uneasily at the battered old house. Nicholls cut the motor, got out and walked at once to the back of the car.

"Come on," he said, dragging things out of the compartment. "Give me a hand with this. I'm not going to carry this stuff all by myself."

Harley came around reluctantly, regarded the curious assortment of bundles of dried faggots, lengths of colored cord, chalk pencils, ugly little bunches of wilted weeds, bleached bones of small animals and a couple of less pleasant things without pleasure.

Pat. HISS. Pat. HISS—

"He's here!" Harley yelped. "Listen! He's someplace around here watching us."

"Ha!"

The laugh was deep, unpleasant and—bodiless. Harley looked around desperately for the tell-tale trickle of blood. And he found it; from the air it issued, just beside the car, sinking gracefully to the ground and sizzling, vanishing, there.

"I'm watching you, all right," the voice said grimly. "Russell, you worthless piece of corruption, I've got no more use for you than you used to have for me. Dead or alive, this is my land! I shared it with your uncle, you young scalawag, but I won't share it with you. Get out!"

Harley's knees weakened and he tottered dizzily to the rear bumper, sat on it. "Nicholls—" he said confusedly.

"Oh, brace up," Nicholls said with irritation. He tossed a ball of gaudy twine, red and green, with curious knots tied along it, to Harley. Then he confronted the trickle of blood and made a few brisk passes in the air before it. His lips were moving silently, Harley saw, but no words came out.

There was a gasp and a chopped-off squawk from the source of the blood drops. Nicholls clapped his hands sharply then turned to young Harley.

"Take that cord you have in your hands and stretch it around the house," he said. "All the way around, and make sure it goes right across the middle of the doors and windows. It isn't much, but it'll hold him till we can get the good stuff set up."

Harley nodded, then pointed a rigid finger at the drops of blood, now sizzling and fuming more angrily than before. "What about *that*?" he managed to get out.

Nicholls grinned complacently. "It'll hold him here till the cows come home," he said. "Get moving!"

Harley inadvertently inhaled a lungful of noxious white smoke and coughed till the tears rolled down his cheeks. When he recovered he looked at Nicholls, who was reading silently from a green leather book with dog-eared pages. He said, "Can I stop stirring this now?"

Nicholls grimaced angrily and shook his head without looking at him. He went on reading, his lips contorting over syllables that were not in any language Harley had ever heard, then snapped the book shut and wiped his brow.

"Fine," he said. "So far, so good." He stepped over to leeward of the boiling pot Harley was stirring on the hob over the fireplace, peered down into it cautiously.

"That's about done," he said. "Take it off the fire and let it cool a bit."

Harley lifted it down, then squeezed his aching biceps with his left hand. The stuff was the consistency of sickly green fudge.

Nicholls didn't answer. He looked up in mild surprise at the sudden squawk of triumph from outside, followed by the howling of a chill wind.

"Hank must be loose," he said casually. "He can't do us any harm, I think, but we'd better get a move on." He rummaged in the dwindled pile of junk he'd brought from the car, extracted a paint-brush. "Smear this stuff around all the windows and doors. All but the front door. For that I have something else." He pointed to what seemed to be the front axle of an old Model-T. "Leave that on the doorsill. Cold iron. You can just step over it, but Hank won't be able to pass it. It's been properly treated already with the very best thaumagurgy."

"Step over it," Harley repeated. "What would I want to step over it for? *He's* out there."

"He won't hurt you," said Nicholls. "You will carry an amulet with you—that one, there—that will keep him away. Probably he couldn't really hurt you anyhow, being a low-order ghost who can't materialize to any great density. But just to take no chances, carry the amulet and don't stay out too long. It won't hold him off forever, not for more than half an hour. If you ever have to go out and stay for any length of time, tie that bundle of herbs around your neck." Nicholls smiled. "That's only for emergencies, though. It works on the asafoetida principle. Ghosts can't come anywhere near it—but you won't like it much yourself. It has—ah—a rather definite odor."

He leaned gingerly over the pot again, sniffing. He sneezed.

"Well, that's cool enough," he said. "Before it hardens, get moving. Start spreading the stuff upstairs—and make sure you don't miss any windows."

"What are you going to do?"

"I," said Nicholls sharply, "will be here. Start."

But he wasn't. When Harley finished his disagreeable task and came down he called Nicholls' name, but the man was gone. Harley stepped to the door and looked out; the car was gone too.

He shrugged. "Oh, well," he said, and began taking the dust-clothes off the furniture.

II

Somewhere within the cold, legal mind of Lawyer Turnbull, he weighed the comparative likeness of nightmare and insanity.

He stared at the plush chair facing him, noted with distinct uneasiness how the strangely weightless, strangely sourceless trickle of redness disappeared as it hit the floor, but left long, mud-ochre streaks matted on the upholstery. The sound was unpleasant too; *Pat. HISS. Pat. HISS—*

The voice continued impatiently, "Damn your human stupidity! I may be a ghost, but heaven knows I'm not trying to haunt you. Friend, you're not that important to me. Get this—I'm here on business."

Turnbull learned that you cannot wet lips with a dehydrated tongue. "Legal business?"

"Sure. The fact that I was once killed by violence, and have to continue my existence on the astral plane, doesn't mean I've lost my legal right. Does it?"

The lawyer shook his head in bafflement. He said, "This would be easier on me if you weren't invisible. Can't you do something about it?"

There was a short pause. "Well, I could materialize for a minute," the voice said. "It's hard work—damn hard, for me. There are a lot of us astral entities that can do it easy as falling out of bed, but—Well, if I have to I shall try to do it once."

There was a shimmering in the air above the armchair, and a milky, thing smoke condensed into an intangible seated figure. Turnbull took no delight in noting that, through the figure, the outlines of the chair were still hazily visible. The figure thickened. Just as the features took form—just as Thornbull's bulging eyes made out a prominent hooked nose and a crisp beard—it thinned and exploded with a soft pop.

The voice said weakly, "I didn't think I was that bad. I'm way out of practice. I guess that's the first daylight materialization I've made in seventy-five years."

The lawyer adjusted his rimless glasses and coughed. *Hell's hinges*, he thought, *the worst thing about this is that I'm believing it!*

"Oh, well," he said aloud. Then he hurried on before the visitor could take offense: "Just what did you want? I'm just a small-town lawyer, you know. My business is fairly routine—"

"I know all about your business," the voice said. "You can handle my case—it's a land affair. I want to sue Russell Harley,"

"Harley?" Turnbull fingered his cheek, "Any relation to Zeb Harley?"

"His nephew—and his heir, too."

Turnbull nodded. "Yes, I remember now. My wife's folks live in Rebel Butte, and I've been there. Quite a coincidence you should come to me—"

The voice laughed. "It was no coincidence," it said softly.

"Oh." Turnbull was silent for a second. Then, "I see," he said. He cast a shrewd glance at the chair. "Lawsuits cost money, Mr.— I don't think you mentioned your name?"

"Hank Jenkins," the voice prompted. "I know that. Would— let's see. Would six hundred and fifty dollars be sufficient?"

Turnbull swallowed. "I think so," he said in a relatively unemotional tone—relative to what he was thinking.

"Then suppose we call that your retainer. I happen to have cached a considerable sum in gold when I was—that is to say, before I became an astral entity. I'm quite certain it hasn't been disturbed. You will have to call it treasure trove, I guess, and give half of it to the state, but there's thirteen hundred dollars altogether."

Turnbull nodded judiciously. "Assuming we can locate your trove," he said, "I think that would be quite satisfactory." He leaned back in his chair and looked legal. His aplomb had returned.

And half an hour later he said slowly, "I'll take your case."

Judge Lawrence Gimbel had always liked his job before. But his thirteen honorable years on the bench lost their flavor for him as he grimaced wearily and reached for his gavel. This case was far too confusing for his taste.

The clerk made his speech, and the packed courtroom sat down en masse. Gimbel held a hand briefly to his eyes before he spoke.

"Is the counsel for the plaintiff ready?"

"I am your honor." Turnbull, alone at his table, rose and bowed.

"The counsel for the defendant?"

"Ready, your honor!" Fred Wilson snapped. He looked with a hard flicker of interest at Turnbull and his solitary table, then leaned over and whispered in Russell Harley's ear. The youth nodded glumly, then shrugged.

Gimbel said, "I understand the attorneys for both sides have waived jury trial in this case of Henry Jenkins versus Russell Joseph Harley."

Both lawyers nodded. Gimbel continued, "In view of the unusual nature of this case, I imagine it will prove necessary to conduct it with a certain amount of informality. The sole purpose of this court is to arrive at the true facts at issue, and to deliver a verdict in accord with the laws pertaining to these facts. I will not stand on ceremony. Nevertheless, I will not tolerate any disturbances or unnecessary irregularities. The spectators will kindly remember that they are here on privilege. Any demonstration will result in the clearing of the court."

He looked severely at the white faces that gleamed unintelligently up at him. He suppressed a sigh as he said, "The counsel for the plaintiff will begin."

Turnbull rose quickly to his feet, faced the judge.

"Your honor," he said, "we propose to show that my client, Henry Jenkins, has been deprived of his just rights by the defendant. Mr. Jenkins, by virtue of a sustained residence of more than twenty years in the house located on Route 22, eight miles north of the town of Rebel Butte, with the full knowledge of its legal owner, has acquired certain rights. In legal terminology we define these as the rights of adverse possession. The layman would call them common-law rights—squatters' rights."

Gimbel folded his hands and tried to relax. Squatters' rights—for a ghost! He sighed, but listened attentively as Turnbull went on.

"Upon the death of Zebulon Harley, the owner of the house involved—it is better known, perhaps, as Harley Hall—the defendant inherited title to the property. We do not question his right to it. But my client has an equity in Harley Hall; the right to free and full occupation of it for the duration of his existence. The defendant has forcefully evicted my client, by means which have caused my client great mental distress, and have even endangered his very existence."

Gimbel nodded. If the case only had a precedent somewhere . . . But it hadn't; he remembered grimly the hours he'd spent thumbing through all sorts of unlikely law books, looking for anything that might bear on the case. It had been his better judgment that he throw the case out of court outright—a judge couldn't afford to have himself laughed at, not if he were ambitious. And public laughter was about the only certainty there was to this case. But Wilson had put up such a fight that the judge's temper had taken over. He never did like Wilson, anyhow.

"You may proceed with your witnesses," he said.

Turnbull nodded. To the clerk he said, "Call Henry Jenkins to the stand."

Wilson was on his feet before the clerk opened his mouth.

"Objection!" he bellowed. "The so-called Henry Jenkins cannot qualify as a witness!"

"Why not?" demanded Turnbull.

"Because he's dead!"

The judge clutched his gavel with one hand, forehead with the other. He banged on the desk to quiet the courtroom.

Turnbull stood there, smiling. "Naturally," he said, "you'll have proof of that statement."

Wilson snarled. "Certainly." He referred to his brief. "The so-called Henry Jenkins is the ghost, spirit of specter of one Hank Jenkins, who prospected for gold in this territory a century ago. He was killed by a bullet through the throat from the gun of one Long Tom Cooper, and was declared legally dead on September 14, 1850. Cooper was hung for his murder. No matter what hocus-pocus you produce for evidence to the contrary now, that status of legal death remains completely valid."

"What evidence have you of the identity of my client with this Hank Jenkins?" Turnbull asked grimly.

"Do you deny it?"

Turnbull shrugged. "I deny nothing. I'm not being cross-examined. Furthermore, the sole prerequisite of a witness is that he understand the value of an oath. Henry Jenkins was tested by John Quincy Fitzjames, professor of psychology at the University of Southern California. The results—I have Dr. Fitzjames' sworn statement of them here, which I will introduce as an exhibit—show clearly that my client's intelligence quotient is well above normal, and that a psychiatric examination discloses no important aberrations which would injure his validity as a witness. I insist that my client be allowed to testify on his own behalf."

"But he's dead!" squawked Wilson. "He's invisible right now!"

"My client," said Turnbull stiffly, "is not present just now. Undoubtedly that accounts for what you term his invisibility."

He paused for the appreciative murmur that swept through the court. Things were breaking perfectly, he thought, smiling. "I have here another affidavit," he said. "It is signed by Elihu James and Terence MacRae, who respectively head the departments of physics and biology at the same univeristy. It states that my client exhibits all the vital phenomena of life. I am prepared to call all three of my expert witnesses to the stand, if necessary."

Wilson scowled but said nothing. Judge Gimbel leaned forward.

"I don't see how it is possible for me to refuse the plaintiff the right to testify," he said. "If the three experts who prepared these reports will testify on the stand to the facts contained in them, Henry Jenkins may then take the stand."

Wilson sat down heavily. The three experts spoke briefly—and dryly. Wilson put them through only the most formal of cross-examinations.

The judge declared a brief recess. In the corridor outside, Wilson and his client lit cigarettes and looked unsympathetically at each other.

"I feel like a fool," said Russell Harley. "Bringing suit against a ghost."

"The ghost brought the suit," Wilson reminded him. "If only we'd been able to hold fire for a couple more weeks, till another judge came on the bench, I could've got this thing thrown right out of court."

"Well, why couldn't we wait?"

"Because you were in such a damn hurry!" Wilson said. "You and that idiot Nicholls—so confident that it would never come to trial."

Harley shrugged, and thought unhappily of their failure in completely exorcising the ghost of Hank Jenkins. That had been a mess. Jenkins had somehow escaped from the charmed circle they'd drawn around him, in which they'd hoped to keep him till the trial was forfeited by non-appearance.

"That's another thing," said Wilson. "Where is Nicholls?"

Harley shrugged again. "I dunno. The last I saw of him was in your office. He came around to see me right after the deputy slapped the show-cause order on me at the house. He brought me down to you—said you'd been recommended to him. Then you and him and I talked about the case for a while. He went out, after he lent me a little money to help meet your retainer. Haven't seen him since."

"I'd like to know who recommended me to him," Wilson said grimly. "I don't think he'd ever recommend anybody else. I don't like this case—and I don't much like you."

Harley growled but said nothing. He flung his cigarette away. It tasted of the garbage that hung around his neck—everything did. Nicholls had told no lies when he said Harley wouldn't much like the bundle of herbs that would ward off the ghost of old Jenkins. They smelled.

The court clerk was in the corridor, bawling something, and people were beginning to trickle back in. Harley and his attorney went with them.

When the trial had been resumed, the clerk said, "Henry Jenkins!"

Wilson was on his feet at once. He opened the door of the judge's chamber, said something in a low tone. Then he stepped back, as if to let someone through.

Pat, HISS. Pat. HISS—

There was a concerted gasp from the spectators as the weirdly appearing trickle of blood moved slowly across the open space to the witness chair. This was the ghost—the plaintiff in the most eminently absurd case in the history of jurisprudence.

"All right, Hank," Turnbull whispered. "You'll have to materialize long enough to let the clerk swear you in."

The clerk drew back nervously at the pillar of milky fog that appeared before him, vaguely humanoid in shape. A phantom hand, half transparent, reached out to touch the Bible. The clerk's voice shook as he administered the oath, and heard the response come from the heart of the cloud-pillar.

The haze drifted into the witness chair, bent curiously at about hip-height, and popped into nothingness.

The judge banged his gavel wildly. The buzz of alarm that had arisen from the spectators died out.

"I'll warn you again," he declared, "that unruliness will not be tolerated. The counsel for the plaintiff may proceed."

Turnbull walked to the witness chair and addressed its emptiness.

"Your name?"

"My name is Henry Jenkins."

"Your occupation?"

There was a slight pause. "I have none. I guess you'd say I'm retired."

"Mr. Jenkins, just what connection have you with the building referred to as Harley Hall?"

"I have occupied it for ninety years."

"During this time, did you come to know the late Zebulon Harley, owner of the Hall?"

"I knew Zeb quite well."

Turnbull nodded. "When did you make his acquaintance?" he asked.

"In the spring of 1907. Zeb had just lost his wife. After that, you see, he made Harley Hall his year-round home. He became—well, more or less of a hermit. Before that we had never met, since he was only seldom at the Hall. But we became friendly then."

"How long did this friendship last?"

"Until he died last fall. I was with him when he died. I still have a few keepsakes he left me then." There was a distinct nostalgic sigh from the witness chair, which by now was liberally spattered with muddy red liquid. The falling drops seemed to hesitate for a second, and their sizzling noise was muted as with a strong emotion.

Turnbull went on, "Your relations with him were good, then?"

"I'd call them excellent," the emptiness replied firmly. "Every night we sat up together. When we didn't play pinochle or chess or cribbage, we just sat and talked over the news of the day. I still have the book we used to keep records of the chess and pinochle games. Zeb made the entries himself, in his own handwriting."

Turnbull abandoned the witness for a moment. He faced the judge with a smile. "I offer in evidence," he said, "the book mentioned. Also a ring given to the plaintiff by the late Mr. Harley, and a copy of the plays of Gilbert and Sullivan. On the flyleaf of this book is inscribed, 'To Old Hank,' in Harley's own hand."

He turned again to the empty, blood-leaking witness chair.

He said, "In all your years of association, did Zebulon Harley ever ask you to leave, or to pay rent?"

"Of course not. Not Zeb!"

Turnbull nodded. "Very good," he said. "Now, just one or two more questions. Will you tell in your own words what occurred, after the death of Zebulon Harley, that caused you to bring this suit?"

"Well, in January young Harley—"

"You mean Russell Joseph Harley, the defendant?"

"Yes. He arrived at Harley Hall on January fifth. I asked him to leave, which he did. On the next day he returned with another man. They placed a talisman upon the threshold of the main entrance, and soon after sealed every threshold and window sill in the Hall with a substance which is noxious to me. These activities were accompanied by several of the most deadly spells in the Ars Magicorum. He further added an Exclusion Circle with a radius of a little over a mile, entirely surrounding the Hall."

"I see," the lawyer said. "Will you explain to the court the effects of these activities?"

"Well," the voice said thoughtfully, "it's a little hard to put in words. I can't pass the Circle without a great expenditure of energy. Even if I did I couldn't enter the building because of the talisman and the seals."

"Could you enter by air? Through a chimney, perhaps?"

"No. The Exclusion Circle is really a sphere. I'm pretty sure the effort would destroy me."

"In effect, then, you are entirely barred from the house you have occupied for ninety years, due to the wilful acts of Russell Joseph Harley, the defendant, and an unnamed accomplice of his."

"That is correct."

Turnbull beamed. "Thank you. That's all."

He turned to Wilson, whose face had been a study in dourness throughout the entire examination. "Your witness," he said.

Wilson snapped to his feet and strode to the witness chair.

He said belligerently, "You say your name is Henry Jenkins?"

"Yes."

"That is your name now, you mean to say. What was your name before?"

"Before?" There was surprise in the voice that emanated from above the trickling blood-drops. "Before when?"

Wilson scowled. "Don't pretend ignorance," he said sharply. "Before you *died*, of course."

"Objection!" Turnbull was on his feet, glaring at Wilson. "The counsel for the defense has no right to speak of some hypothetical death of my client!"

Gimbel raised a hand wearily and cut off the words that were forming on Wilson's lips. "Objection sustained," he said. "No evidence has been presented to identify the plaintiff as the prospector who was killed in 1850—or anyone else."

Wilson's mouth twisted into a sour grimace. He continued on a lower key. "You say, Mr. Jenkins, that you occupied Harley Hall for ninety years."

"Ninety-two years next month. The Hall wasn't built—in its present form, anyhow—until 1876, but I occupied the house that stood on the site previously."

"What did you do before then?"

"Before then?" The voice paused, then said doubtfully, "I don't remember."

"You're under oath!" Wilson flared.

The voice got firmer. "Ninety years is a long time," it said. "I don't remember."

"Let's see if I can't refresh your memory. Is is true that ninety-one years ago, in the very year in which you claim to have begun your occupancy of Harley Hall, Hank Jenkins was killed in a gun duel?"

"That may be true, if you say so. I don't remember."

"Do you remember that the shooting occurred not fifty feet from the present site of Harley Hall?"

"It may be."

"Well, then," Wilson thundered, "is it not a fact that when Hank Jenkins died by violence his ghost assumed existence? That it was then doomed to haunt the site of its slaying throughout eternity?"

The voice said evenly, "I have no knowledge of that."

"Do you deny that it is well known throughout that section that the ghost of Hank Jenkins haunts Harley Hall?"

"Objection!" shouted Turnbull. "Popular opinion is not evidence."

"Objection sustained. Strike the question from the record."

Wilson, badgered, lost his control. In a dangerously uneven voice, he said, "Perjury is a criminal offense. Mr. Jenkins, do you deny that you are the ghost of Hank Jenkins?"

The tone was surprised. "Why, certainly."

"You *are* a ghost, aren't you?"

Stiffly, "I'm an entity on the astral plane."

"That, I believe, is what is called a ghost?"

"I can't help what it's called. I've heard you called a lot of things. Is that proof?"

There was a surge of laughter from the audience. Gimbel slammed his gavel down on the bench.

"The witness," he said, "will confine himself to answering questions."

Wilson bellowed, "In spite of what you say, it's true, isn't it, that you are merely the spirit of a human being who had died through violence?"

The voice from above the blood drops retorted, "I repeat that I am an entity of the astral plane. I am not aware that I was ever a human being."

The lawyer turned an exasperated face to the bench.

"Your honor," he said, "I ask that you instruct the witness to cease playing verbal hide-and-seek. It is quite evident that the witness is a ghost, and that he is therefore the relict of some human being, ipso facto. Circumstantial evidence is strong that he is the ghost of the Hank Jenkins who was killed in 1850. But this is a non-essential point. What is definite is that he is the ghost of someone who is dead, and hence is unqualified to act as witness! I demand his testimony be stricken from the record!"

Turnbull spoke up at once. "Will the counsel for the defense quote his authority for branding my client a ghost—in the face of my client's repeated declaration that he is an entity of the astral plane? What is the legal definition of a ghost?"

Judge Gimbel smiled. "Counsel for the defense will proceed with the cross-examination," he said.

Wilson's face flushed dark purple. He mopped his brow with a large bandanna, then glared at the dropping, sizzling trickle of blood.

"Whatever you are," he said, "answer me this question. Can you pass through a wall?"

"Why, yes. Certainly." There was a definite note of surprise in the voice from nowhere. "But it isn't as easy as some people think. It definitely requires a lot of effort."

"Never mind that. You can do it?"

"Yes."

"Could you be bound by any physical means? Would handcuffs hold you? Or ropes, chains, prison walls, a hermetically sealed steel chest?"

Jenkins had no chance to answer. Turnbull, scenting danger, cut in hastily. "I object to this line of questioning. It is entirely irrelevant."

"On the contrary," Wilson cried loudly, "it bears strongly on the qualifications of the so-called Henry Jenkins as a witness! I demand that he answer the question."

Judge Gimbel said, "Objection overruled. Witness will answer the question."

The voice from the air said superciliously, "I don't mind answering. Physical barriers mean nothing to me, by and large."

The counsel for the defense drew himself up triumphantly.

"Very good," he said with satisfaction. "*Very* good." Then to the judge, the words coming sharp and fast, "I claim, your honor, that the so-called Henry Jenkins has no legal status as a witness in court. There is clearly no value in understanding the nature of an oath if a violation of the oath can bring no punishment in its wake. The statements of a man who can perjure himself freely have no worth. I demand they be stricken from the record!"

Turnbull was at the judge's bench in two strides.

"I had anticipated that, your honor," he said quickly. "From the very nature of the case, however, it is clear that my client can be very definitely restricted in his movements—spells, pentagrams, talismans, amulets,

Exclusion Circles and what-not. I have here—which I am prepared to deliver to the bailiff of the court—a list of the various methods of confining an astral entity to a restricted area for periods ranging from a few moments to all eternity. Moroever, I have also signed a bond for five thousand dollars, prior to the beginning of the trial, which I stand ready to forfeit should my client be confined and make his escape, if found guilty of any misfeasance as a witness."

Gimbel's face, which had looked startled for a second, slowly cleared. He nodded. "The court is satisfied with the statement of the counsel for the plaintiff," he declared. "There seems no doubt that the plaintiff can be penalized for any misstatements, and the motion of the defense is denied."

Wilson looked choleric, but shrugged. "All right," he said. "That will be all."

"You may step down, Mr. Jenkins," Gimbel directed, and watched in fascination as the blood-dripping column rose and floated over the floor, along the corridor, out the door.

Turnbull approached the judge's bench again. He said, "I would like to place in evidence these notes, the diary of the late Zebulon Harley. It was presented to my client by Harley himself last fall. I call particular attention to the entry for April sixth, nineteen seventeen, in which he mentions the entrance of the United States into the First World War, and records the results of a series of eleven pinochle games played with a personage identified as 'Old Hank.' With the court's permission, I will read the entry for that day, and also various other entries for the next four years. Please note the references to someone known variously as 'Jenkins,' 'Hank Jenkins' and—in one extremely significant passage—'Old Invisible.'"

Wilson stewed silently during the slow reading of Harley's diary. There was anger on his face, but he paid close attention, and when the reading was over he leaped to his feet.

"I would like to know," he asked, "if the counsel for the plaintiff is in possession of any diaries *after* nineteen twenty?"

Turnbull shook his head. "Harley apparently never kept a diary, except during the four years represented in this."

"Then I demand that the court refuse to admit this diary as evidence on two counts," Wilson said. He raised two fingers to tick off the points. "In the first place, the evidence presented is frivolous. The few vague and unsatisfactory references to Jenkins nowhere specifically describe him as what he is—ghost, astral entity or what you will. Second, the evidence, even were the first point overlooked, concerns only the years up to nineteen twenty-one. The case concerns itself only with the supposed occupation of Harley Hall by the so-called Jenkins in the last twenty years—*since* 'twenty-one. Clearly, the evidence is therefore irrelevant."

Gimbel looked at Turnbull, who smiled calmly.

"The reference to 'Old Invisible' is far from vague," he said. "It is a definite indication of the astral character of my client. Furthermore, evidence as to the friendship of my client with the late Mr. Zebulon Harley before nineteen twenty-one is entirely relevant, as such a friendship, once established, would naturally be presumed to have continued indefinitely. Unless of course, the defense is able to present evidence to the contrary."

Judge Gimbel said, "The diary is admitted as evidence."

Turnbull said, "I rest my case."

There was a buzz of conversation in the courtroom while the judge looked over the diary, and then handed it to the clerk to be marked and entered.

Gimbel said, "The defense may open its case."

Wilson rose. To the clerk he said, "Russell Joseph Harley."

But young Harley was recalcitrant. "Nix," he said, on his feet, pointing at the witness chair. "That thing's got blood all over it! You don't expect me to sit down in that large puddle of blood, do you?"

Judge Gimbel leaned over to look at the chair. The drip-drop trickle of blood from the apparition who'd been testifying had left its mark. Muddy brown all down the front of the chair. Gimbel found himself wondering how the ghost managed to replenish its supply of the fluid, but gave it up.

"I see your point," he said. "Well, it's getting a bit late anyhow. The clerk will take away the present witness chair and replace it. In the interim, I declare the court recessed till tomorrow morning at ten o'clock."

III

Russell Harley noticed how the elevator boy's back registered repulsion and disapproval, and scowled. He was not a popular guest in the hotel, he knew well. Where he made his mistake, though, was in thinking that the noxious bundle of herbs about his neck was the cause of it. His odious personality had a lot to do with the chilly attitude of the management and his fellow guests.

He made his way to the bar, ignoring the heads that turned in surprise to follow the reeking comet-tail of his passage. He entered the red-leather-and-chromium drinking room, and stared about for Lawyer Wilson.

And blinked in surprise when he saw him. Wilson wasn't alone. In the booth with him was a tall, dark figure, with his back to Harley. The back alone was plenty of recognition. Nicholls!

Wilson had seen him. "Hello, Harley," he said, all smiles and affability in the presence of the man with the money. "Come on and sit down. Mr. Nicholls dropped in on me a little while ago, so I brought him over."

"Hello," Harley said glumly, and Nicholls nodded. The muscles of his cheeks pulsed, and he seemed under a strain, strangely uncomfortable in Harley's presence. Still there was a twinkle in the look he gave young Harley, and his voice was friendly enough—though supercilious—as he said:

"Hello, Harley. How is the trial going?"

"Ask him," said Harley, pointing a thumb at Wilson as he slid his knees under the booth's table and sat down. "He's the lawyer. He's supposed to know these things."

"Doesn't he?"

Harley shrugged and craned his neck for the waitress. "Oh, I guess so . . . . Rye and water!" He watched the girl appreciatively as she nodded and went off to the bar, then turned his attention back to Nicholls. "The trouble is," he said, "Wilson may think he knows, but I think he's all wet."

Wilson frowned. "Do you imply—" he began, but Nicholls put up a hand.

"Let's not bicker," said Nicholls. "Suppose you answer my question. I have a stake in this, and I want to know. How's the trial going?"

Wilson put on his most open-faced expression. "Frankly," he said, "not too well. I'm afraid the judge is on the other side. If you'd listened to me and stalled till another judge came along—"

"I had no time to stall," said Nicholls. "I have to be elsewhere within a few days. Even now, I should be on my way. Do you think we might lose the case?"

Harley laughed sharply. As Wilson glared at him he took his drink from the waitress' tray and swallowed it. The smile remained on his face as he listened to Wilson say smoothly:

"There is a good deal of danger, yes."

"Hum." Nicholls looked interestedly at his fingernails. "Perhaps I chose the wrong lawyer."

"Sure you did." Harley waved at the waitress, ordered another drink. "You want to know what else I think? I think you picked the wrong client, spelled s-t-o-o-g-e. I'm getting sick of this. This damn thing around my neck smells bad. How do I know it's any good, anyhow? Far as I can see, it just smells bad, and that's all."

"It works." Nicholls said succinctly. "I wouldn't advise you to go without it. The late Hank Jenkins is not a very strong ghost—a strong one would tear you apart and chew up your herbs for dessert—but without the protection of what you wear about your neck, you would become a very uncomfortable human as soon as Jenkins heard you'd stopped wearing it."

He put down the glass of red wine he'd been inhaling without drinking, looked intently at Wilson. "I've put up the money in this," he said. "I had hoped you'd be able to handle the legal end. I see I'll have to do more. Now listen intently, because I have no intention of repeating this. There's an angle to his case that's got right by your blunted legal acumen. Jenkins claims to be an astral entity, which he undoubtedly is. Now, instead of trying to prove him a ghost, and legally dead, and therefore unfit to testify, which you have been doing, suppose you do this . . ."

He went on to speak rapidly and to the point.

And when he left them a bit later, and Wilson took Harley up to his room and poured him into bed, the lawyer felt happy for the first time in days.

Russell Joseph Harley, a little hung over and a lot nervous, was called to the stand as first witness in his own behalf.

Wilson said, "Your name?"

"Russell Joseph Harley."

"You are the nephew of the late Zebulon Harley, who bequeathed the residence known as Harley Hall to you?"

"Yes."

Wilson turned to the bench. "I offer this copy of the late Mr. Zebulon Harley's will in evidence. All his possessions are left to his nephew and only living kin, the defendant."

Turnbull spoke from his desk. "The plaintiff in no way disputes the defendant's equity in Harley Hall."

Wilson continued, "You passed part of your childhood in Harley Hall, did you not, and visited it as a grown man on occasion?"

"Yes."

"At any time, has anything in the shape of a ghost, specter of astral entity manifested itself to you in Harley Hall?"

"No. I'd remember it."

"Did your late uncle ever mention any such manifestation to you?"

"Him? No."

"That's all."

Turnbull came up for the cross-examination.

"When, Mr. Harley, did you last see your uncle before his death?"

"It was in 1938. In September, some time—around the tenth or eleventh of the month."

"How long a time did you spend with him?"

Harley flushed unaccountably. "Ah—just one day," he said.

"When before that did you see him?"

"Well, not since I was quite young. My parents moved to Pennsylvania in 1920."

"And since then—except for that one-day visit in 1938—has any communication passed between you uncle and yourself?"

"No, I guess not. He was a rather queer duck—solitary. A little bit balmy, I think."

"Well, you're a loving nephew. But in view of what you've just said, does it sound surprising that your uncle never told you of Mr. Jenkins? He never had much chance to, did he?

"He had a chance in 1938, but he didn't," Harley said defiantly.

Turnbull shrugged. "I'm finished," he said.

Gimbel began to look bored. He had anticipated something more in the way of fireworks. He said, "Has the defense any further witnesses?"

Wilson smiled grimly. "Yes, your honor," he said. This was his big moment, and he smiled again as he said gently, "I would like to call Mr. Henry Jenkins to the stand."

In the amazed silence that followed, Judge Gimbel leaned forward. "You mean you wish to call the plaintiff as a witness for the defense?"

Serenely, "Yes, your honor."

Gimbel grimaced. "Call Henry Jenkins," he said wearily to the clerk, and sank back in his chair.

Turnbull was looking alarmed. He bit his lip, trying to decide whether to object to this astonishing procedure, but finally shrugged as the clerk bawled out the ghost's name.

Turnbull sped down the corridor, out the door. His voice was heard in the anteroom, then he returned more slowly. Behind him came the trickle of blood drops: *Pat. HISS. Pat. HISS—*

"One moment," said Gimbel, coming to life again. "I have no objection to your testifying, Mr. Jenkins, but the State should not be subjected to the needless expense of reupholstering its witness chair every time you do. Bailiff, find some sort of a rug or something to throw over the chair before Mr. Jenkins is sworn in."

A tarpaulin was hurriedly procured and adjusted to the chair; Jenkins materialized long enough to be sworn in, then sat.

Wilson began in an amiable enough tone.

"Tell me, Mr. Jenkins," he said, "just how many 'astral entities'—I believe that is what you call yourself—are there?"

"I have no way of knowing, Many billions."

"As many, in other words, as there have been human beings to die by violence?"

Turnbull rose to his feet in sudden agitation, but the ghost neatly evaded the trap. "I don't know. I only know there are billions."

The lawyer's cat-who-ate-canary smile remained undimmed "And all these billions are constantly about us, everywhere, only remaining invisible. Is that it?"

"Oh, no. Very few remain on Earth. Of those, still fewer have anything to do with humans. Most humans are quite boring to us."

"Well, how many would you say are on Earth? A hundred thousand?"

"Even more, maybe. But that's a good guess."

Turnbull interrupted suddenly. "I would like to know the significance of these questions. I object to this whole line of questioning as being totally irrelevant."

Wilson was a study in legal dignity. He retorted, "I am trying to elicit some facts of major value, your honor. This may change the entire character of the case. I ask your patience for a moment or two."

"Counsel for the defense may continue," Gimbel said curtly.

Wilson showed his canines in a grin. He continued to the blood-dripping before him. "Now, the contention of your counsel is that the late Mr. Harley allowed an 'astral entity' to occupy his home for twenty years or more, with his full knowledge and consent. That strikes me as being entirely improbable, but shall we for the moment assume it to be the case?"

"Certainly! It's the truth."

"Then tell me, Mr. Jenkins, have you fingers?"

"Have I—what?"

"You heard me!" Wilson snapped. "Have you fingers, flesh-and-blood fingers, capable of making an imprint?"

"Why, no. I—"

Wilson rushed on. "Or have you a photograph of yourself—or specimens of your handwriting—or any sort of material identification? Have you any of these?"

The voice was definitely querulous. "What do you mean?"

Wilson's voice became harsh, menacing. "I mean, can you prove that *you* are the astral entity alleged to have occupied Zebulon Harley's home. Was it you—or was it another of the featureless, faceless, intangible unknowns— one of the hundreds of thousands of them that, by your own admission, are all over the face of the earth, rambling where they choose, not halted by any locks or bars? Can you prove that *you* are anyone in particular?"

"Your honor!" Turnbull's voice was almost a shriek as he found his feet at last. "My client's identity was never in question!"

"It is now!" roared Wilson. "The opposing counsel has presented a personage whom he styles 'Henry Jenkins.' Who is this Jenkins? What is he? Is he even an individual—or a corporate aggregation of these mysterious 'astral entities' which we are to believe are everywhere, but which we never see? If he is an individual, is he *the* individual? And how can we know that even if he says he is? Let him produce evidence—photographs, a birth certificate, fingerprints. Let him bring in identifying witnesses who have known both ghosts, and are prepared to swear that these ghosts are the same ghost. Failing this, there is no case! Your honor, I demand the court declare an immediate judgment in favor of the defendant!"

Judge Gimbel stared at Turnbull. "Have you anything to say?" he asked. "The argument of the defense would seem to have every merit with it. Unless you can produce some sort of evidence as to the identity of your client, I have no alternative but to find for the defense."

For a moment there was a silent tableau. Wilson triumphant, Turnbull furiously frustrated.

How could you identify a ghost?

And then came the quietly amused voice from the witness chair.

"This thing has gone far enough," it said above the sizzle and splatter of its own leaking blood. "I believe I can present proof that will satisfy the court."

Wilson's face fell with express-elevator speed. Turnbull held his breath, afraid to hope.

Judge Gimbel said, "You are under oath. Proceed."

There was no other sound in the courtroom as the voice said, "Mr. Harley, here, spoke of a visit to his uncle in 1938. I can vouch for that. They spent a night and a day together. They weren't alone. I was there."

No one was watching Russell Harley, or they might have seen the sudden sick pallor that passed over his face.

The voice, relentless, went on, "Perhaps I shouldn't have eavesdropped as I did, but old Zeb never had any secrets from me anyhow. I listened to

what they talked about. Young Harley was working for a bank in
Philadelphia at the time. His first big job. He needed money, and needed it
bad. There was a shortage in his department. A woman named Sally—"

"Hold on!" Wilson yelled. "This has nothing to do with your identification
of yourself, Keep to the point!"

But Turnbull had begun to comprehend. He was shouting too, almost too
excited to be coherent. "Your honor, my client must be allowed to speak. If
he shows knowledge of an intimate conversation between the late Mr.
Harley and defendant, it would be certain proof that he enjoyed the late Mr.
Harley's confidence, and thus, Q.E.D., that he is no other than the astral
entity who occupied Harley Hall for so long!"

Gimbel nodded sharply. "Let me remind counsel for defense that this is
his own witness. Mr. Jenkins, continue."

The voice began again. "As I was saying, the woman's name—"

"Shut up, damn you!" Harley yelled. He sprang upright, turned
beseechingly toward the judge. "He's twisting it! Make him stop! Sure, I
knew my uncle had a ghost. He's it, all right, curse his black soul! He can
have the house if he wants it—I'll clear out. I'll clear out of the whole
damned state!" He broke off into babbling and turned about wildly. Only
the intervention of a marshal kept him from hurtling out of the courtroom.

Banging of the gavel and hard work by the court clerk and his staff
restored order in the courtroom. When the room had returned almost to
normalcy, Judge Gimbel, perspiring and annoyed, said. "As far as I am
concerned, identification of the witness is complete. Has the defense any
further evidence to present?"

Wilson shrugged morosely. "No, your honor."

"Counsel for the plaintiff?"

"Nothing, your honor. I rest my case."

Gimbel plowed a hand through his sparse hair and blinked. "In that case,"
he said, "I find for the plaintiff. An order is entered hereby that the
defendant, Russell Joseph Harley, shall remove from the premises of Harley
Hall all spells, pentagrams, talismans and other means of exorcism
employed; that he shall cease and desist from making any attempts, of
whatever nature, to evict the tenant in the future; and that Henry Jenkins,
the plaintiff, shall be permitted the full use and occupancy of the premises
designated as Harley Hall for the full term of his natural—ah—existence."

The gavel banged. "The case is closed."

"Don't take it so hard," said a mild voice behind Russell Harley. He
whirled surlily. Nicholls was coming up the street after him from the
courthouse, Wilson in tow.

Nicholls said. "You lost the case, but you've still got your life. Let me buy
you a drink. In here, perhaps."

He herded them into a cocktail lounge, sat them down before they had a
chance to object. He glanced at his expensive wrist watch. "I have a few
minutes," he said. "Then I really must be off. It's urgent."

He hailed a barman, ordered for all. Then he looked at young Harley and smiled broadly as he dropped a bill on the counter to pay for the drinks.

"Harley," he said, "I have a motto that you would do well to remember at times like these. I'll make you a present of it, if you like."

"What is it?"

"'The worst is yet to come.'"

Harley snarled and swallowed his drink without replying. Wilson said, "What gets me is why didn't they come to us before the trial with that stuff about this charmingly illicit client you wished on me? We'd have had to settle out of court."

Nicholls shrugged. "They had their reasons," he said. "After all one case of exorcism, more or less, doesn't matter. But lawsuits set precedents. You're a lawyer, of sorts, Wilson; do you see what I mean?"

"Precedents?" Wilson looked at him slackjawed for a moment; then his eyes widened.

"I see you understand me." Nicholls nodded. "From now on in this state—and by virtue of the full-faith-and-credence clause of the Constitution, in *every* state of the country—a ghost has a legal right to haunt a house!"

"Good Lord!" said Wilson. He began to laugh, not loud, but from the bottom of his chest.

Harley stared at Nicholls. "Once and for all," he whispered, "tell me—what's your angle on all this?"

Nicholls smiled again.

"Think about it a while," he said lightly. "You'll begin to understand." He sniffed his wine once more, then sat the glass down gently—

And vanished.

NEW HAMPSHIRE

The Devil and Daniel Webster
by Stephen Vincent Benét

It's a story they tell in the border country, where Massachusetts joins Vermont and New Hampshire.

Yes, Dan'l Webster's dead—or at least, they buried him. But every time there's a thunderstorm around Marshfield, they say you can hear his rolling voice in the hollows of the sky. And they say that if you go to his grave and speak loud and clear, "Dan'l Webster—Dan'l Webster!" the ground'll begin to shiver and the trees begin to shake. And after a while you'll hear a deep voice saying, "Neighbor, how stands the Union?" Then you better answer the Union stands as she stood, rock-bottomed and copper-sheathed, one and indivisible, or he's liable to rear right out of the ground. At least, that's what I was told when I was a youngster.

You see, for a while, he was the biggest man in the country. He never got to be President, but he was the biggest man. There were thousands that trusted in him right next to God Almighty, and they told stories about him that were like the stories of patriarchs and such. They said, when he stood up to speak, stars and stripes came right out in the sky, and once he spoke against a river and made it sink into the ground. They said, when he walked the woods with his fishing rod, Killall, the trout would jump out of the streams right into his pockets, for they knew it was not use putting up a fight against him; and, when he argued a case, he could turn on the harps of the blessed and the shaking of the earth underground. That was the kind of man he was, and his big farm up at Marshfield was suitable to him. The chickens he raised were all white meat down through the drumsticks, the cows were tended like children, and the big ram he called Goliath had horns with a curl like a morning-glory vine and could butt through an iron door. But Dan'l wasn't one of your gentlemen farmers; he knew all the ways of the land, and he'd be up by candlelight to see that the chores got done. A man with a mouth like a mastiff, a brow like a mountain and eyes like burning anthracite—that was Dan'l Webster in his prime. And the biggest case he argued never got written down in the books, for he argued it against the devil, nip and tuck and no holds barred. And this is the way I used to hear it told.

There was a man named Jabez Stone, lived at Cross Corners, New Hampshire. He wasn't a bad man to start with, but he was an unlucky man. If he planted corn, he got borers; if he planted potatoes, he got blight. He had good-enough land, but it didn't prosper him; he had a decent wife and children, but the more children he had, the less there was to feed them. If stones cropped up in his neighbor's field, boulders boiled up in his; if he had a horse with the spavins, he'd trade it for one with the staggers and give something extra. There's some folks bound to be like that, apparently. But one day Jabez Stone got sick of the whole business.

He'd been plowing that morning and he'd just broke the plowshare on a rock that he could have sworn hadn't been there yesterday. And, as he stood looking at the plowshare, the off horse began to cough—that ropy kind of cough that means sickness and horse doctors. There were two children down with the measles, his wife was ailing, and he had a whitlow on his thumb. It was about the last straw for Jabez Stone. "I vow," he said, and he looked around him kind of desperate—"I vow it's enough to make a man want to sell his soul to the devil! And I would, too, for two cents!"

Then he felt a kind of queerness come over him at having said what he'd said; though, naturally, being a New Hampshireman, he wouldn't take it back. But, all the same, when it got to be evening and, as far as he could see, no notice had been taken, he felt relieved in his mind, for he was a religious man. But notice is always taken, sooner or later, just like the Good Book says. And, sure enough, next day, about suppertime, a soft-spoken, dark-dressed stranger drove up in a handsome buggy and asked for Jabez Stone.

Well, Jabez told his family it was a lawyer, come to see him about a legacy. But he knew who it was. He didn't like the looks of the stranger, nor the way he smiled with his teeth. They were white teeth, and plentiful—some say they were filed to a point, but I wouldn't vouch for that. And he didn't like it when the dog took one look at the stranger and ran away howling, with his tail between his legs. But having passed his word, more or less, he stuck to it, and they went out behind the barn and made their bargain. Jabez Stone had to prick his finger to sign, and the stranger lent him a silver pin. The wound healed clean, but it left a little white scar.

After that, all of a sudden, things began to pick up and prosper for Jabez Stone. His cows got fat and his horses sleek, his crops were the envy of the neighborhood, and lightning might strike all over the valley, but it wouldn't strike his barn. Pretty soon, he was one of the prosperous people of the county; they asked him to stand for selectman, and he stood for it; there began to be talk of running him for state senate. All in all, you might say the Stone family was as happy and contented as cats in a dairy. And so they were, except for Jabez Stone.

He'd been contented enough, the first few years. It's a great thing when bad luck turns; it drives most other things out of you head. True, every now and then, especially in rainy weather, the little white scar on his finger would give him a twinge. And once a year, punctual as clockwork, the stranger with the handsome buggy would come driving by. But the sixth year, the stranger lighted, and, after that, his peace was over for Jabez Stone.

The stranger came up through the lower field, switching his boots with a cane—they were handsome black boots, but Jabez Stone never liked the look of them, particularly the toes. And, after he'd passed the time of day, he said, "Well, Mr. Stone, you're a hummer! It's a very pretty property you've got here, Mr. Stone."

"Well, some might favor it and others might not," said Jabez Stone, for he was a New Hampshireman.

"Oh, no need to decry your industry!" said the stranger, very easy, showing his teeth in a smile. "After all, we know what's been done, and it's been according to contract and specifications. So when—ahem—the mortgage falls due next year, you shouldn't have any regrets."

"Speaking of that mortgage, mister," said Jabez Stone, and he looked around for help to the earth and the sky, "I'm beginning to have one or two doubts about it."

"Doubts?" said the stranger, not quite so pleasantly.

"Why, yes," said Jabez Stone. "This being the U.S.A. and me always having been a religious man." He cleared his throat and got bolder. "Yes, sir," he said "I'm beginning to have considerable doubts as to that mortgage holding in court."

"There's courts and courts," said the stranger, clicking his teeth. "Still, we might as well have a look at the original document." And he hauled out a big black pocketbook, full of papers. "Sherwin, Slater, Stevens, Stone," he muttered. "I, Jabez Stone, for a term of seven years—Oh, it's quite in order, I think."

But Jabez Stone wasn't listening, for he saw something else flutter out of the black pocketbook. It was something that looked like a moth, but it wasn't a moth. And as Jabez Stone stared at it, it seemed to speak to him in a small sort of piping voice, terrible small and thin, but terrible human. "Neighbor Stone!" it squeaked. "Neighbor Stone! Help me! For God's sake, help me!"

But before Jabez Stone could stir hand or foot, the stranger whipped out a big bandanna handkerchief, caught the creature in it, just like a butterfly, and started tying up the ends of the bandanna.

"Sorry for the interruption," he said. "As I was saying—"

But Jabez Stone was shaking all over like a scared horse.

"That's Miser Stevens' voice!" he said, in a croak. "And you've got him in your handkerchief!"

The stranger looked a little embarrassed.

"Yes, I really should have transferred him to the collecting box," he said with a simper, "but there were some rather unusual specimens there and I didn't want them crowded. Well, well, these little contretemps will occur."

"I don't know what you mean by contertan," said Jabez Stone, "but that was Miser Stevens' voice! And he ain't dead! You can't tell me he is! He was just as spry and mean as a woodchuck, Tuesday!"

"In the midst of life—" said the stranger, kind of pious. "Listen!" Then a bell began to toll in the valley and Jabez Stone listened, with the sweat running down his face. For he knew it was tolled for Miser Stevens and that he was dead.

"These long-standing accounts," said the stranger with a sigh; "one really hates to close them. But business is business."

He still had the bandanna in his hand, and Jabez Stone felt sick as he saw the cloth struggle and flutter.

"Are they all as small as that?" he asked hoarsely.

"Small?" said the stranger. "Oh, I see what you mean. Why, they vary." He measured Jabez Stone with his eyes, and his teeth showed. "Don't worry, Mr. Stone," he said. "You'll go with a very good grade. I wouldn't trust you outside the collecting box. Now, a man like Dan'l Webster, of course—well, we'd have to build a special box for him, and even at that, I imagine the wing spread would astonish you. But, in your case, as I was saying—"

"Put that handkerchief away!" said Jabez Stone, and he began to beg and to pray. But the best he could get at the end was a three years' extension, with conditions.

But till you make a bargain like that, you've got no idea of how fast four years can run. By the last months of those years, Jabez Stone's known all over the state and there's talk of running him for governor— and it's dust and ashes in his mouth. For every day, when he gets up, he thinks, "There's one more night gone," and every night when he lies down, he thinks of the black pocketbook and the soul of Miser Stevens, and it makes him sick at heart. Till, finally, he can't bear it any longer, and, in the last days of the last year, he hitches up his horse and drives off to seek Dan'l Webster. For Dan'l was born in New Hampshire, only a few miles from Cross Corners, and it's well known that he has a particular soft spot for old neighbors.

It was early in the morning when he got to Marshfield, but Dan'l was up already, talking Latin to the farm hands and wrestling with the ram, Goliath, and trying out a new trotter and working up speeches to make against John C. Calhoun. But when he heard a New Hampshireman had come to see him, he dropped everything else he was doing, for that was Dan'l's way. He gave Jabez Stone a breakfast that five men couldn't eat, went into the living history of every man and woman in Cross Corners, and finally asked him how he could serve him.

Jabez Stone allowed that it was a kind of mortgage case.

"Well, I haven't pleaded a mortgage case in a long time, and I don't generally plead now, except before the Supreme Court," said Dan'l, "but if I can, I'll help you."

"Then I've got hope for the first time in ten years," said Jabez Stone, and told him the details.

Dan'l walked up and down as he listened, hands behind his back, now and then asking a question, now and then plunging his eyes at the floor, as if they'd bore through it like gimlets. When Jabez Stone had finished, Dan'l puffed out his cheeks and blew. Then he turned to Jabez Stone and a smile broke over his face like the sunrise over Monadnock.

"You've certainly given yourself the devil's own row to hoe, Neighbor Stone," he said, "But I'll take your case."

"You'll take it?" said Jabez Stone, hardly daring to believe.

"Yes," said Dan'l Webster. "I've got about seventy-five other things to do and the Missouri Compromise to straighten out, but I'll take your case. For if two New Hampshiremen aren't a match for the devil, we might as well give the country back to the Indians."

Then he shook Jabez Stone by the hand and said, "Did you come down here in a hurry?"

"Well, I admit I made time," said Jabez Stone.

"You'll go back faster," said Dan'l Webster, and he told 'em to hitch up Constitution and Constellation to the carriage. They were matched grays with one white forefoot, and they stepped like greased lightning.

Well, I won't describe how excited and pleased the whole Stone family was to have the great Dan'l Webster for a guest, when they finally got there. Jabez Stone had lost his hat on the way, blown off when they overtook a wind, but he didn't take much account of that. But after supper he sent the family off to bed, for he had most particular business with Mr. Webster. Mrs. Stone wanted them to sit in the front parlor, but Dan'l Webster knew front parlors and said he preferred the kitchen. So it was there they sat, waiting for the stranger, with a jug on the table between them and a bright fire on the hearth—the stranger being scheduled to show up on the stroke of midnight, according to specifications.

Well, most men wouldn't have asked for better company than Dan'l Webster and a jug. But with every tick of the clock Jabez Stone got sadder and sadder. His eyes roved round, and though he sampled the jug you could see he couldn't taste it. Finally on the stroke of 11:30 he reached over the grabbed Dan'l Webster by the arm.

"Mr. Webster, Mr. Webster!" he said, and his voice was shaking with fear and a desperate courage. "For God's sake, Mr. Webster, harness your horses and get away from this place while you can!"

"You've brought me a long way, neighbor, to tell me you don't like my company," said Dan'l Webster, quite peaceable, pulling at the jug.

"Miserable wretch that I am!" groaned Jabez Stone. "I've brought you a devilish way, and now I see my folly. Let him take me if he wills. I don't hanker after it, I must say, but I can stand it. But you're the Union's stay and New Hampshire's pride! He mustn't get you, Mr. Webster! He mustn't get you!"

Dan'l Webster looked at the distracted man, all gray and shaking in the firelight, and laid a hand on his shoulder.

"I'm obliged to you, Neighbor Stone," he said gently. "It's kindly thought of. But there's a jug on the table and a case in hand. And I never left a jug or a case half finished in my life."

And just at that moment there was a sharp rap on the door.

"Ah," said Dan'l Webster, very coolly, "I thought your clock was a trifle slow, Neighbor Stone." He stepped to the door and opened it. "Come in!" he said.

The stranger came in—very dark and tall he looked in the firelight. He was carrying a box under his arm—a black, japanned box with little air holes in the lid. At the sight of the box, Jabez Stone gave a low cry and shrank into a corner of the room.

"Mr. Webster, I presume," said the stranger, very polite, but with his eyes glowing like a fox's deep in the woods.

"Attorney of record for Jabez Stone," said Dan'l Webster, but his eyes were glowing too. "Might I ask about your name?"

"I've gone by a good many," said the stranger carelessly. "Perhaps Scratch will do for the evening. I'm often called that in these regions."

Then he sat down at the table and poured himself a drink from the jug. The liquor was cold in the jug, but it came steaming into the glass.

"And now," said the stranger, smiling and showing his teeth, "I shall call upon you, as a law-abiding citizen, to assist me in taking possession of my property."

Well, with that the argument began—and it went hot and heavy. At first, Jabez Stone had a flicker of hope, but when he saw Dan'l Webster being forced back at point after point, he just scrunched in his corner, with his eyes on that japanned box. For there wasn't any doubt as to the deed or the signature—that was the worst of it. Dan'l Webster twisted and turned and thumped his fist on the table, but he couldn't get away from that. He offered to compromise the case; the stranger wouldn't hear of it. He pointed out the property had increased in value, and state senators ought to be worth more; the stranger stuck to the letter of the law. He was a great lawyer, Dan'l Webster, but we know who's the King of Lawyers, as the Good Book tells us, and it seemed as if, for the first time, Dan'l Webster had met his match.

Finally, the stranger yawned a little. "Your spirited efforts on behalf of your client do you credit, Mr. Webster," he said, "but if you have no more arguments to adduce, I'm rather pressed for time"— and Jabez Stone shuddered.

Dan'l Webster's brow looked dark as a thunder-cloud.

"Pressed or not, you shall not have this man!" he thundered. "Mr. Stone is an American citizen, and no American citizen may be forced into the service of a foreign prince. We fought England for that in '12 and we'll fight all hell for it again!"

"Foreign?" said the stranger. "And who calls me a foreigner?"

"Well, I never yet heard of the dev—of your claiming American citizenship," said Dan'l Webster with surprise.

"And who with better right?" said the stranger, with one of his terrible smiles. "When the first wrong was done to the first Indian, I was there. When the first slaver put out for the Congo, I stood on her deck. Am I not in your books and stories and beliefs, from the first settlements on? Am I not spoken of, still, in every church in New England? 'Tis true the North claims me for a Southerner and the South for a Northerner, but I am neither. I am merely an honest American like yourself—and of the best descent—for, to tell the truth, Mr. Webster, though I don't like to boast of it, my name is older in this country than yours."

"Aha!" said Dan'l Webster, with the veins standing out in his forehead. "Then I stand on the Constitution! I demand a trial for my client!"

"The case is hardly one for an ordinary court," said the stranger, his eyes flickering. "And, indeed, the lateness of the hour—"

"Let it be any court you choose, so it is an American judge and an American jury!" said Dan'l Webster in his pride. "Let it be the quick or the dead; I'll abide the issue!"

"You have said it," said the stranger, and pointed his finger at the door. And with that, and all of a sudden, there was a rushing of wind outside and a noise of footsteps. They came, clear and distinct, through the night. And yet, they were not like the footsteps of living men.

"In God's name, who comes by so late?" cried Jabez Stone, in an ague of fear.

"The jury Mr. Webster demands," said the stranger, sipping at his boiling glass. "You must pardon the rough appearance of one or two; they will have come a long way."

And with that the fire burned blue and the door blew open and twelve men entered, one by one.

If Jabez Stone had been sick with terror before, he was blind with terror now. For there was Walter Butler, the loyalist, who spread fire and horror through the Mohawk Valley in the times of the Revolution; and there was Simon Girty, the renegade, who saw white men burned at the stake and whooped with the Indians to see them burn. His eyes were green, like a catamount's, and the stains on his hunting shirt did not come from the blood of the deer. King Philip was there, wild and proud as he had been in life, with the great gash in his head that gave him his death wound, and cruel Governor Dale, who broke men on the wheel. There was Morton of Merry Mount, who so vexed the Plymouth Colony, with his flushed, loose, handsome face and his hate of the godly. There was Teach, the bloody pirate, with his black beard curling on his breast. The Reverend John Smeet, with his strangler's hands and his Geneva gown, walked as daintily as he had to the gallows. The red print of the rope was still around his neck, but he carried a perfumed handkerchief in one hand. One and all, they came into the room with the fires of hell still upon them, and the stranger named their names and their deeds as they came, till the tale of twelve was told. Yet the stranger had told the truth—they had all played a part in America.

"Are you satisfied with the jury, Mr. Webster?" said the stranger mockingly, when they had taken their places.

The sweat stood upon Dan'l Webster's brow, but his voice was clear.

"Quite satisfied," he said. "Though I miss General Arnold from the company."

"Benedict Arnold is engaged upon other business," said the stranger, with a glower. "Ah, you asked for a justice, I believe."

He pointed his finger once more, and a tall man, soberly clad in Puritan garb, with the burning gaze of the fanatic, stalked into the room an took his judge's place.

"Justice Hathorne is a jurist of experience," said the stranger. "He presided at certain witch trials once held in Salem. There were others who repented of the business later, but not he."

"Repent of such notable wonders and undertakings?" said the stern old justice. "Nay, hang them—hang them all!" And he muttered to himself in a way that struck ice into the soul of Jabez Stone.

Then the trial began, and, as you might expect, it didn't look anyways good for the defense. And Jabez Stone didn't make much of a witness in his own behalf. He took one look at Simon Girty and screeched, and they had to put him back in his corner in a kind of swoon.

It didn't halt the trial, though; the trial went on, as trials do. Dan'l Webster had faced some hard juries and hanging judges in his time, but this was the hardest he'd ever faced, and he knew it. They sat there with a kind of glitter in their eyes, and the stranger's smooth voice went on and on. Every time he'd raise an objection, it'd be "Objection sustained," but whenever Dan'l objected, it'd be "Objection denied." Well, you couldn't expect fair play from a fellow like this Mr. Scratch.

It got to Dan'l in the end, and he began to heat, like iron in the forge. When he got up to speak he was going to flay that stranger with every trick known to the law, and the judge and jury too. He didn't care if it was contempt of court or what would happen to him for it. He didn't care any more what happened to Jabez Stone. He just got madder and madder, thinking of what he'd say. And yet, curiously enough, the more he thought about it, the less he was able to arrange his speech in his mind.

Till, finally, it was time for him to get up on his feet, and he did so, all ready to bust out with lightnings and denunciations. But before he started he looked over the judge and jury for a moment, such being his custom. And he noticed the glitter in their eyes was twice as strong as before, and they all leaned forward. Like hounds just before they get the fox, they looked, and the blue mist of evil in the room thickened as he watched them. Then he saw what he'd been about to do, and he wiped his forehead, as a man might who's just escaped falling into a pit in the dark.

For it was him they'd come for, not only Jabez Stone. He read it in the glitter of their eyes and in the way the stranger hid his mouth with one hand. And if he fought them with their own weapons, he'd fall into their power; he knew that, though he couldn't have told you how. It was his own anger and horror that burned in their eyes; and he'd have to wipe that out or the case was lost. He stood there for a moment, his black eyes burning like anthracite. And then he began to speak.

He started off in a low voice, though you could hear every word. They say he could call on the harps of the blessed when he chose. And this was just as simple and easy as a man could talk. But he didn't start out by condemning or reviling. He was talking about the things that make a country a country, and a man a man.

And he began with the simple things that everybody's known and felt—the freshness of a fine morning when you're young, and the taste of food when you're hungry, and the new day that's every day when you're a child. He took them up and he turned them in his hands. They were good things for any man. But without freedom, they sickened. And when he talked of those enslaved, and the sorrows of slavery, his voice got like a big bell. He talked of the early days of America and the men who had made those days. It wasn't a spread-eagle speech, but he made you see it. He admitted all the wrong that had ever been done. But he showed how, out of the wrong and the right, the suffering and the starvations, something new had come. And everybody had played a part in it, even the traitors.

Then he turned to Jabez Stone and showed him as he was—an ordinary man who'd had hard luck and wanted to change it. And, because he'd wanted to change it, now he was going to be punished for all eternity. And yet there was good in Jabez Stone, and he showed that good. He was hard and mean, in some ways, but he was a man. There was sadness in being a man, but it was a proud thing too. And he showed what the pride of it was till you couldn't help feeling it. Yes, even in hell, if a man was a man, you'd know it. And he wasn't pleading for any one person any more, though his voice rang like an organ. He was telling the story and the failures and the endless journey of mankind. They got tricked and trapped and bamboozled, but it was a great journey. And no demon that was ever foaled could know the inwardness of it—it took a man to do that.

The fire began to die on the hearth and the wind before morning to blow. The light was getting gray in the room when Dan'l Webster finished. And his words came back at the end to New Hampshire ground, and the one spot of land that each man loves and clings to. He painted a picture of that, and to each one of that jury he spoke of things long forgotten. For his voice could search the heart, and that was his gift and his strength. And to one, his voice was like a forest and its secrecy, and to another like the sea and the storms of the sea; and one heard the cry of his lost nation in it, and another saw a little harmless scene he hadn't remembered for years. But each saw something. And when Dan'l Webster finished he didn't know whether or not he'd saved Jabez Stone. But he knew he'd done a miracle. For the glitter was gone from the eyes of judge and jury, and, for the moment, they were men again, and knew they were men.

"The defense rests," said Dan'l Webster, and stood there like a mountain. His ears were still ringing with his speech, and he didn't hear anything else till he heard Judge Hathorne say, "The jury will retire to consider its verdict."

Walter Butler rose in his place and his face had a dark, gay pride on it.

"The jury has considered its verdict," he said, and looked the stranger full in the eye. "We find for the defendant, Jabez Stone."

With that, the smile left the stranger's face, but Walter Butler did not flinch.

"Perhaps 'tis not strictly in accordance with the evidence," he said, "but even the damned may salute the eloquence of Mr. Webster."

With that, the long crow of a rooster split the gray morning sky, and judge and jury were gone from the room like a puff of smoke and as if they had never been there. The stranger turned to Dan'l Webster, smiling wryly.

"Major Butler was always a bold man," he said. "I had not thought him quite so bold. Nevertheless, my congratulations, as between two gentlemen."

"I'll have that paper first, if you please," said Dan'l Webster, and he took it and tore it into four pieces. It was queerly warm to the touch. "And now," he said, "I'll have you!" and his hand came down like a bear trap on the stranger's arm. For he knew that once you bested anybody like Mr. Scratch in fair fight, his power on you was gone. And he could see that Mr. Scratch knew it too.

The stranger twisted and wriggled, but he couldn't get out of that grip. "Come, come, Mr. Webster," he said, smiling palely. "This sort of thing is ridic—ouch!—is ridiculous. If you're worried about the costs of the case, naturally, I'd be glad to pay—"

"And so you shall!" said Dan'l Webster, shaking him till his teeth rattled. "For you'll sit right down at that table and draw up a document, promising never to bother Jabez Stone nor his heirs or assigns nor any other New Hampshireman till doomsday! For any hades we want to raise in this state, we can raise ourselves, without assistance from strangers."

"Ouch!" said the stranger. "Ouch! Well, they never did run very big to the barrel, but—ouch!—I agree!"

So he sat down and drew up the document. But Dan'l Webster kept his hand on his coat collar all the time.

"And, now, may I go?" said the stranger, quite humble, when Dan'l'd seen the document was in proper and legal form.

"Go?" said Dan'l, giving him another shake. "I'm still trying to figure out what I'll do with you. For you've settled the costs of the case, but you haven't settled with me. I think I'll take you back to Marshfield," he said, kind of reflective. "I've got a ram there named Goliath that can butt through an iron door. I'd kind of like to turn you loose in his field and see what he'd do."

Well, with that the stranger began to beg and to plead. And he begged and he pled so humble that finally Dan'l, who was naturally kindhearted, agreed to let him go. The stranger seemed terrible grateful for that and said, just to show they were friends, he'd tell Dan'l's fortune before leaving. So Dan'l agreed to that, though he didn't take much stock in fortune-tellers ordinarily. But, naturally, the stranger was a little different.

Well, he pried and he peered at the lines in Dan'l's hands. And he told him one thing and another that was quite remarkable. But they were all in the past.

"Yes, all that's true, and it happened," said Dan'l Webster. "But what's to come in the future?"

The stranger grinned, kind of happily, and shook his head.

"The future's not as you think it," he said. "It's dark. You have a great ambition, Mr. Webster."

"I have," said Dan'l firmly, for everybody knew he wanted to be President.

"It seems almost within your grasp," said the stranger, "but you will not attain it. Lesser men will be made President and you will be passed over."

"And, if I am, I'll still be Daniel Webster," said Dan'l. "Say on."

"You have two strong sons," said the stranger, shaking his head. "You look to found a line. But each will die in war and neither reach greatness."

"Live or die, they are still my sons," said Dan'l Webster. "Say on."

"You have made great speeches," said the stranger. "You will make more."

"Ah," said Dan'l Webster.

"But the last great speech you make will turn many of you own against you," said the stranger. "They will call you Ichabod; they will call you by other names. Even in New England, some will say you have turned your coat and sold your country, and their voices will be loud against you till you die."

"So it is an honest speech, it does not matter what men say," said Dan'l Webster. Then he looked at the stranger and their glances locked.

"One question," he said. "I have fought for the Union all my life. Will I see that fight won against those who would tear it apart?"

"Not while you live," said the stranger, grimly, "but it will be won. And after you are dead, there are thousands who will fight for your cause, because of words that you spoke."

"Why, then, you long-barreled, slab-sided, lantern-jawed, forture-telling note shaver!" said Dan'l Webster, with a great roar of laughter, "be off with you to your own place before I put my mark on you! For, by the thirteen original colonies, I'd go to the Pit itself to save the Union!"

And with that he drew back his foot for a kick that would have stunned a horse. It was only the tip of his shoe that caught the stranger, but he went flying out of the door with his collecting box under his arm.

"And now," said Dan'l Webster, seeing Jabez Stone beginning to rouse from his swoon, "let's see what's left in the jug, for it's dry work talking all night. I hope there's pie for breakfast, Neighbor Stone."

But they say that whenever the devil comes near Marshfield, even now, he gives it a wide berth. And he hasn't been seen in the state of New Hampshire from that day to this. I'm not talking about Massachusetts or Vermont.

NEW JERSEY

The Master of The Hounds
by Algis Budrys

THE WHITE sand road led off the state highway through the sparse pines. There were no tire tracks in the road, but, as Malcolm turned the car onto it, he noticed the footprints of dogs, or perhaps of only one dog, running along the middle of the road toward the combined general store and gas station at the intersection.

"Well, it's far enough away from everything, all right," Virginia said. She was lean and had dusty black hair. Her face was long, with high cheekbones. They had married ten years ago, when she had been girlish and very slightly plump.

"Yes," Malcolm said. Just days ago, when he'd been turned down for a Guggenheim Fellowship that he'd expected to get, he had quit his job at the agency and made plans to spend the summer, somewhere as cheap as possible, working out with himself whether he was really an artist or just had a certain commercial talent. Now they were here.

He urged the car up the road, following a line of infrequent and weathered utility poles that carried a single strand of power line. The real-estate agent already had told them there were no telephones. Malcolm had taken that to be a positive feature, but somehow he did not like the looks of that one thin wire sagging from pole to pole. The wheels of the car sank in deeply on either side of the dog prints, which he followed like a row of bread crumbs through a forest.

Several hundred yards farther along, they came to a sign at the top of a hill:

MARINE VIEW SHORES! NEW JERSEY'S NEWEST, FASTEST-GROWING

RESIDENTIAL COMMUNITY. WELCOME HOME! FROM $9,990.
NO DN PYT FOR VETS.

Below them was a wedge of land—perhaps ten acres altogether that
pushed out into Lower New York Bay. The road became a gullied, yellow
gravel street, pointing straight toward the water and ending in three
concrete posts, one of which had fallen and left a gap wide enough for a car
to blunder through. Beyond that was a low drop-off where the bay ran
northward to New York City and, in the other direction, toward the open
Atlantic.

On either side of the roughed-out street, the bulldozed land was
overgrown with scrub oak and sumac. Along the street were rows of roughly
rectangular pits—some with half-finished foundation walls in them—piles of
excavated clay, and lesser quantities of sand, sparsely weed-grown and
washed into ravaged mounds like Dakota Territory. Here and there were
houses with half-completed frames, now silvered and warped.

There were only two exceptions to the general vista. At the end of the
street, two identically designed, finished houses faced each other. One
looked shabby. The lot around it was free of scrub, but weedy and
unsodded. Across the street from it stood a house in excellent repair.
Painted a charcoal gray and roofed with dark asphalt shingles, it sat in the
center of a meticulously green and level lawn, which was in turn surrounded
by a wire fence approximately four feet tall and splendid with fresh
aluminum paint. False shutters, painted stark white, flanked high, narrow
windows along the side Malcolm could see. In front of the house, a line of
whitewashed stones the size of men's heads served as curbing. There wasn't
a thing about the house and its surroundings that couldn't have been
achieved with a straight string, a handsaw, and a three-inch brush. Malcolm
saw a chance to cheer things up. "There now, Marthy!" he said to Virginia.
"I've led you safe and sound through the howlin' forest to a snug home in the
shadder of Fort Defiance."

"It's orderly," Virginia said. "I'll bet it's no joke, keeping up a place like
that out here."

As Malcolm was parking the car parallel to where the curb would have
been in front of their house, a pair of handsome young Doberman pinschers
came out from behind the gray house across the street and stood together on
the lawn with their noses just short of the fence, looking out. They did not
bark. There was no movement at the front window, and no one came out
into the yard. The dogs simply stood there, watching, as Malcolm walked
over the clay to his door.

The house was furnished—that is to say, there were chairs in the living
room, although there was no couch, and a chromium-and-plastic dinette set
in the area off the kitchen. Though one of the bedrooms was completely
empty, there was a bureau and a bed in the other. Malcolm walked through
the house quickly and went back out to the car to get the luggage and

groceries. Nodding toward the dogs, he said to Virginia, "Well! The latest thing in iron deer." He felt he had to say something light, because Virginia was staring across the street.

He knew perfectly well, as most people do and he assumed Virginia did, that Doberman pinschers are nervous, untrustworthy, and vicious. At the same time, he and his wife did have to spend the whole summer here. He could guess how much luck they'd have trying to get their money back from the agent now.

"They look streamlined like that because their ears and tails are trimmed when they're puppies," Virginia said. She picked up a bag of groceries and carried it into the house.

When Malcolm had finished unloading the car, he slammed the trunk lid shut. Although they hadn't moved until then, the Dobermans seemed to regard this as a sign. They turned smoothly, the arc of one inside the arc of the other, and keeping formation, trotted out of sight behind the gray house.

Malcolm helped Virginia put things away in the closets and in the lone bedroom bureau. There was enough to do to keep both of them busy for several hours, and it was dusk when Malcolm happened to look out through the living-room window. After he had glanced that way, he stopped.

Across the street, floodlights had come on at the four corners of the gray house. They poured illumination downward in cones that lighted the entire yard. A crippled man was walking just inside the fence, his legs stiff and his body bent forward from the waist, as he gripped the projecting handles of two crutch-canes that supported his weight at the elbows. As Malcolm watched, the man took a precise square turn at the corner of the fence and began walking along the front of his property. Looking straight ahead, he moved regularly and purposefully, his shadow thrown out through the fence behind the composite shadow of the two dogs walking immediately ahead of him. None of them was looking in Malcolm's direction. He watched as the man made another turn, followed the fence toward the back of his property, and disappeared behind the house.

Later Virginia served cold cuts in the little dining alcove. Putting the house in order seemed to have had a good effect on her morale.

"Listen, I think we're going to be all right here, don't you?" Malcolm said.

"Look," she said reasonably, "any place you can get straightened out is fine with me."

This wasn't quite the answer he wanted. He had been sure in New York that the summer would do it—that in four months a man would come to *some* decision. He had visualized a house for them by the ocean, in a town with a library and a movie and other diversions. It had been a shock to discover how expensive summer rentals were and how far in advance you had to book them. When the last agent they saw described this place to them and told them how low the rent was, Malcolm had jumped at it immediately. But so had Virginia, even though there wasn't anything to do for distraction.

In fact, she had made a point of asking the agent again about the location of the house, and the agent, a fat, gray man with ashes on his shirt, had said earnestly, "Mrs. Lawrence, if you're looking for a place where nobody will bother your husband from working, I can't think of anything better." Virginia had nodded decisively.

It had bothered her, his quitting the agency; he could understand that. Still, he wanted her to be happy, because he expected to be surer of what he wanted to be the end of the summer. She was looking at him steadily now. He cast about for something to offer her that would interest her and change the mood between them. Then he remembered the scene he had witnessed earlier that evening. He told her about the man and his dogs, and this did raise her eyebrows.

"Do you remember the real-estate agent telling us anything about him?" she asked. "I don't."

Malcolm, searching through his memory, did recall that the agent had mentioned a custodian they could call on if there were any problems. At the time he had let it pass, because he couldn't imagine either agent or custodian really caring. Now he realized how dependent he and Virginia were out here if it came to things like broken plumbing or bad wiring, and the custodian's importance altered accordingly. "I guess he's the caretaker," he said.

"Oh."

"It makes sense—all this property has got to be worth something. If they didn't have someone here, people would just carry stuff away or come and camp or something."

"I suppose they would. I guess the owners let him live here rent-free, and with those dogs he must do a good job."

"He'll get to keep it for a while, too," Malcolm said. "Whoever started to build here was a good ten years ahead of himself. I can't see anybody buying into these places until things have gotten completely jammed up closer to New York."

"So, he's holding the fort," Virginia said, leaning casually over the table to put a dish down before him. She glanced over his shoulder toward the living-room window, widened her eyes, and automatically touched the neckline of her housecoat, and then snorted at herself.

"Look, he can't possibly see in here," Malcolm said. "The living room, yes, but to look in here he'd have to be standing in the far corner of his yard. And he's back inside his house." He turned his head to look, and it was indeed true, except that one of the dogs was standing at that corner looking toward their house, eyes glittering. Then its head seemed to melt into a new shape, and it was looking down the road. It pivoted, moved a few steps away from the fence, turned, soared, landed in the street, and set off. Then, a moment later, it came back down the street running side by side with its companion, whose jaws were lightly pressed together around the rolled-over neck of a small paper bag. The dogs trotted together companionably and briskly, their flanks rubbing against one another, and when they were a few steps from the fence they leaped over it in unison and continued across the lawn until they were out of Malcolm's range of vision.

"For heaven's sake! He lives all alone with those dogs!" Virginia said.

Malcolm turned quickly back to her. "How do you come to think that?"

"Well, it's pretty plain. You saw what they were doing out there just now. They're his servants. He can't get around himself, so they run errands for him. If he had a wife, she would do it."

"You learned all that already?"

"Did you notice how happy they were?" Virginia asked.

"There was no need for that other dog to go meet its friend. But it wanted to. They can't be anything but happy." Then she looked at Malcolm, and he saw the old, studying reserve coming back into her eyes.

"For Pete's sake! They're only dogs—what do they know about anything?" Malcolm said.

"They know about happiness," Virginia said. "They know what they do in life."

Malcolm lay awake for a long time that night. He started by thinking about how good the summer was going to be, living here and working, and then he thought about the agency and about why he didn't seem to have the kind of shrewd, limited intuition that let a man do advertising work easily. At about four in the morning he wondered if perhaps he wasn't frightened, and had been frightened for a long time. None of this kind of thinking was new to him, and he knew that it would take him until late afternoon the following day to reach the point where he was feeling pretty good about himself.

When Virginia tried to wake him early the next morning he asked her to please leave him alone. At two in the afternoon, she brought him a cup of coffee and shook his shoulder. After a while, he walked out to the kitchen in his pajama pants and found that she had scrambled up some eggs for the two of them.

"What are your plans for the day?" Virginia said when he had finished eating.

He looked up. "Why?"

"Well, while you were sleeping, I put all your art things in the front bedroom. I think it'll make a good studio. With all your gear in there now, you can be pretty well set up by this evening."

At times she was so abrupt that she shocked him. It upset him that she might have been thinking that he wasn't planning to do anything at all today. "Look," he said, "you know I like to get the feel of a new thing."

"I know that. I didn't set anything up in there. I'm no artist. I just moved it all in."

When Malcolm had sat for a while without speaking, Virginia cleared away their plates and cups and went into the bedroom. She came out wearing a dress, and she had combed her hair and put on lipstick. "Well, you do what you want to," she said.

"I'm going to go across the street and introduce myself."

A flash of irritability hit him, but then he said, "If you'll wait a minute, I'll get dressed and go with you. We might as well both meet him."

He got up and went back to the bedroom for a T-shirt and blue jeans and a pair of loafers. He could feel himself beginning to react to pressure. Pressure always made him bind up; it looked to him as if Virginia had already shot the day for him.

They were standing at the fence, on the narrow strip of lawn between it and the row of whitewashed stones, and nothing was happening. Malcolm saw that although there was a gate in the fence, there was no break in the little grass border opposite it. And there was no front walk. The lawn was lush and all one piece, as if the house had been lowered onto it by helicopter. He began to look closely at the ground just inside the fence, and when he saw the regular pockmarks of the man's crutches, he was comforted.

"Do you see any kind of bell or anything?" Virginia asked.

"No."

"You'd think the dogs would bark."

"I'd just as soon they didn't."

"Will you look?" she said, fingering the gate latch. "The paint's hardly scuffed. I'll bet he hasn't been out of his yard all summer." Her touch rattled the gate lightly, and at that the two dogs came out from behind the house. One of them stopped, turned, and went back. The other dog came and stood by the fence, close enough for them to hear its breathing, and watched them with its head cocked alertly.

The front door of the house opened. At the doorway there was a wink of metal crutches, and then the man came out and stood on his front steps. When he had satisfied himself as to who they were, he nodded, smiled, and came toward them. The other dog walked beside him. Malcolm noticed that the dog at the fence did not distract himself by looking back at his master.

The man moved swiftly, crossing the ground with nimble swings of his body. His trouble seemed to be not in the spine, but in the legs themselves, for he was trying to help himself along with them. It could not be called total helplessness either.

Although the man seemed to be in his late fifties, he had not gone to seed any more than his property had. He was wiry and clean-boned, and the skin on his face was tough and tanned. Around his small blue eyes and at the corners of his thin lips were many fine, deep-etched wrinkles. His yellowish-white hair was brushed straight back from his temples in the classic British military manner. And he even had a slight mustache. He was wearing a tweed jacket with leather patches at the elbows, which seemed a little warm for this kind of day, and a light flannel pale-gray shirt with a pale-blue bow tie. He stopped at the fence, rested his elbows on the crutches, and held out a firm hand with short nails the color of old bones.

"How do you do," he said pleasantly, his manner polished and well-bred. "I have been looking forward to meeting my new neighbors. I am Colonel

Ritchey. "The dogs stood motionless, one to each side of him, their sharp black faces pointing outward.

"How do you do," Virginia said. "We are Malcolm and Virginia Lawrence."

"I am very happy to meet you," Colonel Ritchey said. "I was prepared to believe Cortelyou would fail to provide anyone this season."

Virginia was smiling. "What beautiful dogs," she said. "I was watching them last night."

"Yes. Their names are Max and Moritz. I'm very proud of them."

As they prattled on, exchanging pleasantries, Malcolm wondered why the Colonel had referred to Cortelyou, the real-estate agent, as a provider. There was something familiar, too, about the colonel.

Virginia said, "You're the famous Colonel Ritchey."

Indeed he was Malcolm now realized, remembering the big magazine series that had appeared with the release of the movie several years before.

Colonel Ritchey smiled with no trace of embarrassment. "I am the famous Colonel Ritchey, but you'll notice I certainly don't look much like that charming fellow in the motion picture."

"What in hell are you doing *here*?" Malcolm asked.

Ritchey turned his attention to him. "One has to live somewhere, you know."

Virginia said immediately, "I was watching the dogs last night, and they seemed to do very well for you. I imagine it's pleasant having them to rely on."

"Yes, it is, indeed. They're quite good to me, Max and Moritz. But it is much better with people here now. I had begun to be quite disappointed in Cortelyou."

Malcolm began to wonder whether the agent would have had the brass to call Ritchey a custodian if the colonel had been within earshot.

"Come in, please," the colonel was saying. The gate latch resisted him momentarily, but he rapped it sharply with the heel of one palm and then lifted it. "Don't be concerned about Max and Moritz—they never do anything they're not told."

"Oh, I'm not the least bit worried about them," Virginia said.

"Ah, to some extent you should have been," the colonel said. "Dobermans are not to be casually trusted, you know. It takes many months before one can be at all confident in dealing with them."

"But you trained them yourself, didn't you?" Virginia said.

"Yes, I did," Colonel Ritchey said, with a pleased smile. "From imported pups." The voice in which he now spoke to the dogs was forceful, but as calm as his manner had been to Virginia. "Kennel," he said, and Max and Moritz stopped looking at Malcolm and Virginia and smoothly turned away.

The colonel's living room, which was as neat as a sample, contained beautifully cared for, somewhat old-fashioned furniture. The couch, with its needle-point upholstery and carved framing, was the sort of thing Malcolm would have expected in a lady's living room. Angling out from one wall was a Morris chair, placed so that a man might relax and gaze across the street or, with a turn of his head, rest his eyes on the distant lights of New York. Oil paintings in heavy gilded frames depicted landscapes, great eye-stretching vistas of rolling, open country. The furniture in the room seemed sparse to Malcolm until it occurred to him that the colonel needed extra clearance to get around in and had no particular need to keep additional chairs for visitors.

"Please do sit down," the colonel said. "I shall fetch some tea to refresh us."

When he had left the room, Virginia said, "Of all people! Neighborly, too."

Malcolm nodded. "Charming," he said.

The colonel entered holding a silver tray perfectly steady, its edges grasped between his thumbs and forefingers, his other fingers curled around each of the projecting black-rubber handgrips of his crutches. He brought tea on the tray and, of all things, homemade cookies. "I must apologize for the tea service," he said, "but it seems to be the only one I have."

When the colonel offered the tray, Malcolm saw that the utensils were made of the common sort of sheet metal used to manufacture food cans. Looking down now into his cup, he saw it had been enameled over its original tinplate, and he realized that the whole thing had been made literally from a tin can. The teapot—handle, spout, vented lid, and all—was the same. "Be damned—you made this for yourself at the prison camp, didn't you?"

"As a matter of fact, I did, yes. I was really quite proud of my handiwork at the time, and it still serves. Somehow, living as I do, I've never brought myself to replace it. It's amazing, the fuddy-duddy skills one needs in a camp and how important they become to one. I find myself repainting these poor objects periodically and still taking as much smug pleasure in it as I did when that attitude was quite necessary. One is allowed to do these things in my position, you know. But I do hope my *ersatz* Spode isn't uncomfortably hot in your fingers."

Virginia smiled. "Well, of course, it's trying to be." Malcolm was amazed. He hadn't thought Virginia still remembered how to act so coquettish. She hadn't grown apart from the girl who'd always attracted a lot of attention at other people's gallery openings; who had simply put that part of herself away somewhere else.

Colonel Ritchey's blue eyes were twinkling in response. He turned to Malcolm. "I must say, it will be delightful to share this summer with someone as charming as Mrs. Lawrence."

"Yes," Malcolm said, preoccupied now with the cup, which was distressing his fingers with both heat and sharp edges. "At least, I've always been well satisfied with her," he added.

"I've been noticing the inscription here," Virginia said quickly, indicating the meticulous freehand engraving on the tea tray. She read out loud, "'To Colonel David N. Ritchey, R.M.E., from his fellow officers at *Oflag* XXXI*b*, on the occasion of their liberation, May 14, 1945. Had he not been there to lead them, many would not have been present to share of this heartfelt token.'" Virginia's eyes shone, as she looked up at the colonel. "They must all have been very fond of you."

"Not all," the colonel said, with a slight smile. "I was senior officer over a very mixed bag. Mostly younger officers gathered from every conceivable branch. No followers at all— just budding leaders, all personally responsible for having surrendered once already, some apathetic, others desperate. Some useful, some not. It was my job to weld them into a disciplined, responsive body, to choose whom we must keep safe and who was best suited to keeping the Jerries on the jump. And we were in, of course, from the time of Dunkirk to the last days of the war, with the strategic situation in the camp constantly changing in various ways. All most of them understood was tactics—when they understood at all."

The colonel grimaced briefly, then smiled again. "The tray was presented by the survivors, of course. They'd had a tame Jerry pinch it out of the commandant's sideboard a few days earlier, in plenty of time to get the inscription on. But even the inscription hints that not all survived."

"It wasn't really like the movie, was it?" Virginia said.

"No, and yet—" Ritchey shrugged, as if remembering a time when he had accommodated someone on a matter of small importance. "That was a question of dramatic values, you must realize, and the need to tell an interesting and exciting story in terms recognizable to a civilian audience. Many of the incidents in the motion picture are literally true—they simply didn't happen in the context shown. The Christmas tunnel was quite real, obviously. I did promise the men I'd get at least one of them home for Christmas if they'd pitch in and dig it. But it wasn't a serious promise, and they knew it wasn't. Unlike the motion picture actor, I was not being fervent; I was being ironic.

"It was late in the war. An intelligent man's natural desire would be to avoid risk and wait for liberation . A great many of them felt exactly that way. In fact, many of them had turned civilian in their own minds and were talking about their careers outside, their families—all that sort of thing. So by couching in sarcasm trite words about Christmas tunnels, I was reminding them what and where they still were. The tactic worked quite well. Through devices of that sort, I was able to keep them from going to seed and coming out no use to anyone." The colonel's expression grew absent. "Some of them called me 'The Shrew,'" he murmured. "*That* was in the movie, too, but they were all shown smiling when they said it."

"But it was your duty to hold them all together any way you could," Virginia said encouragingly.

Ritchey's face twisted into a spasm of tension so fierce that there might have been strychnine in his tea. But it was gone at once. "Oh, yes, yes, I held them together. But the expenditure of energy was enormous. And demeaning. It ought not to have made any difference that we were cut off from higher authority. If we had all still been home, there was not a man among the prisoners who would have dared not jump to my simplest command. But in the camp they could shilly-shally and evade; they could settle down into little private ambitions. People will do that. People will not hold true to common purposes unless they are shown discipline." The colonel's uncompromising glance went from Virginia to Malcolm. "It's no good telling people what they ought to do. The only surety is in being in a position to tell people what they *must* do."

"Get some armed guards to back you up. That the idea, Colonel? Get permission from the Germans to set up your own machine-gun towers inside the camp?" Malcolm liked working things out to the point of absurdity.

The colonel appraised him imperturbably. "I was never quite that much my own man in Germany. But there is a little story I must tell you. It's not altogether off the point. "He settled back, at ease once again.

"You may have been curious about Max and Moritz. The Germans, as you know, have always been fond of training dogs to perform all sorts of entertaining and useful things. During the war the Jerries were very much given to using Dobermans for auxiliary guard duty at the various prisoner-of-war camps. In action, Mr. Lawrence, or simply in view, a trained dog is far more terrifying than any soldier with a machine pistol. It takes an animal to stop a man without hesitation, no matter if the man is cursing or praying.

"Guard dogs at each camp were under the charge of a man called the *Hundführer*—the master of the hounds, if you will—whose function, after establishing himself with the dogs as their master and director, was to follow a few simple rules and to take the dogs to wherever they were needed. The dogs had been taught certain patrol routines. It was necessary only for the *Hundführer* to give simple commands such as 'Search' or 'Arrest,' and the dogs would know what to do. Once we had seen them do it, they were very much on our minds, I assure you.

"A Doberman, you see, has no conscience, being a dog. And a trained Doberman has no discretion. From the time he is a puppy, he is bent to whatever purpose has been preordained for him. And the lessons are painful—and autocratic. Once an order has been given, it must be enforced at all costs, for the dog must learn that all orders are to be obeyed unquestioningly. That being true, the dog must also learn immediately and irrevocably that only the orders from one particular individual are valid. Once a Doberman has been trained, there is no way to retrain it. When the American soldiers were seen coming, the Germans in the machine-gun towers threw down their weapons and tried to flee, but the dogs had to be shot. I watched from the hospital window, and I shall never forget how they continued to leap at the kennel fencing until the last one was dead. Their *Hundführer* had run away. . . ."

Malcolm found that his attention was wandering, but Virginia asked, as if on cue, "How did you get into the hospital—was that the Christmas tunnel accident?"

"Yes," the colonel said to Virginia, gentleman to lady. "The sole purpose of the tunnel was, as I said, to give the men a focus of attention. The war was near enough its end. It would have been foolhardy to risk actual escape attempts. But we did the thing up brown, of course. We had a concealed shaft, a tunnel lined with bed slats, a trolley for getting to and from the tunnel entrance, fat lamps made from shoe-blacking tins filled with margarine—all the normal appurtenances. The Germans at that stage were quite experienced in ferreting out this sort of operation, and the only reasonable assurance of continued progress was to work deeply and swiftly. Tunneling is always a calculated risk—the accounts of that sort of operation are biased in favor of the successes, of course.

"At any rate, by the end of November, some of the men were audibly thinking it was my turn to pitch in a bit, so one night I went down and began working. The shoring was as good as it ever was, and the conditions weren't any worse than normal. The air was breathable, and as long as one worked—ah—unclothed, and brushed down immediately on leaving the tunnel, the sand was not particularly damaging to one's skin. Clothing creates chafes in those circumstances. Sand burns coming to light at medical inspections were one of the surest signs that such an operation was under way.

"However that may be, I had been down there for about an hour and a half, and was about to start inching my way back up the tunnel, feetfirst on the trolley like some Freudian symbol, when there was a fall of the tunnel roof that buried my entire chest. It did not cover my face, which was fortunate, and I clearly remember my first thought was that now none of the men would be able to feel the senior officer hadn't shared their physical tribulations. I discovered, at once, that the business of clearing the sand that had fallen was going to be extremely awkward. First, I had to scoop some extra clearance from the roof over my face. Handfuls of sand began falling directly on me, and all I could do about that was to thrash my head back and forth. I was becoming distinctly exasperated at that when the fat lamp attached to the shoring loosened from its fastenings and spilled across my thighs. The hot fat was quite painful. What made it rather worse was that the string wick was not extinguished by the fall, and accordingly, the entire lower part of my body between navel and knees, having been saturated with volatile fat. . . ." The colonel grimaced in embarrassment.

"Well, I was immediately in a very bad way, for there was nothing I could do about the fire until I had dug my way past the sand on my chest. In due course, I did indeed free myself and was able to push my way backward up the tunnel after extinguishing the flames. The men at the shaft head had seen no reason to become alarmed—tunnels always smell rather high and sooty, as you can imagine. But they did send a man down when I got near the entrance shaft and made myself heard.

"Of course, there was nothing to do but tell the Jerries, since we had no facilities whatever for concealing my condition or treating it. They put me in the camp hospital, and there I stayed until the end of the war with plenty of time to lie about and think my thoughts. I was even able to continue exercising some control over my men. I shouldn't be a bit surprised if that hadn't been in the commandant's mind all along. I think he had come to depend on my presence to moderate the behavior of the men.

"That is really almost the end of the story. We were liberated by the American Army, and the men were sent home. I stayed in military hospitals until I was well enough to travel home, and there I dwelt in hotels and played the retired, invalided officer. After that journalist's book was published and the dramatic rights were sold, I was called to Hollywood to be the technical adviser for the movie. I was rather grateful to accept the employment, frankly—an officer's pension is not particularly munificent—and what with selectively lending my name and services to various organizations while my name was still before the public, I was able to accumulate a sufficient nest egg.

"Of course, I cannot go back to England, where the Inland Revenue would relieve me of most of it, but, having established a relationship with Mr. Cortelyou and acquired and trained Max and Moritz, I am content. A man must make his way as best he can and do whatever is required for survival." The colonel cocked his head brightly and regarded Virginia and Malcolm. "Wouldn't you say?"

"Y—es," Virginia said slowly. Malcolm couldn't decide what the look on her face meant. He had never seen it before. Her eyes were shining, but wary. Her smile showed excitement and sympathy, but tension too. She seemed caught between two feelings.

"Quite!" the colonel said, smacking his hands together. "It is most important to me that you fully understand the situation." He pushed himself up to his feet and, with the same move, brought the crutches out smoothly and positioned them to balance him before he could fall. He stood leaning slightly forward, beaming. "Well, now, having given my story. I imagine the objectives of this conversation are fully attained, and there is no need to detain you here further. I'll see you to the front gate."

"That won't be necessary," Malcolm said.

"I insist," the colonel said in what would have been a perfectly pleasant manner if he had added the animated twinkle to his eyes. Virginia was staring at him, blinking slowly.

"Please forgive us," she said. "We certainly hadn't meant to stay long enough to be rude. Thank you for the tea and cookies. They were very good."

"Not at all, my dear," the colonel said. "It's really quite pleasant to think of looking across the way, now and then, and catching glimpses of someone so attractive at her domestic preoccupations. I cleaned up thoroughly after the last tenants, of course, but there are always little personal touches one

THE MASTER OF THE HOUNDS

wants to apply. And you will start some plantings at the front of the house, won't you? Such little activities are quite precious to me—someone as charming as you, in her summer things, going about her little fussings and tendings, resting in the sun after summer. I assume there was never any question you wouldn't stay all summer. Cortelyou would hardly bother with anyone who could not afford to pay him that much. But little more, eh?" The urbane, shrewd look returned to the colonel's face. "Pinched resources and few ties, eh? Or what would you be doing here, if there were somewhere else to turn to?"

"Well, good afternoon, Colonel," Virginia said with noticeable composure. "Let's go, Malcolm."

"Interesting conversation, Colonel," Malcolm said.

"Interesting and necessary, Mr. Lawrence," the colonel said, following them out onto the lawn. Virginia watched him closely as she moved toward the gate, and Malcolm noticed a little downward twitch at the corners of her mouth.

"Feeling a bit of a strain, Mrs. Lawrence?" the colonel asked solicitously. "Please believe that I shall be as considerate of your sensibilities as intelligent care of my own comfort will permit. It is not at all in my code to offer offense to a lady, and in any case—" the colonel smiled deprecatingly "—since the mishap of the Christmas tunnel, one might say the spirit is willing but . . ." The colonel frowned down absently at his canes. "No, Mrs. Lawrence," he went on, shaking his head paternally, "is a flower the less for being breathed of? And is the cultivated flower, tended and nourished, not more fortunate than the wild rose that blushes unseen? Do not regret your present social situation too much, Mrs. Lawrence—some might find it enviable. Few things are more changeable than points of view. In the coming weeks your viewpoint might well change."

"Just what the hell are you saying to my wife?" Malcolm asked.

Virginia said quickly, "We can talk about it later."

The colonel smiled at Virginia. "Before you do that, I have something else to show Mr. Lawrence." He raised his voice slightly: "Max! Moritz! Here!"— and the dogs were there. "Ah, Mr. Lawrence, I would like to show you first how these animals respond, how discriminating they can be." He turned to one of the dogs. "Moritz," he said sharply, nodding toward Malcolm, "Kill."

Malcolm couldn't believe what he had heard. Then he felt a blow on his chest. The dog was on him, its hind legs making short, fast, digging sounds in the lawn as it pressed its body against him. It was inside the arc of his arms, and the most he could have done was to clasp it closer to him. He made a tentative move to pull his arms back and then push forward against its rib cage, but the minor shift in weight made him stumble, and he realized if he completed the gesture he would fall. All this happened in a very short time, and then the dog touched open lips with him. Having done that, it dropped down and went back to stand beside Colonel Ritchey and Max.

"You see, Mr. Lawrence?" the colonel asked conversationally. "A dog does not respond to literal meaning. It is conditioned. It is trained to perform a certain action when it hears a certain sound. The cues one teaches a dog with pain and patience are not necessarily cues an educated organism can understand. Pavlov rang a bell and a dog salivated. Is a bell food? If he had rung a different bell, or said, 'Food, doggie,' there would have been no response. So, when I speak in a normal tone, rather than at command pitch, 'kill' does not mean 'kiss,' even to Moritz. It means nothing to him—unless I raise my voice. And I could just as easily have conditioned him to perform that sequence in association with some other command—such as, oh, say, 'gingersnaps'—but then you might not have taken the point of my little instructive jest. There is no way anyone but myself can operate these creatures. Only when I command do they respond. And now you respond, eh, Mr. Lawrence? I dare say. . . . Well, good day. As I said, you have things to do."

They left through the gate, which the colonel drew shut behind them. "Max," he said, "watch," and the dog froze in position. "Moritz, come." The colonel turned, an he and the other dog crossed the lawn and went into his house.

Malcolm and Virginia walked at a normal pace back to the rented house, Malcolm matching his step to Virginia's. He wondered if she were being so deliberate because she wasn't sure what the dog would do if she ran. It had been a long time since Virginia hadn't been sure of something.

In the house, Virginia made certain the door was shut tight, and then she went to sit in the chair that faced away from the window. "Would you make me some coffee, please?" she said.

"All right, sure. Take a few minutes. Catch your breath a little."

"A few minutes is what I need," she said. "Yes, a few minutes, and everything will be fine." When Malcolm returned with the coffee, she continued. "He's got some kind of string on Cortelyou, and I bet those people at the store down at the corner have those dogs walking in and out of there all the time. He's got us. We're locked up."

"Now, wait," Malcolm said, "there's the whole state of New Jersey out there, and he can't—"

"Yes, he can. If he thinks he can get away with it, and he's got good reasons for thinking he can. Take it on faith. There's no bluff in *him*."

"Well, look," he said, "just what can he do to us?"

"Any damn thing he pleases."

"That can't be right." Malcolm frowned. "He's got us pretty well scared right now, but we ought to be able to work out some way of—"

Virginia said tightly, "The dog's still there, right?" Malcolm nodded. "Okay," she said. "What did it feel like when he hit you? It looked awful. It looked like he was going to drive you clear onto your back. Did it feel that way? What did you *think*?"

"Well, he's a pretty strong animal," Malcolm said. "But, to tell you the truth, I didn't have time to believe it. You know, a man just saying 'kill' like that is a pretty hard thing to believe. Especially just after tea and cookies."

"He's very shrewd," Virginia said. "I can see why he had the camp guards running around in circles. He deserved to have a book written about him."

"All right, and then they should have thrown him into a padded cell."

"Tried to throw," Virginia amended.

"Oh, come on. This is his territory, and he dealt the cards before we even knew we were playing. But all he is is a crazy old cripple. If he wants to buffalo some people in a store and twist a two-bit real-estate salesman around his finger, fine—if he can get away with it. But he doesn't own us. We're not in his army."

"We're inside his prison camp," Virginia said.

"Now, look," Malcolm said. "When we walk in Cortelyou's door and tell him we know all about the colonel, there's not going to be any trouble about getting the rent back. We'll find someplace else, or we'll go back to the city. But whatever we do to get out of this, it's going to work out a lot smoother if the two of us think about it. It's not like you to be sitting there and spending a lot of time on how we can't win."

"Well, Malcolm. Being a prisoner certainly brings out your initiative. Here you are, making noises just like a senior officer. Proposing escape committees and everything."

Malcolm shook his head. Now of all times, when they needed each other so much, she wouldn't let up. The thing to do was to move too fast for her.

"All right," he said, "let's get in the car." There was just the littlest bit of sweat on his upper lip.

"*What*?" He had her sitting up straight in the chair, at least. "Do you imagine that that dog will let us get anywhere near the car?"

"You want to stay here? All right. Just keep the door locked. I'm going to try it, and once I'm out I'm going to come back here with a nice healthy state cop carrying a nice healthy riot gun. And we're either going to do something about the colonel and those two dogs, or we're at least going to move you and our stuff out of here."

He picked up the car keys, stepped through the front door very quickly, and began to walk straight for the car. The dog barked sharply, once. The front door of Ritchey's house opened immediately, and Ritchie called out, "Max! Hold!" The dog on the lawn was over the fence and had its teeth thrust carefully around Malcolm's wrist before he could take another eight steps, even though he had broken into a run. Both the dog and Malcolm stood very still. The dog was breathing shallowly and quietly, its eyes shining. Ritchey and Moritz walked as far as the front fence. "Now, Mr. Lawrence," Ritchey said, "in a moment I am going to call to Max, and he is to bring you with him. Do not attempt to hold back, or you will lacerate your wrist. Max! Bring here!"

Malcolm walked steadily toward the colonel. By some smooth trick of his neck, Max was able to trot alongside him without shifting his grip. "Very good, Max," Ritchey said soothingly when they had reached the fence. "Loose now," and the dog let go of Malcolm's wrist. Malcolm and Ritchey looked into each other's eyes across the fence, in the darkening evening.

"Now Mr. Lawrence," Ritchey said, "I want you to give me your car keys." Malcolm held out the keys, and Ritchey put them into his pocket. "Thank you." He seemed to reflect on what he was going to say next, as a teacher might reflect on his reply to a child who has asked why the sky is blue. "Mr. Lawrence, I want you to understand the situation. As it happens, I also want a three-pound can of Crisco. If you will please give me all the money in your pocket, this will simplify matters."

"I don't have any money on me," Malcolm said. "Do you want me to go in the house and get some?"

"No, Mr. Lawrence, I'm not a thief. I'm simply restricting your radius of action in one of the several ways I'm going to do so. Please turn out your pockets."

Malcolm turned out his pockets.

"All right, Mr. Lawrence, if you will hand me your wallet and your address book and the thirty-seven cents, they will all be returned to you whenever you have a legitimate use for them." Ritchey put the items away in the pockets of his jacket. "Now, a three-pound can of Crisco is ninety-eight cents. Here is a dollar bill. Max will walk with you to the corner grocery store, and you will buy the Crisco for me and bring it back. It is too much for a dog to carry in a bag, and it is three days until my next monthly delivery of staples. At the store you will please tell them that it will not be necessary for them to come here with monthly deliveries any longer—that you will be in to do my shopping for me from now on. I expect you to take a minimum amount of time to accomplish all this and to come back with my purchase, Mr. Lawrence. Max!" The colonel nodded toward Malcolm. "Guard. Store." The dog trembled and whined. "Don't stand still, Mr. Lawrence. Those commands are incompatible until you start toward the store. If you fail to move, he will grow increasingly tense. Please go now. Moritz and I will keep Mrs. Lawrence good company until you return."

The store consisted of one small room in the front of a drab house. On unpainted pine shelves were brands of goods that Malcolm had never heard of. "Oh! You're with one of those nice dogs," the tired, plump woman behind the counter said, leaning down to pat Max, who had approached her for that purpose. It seemed to Malcolm that the dog was quite mechanical about it and was pretending to itself that nothing caressed it at all. He looked around the place, but he couldn't see anything or anyone that offered any prospect of alliance with him.

"Colonel Ritchey wants a three-pound can of Crisco," he said, bringing the name out to check the reaction.

"Oh, you're helping him?"

"You could say that."

"Isn't he brave?" the woman said in low and confidential tones, as if concerned that the dog would overhear. "You know, there are some people who would think you should feel sorry for a man like that, but I say it would be a sin to do so. Why, he gets along just fine, and he's got more pride and spunk than any whole man I've ever seen. Makes a person proud to know him. You know, I think it's just wonderful the way these dogs come and fetch little things for him. But I'm glad he's got somebody to look out for him now. 'Cept for us, I don't think he sees anybody from one year to the next—'cept summers, of course."

She studied Malcolm closely. "You're summer people too, aren't you? Well, glad to have you, if you're doin' some good for the colonel. Those people last year were a shame. Just moved out one night in September, and neither the colonel nor me or my husband seen hide nor hair of them since. Owed the colonel a month's rent, he said when we was out there."

"Is he the landlord?" Malcolm asked.

"Oh, sure, yes. He owns a lot of land around here. Bought it from the original company after it went bust."

"Does he own this store, too?"

"Well, we lease it from him now. Used to own it, but we sold it to the company and leased it from them. Oh, we was all gonna be rich. My husband took the money from the land and bought a lot across the street and was gonna set up a real big gas station there—figured to be real shrewd—but you just can't get people to live out here. I mean, it isn't as if this was *ocean*-front property. But the colonel now, he's got a head on his shoulders. Value's got to go up someday, and he's just gonna hold on until it does."

The dog was getting restless, and Malcolm was worried about Virginia. He paid for the can of Crisco, and he and Max went back up the sand road in the dark. There really, honestly, didn't seem to be much else to do.

At his front door, he stopped, sensing that he should knock. When Virginia let him in, he saw that she had changed to shorts and a halter. "Hello," she said, and then stood aside quietly for him and Max. The colonel, sitting pertly forward on one of the chairs, looked up. "Ah, Mr. Lawrence, you're a trifle tardy, but the company has been delightful, and the moments seemed to fly."

Malcolm looked at Virginia. In the past couple of years, a little fat had accumulated above her knees, but she still had long, good legs. Colonel Ritchey smiled at Malcolm. "It's a rather close evening. I simply suggested to Mrs. Lawrence that I certainly wouldn't be offended if she left me for a moment and changed into something more comfortable."

It seemed to Malcolm that she could have handled that. But apparently she hadn't.

"Here's your Crisco," Malcolm said. "The change is in the bag."

"Thank you very much," the colonel said. "Did you tell them about the grocery deliveries?"

Malcolm shook his head. "I don't remember. I don't think so. I was busy getting an earful about how you owned them, lock, stock, and barrel."

"Well, no harm. You can tell them tomorrow."

"Is there going to be some set time for me to run your errands every day, Colonel? Or are you just going to whistle whenever something comes up?"

"Ah yes. You're concerned about interruptions in your mood. Mrs. Lawrence told me you were some sort of artist. I'd wondered at your not shaving this morning." The colonel paused and then went on crisply. "I'm sure we'll shake down into whatever routine suits best. It always takes a few days for individuals to hit their stride as a group. After that, it's quite easy—regular functions, established duties, that sort of thing. A time to rise and wash, a time to work, a time to sleep. Everything and everyone in his proper niche. Don't worry, Mr. Lawrence, you'll be surprised how comfortable it becomes. Most people find it a revelation." The colonel's gaze grew distant for a moment. "Some do not. Some are as if born on another planet, innocent of human nature. Dealing with that sort, there comes a point when one must cease to try; at the camp, I found that the energy for over-all success depended on my admitting the existence of the individual failure. No, some do not respond. But we needn't dwell on what time will tell us."

Ritchey's eyes twinkled. "I have dealt previously with creative people. Most of them need to work with their hands; do stupid, dull, boring work that leaves their minds free to soar in spirals and yet forces them to stay away from their craft until the tension is nearly unbearable." The colonel waved in the direction of the unbuilt houses. "There's plenty to do. If you don't know how to use a hammer and saw as yet, I know how to teach that. And when from time to time I see you've reached the proper pitch of creative frustration, then you shall have what time off I judge will best serve you artistically. I think you'll be surprised how pleasingly you'll take to your studio. From what I gather from your wife, this may well be a very good experience for you."

Malcolm looked at Virginia. "Yes. Well, that's been bugging her for a long time. I'm glad she's found a sympathetic ear."

"Don't quarrel with your wife, Mr. Lawrence. That sort of thing wastes energy and creates serious morale problems." The colonel got to his feet and went to the door. "One thing no one could ever learn to tolerate in a fellow *Kriegie* was pettiness. That sort of thing was always weeded out. Come, Max. Come, Moritz. Good night!" He left.

Malcolm went over to the door and put the chain on. "Well?" he said.

"All right, now, look—"

Malcolm held up one finger. "Hold it. Nobody likes a quarrelsome *Kriegie*. We're not going to fight. We're going to talk, and we're going to think." He found himself looking at her halter and took his glance away. Virginia blushed.

"I just want you to know it was exactly the way he described it," she said. "He said he wouldn't think it impolite if I left him alone in the living room while I went to change. And I wasn't telling him our troubles. We were talking about what you did for a living, and it didn't take much for him to figure out—"

"I don't want you explaining," Malcolm said. "I want you to help me tackle this thing and get it solved."

"How are you going to solve it? This is a man who always uses everything he's got! He never quits! How is somebody like *you* going to solve that?"

All these years, it occurred to Malcolm, at a time like this, now, she finally had to say the thing you couldn't make go away.

When Malcolm did not say anything at all for a while but only walked around frowning and thinking, Virginia said she was going to sleep. In a sense, he was relieved; a whole plan of action was forming in his mind, and he did not want her there to badger him.

After she had closed the bedroom door, he went into the studio. In a corner was a carton of his painting stuff, which he now approached, detached but thinking. From this room he could see the floodlights on around the colonel's house. The colonel had made his circuit of the yard, and one of the dogs stood at attention, looking across the way. The setting hadn't altered at all from the night before. Setting, no, Malcolm thought, bouncing a jar of brown tempera in his hand; mood, *si*. His arm felt good all the way down from his shoulder, into the forearm, wrist, and fingers.

When Ritchey had been in his house a full five minutes, Malcolm said to himself aloud, "Do first, analyze later." Whipping open the front door, he took two steps forward on the bare earth to gather momentum and pitched the jar of paint in a shallow arc calculated to end against the aluminum fence.

It was going to fall short, Malcolm thought, and it did, smashing with a loud impact against one of the whitewashed stones and throwing out a fan of gluey, brown spray over the adjacent stones, the fence, and the dog, which jumped back but, lacking orders to charge, stood its ground, whimpering. Malcolm stepped back into his open doorway and leaned in it. When the front door of Ritchey's house opened he put his thumbs to his ears and waggled his fingers, "*Gute Nacht, Herr Kommandant*," he called, then stepped back inside and slammed and locked the door, throwing the spring-bolt latch. The dog was already on its way. It loped across the yard and scraped its front paws against the other side of the door. Its breath sounded like giggling.

Malcolm moved over to the window. The dog sprang away from the door with a scratching of toenails and leaped upward, glancing off the glass. It turned, trotted away for a better angle, and tried again. Malcolm watched it; this was the part he'd bet on.

The dog didn't make it. Its jaws flattened against the pane, and the whole sheet quivered, but there was too much going against success. The window was pretty high above the yard, and the dog couldn't get a proper combination of momentum and angle of impact. If he did manage to break it, he'd never have enough momentum left to clear the break; he'd fall on the sharp edges of glass in the frame while other chunks fell and cut his neck, and then the colonel would be down to one dog. One dog wouldn't be enough; the system would break down somewhere.

The dog dropped down, leaving nothing on the glass but a wet brown smear.

It seemed to Malcolm equally impossible for the colonel to break the

window himself. He couldn't stride forward to throw a small stone hard
enough to shatter the pane, and he couldn't balance well enough to heft a
heavy one from nearby. The lock and chain would prevent him from
entering through the front door. No, it wasn't efficient for the colonel any
way you looked at it. He would rather take a few days to think of something
shrewd and economical. In fact, he was calling the dog back now. When the
dog reached him, he shifted one crutch and did his best to kneel while
rubbing the dog's head. There was something rather like affection in the
scene. Then the colonel straightened up and called again. The other dog
came out of the house and took up its station at the corner of the yard. The
colonel and the dirty dog went back into the colonel's house.

Malcolm smiled, then turned out the lights, double-checked the locks,
and went back through the hall to the bedroom. Virginia was sitting up in
bed, staring in the direction from which the noise had come.

"What did you do?" she asked.

"Oh, changed the situation a little," Malcolm said, grinning. "Asserted
my independence. Shook up the colonel. Smirched his neatness a little bit.
Spoiled his night's sleep for him, I hope. Standard *Kriegie* tactics. I hope he
likes them."

Virginia was incredulous. "Do you know what he could do to you with
those dogs if you step outside this house?"

"I'm not going to step outside. Neither are you. We're just going to wait a
few days."

"What do you mean?" Virginia said, looking at him as if he were a maniac.

"Day after tomorrow, maybe the day after that," Malcolm explained,
"he's due for a grocery delivery I didn't turn off. Somebody's going to be
here with a car then, lugging all kinds of things. I don't care how beholden
those storekeepers are to him; when we come out the door, he's not going to
have those dogs tear us to pieces right on the front lawn in broad daylight and
with a witness. We're going to get into the grocery car, and sooner or later
we're going to drive out in it, because *that* car and driver have to turn up in
the outside world again."

Virginia sighed. "Look," she said with obvious control, "all he has to do is
send a note with the dogs. He can stop the delivery that way."

Malcolm nodded. "Uh-huh. And so the groceries don't come. Then what?
He starts trying to freight flour and eggs in here by dog back? By remote
control? What's he going to do? All right, so it doesn't work out so neatly in
two or three days. But we've got a fresh supply of food, and he's almost out.
Unless he's planning to live on Crisco, he's in a bad way. And even so, he's
only got three pounds of that." Malcolm got out of his clothes and lay down
on the bed. "Tomorrow's another day, but I'll be damned if I'm going to
worry any more about it tonight. I've got a good head start on frustrating the
legless wonder, and tomorrow I'm going to have a nice clear mind, and I'm
going to see what other holes I can pick in his defense. I learned a lot of snide
little tricks from watching jolly movies about clever prisoners and dumb

guards." He reached up and turned out the bed light. "Good night, love," he said. Virginia rolled away from him in the dark. "Oh, my God," she said in a voice with a brittle edge around it.

It was a sad thing for Malcolm to lie there thinking that she had that kind of limitation in her, that she didn't really understand what had to be done. On the other hand, he thought sleepily, feeling more relaxed than he had in years, he had his own limitations. And she had put up with them for years. He fell asleep wondering pleasantly what tomorrow would bring.

He woke to a sound of rumbling and crunching under the earth, as if there were teeth at the foundations of the house. Still sleeping in large portions of his brain, he cried out silently to himself with a madman's lucidity, "Ah, of course, he's been tunneling!" And his mind gave him all the details—the careful transfer of supporting timber from falling houses, the disposal of the excavated clay in the piles beside the other foundations, too, for when the colonel had more people. . . .

Now one corner of the room showed a jagged line of yellow, and Malcolm's hands sprang to the light switch. Virginia jumped from sleep. In the corner was a trap door, its uneven joints concealed by boards of different angles. The trap door crashed back, releasing a stench of body odor and soot.

A dog popped up through the opening and scrambled into the bedroom. Its face and body were streaked, and it shook itself to get the sand from its coat. Behind it, the colonel dragged himself up, naked, and braced himself on his arms, half out of the tunnel mouth. His hair was matted down with perspiration over his narrow-boned skull. He was mottled yellow–red with dirt, and half in the shadows. Virginia buried her face in her hands, one eye glinting out between spread fingers, and cried to Malcolm, "Oh my God, what have you done to us?"

"Don't worry, my dear," the colonel said crisply to her. Then he screamed at Malcolm, "I will not be abused!" Trembling with strain as he braced on one muscle-corded arm, he pointed at Malcolm. He said to the dog at command pitch: "Kiss!"

NEW MEXICO

The Devil of the Picuris
by Edwin L. Sabin

A YEAR or two ago there customarily sat in a bare little yard of an old-time outskirts adobe of older Santa Fe, New Mexico, an aged, wrinkled señor. All the fairweather days he sat here, huddled in a chair, with a plaid shawl in lieu of a striped serape over his shoulders; and upon many days Indian visitors from the pueblos north or south bore him respectful company.

Frequently marking him, swart, leathery, gray-locked and silent and noting his strange guests, I said to myself: "Here is a venerable with history behind his lips." So I vented cautious queries in the neighborhood.

"His name?"

"Miguel García, señor."

"He is very old?"

"*Quién sabe?* Very old, señor."

"He is an Indian?"

"No, no, señor. He is Spanish."

"Then why do the Indians visit him so often?"

"*Sabe Dios, señor.* But he is an old Indian fighter."

"He must have been a good one," thought I. "The Indians do him homage even at this late date." Whereby my curiosity was further piqued, and out of my occasional polite "*Buenos dias, señor,*" and felicitation upon the weather, there arrived a day when I might enter the yard and stand uncovered beside his chair. Just in right time, too; for another of his constant visitors shuffled in, looking only straight ahead (as is Indian trait), bringing a quarter of venison wrapped in the hide.

"*Cómo 'stá?*" my old man grunted.

"*Cómo 'stá?*" The Indian gave me one sharp glance and with that

425

dismissed me. I could see that he was a Pueblo, by virtue of his blanket and white leggins, but was darker, more wiry, more savage in lineaments than the average Pueblo; a very Indian of romance.

He shifted the quarter of deer.

"For the Captain," he announced.

My old man called with the voice of authority: "María! Here!"

An ancient dame scuttled from the house, took the venison superciliously delivered to her, and scuttled back.

"'stá bueno," my old man shortly acknowledged.

"Bueno," the Indian responded. "Adiós."

He went as swiftly as he had come.

"A Pueblo, señor?" I asked.

"Sí."

"Of Taos? Of Tesuque?"

"No, no. Of Picuris." His tone held testy rebuke, but how was I to know? "Of Picuris where they yet have scalps strung on their roofs. What think you of that?"

"You are an old Indian fighter, I hear, señor."

"Sí, Sí! I have fought them, in my day; the Apache, the Navajo, the Comanche—all."

"You are an old Indian fighter," I pursued. "Now the Indians visit you, they bring you gifts, you are called Captain by them. The Picuris Pueblos have not been friendly to the white people. There must be a story."

"Dios! There is a story." He meditated, rubbing his grizzled chin. "Así es. You are an American, but you are civil. Well, some day; maybe some day."

He was a chronicler not to be hurried; but by dint of salutation and expectancy I at last swung him to an appointment.

At the hour he was not alone. A Pueblo sat upon the ground beside him. The former venison bringer, I opined. And when to my "Muy buenos días, Señor Capitán," he fastened his somber hawk eyes upon me, I saw indeed that it was the same stately Pueblo of Picuris.

"You have come to hear the story of the thunder-devil bird?" my old man addressed me, when I had been seated.

"Of the—what, señor?" said I, puzzled. And this put him to cackling; a rare event which apprised me that he was in good humor.

"Oh-ho! What is that, you ask? Not knowing, maybe you will not believe, like all Americans who will not believe that which they do not see."

"Try me, señor," I pleaded. "I wish to hear of the thunder-devil bird. You have many years; you were there, and you know."

"Many years? Santo Dios! I think one hundred. On a cold day I think one thousand," he grumbled. "Yes, I was there. And that you may believe, I have invited another captain (and he indicated the Indian) whose Christian name is Antonio, to hear also. For I am his godfather and he has received the story from his father who was there when I was there. He is the war captain of the Picuris."

The Indian looked upon me and I looked upon him; but he was red and I was white, and we had no words to exchange.

"And because you speak my language and have treated me as if I were somebody and not an old simple, I will tell you," my host proceeded. "Now I must get on with it or I shall have no breath."

Whereat he huddled more warmly, swathed his withered hands in his shawl, and launched his narrative upon the full strong tide of measured, sonorous Spanish.

It was the second year before the conquest (he said), and I was then young and active and a buffalo-hunter out of Abiquiu. We traveled far east, twice a year, to hunt the buffalo in the country of the Comanches and to trade the robes and meat with the caravans of the North Americans. All this is nothing, except that it shows I learned to fight the savages.

Well, one night I had a little trouble over a girl at a ball—here in Santa Fe, and the family and friends of the young man made me take to the road. His father was a *rico*; there were masses for his soul: God no doubt forgave me, but I knew enough to go.

I went to Picuris, and asked the *cacique* for sanctuary. He ordered me a room of my own. It was with the grandfather of this very Antonio. These tame Indians, as we Spanish call the Pueblos, live comfortably in great houses. They can shut themselves up from their enemies. So here I shut myself up, too, from my enemies; and I became as a son to my new father.

A people very proud and fierce, the Picuris Pueblos; but not many. They numbered only about three hundred. And today—*quién sabe?* But they were strong in hearts, fine warriors and hunters; their men preferred the bow to the hoe. They have Apache blood. They were different from the other Pueblos, so that between them and even the Taos Pueblo, only two hours by horse, there was scarcely any visiting.

The Pueblos do not like to have their children marry outsiders. But I was told I ought to take a wife, and I married one of my adopted sisters, which was all right. Her Spanish name was Felicia. Her home name was something that means cornsilk. And she had a sacred name given by the Picuris priests, which nobody else knew except her and her mother.

We set up housekeeping. *Dios*, how proud we were when a baby arrived! Now I was a man in earnest. That did not make me a Picuris, though. True, I might dance with the others in the *fiestas*, but I was not admitted to the councils. What was said and done in the *estufas*, the underground chambers of the clans, I had too much sense to ask. When, twice, almost the whole town went away toward the mountains, I was left behind. All I heard was, that they had gone to pay a visit to the thunder-devil bird. But being Spanish and a Christian I did not care; I laughed to myself at the foolishness of the Picuris.

"What is that thunder-devil bird they go to see?" said I to my little wife.

"Oh, you must not mention it," said she, looking frightened.

"But what is he? Tell me?"

"He is a great bad god. He makes the thunder that can strike us dead."

"Where does he live?"

"On the Sacred Mountain."

"Did anyone ever see him?"

"Oh, yes, yes!"

"Did you ever see him?"

"You must not ask."

"Did you see him this time when you went away from me, and came back?"

"You must not ask, you must not ask."

"I have a right to know where my wife goes," said I.

"No. The priests forbid. It is against the laws. Only the priests may speak of the thunder-devil bird. Please do not force me; and please, please ask nothing of anybody, for it will bring you danger."

That had been the first time when she had gone, with the others—everybody except the children and a few very old men and women. The second time she did not go, because she was about to be delivered of our baby. And I was glad. That thunder-devil business seemed to make unhappiness among the women. There always were some of them who cried. Under the blessings of God, I thought, my little wife shall never cry.

Then, one day when our baby had about six months, and from the talk that I had pretended not to hear, I knew that the thunder-devil bird time was arrived again; when I came home from the field I found my little wife crying indeed.

"What is the matter with you?" I asked.

"Do not ask me."

"But I will ask you," I said. "Are you sick?"

"No, no."

"Has somebody harmed you?"

"No, no."

"You are not happy with me?"

"Yes, yes."

"Then don't sit there crying. Is it the thunder-devil time again?"

"Yes, it is the thunder-devil time again, and I am afraid."

"Afraid of what?"

"Do not ask me. Your food is ready."

That was all I could get out of her, except the tears. After I had eaten and had petted our *niño*, I went out and found my brother Antonio, who was this Antonio's father.

"Let us walk by the river," I said. "I have something to say."

So we pulled our blankets over our heads, in sign that we did not wish to be known; and when we were in the willows out of sight of even the persons standing on the rooftops (you know señor, that in the pueblos which look for Montezuma there always is somebody on the rooftops, morning and evening) I spoke.

"What is all this nonsense about the thunder-devil bird, that is making my wife cry, and makes the other women cry?"

"Hush!" he answered. "It is not for you to know."

"I am a man," said I. "My woman is unhappy, I want to know."

"If you ask questions you will be in danger. You are not a member of any clan, yet. You meddle with sacred matters."

"I am a man," said I again. "I am not afraid of danger. But my woman cries about the thunder-devil bird, and I will know why."

"No man may always know why a woman cries," he said. "And it is forbidden us to talk of the thunder-devil bird."

"You are my brother," I replied. "If my brother will not tell me what I wish to know, then I will ask and listen until I do find things out. Maybe," I said, "I can make her tell me. She is my wife."

"No." And he gazed all around, frightened. "That would ruin you both. The priests would know—she would have to die, you would be killed. It is better that I tell you a little, so you will understand. Now, if I tell you a little, do you swear by your Christian God, and by all Those Above, that you will never, never reveal one word?"

"I swear, by the Christian God and by Those Above," I promised.

"Or betray me?"

"I swear it, my brother," I promised.

"Let us sit down close together," he bade. "You may ask me questions." We sat down, close together.

"What is this thunder-devil bird?" I asked.

"He is the thunder-devil bird. A very large bird, who makes the thunder."

"How do you know?"

"We know because we have seen him."

"Where have you seen him?"

"On the mountain."

"The Sacred Mountain?"

"Yes."

"What does he do there?"

"He lives there. He makes the thunder. In the winter he sleeps."

"What kind of bird?"

"A great bird; a bad god bird—like a bird and snake both. There is no such other bird anywhere."

"You have seen him, yourself, my brother?"

"Yes, many times."

"By yourself?"

"With the others."

"Is that where the people go, when they leave the pueblo and stay away two days?"

"That is where they go."

"Why?"

"To feed him."

"Do you feed him only twice a year?"

"No. Things are left for him. But twice a year we all must visit him, with sacred food, and the priests make medicine to him so he will be good to us and not send the thunder to burn us up."

"Are the people getting ready to go again?"

"It is the time. We go tomorrow. Tonight we get ready."

"Is that why my wife cries?"

"I cannot tell you. I suppose it is. At thunder-devil bird time women cry."

"Why? Is the way dangerous? Is he such a bad bird?"

"He is a devil bird. He will be bad unless we keep him good toward us. When he is angry with any of us he kills us."

"That sounds foolish to me, my brother," I said.

"No. You do not understand. You have never seen him. But he is there: He has been there many, many years. He was there when my grandfather was a boy. He has always been there. He is stronger than the God of your Spanish priests. They have tried to stop our going, and the thunder came and killed us in our houses."

"Still, you do not tell me why my woman cries now, and why other women cry."

"I do not tell you."

"I will go, and maybe I will find out."

"Go where?"

"With the pueblo people tomorrow."

My brother caught me by the arm.

"You cannot. They would not let you."

"Why?"

"You are no Picuris."

"I have married a Picuris, and I live here."

"You are white, just the same."

"I will follow. I will look like a Picuris. They would not know me until too late."

"That is impossible. You do not understand. You would be found out, and the priests would have you killed. It is death for any stranger to be caught on the Sacred Mountain."

"For all that," I said, "I do not like to have my wife cry, and I shall learn what makes her cry now at thunder-devil bird time. Some evil threatens her."

"Listen," he said. "I love you, my brother; and I love my sister. Some evil does threaten you both. She will accept it, because she is of the Picuris, and it is for the good of the pueblo. But you are Spanish, and you do not believe as we do. Maybe the evil will not happen; I know nothing one way or the other. It all lies with the priests; but the priests are not friendly toward you, yet, and I fear for you. They may try you, to see whether you are going to be Picuris or Spanish. Listen, my brother. Will you swear again by your God and by Those Above, never to betray me if I show you what is in my secret heart?"

"I swear, by my God and by Those Above," I answered.

"I have sometimes thought, to myself," he said (he was a wise young man, that Antonio, father to this Antonio), "that if we could only get rid of the thunder-devil bird we all would be much better off."

"Yes," I answered. "Women who cry and won't tell are not pleasant things. There seems to be some evil hanging over this pueblo. Have you ever tried getting rid of the thunder-devil bird?"

"No. How can we get rid of him? We feed him and he lives forever. He is strong, and it will take stronger medicine than anything we have to overcome him. And the priests do not wish him out of the way. He is one of the gods; they learn things from him. But, my brother, you may know of a medicine so strong that it will shrivel him up. I have heard from the old men that your priests have worked wonders against devils. They speak names and touch with a cross, and the sick get well. That happened a long time ago, when they first came into our country. The last padre we had here did not do it. Do you known anything about that medicine?"

"The name of God, and the Virgin, and the sign of the cross will conquer any devil," I said.

"Would they conquer the thunder-devil bird?"

"If he is a devil," I said. "Yes, if he is a devil one of our good padres would shrivel him up in a moment."

"But there is no one of the padres here; and besides, our priests would not let him see the thunder-devil bird. They do not wish to lose the thunder-devil bird. Now, my brother, if you know anything about that power, and are brave enough to try, I will help you."

"How?" I asked.

"I will guide you on a trail to the thunder-devil bird place."

"When?"

"Tomorrow early, so you will be there to see him. He comes out only at night, except twice a year when we call him. And if you wait longer you may be too late to save yourself from the evil that is making your wife cry."

"That is good," I said. "I will go and see the thunder-devil bird and shrivel him up."

"You can work the magic of the Christian priests?" he asked.

"I can speak the words and make the sign. With the help of God and the Holy Mother Mary that will be enough, if he is a devil."

"If it is not enough, then you will die by thunder or by the priests. But I think this, too: If you rid the pueblo of that thunder-devil bird, you will be a great man. I hate to have you go, though, my brother. When you are there, there will be no backing out."

"I will go," said I. "I will go, to stop the women's crying. As for the evil that threatens me and my woman. I ought to know about it."

My brother stood up.

"We must return to the pueblo," he said. "You go by one way and I by another, so we will not be seen together. I will meet you in the morning when the morning star is brightest. You remember where we killed the deer day before yesterday?"

"Yes."

"I will meet you there. And when I have shown you the way I shall leave you, for I have to travel to the thunder-devil bird place with the other people."

"Wait," I asked. "You have not told me what the evil is, or why my little Felicia cries."

"When you have been to the thunder-devil bird place you will know," he answered. Then he went in one direction and I went in another.

The sun had set, señor, and all the pueblo was getting ready for thunder-devil bird day. Men were singing the thunder-devil chant, and women were wailing, and a drum was beating the call for a meeting in the *estufa*. There was evil in the air—the evil that made my wife cry, and the other women cry. But most I cared about my wife. My brother would not tell me what that evil might be. So I did a reckless thing. I followed into the principal *estufa*, to hear and see what I could.

You know that these *estufas* are sacred chambers where the men gather for rest and to make ceremonies. They are hollowed under ground and surrounded by a wall, at the mouth; and to enter, you climb over by one ladder and down in by another. No outsider is permitted in an *estufa*; the penalty is death. Yes, those priests would have been very glad to catch me. But by help of the dusk and my blanket over my head, I went in with the others. God be thanked, a great crowd of all the men of the pueblo was here, sitting close together in the dark, which made it the safer for me. The only light was that of a fire. The priests were in front, at the fire, and there were singing and drum beating, belonging to the thunder-devil ceremony.

Well, the priests had things to do, connected with the thunder-devil business; and although I understand the Picuris language and I listened with both ears and at the same time I pretended to sing like the rest, what the priests were doing I could not find out, except that they were praying to their gods to show them the way.

After a long time the chief-priest stood up and said: "It is chosen." That is all he said. Then the men began to leave as thick as they had come in, and I went, too. As for me, I had found out nothing, but I was very glad to get away and slip into my house before being caught.

"Where have you been?" my wife asked me.

"I have been walking, so as not to hear you cry," I said.

"I do not mean to drive you out," said she. "You are good to me, but I am afraid."

"Afraid of what?"

"I cannot tell you. Perhaps I am foolish. After thunder-devil bird day I shall be all right."

"You fear evil?"

"Yes, I fear evil, but it may not happen."

"I feel an evil but I do not fear it," I said. "I am your man and I will protect you. Do you go away from me tomorrow?"

"I go away. I have to. We all have to. But I shall be back."

"Then I shall go with you. It is not right for a married woman to leave her husband and go off with the other men."

"You cannot. They would not let you. You are not a Picuris."

So I thought best not to tell her that I would be there at the thunder-devil bird place; and I tried to sleep. Outside, all the pueblo was humming with the thunder-devil chant; people hurried about, to and from the *kivas*, which is another name for the *estufas*; and evil seemed to press close.

Pretty soon somebody scratched at the mat which shut the doorway of our room; so I arose and went and asked:

"What is wanted?"

It was one of the priests.

"I want to speak with your woman," he said. "Send her out to me."

My Felicia had heard; for she made a sound in her throat and went out past me. She was gone a little time; and when she came in, it was to crouch in a corner and moan under her shawl. I knew that the evil had fallen.

"What did that priest wish?" I asked.

"No, no!"

"But I ask you."

"No, no!"

"What is the matter, then?"

"No, no!"

"Has the evil fallen?"

"Oh, yes."

"As you feared?"

"Yes."

"Has it something to do with the thunder-devil bird?"

"Yes, yes!"

That was very irritating: a woman who wept and said only, "No, no," and "Yes, yes."

"I am your husband. I say that you shall tell me."

"I cannot. Do not ask."

"Shall I ever know?"

"Yes, you shall know. When it is over with, you shall know."

"Why cannot I know now, to help you?"

"You would not understand. You would ruin us. I must do as the priest says. You cannot help."

And all the night she moaned under her shawl in the corner, and all the night the thunder-devil chant sounded; and though I was a Christian I now feared the evil thing that had fallen upon us.

Well, early in the morning she was quiet, and breathing as if asleep, with our *niño* in her arms. Then I arose, and took my gun, and slipped away; and if anyone spoke to me I would say that I was going hunting. But the town was tired, at this hour; not yet was there any watcher on the rooftops, and nobody saw me, for the dawn was scarcely breaking and the morning star was at its brightest.

At the place up the river, where we had killed the deer, I found my brother waiting. It seemed to me that he might have been here many hours, he looked so fierce and heavy-eyed.

"Am I on time?" I asked.

"You are on time, brother. Come; we must travel fast."

We set out. He, too, had arms of bow and quiver, as if he were going hunting. Travel fast we did, without speaking, to save our breath until were clear of the town. Then he said, at last:

"What do you know now of the evil that threathened, brother?"

"It has fallen," I replied. "A priest brought it. My wife cried all night, but she would not tell me. I ask you again, what is it?"

"You shall know."

"When?"

"Tomorrow."

"Where?"

"At the thunder-devil bird place, where we are going."

"On the Sacred Mountain?"

"On the Sacred Mountain."

"You will surely show me, before you leave me?"

"I shall go to the place with you."

"That is good," I said. "I thank you, my brother. We will hasten, so you will not be missed."

"I do not care if I am missed," he said. "I will stay with you and we will conquer the thunder-devil bird or we will die; for the evil has fallen upon me also."

"The evil? The same evil?"

"The same evil. The priests brought it to you because you are a foreigner and a Christian. They brought it to me because I am your brother and they know I love you. Now my woman, and my sister who is your woman, both are crying; and you and I go together to face the thunder-devil bird and undo this evil if we may."

"Then tell me what this evil is that we share," I begged again.

"No. Your medicine must be strong and your heart newly hot. If I tell you now you will throw your strength away. You will be weak and scattered. It is better that you wait for the great moment."

As you know, señor, the Sacred Mountain of the Pueblos lies beyond the pueblo of Taos which is eighteen miles from the pueblo of Picuris; therefore we had more than thirty miles to travel afoot before we reached it by the trail we took. It is a mountain very large and very beautiful, señor; and for many years, back farther than the memory of the oldest Indian, the Pueblos of the country have gone up into the mountain to worship. I think that even yet no white man has visited all of the mountain; there are places kept secret by the Pueblos.

When the morning star was fading in the dawn we were three leagues out; and from a little hill we might look back and see Picuris. The people had begun to move busily; watchers in white were waiting on the rooftops for the rising sun; there was smoke of breakfast fires; it did not look like evil, but I remembered the crying of my little Felicia, and I knew that when the sun rose, then all the pueblo would start for the Sacred Mountain and the thunder-devil bird. Was the evil behind us, or was it before? *Sabe Dios.* That was for me to find out.

Well, we traveled fast, so as to keep ahead out of sight: across the mesas and the arroyos and through among the little hills, with the sun growing hotter and the piñones and the cedars warm and sweet. My brother led far around the great pueblo of Taos, and the Sacred Mountain now stood high and beautiful, wooded clear to the top, you know, señor, and covered all with the blue haze which is the sign of the spirits. It was more distant than it seemed to be, too, so that when at last we reached its base beyond the smaller hills, the sun was nearing noon.

"We will camp at the thunder-devil bird place tonight," my brother said. "And wait. Are you strong?"

"I am strong," said I.

Then we commenced to climb indeed; up, and up, and up, in trees and bushes very thick, and around cliffs and rocks, and across fine parks where there were deer and turkeys. But we did not pause for deer and turkeys. Strange things I saw, señor, as we got higher: rocks painted with sacred signs, and prayer altars, and other medicine tokens left by the Pueblos to win the favor of Those Above. Some were very old. But we did not pause for these, either. After a time we arrived at a bench of rocks, far up on this Sacred Mountain. The bench faced to the south. Grass grew among the rocks, and sun made comfort, and there was a cold spring blessing the spot.

"We have done well," spoke my brother. "Now we can rest, so as to be strong when we reach the thunder-devil bird place."

We drank, and lay down.

"It is far, yet, my brother?" I asked.

"It is far, by the way we go; but not so far as we have come. Look," he pointed.

My eyes were good, in those days, señor. Now below us we could see all the country flattened out; there was nothing between us and Picuris. The pueblo of Taos sat small, although its *casas grandes* are five and seven stories high. Picuris we could not see, because its houses mingled with the earth; but what I did see, when he pointed, was the Picuris people coming, like ants at our feet, to the mountain.

"That is they?"

436

EDWIN L. SABIN

"That is they. Do you feel the evil?"

"No," I answered, "I do not feel the evil now." And it was difficult, señor, to feel any evil, here, in the sun, high on the beautiful mountain, near to God. "Do they bring it?"

"Yes, they bring it. You shall feel it again, and you shall see it," he said. "As for me, I hear it; I hear my woman and my sister crying. But we may rest; we have plenty of time to meet the evil when it comes, and to uncover its face."

We rested here a little time, until the Picuris ants had disappeared in the foothills; they had traveled more slowly than we, because of the old persons and the women, and also to search the country for the enemy Apaches. When the sun was about an hour lower my brother arose.

"We shall go," he said. "It will not be good to arrive at the thunder-devil bird place in the dark."

Now we climbed again. We climbed to the very top of the mountain, where the trees were shorter and the rocks larger. The sun had set for the world below, but it was still bright up here, when by brother stopped.

"We are here," he whispered.

"At the thunder-devil bird place?"

"Yes, brother."

As soon as the blood cleared out of my eyes, for we had hurried fast, I began to believe that there might be something in the thunder-devil bird business after all. It was a devil place, sure enough: a black lake, not large, señor, sunk into black rock, walling it all about except at the end where we lay. The walls rose forty and fifty feet high, in almost a circle, and hollowed with caves; and at the farther end the mountaintop showed, black and gray and snow-patched, in the sun.

The sun shone on it, señor, but not on the little lake, so that the water was like thin tar, and seemed to have no bottom. Back of us were trees that we had left; in front of us there were no trees, only the lake, ten feet below us, and beyond the lake, the walls, pitted like spoiled wild honeycomb. We could hear not a sound: the water seemed to have no ripples and no voice; the place had no breeze, no life; the sun had no power. It was a place very black, very dead, and very evil.

At our end the lake narrowed, with a tongue that licked silently into a piece of low shore. The shore was lowest almost opposite us, and ran around this open end from cliffs to cliffs. There were white things scattered on the low shore, and splashes of white upon the cliff faces, and in the air a smell of death—a strange, bad smell, very disagreeable.

"Do you feel anything now, brother?" Antonio asked me, whispering.

"I feel an evil, but you say that our evil is coming," I whispered back.

"You feel the evil that has been done here for the thunder-devil."

"I smell it," I said. "Do I smell it?"

"You smell it. Listen, now. I will tell you. You see that hole, in the wall across the lake and up?"

"Which hole? There are many."

"The large hole, with a shelf in front of it, and a white streak staining the wall face below it."

"I see it."

"That is the house of the thunder-devil bird. He lives inside."

"You know?"

"I know. I have seen him on the shelf. The white stain is his droppings. The stain is broader than it looks to be from here, and the hole is larger than any room at the pueblo. And he himself is greater in size than a buffalo."

"What is his kind?" I asked.

"I cannot tell you. You shall see him for yourself, I think; but I have said that he is part bird and part snake. When he plunges into the lake the water rises and the thunder sounds. He can make the lake overflow down the mountain, the priests say, and there is water enough to cover all the world. So we feed him, that he may not have to hunt."

"Does he always stay here, then?"

"Yes, he stays here while he is content."

"Can he fly?"

"His wings are short, but he can fly on the thunder. The priests have seen him in the clouds. He likes the water best; and some day he may ride the water, when it overflows to drown the world. He does not see well except in blackness. That is why the lake is black, and the rocks are black, to make the nights black."

"And those other white things. What are they?"

"They are his droppings, and the bones of things that he has eaten. Sometimes he comes to the shore, at night, to eat what he finds. He can cling to the walls like a bat, too, with his wings."

"Now tell me of the evil that threatens us, my brother," I besought.

"No, not yet. You will see. We are here. Let us stay where we are till morning, and Those Above will guard us. I got a good sign when I prayed."

The rocks between which we lay were taller than we. They, and the other rocks, were like rocks that had been melted black in a hot fire. We ate a little dried meat. Now the sun was just touching the mountaintop, before he sank entirely. To the world below he had been sunk some time. The lake was growing blacker, and the blackness was rising up the walls, and we could scarcely see the hole in which the thunder-devil lived. Night gathered swiftly here, señor, so that soon we two were lying all in the blackness, and even the mountaintop had been swallowed. The sense of evil was very strong. I had little doubt, now, but that it was the place of some devil.

A change of air came blowing toward us from up the lake, and with it that smell. Yes, señor, the breeze carried a stench like the stench of a den of rattlesnakes, truly a devil stench and a death stench, enough to make a man sicken and fear. My brother and I lay pressed close for warmth and company, but we did not speak. It seemed to me that something was about to happen, in the stench and the stillness.

Then we heard a sound, breaking the night in two. It was a sound that I cannot describe—a harsh sound, harsher than the sound of locked wagon-wheels grating over rocks. That is the only way I can tell you of it, but it was a sound terrible, made by a voice, in the darkness.

I felt my brother tremble.

"The thunder-devil is out," he whispered. "That is he. Listen."

We listened, and smelled the evil stench. Again the thunder-devil called, with his loud croak; and up the lake, toward where he lived, we heard a scratching in the blackness. That brought out the sweat, señor, cold and sticky. My brother muttered, praying to his Those Above.

"Try your medicine," he said, to me. "But only a little of it. Do not throw it away. We shall need it in the morning."

"In the name of God and the Most Holy Virgin, stay where you are, devil," I cried.

Whether the words reached him I did not know; but we heard nothing more, then.

"He is hungry, and waiting," my brother whispered. "I think we are safe, for tomorrow he will be fed, and he knows. It is the time. Twice a year, on thunder-devil bird day, he is fed full. It lasts him a long time; his throat is small, and when he is full, he sleeps. He is never allowed to get too hungry."

We lay there. The stars were very bright above, but the darkness around was very thick, and through our blankets the night was very cold and the rocks hard. The stench continued. Once again we heard the thunder-devil call, and he rattled his claws; he was no nearer, though, and seeing that he kept his distance we grew less afraid.

"He is waiting for tomorrow," my brother said.

"Then the people from the pueblo come?"

"At sunrise. And I look to you to shrivel the thunder-devil bird. That is the only way to kill the evil that they bring."

"The evil that threatens and makes our women cry?"

"So I have said. It is in the priests' hands, not far. What we have smelt and heard is only a sign."

Well, the night seemed long, señor, while we lay and tried not to shiver, and the stars slowly passed. I think that we slept a little; but when the darkness paled I was awake, and so was he. Pretty soon we sat up, in our blankets; we ate a few mouthfuls of our meat, and watched the mountaintop brighten, until the time when we might see the thunder-devil bird hole. Thanks to God, the day had arrived and we were safe; for when the gray had crept down into the place, we saw nothing but the cliffs and the lake. The thunder-devil bird cave looked empty, all the lake was quiet; he had gone inside his house, away from the day.

The sunshine struck the mountaintop first, and began to flow downward. Then my brother bade:

"Listen!"

I listened, and I heard a singing in the distance. It was the thunder-devil chant. The singing grew louder, and I knew that the pueblo people were coming. My brother sat straighter and threw off his blanket.

"They are coming, and the evil," he said. "Let us be ready to face the evil and the thunder-devil with your medicine. Are you strong?"

"With the help of God I am strong," said I. "I want to know what that evil is."

"You shall know," he answered. "And very soon. And while you work your medicine I will stand by you, for it is an evil that we share, and perhaps Those Above will help us also."

The singing drew nearer, from beyond the end of the lake. And we looked, and just as the sunshine reached us, there they came, into the open, out of the trees, with their priests leading, bearing a canopy, señor. As a procession they came, singing the thunder-devil chant—and in the name of God, señor, that was a sight; for every man and woman was without clothing, as naked as when born.

This was evil enough. I had seen naked Indians before, but never so many at once. However, it was a custom, and not wrong in the sight of their gods, Those Above.

"Shall we wait?" I asked.

"Wait," he said. "You shall see; there will be more for you."

"What is under the canopy?"

"The evil." And the voice of my brother was so fierce that I feared.

Then I heard the sound of the night. The chanting filled all the place, and the sound had answered, harsh and grating and glad—the call from the thunder-devil. It made me gaze quickly; and I saw him. He was coming out of his hole, into the sunshine, for the hole faced the east. *Santo Dios*, señor, you may not wish to believe, but he it was, the thunder-devil bird. (I heard the squatted Antonio breathing quickly, all intent, and I felt the truth of the earnest old señor.) A devil indeed, as he emerged, part bird, part snake, just as I had been told. First there came his bird bill and snake head, with round, staring eyes; then his long, scaly snake neck, as long as my body, but thin and round; then his scaly bird body, on short legs with clawed feet. A body as large as that of a cow, señor, having no tail, and ending suddenly. He called again, opening his mouth, which had teeth; and he flapped his wings; short wings; but he did not fly. He sat there, holding fast on the edge of his shelf, weaving his neck and answering the people, with his eyes (as large as saucers, señor) open to the sun. They had no lids, señor; no lids any more than the eyes of a snake; and whether he could see or not, *quién sabe?* But it was terrible to witness him gazing into the sun.

And such a stench from his body and his breath! The stench of the night, only worse. Truly an evil stench.

"*Santísima!* Guard us!" I cried.

"He hears. He is ready," my brother said in a strange voice. "Look! They are making ready, too, and bringing what you are here to see. Now you shall know the evil thing that is upon us."

When the thunder-devil bird had answered, the people had answered back, shouting; they were singing the chant and dancing like mad, at the end of the lake almost across from us—dancing all except the priests and two who were women. But the two women were flat upon their faces, and the priests were taking out what had been carried under the canopy. Now they held the things up; held them up toward the thunder-devil bird, señor; but no evil things, only two naked little babies, which moved not, as if asleep.

Nombre de Dios! I heard my brother speaking fast.

"Brother! It is the offering to the thunder-devil bird. Your *niño* and my *niño*: Twice a year two babies to the thunder-devil bird. Now you know why the women cry, and what the evil is that has come upon us. Those Above have permitted it, because the people have permitted it, and fear is great and the priests strong. In a moment they will throw the *niños* where the thunder-devil will smell them, out in the water; and they will go. Quick! If your medicine is stronger, shrivel the thunder-devil."

Then I think I turned a little crazy, señor, with all my blood bursting my head and blinding me. I cared nothing for the thunder-devil; I wished only to save those babies from the water. I stood up, and shouted, and not waiting I leaped straight out, down into the lake. Waist deep it happened to be, at this place, and I held my gun high and, shouting, I plowed across. Right behind me there came my brother, Antonio, who was this Antonio's father—the father of the little Antonio in the arms of a priest. Yes; this Antonio and my own *niño* were to be offered to the thunder-devil bird.

The people saw us, and they heard us; and the priests knew.

"Kill, kill!" they cried. "A stranger is in the thunder-devil bird place. He shall die, and he who brought him. It is more food for the thunder-devil."

We were in the water and they all were on the shore. The men shouted together; they ran; they picked up rocks, and the thunder-devil was squawking and stenching; but I saw my *niño*, and I saw my wife lifting her face, and I called.

"Friends! You are doing me an evil thing. That is my baby and that is my brother's baby. Shame on you! I am here. You know me. I have lived with you. Be careful now, or some of *you* shall go to feed the thunder-devil."

"Kill, kill!" the priests ordered; and the rocks began to fly.

"Quick, with you medicine! Shrivel them all except yours and mine," Antonio begged, breathing hard beside me.

"Wait!" I shouted again. "Let us talk."

"No. The time has come," said the chief priest. And they raised the little babies, to throw them; but I called, and they saw my gun pointed at them. You remember that I had taken my gun, thanks to God, señor.

"Stop! Listen, or one of your priests shall die and be thunder-devil meat," I warned.

That halted them indeed. The priests had no power against good powder and lead.

"What do you want?" they asked.

"I want the babies. Leave them safe, and go."

"No. That is impossible. The thunder-devil bird has been promised. You see him. He is waiting. It is commanded by Those Above, or we all shall die by the thunder."

"I will shrivel the thunder-devil, then," I said. "He shall live no longer."

At that, señor, the women cried out. *Dios*, how they cried out!

"He will shrivel the thunder-devil! Our brother says he will shrivel the thunder-devil!"

"He lies," the priests shouted. "Who can shrivel the thunder-devil bird? It is a god. It will live forever. Kill him before the thunder-devil burns us up for listening to the lie. Kill him, and the other who stands beside him, so we can make the sacrifice and go."

But the women cried louder:

"No, no. Let him try. We hate the thunder-devil that takes our babies. It is time that he should die, or else we would die."

And señor, they ran forward, themselves, and they fought back the men, on the shore, who were stoning us. Yes, it was wonderful to see the women, even the old ones, fighting back the men—and to see the women, even the old ones, fighting back the men—and all clothesless, but not ashamed, like animals. Some of the men, too, were shouting for us; and others were angry, the same as the priests.

"Shrivel him quick," spoke Antonio, to me, "if you can; for time is short. I will protect you." And now he also shouted, bending his bow at the priests, "Our brother can do it. I say so. Stand where you are, priests. We are here to destroy the thunder-devil or die."

The thunder-devil had been squawking, as I have said, señor; but now a greater shout yet arose, making me look. *Dios*, he had grown impatient; he had lowered his snake neck, stretching it down from his shelf; and, *caramba*, he was about to plunge!

"Save us! Save us!" the people cried. "He is coming." And the women called: "Shrivel him, brother!" And the men called: "Give him the meat!"

"Meat for the thunder-devil bird," shouted the priests. "Meat he shall have. Back from the shore!"

Todos los santos! The lake was no place for the thunder-devil bird and us, at the same time. I not being a padre, I doubted if any of my words would travel fast enough through that hubbub to catch him: something more certain must be done; and in the instant, while he teetered, I raised my gun—

"*Sí, sí*" the squatting Antonio uttered. His black eyes blazed.

"*El escopeta!*" Evidently temporal weapons appealed to him more than spiritual. He was war captain.

The old señor paused, to summon: "María! Here! Bring the gun."

The wrinkled María appeared at once, running out with a gun. An ancient, battered fusil it was, its lock tied fast with flinty rawhide. The old señor eagerly seized it.

"This very gun I raised. It is a poor piece, señor, but it was my best; and a good gun, in those days. I raised it—so." He aimed, strong again with youth . . .

"I called upon all the saints to help the bullet through the thunder-devil's coat of mail, and I fired—Bang!" The imaginary recoil drove him back into his chair. "It was that, or nothing. The priests howled: but the thunder-devil, he howled too. *Mira!* See him! By the will of God the ball had gone home into him. He had fallen over, he flopped—"

"*Viva! Muy bien!*" our Antonio panted.

"Thanks to God!" old María exclaimed. "'*Stá bueno, bueno!*"

"Hurrah!" I encouraged.

He flopped about, screaming and scattering blood and stench so that you could scarcely see the cave. Over the edge of the shelf he slipped; there he hung, on the face of the cliff, with one wing hooked like a bat's into the rock. Like a bat's it was, señor, leathery, and longer than I had thought. He extended from the shelf clear to the water, señor, and his blood hissed when it struck. Then his strength failed him; he let go; he landed with a great splash, he disappeared, and all the lake behan to boil red with his struggles. Once his neck writhed out. *En el nombre*, señor, it was time for us to get our legs away. I tell you, in half a minute we were on the shore. That was another scene. The women were dancing and singing—"He has killed the thunder-devil!" they cried. "With his magic bullet he has killed the thunder-devil bird!" The men were staring at the lake; and the priests had their mouths open but nothing to say.

No thunder came; pretty soon the lake quieted. Then my woman and my brother's woman walked straight to the priests. "The thunder-devil is dead," they said. "We will take our babies." So they took them, and breathed upon them, and coaxed them back to life, for they had been put asleep with medicine.

Then the men came to me and one after another grasped my hand. "You are a great man," they said. "The bad god lost his power to you. Stay with us and keep us from further evil."

"No!" said the chief priest. "The thunder-devil is not dead. He was weak. The magic bullet surprised him. He is resting at the bottom of the lake, a mile deep. He will be well in one day, and very hungry. Unless we throw this man in to him he will ride the water down upon us and destroy us all."

"That is a lie," I said "Who will wait here with me and watch?"

"I will," spoke my brother. And there were others. Then the people went back down to the pueblo; and my brother and I, and our women and three men waited beside the lake for three days. On the third day the carcass of the thunder-devil bird floated to the top. He was still dead, and he stunk very badly, for he was flesh and blood. We took signs from him, and we went down to the town; and from that time to this, señor, I have been well thought of by the Picuris. Yes, as you have seen, and as Antonio, here, was a baby then and is war captain now, can tell you.

My old señor settled into his shawl, tired out.

"You are an American, señor," he added. "You read in books. Now, what do you say that the thunder-devil was?"

"I believe, but I cannot say," I answered. "You took a sign?"

"María!" he bade. "The devil sign."

María scuttled in, she scuttled out, and handed something to him. He passed it to me.

"This is one, señor."

It was a fragment of parchment skin, about the size of one's palm, set with scales like mica dollars, and with a round hole through it.

"That," said he, "is where the good God and Mary directed my bullet. The head I could show you at Picuris."

"Perhaps an extinct kind of pterodactyl, señor," I ventured wisely. I tried to find the words. "*Un dragón alado y furioso*—a terrible winged dragon."

"Indeed, yes. So the padre said, to whom I made confession. A devil, sure enough. Now I have finished."

The squatting Antonio arose. He stood tall and straight, older than I had at first supposed.

"*Bueno,*" he muttered. "It is all true. I was there." He shook hands with me. "*Adiós.*" He drew his blanket over his shoulders and stalked out.

NEW YORK

The Garrison
by Donald A. Wollheim

YOU MAY recall reading of the discovery several years ago of an ancient temple of Mithra being uncovered strictly by accident in the business city of London during the excavations for a new building. It made a bit of a sensation for a while—not that it was any secret that there had been such a faith during the Roman days, but that somehow this temple, basically untouched—if you disregard having been filled with silt and many feet of dirt—had been there all the past seventeen centuries without anyone suspecting its existence.

It brought home to some of us just how many wonders and secrets are buried from sight beneath the busy everyday feet of men and women. Surely all the towns and cities, the farmers' fields, and the scenic mountains of old Europe and Asia must conceal beneath their folds innumerable fragments of human meanderings over the past thousands of years. The fact that there was once a major empire that rivaled Egypt and Babylon for power and size which had been very nearly totally forgotten until only the past dozen years is something that still staggers historians. I refer, of course, to the Hittites, mentioned once in the Bible and then forgotten.

Of course, for Americans like myself there is an extra marvel in this evidence of antiquities untold. We live in such a new country, inhabited before us only by nomadic savages, so that when a building is a mere hundred and fifty years old we put a plaque on it and visitors come to stand in the street and stare at it. I was driving along a road in New England when I saw one of those markers. It said something about somebody having erected a grist mill there in 1712. Big thing for us! But tell me, how many mills in Europe and Asia still standing and operating were already old when this American thing was first built?

That's what confounds me as an American. In Europe a house less than five hundred years old wouldn't get a second glance. Why, there must be slums all over the Old World whose dirty old hovels are a thousand years standing! But I'm getting away from what I started out to tell. About that temple in London having gone unnoticed. I can tell you now that there's something like that in New York, too.

I know it seems impossible, for after all there were no Romans here. That's true and I'm not going to claim otherwise. But still there was a structure uncovered in Manhattan Borough once that gave the archeologists a start. How is it that you've never heard of it? Well, that's my story.

I never heard of it either and I've lived here all my life. I've been a magazine feature writer for many years now and I've probed into a lot of odd places about this city for stories. But this is a part of one such story that I never did write up. I'm only putting it down now, just for the record, as it were.

Oh, the main story was written long ago and sold, and the magazine containing it will be found now only in secondhand stores, if anyone still wants it, which I doubt. It was about the subways of New York and mostly about the first subways and the old ones.

I covered the well-known subways, to be sure. The story of the IRT and the BMT and of the tunnels they dug and discarded—there are a couple such way down near the Battery—and the story of the original plans and the difficulties that were encountered—underground streams and suchlike. The subway management cooperated with me. I walked the rails under the East River and I poked through their old blueprints and files, talked with engineers, and took pictures of some old tunnels.

Then one old-timer, a dispatcher he was, mentioned that there was a private subway in New York practically nobody knew about. Not any of the big three. It ran—and still runs, as a matter of fact—from the Manhattan office of the gas works under the river to Randalls Island where the gas company maintains a pumping station and storage tank. That was news to me and sounded like just the ticket to round off my article.

I called up the gas company and after beating my way through a dozen officials finally found one who thought he could help me. I went up there to his office and told him what I had heard. He nodded, confirmed it. Yes, there really was a subway that had been built by the gas company about seventy years ago. They'd built it because there was no convenient ferry or bridge at that end of Manhattan to reach their works—Randalls Island being a small, uninhabited isle in the middle of the East River with Queensborough on the far side. Some company bigwig had money to burn and an idea. It wasn't such a hot idea.

The fact was, the man said, it was never officially put into use. It was a regular boring, a full-size single-track tunnel running underground and under the river bottom. But after it had been built and the track laid, it just turned out to be unnecessary.

Was it still passable? Could I get to see it?

The official scratched his head. He didn't know for sure. The matter had never come up. So he gave me a note to the superintendent of the works up at 135th Street and the riverfront and asked him to look into it with me.

I went up there and found the super. He knew about the private subway all right. Its Manhattan station, if you could call it that, was right here in this building, in the basement, he said. In fact, and what was more, the subway was clear and it was actually used. One man used it, once a day.

That man was the watchman of the Randalls Island installation. He lived in Manhattan in the neighborhood and each morning he would take his lunch box, go down to the basement, climb aboard a little hand-driven truck standing on the rails and go on down that long, dark tunnel under the river to Randalls Island. In the evening when his duties were done, he'd get aboard it and run it back again. Just one man, imagine! A whole subway line to serve one man!

Nothing would suffice but that I'd have to make that trip with him. Well, he was out at the island now, I'd have to wait until he returned. I did that, too. Went down to the basement, under the gas works, and found a little tiled room at one end of it. Sure enough, there were the end of tracks running out of a whopping big wide round hole in the wall. Look down into it—total darkness.

I sat down there on a small bench and looked down that hole around five o'clock and after awhile I heard a faint humming in the tracks. Then I saw a tiny light way off down the huge rat hole and by and by it came closer and there was this little hand truck with an old guy standing on it pumping the handles up and down vigorously, the light coming from a battery lamp set on the truck.

When the truck pulled up and stopped, I asked the old fellow whether he'd take me along tomorrow morning. He was quite pleased, talked a good deal about the trip. Most of the men who worked in the plant were scared stiff at the thought of it. It didn't bother him, for he'd been doing it for thirty years already.

But I'm not going to tell you about this—I've already written about that weird trip down the pitch-black hole with nobody but the old man and the crazy shadows as he bobbed up and down on that pump and the single light pushing into that absolute darkness. It was damp and silent and spooky as all hell—and yet, in a way, fun.

I'd taken a big flashlight of my own along and searched the old walls, the grimy tiling, the ancient piping, and you know, it was in pretty good condition still. When we got to Randalls Island, I saw something interesting. There was a branch of the subway going off in a side direction, but no tracks.

Later on, I asked the old watchman about it. He said finally, "I never pay no attention to it. When they first built this thing they was going to extend it across the island and connect it up with the Queens side. But that there section of side tunnel is as far as they got. They changed their minds fast after they'd got a little way along it."

"How's that? What made them stop?" I asked, sensing a story.

"They never right said. I've heard stories, of course. My father, who worked for the company in those days, once told me they'd run into some old diggings and decided not to bust them up."

"Old diggings? Dutch? Indian? I never heard of any discoveries having been made here," I said.

"Well, I wouldn't know. I never paid no attention to that sort of museum stuff. I supposed the professors had found what they wanted and put it in books and all that. Maybe they didn't, though. Maybe they didn't at that. My pa did say they was sort of quiet about it all." The old fellow was enjoying himself. He had visions of seeing himself in print. I pressed my luck.

"Could you stop at that side tunnel going back and wait for me to walk along it to where they stopped excavating?"

The old fellow thought awhile, then said he'd accommodate me. Sometimes I wish he hadn't been so helpful.

That evening we got back on the handcart and pumped our way a little bit down the track until we found the dark branch-off. We stopped the truck and I got down with my flashlight. The watchman said he'd stay on the truck and wait for my return.

So I walked down that pitch-black tunnel by myself, my steps echoing hollowly in that pipe, big enough for a subway car to fit through. The tunnel turned sharply and the light of the handtruck was cut off. I flashed my light ahead, saw where the diggers had stopped.

There was an abrupt end of the tiling and piping. Beyond was a stretch of several yards of raw stone cut through with pick and drill. Beyond that there were some black breaks and loose masses of small rocks and debris. I walked as far as I could, flashed my beam and saw that what had happened was that they'd broken into what was apparently an underground cavern or hole.

I started to climb over the piles of rock to reach the lips of the breakthrough and when I'd stretched out my body through the opening to look through, I noticed something. I wasn't lying on dirt and rock any more—I was lying, at least my chest and elbows, on smooth, chiseled rock, rock that had been squared off and joined to blocks of other rock by angles cut like a jigsaw puzzle. This rock was different than the kind in the passage outside—it looked as if it were something that had been constructed, like part of a wall.

And that's what it was, a thick wall. An artificially constructed wall, several feet thick, beyond which was the dark expanse of a buried structure. The excavators had broken into a room of this structure, a room still standing, whose ceiling had not crumpled.

I flashed my light around. The walls were smooth and undecorated. I couldn't place the style, but it was old, it had to be old to have been under all that soil and so forgotten.

I climbed through, stood up in that damned lightless room and figured I'd made the find of the century. I'd be famous. I knew no Dutchman could have built that place, it was long before their time; they weren't building stone fortresses without cement. It reminded me of what I'd read of the Inca walls, but I was willing to bet this was older even than any Inca structure.

I crossed that empty room—a watchtower, I think now that it must have been, and at the end of it was a dark hole. It was probably meant for a ladder, but there was nothing there now. I knelt down beside that hole and looked down to see what was below.

It was vast down there. That much I knew. I realized that I was high up above the next landing. I felt it, I sensed it, that down below me was a drop of hundreds of feet. I flashed my light down and it barely shone on a smooth stone surface far, far below. I was beginning to get frightened then, and I don't scare easily. How big was this place, I thought to myself. If it was a fortress, who built it and when and against what enemy?

For it was a fortress, of that I'm convinced. It was made to stand age and siege and fire and sword. It was made to stand tons of rock piled on it; it was made impregnable to man and nature.

And then I wondered why the tunnel diggers had kept mum about it. I wondered that while staring down that hole into the unknown depths of the fortress below me. And by and by, I suspected something. I suspected the answer. And when I was sure of it, I got up, kept my flashlight away from that hole and made my way out. I got back to the watchman and we went back to Manhattan and I made my way home through the electric lights and the hurly-burly and the mobs in the streets and I was near crazy with wonder and the mystery of the universe. I looked up at the sky and I saw a million stars shining down and knew that to them and their mysteries all this clamor and bustle was tinsel and junk.

I knew why the excavators had shut up about the old fortress they'd dug into under the surface of the metropolis. The Temple of Mithra in London was ruined and abandoned. The catacombs of Rome have served their purpose and have been left to the curious. The great city of Angkor has been deserted by its citizens and left to the jungle.

But when I looked down that hole in the buried watchtower's floor, down into the keep of the fortress, into the darkness there, I saw a light appear. I saw a sentinel go his rounds. I saw a member of the garrison still keeping up the vigil against an enemy that would not be one of the insignificant cloth-covered biped scramblers of the surface, but something that would be coming some day from the place that fortress was built to oppose, something worthy of that monstrous trooper's steel.

There are still some things that it is necessary to conceal for the sake of human pride. One of them is that that fortress, which is older than our entire geological epoch, has never been abandoned.

NORTH CAROLINA

The Desrick on Yandro
by Manly Wade Wellman

THE FOLKS at the party clapped me such an encore, I sang that song.

The lady had stopped her car when she saw my thumb out and my silver-strung guitar under my arm. Asked where I was headed, I told her nowhere special. Asked could I play the guitar, I played it as we rolled along. Asked me my name, I told her John. Then she invited me, most kindly, to her big country house to sing to her friends. They'd be obliged, she said. So I went there with her.

The people were fired up with what they'd drunk, lots of ladies and men in costly clothes, and I had my bothers not getting drunk myself. But, too, they liked what I played and sang. Staying off the worn-out songs, I smote out what they'd never heard before—*Rebel Soldier* and *Well I Know That Love Is Pretty* and *When the Stars Begin to Fall*. When they clapped me and hollered me for more, I sang the Yandro song, like this:

> *"I'll build me a desrick on Yandro's high hill*
> *Where the wild beasts can't reach me nor hear my sad cry,*
> *For you've gone away, gone to stay a while,*
> *But you'll come back if you come ten thousand miles . . ."*

Then they strung all round and made me more welcome than just any stranger could call for, and the hostess lady said I must stay for supper and sleep there that night. But at that moment, everybody sort of pulled back, and one man came up and sat down by me.

I'd been aware that, when first he came in, things stilled down. It was like when a big bully shows himself among little boys. He was built short and

451

broad, his clothes were cut handsome and costly. His buckskin hair was combed across his head to baffle folks he wasn't getting bald. His round pink face wasn't soft, and his big smiling teeth reminded you he had a skull under the meat. His pale eyes, like two gravel bits, made me recollect I needed a haircut and a shoe shine.

"You said Yandro, young man," said this fellow, almost like a charge in court, with me the prisoner.

"Yes, sir. The song's not too far from the Smokies. I heard it in a valley, and the highest peak over that valley's named Yandro. Now," I said, "I've had scholarfolks argue me it really means yonder, yonder high hill. But the peak's named Yandro, not a usual name."

"No," and he smiled toothy and fierce, "not a usual name. I'm like the peak. I'm named Yandro, too."

"How you, Mr. Yandro?" I said.

"I've never heard of that valley or peak, nor, I imagine, did my father. But my grandfather—Joris Yandro—came from the Southern mountains. He was young, with small education, but lots of energy and ambition." Mr. Yandro swelled up inside his fancy clothes. "He went to New York, then Chicago. His fortunes prospered. His son—my father—and then I, we contrived to make them prosper still more."

"You're to be honored," I said, my politest; but I judged, with no sure reason, that he might could not be too honorable about how he made his money, or either used it. How the others pulled back from him made me reckon he scared them, and that breed of folks scares worst where their money-pocket's located.

"I've done all right," he said, not caring who heard the brag. "I don't think anybody for a hundred miles around here can turn a deal or make a promise without asking me first. John, I own this part of the world."

Again he showed his teeth.

"You're the first one ever to tell me where my grandfather might have come from. Yandro's high hill, eh? How do we get there, John?"

I tried to recollect the way from highway to side way, side way to trail, and so in and round and over. "I fear I could show you better than I could tell you," I said.

"All right, you'll show me," he said, with no notion I might could have something different to do. "I can afford to make up my mind on a moment's notice, like that. I'll call the airport and charter a plane and we'll leave right now."

"I've asked John to stay here tonight," said my hostess lady.

"We leave now," said Mr. Yandro, and she hushed right up, and I saw how everybody was scared of him. Maybe they'd be pleasured if I got him out of there for a spell.

"Get your plane," I said. "I'll go with you."

He meant that thing he'd said. Not many hours had died before the hired plane set us down at the airport betwixt Asheville and Hendersonville. A taxi rode us into Hendersonville. Mr. Yandro found a used car man still at his place, and bought a fair car from him. Then, on my guiding, Mr. Yandro took out in the dark for that part of the mountains I told him about.

The sky stretched over us with no moon at all, only a many stars like little stitches of blazing thread in a black quilt. For sure-enough light, only our headlamps—first on a paved road twining round one slope and over another and behind a third, then a pretty good gravel road, then a pretty bad dirt road.

"What a stinking country!" said Mr. Yandro as we chugged along a ridge top as lean as a butcher knife.

I didn't say how I resented that word about a country that stoops to none on earth for prettiness. "Maybe we should ought to have waited for daytime," was all I said.

"I don't ever wait," he sniffled. "Where's the town?"

"There's nary town. Just the valley. Three-four hours away, I judge. We'll be there by midnight."

"Oh, God. Let's have some more of that whiskey I brought," and he reached for the glove compartment, but I pushed his hand away.

"Not if you're driving these mountain roads, Mr. Yandro."

"Then you drive and I'll take a drink."

"I don't know how to drive a car."

"Oh, God," he said again, and couldn't have scorned me more if I'd said I didn't know how to wash my face. "What's a desrick, exactly?"

"That's a word only old-timey folks use these days. It's the kind of cabin they used to make, strong logs and a door you can bar, and loophole windows. So maybe you might could stand off Indians."

"Or the wild beasts can't reach you," he quoted, and snickered. "What wild beasts do you have up here in the Forgotten Latitudes?"

"Can't rightly say all of them. A few bears, a wildcat or two. Used to be wolves, and a bounty for killing them. And so on."

True enough, I wasn't certain sure about the tales I'd heard, and didn't love to tell them if Mr. Yandro would say they were foolish for the lack of sense.

The narrow road climbed a great rocky slant one way, then doubled back to climb the other way, and petered out into just a double rut with an empty, scary-as-hell drop thousands of feet beside the car. Finally Mr. Yandro edged us onto a sort of notch beside the trail and cut off the power. He shook. Fear must have been a new feel to his bones.

"Want some of this whiskey, John?" he asked, and drank.

"No, I thank you. We walk from here, anyway. Beyond's the valley."

He grumped about that, but out he got. I took a flashlight and my guitar and led out. It was a down way from there, on a narrow trail where even a mule would be nervish. And not quiet enough to be an easy trip.

You don't get used to that breed of mountain night noises, not even if you're born and raised there and live and die there. Noises too soft and sneaky to be real whispering voices. Noises like big slow wings, far off and then near. And, above and below the trail, noises like heavy soft paws keeping pace with you, sometimes two paws, sometimes four, sometimes many. They stay with you, such noises as that, all the hours you grope the night trail, all the way down to the valley so low, till you're ready to bless God for the little bitty crumb of light that means a human home, and you ache and pray to get to that home, be it ever so humble, so you can be safe inside with the light.

It's wondered me since if Mr. Yandro's constant chatter was a string of curses or, for maybe the first time in his proud life, a string of prayers.

The light we saw was a pine-knot fire inside a little cabin above the stream that giggled along the valley bottom. The door was open and somebody sat on the stoop.

"Is that a desrick?" panted and puffed Mr. Yandro.

"No, sir, it's newer made. Yonder's Miss Tully at the door, sitting up to think."

Miss Tully recollected me and welcomed us. She was eighty or ninety, without any tooth in her mouth to clamp her stone-bowl pipe, but she stood straight as a pine on the split-slab floor, and the firelight showed no gray to her neatly combed black hair. "Rest your hats," she bade us. "So this here stranger man is named Yandro. Funny, sir, you coming just now. You looking for the desrick on Yandro? It's right where it's been," and she pointed with her pipe stem off across the valley and up the far side.

She gave us two chairs bottomed with juniper bark by the fire, and sat on a stool next the shelf with herbs in pots and one-two old paper books, *The Long Lost Friend* and *Egyptian Secrets*, and *Big Albert*, the one they tell you can't be flung away or given away or burnt, only to be got rid of by burying with a funeral prayer, like a human corpse.

"Funny," she said again, not laughing, "you coming along just as the seventy-five years run out."

We inquired her, and she told us what we'd come to hear:

"I was just a pigtail girl back then, when Joris Yandro courted Polly Wiltse, the witch girl. Mr. Yandro, you favor your grandsire a right much. He wasn't nowhere as stout-built as you, and younger by years when last I saw him, though."

Though I'd heard it all before. I harked at it. It was like a many such tale at the start. Polly Wiltse was sure enough a witch, not just a study-witch like Miss Tully, and Poly Wiltse's beauty would melt the heart of nature and make a dumb man cry out, "Praise God Who made her!" But none dared court her save only Joris Yandro, who was handsome for a man as she was lovely for a woman. For it was his wish to get her to show him the gold on top of the mountain named for his folks, that only Polly Wiltse and her witchings could find.

"Sure enough there's gold in these mountains," I answered Mr. Yandro's interrupting question. "The history books tell that before even the California rush, folks mined and minted gold in these parts."

"Gold," he repeated me, both respectful and greedy. "I was right to come."

Miss Tully told that Joris Yandro coaxed Polly Wiltse to fetch down gold to him, and he carried it off and never came back. And Polly Wiltse pined and mourned like a sick bird, and on Yandro's top she built her desrick. She sang the song, the one I'd sung, it was part of a long charm-spell. Three quarters of a century would pass, seventy-five years, and her love would come back.

"But he didn't," said Mr. Yandro. "My grandfather died up North."

"He sent his grand-boy, who favors him," Miss Tully thumbed tobacco into her pipe. "All the Yandros moved out, purely scared of Polly Wiltse's singing. But the song fetched you back here, just at the right time, to where maybe she's waiting."

"In her desrick, where the wild beasts can't reach her," Mr. Yandro quoted, and laughed. "John says they have bears and wildcats up here." He expected her to say I was wrong.

"Other things, too. Scarced-out animals like the Toller."

"The Toller?" he said.

"The hugest flying thing there is, I reckon," said Miss Tully. "It tolls its voice like a bell, to tell other creatures their feed is come near. And there's the Flat. It lies level with the ground and not much higher, and it can wrop you like a blanket." She lighted the pipe with a splinter from the fire. "And the Bammat. Big, the Bammat is."

"You mean the Behemoth," he suggested.

"No, the Behemoth was in Bible times. The Bammat's hairy-like, with big ears and a long wiggly snaky nose and twisty white teeth sticking out its mouth."

"Oh!" and Mr. Yandro trumpeted his laugh. "You've heard some story about the Mammoth. Why, it's been extinct for thousands of years."

"Not for such a long time, I hear tell," she said, puffing.

"Anyway," he argued on, "the Mammoth, the Bammat as you call it, was of the elephant family. How would it get up in these mountains?"

"Maybe folks hunted it up here," said Miss Tully, "and maybe it stays here so folks'll reckon it's dead and gone these thousand years. Then there's the Behinder."

"And what," inquired Mr. Yandro, "might the Behinder look like?"

"Can't rightly say. For it's always behind the one it's a-fixing to grab. And there's the Skim, it kites through the air. And the Culverin, that can shoot pebbles with its mouth."

"And you believe all that?" sneered Mr. Yandro, the way he always sneered at everything, everywhere.

"Why else do I tell it? Well, sir, you're back where your kin used to live, in the valley where the mountain was named for them. I can let youins sleep here on my front stoop this night."

"I came to climb the mountain and see the desrick," said Mr. Yandro with that anxious hurry to him I kept wondering on.

"You can't climb there till it's light," she said, and she made us up two quilt pallets on the stoop.

I was tired, glad to stretch out, but Mr. Yandro fussed, as if it was wasting time. At sunup, Miss Tully fried us some side meat and some slices of cold-set hominy grits and fixed us a snack to carry, and a gourd, for water. Mr. Yandro held out a ten-dollar bill.

"No, I thank you," said Miss Tully. "I bade you stay. I don't take money for such as that."

"Oh, everybody takes money from me," he snickered, and flung it on the door sill at her feet. "Go on, it's yours."

Quick as a weasel, her hand grabbed a big stick of stove wood. "Stoop down and take that money bill back, Mr. Yandro," she said.

He did as she said to do. She pointed the stick out across the stream in the thickets below, and up the height beyond. She acted as if there'd been no trouble a second before.

"That's Yandro Mountain," she said, "and up at the top, where it looks like the crown of a hat, thick with trees all the way up, stands the desrick by Polly Wiltse. Look close with the sun rising, and you can maybe make it out."

I looked hard. There for sure it was, far off and high up. It looked a lean sort of building. "How about trails up?" I asked.

"There's trails up, John, but nobody walks them."

"Now, now," said Mr. Yandro. "If there's a trail somebody walks it."

"Maybe, but I don't know any soul in this here valley would set foot to such a trail, not with what they say's up there."

He laughed, as I wouldn't have dared. "You mean the Bammat," he said. "And the Flat and the Skim and the Culverin."

"And the Toller," she added for him, "and the Behinder. Only a gone gump would climb up yonder."

We headed down to the waterside, and crossed on a log. On the far bank led a trail along, and when the sun was an hour up we were at the foot of Yandro's hill and a trail went up there too.

We rested. He needed rest worse than I did. Moving most of the night before, unused to walking and climbing, he had a gaunted look to his heavy face and his clothes were sweated and dust dulled out his shiny shoes. But he grinned at me.

"So she's waited seventy-five years," he said, "and so I look like the man she's waiting for, and so there's gold up there. Gold my grandfather didn't carry off."

"You truly believe what you heard," I said, surprised.

"John, a wise man knows when to believe the unusual, and knows how it will profit him. She's waiting up there, and so is the gold."

"What when you find it?" I inquired him.

"My grandfather went off and left her. Sounds like a good example to me."
He grinned toothier. "I'll give you some of the gold."

"No, I thank you, Mr. Yandro."

"You don't want pay? Why did you come here with me?"

"Just made up my mind in a moment, like you."

He scowled up the height. "How long will it take to climb?"

"Depends on how fast we keep the pace."

"Let's go," and he started up.

Folks' feet hadn't worn that trail. We saw a hoof mark.

"Deer," grunted Mr. Yandro, and I said, "Maybe."

We scrambled up a rightward slant, then leftward. The trees marched in close with us and their branches filtered just a soft green light. Something rustled. A brown furry shape, bigger than a big cat, scuttled out of sight.

"Woodchuck," wheezed Mr. Yandro, and again I said, "Maybe."

After working up for an hour we rested, and after two hours more we rested again. Around 10 o'clock we got to an open space with clear light, and sat on a log to eat the corn bread and smoked meat Miss Tully had fixed. Mr. Yandro mopped his face with a fancy handkerchief and gobbled food and glittered his eye at me.

"What are you glooming about?" he said. "You look as if you'd call me a name if you weren't afraid to."

"I've held my tongue by way of manners, not fear," I said. "I'm just thinking how and why we came so far and sudden to this place."

"I heard that song you sang and thought I'd see where my people originated. Now I've a hunch about profit. That's enough for you."

"You're more than rich enough without that gold," I said.

"I'm going up," said Mr. Yandro, "because, by God, that old hag down there said everyone's afraid to. And you said you'd go with me."

"Right to the top with you," I promised.

I forebore to say that something was looking from among the trees right behind him. It was big and broad-headed, with elephant ears, and white tusks like banisters on a spiral staircase, but it was woolly-shaggy, like a buffalo bull. How could a thing as big as the Bammat move without making noise?

Mr. Yandro drank from his whiskey bottle, and on we climbed. We heard noises from the woods and brush, behind rocks and down little draws, as if the mountain side thronged with live things, thick as fleas on a possum dog and another sight sneakier.

"Why are you singing under your breath?" he grunted.

"I'm not singing. I need my wind for climbing."

"But I hear it." We stopped on the trail, and I heard it too.

Soft, almost like a half-remembered song in your mind, it was the Yandro song, all right:

"*Look away, look away, look away over Yandro*
Where them wild things are a-flyin',

From bough to bough, and a-mating with their mates,
So why not me with mine? . . ."

"It comes from above us," I said.

"Then we must be nearly at the top."

As we started to climb again, I heard the noises to right and left, and realized they'd gone quiet when we stopped. They moved when we moved, they waited when we waited. Soft noises, but lots of them.

Which is why I, and Mr. Yandro probably, didn't pause any more on the way up, even on a rocky stretch where we had to climb on all fours. It was about an hour before noon when we got to the top.

There was a circle-shaped clearing, with trees thronged all the way round except toward the slope. Those trees had mist among and betwixt them, quiet and fluffy, like spider webbing. And at the open space, on the lip of the way down, perched the desrick.

Old-aged was how it looked. It stood high and looked higher, because it was so narrow built of unnotched logs, four set above four, hogpen fashion, tall as a tall tobacco barn. Betwixt the logs was clinking, big masses and wads of clay. The steep roof was of long-cut, narrow shingles, and there was one big door of one axe-chopped plank, with hinges inside, for I saw none. And one window, covered with what must have been rawhide scraped thin, with a glow of soft light soaking through.

"That's the desrick," puffed Mr. Yandro.

Looking at him then, I know what most he wanted on this earth. To be boss. Money just greatened him. His greatness was bigness. He wanted to do all the taking and have everybody else do all the listening. He licked his lips, like a cat over a dish of cream.

"Let's go in," he said.

"Not where I'm not invited," I told him, flat. "I said I'd come with you to the top, and I've done that."

"Come with me. My name's Yandro, and this mountain's name is Yandro. I can buy and sell every man, woman and child in this part of the country. If I say it's all right to go in, it's all right."

He meant that thing. The world and all in it was just there to let him walk on it. He took a step toward the desrick. Somebody hummed inside, not the words of the song, just the tune. Mr. Yandro snorted at me, to show how small he reckoned me to hold back, and headed toward the big door.

"She's going to show me the gold," he said.

Where I stood at the clearing's edge, I was aware of a sort of closing in round the edge, among the trees and brush. Not that it could be seen, but there was a *gong-gong* somewhere, the voice of the Toller saying to the other creatures their feed was near. Above the treetops sailed a round flat thing like a big plate being flung high. A Skim. Then another Skim. And the blood in my body was as solid cold as ice, and for voice I had a handful of sand in my throat.

Plain as paint I knew that if I tried to back up, to turn round even, my legs would fail and I'd fall down. With fingers like sleety twigs I dragged forward my guitar to touch the silver strings, for silver is protection against evil.

But I never did. For out of some bushes near me the Bammat stuck its broad woolly head and shook it at me once, for silence. It looked me betwixt the eyes, steadier than a beast should ought to look at a man, and shook its head again. I wasn't to make any noise, and I didn't. Then the Bammat paid me no more mind, and I saw I wasn't to be included in what would happen then.

Mr. Yandro knocked at the big plank door. He waited, and knocked again. I heard him rough out that he wasn't used to waiting for his knock to be answered.

The humming had died inside. Mr. Yandro moved around to the window and picked at that rawhide.

I saw, but he couldn't, how around from back of the desrick flowed something. It lay on the ground like a broad, black, short-furred carpet rug. It humped and then flattened, the way a measuring worm moves. It came up pretty fast behind Mr. Yandro. The Toller said *gong-gong-gong*, from closer to us.

"Anybody home?" bawled Mr. Yandro. "Let me in!"

That crawling carpet brushed its edge on his foot. He looked down at it, and his eyes stuck out like two doorknobs. He knew what it was, he named it at the top of his voice.

"The Flat!"

Humping against him, it tried to wrap round his foot and leg. He gobbled out something I'd never want written down for my last words, and pulled loose and ran toward the edge of the clearing.

Gong-gong, said the Toller, and just in front of Mr. Yandro the Culverin slid into sight on its many legs. It pointed its needly mouth and spit a pebble. I heard the pebble ring on Mr. Yandro's head. He staggered and half fell. And I saw what nobody's ever supposed to see.

The Behinder flung itself on his shoulders. Then I knew why nobody's supposed to see one. I wish I hadn't. To this day I can see it, plain as a fence at noon, and forever I'll be able to see it. But telling about it is another matter. Thank you, gentlemen, I won't try.

Everything else was out—the Bammat, the Culverin, all the others—hustling Mr. Yandro across toward the desrick, and the door moved slowly and quietly open to let him in.

As for me, I hoped and prayed they won't mind if I just went down the trail as fast as I could put one foot below the other.

Scrambling down, without a noise to keep me company, I reckoned I'd probably had my unguessed part in the whole thing. Seventy-five years had to pass, and then Mr. Yandro return to the desrick. It needed me, or somebody like me, to put it in his head and heart to come to where his grandsire had courted Polly Wiltse, just as though it was his own whim.

I told myself this would be a good time to go searching for another valley, a valley where there was a song I wanted to hear and learn, a right pretty song named *Vandy, Vandy*. But meanwhile—

No. No, of course Mr. Yandro wasn't the one who'd made Polly Wiltse love him and then had left her. But he was the man's grand-boy, of the same blood and the same common, low-down, sorry nature that wanted the power of money and never cared who was hurt so he could have his wish. And he looked enough like Joris Yandro so that Polly Wiltse would recognize him.

So I headed out of the valley. I was gone by sundown.

I've never studied much about what Polly Wiltse might could be like, welcoming him into her desrick on Yandro, after waiting there inside for three quarters of a hundred years. Anyway, I never heard that he followed me down. Maybe he's been missed by those who knew him. But I'll lay you any amount of money you name that he's not been mourned.

NORTH DAKOTA

Shaggy Vengeance
by Robert Adams

"IT WAS back in the late 1880s," Professor Bauer began, "that the last sizable herd of Northern Plains Bison was located along the banks of Blutig Creek, where it twisted its course through what came to be called *das Schlacht-haustal*."

Peggy, my wife, seated on the couch beside me with her legs tucked under her like the graceful feline she often resembled in movement, shivered suddenly and pressed closer to my side. A gust of the storm blowing down from Canada chose that moment to strike our cozy, if rented, house with a force that rattled doors and windows and shot tiny darts of icy air in an erratic pattern through the room, like a volley of phantom arrows from the bows of long-dead Indian warriors.

"Can't we talk about something else?" she asked. "If this keeps up, I won't get a wink of sleep, and I have to teach tomorrow, too, if you'll remember."

I was in the second semester of my first year at Buffalo Mountain Agricultural College back then, and Peggy was teaching second grade at Lost Herd Elementary School. While she was earning a bit less than she had back east, I was earning enough more to make up the difference and, moreover, I was doing what I wanted to do—teaching college-level English to kids who really had a desire to learn something. And after two years of attempting to teach high-school English to roomsful of dead-end kids whose only interests were discussing the finer points of constructing zip-guns, smoking reefers in the boys' rooms and carving their initials into anything within reach—mineral, vegetable or animal—with the switchblade knives, which items were *de rigueur* for school dress in their primitive, savage sub-culture.

Each time I had forced myself to enter East Yorkville High, I had felt less like a teacher than like Clyde Beatty, with chair and whip and blank pistol, endeavoring to put wild, killer animals through the prescribed paces. Now, I was happy. I often found myself whistling something light and jolly as I drove my battered eleven-year-old Rambler the six or so miles from the outskirts of Lost Herd along the new and almost arrow-straight road to the college six miles away, even on mornings I had to follow the snowplow to get there.

Peggy, bless her, was content anywhere there were lots and lots of children, but she also was city-born-and-bred and she missed the appurtenances of big-city life—museums, theaters, ballet, symphony. But she loved me and did not complain . . . often or much.

There were comparatively few men involved in elementary or even in secondary education in those days, but such few as there were at Lost Herd School—from the courtly-mannered, stylish Principal Frederick Räbel to the strapping, likeable assistant athletic director, Rudi Keilermann—moved in a worshipful attendance upon my petite, vivacious, blonde wife. Since this sort of thing had been happening to Peggy for most of her twenty-six years, she took it all in stride, easily negotiating the tightly constricted and hazard-strewn path that such open masculine adulation set for her.

She got the same reaction from the fathers of most of her pupils, too. But, as she was really good at her chosen work—the kids liked her and she could get through to them—her relations with the other female teachers and the mothers were close and unstrained.

She had never learned to drive and, on those rare mornings when it was feasible, she pedaled her bike the eight blocks down Büffel Street to the school, but most of the time she rode in on the rickety bus on its return from the northwestern farms with its load of kids.

There were four of these ancient, rattletrap conveyances in Lost Herd—well, six actually, but the other two were no longer in working order and were being used as parts reservoirs at the behest of the tightfisted school board, its members worthy descendants of the more-than-thrifty, Germanic peasants who had settled this area eighty or so years back. I shuddered every time I saw my sweet, little Peggy climb aboard one of the automotive nightmares and watched it chug off, usually emitting backfires as loud as the reports of a 20mm Bofors and invariably trailing an opaque cloud of coal-black smoke.

My little Rambler coupe *looked* every bit as bad as a typical Lost Herd school bus, but I maintained it in its optimum condition, driving into Lost Herd at least one night in every couple of weeks to Wolff Knipsengeldt's service station, where that worthy would allow me to use his tools and lift, sell me whatever I needed at cost and even order parts he did not stock. The price of this largesse being that I give ear to his endless, often bloodcurdling anecdotes of his days as a driver for Dutch Schultz in the Chicago area of the twenties. The townsfolk had heard these tales reiterated for years and would no longer sit still for them, so the rare newcomers or the transients were Wolff's only audience.

Professor Olaf Bauer, a jovial little gnome of a man, was easily twice my age and, with his round, rosy cheeks, thick moustache and drooping meerschaum hunter's pipe, more resembled one of those jolly figures found on "Souvenir of München" *bierkrugen* than he did a professor of agrology and agronomy. Through his father, he was a grandson of one of the founders of Lost Herd. He had leapt at the chance to return when the state had decided to build one of the strategically located branch colleges hereabouts, acted as sort of an unofficial liaison between the college and the town, and had become my fast friend within weeks of my arrival.

Olaf was a widower and seldom saw his children, who were scattered about the county with families of their own now, so he took to dropping in on Peggy and me on a semi-regular, twice-weekly basis, always bringing several long, green or brown bottles of wine to accompany the dinner. He and Peggy got along fabulously, chattering happily away in German (her maiden name was von Annweiler) or, haltingly, in the Norwegian he had absorbed with his Norse mother's milk and was, at Peggy's request, teaching her.

That particular night, with the dishes stacked in the kitchen, our bellies full of hearty, Germanic fare cooked by Peggy in her superlative manner, three bottles of an incomparable Wehlener Sonnenuhr Moselle and vanilla ice cream, we had congregated before the coal grate in the small living room of our frame house, Olaf and I with our pipes and all three of us with scalding black coffee and snifters of brandy.

Mausi, the huge, rangy, grey tomcat, was apparently a fixture of the house, since he was resident on the premises when Peggy and I arrived. He had remained because he earned his keep, waging constant, no-quarter war against the horde of field mice and voles which seemed to prefer a heated house to a frozen, and usually snow-covered, prairie for their winter habitat. Mausi was also an infallible prophet of coming blizzards or deep snows. Any night he refused to go out we always could expect bad weather by morning, no matter what some glib meteorologist might declare on the radio.

As I faced him across Mausi's hearth rug, I remarked, "Olaf, how did the town ever get the name, Lost Herd. This certainly isn't ranching country and I didn't think the old trail-herds ever got this far north."

Olaf had raised his bushy eyebrows a notch. "You drive from here to the college every day, Frank; haven't you ever stopped and read that state marker-sign just beyond the first bridge where the road curves around the base of Buffalo Mountain?"

When I admitted I had not, he began the tale.

"In those days there were very few Indians hereabouts. Those who later were brought back here and settled on the Buffalo Mountain Reservation were then still living under guard in the south, Oklahoma Territory, I think. But one very old Indian lived on the mountain and sometimes came into the town, which then was called 'Freiheitburgh,' to trade a few skins and furs for tobacco, dried beans and the odd bit of hardware.

"My own *Grossvater* Bauer often saw him and was several times in Messerschmidt's store when the old Indian came in. *Grossvater* used to say that he looked as old as the mountain itself, that Indian, with snow-white hair and teeth worn almost to the gums, hands like bony claws covered with dark parchment and beady, black eyes sunk deep into the sockets.

"Those few who could speak his language said that he called the mountain on which he lived 'The Mother of Buffalo' and claimed that the mountain had given birth to the ancestors of the buffalo, long ago, before even the Indians came here.

"*Grossvater* knew the old man's Indian name and used to tell it to me, but I confess I've forgotten it, now. The translation from whatever tongue it was into English by way of *Grossvater*'s Plattdeutsch would be something on the order of 'Guardian-Priest of the Mother of Buffalo.'

"The folks from Freiheitburgh and round about had known of the small herd in the little valley or *Tal* as long as they had been settled here, but the valley's creek was subject to annual floodings of meltwater from the mountain and was too narrow, anyway, for farming, so the bison were left alone except when one or two men rode over and shot the occasional animal for meat. But not just the meat, either, for they were frugal folks and, like the Indians, they used every part of a carcass.

"Another reason they kept close about the bison herd was that they wanted no part of professional buffalo hunters, not around their town and farms and womenfolk.

"Buffalo hunters have often been glamorized, but there was nothing glamorous about the real article. They were a class made up of the utter dregs of frontier society—brutal, vicious, filthy men. They seldom washed, wore clothes until they rotted off, and carried with them everywhere the stench of blood and death.

"Indians killed them on sight, peaceable towns that wanted to stay that way hired mankillers to keep the buffalo hunters and similar riffraff out; only the Army tolerated these pariahs, and then only because their extermination of the bison was helping the Army by eliminating the natural larder of the Plains Tribes.

"Well, all through the seventies and early eighties while the bison fell in their millions under the big-bore rifles of the hunters, who took only the hides and sometimes the tongues, leaving billions of tons of meat to rot, the small herd thrived in its little valley, showing little proclivity to stray far from the mountain, and not threatening crops enough to warrant exterminating it.

"By the late eighties, the buffalo hunters' grisly time was over; they had done their chosen work too well and too completely. The Plains Bison was considered extinct by the scholars of that time, and the species very narrowly missed that classification.

"Such few hunters as were still in the field spent more time gathering wagonloads of buffalo bones and carting them to the railheads than they did shooting their rifles.

"Therefore, when a big-mouthed railroad employee who had been served a fresh bison steak in the town of Freiheitburgh mentioned the fact, the hunters converged on this area like buzzards to a dead horse."

"But," I interjected, "hadn't any of them passed through here earlier? I thought they scoured the territories after the larger herds were slaughtered."

Olaf shrugged and took a sip of his brandy. "I suppose those who passed nearby thought that, as the land was mostly farms, the bison had all been killed off by the farmers. But when they heard the truth, dozens came—by rail, by horse, by wagon and Red River cart. They didn't waste much time in the town, but headed straight for Buffalo Mountain.

"None of the folks hereabouts liked thinking of what was going to happen to the bison, but they were hard-working, peace-loving people and they didn't consider the shooting of a few score wild beasts sufficient reason to rile the hair-trigger tempers of a group of fifty or sixty rough, cruel men. The town marshall, Horst Zeuge, gave notice that he and his three regular deputies would protect the town, but that anybody who went out to the hunters' camp was on his own.

"The first night after most of the hunters arrived, they set up camp, brought whiskey and started a drinking bout that ended in a pitched battle between three or four different groups of them. The next morning, the survivors were too hung over to do any shooting so they just scouted out the herd. They boozed the second night, too, and somehow the wagon containing most of the ammunition for the big rifles caught fire and burned to the axles.

"Three of the leaders took what money hadn't been spent on whiskey into town and bought out Messerschmidt's small stock of heavy caliber ammunition, placing orders for more as soon as the railroad could get it up to Freiheitburgh.

"*Grossvater* said that from noon until it was too dark to see, all the town could hear the booming cracks of the big rifles. There were not many shots though the next day, for most of the ammunition was by then gone and the hunters had no more money to buy the lead and powder and primers they would have needed to make more cartridges.

"When the three hunter leaders finally came into town on the day the train was due with their ordered ammunition, they brought two wagons piled high with scraped, green hides and a cart with two barrels of fresh tongues. Old Messerschmidt got all three loads, giving the hunters what value they didn't get in ammunition in whiskey.

"*Grossvater* was then one of the town marshall's regular deputies and he berated Messerschmidt for selling more whiskey to the hunters, but the old merchant said that if they should get drunk and kill a few more of each other, why then that would be that many fewer for the federal marshall the town had sent for after the first shootout to handle.

"After the hunters had left for their camp with the new stocks of ammunition, one of the earliest settlers, who could speak the Indian language, came to the marshall's office, and with him was the old Indian. Through the translator, Guardian-Priest of the Mother of Buffalo implored Marshall Zeuge to stop the strangers from killing more bison, but Zeuge gave the same answer he had given to the white folks. Then he advised the old man to go up on his mountain and stay there until the territorial marshall came and brought things back to normal.

"*Grossvater* was there that afternoon, and he said that Guardian-Priest just stood and stared at the marshall and the rest of them for two or three minutes; then he started to speak . . . *in good German*.

"'The Mother of Buffalo has been good to you who have come from a far land, as she was good to those who lived in this land before you, as she was good to the ones who preceded them. Her children's bodies have given you sustenance, warm hides, horn and bone and sinew for your tools, chips for your fires. Nor have the Mother's children gone forth from their valley to eat or despoil your maize or the strange grasses you grow for the tiny seeds.

"'Yet now you see strangers come to kill all The Mother's children, not for food and tools, but only for hides and the evil joy of killing for the sake of killing. The Mother has given of her children to help you in your times of need. In this, her time of need, you turn away your faces from her.

"'I am a very old man. I have done and will do all that one old man can do to protect The Mother's children, while you many and far younger men will do nothing.

"'But be warned: The Mother will neither forget nor forgive your perfidy. As her children are dying in their little valley, so too will the get of your loins die there, one day. Skinless and tongueless and dead will your children lie in that valley, even as The Mother's children now lie there.'"

Olaf had emptied his pipe of ashes and now he began to stuff it afresh with the dark mixture from his old, cracked pouch.

Peggy gulped half her brandy and shivered. "I thought you weren't going to tell ghost stories tonight, Olaf? You lied to me."

The old man eyed her from beneath his shaggy brows. "I lied to you, *liebchen?* I did not lie to you. I have told nothing but the truth as it was told to me, and my *Grossvater* was known all his life as a truthful man, not given to exaggeration or embroidery."

Peggy shivered yet again. "But that curse, Olaf, that poor Indian's curse, I'm all gooseflesh from it."

Olaf chuckled. "Now, *liebchen,* you know how and why voodoo works against primitives and not, usually, against civilized people. It is necessary to believe in curses, to be superstitious. You are clearly superstitious.

"So, too, were my ancestors, but only in a European variety of superstition, so the old Indian's curse had no effect upon them, as it certainly would have upon other Indians."

Peggy shook her tiny head, gripping the snifter so tightly that her knuckles shone white and I was sure that any minute the stem would snap off or the globe break.

"No, Olaf, the curse was not directed at them, but at their children and grandchildren, at all those children who descended from them."

Olaf finished stuffing his huge pipe, struck a match and went through the meticulous routine of lighting it before he answered.

"Well, if so, the curse has had no effect to date, not one that I know of anyway."

I still wanted to hear the conclusion of the story, so I said, "Did they kill the rest of the herd the next day?"

He shook his head. "No, what with the whiskey, they had another drinking bout and, instead of shooting the next day, they moved their camp further from town, into the valley itself, which was a fatal mistake, as it turned out. With the marshall's warning and all, nobody rode out there until the territorial marshall came in on the train with a platoon of the Tenth Cavalry. He and Zeuge and *Grossvater* rode out with the soldiers, but there were no hunters to arrest.

"Somehow or other, they'd managed to stampede the herd, what was left of it. The bison had apparently run right over the camp in the middle of the night, since most of the bodies found were still rolled in their blankets. That camp was a gruesome sight, *Grossvater* averred.

"The only survivor was found a couple of days later by a farmer. He wasn't quite right in the head and didn't live long, but the story he told was that the first night in the new camp, they had caught an old Indian skulking about. The hunters hated Indians as much as Indians hated them. They skinned him alive before they finally killed him.

"That night the bison came. As I said, the one survivor was mentally unbalanced by it all. He repeatedly swore that the herd that struck the camp was led by an Indian on a pony, but of course no one believed him.

"But the strangest thing of all is that no one ever saw the herd after that, to this very day. Soldiers and settlers rode up and down that valley and all over the mountain, but never found even a fresh buffalo chip. The federal marshall, who had been a plainsman in his youth, was of the opion that the herd, after it overran the camp, kept going north and passed on into Canada. *Grossvater* agreed with him.

"During the First World War, when things and people were suspect if German, it was decided to change the name of Freiheitburgh and the name finally decided upon was Lost Herd. It is as simple as that, my good, young friends."

Peggy, with her prescience, must have known of the horror that was coming, for she awakened me that night and many another for several weeks with her nightmare-spawned screams. I must confess that I, too, felt a little prickle up the back of my neck each time I drove past Buffalo Mountain, after that, or crossed the fine, new concrete bridge over Blutig Creek, but being a sane, well-educated man, I rationalized it to the point at which it no longer bothered me on a conscious level.

In early March we had a week of unseasonal warmth, followed by a howling storm and freezing rain that left everything for miles coated with ice, including the nice, new road. That was the night on which two of our college boys were coming back from a weekend visit to their families on farms just the other side of Lost Herd.

Hansi Zeuge was known to be a good, careful driver and his almost-new Triumph sportscar was equipped with chains and said to have been in perfect mechanical condition. Nonetheless, a county roadcrew found the Triumph smashed into the rail of Blutig Creek bridge around dawn of a Monday morning. The two bodies were found atop the ice of the creek, below. Hansi and Wilhelm Hüter were buried in sealed caskets, not unusual in bad smashups.

The next accident was less than a month later and at almost the same spot. There were four fatalities in the second mishap, three of them locals, one a boy from downstate. Strangely, in the wake of the second accident, a bevy of law-enforcement types descended on Lost Herd, poked and pried about the town and the area, and questioned a number of residents.

The resident MD at the college, Herman Blaurig, had done his residency in New York and welcomed my occasional visits to his clinic. His cousin was county coroner and as we sat in his office one afternoon sipping tea laced with dark rum, "Frank," he said, "have you wondered why the state cops have been nosing around here?"

I nodded. "Sure, Doc, everybody has."

He glanced about the room with a conspiratorial eye, then lowered his voice. "Now don't go spreading this around. We don't want to scare folks, Frank, but they was some damn peculiar things about the four kids that was killed week before last. And the two boys before them, for that matter.

"My cousin, Doc Egon, is the main reason the cops is here. The first two, the Zeuge boy and Willi Hüter, was thrown clear through the convertible top, prob'ly parts of them went through the windshield, too, and they must've slid some way on the ice and they likely laid down there for some hours, so Egon figgered what all was done to them could be explained by the accident itself or by animals getting at the bodies, 'fore they was found.

"But in this last one, Frank, it was a four-door seedan. The driver seems to of lost control right where the road starts to curve 'round the mountain. The car skidded, flipped end over end a couple of times and wound up burning in the creek. All four kids was flung out while it was still moving. Some drummer seen the fire and all and barrelassed into town and the sheriff and rescue squad and fire company and all got they no more'n a hour after it happened.

"And that's where the funny part starts. All four of them kids was thrown into snowbanks on the sides of the road. The clothes of three of them was torn off in pieces, even their boots, the skin had been torn or abraded off all three of them and some critter had torn out their tongues. Aside from the tongues being gone, their faces and heads hadn't been touched."

As he added hot tea and dollops of rum to our cups, I asked, "You said three, what happened to the fourth one?"

He sucked at his prominent incisors for a moment, then shook his head. "Nothing, Frank, not one dang think! It was that Garrity boy from downstate. His neck was broke clean and he had some more broken bones and accompanying contusions, but he was fully dressed. His nose had been mashed flat, his front teeth were broken off and his face generally torn up some, but he still had his tongue."

The doctor blew hard on his tea, then sipped it noisily. "Egon figgers that any animals would've got to three of them kids would've got to the othern, too. So he figgers warn't a four-legged critter, that's why he called in the state on it.

"Now, Frank, don't you go tellin' all this here to your pretty little wife and scare her half to death. But you be dang sure you lock up tight at night until they catch this lunatic."

I didn't tell Peggy any of it. Maybe I should've; she thinks so . . . now. Maybe, if I had, none of the worst part would have happened. But Hell, you can "if" and "maybe" yourself into a straitjacket and a soft room. I didn't tell her because I love her and I knew she was sensitive as all Hell and I didn't want to upset her.

Grimfaced, well-armed men tramped and drove and rode horses all over the area, working outward from Buffalo Mountain in wide spirals, but they never found much of anything. Some hoofprints in the snow down by the creek that some said were bison, but were felt to be simply strayed cattle from one of the small-scale, local dairy-beef operations.

I did buy a pistol—an elderly Colt Peacemaker with a four-inch barrel, which I loaded with five of the huge cartridges and hid in the glove compartment of the car, so as not to alarm Peggy, who was terrified of firearms of any description.

Spring came in without any more deaths and the community settled down into its usual pursuits. Olaf began to drive over for the twice-weekly dinners again; I recommenced my evenings at Wolff Knipsengeldt's automotive infirmary.

At the college, the faculty and students returned from spring break to stare in wonder at the five bison which had, after knocking down some yards of fencing, joined the dairy herd in its pasture. They all were young, healthy animals—two heifers and three immature bulls. The Canadian Government was known to maintain a herd of bison in the province just north of us, and the initial supposition was that these were strays from that herd.

When I told Peggy about the bison she was thrilled and, two nights later at the first of our dinners since the break, she and Olaf cooked up the idea for a couple of bus loads of the children from Lost Herd Elementary coming out to see these first bison to reappear in these parts since the 1880s.

I had misgivings about the whole affair, principally because I feared that if those decrepit busses tried to maintain any speed in excess of twenty-five miles per hour for some six whole miles, they would rapidly disintegrate right there on the highway, held together as all four were with rust, peeling paint, rubberbands, masking tape and prayer.

The outing was cleared with the school board and set for a Thursday afternoon. It was decided that the second and third grades would go: Peggy's class and the one taught by a Miss Irunn Gustafsson, who was also a school bus driver. The forty-odd children were to go in two buses—apparently the board members had no more faith in their four automotive abortions than did I.

On the Wednesday evening before that hellish day, I had driven in to Wolff Knipsengeldt's, immediately after dinner. He had sent word that that day's mail had finally brought a part we had ordered from the closest Nash-Rambler dealer, far downstate. When, at length, the old mechanic and I had finished the installation, washed up a bit and were sharing a couple of bottles of cold beer, while relaxing in the tilt-back front seats of my car, Wolff lolled his grizzled head back and reached up to ring his scarred knuckles on the horizontal section of the two-inch steel rollbar—sometime in its checkered past, my little car had apparently been used as a stockcar or a dragster, of which period the rollbar welded to the frame was the only souvenir, aside from an extremely heavy suspension.

After another pull at his beer bottle, Wolff said, "Franky, tinny as they makes cars today, you'uz shore smart to leave this-here bar on. Ef this-here little sweetie-pie ever comes to roll 'r flip, that-there bar'll save your life, likely.

"You mark my words, Franky, the day's gonna come, and not too long a-comin' neither, whin the friggin' in-surance comp'nies or eyun the Guv'mint's gonna make the folks builds cars—Ford and Chrysler and Gen'rul Motors and all—put in stuff like rollbars and steerin' wheels won't bust up your ribs, and rubber or suthin to pad the dashboards and a whole lotta stuff like thet, just like they made 'em all put in safety glass in windshields, a while back.

"Hell, prob'ly won't be long 'fore near ever car you see'll have seat belts, too. Standard!"

This was a new one on me. "Seat belts, Wolff? Such as airplanes use? That kind? What earthly good would they be in a car?"

Without answering me, he set his half-full bottle on the floorboards and got out of the car. I assumed he was going around to the john, but I was wrong. Presently, he returned bearing a paper-wrapped parcel. Sitting back down and holding his bottle tightly between his bony knees, he delved under the wrappings and extracted two pieces of black webbing each about two inches wide and obviously of some length, though folded upon themselves several laps and secured with thick rubber bands; each dangled metal fittings from the ends and the centers of each mounted a thick, square piece of chrome a bit wider than the webbing and bearing some automotive hallmark I could not make out in the dim interior of the Rambler.

Wolff handed one of the things to me and said, "These-here is seat belts, Franky. Old man Zeuge got me to order 'em for to go on poor little Hansi's TR. An' you know, Hansi an' Willi seen my light—I'z workin' late on ol' Miz Heidi Wagner's '47 Hudson—an' they drove in here to get gas, thet same night they'z kilt. I tol' him then I'd done got these-here in an' I could put 'em on right then, wouldn' a took more'n twenny, thirty minits, but them poor *Burschen*, they dint wanta take the time, then. Chances are if they hadn' been in sich a all-fired hurry," he sighed, belched, and sniffed strongly, then hawked and spit out the window.

But his story had told me what I wanted to know. I could see the value of the strips of webbing. If the two boys had been belted into the sportscar, the impact would not have hurled their bodies through roof or windshield and twenty long feet down onto a hard-frozen creek. They still might have been injured, but they, most likely, would still be alive, at least.

Knowing Wolff's frugality—though he'd do almost anything for someone he considered a friend, the wag throughout Lost Herd was to the effect that he was capable of extracting blood from turnips and of squeezing a silver dollar until the eagle defecated—I asked, "These things must be damned expensive, Wolff, anything that goes on a sportscar is. Why haven't you sent them back for a refund?"

"*Englische Dummköpfe!*" he exclaimed, with feeling. "I tried to, Franky. You know I don't write letters too good, but I tol' thet sweet Miss Gustafsson whatall I wanted to say, one day an' she writ the purties' letter you ever did see an' done it with a typewriter, t'boot. She tol' the dealer I got these-here belts from in Ch'cago all 'bout them *Jungen* a getting kilt an' all, but it dint do no damn good.

"Them bastids, they sint 'em back to me, *postage due*, along of this-here snotty letter, said I'd bought the fuckers an' now they'uz mine! So they jest been layin' back in the office closit with a bunch of old Hupmobile and Maxwell parts was in there whin I bought this-here place."

To shorten a long story, when I drove back home that night, the Triumph seat belts had been installed in my car. I knew that Peggy would not like the extra expense, but I thought the added safety feature might win over her cautious nature. May God bless and keep old Wolff Knipsengeldt, wherever he may be today, for those seat belts saved our lives, Peggy's and mine.

Wednesday had been rainy and Wednesday night had been cold and drizzly with a brisk wind from the northwest making it downright chilly. But Thursday morning dawned clear and bright, with only a few high, wispy clouds drifting like cotton candy across the rich, light-blue of the sky. The air was almost balmy and filled with the promise of the prairie summer to come. There was no hint, that morning, of the cold, grim, Hell-spawned horror that would lie under that sun before the day had ended.

The busses from Lost Herd were scheduled to arrive at the college at nine that morning and I had made arrangements to be free for most of the time the kids would be on campus—not a difficult thing for me within the small, friendly, easy-going college. They were not there at nine, nor yet at ten and I was worried sick about Peggy by the time the two aged vehicles chugged and spluttered up the cursive drive, each trailing its inevitable cloud of thick, oily fumes.

Peggy and her twenty-three little second-graders were on the first bus, driven by blond, handsome Rudi Keilermann. The second automotive antique was driven by plump, red-haired Irunn Gustafsson, leading her twenty-seven third-graders in a round of *Volkslieder*.

Olaf Bauer had outdone himself in preparations for the visiting children. Since most of them were farm kids and many would eventually be students at Buffalo Mountain Ag., he had set up a Cook's tour of all of the varied facilities and some of the classes, a cafeteria lunch, with the dairy herd and bison for dessert. The delayed arrival naturally forced him to reshuffle his schedule somewhat, but the program worked out just fine, with the children all suitably impressed throughout. But, at the end, they ignored the prize cattle to ooh and ahh and bombard poor, patient Olaf with their endless questions concerning the huge, shaggy, dark-brown bovines.

Doctor Wallace Churchill, the Administrator, had wired an inquiry to the Canadians regarding our five young *bison bison* and had received a return wire to the effect that none of the small herd seemed to be AWOL but, nonetheless, had included examples of the series of numbers which would be found tattooed inside the left ear of any Canadian-type bison.

The five shaggy strangers had proven amazingly tame and cooperative— which reinforced the suppositions that they were not truly wild. But when they were all chuted and examined, no man-made markings of any description were found.

The children were loaded aboard the busses a little after two PM, but then the third-grader bus refused to start. Two of our mechanics were hastily summoned from the college tractor garage. After extensive examinations of the grease-caked, oil-dripping engines of both busses, accompanied by exclamations and crudities that would have made even Wolff Knipsengeldt blush, the mechanics announced that, considering the abominable conditions of the engines, it was a divine miracle that either bus had even made it to the college and that the only way the one would make it off the campus would be behind a tow truck.

After some discussion, it was decided to put all the kids aboard the one operative bus, three instead of two to a seat. I offered to follow in my car and, since the bus was rather crowded, it was not difficult to persuade

With a roar and a clatter of loose parts, backfiring deafeningly and laying its usual smoke screen, the single, jam-packed bus swung around the drive and headed for the road back to Lost Herd.

Peggy had been sleeping when I had come in the night before and I had forgotten to tell her about the new seat belts earlier, so it took me a few minutes to explain to her how to fasten and tighten them. Then a student came running over to the car to bring Olaf the pipe he had left behind somewhere on the tour and to have a few words with the professor about something academic. By the time I finally got down to the highway, the bus was minuscule with distance on the straight, almost flat road.

Going a little faster than I liked to push my aging car, I took up pursuit, trying to at least close some of the lead. But young Rudi Keilermann seemed to think he was Raymond Mays, he was firewalling the bus as it started the long, looping curve around the flank of Buffalo Mountain. The mountain— all dark-green conifers and black rock outcrops—stood like a monstrous, shaggy-flanked beast in the midst of the flat or gently-rolling prairie lands and I suddenly realized how it had likely acquired its Indian name and legends: from this angle, its ridgecrest did bear a resemblance to a bison's silhouette—the glaciers of Pleistocene times had so carved it that the rounded peak took a sharp downslope on the long side and fell into a saddle on the other before rising back to another slightly lower round summit. Viewed imaginatively, this lone sentinel of the plains could easily be likened to a gigantic bison.

Nonetheless, I had closed the gap sufficiently to hear the sudden screaming of tortured rubber, followed almost immediately by a tearing, rending metallic crash!

"No! Oh, dear God, no!" screamed Peggy.

Not knowing just what lay ahead, I geared down as I rounded the mountain and started down the long, gentle slope into Slaughterhouse Valley, toward the bridge over Bloody Creek. All that was visible of the bus from that angle was the red-rust undercarriage and the smoking, still-spinning wheels. I could hear Peggy sobbing and Olaf muttering German prayers.

Then, as I neared the bridge, up the steep bank from the bed of Bloody Creek came the bison, a dozen or more of the huge beasts, all shining, curved horns and little red-glowing eyes. Each of the ton-weight monsters seemed to span the width of the road and I knew the Rambler would fold into itself like an accordion if it hit one. Nor was I the only one who saw them, for Olaf was leaning past me, pointing his finger at the animals while he shouted something incomprehensible in my ear.

I slammed on the brakes and it seemed for a moment that I might make it safely. But then the rear end fishtailed far, far to the right and both left wheels rose up and then it all was a kaleidoscope of blue sky below and black macadam above and gut-wrenching terror for myself and for Peggy and Oh-God-take-me-if-you-must-but-please-spare-Peggy. The screams were as deafening as the grinding-tearing of rending metal and the bone-jarring, slamming thuds. And it seemed to go on forever, yet was over immediately.

I'll never know just how many times the little car rolled, but when I came to realize that I was alive, the Rambler was upright again and still on the roadway, just beyond the wrecked bus. The Rambler's hood was gone, along with the windshield, all the other windows and most of the roof . . . and poor old Olaf. I could see his grotesquely sprawled body in the middle of the road.

At first, I thought Peggy was gone, too, but she still was strapped safely beside me. As it developed, she actually had come out of it all with fewer physical injuries than had I, since the long-defective lock on her side of the seat-back had failed early-on and centrifugal force had held her prone, affording her body the added protection of the stronger sides of the car.

From far back the road, the broad, multiple skid marks showed the distance the bus had skidded before slamming over on its left side. The sliding bus had struck the strong, thick steel pole that held the state's **Slaughterhouse Valley—Lost Herd** sign at windshield level *and torn back almost the entire length* of the weak, rusty metal. The bus lay open like a discarded can of sardines and part of its contents spilled down the green, grassy slope into the old level of Slaughterhouse Valley.

And among those too-still little shapes, the bison moved. In twos and threes, the brown-and-black-nightmare monsters went from one battered small body to another, leaving in their wake . . . pure, screaming horror. The huge, primeval heads went down and when they arose, the small corpses lay stripped of both clothing and skin.

Other bison were grouped about Olaf, up the road. And then I saw a rider approaching—a white-haired, wrinkled Indian on a runty, big-headed, claybank horse. The pony-sized equine was devoid of saddle, only a faded blanket hung over his back and withers; and his "bridle" was a length of braided rawhide tied around his lower jaw. The old Indian bore no feathers or other ornaments, and his clothing was roughly fashioned of buckskin.

Though the oldster looked as if the wind would blow him away, he dropped lightly from his mount at Olaf's now bare and skinless body. The sun glinted on the blade of the curved knife he drew from a hide sheath. He bent and grabbed something that distance denied me sight of, and his knife moved downward in a swift blur. Then he remounted and rode on toward the bus.

I must have passed out then—I was seriously injured, although I was not then aware of the fact. But Peggy's terrified shrieks aroused me. My wrecked car was surrounded by bison. Still prone, Peggy was frantically working the chrome handle in a vain attempt to roll up the smashed-out window.

Then I thought of the old Colt revolver. I didn't think that even so massive a pistol as the Peacemaker would kill one of the shaggy behemoths, but the noise—with its big, .45-caliber cartridges and its shortened barrel, made a Hellacious racket—might panic the mammoth creatures into a long-distance run . . . away from us. Miracles still happen. The glove compartment had not come open during the demolition of the rest of the car, yet it opened easily for me.

One of the hideous, red-eyed heads had intruded over the edge of the buckled door on Peggy's side and, screaming mindlessly, she threw up her arms to fend it off. I saw the mouth open, the tremendous tongue come out and lick along the upper surface of her right arm, removing the skin almost from elbow to wrist. That was when I cocked, levelled and fired the big pistol, point-blank!

The bison just rolled one of those red hell-eyes at me, and made to lower head and flaying tongue toward the now-unconscious body of my wife. But, suddenly, the old Indian was there, sitting on his horse.

His lips moved in the shaping of words that could not have been English or any other language I spoke, yet I could clearly understand him.

"No, Children of The Mother, these two are not accursed of Her."

I wasn't fully conscious or rational for weeks and, of course, no one believed a word of my account of what happened. All of it was blamed on shock and my concussion. The various law-enforcement types were of the opinion that the fact I had a pistol and had fired a "warning shot" had kept the maniacs who had mutilated all the bodies from the bus and poor Olaf's away from me and Peggy. Nor could her story corroborate my own since her mind had mercifully blanked out the horrors of that day.

The coroner's inquest decided that the bus had been driven too fast and that the bodies had been mutilated by "person or persons unknown."

The copious cloven-hoofprints pressed into the rain-softened earth up and down the length and width of Slaughterhouse Valley were said to have been there before the accident, caused by a herd of reservation cattle surreptitiously driven by Indians from their own barren ranges of wiregrass to feed the night long on the verdant, state-owned roadsides before being driven back to the reservation before dawn. This was known to be fact because only the dirt-poor Reservation Indians did not shoe their starveling nags, and the prints of unshod horsehooves had been found here and there.

By the time I was released from the hospital in Regen, the county seat, thirty-five miles from Lost Herd, the summer was well along. So that she could more easily visit me during my protracted confinement, Peggy had gotten Wolff Knipsengeldt to teach her to drive and then had bought Olaf Bauer's Bel-Air sedan from her instructor, who acted as agent in most of the used car sales in Lost Herd.

Old Wolff was, as well, the source of most of what follows, since he was the only townsperson who did not show acute discomfort whenever I came around and who did not change the subject, clam up or walk rapidly away when an outsider broached the subject of the sinister tragedy in Slaughterhouse Valley.

Not only had the state police investigators come back to Lost Herd, but various federal officials, as well. The Governor, himself, had been in town for a few days, and most of his entourage had remained when he did leave—a mixed bag of experts in specialties ranging from forensic medicine and game management through highway engineering and psychology.

Within the seven days which followed the "accident," every square inch of land surface, every building, construction or excavation of any nature was covered and re-covered by posses of townsmen and farmers under the sheriff and his deputies, two full battalions of National Guardsmen trucked up from the state capital, a busload of federal marshals and FBI agents, most of the male students and staff from the college and even a contingent of mounted Indians from Buffalo Mountain Reservation. They searched a fifteen-mile radius of Lost Herd, by day and by night. Crop dusters flew their light planes at almost treetop level, keeping in touch with the ground parties by radio.

A farmer some miles northeast of Lost Herd had a fine Holstein bull killed when the animal made the fatal error of charging a group of Guardsmen crossing his pasture one night; he fell under a hail of rifle and sub-machine gun fire. Several coyotes were shot, here and there; and a couple of deer poachers apprehended. A hired hand on Otto Kleist's dairy farm was determined to be an Army deserter, arrested, and returned to some post clear down in Texas. But his and those of the poachers were the only arrests ever made. No slightest trace was ever discovered of the maniac or maniacs responsible for the mutilations.

Wolff did say that, high up on Buffalo Mountain, a cave had been discovered, its mouth almost closed by an old rock slide all overgrown with trees that had stood there at least fifty years. Two skeletons were found far back in the cave. One was that of a small horse and the other that of a man.

Those forensic types still in Lost Herd determined that the horse had most likely starved to death, as there were no marks of violence on the desiccated skin stretched over the bones and since marks of equine teeth were found in the partially-chewed-away poles which had formed the creature's stall.

There was no question what had killed the man, what with a round hole half of an inch in diameter in the forehead and most of the back of the skull missing. What was questioned was why no skin was found stretched over the human bones, save on the hands, feet and portions of the lower face. The dry, cool air of the cave had preserved the horse's skin, so why not the man's?

Another unanswered question was how, among a collection of rusty, antique pots and small hardware, had come to rest an antler-hilted knife. Its curved blade was bright and shiny, where it was not blotched with blood determined, by testing, to be of several different *human* types and no more than a few days old!

Wolff had only heard bits and pieces of my own story, third and fourth hand from people who did not believe it . . . or could not allow themselves to do so. When he asked me to tell him, I did; I told him all of it on the August evening he checked over the Bel-Air the last time. Peggy and I were to start the long drive east, to Ohio and the new positions we had accepted, the next day.

When I had finished, Wolff just stared at his bottle of beer for some minutes, then he shook his grizzled head and said, softly, "It's some things happens in this-here old worl', Franky, cain't nobody ever figger. So mos' folks jest swears them things dint never happen, nohow, an' the folks what see them things wuz teched or drunk or jest plain lyin'. They *has* to do thet way, Franky, elst they couldn' sleep nights. But jest 'cause them as dint see won't an' caint b'lieve, don't allus mean them p'culiar things dint happun."

Arising and setting down his beer bottle, he took a big flashlight from a shelf and walked toward the door, saying "C'mon, Franky. It's sumpin back in the junkyard you needs to see."

The Rambler had long-since been stripped of any usable parts and its crumpled, jaggedly ripped and scraped body was red with rust except in those rare patches where a bit of paint remained. Wolff lifted off the passenger side door and laid it atop the crumbled fender, then opened the glove compartment and shone his light in.

"Franky, look in the left-han' back corner, there. See that-there hole? Now, looky here."

From beneath the seat, he pulled a rumpled and water-stained brown paper bag, delved a hand into it, then shone the beam on that palm. Across the grimy palm lay about five inches of a broad, sharp-pointed horn. At the wider end, it was raggedly shattered.

"Is this-here yours, Franky, or Miz Peggy's?"

I tried to answer but couldn't and ended shaking my head.

Wordlessly, Wolff put his hand into the still-open glove compartment and stuck the pointed end of the piece of horn in the peculiar hole. It fitted perfectly.

"When I towed this-here car in," he explained, "I natcherly put it in the locked lot over there, so wouldn' nobody mess with it 'til after Dep'ty Kalb an' th' Sher'f an' all had done pokin' at it. But, since you's my frien', Franky, I figgered to clean out the trunk an' glove c'mpartmunt, cause—nothin' 'ginst Karl Kalb, y'unnerstan'—it's some dep'ties got sticky fingers.

"After I'd done got ever'thin' out'n the trunk an' got the glove c'mpartmunt empty, I felt aroun' in there an' come out with thet. An', Franky, I purely had to pull to get'er out, too, she'd really dug in. How you reckon the end of some critter's horn come to be stuck th'ough there, enyhow, Franky?"

Again, I could picture the huge, shaggy, horned head of the monster bison, the red fires of hell flickering in its eyes. Again, I could feel myself jerking open the glove compartment to get to the old Colt, painfully cocking the hammer, then trying to force my tremulous hands to hold the heavy weapon level with a big, flaming eye. I figured, there in Wolff Knipsengeldt's junkyard, that it was entirely possible that the massive slug had missed the eye and struck the horn, propelling the splintered-off tip with sufficient force to imbed itself in the still-open glove compartment.

Neither Wolff nor I spoke as we picked our way between the rusty hulks and stacks of old tires, back to the grubby office and the bottles of warm beer, nor did we talk much as we finished that last beer together. But, after he had filled the Bel Air's tank, just before he extended his thick, grimy hand in farewell, he pressed the crumpled sack on me.

"Franky, most folks in town an' here' bouts cain' even stan' to think on *what* was done to them poor kids, much less *how* it mighta happund. That's why folks all wants you to think you dint see what really come down out there in *das Schlachthaustal*. It'll be the same wherever you goes, too, an' after while, you'll likely start wonderin' if they ain't right an' you wrong.

"Ever'time you start thinkin' like thet, Franky, you jest take out that there an' look at it, an' squeeze on it hard an' r'member that whutall folks says, you knows the truth . . . an' so does old Wolff Knipsengeldt, too."

I still have that old bit of horn. It's tucked away with a yellowed clipping from a Cincinnati paper, dated in early September of that year, a few weeks after Peggy and I came back east.

> LOST HERD, N. DAK. (AP) This small farming community is once more in the news. On the first day of the current school year, yesterday morning, no children could be found in the yard of Lost Herd Elementary School, for the yard was crowded with a milling herd of buffalo, 53 of the huge wild cattle. No one here seems to know when or how they came into town, since residents did not see or hear them in the streets and none of the farmlands completely surrounding the town appear to have been recently crossed by so many large animals.
>
> Deputy Sheriff K. S. Kalb states that five buffalo were found on the campus of a nearby college more than six months ago. Along with most other townspeople interviewed, Deputy Kalb thinks that the herd are part of a larger herd known to roam a park in Saskatchewan, which province borders on this state only bare miles north of Lost Herd.
>
> Readers may recall that this little town was visited by tragedy last spring when 50 second and third grade children and three adults were killed in the wreck of a school bus two miles west of Lost Herd.

OHIO

The Horsehair Trunk
by Davis Grubb

To MARIUS the fever was like a cloud of warm river fog around him. Or like the blissful vacuum that he had always imagined death would be. He had lain for nearly a week like this in the big corner room while the typhoid raged and boiled inside him. Mary Ann was a dutiful wife. She came and fed him his medicine and stood at the foot of the brass bed when the doctor was there, clasping and unclasping her thin hands; and sometimes from between hot, heavy lids Marius could glimpse her face, dimly pale and working slowly in prayer. Such a fool she was, a praying, stupid fool that he had married five years ago. He could remember thinking that even in the deep, troubled delirium of the fever.

"You want me to die," he said to her one morning when she came with his medicine. "You want me to die, don't you?"

"Marius! Don't say such a thing! Don't ever—"

"It's true, though," he went on, hearing his voice miles above him at the edge of the quilt. "You want me to die. But I'm not going to. I'm going to get well, Mary Ann. I'm not going to die. Aren't you disappointed?"

"No! No! It's not true! It's not!"

Now, though he could not see her face through the hot blur of fever, he could hear her crying; sobbing and shaking with her fist pressed tight against her teeth. Such a fool.

On the eighth morning Marius woke full of a strange, fiery brilliance as if all his flesh were glass not yet cool from the furnace. He knew the fever was worse, close to its crisis, and yet it no longer had the quality of darkness and mists. Everything was sharp and clear. The red of his necktie hanging in the corner of the bureau mirror was a flame. And he could hear the minutest stirrings down in the kitchen, the breaking of a match stick in Mary Ann's fingers as clear as pistol shots outside his bedroom window. It was a joy.

Marius wondered for a moment if he might have died. But if it was death it was certainly more pleasant than he had ever imagined death would be. He could rise from the bed without any sense of weakness and he could stretch his arms and he could even walk out through the solid door into the upstairs hall. He thought it might be fun to tiptoe downstairs and give Mary Ann a fright, but when he was in the parlor he remembered suddenly that she would be unable to see him. Then when he heard her coming from the kitchen with his medicine he thought of an even better joke. With the speed of thought Marius was back in his body under the quilt again, and Mary Ann was coming into the bedroom with her large eyes wide and worried.

"Marius," she whispered, leaning over him and stroking his hot forehead with her cold, thin fingers. "Marius, are you better?"

He opened his eyes as if he had been asleep.

"I see," he said, "that you've moved the pianola over to the north end of the parlor."

Mary Ann's eyes widened and the glass of amber liquid rattled against the dish.

"Marius!" she whispered. "You haven't been out of bed! You'll kill yourself! With a fever like—"

"No," said Marius faintly, listening to his own voice as if it were in another room. "I haven't been out of bed, Mary Ann."

His eyelids flickered weakly up at her face, round and ghost-like, incredulous. She quickly set the tinkling glass of medicine on the little table.

"Then how—?" she said. "Marius, how could you know?"

Marius smiled weakly up at her and closed his eyes, saying nothing, leaving the terrible question unanswered, leaving her to tremble and ponder over it forever if need be. She was such a fool.

It had begun that way, and it had been so easy he wondered why he had never discovered it before. Within a few hours the fever broke in great rivers of sweat, and by Wednesday, Marius was able to sit up in the chair by the window and watch the starlings hopping on the front lawn. By the end of the month he was back at work as editor of the *Daily Argus*. But even those who knew him least were able to detect in the manner of Marius Lindsay that he was a changed man—and a worse one. And those who knew him best wondered how so malignant a citizen, such a confirmed and studied misanthrope as Marius could possibly change into anything worse than he was. Some said that typhoid always burned the temper from the toughest steel and that Marius' mind had been left a dark and twisted thing. At prayer meeting on Wednesday nights the wives used to watch Marius' young wife and wonder how she endured her cross. She was such a pretty thing.

One afternoon in September, as he dozed on the bulging leather couch of his office, Marius decided to try it again. The secret, he knew, lay somewhere on the brink of sleep. If a man knew that—any man—he would know what Marius did. It wasn't more than a minute later that Marius knew that all he would have to do to leave his body was to get up from the couch. Presently he was standing there, staring down at his heavy, middle-aged figure sunk deep into the cracked leather of the couch, the jowls of the face under the close-cropped mustache sagging deep in sleep, the heart above his heavy gold watch chain beating solidly in its breast.

I'm not dead, he thought, delighted. But here is my soul—my damned, immortal soul standing looking at its body!

It was as simple as shedding a shoe. Marius smiled to himself, remembering his old partner Charlie Cunningham and how they used to spend long hours in the office, in this very room, arguing about death and atheism and the whither of the soul. If Charlie were still alive, Marius thought, I would win from him a quart of the best Kentucky bourbon in the county. As it was, no one would ever know. He would keep his secret even from Mary Ann, especially from Mary Ann, who would go to her grave with the superstitious belief that Marius had died for a moment, that for an instant fate had favored her; that she had been so close to happiness, to freedom from him forever. She would never know. Still, it would be fun to use a trick, a practical joke to set fools like his wife at their wits' edge. If only he could *move* things. If only the filmy substance of his soul could grasp a tumbler and send it shattering at Mary Ann's feet on the kitchen floor some morning. Or tweak a copy boy's nose. Or snatch a cigar from the teeth of Judge John Robert Gants as he strolled home some quiet evening from the fall session of the district court.

Well, it was, after all, a matter of will, Marius decided. It was his own powerful and indomitable will that had made the trick possible in the first place. He walked to the edge of his desk and grasped at the letter opener on the dirty, ancient blotter. His fingers were like wisps of fog that blew through a screen door. He tried again, willing it with all his power, grasping again and again at the small brass dagger until at last it moved a fraction of an inch. A little more. On the next try it lifted four inches in the air and hung for a second on its point before it dropped. Marius spent the rest of the afternoon practicing until at last he could lift the letter opener in his fist, fingers tight around the haft, the thumb pressing the cold blade tightly, and drive it through the blotter so deeply that it bit into the wood of the desk beneath.

Marius giggled in spite of himself and hurried around the office picking things up like a pleased child. He lifted a tumbler off the dusty water cooler and stared laughing at it, hanging there in the middle of nothing. At that moment he heard the copy boy coming for the proofs of the morning editorials and Marius flitted quickly back into the cloak of his flesh. Nor was he a moment too soon. Just as he opened his eyes, the door opened and he heard the glass shatter on the floor.

"I'm going to take a nap before supper, Mary Ann," Marius said that evening, hanging his black hat carefully on the elk-horn hatrack.

"Very well," said Mary Ann. He watched her young, unhappy figure disappearing into the gloom of the kitchen and he smiled to himself again, thinking what a fool she was, his wife. He could scarcely wait to get to the davenport and stretch out in the cool, dark parlor with his head on the beaded pillow.

Now, thought Marius. Now.

And in a moment he had risen from his body and hurried out into the hallway, struggling to suppress the laughter that would tell her he was coming. He could already anticipate her white, stricken face when the pepper pot pulled firmly from between her fingers cut a clean figure eight in the air before it crashed against the ceiling.

He heard her voice and was puzzled.

"You must go," she was murmuring. "You mustn't ever come here when he's home. I've told you that before, Jim. What would you do if he woke up and found you here!"

Then Marius, as he rushed into the kitchen, saw her bending through the doorway into the dusk with the saucepan of greens clutched in her white knuckles.

"What would you do? You must go!"

Marius rushed to her side, careful not to touch her, careful not to let either of them know he was there, listening, looking, flaming hatred growing slowly inside him.

The man was young and dark and well built and clean-looking. He leaned against the half-open screen door, holding Mary Ann's free hand between his own. His round, dark face bent to hers, and she smiled with a tenderness and passion that Marius had never seen before.

"I know," the man said. "I know all that. But I just can't stand it no more, Mary Ann. I just can't stand it thinking about him beating you up that time. He might do it again, Mary Ann. He might! He's worse, they say, since he had the fever. Crazy, I think. I've heard them say he's crazy."

"Yes. Yes. You must go away now, though," she was whispering frantically, looking back over her shoulder through Marius' dark face. "We'll have time to talk it all over again, Jim. I—I know I'm going to leave him but— Don't rush me into things, Jim dear. Don't make me do it till I'm clear with myself."

"Why not now?" came the whisper. "Why not tonight? We can take a steamboat to Lou'ville and you'll never have to put up with him again. You'll be shed of him forever, honey. Look! I've got two tickets for Lou'ville right here in my pocket on the *Nancy B. Turner*. My God, Mary Ann, don't make me suffer like this—lyin' abed nights dreaming about him comin' at you with his cane and beatin' you—maybe killin' you!"

The woman grew silent and her face softened as she watched the fireflies dart their zigzags of cold light under the low trees along the street. She opened her mouth, closed it, and stood biting her lip hard. Then she reached up and pulled his face down to hers, seeking his mouth.

"All right," she whispered then. "All right. I'll do it! Now go! Quick!"

"Meet me at the wharf at nine," he said. "Tell him that you're going to prayer meeting. He'll never suspicion anything. Then we can be together without all this sneakin' around. Oh, honey, if you ever knew how much I—"

The words were smeared in her kiss as he pulled her down through the half-open door and held her.

"All right. All right," she gasped. "Now go! Please!"

And he walked away, his heels ringing boldly on the bricks, lighting a cigarette, the match arching like a shooting star into the darkness of the shrubs. Mary Ann stood stiff for a moment in the shadow of the porch vines, her large eyes full of tears, and the saucepan of greens grown cold in her hands. Marius drew back to let her pass. He stood then and watched her for a moment before he hurried back into the parlor and lay down again within his flesh and bone in time to be called for supper.

Captain Joe Alexander of the *Nancy B. Turner* was not curious that Marius should want a ticket for Louisville. He remembered years later that he had thought nothing strange about it at the time. It was less than two months till the elections and there was a big Democratic convention there.

Everyone had heard of Marius Lindsay and the power he and his *Daily Argus* held over the choices of the people. But Captain Alexander did remember thinking it strange that Marius should insist on seeing the passenger list of the *Nancy B.* that night and that he should ask particularly after a man named Jim. Smith, Marius had said, but there was no Smith. There was a Jim though, a furniture salesman from Wheeling: Jim O'Toole, who had reserved two staterooms, No. 3 and No. 4.

"What do you think of the Presidential chances this term, Mr. Lindsay?" Captain Alexander had said. And Marius had looked absent for a moment (the captain had never failed to recount that detail) and then said that it would be Cleveland, that the Republicans were done forever.

Captain Alexander had remembered that conversation and the manner of its delivery years later and it had become part of the tale that rivermen told in wharf boats and water-street saloons from Pittsburgh to Cairo long after that night had woven itself into legend.

Then Marius had asked for stateroom No. 5, and that had been part of the legend, too, for it was next to the room that was to be occupied by Jim O'Toole, the furniture salesman from Wheeling.

"Say nothing," said Marius, before he disappeared down the stairway from the captain's cabin, "to anyone about my being aboard this boat tonight. My trip to Louisville is connected with the approaching election and is, of necessity, confidential."

"Certainly, sir," said the captain, and he listened as Marius made his way awkwardly down the gilded staircase, lugging his small horsehair trunk under his arm. Presently the door to Marius' stateroom snapped shut and the bolt fell to.

At nine o'clock sharp, two rockaway buggies rattled down the brick pavement of Water Street and met at the wharf. A man jumped from one, and a woman from the other.

"You say he wasn't home when you left," the man was whispering as he helped the woman down the rocky cobbles, the two carpetbags tucked under his arms.

"No. But it's all right," Mary Ann said. "He always goes down to the office this time of night to help set up the morning edition."

"You reckon he suspicions anything?"

The woman laughed, a low, sad laugh.

"He always suspicions everybody," she said. "Marius has the kind of a mind that always suspicions; and the kind of life he leads, I guess he has to. But I don't think he knows about us—tonight. I don't think he ever *knew* about us—ever."

They hurried up the gangplank together. The water lapped and gurgled against the wharf, and off over the river, lightning scratched the dark rim of mountains like the sudden flare of a kitchen match.

"I'm Jim O'Toole," Jim said to Captain Alexander, handing him the tickets. "This is my wife—"

Mary Ann bit her lip and clutched the strap of her carpetbag till her knuckles showed through the flesh.

"—she has the stateroom next to mine. Is everything in order?"

"Right, sir," said Captain Alexander, wondering in what strange ways the destinies of this furniture salesman and his wife were meshed with the life of Marius Lindsay.

They tiptoed down the worn carpet of the narrow, white hallway, counting the numbers on the long, monotonous row of doors to either side.

"Good night, dear," said Jim, glancing unhappily at the Negro porter dozing on the split-bottom chair under the swinging oil lantern by the door. "Good night, Mary Ann. Tomorrow we'll be on our way. Tomorrow you'll be shed of Marius forever."

Marius lay in his bunk, listening as the deepthroated whistle shook the quiet valley three times. Then he lay smiling and relaxed as the great drive shafts tensed and plunged once forward and backward, gathering into their dark, heavy rhythm as the paddles bit the black water. The *Nancy B. Turner* moved heavily away into the thick current and headed downstream for the Devil's Elbow and the open river. Marius was stiff. He had lain for nearly four hours waiting to hear the voices. Every sound had been as clear to him as the tick of his heavy watch in his vest pocket. He had heard the dry, rasping racket of the green frogs along the shore and the low, occasional words of boys fishing in their skiffs down the shore under the willows.

Then he had stiffened as he heard Mary Ann's excited murmur suddenly just outside his stateroom door and the voice of the man answering her, comforting her. Lightning flashed and flickered out again over the Ohio hills and lit the river for one clear moment. Marius saw all of his stateroom etched suddenly in silver from the open porthole. The mirror, washstand, bowl and pitcher. The horsehair trunk beside him on the floor. Thunder rumbled in the dark and Marius smiled to himself, secure again in the secret darkness, thinking how easy it would be, wondering why no one had thought of such a thing before. Except for the heavy pounding rhythm of the drive shafts and the chatter of the drinking glass against the washbowl as the boat shuddered through the water, everything was still. The Negro porter dozed in his chair under the lantern by the stateroom door. Once Marius thought he heard the lovers' voices in the next room, but he knew then that it was the laughter of the cooks down in the galley.

Softly he rose and slipped past the sleeping porter, making his way for the white-painted handrail at the head of the stairway. Once Marius laughed aloud to himself as he realized that there was no need to tiptoe with no earthly substance there to make a sound. He crept down the narrow stairway to the galley. The Negro cooks bent around the long wooden table eating their supper. Marius slid his long shadow along the wall toward the row of kitchen knives lying, freshly washed and honed, on the zinc table by the pump. For a moment, he hovered over them, dallying, with his finger in his mouth, like a child before an assortment of equally tempting sweets, before he chose the longest of them all, and the sharpest, a knife that would shear the ham clean from a hog with one quick upward sweep. There was, he realized suddenly, the problem of getting the knife past human eyes even if he himself was invisible. The cooks laughed then at some joke one of them had made and all of them bent forward, their heads in a dark circle of merriment over their plates.

In that instant Marius swept the knife soundlessly from the zinc table and darted into the gloomy companionway. The Negro porter was asleep still, and Marius laughed to himself to imagine the man's horror at seeing the butcher knife, its razor edge flashing bright in the dull light, inching itself along the wall. But it was a joke he could not afford. He bent at last and slipped the knife cautiously along the threadbare rug under the little ventilation space beneath the stateroom door; and then, rising, so full of hate that he was half afraid he might shine forth in the darkness, Marius passed through the door and picked the knife up quickly again in his hand.

Off down the Ohio the thunder throbbed again. Marius stepped carefully across the worn rug toward the sleeping body on the bunk. He felt so gay and light he almost laughed aloud. In a moment it would be over and there would be one full-throated cry, and Mary Ann would come beating on the locked door. And when she saw her lover . . .

With an impatient gesture, Marius lifted the knife and felt quickly for the sleeping, pulsing throat. The flesh was warm and living under his fingers as he held it taut for the one quick stroke. His arm flashed. It was done. Marius, fainting with excitement, leaned in the darkness to brace himself. His hand came to rest on the harsh, rough surface of the horsehair trunk.

"My God!" screamed Marius. "My God!"

And at his cry the laughing murmur in the galley grew still and there was a sharp scrape of a chair outside the stateroom door.

"The wrong room!" screamed Marius. "The wrong room!" And he clawed with fingers of smoke at the jetting fountain of his own blood.

OKLAHOMA

The Curse of Yig
by Zealia Brown Reed Bishop

IN 1925 I went into Oklahoma looking for snake lore, and I came out with a fear of snakes that will last me the rest of my life. I admit it is foolish, since there are natural explanations for everything I saw and heard, but it masters me none the less. If the old story had been all there was to it, I would not have been so badly shaken. My work as an American Indian ethnologist has hardened me to all kinds of extravagant legendry, and I know that simple white people can beat the redskins at their own game when it comes to fanciful inventions. But I can't forget what I saw with my own eyes at the insane asylum in Guthrie.

I called at that asylum because a few of the oldest settlers told me I would find something important there. Neither Indians nor white men would discuss the snake-god legends I had come to trace. The oil-boom new-comers, of course, knew nothing of such matters, and the red men and old pioneers were plainly frightened when I spoke to them. Not more than six or seven people mentioned the asylum, and those who did were careful to talk in whispers. But the whisperers said that Dr. McNeill could show me a very terrible relic and tell me all I wanted to know. He could explain why Yig, the half-human father of serpents, is a shunned and feared object in central Oklahoma, and why old settlers shiver at the secret Indian orgies which make the autumn days and nights hideous with the ceaseless beating of tom-toms in lonely places.

It was with the scent of a hound on the trail that I went to Guthrie, for I had spent many years collecting data on the evolution of serpent-worship among the Indians. I had always felt, from well-defined undertones of legend and archeology, that great Quetzalcoatl—benign snake-god of the

Mexicans—had had an older and darker prototype; and during recent months I had well-nigh proved it in a series of researches stretching from Guatemala to the Oklahoma plains. But everything was tantalizing and incomplete, for above the border the cult of the snake was hedged about by fear and furtiveness.

Now it appeared that a new and copious source of data was about to dawn, and I sought the head of the asylum with an eagerness I did not try to cloak. Doctor McNeill was a small clean-shaven man of somewhat advanced years, and I saw at once from his speech and manner that he was a scholar of no mean attainments in many branches outside his profession. Grave and doubtful when I first made known my errand, his face grew thoughtful as he carefully scanned my credentials and the letter of introduction which a kindly old ex-Indian agent had given me.

"So you've been studying the Yig-legend, eh?" he reflected sententiously. "I know that many of our Oklahoma ethnologists have tried to connect it with Quetzalcoatl, but I don't think any of them have traced the intermediate steps so well. You've done remarkable work for a man as young as you seem to be, and you certainly deserve all the data we can give.

"I don't suppose old Major Moore or any of the others told you what it is I have here. They don't like to talk about it, and neither do I. It is very tragic and very horrible, but that is all. I refuse to consider it anything supernatural. There's a story about it that I'll tell you after you see it—a devilish sad story, but one that I won't call magic. It merely shows the potency that belief has over some people. I'll admit there are times when I feel a shiver that's more than physical, but in daylight I set all that down to nerves. I'm not a young fellow any more, alas!

"To come to the point, the thing I have is what you might call a victim of Yig's curse—a physically living victim. We don't let the bulk of the nurses see it, although most of them know it's here. There are just two steady old chaps whom I let feed it and clean out its quarters—used to be there, but good old Stevens passed on a few years ago. I suppose I'll have to break in a new group pretty soon; or change much, and we old boys can't last forever. Maybe the ethics of the near future will let us give it a merciless release, but it's hard to tell.

"Did you see that single ground-glass basement window over in the east wing when you came up the drive? That's where it is. I'll take you there myself now. You needn't make any comment. Just look through the movable panel in the door and thank God the light isn't any stronger. Then I'll tell you the story—or as much as I've been able to piece together."

We walked downstairs very quietly, and did not talk as we threaded the corridors of seemingly deserted basement. Doctor McNeill unlocked a gray-painted steel door, but it was only a bulkhead leading to a further stretch of hallway. At length he paused before a door marked B 116, opened a small observation panel which he could use only by standing on tiptoe, and pounded several times upon the painted metal, as if to arouse the occupant, whatever it might be.

A faint stench came from the aperture as the doctor unclosed it, and I fancied his pounding elicited a kind of low, hissing response. Finally he motioned me to replace him at the peep-hole, and I did so with a causeless and increasing tremor. The barred, ground-glass window, close to the earth outside, admitted only a feeble and uncertain pallor; and I had to look into the malodorous den for several seconds before I could see what was crawling and wriggling about on the straw-covered floor, emitting every now and then a weak and vacuous hiss. Then the shadowed outlines began to take shape, and I perceived that the squirming entity bore some remote resemblance to a human form laid flat on its belly. I clutched at the door-handle for support as I tried to keep from fainting.

The moving object was almost of human size, and entirely devoid of clothing. It was absolutely hairless, and its tawny-looking back seemed subtly squamous in the dim ghoulish light.

Around the shoulders it was rather speckled and brownish, and the head was very curiously flat. As it looked up to hiss at me I saw that the beady little black eyes were damnably anthropoid, but I could not bear to study them long. They fastened themselves on me with a horrible persistence, so that I closed the panel graspingly and left the creature to wriggle about unseen in its matted straw and spectral twilight. I must have reeled a bit, for I saw that the doctor was gently holding my arm as he guided me away. I was stuttering over and over again:

"B-but for God's sake, what is it?"

Doctor McNeill told me the story in his private office as I sprawled opposite him in an easy-chair. The gold and crimson of late afternoon changed to the violet of early dusk, but still I sat awed and motionless. I resented every ring of the telephone and every whir of the buzzer, and I could have cursed the nurses and internes whose knocks now and then summoned the doctor briefly to the outer office. Night came, and I was glad my host switched on all the lights. Scientist though I was, my zeal for research was half forgotten amid such breathless ecstasies of fright as a small boy might feel when whispered witch-tales go the rounds of the chimney-corner.

It seems that Yig, the snake-god of the central plains tribes—presumably the primal source of the more southerly Quetzalcoatl or Kukulcan—was an odd, half-anthropomorphic devil of highly arbitrary and capricious nature. He was not wholly evil, and was usually quite well disposed toward those who gave proper respect to him and his children, the serpents; but in the autumn he became abnormally ravenous and had to be driven away by means of suitable rites. That was why the tom-toms in the Pawnee, Wichita, and Caddo country pounded ceaselessly week in and week out in August, September, and October; and why the medicine-men made strange noises with rattles and whistles curiously like those of the Aztecs and Mayas.

Yig's chief trait was a relentless devotion to his children—a devotion so great that the redskins almost feared to protect themselves from the venomous rattlesnakes which thronged the region. Frightful clandestine tales hinted of his vengeance upon mortals who flouted him or wreaked harm upon his wriggling progeny; his chosen method being to turn his victim, after suitable tortures, to a spotted snake.

In the old days of the Indian Territory, the doctor went on, there was not quite so much secrecy about Yig. The plains tribes, less cautious than the desert nomads and Peublos, talked quite freely of their legends and autumn ceremonies with the first Indian agents, and let considerable of the lore spread out through the neighboring regions of white settlement. The great fear came in the land-rush days of eighty-nine, when some extraordinary incidents had been rumored, and the rumors sustained, by what seemed to be hideously tangible proofs. Indians said that the new white men did not know how to get on with Yig, and afterward the settlers came to take that theory at face value. Now no old-timer in middle Oklahoma, white or red, could be induced to breathe a word about the snake-god except in vague hints. Yet after all, the doctor added with almost needless emphasis, the only truly authenticated horror had been a thing of pitiful tragedy rather than of bewitchment. It was all very material and cruel—even that last phase which had caused so much dispute.

Doctor McNeill paused and cleared his throat before getting down to his special story, and I felt a tingling sensation as when a theatre curtain rises. The thing had begun when Walker Davis and his wife Audrey left Arkansas to settle in the newly opened public lands in the spring of 1889, and the end had come in the country of the Wichitas—north of the Wichita River, in what is at present Caddo Country. There is a small village called Binger there now, and the railway goes through; but otherwise the place is less changed than other parts of Oklahoma. It is still a section of farms and ranches—quite productive in these days—since the great oil-fields do not come very close.

Walker and Audrey had come from Franklin County in the Ozarks with a canvas-topped wagon, two mules, an ancient and useless dog called Wolf, and all their household goods. They were typical hill-folk, youngish and perhaps a little more ambitious than most, and looked forward to a life of better returns for their hard work than they had had in Arkansas. Both were lean, raw-boned specimens; the man sandy, and gray-eyed, and the woman short and rather dark, with a black straightness of hair suggesting a slight Indian admixture.

In general, there was very little of distinction about them, and but for one thing their annals might not have differed from those thousands of other pioneers who flocked into the new country at that time. That thing was Walker's almost epileptic fear of snakes, which some laid to prenatal causes, and some said came from a dark prophecy about his end with which an old Indian squaw had tried to scare him when he was small. Whatever the cause, the effect was marked indeed; for despite his strong general courage the very mention of a snake would cause him to grow faint and pale, while the sight of even a tiny specimen would produce a shock sometimes bordering on a convulsion seizure.

The Davises started out early in the year, in the hope of being on their new land for the spring plowing. Travel was slow; for the roads were bad in Arkansas, while in the Territory there were great stretches of rolling hills and red, sandy barrens without any roads whatever. As the terrain grew flatter, the change from their native mountains depressed them more, perhaps, than they realized, but they found the people at the Indian agencies very affable, while most of the settled Indians seemed friendly and civil. Now and then they encountered a fellow-pioneer, with whom crude pleasantries and expressions of amiable rivalry were generally exchanged.

Owing to the season, there were not many snakes in evidence, so Walker did not suffer from his special temperamental weakness. In the earlier stages of the journey, too, there were no Indian snake legends to trouble him; for the transplanted tribes from the southeast do not share the wilder beliefs of their western neighbors. As fate would have it, it was a white man at Okmulgee in the Creek country who gave the Davises the first hint of the Yig beliefs; a hint which had a curiously fascinating effect on Walker, and caused him to ask questions very freely after that.

Before long Walker's fascination had developed into a bad case of fright. He took the most extraordinary precautions at each of the nightly camps, always clearing away whatever vegetation he found, and avoiding stony places whenever he could. Every clump of stunted bushes and every cleft in the great, slab-like rocks seemed to him now to hide malevolent serpents, while every human figure not obviously part of a settlement or emigrant train seemed to him a potential snake-god till nearness had proved the contrary. Fortunately no troublesome encounters came at this stage to shake his nerves still further.

As they approached the Kickapoo country they found it harder and harder to avoid camping near rocks. Finally it was no longer possible, and poor Walker was reduced to the puerile expedient of droning some of the rustic anti-snake charms he had learned in his boyhood. Two or three times a snake was really glimpsed, and these sights did not help the sufferer in his efforts to preserve composure.

On the twenty-second evening of the journey a savage wind made it imperative, for the sake of the mules, to camp in as sheltered a spot as possible; and Audrey persuaded her husband to take advantage of a cliff which rose uncommonly high above the dried bed of a former tributary of the Canadian River. He did not like the rocky cast of the place, but allowed himself to be overruled this once; leading the animals sullenly toward the protecting slope, which the nature of the ground would not allow the wagon to approach.

Audrey, examining the rocks near the wagon, meanwhile noticed a singular sniffing on the part of the feeble old dog. Seizing a rifle, she followed his lead, and presently thanked her stars that she had forestalled Walker in her discovery. For there, snugly nested in the gap between two boulders, was a sight it would have done him no good to see. Visible only as one convoluted expanse, but perhaps comprising as many as three or four separate units, was a mass of lazy wriggling which could not be other than a brood of newborn rattlesnakes.

Anxious to save Walker from a trying shock, Audrey did not hesitate to act, but took the gun firmly by the barrel and brought the butt down again and again upon the writhing objects. Her own sense of loathing was great, but it did not amount to a real fear. Finally she saw that her task was done, and turned to cleanse the improvised bludgeon in the red sand and dry, dead grass near by. She must, she reflected, cover the nest up before Walker got back from tethering the mules. Old Wolf, tottering relic of mixed shepherd and coyote ancestry that he was, had vanished, and she feared he had gone to fetch his master.

Footsteps at that instant proved her fear well founded. A second more, and Walker had seen everything. Audrey made a move to catch him if he should faint, but he did no more than sway. Then the look of pure fright on his bloodless face turned slowly to something like mingled awe and anger, and he began to upbraid his wife in trembling tones.

"Gawd's sake, Aud, but why'd ye go for to do that? Hain't ye heerd all the things they've ben tellin' about this snake-devil Yig? Ye'd ought to a told me, and we'd a moved on. Don't ye know they's a devil-god what gets even if ye hurts his children? What d'ye think the Injuns all dances and beats their drums in the fall about? This land's under a curse, I can tell ye—nigh every soul we've a-talked to sence we come in's said the same. Yig rules here, an' he comes out every fall for to git his victims and turn 'm into snakes. Why, Aud, they won't none of them Injuns acrost the Canayjin kill a snake for love nor money!

"Gawd knows what ye done to yourself, gal, a-stompin' out a hull brood o' Yig's chillen. He'll git ye, sure, sooner or later, unlessen I kin buy a charm offen some o' the Injun medicine-men. He'll git ye, Aud, as sure's they's a Gawd in heaven—he'll come outa the night and turn ye into a crawlin' spotted snake!"

All the rest of the journey Walker kept up the frightened reproofs and prophecies. They crossed the Canadian near Newcastle, and soon afterward met with the first of the real plains Indians they had seen—a party of blanketed Wichitas, whose leader talked freely under the spell of the whisky offered him, and taught poor Walker a long-winded protective charm against Yig in exchange for a quart bottle of the same inspiring fluid. By the end of the week the chosen site in the Wichita country was reached, and the Davises made haste to trace their boundaries and perform the spring plowing before even beginning the construction of a cabin.

The region was flat, drearily windy, and sparse of natural vegetation, but promised great fertility under cultivation. Occasional outcroppings of granite diversified a soil of decomposed red sandstone, and here and there a great flat rock would stretch along the surface of the ground like a man-made floor. There seemed to be very few snakes, or possible dens for them; so Audrey at last persuaded Walker to build the one-room cabin over a vast, smooth slab of exposed stone. With such a flooring and with a good-sized fireplace the wettest weather might be defied—though it soon became evident that dampness was no salient quality of the district. Logs were hauled in the wagon from the nearest belt of woods, many miles toward the Wichita Mountains.

Walker built his wide-chimneyed cabin and crude barn with the aid of the other settlers, though the nearest one was over a mile away. In turn, he helped his helpers at similar hourse-raisings, so that many ties of friendship sprang up between the new neighbors. There was no town worthy the name nearer than El Reno, on the railway thirty miles or more to the northeast; and before many weeks had passed, the people of the section had become very cohesive despite the wideness of their scattering. The Indians, a few of whom had begun to settle down on ranches, were for the most part harmless, though somewhat quarrelsome when fired by the liquid stimulation which found its way to them despite all Government bans.

Of all the neighbors the Davises found Joe and Sally Compton, who likewise hailed from Arkansas, the most helpful and congenial. Sally is still alive, known now as Grandma Compton; and her son Clyde, then an infant in arms, has become one of the leading men of the State. Sally and Audrey used to visit each other often for their cabins were only two miles apart; and in the long spring and summer afternoons they exchanged many a tale of old Arkansas and many a rumor about the new country.

Sally was very sympathetic about Walker's weakness regarding snakes, but perhaps did more to aggravate than cure the parallel nervousness which Audrey was acquiring through his incessant praying and prophesying about the curse of Yig. She was uncommonly full of gruesome snake stories, and produced a direfully strong impression with her acknowledged masterpiece —the tale of a man in Scott County who had been bitten by a whole horde of rattlers at once, and had swelled so monstrously from poison that his body had finally burst with a pop. Needless to say, Audrey did not repeat this anecdote to her husband, and she implored the Comptons to beware of starting it on the rounds of the countryside. It is to Joe's and Sally's credit that they heeded this plea with the utmost fidelity.

Walker did his corn-planting early, and in midsummer improved his time by harvesting a fair crop of the native grass of the region. With the help of Joe Compton he dug a well which gave a moderate supply of very good water, though he planned to sink an artesian later on. He did not run into many serious snake scares, and made his land as inhospitable as possible for wriggling visitors. Every now and then he rode over to the cluster of thatched, conical huts which formed the main village of the Wichitas, and talked along with the old men and shamans about the snake-god and how to nullify his wrath. Charms were always ready in exchange for whisky, but much of the information he got was far from reassuring.

Yig was a great god. He was bad medicine. He did not forget things. In the autumn his children were hungry and wild, and Yig was hungry and wild, too. All the tribes made medicine against Yig when the corn harvest came. They gave him some corn, and danced in proper regalia to the sound of whistle, rattle, and drum. They kept the drums pounding to drive Yig away, and called down the aid of Tirawa, whose children men are, even as the snakes are Yig's children. It was bad that the squaw of Davis killed the children of Yig. Let Davis say the charms many times when the corn harvest comes. Yig is Yig. Yig is a great god.

By the time the corn harvest did come, Walker had succeeded in getting his wife into a deplorably jumpy state. His prayers and borrowed incantations came to be a nuisance; and when the autumn rites of the Indians began, there was always a distant wind-borne pounding of tom-toms to lend an added background of the sinister. It was maddening to have the muffled clatter always stealing over the wide, red plains. Why would it never stop? Day and night, week on week, it was always going in exhaustless relays, as persistently as the red dusty winds that carried it. Audrey loathed it more than her husband did, for he saw in it a compensating element of protection. It was with this sense of a mighty, intangible bulwark against evil that he got in his corn crop and prepared cabin and stable for the coming winter.

The autumn was abnormally warm, and except for their primitive cookery the Davises found scant use for the stone fireplace Walker had built with such care. Something in the unnaturalness of the hot dust-clouds preyed on the nerves of all the settlers, but most of all on Audrey's and Walker's. The notions of a hovering snake-curse and the weird, endless rhythm of the distant Indian drums formed a bad combination which any added element of the bizarre went far to render utterly unendurable.

Notwithstanding this strain, several festive gatherings were held at one or another of the cabins after the crops were reaped; keeping naively alive in modernity those curious rites of the harvest-home which are as old as human agriculture itself. Lafayette Smith, who came from southern Missouri had a cabin about three miles east of Walker's, was a very passable fiddler; and his tunes did much to make the celebrants forget the monotonous beating of the distant tom-toms. Then Halloween drew near, and the settlers planned another frolic—this time, had they but known it, of a lineage older than even agriculture; the dread Witch-Sabbath of the primal pre-Aryans, kept alive through ages in the midnight blackness of secret woods, and still hinting at vague terrors under its latterday mask of comedy and lightness. Halloween was to fall on a Thursday, and the neighbors agreed to gather for their first revel at the Davis cabin.

It was on that thirty-first of October that the warm spell broke. The morning was gray and leaden, and by noon the incessant winds had changed from searingness to rawness. People shivered all the more because they were not prepared for the chill, and Walker Davis's old dog, Wolf, dragged himself wearily indoors to a place beside the hearth. But the distant drums still thumped on, nor were the white citizenry less inclined to pursue their chosen rites. As early as four in the afternoon the wagons began to arrive at Walker's cabin; and in the evening, after a memorable barbecue, Lafayette Smith's fiddle inspired a very fair-sized company to great feats of saltatory grotesqueness in the one good-sized but crowded room. The younger folk indulged in the amiable inanities proper to the season, and now and then old Wolf would howl with doleful and spine-tickling ominousness at some especially spectral strain from Lafayette's squeaky violin—a device he had never heard before. Mostly, though, this battered veteran slept through the merriment, for he was past the age of active interests and lived largely in his dreams. Tom and Jennie Rigby had brought their collie Zeke along, but the canines did not fraternize. Zeke seemed strangely uneasy over something, and nosed around curiously all the evening.

Audrey and Walker made a fine couple on the floor, and Grandma Compton still likes to recall her impression of their dancing that night. Their worries seemed forgotten for the nonce, and Walker was shaved and trimmed into a surprising degree of spruceness. By ten o'clock all hands were healthily tired, and the guests began to depart family by family with many handshakings and bluff assurances of what a fine time everybody had had. Tom and Jennie thought Zeke's eery howls as he followed them to their wagon were marks of regret at having to go home; though Audrey said it must be the far-away tom-toms which annoyed him, for the distant thumping was surely ghastly enough after the merriment within.

The night was bitterly cold, and for the first time Walker put a great log in the fireplace and banked it with ashes to keep it smoldering till morning. Old Wolf dragged himself within the ruddy glow and lapsed into his customary coma. Audrey and Walker, too tired to think of charms or curses, tumbled into the rough pine bed and were asleep before the cheap alarm-clock on the mantel had ticked out three minutes. And from far away, the rhythmic pounding of those hellish tom-toms still pulsed on the chill night wind.

Doctor McNeill paused here and removed his glasses, as if a blurring of the objective world might make the reminiscent vision clearer.

"You'll soon appreciate," he said, "that I had a great deal of difficulty in piecing out all that happened after the guests left. There were times, though—at first—when I was able to make a try at it." After a moment of silence he went on with the tale.

Audrey had terrible dreams of Yig, who appeared to her in the guise of Satan as depicted in cheap engravings she had seen. It was, indeed, from an absolute ecstasy of nightmare that she started suddenly awake to find Walker already conscious and sitting up in bed. He seemed to be listening intently to something and silenced her with a whisper when she began to ask what had aroused him.

"Hark, Aud!" he breathed. "Don't ye hear somethin' a-singin' and buzzin' and rustlin'? D'ye reckon it's the fall crickets?"

Certainly, there was distinctly audible within the cabin such a sound as he had described. Audrey tried to analyze it, and was impressed with some element at once horrible and familiar, which hovered just outside the rim of her memory. And beyond it all, waking a hideous thought, the monotonous beating of the distant tom-toms came incessantly across the black plains on which a cloudy half-moon had set.

"Walker—s'pose it's—the—the—curse o' Yig?"

She could feel him tremble.

"No, gal, I don't reckon he comes that way. He's shapen like a man, except ye look at him closet. That's what Chief Gray Eagle says. This here's some varmints come in outen the cold—not crickets, I calc'late, but summat like 'em. I orter git up and stomp 'em out afore they make much headway or git at the cupboard."

He rose, felt for the lantern that hung within easy reach, and rattled the tin match-box nailed to the wall beside it. Audrey sat up in bed and watched the flare of the match grow into the steady glow of the lantern. Then, as their eyes began to take in the whole of the room, the crude rafters shook with the frenzy of their simultaneous shriek. For the flat, rocky floor, revealed in the new-born illumination, was one seething, brown-speckled mass of wriggling rattlesnakes, slithering toward the fire, and even now turning their loathsome heads to menace the fright-blasted lantern-bearer.

It was only for an instant that Audrey saw the things. The reptiles were of every size, of uncountable numbers, and apparently of several varieties; and even as she looked, two or three of them reared their heads as if to strike at Walker. She did not faint—it was Walker's crash to the floor that extinguished the lantern and plunged her into blackness. He had not screamed a second time—fright had paralyzed him, and he fell as if shot by a silent arrow from no mortal's bow. To Audrey the entire world seemed to whirl about fantastically, mingling with the nightmare from which she had started.

Voluntary motion of any sort was impossible, for will and the sense of reality had left her. She fell back inertly on her pillow, hoping that she would wake soon. No actual sense of what had happened penetrated her mind for some time. Then, little by little, the suspicion that she was really awake began to dawn on her; and she was convulsed with a mounting blend of panic and grief which made her long to shriek out despite the inhibiting spell which kept her mute.

Walker was gone and she had not been able to help him. He had died of snakes, just as the old witch-woman had predicted when he was a little boy. Poor Wolf had not been able to help, either—probably he had not even awakened from his senile stupor. And now the crawling things must be coming for her, writhing closer and closer every moment in the dark, perhaps even now twining slipperily about the bedposts and oozing up over the coarse woolen blankets. Unconsciously she crept under the clothes and trembled.

It must be the curse of Yig. He had sent his monstrous children on

All-Hallow's Night, and they had taken Walker first. Why was that—wasn't he innocent enough? Why not come straight for her—hadn't she killed those littler rattlers alone? Then she thought of the curse's form as told by the Indians. She wouldn't be killed—just turned to a spotted snake. Ugh! So she would be like those things she had glimpsed on the floor—those things which Yig had sent to get her and enroll her among their number! She tried to mumble a charm that Walker had taught her, but found she could not utter a single sound.

The noisy ticking of the alarm-clock sounded above the maddening beat of the distant tom-toms. The snakes were taking a long time—did they mean to delay on purpose to play on her nerves? Every now and then she thought she felt a steady, insidious pressure on the bedclothes, but each time it turned out to be only the automatic twitchings of her over-wrought nerves. The clock ticked on in the dark, and a change came slowly over her thoughts.

Those snakes couldn't have taken so long! They couldn't be Yig's messengers after all, but just natural rattlers that were nested below the rock and had been drawn there by the fire. They weren't coming for her, perhaps—perhaps they had sated themselves on poor Walker. Where were they now? Gone? Coiled by the fire? Still crawling over the prone corpse of their victim? The clock ticked, and the distant drums throbbed on.

At the thought of her husband's body lying there in the pitch blackness a thrill of purely physical horror passed over Audrey. That story of Sally Compton's about the man back in Scott County! He, too, had been bitten by a whole bunch of rattlesnakes, and what had happened to him? The poison had rotted the flesh and swelled the whole corpse, and in the end the bloated thing had burst horribly—burst horribly with a detestable popping noise. Was that what was happening to Walker down there on the rock floor? Instinctively she felt she had begun to listen for something too terrible even to name to herself.

The clock ticked on, keeping a kind of mocking, sardonic time with the far-off drumming that the night wind brought. She wished it were a striking clock, so that she could know how long this eldritch vigil must last. She cursed the toughness of fiber, that kept her from fainting, and wondered what sort of relief the dawn could bring, after all. Probably neighbors would pass—no doubt somebody would call—would they find her still sane? Was she still sane now?

Morbidly listening, Audrey all at once became aware of something which she had to verify with every effort of her will before she could believe it; and which, once verified, she did not know whether to welcome or dread. The distant beating of the Indian tom-toms had ceased.

She did not relish this new and sudden silence, after all! There was something sinister about it. The loud-ticking clock seemed abnormal in its new loneliness. Capable at last of conscious motion, she shook the covers from her face and looked into the darkness toward the window. It must have cleared after the moon set, for she saw the square aperture distinctly against the background of stars.

Then without warning came that shocking, unutterable sound—ugh!—
that dull pop of cleft skin and escaping poison in the dark. God!—the bonds
of muteness snapped, and the black night waxed reverberant with Audrey's
screams of stark, unbridled frenzy.

Consciousness did not pass away with the shock. How merciful if only it
had! Amidst the echoes of her shrieking Audrey still saw the star-sprinkled
square of window ahead, and heard the doom-boding ticking of that frightful
clock. Did she hear another sound? Was that square window still a perfect
square? She was in no condition to weigh the evidence of her sense or
distinguish between fact and hallucination.

No—that window was not a perfect square. Something had encroached on
the lower edge. Nor was the ticking of the clock the only sound in her room.
There was, beyond dispute, a heavy breathing neither her own nor poor
Wolf's. Wolf slept very silently, and his wakeful wheezing was unmistakable. Then Audrey saw against the stars the black, demoniac silhouette of
something anthropoid—the undulant bulk of a gigantic head and shoulders
fumbling slowly toward her.

"Y'aaaah! Y'aaaah! Go away! Go away! Go away, snake devil! Go'way,
Yig! I didn't mean to kill 'em—I was feared he'd be scairt of 'em. Don't Yig,
don't! I didn't go for to hurt yore chillen—don't come nigh me—don't come
nigh me—don't change me into no spotted snake!"

But the half-formless head and shoulders only lurched onward toward the
bed very silently.

Everything snapped at once inside Audrey's head, and in a second she had
turned from a cowering child to a raging madwoman. She knew where the ax
was—hung against the wall on those pegs near the lantern. It was within easy
reach, and she could find it in the dark. Before she was conscious of anything
further it was in her hands, and she was creeping toward the foot of the
bed—toward the monstrous head and shoulders that every moment groped
their way nearer. Had there been any light, the look on her face would not
have been pleasant to see.

"Take that, you! And that, and that, and that!"

She was laughing shrilly now, and her crackles mounted higher as she saw
that the starlight beyond the window was yielding to the dim prophetic pallor
of coming dawn.

Doctor McNeill wiped the perspiration from his forehead and put on his
glasses again. I waited for him to resume, and as he kept silent, I spoke
softly.

"She lived? She was found? Was it ever explained?"

The doctor cleared his throat.

"Yes—she lived, in a way. And it was explained. I told you there was no
bewitchment—only cruel, pitiful, material horror."

It was Sally Compton who had made the discovery. She had ridden over to
the Davis cabin the next afternoon to talk over the party with Audrey, and
had seen no smoke from the chimney. That was queer. It had turned very
warm again, yet Audrey was usually cooking something at that hour. The

mules were making hungry-sounding noises in the barn, and there was no sign of old Wolf sunning himself in the accustomed spot by the door.

Altogether, Sally did not like the look of the place, so was very timid and hesitant as she dismounted and knocked. She got no answer, but waited some time before trying the crude door of split logs. The lock, it appeared, was unfastened; and she slowly pushed her way in. Then, perceiving what was there, she reeled back, gasped, and clung to the jamb to preserve her balance.

A terrible odor had welled out as she opened the door, but that was not what had stunned her. It was what she had seen. For within that shadowy cabin monstrous things had happened and three shocking objects remained on the floor to awe and baffle the beholder.

Near the burned-out fireplace was the great dog—purple decay on the skin left bare by mange and old age, and the whole carcass burst by the puffing effect of rattlesnake poison. It must have been bitten by a veritable legion of the reptiles.

To the right of the door was the ax-hacked remnant of what had been a man—clad in a nightshirt, and with the shattered bulk of a lantern clenched in one hand. He was totally free from any sign of snake-bite. Near him lay the ensanguined ax, carelessly discarded.

And wriggling flat on the floor was a loathsome, vacant-eyed thing that had been a woman, but was now only a mute mad caricature. All that this thing could do was to hiss, and hiss, and hiss.

Both the doctor and I were brushing cold drops from our foreheads by this time. He poured something from a flask on his desk, took a nip, and handed another glass to me. I could only suggest tremulously and stupidly:

"So Walker had only fainted that first time—the screams roused him, and the ax did the rest?"

"Yes." Doctor McNeill's voice was low. "But he met his death from snakes just the same. It was his fear working in two ways—it made him faint, and it made him fill his wife with the wild stories that caused her to strike out when she thought she saw the snake devil."

I thought for a moment.

"And Audrey—wasn't it queer how the curse of Yig seemed to work itself out on her? I suppose the impression of hissing snakes had been fairly ground into her."

"Yes. There were lucid spells at first, but they got to be fewer and fewer. Her hair came white at the roots as it grew, and later began to fall out. The skin grew blotchy, and when she died—"

I interrupted with a start.

"Died? Then what was that—that thing downstairs?"

Doctor McNeill spoke gravely.

"That is what was born to her three-quarters of a year afterwards. There were three more of them—two were even worse—but this is the only one that lived."

OREGON

Peekaboo
by Bill Pronzini

ROPER CAME awake with the feeling that he wasn't alone in the house.

He sat up in bed, tense and wary, a crawling sensation on the back of his scalp. The night was dark, overcast; the rain that seemed always to dampen the Oregon seacoast had quit for the time being and the clotted black that surrounded him was cold and silent. He rubbed sleep-mucus from his eyes, blinking, until he could make out the vague grayish outlines of the window in one wall.

Ears straining, he listened. But there wasn't anything to hear. The house seemed almost graveyard still, void of even the faintest of night sounds.

What was it that had awakened him? A noise of some kind? An intuition of danger? It might only have been a bad dream, except that the feeling of not being alone was strong and urgent.

There's somebody in the house, he thought.

Or some *thing* in the house?

In spite of himself Roper remembered the story the nervous real estate agent in White River had told him about this place. It had been built in the early 1900s by a local family, and when the last of them died off a generation later it was sold to a man named Lavolle who had come to Oregon from some place back east and who had lived here for forty years. Lavolle had been a recluse whom the locals considered strange and probably evil; they hadn't had anything to do with him. But then he'd died five years ago, of natural causes, and evidence had been found by county officials that he'd been "some kind of devil worshiper" who had "practiced all sorts of dark rites." That was all the real estate agent would say about it.

Word had gotten out about that and a lot of people seemed to believe the

501

house was haunted or cursed or something. For that reason, and becaused it was isolated and in ramshackle condition, it had stayed empty until a couple of years ago. Then a man called Garber, who was an amateur parapsychologist, leased the place and lived in it for ten days. At the end of that time somebody came out from White River to deliver groceries and found Garber dead. Murdered. The real estate agent wouldn't talk about how he'd been killed; nobody else would talk about it either.

Some people thought it was ghosts or demons that had murdered Garber. Others figured it was a lunatic—maybe the same one who'd killed half a dozen people in this sparsely populated section of southern Oregon over the past couple of years. Roper didn't belive in ghosts or demons or things that went bump in the night; that kind of supernatural stuff was for rural types like the ones in White River. He believed in psychotic killers, all right, but he wasn't afraid of them; he wasn't afraid of anybody or anything. He'd made his living with a gun too long for that. And the way things were for him now, since the bank job in Portland had gone sour two weeks ago, an isolated back-country place like this was just what he needed for a few months.

So he'd leased the house under a fake name, claiming to be a writer, and he'd been here for eight days. Nothing had happened in that time: no ghosts, no demons, no strange lights or wailings or rattling chains—and no lunatics or burglars or visitors of any kind. Nothing at all.

Until now.

Well, if he *wasn't* alone in the house, it was because somebody human had come in. And he sure as hell knew how to deal with a human intruder. He pushed the blankets aside, swung his feet out of bed, and eased open the nightstand drawer. His fingers groped inside, found his .38 revolver and the flashlight he kept in there with it; he took them out. Then he stood, shrugged into his robe; made his way carefully across to the bedroom door, opened it a crack, and listened.

The same heavy silence.

Roper pulled the door wide, switched on the flash, and probed the hallway with its beam. No one there. He stepped out, moving on the balls of his bare feet. There were four other doors along the hallway: two more bedrooms, a bathroom, and an upstairs sitting room. He opened each of the doors in turn, swept the rooms with the flash, then put on the overhead lights.

Empty, all of them.

He came back to the stairs. Shadows clung to them, filled the wide foyer below. He threw the light down there from the landing. Bare redwood walls, the lumpish shapes of furniture, more shadows crouching inside the arched entrances to the parlor and the library. But that was all: no sign of anybody, still no sounds anywhere in the chilly dark.

He went down the stairs, swinging the light from side to side. At the bottom he stopped next to the newel post and used the beam to slice into the blackness in the center hall. Deserted. He arced it around into the parlor, followed it with his body turned sideways to within a pace of the archway. More furniture, the big fieldstone fireplace at the far wall, the parlor windows reflecting glints of light from the flash. He glanced back at the heavy darkness inside the library, didn't see or hear any movement over that way, and reached out with his gun hand to flick the switch on the wall inside the parlor.

Nothing happened when the electric bulbs in the old-fashioned chandelier came on; there wasn't anybody lurking in there.

Roper turned and crossed to the library arch and scanned the interior with the flash. Empty bookshelves, empty furniture. He put on the chandelier. Empty room.

He swung the cone of the light past the staircase, into the center hall—and then brought it back to the stairs and held it there. The area beneath them had been walled on both sides, as it was in a lot of these old houses in the Pacific Northwest, to form a coat or storage closet; he'd found that out when he first moved in and opened the small door that was set into the staircase on this side. But it was just an empty space now, full of dust—

The back of his scalp tingled again. And a phrase from when he was a kid playing hide-and-seek games popped into his mind.

Peekaboo, I see you. Hiding under the stair.

His fingers tightened around the butt of the .38. He padded forward cautiously, stopped in front of the door. And reached out with the hand holding the flash, turned the knob, jerked the door open, and aimed the light and the gun inside.

Nothing.

Roper let out a breath, backed away to where he could look down the hall again. The house was still graveyard quiet; he couldn't even hear the faint grumblings its old wooden joints usually made in the night. It was as if the whole place was wrapped in a breathless waiting hush. As if there was some kind of unnatural presence at work here—

To hell with that, he told himself angrily. No such things as ghosts and demons. There seemed to be a presence here, all right—he could feel it just as strongly as before—but it was a human presence. Maybe a burglar, maybe a tramp or some long-haired kid on his way south to California, maybe even a goddamn lunatic. But *human*.

He snapped on the hall lights and went along there to the archway that led into the downstairs sitting room. First the flash and then the electric wall lamps told him it was deserted. The dining room off the parlor next. And the kitchen. And the rear porch.

Still nothing.

Where was he, damn it? Where was he hiding?

The cellar? Roper thought.

It didn't make sense that whoever it was would have gone down there. The cellar was a huge room, walled and floored in stone, that ran under most of the house; there wasn't anything in it except spiderwebs and stains on the

floor that he didn't like to think about, not after the real estate agent's story
about Lavolle and his dark rites. But it was the only place left that he hadn't
searched.

In the kitchen again, Roper crossed to the cellar door. Outside the rain
started up, making a dull hollow drumbeat on the roof. Damn rain. No
wonder Oregon was green the year round. He should have gone south
himself, to where it was warm and dry. Well, maybe that was what he'd do
after all. And soon.

The door knob turned soundlessly under his hand. With the door open a
crack, he peered into the thick darkness below and listened. But there
wasn't anything to hear, not with that rain thumping down.

He started to reach inside for the light switch. Then he remembered that
there wasn't any bulb in the socket above the stairs; he'd explored the cellar
by flashlight before, and he hadn't bothered to buy a bulb. He widened the
opening and aimed the flash downward, fanning it slowly from left to right
and up and down over the stone walls and floor. Shadowy shapes appeared
and disappeared in the bobbing light: furnace, storage shelves, a wooden
wine rack, the blackish gleaming stains at the far end, spiderwebs like
tattered curtains hanging from the ceiling beams.

Roper hesitated, feeling the damp chill that came up from below. Nobody
down there either, he thought. Nobody in the house after all? The feeling
that he wasn't alone kept nagging at him—but it *could* be nothing more than
imagination. All that business about devil worshiping and ghosts and
demons and Garber being murdered and psychotic killers on the loose might
have affected him more than he'd figured. Might have jumbled together in
his subconscious all week and finally come out tonight, making him imagine
menace where there wasn't any. Sure, maybe that was it.

But he had to make certain. He couldn't see all of the cellar from up here;
he had to go down and give it a full search before he'd be satisfied that he
really was alone. Otherwise he'd never be able to get back to sleep tonight.

Playing the light again, he descended the stairs in the same wary
movements as before. The beam showed him nothing. Except for the faint
whisper of his breathing, the creak of the risers when he put his weight on
them, the stillness remained unbroken; he couldn't even hear the rain down
here. The odors of dust and decaying wood and subterranean dampness
dilated his nostrils, made him breathe through his mouth.

When he came off the last of the steps he took a half-dozen strides into the
middle of the cellar. The stones were cold and clammy against the soles of his
bare feet; he shivered in spite of himself. Turning to the right, he let the
beam and his body transcribe a slow circle until he was facing the stairs.

Nothing to see, nothing to hear.

But with the light on the staircase, he realized that part of the wide, dusty
area beneath them was invisible from where he stood—a mass of clotted
shadow. The vertical boards between the risers kept the beam from reaching
all the way under there.

The phrase from when he was a kid repeated itself in his mind: *Peekaboo, I see you. Hiding under the stair.*

With the gun and the flash extended at arms' length, he went diagonally to his right. The light cut away some of the thick gloom under the staircase, letting him see naked stone draped with more gray webs. He moved closer to the stairs, ducked under them, and put the beam full on the far joining of the walls.

Empty.

For the first time Roper began to relax. Imagination, no doubt about it now. No ghosts or demons, no burglars or lunatics hiding under the stair. A thin smile curved the corners of his mouth. Hell, the only one hiding under the stair was himself—

"Peekaboo," a voice behind him said.

PENNSYLVANIA

Bird of Prey
by Nelson S. Bond

THIS IS not a nice story. This is a grim and dark and ugly story, and if it is fine tales of high adventure you would be reading, and they dealing with grand strong men that do meet the buffets of the world with a flashing blade and a ready wit and the roar of laughter on their lips, then you had best be picking up some other book, a happier romance prepared for your entertainment by someone who has nought on his mind but the telling of such gay tales. For this is a strange and, it may be, an unpleasant story. But it is most terribly a true one. . . .

From the green hills of Eire came my Uncle Michael to dwell with us in the red brick city of Philadelphia. He came in the dung-reeking hold of a cattle boat, one hop and a skip and only a part of a jump ahead of the Black and Tan to the City of Brotherly Love, for it was there that my father, his brother, had made his home and his livelihood since a decade of years. There too had my father raised a family of five lad, for 'tis the way of the O'Hallorans, if mayhap a wee sorrow to the women they do make their wives, to run largely to boy children. Why this should be so I do not rightly know. The biologists speak sagely of chromosomes, and of cells called x and y. Let these matters be their concern. I know only that the O'Halloran children run for the most part to males, and that when rarely a colleen is born to one of our name it is a cause for great celebration, for much dancing and singing and drinking, and perhaps even for a darkling shred of suspicion.

But let that pass. I had not meant to speak here of my uncle Rory and aunt Kathleen, and of that handsome young boarder to whom in later years my uncle took so oddly violent a dislike. This tale is of Michael O'Halloran,

507

who came from the Emerald Isle to live with us in the red brick city of Philadelphia.

That we were all of us glad to see him is a thing that needs no questioning. That we were still glad to have him with us after a spring had passed, and a fall, and the greater part of a year, is another matter entirely. My father, yes. There was never the time he was not proud to have a bed in his home for his brother. We children, too, were happier for his presence. For he was not a worldly man, my uncle Michael, but he was a man who knew much about those things which are the marvels of this world; the things that are important to the young. To walk with him in those patches of woodland which in the year 1919 still girdled even the great cities was a wonder and a revelation and a joy. Because my uncle Michael was wise in those ways of which the average man knows nothing.

The trees were his friends; by their green he could name them in the season of leaf, and by their bark in the wintertime. He showed us how to grind the coarse crust of the shagbark hickory between our palms and make of it a redolent magic powder: "fairy dust" he called it. He could cut a slim finger-length of willow, slip its smooth skin from the green wood beneath as slick as an eel's hide, cut a sliver from the wood and properly notch the bark, then put both together again to make for a lad the loveliest whistle as ever the ear might hear. From the green-bleeding bole of tall pines he dug us thick chunks of savory gum to chew, while from the thin, white, peeling skin of the silver birch he made us the finest parchment rolls young pirates could ask to draw their maps of buried treasure.

The plants, too, were his intimates, and there was no shrub but that he knew its faults and virtues. He taught us which bright berries might be eaten, and which not; made us familiar with the healing power of the slender witches' hazel, and the fine, strong, aromatic flavor of sassafras that, brewed to a tea, will ward off nightmares and baldness. He had the green touch, had my uncle Michael, and even in that thwarted square of pebbly clay which was the back yard of our row house did he succeed in growing (to my mother's delight and to the everlasting amazement of our neighbors) a miniature paradise of color.

So the wild things that grow with sap for blood. But his province was the knowledge, too, of breathing things, and it was from my uncle Michael that we lads learned early the ways and haunts and secrets of the animals. For he knew how to find by its rift in the hedge the secret lair of the groundhog, and the tangled bramble patch was no maze to him who knew by an unfathomable instinct where the coney would build its burrow. He could point out the tunnel of the shovel-pawed mole, and it humping its wee blind way beneath the grassy layer of earth's skin; he knew in which trees nested the gray squirrels and the red, and it was from him we learned why these hated each other with so deadly a ferocity.

All this and so much more. The birds would answer his call, and the fish would strike at his lures when those of others dangled untouched in the water. He could tell of the weather tomorrow by the look of the moon tonight or the vagrant shifting of yesterday's wind. These were all a part of the tremendous and enviable knowledge held by my uncle Michael.

And of course all these things were good, but they did not cut much ice with my mother. For he was a man who knew the wonders of this world, was my uncle Michael, but he was not a worldly man. And it is sorry truth to tell that after a time his living at our home became a burden on us. For my father was far from a wealthy man. And when there are five young healthy bodies to feed, as well as the head of the house and his good wife, and they not one of them lending an ear to newfangled fiddle-faddle on the virtue of vegetable diets and green salads and suchlike slimming nonsense; when there are these mouths to feed, then an extra one, no matter how delightful the words of wisdom that do be flowing from it between meals, becomes a cause to furrow the brow when the cost of the food is considered.

"'Tis not, Tim, that I dislike your brother," my mother would plead, "nor that I diswant him in our home. But the carter's horse must pull its own weight. And when the man cannot even hold a job——"

"Now, Molly," my father would say, "do you not be condemning him out of hand, but try for a little patience with him. For 'tis new to our country he is, and not yet has he learned our ways."

"He knows the ways to the fishing streams," my mother retorted, "and the whistling ways to the hills, with the boys at his heels like a pack of young savages. And the way to Clancy's bar on the corner he knows, too, and the way to the sugarbowl in my kitchen, where he filches the silver to set up a round for the lads. Can he not, then, find the way to an employment office and a steady job, and himself the owner of a horse's appetite that is eating us out of house and home?"

"'Tis the man's small weakness that he dislikes routine work," placated my father. "But there's a genius in him all his own. If you'll be patient——"

"Patient! And have I not been patient these more than fifteen months? Tim *bach*, dear Timothy," wailed my mother, "sure and it's myself would be the last to come between you and your own blood kin. But the man must find work. Not only because of the expense—which God knows we can ill afford—but because it's the day long, the week 'round, that he's under foot in the house, and me not able to get a lick of work done for the endless yammer of him filling the lads' heads with superstitious nonsense."

Because this last, you see, was another grievance, and it no small one, that my mother held against my uncle Michael. For as he had learning of the things of nature, so had he also understanding of those things which some declare unnatural. And it was not to my mother's liking (though it was greatly to ours) that he should sit by the hour and tell us tales of those creatures and folk who invisibly cohabit this world with the race of man.

All manner of tales, both gay and grim, would he tell us of the ways and doings of the Little People: the diligent brownies, the mischievous pixies, and the fairies bedecked with their gossamer wings.

He would speak—and why not, having seem them?—of the tricks of the kelpies and nixies, of the curious games pigwidgeons play in their magic rings on the midsummer's eve. He had once grasped the bottlegreen coattails of a leprechaun, had my uncle Michael, and it was the sorriest mischance and a great bewailment to him that of overeagerness his fingers had slipped. Else, he told us with a sigh and a shake of the head, it was not himself that would be this day a penniless man, and him slyly lifting a poor dime or two from the sugarbowl now and again to slake his parching thirst. But had he held tight to the squealing little cobbler, then his would have been three fine wishes, along with that pot of gold which is buried in a place known to each whiskered little bogle.

He told us enchanting tales of the gnomes and imps and flibbertigibbets: gay creatures, each of them, and friends to man, if mayhap a mite mischievous. Yet others there were that were not so friendly-like, and it's make the small hairs at the back of our necks rise and creep he would with his tales of the plotting of goblins that do lay their own changeling spawn in the cradles of honest folk; of the wailing of gray banshees in the ominous shadows of nightfall; spine-tingling tales of the Women of the Shee, whose keening cry in the twilight is the telling of future trouble; and of the Bird of Prey, that terrible and monstrous white bird who comes to the bedside of dying folk to bear their souls away to a questionable peace in the heaven of Tirna nOg.

To us the hearing of these tales was a delicious and trembly sort of delight, the more so because we knew the stories to be true. For had not my uncle Michael seen these things with his own eyes? But to my mother, who held no truck with his nonsense, it was a great annoyance that my uncle Michael should make our hides crawl with their telling. And in simple candor, there was much justice to my mother's complaining. For this was the March of 1919, and if you are old enough to do so, you will recall that in that first postwar springtime there were jobs and aplenty for any man with a will to work. There was a crying demand for goods scarce these three long lateliest years, the construction of new homes was booming, and wages were as high as workmen were scarce. For also in that spring of 1919 there was sweeping this country (along with all others) that second wave of the Spanish influenza which left untouched scarce a household in the nation.

It was a dread of the flu as much as anything else that made my mother uncommonly irritable. For when there are people tumbling in the streets and being carted away to overcrowded hospitals in hastily summoned ambulances, when there are crude pine boxes stacked two storeys high on the sidewalks before undertaking establishments, when on the streets old friends wave cheery greeting to you, then walk into their homes never to be seen again save at the wake, and then lying cold and strange and waxenly unreal in their coffins; then it is that with five young sons, and they all of school age, any mother is like to find herself wrinkling a mite more at the forehead and silvering at the temples.

Like the others of our schoolmates we took the precautions of the day. We wore to our classrooms white oblong masks of sterile gauze tied bandit fashion over the nose and mouth and about the back of the head; we carried medallions and wore small, strong-smelling bags of the asafoetida about our necks. But the precautions were not enough. There was no day but that several of our playmates were missing from their desks. Some were to return days or weeks later, paler and thinner and older in the eyes; other were not ever to return.

So my mother was worried, and being worried was fretful, and being fretful spoke more sharply than was her way against the happy-go-lucky sloth of my uncle Michael. So sharply, indeed, that at the last her words were no complaint nor admonishment, but an ultimatum.

"Brother or no brother," one evening she told my father, "I am weary of his everlasting loafing. One more week, and one only, will I give him. If in that time he has not found a job, and a job he can hold, then it's out he goes, and a good riddance to him."

"But, Molly——" said my father, sorely troubled.

"A week," repeated my mother.

And there is no doubt in my mind but that she meant it; that at the end of a week's time she would have made good her threat. But before that week was up happened that which caused her quite to forget her impatience with uncle Michael and, indeed, all other things of trifling importance. For in that time it was that her second son, Dennis, fell ill of influenza. . . .

Now in this day of miracle drugs, and of great clean-corridored hospitals, and they awesome with the last word in every modern medical device, such illnesses are handled in ways that do not throw a household into chaos. But thirty-odd years ago the medical value of sulphur was known only to the old wives, and they mixing it strong and burny with thick black molasses when the strange spring slowness took the children. Then the life-giving penicillin was nought but a blue mold on the drying crusts of yesterday's bread. And in those days, too, were the hospitals so crammed to overflowing that the sick were best cared for at home. So into the back bedroom went Dennis, there to lie in a room darkened with drawn shades, while his father and four brothers were barred from the contagion of the isolation ward.

They five, so. But not my mother, who was in and out of the room a hundred times a day; now to take a fresh, fearful reading of the clinical thermometer, now to change the soaked sheets and pillow cases, again to bathe the poor burning body in alcohol applied with hands that for all their Monday-wash coarseness were astonishingly soft and tender, or to administer those elixirs and powders with which the inadequate medical science of the day strove to combat a plague about which it knew next to nothing.

And this was a task which, despite her willingness, would have been altogether too great for her had there not unexpectedly come to her aid another pair of hands. For it was in this hour of need that my uncle Michael came through to prove his place in our household.

He it was who forsook his woodland walks and his gabfests with his cronies at Clancy's saloon to sit for long hours in the sick lad's room, moving closer to the bed to narrate in his soothing voice beguiling stories whensoever it appeared that the patient in his fevered fretfulness might be able to understand some portion of what was being told him. He it was who most anxiously watched the grip of sickness tightening on Dennis, for he saw in its every stage the way this creeping disease attacked the boy's body.

He watched his patient through those first hot days of the fever, diligent to keep the patient covered in his bed when in delirium Dennis would claw back the blankets and comforters in unreasoned impulse to struggle from his bed; later, when drugged languor took the lad, withdrawing to the window-side, there to rock slowly back and forth, musing and thinking his own thoughts, unspeaking and silent, sucking on the cold bit of his pipe, and it untouched by match lest the pungent fumes of tobacco annoy the ailing lad.

He it was, too, who more closely than any other watched with grave anxiety as the thin red thread of the thermometer mounted daily ever higher and higher to that dangerous point which doctors call the crisis. He knew that very soon would come that moment when one of two things must happen—either the straining body must prove itself strong enough to fight the germs attacking it, or those tiny invaders must have their own way and claim the conquered body as their booty.

So he waited and watched, and curiously enough not all his watchful eyeing was of the sick lad himself, but an equal time or greater would my uncle Michael sit beside the small window of the shaded room rocking back and forth, back and forth, peering ever and again around the lifted corner of the blind into the daylight or darkness outside, as if in search of something.

So a third day passed, and a fourth, and dawned the fifth. And on that day there happened a strange thing. For my mother was in the sick room changing again the damp and fever-smelling sheets of the patient, and my uncle was at his usual post by the window. Then, as my mother tells it, a great grunt broke from the man, and she turned to see him lowering that corner of the shade which but a moment before he had been lifting. He rose from his chair, a curious dark look in his eyes, one of a thoughtful doubt not wholly free of fear. Then with a slow determination he pressed down the sash of the window.

"Michael," began my mother, "what——"

"'Tis blowing up sharper," he said. "The cold air might harm the lad. I'll be back in a minute, Molly." And he turned and walked swiftly from the room. She heard him rummaging about the house, first in his own bedroom, then in the cellar. When he returned a few minutes later he carried in his left hand a stick of kindling; in his right he held a caseknife with a murderous long blade. He settled himself again at his post beside the window, essayed a brief smile in my mother's direction, and mumbled a thin apology.

"It does get weary, the sitting," he said. "I thought a wee spell of whittling to let the hands think——"

My mother nodded absently. "As it pleases you, Michael. But a bit of paper on the floor to catch the shavings——?"

And there he sat that livelong day, beside the lowered window. But they were precious few shavings that fell from that strip of wood. My uncle Michael spent most of those hours sweeping that long and gleaming knifeblade back and forth, back and forth, in a tempo to match his rocking, on a whetstone he had carried from the kitchen.

It was so he sat at tea time when the doctor bustled in, all nerves and shadowed eyes and the smell of perspiration dried on clothes worn overlong. It is little blame to the man that he was brusque and edgy and irritable. These were fretful days for a man of medicine, and on this day he had seen much sorrow.

"Well," he greeted, "how is our young patient today?"

My mother ventured timidly, "About the same, doctor. His temperature is up a bit. But he hasn't been quite so restless."

The doctor's practiced hand fingered the patient's pulse while its mate traveled from brow to temple and lifted a drowsy eyelid that he might gauge the lad's condition.

"Then we can only wait," he said. "Continue the treatments and wait to see what course the fever takes. It may be several days yet; perhaps as much as a week."

My uncle Michael spoke from beside the window. "The lad," he said quietly, "will reach his crisis tonight."

The doctor turned, startled and surprised, to stare at him. "Indeed?" he snapped. "And who are you to say so?"

"'Tis my brother-in-law, Michael O'Halloran," said my mother hastily. "My husband's brother, that is lately come from the old country. He—he's been a great help to me, doctor."

"No doubt." The physician glanced contemptuously at my uncle's unpressed trousers, at the scarred and gnarly clumps that were his hands, and at his day's growth of beard. "You are a medical man, then? *Doctor* O'Halloran it is, I take it?"

"If you please, doctor," agonized my mother, "I'm sure he meant no harm. It's just that he's so concerned, as are we all."

"'Tis no doctor I am," said my uncle Michael, "but I'm telling you simple truth. The lad will come to his crisis tonight."

"Really, sir? And how do you know that?"

"Because——" began uncle Michael, and stopped. He shook his head, and his lips tightened. "Just—because," he repeated.

"Now, it is a great shame," said the doctor with a bit of a sneer in his voice, "that you cannot give me more of a hint than that. For it is a vital piece of information you're withholding from the medical profession, Mr. O'Halloran, if of all men you alone can tell when this baffling disease is due to reach its crisis. It would save us much time and trouble, and we as busy as we are."

Again there was that derisive sidelong glance at my uncle's rocking-chair, and at the carpet slippers dangling from his feet, and at the little heap of shavings to which, with a claspknife now honed to razor sharpness, my uncle was adding slowly and mechanically and doggedly.

"Well, then," said the doctor, turning to my mother, "If your wise kinsman will not share his knowledge, we must assume my treatment is correct. See that the lad gets his medicine regularly, feed him such liquids as you can get into him, keep him well covered and warm and supplied with plenty of fresh air. I'll be back at this time tomorrow. Good day to you. And to you, *Mister* O'Halloran," he crisped—and was off down the steps, his footsteps an indignant tattoo.

My mother busied herself with arranging the bedclothes until the front door had closed with a petulant slam. She was of no mind to be harsh with my uncle Michael these days, and him the great help he had been to her in her hour of trouble. Yet there was an annoyance on her, and she was never one to let her mind fester with an unspoken grievance.

She said at last reproachfully, "I would thank you, Michael, to hold your tongue when you're talking to learned men on things that do not concern you. 'Tis not for myself I ask it, but for the boy's own sake, and him lying helpless here, in need of the best care a doctor can give, and not the haphazard attention of an angered man."

Uncle Michael mumbled, "I'm sorry, Molly *beg*, little Molly. I was only trying to help. I didn't guess the man would take it amiss."

"But to advise a man in his own field——"

"Let him stick to his field, then, and me to mine. If his medical science cannot tell him the things my sense tells me——"

Uncle Michael stroked a long white sliver of shaving from his pine strip. Then carefully: "Believe me, Molly, I know what I say is true. Doctor or no doctor, this midnight is Dennis' crucial time."

"And how——" cried my mother, goaded finally beyond endurance—— "and how could you be after knowing that? You that have not a grade school diploma, let alone a letter to write after your name?"

"I know," said uncle Michael heavily. "I have a way of knowing. Is that not enough for you, Molly? Must a man always be telling everything he knows?"

"On matters of such importance, yes. If you know, then how! Is it something about the lad? The look in his eyes or something he said? The flush of his cheeks or the feel of his flesh?"

"'Tis none of those," said my uncle. "'Tis——" He drew a long, uncertain breath—— "If I told you, Molly," he said plaintively, "you wouldn't be believing me."

"Speak, man! What is it?"

Again my uncle Michael sighed wearily. His troubled eyes sought hers briefly, then turned away.

"'Tis the white bird, Molly. I saw him with my own eyes some hours since.

I saw him hovering and wheeling and curving above this house like a great, shining vulture, marking the place where he must come this night."

"White bird," cried my mother, uncomprehending. "*What* white bird?"

"The Bird of Prey, Molly darling. The white bird of death that does be coming from the dark country to bear away the poor, weak souls of them that have ended their time on earth." He hesitated, scrubbing one course-knuckled hand with the palm of the other. Then gently: "Forgive me, Molly, I meant to say nothing to fret you. But yourself forced me to say it. Would to God I had not seen the bird and known him for what he is."

But if he expected dismay of my mother, it was himself that got the surprise. For there was only outrage in her answer.

"White bird, Michael O'Halloran! Bird of Prey, indeed! Then it's on the fear of a silly superstition you'd be setting yourself up as an authority against the men of learning? Now *pogue ma hone* to you and your eternal tales of bogies and hobgoblins. 'Tis bad enough that for months you've been filling the children's heads with such nonsense. Do you not now be plaguing me with more of the same, when there are great needy things to be done."

"I saw him, Molly. The great white bird with the crimson eyes, and the slow, strong wings of silver. 'Tis the fey in me that lets me see such things."

"Fey! 'Tis the fool in you!" My mother flounced petulantly past him to unfasten and raise the window he had lowered some hours since. "Enough of such talk!" she cried. "So that's what caused you to close the sash, and you telling lies that the cool, fresh breeze might harm the lad?"

"Molly *bach*," begged my uncle Michael. "Molly darling, please lower the window again."

"Hush! Did you not hear what the doctor said? Plenty of fresh air."

"But the bird. It must be closed against him."

"As your mind is closed against wisdom? Tosh, Michael O'Halloran. Now, leave be!" she said sternly as he reached for the upraised sash. "And do you not again be lowering it one inch, do you hear?

"Or perhaps," she suggested, "you'd rather leave this room and this house and let someone with a clear head tend the child?"

My uncle Michael sighed and settled back into the chair from which he had half risen. "Very well, Molly," he said. "Have it as you will. I'll stay."

"And you'll not again lower the window?"

"Did I not give you my word?"

My mother said more kindly, "Very well, then. And Michael—do not be thinking I mean to be hard on you. 'Tis a simple difference of opinion, is all. Our ways in this new land are not old country ways, and it's to science and learning we look for advice, rather than to the folklore and the stories of the old wives.

"And sure, brother Michael," she went on more kindly yet, "it's overwrought and tired like myself you must be at having sat these five long anxious days in one little room. Would you not now like to go out a short while and make an evening of it with the friends you have not seen for nigh a week?"

Uncle Michael shook his head quietly. "No, thank you, Molly. I'd rather be here with the lad."

"I know your heart's with the boy," said my mother. "But it's myself can be taking care of him till you get back. And it comes to my mind there's a bit of silver in the sugarbowl that the groceryman could be sparing——"

My uncle Michael smiled a curious half smile, but shook his head. And he would not go out that night.

Now, I do not know how best to end this tale. There is an end to it, but not one to be reached in the proper way of authors. For it's they that do build their tales carefully, with the suspense mounting word by word and each incident more dramatic than the last until at the end there's such a grip on your heart and mind as glues your very eyes to the page. And it is tales the like of these you would have found had you turned, as I bade you long since, to another story in another book: to a gay tale of high adventure, perhaps, with a beautiful woman in it, and a strong and clear-eyed man, and them living happy every after with their mouths meeting warm and sweet.

But there's not that kind of ending to this story. This story dwindles off in silence and unsureness, and I am the sorrier for it. For more than yourself would I like to be certain what happened that night in the room of the fevered Dennis.

This only do I know: that my uncle Michael would not leave that room for a single instant of that night. There he sat and munched his lonely supper in the early hours of evening; there as darkness gathered he sat and rocked and chatted a brief while with my mother when she came to settle her son for the long night's rest, sat and chatted the while he stroked back and forth, back and forth in tempo to his chair's slow rocking, the wicked edge of his shiny whittling knife.

Then it was deep night, and the family was abed. All but my uncle Michael. He would not turn in for yet a while when at past ten o'clock my mother brought him a cup of steaming tea. He was that wide awake, he said, that his nerves were like wee red ants, and would she leave the hall light burning, there's the darling, and be off to bed now and not worrying her sweet head about him?

My mother said softly, "'Tis a good man you are, Michael O'Halloran. Could I say now I'm sorry that once I thought of asking you to leave this house?"

"Did you so, ever?" asked my uncle Michael wonderingly. "Well, and 'tis sure I am you had your own good reasons."

"If I had, they're forgotten now," said my mother, gently brushing her brother-in-law's forehead with her lips as she rose to go. "You'll not stay up too late, Michael?"

"We shall see."

"It's still thinking of the white bird you are."

"Perhaps," said my uncle Michael. "And then again, perhaps not."

"You're a good man," repeated my mother, "but a foolish one. The white bird is a myth, Michael; a fancy of idle people. No harm will come to the lad."

Once again my uncle smiled that curious half smile, and on his lips there was a tenderness and a tightness. "There at least we are agreed, Molly," he said. "No harm will come to the lad."

My mother went to her bed, then. And of what happened after, there is no sure fact I can tell you. In later days she said that the sound which lulled her to sleep was the slow purring of my uncle Michael's knifeblade moving back and forth, back and forth on his whetstone. Later yet, at some unknown hour between midnight and dawn, she woke for the briefest of troubled instants with a curious feeling on her that in this house there was something gone amiss. So strong was the feeling, said she, that she sat bolt upright in the bed for a second or two to hear if there were movement in the house. But hearing nothing went back to her sleep.

And the youngest of my brothers since has claimed that he, too, was awakened in the dark hours before dawn by a sound he could not then nor afterwards describe. It was, he claims, a rushing sort of noise with a feeling of heaviness to it, of darkness and of movement and of dread. It frightened him so that for a time he lay in his bed atremble with a terror of something he could not name. But then the feeling passed, and being young he fell again into a deep, untroubled slumber.

So it is only the sick Dennis who, if anyone, knows what took place at the open window of that bedroom on that dreadful night. And what may be believed of Dennis's tale is hard to say. For my uncle Michael had guessed more rightly than the doctor. That night was indeed the night Dennis touched the crisis of his fever, and at such times the mind roams in a strange world of fancy peopled by creatures unlike any known to this earth. In this feverland of delirium dwelt Dennis that night, for in the morning my mother found him awake in his bed, clear-eyed and cool, and demanding food and drink.

It was not until long afterward that he recalled and tried to tell of the wicked dream he had dreamed that night, a dream that came and went in fitful snatches. Of his uncle Michael seated before the open window, rocking ceaselessly back and forth, back and forth. Then of a curious whiteness at that window, a shining in the night that was not moonlight because there was no moon.

Then there was darkness outlined against that lighter form, and the dark shape was my uncle Michael. And to Dennis it seemed they struggled in that window, they two, the one against the other, each silent and each grim, each determined to his own way, the one that it should enter and bear away from this house the life it had come to claim, the other equally determined it should not.

And the strangest part of this dream, remembers Dennis, is that for all the bitter fury of that contest there was no sound loud enough really to be called such. There was only the labored panting of my uncle Michael as, like the great mad Jacob that it tells of in the holy book, he wrestled with a Being stronger than himself. Only, says Dennis, there was nothing angelic about this Being, for in its cruel beaked visage there was only a frightful evil. Yet it uttered no sound, and his memory of it is only that its great strong wings made a muffled thrumming as they beat against the casement, or on the solid flesh of its antagonist.

Then it seemed that the struggling bodies were perilously close to the window ledge itself. And at that time Dennis saw my uncle's arm raise once, and twice, and yet again, and with a clenched fist beat upon the breast of the white thing, till suddenly that clean-shining expanse was no longer spotless but mottled with a dark and ugly stain. Then it was he heard the only sound to be born of that curious struggle. For then from the thing my uncle Michael wrestled broke a sharp and plaintive rasping, as of an animal that had never before known pain, and now in anger and surprise felt the unexpected bit of steel.

Then of a sudden its great wings beat stronger and more swiftly, and the creature was in flight. So for an instant they teetered there, they two, at the precarious windowsill two storeys from the ground. Then both of them were gone, white form and dark, and a sudden giddiness assailed the ailing lad. His head reeled with a sense of dark oppression abruptly lifted, a cold sweat broke out on his brow and on his lips and on his no longer fevered body. And it may be that he fainted, or it may be that he slept. Or it may be that it was all delirium. For this was the hour of his crisis, and with the morning he was well again.

And my uncle Michael? There is a matter that will never be explained. Some think that he was weary of this world, and of the failure he had made in it. They point out that for days be had been brooding in the dark and melancholy way of men in middle years whose life is empty. My mother thinks it was the man's great stubborn heart that was his downfall; that in his determination to stay awake and watch over his nephew he had been betrayed by sleep that would not be denied; that he had fallen into a troubled slumber, and doing so had walked to his destruction.

For they found him in the morning lying on the hard earth two floors beneath the open window of the sick lad's bedchamber. There was a stain of blood on the claspknife in his right hand, yet there was neither prick nor wound on his twisted body; only some gouges on his arms and face as if great talons had clawed him. There was a curious half smile of triumph on his lips. And in the fingers of his cold left hand were clenched two shining feathers. . . .

So, as I said before, this is not a nice story. It is a grim and dark and ugly story, and a most unsatisfying one, for to it there is no certain ending. Of it you may believe what you will, and your guess will be as good as any man's.

My uncle Michael was a fey man, and it was his to see strange things invisible to most men's eyes. It may be that the legends he believed were false. But I know what *I* believe—for with a dreadful clarity still I remember what I saw.

I think the great white bird *did* come to a house where death was fated, and took away a soul, as was ordained.

This I believe as surely as my name is Dennis O'Halloran.

RHODE ISLAND

The Haunter of the Dark
by H. P. Lovecraft

(Dedicated to Robert Bloch)

CAUTIOUS INVESTIGATORS will hesitate to challenge the common belief that Robert Blake was killed by lightning, or by some profound nervous shock derived from an electrical discharge. It is true that the window he faced was unbroken, but nature has shown herself capable of many freakish performances. The expression on his face may easily have arisen from some obscure muscular source unrelated to anything he saw, while the entries in his diary are clearly the result of a fantastic imagination aroused by certain local superstitions and by certain old matters he had uncovered. As for the anomalous conditions at the deserted church of Federal Hill—the shrewd analyst is not slow in attributing them to some charlatanry, conscious or unconscious, with at least some of which Blake was secretly connected.

For after all, the victim was a writer and painter wholly devoted to the field of myth, dream, terror, and superstition, and avid in his quest for scenes and effects of a bizarre, spectral sort. His earlier stay in the city—a visit to a strange old man as deeply given to occult and forbidden lore as he—had ended amidst death and flame, and it must have been some morbid instinct which drew him back from his home in Milwaukee. He may have known of the old stories despite his statement to the contrary in the diary, and his death may have nipped in the bud some stupendous hoax destined to have a literary reflection.

Among those, however, who have examined and correlated all this evidence, there remain several who cling to less rational and commonplace theories. They are inclined to take much of Blake's diary at its face value, and point significantly to certain facts such as the undoubted genuineness of the old church record, the verified existence of the disliked and unorthodox Starry Wisdom sect prior to 1877, the recorded disappearance of an inquisitive reporter named Edwin M. Lillibridge in 1893, and—above all—the look of monstrous, transfiguring fear on the face of the young writer when he died. It was one of these believers who, moved to fanatical extremes, threw into the bay the curiously angled stone and its strangely adorned metal box found in the old church steeple—the black windowless steeple, and not the tower where Blake's diary said those things originally were. Though widely censured both officially and unofficially, this man—a reputable physician with a taste for odd folklore—averred that he had rid the earth of something too dangerous to rest upon it.

Between these two schools of opinion the reader must judge for himself. The papers have given the tangible details from a skeptical angle, leaving for others the drawing of the picture as Robert Blake saw it—or thought he saw it—or pretended to see it. Now, studying the diary closely, dispassionately, and at leisure, let us summarize the dark chain of events from the expressed point of view of their chief actor.

Young Blake returned to Providence in the winter of 1934—5, taking the upper floor of a venerable dwelling in a grassy court off College Street—on the crest of the great eastward hill near the Brown University campus and behind the marble John Hay Library. It was a cozy and fascinating place, in a little garden oasis of village-like antquity where huge, friendly cats sunned themselves atop a convenient shed. The square Georgian house had a monitor roof, classic doorway with fan carving, small-paned windows, and all the other earmarks of early Nineteenth Century workmanship. Inside were six-paneled doors, wide floor-boards, a curving colonial staircase, white Adam-period mantels, and a rear set of rooms three steps below the general level.

Blake's study, a large southwest chamber, overlooked the front garden on one side, while its west windows—before one of which he had his desk—faced off from the brow of the hill and commanded a splendid view of the lower town's outspread roofs and of the mystical sunsets that flamed behind them. On the far horizon were the open countryside's purple slopes. Against these, some two miles away, rose the spectral hump of Federal Hill, bristling with huddled roofs and steeples whose remote outlines wavered mysteriously, taking fantastic forms as the smoke of the city swirled up and enmeshed them. Blake had a curious sense that he was looking upon some unknown, ethereal world which might or might not vanish in dream if ever he tried to seek it out and enter it in person.

Having sent home for most of his books, Blake bought some antique furniture suitable to his quarters and settled down to write and paint—living alone, and attending to the simple housework himself. His studio was in a north attic room, where the panes of the monitor roof furnished admirable lighting. During that first winter he produced five of his best-known short stories—*The Burrower Beneath, The Stairs in the Crypt, Shaggai, In the Vale of Pnath,* and *The Feaster from the Stars*—and painted seven canvases; studies of nameless, unhuman monsters, and profoundly alien, non-terrestrial landscapes.

At sunset he would often sit at his desk and gaze dreamily off at the outspread west—the dark towers of Memorial Hall just below, the Georgian courthouse belfry, the lofty pinnacles of the downtown section, and that shimmering, spire-crowned mound in the distance whose unknown streets and labyrinthine gables so potently provoked his fancy. From his few local acquaintances he learned that the far-off slope was a vast Italian quarter, though most of the houses were remnants of older Yankee and Irish days. Now and then he would train his field-glasses on that spectral, unreachable world beyond the curling smoke; picking out individual roofs and chimneys and steeples, and speculating upon the bizarre and curious mysteries they might house. Even with optical aid Federal Hill seemed somehow alien, half fabulous, and linked to the unreal, intangible marvels of Blake's own tales and pictures. The feeling would persist long after the hill had faded into the violet, lampstarred twilight, and the court-house floodlights and the red Industrial Trust beacon had blazed up to make the night grotesque.

Of all the distant objects on Federal Hill, a certain huge, dark church most fascinated Blake. It stood out with especial distinctness at certain hours of the day, and at sunset the great tower and tapering steeple loomed blackly against the flaming sky. It seemed to rest on especially high ground; for the grimy façade, and the obliquely seen north side with sloping roof and the tops of great pointed windows, rose boldly above the tangle of surrounding ridgepoles and chimney-pots. Peculiarly grim and austere, it appeared to be built of stone, stained and weathered with the smoke and storms of a century and more. The style, so far as the glass could show, was that earliest experimental form of Gothic revival which preceded the stately Upjohn period and held over some of the outlines and proportions of the Georgian age. Perhaps it was reared around 1810 or 1815.

As months passed, Blake watched the far-off, forbidding structure with an oddly mounting interest. Since the vast windows were never lighted, he knew that it must be vacant. The longer he watched, the more his imagination worked, till at length he began to fancy curious things. He believed that a vague, singular aura of desolation hovered over a place, so that even the pigeons and swallows shunned its smoky eaves. Around other towers and belfries his glass would reveal great flocks of birds, but here they never rested. At least, that is what he thought and set down in his diary. He pointed the place out to several friends, but none of them had even been on Federal Hill or possessed the faintest notion of what the church was or had been.

In the spring a deep restlessness gripped Blake. He had begun his long-planned novel—based on a supposed survival of the witchcult in Maine—but was strangely unable to make progress with it. More and more he would sit at his westward window and gaze at the distant hill and the black, frowning steeple shunned by the birds. When the delicate leaves came out on the garden boughs the world was filled wih a new beauty, but Blake's restlessness was merely increased. It was then that he first thought of crossing the city and climbing bodily up that fabulous slope into the smoke-wreathed world of dream.

Late in April, just before the eon-shadowed Walpurgis time, Blake made his first trip into the unknown. Plodding through the endless downtown streets and the bleak, decayed squares beyond, he came finally upon the ascending avenue of century-worn steps, sagging Doric porches, and blear-paned cupolas which he felt must lead up to the long-known, unreachable world beyond the mists. There were dingy blue-and-white street signs which meant nothing to him, and presently he noted the strange, dark faces of the drifting crowds, and the foreign signs over curious shops in brown, decade-weathered buildings. Nowhere could he find any of the objects he had seen from afar; so that once more he half fancied that the Federal Hill of that distant view was a dream-world never to be trod by living human feet.

Now and then a battered church façade or crumbling spire came in sight, but never the blackened pile that he sought. When he asked a shopkeeper about a great stone church the man smiled and shook his head, though he spoke English freely. As Blake climbed higher, the region seemed stranger and stranger, with bewildering mazes of brooding brown alleys leading eternally off to the south. He crossed two or three broad avenues, and once thought he glimpsed a familiar tower. Again he asked a merchant about the massive church of stone, and this time he could have sworn that the plea of ignorance was feigned. The dark man's face had a look of fear which he tried to hide, and Blake saw him make a curious sign with his right hand.

Then suddenly a black spire stood out against the cloudy sky on his left, above the tiers of brown roofs lining the tangled southerly alleys. Blake knew at once what it was, and plunged toward it through the squalid, unpaved lanes that climbed from the avenue. Twice he lost his way, but he somehow dared not ask any of the patriarchs or housewives who sat on their door-steps, or any of the children who shouted and played in the mud of the shadowy lanes.

At last he saw the tower plain against the southwest, and a huge stone bulk rose darkly at the end of an alley. Presently he stood in a wind-swept open square, quaintly cobblestoned, with a high bank wall on the farther side. This was the end of his quest; for upon the wide, iron-railed, weed-grown plateau which the wall supported—a separate, lesser world raised fully six feet above the surrounding streets—there stood a grim, titan bulk whose identity, despite Blake's new perspective, was beyond dispute.

The vacant church was in a state of great decrepitude. Some of the high stone buttresses had fallen, and several delicate finials lay half lost among the brown, neglected weeds and grasses. The sooty Gothic windows were largely unbroken, though many of the stone mullions were missing. Blake wondered how the obscurely painted panes could have survived so well, in view of the known habits of small boys the world over. The massive doors were intact and tightly closed. Around the top of the bank wall, fully enclosing the grounds, was a rusty iron fence whose gate—at the head of a flight of steps from the square—was visibly padlocked. The path from the gate to the building was completely overgrown. Desolation and decay hung like a pall above the place, and in the birdless eaves and black, ivyless walls Blake felt a touch of the dimly sinister beyond his power to define.

There were very few people in the square, but Blake saw a policeman at the northerly end and approached him with questions about the church. He was a great wholesome Irishman, and it seemed odd that he would do little more than make the sign of the cross and mutter that people never spoke of that building. When Blake pressed him he said very hurriedly that the Italian priests warned everybody against it, vowing that a monstrous evil had once dwelt there and left its mark. He himself had heard dark whispers of it from his father, who recalled certain sounds and rumors from his boyhood.

There had been a bad sect there in the old days—an outlaw sect that called up awful things from some unknown gulf of night. It had taken a good priest to exorcise what had come, though there did be those who said that merely the light could do it. If Father O'Malley were alive there would be many the thing he could tell. But now there was nothing to do but let it alone. It hurt nobody now, and those that owned it were dead or far away. They had run away like rats after the threatening talk in '77, when people began to mind the way folks vanished now and then in the neighbourhood. Some day the city would step in and take the property for lack of heirs, but little good would come of anybody's touching it. Better it be left alone for the years to topple, lest things be stirred that ought to rest for ever in their black abyss.

After the policeman had gone Blake stood staring at the sullen steepled pile. It excited him to find that the structure seemed as sinister to others as to him, and he wondered what grain of truth might lie behind the old tales the bluecoat had repeated. Probably they were mere legends evoked by the evil look of the place, but even so, they were like a strange coming to life of one of his own stories.

The afternoon sun came out from behind dispersing clouds, but seemed unable to light up the stained, sooty walls of the old temple that towered on its high plateau. It was odd that the green of spring had not touched the brown, withered growths in the raised, iron-fenced yard. Blake found himself edging nearer the raised area and examining the bank wall and rusted fence for possible avenues of ingress. There was a terrible lure about the blackened fane which was not to be resisted. The fence had no opening near the steps, but around on the north side were some missing bars. He could go up the steps and walk around on the narrow coping outside the fence till he came to the gap. If the people feared the place so wildly, he would encounter no interference.

He was on the embankment and almost inside the fence before anyone noticed him. Then, looking down, he saw the few people in the square edging away and making the same sign with their right hands that the shopkeeper in the avenue had made. Several windows were slammed down, and a fat woman darted into the street and pulled some small children inside a rickety, unpainted house. The gap in the fence was very easy to pass through, and before long Blake found himself wading amidst the rotting, tangled growths of the deserted yard. Here and there the worn stump of a headstone told him that there had once been burials in this field; but that, he saw, must have been very long ago. The sheer bulk of the church was oppressive now that he was close to it, but he conquered his mood and approached to try the three great doors in the façade. All were securely locked, so he began a circuit of the Cyclopean building in quest of some minor and more penetrable opening. Even then he could not be sure that he wished to enter that haunt of desertion and shadow, yet the pull of its strangeness dragged him on automatically.

A yawning and unprotected cellar window in the rear furnished the needed aperture. Peering in, Blake saw a subterrene gulf of cobwebs and dust faintly litten by the western sun's filtered rays. Debris, old barrels, and ruined boxes and furniture of numerous sorts met his eye, though over everything lay a shroud of dust which softened all sharp outlines. The rusted remains of a hot-air furnace showed that the building had been used and kept in shape as late as Mid-Victorian times.

Acting almost without conscious initiative, Blake crawled through the window and let himself down to the dust-carpeted and debris-strewn con- crete floor. The vaulted cellar was a vast one, without partitions; and in a corner far to the right, amid dense shadows, he saw a black archway eviden- tly leading upstairs. He felt a peculiar sense of oppression at being actually within the great spectral building, but kept it in check as he cautiously scouted about—finding a still-intact barrel amid the dust, and rolling it over to the open window to provide for his exit. Then, bracing himself, he crossed the wide, cobweb-festooned space toward the arch. Half choked with the omnipresent dust and covered with ghostly gossamer fibers, he reached and began to climb the worn stone steps which rose into the darkness. He had no light, but groped carefully with his hands. After a sharp turn he felt a closed door ahead, and a little fumbling revealed its ancient latch. It opened inward, and beyond it he saw a dimly illumined corridor lined with worm-eaten paneling.

Once on the ground floor, Blake began exploring in a rapid fashion. All the inner doors were unlocked, so that he freely passed from room to room. The colossal nave was an almost eldritch place with its drifts and mountains of dust over box pews, altar, hour-glass pulpit, and sounding-board, and its titanic ropes of cobweb stretching among the pointed arches of the gallery and entwining the cluttered Gothic columns. Over all this hushed desolation played a hideous leaden light as the declining afternoon sun sent its rays through the strange, half-blackened panes of the great apsidal windows.

The paintings on those windows were so obscured by soot that Blake could scarcely decipher what they had represented, but from the little he could make out he did not like them. The designs were largely conventional, and his knowledge of obscure symbolism told him much concerning some of the ancient patterns. The few saints depicted bore expressions distinctly open to criticism, while one of the windows seemed to show merely a dark space with spirals of curious luminosity scattered about in it. Turning away from the windows, Blake noticed that the cobwebbed cross above the altar was not of the ordinary kind, but resembled the primordial ankh or crux ansata of shadowy Egypt.

In a rear vestry room beside the apse Blake found a rotting desk and ceiling-high shelves of mildewed, disintegrating books. Here for the first time he received a positive shock of objective horror, for the titles of those books told him much. They were the black, forbidden things which most sane people have never even heard of, or have heard of only in furtive, timorous whispers; the banned and dreaded repositories of equivocal secrets and immemorial formulae which have trickled down the stream of time from the days of man's youth, and the dim, fabulous days before man was. He had himself read many of them—a Latin version of the abhorred *Necronomicon* the sinister *Liber Ivonis,* the infamous *Cultes des Goules* of Comte d'Erlette, the *Unaussprechlichen Kulten* of von Junzt, and old Ludvig Prinn's hellish *De Vermis Mysteriis*. But there were others he had known merely by reputation or not at all—the *Pnakotic Manuscripts,* the *Book of Dzyan*, and a crumbling volume in wholly unidentifiable characters yet with certain symbols and diagrams shudderingly recognizable to the occult student. Clearly, the lingering local rumors had not lied. This place had once been the seat of an evil older than mankind and wider than the known universe.

In the ruined desk was a small leatherbound record-book filled with entries in some odd cryptographic medium. The manuscript writing consisted of the common traditional symbols used today in astronomy and anciently in alchemy, astrology, and other dubious arts—the devices of the sun, moon, planets, aspects, and zodiacal signs—here massed in solid pages of text, with divisions and paragraphings suggesting that each symbol answered to some alphabetical letter.

In the hope of later solving the cryptogram, Blake bore off this volume in his coat pocket. Many of the great tomes on the shelves fascinated him unutterably, and he felt tempted to borrow them at some later time. He wondered how they could have remained undisturbed so long. Was he the first to conquer the clutching, pervasive fear which had for nearly sixty years protected this deserted place from visitors?

Having now thoroughly explored the ground floor, Blake plowed again through the dust of the spectral nave to the front vestibule, where he had seen a door and staircase presumably leading up to the blackened tower and steeple—objects so long familiar to him at a distance. The ascent was a choking experience, for dust lay thick, while the spiders had done their worst in this constricted place. The staircase was a spiral with high, narrow wooden treads, and now and then Blake passed a clouded window looking dizzily out over the city. Though he had seen no ropes below, he expected to find a bell or peal of bells in the tower whose narrow, louver-boarded lancet windows his field-glass had studied so often. Here he was doomed to disappointment; for when he attained the top of the stairs he found the tower chamber vacant of chimes, and clearly devoted to vastly different purposes.

The room, about fifteen feet square, was faintly lighted by four lancet windows, one on each side, which were glazed within their screening of decayed louver-boards. These had been further fitted with tight, opaque screens, but the latter were now largely rotted away. In the center of the dust-laden floor rose a curiously angled stone pillar some four feet in height and two in average diameter, covered on each side with bizarre, crudely incised and wholly unrecognizable hieroglyphs. On this pillar rested a metal box of peculiarly asymmetrical form; its hinged lid thrown back, and its interior holding what looked beneath the decade-deep dust to be an egg-shaped or irregularly spherical object some four inches through. Around the pillar in a rough circle were seven high-backed Gothic chairs still largely intact, while behind them, ranging along the dark-paneled walls, were seven colossal images of crumbling, blackpainted plaster, resembling more than anything else the cryptic carven megaliths of mysterious Easter Island. In one corner of the cobwebbed chamber a ladder was built into the wall, leading up to the closed trap-door of the windowless steeple above.

As Blake grew accustomed to the feeble light he noticed odd bas-reliefs on the strange open box of yellowish metal. Approaching, he tried to clear the dust away with his hands and handkerchief, and saw that the figurings were of a monstrous and utterly alien kind; depicting entities which, though seemingly alive, resembled no known life-form ever evolved on this planet. The four-inch seeming sphere turned out to be a nearly black, red-striated polyhedron with many irregular flat surfaces; either a very remarkable crystal of some sort, or an artificial object of carved and highly polished mineral matter. It did not touch the bottom of the box, but was held suspended by means of a metal band around its center, with seven queerly-designed supports extending horizontally to angles of the box's inner wall near the top. This stone, once exposed, exerted upon Blake an almost alarming fascination. He could scarcely tear his eyes from it, and as he looked at its glistening surfaces he almost fancied it was transparent, with half-formed worlds of wonder within. Into his mind floated pictures of alien orbs with great stone towers, and other orbs with titan mountains and no mark of life, and still remoter spaces where only a stirring in vague blacknesses told of the presence of consciousness and will.

When he did look away, it was to notice a somewhat singular mound of dust in the far corner near the ladder to the steeple. Just why it took his attention he could not tell, but something in its contours carried a message to his unconscious mind. Plowing toward it, and brushing aside the hanging cobwebs as he went, he began to discern something grim about it. Hand and handkerchief soon revealed the truth, and Blake gasped with a baffling mixture of emotions. It was a human skeleton, and it must have been there for a very long time. The clothing was in shreds, but some buttons and fragments of cloth bespoke a man's gray suit. There were other bits of evidence—shoes, metal clasps, huge buttons for round cuffs, a stickpin of bygone pattern, a reporter's badge with the name of the old *Providence Telegram*, and a crumbling leather pocket-book. Blake examined the latter with care, finding within it several bills· of antiquated issue, a celluloid advertising claendar for 1893, some cards with the name "Edwin M. Lillibridge," and a paper covered with penciled memoranda.

This paper held much of a puzzling nature, and Blake read it carefully at the dim westward window. Its disjointed text included such phrases as the following:

"Prof. Enoch Bowen home from Egypt May 1844—buys old Free-Will Church in July—his archaelogical work & studies in occult well known."

"Dr. Drowne of 4th Baptist warns against Starry Wisdom in sermon Dec. 29, 1844."

"Congregation 97 by end of '45."

"1846—3 disappearances—first mention of Shining Trape-zohedron."

"7 disappearances 1848—stories of blood sacrifice begin."

"Investigation 1853 comes to nothing—stories of sounds."

"Fr. O'Malley tells of devil-worship with box found in great Egyptian ruins—says they call up something that can't exist in light. Flees a little light, and banished by strong light. Then has to be summoned again. Probably got this from deathbed confession of Francis X. Feeney, who had joined Starry Wisdom in '49. These people say the Shining Trapezohedron shows them heaven & other worlds, & that the Haunter of the Dark tells them secrets in some way."

"Story of Orrin B. Eddy 1857. They call it up by gazing at the crystal, & have a secret language of their own."

"200 or more in cong. 1863, exclusive of men at front."

"Irish boys mob church in 1869, after Patrick Regan's dis-appearance."

"Veiled article in J. March 14, '72, but people don't talk about it."

"6 disappearances 1876—secret committee calls on Mayor Doyle."

"Action promised Feb. 1877—church closes in April."

"Gang—Federal Hill Boys—threaten Dr. —— and vestrymen in May."

"181 persons leave city before end of '77—mention no names."

"Ghost stories begin around 1880—try to ascertain truth of report that no human being has entered church since 1877."

"Ask Lanigan for photograph of place taken 1851." . . .

Restoring the paper to the pocketbook and placing the latter in his coat, Blake turned to look down at the skeleton in the dust. The implications of the notes were clear, and there could be no doubt but that this man had come to the deserted edifice forty-two years before in quest of a newspaper sensation which no one else had been bold enough to attempt. Perhaps no one else had known of his plan—who could tell? But he had never returned to his paper. Had some bravely-suppressed fear risen to overcome him and bring on sudden heart-failure? Blake stooped over the gleaming bones and noted their peculiar state. Some of them were badly scattered, and a few seemed oddly *dissolved* at the ends. Others were strangely yellowed, with vague suggestions at charring. This charring extended to some of the fragments of clothing. The skull was in a very peculiar state—stained yellow, and with a charred aperture in the top as if some powerful acid had eaten through the solid bone. What had happened to the skeleton during its four decades of silent entombment here Blake could not imagine.

Before he realized it, he was looking at the stone again, and letting its curious influence call up a nebulous pageantry in his mind. He saw processions of robed, hooded figures whose outlines were not human, and looked on endless leagues of desert lined with carved sky-reaching monoliths. He saw towers and walls in nighted depths under the sea, and vortices of space where wisps of black mist floated before thin shimmerings of cold purple haze. And beyond all else he glimpsed an infinte gulf of darkness, where solid and semi-solid forms were known only by their windy stirrings, and cloud patterns of force seemed to superimpose order on chaos and hold forth a key to all the paradoxes and arcana of the worlds we know.

Then all at once the spell was broken by an access of gnawing, indeterminate panic fear. Blake choked and turned away from the stone, conscious of some formless alien presence close to him and watching him with horrible intentness. He felt entangled with something—something which was not in the stone, but which had looked through it at him— something which would ceaselessly follow him with a cognition that was not physical sight. Plainly the place was getting on his nerves—as well it might in view of his gruesome find. The light was waning, too, and since he had no illuminant with him he knew he would have to be leaving soon.

It was then, in the gathering twilight, that he thought he saw a faint trace of luminosity in the crazily angled stone. He had tried to look away from it, but some obscure compulsion drew his eyes back. Was there a subtle phosphorescence of radio-activity about the thing? What was it that the dead man's notes had said concerning a *Shining Trapezohedron*? What, anyway, was his abandoned air of cosmic evil? What had been done here, and what might still be lurking in the bird-shunned shadows? It seemed now as if an elusive touch of fetor had arisen somewhere close by, though its source was not apparent. Blake seized the cover of the long-open box and snapped it down. It moved easily on its alien hinges, and closed completely over the unmistakably glowing stone.

At the sharp click of that closing a soft stirring sound seemed to come from the steeple's eternal blackness overhead, beyond the trap-door. Rats, without question—the only living things to reveal their presence in this accursed pile since he had entered it. And yet that stirring in the steeple frightened him horribly, so that he plunged almost wildly down the spiral stairs, across the ghoulish nave into the vaulted basement, out amidst the gathering dusk of the deserted square, and down through the teeming, fear-haunted alleys and avenues of Federal Hill toward the sane central streets and the home-like brick sidewalks of the college district.

During the days which followed, Blake told no one of his expedition. Instead, he read much in certain books, examined long years of newspaper files downtown, and worked feverishly at the cryptogram in that leather volume from the cobwebbed vestry room. The cipher, he soon saw, was no simple one; and after a long period of endeavor he felt sure that its language could not be English, Latin, Greek, French, Spanish, Italian, or German. Evidently he would have to draw upon the deepest wells of his strange erudition.

Every evening the old impulse to gaze westward returned, and he saw the black steeple as of yore amongst the bristling roofs of a distant and half-fabulous world. But now it held a fresh note of terror for him. He knew the heritage of evil lore it masked, and with the knowledge his vision ran riot in queer new ways. The birds of spring were returning, and as he watched their sunset flights he fancied they avoided the gaunt, lone spire as never before. When a flock of them approached it, he thought, they would wheel and scatter in panic confusion—and he could guess at the wild twitterings which failed to reach him across the intervening miles.

It was in June that Blake's diary told of his victory over the cryptogram. The text was, he found, in the dark Aklo language used by certain cults of evil antiquity, and known to him in a halting way through previous researches. The diary is strangely reticent about what Blake deciphered, but he was patently awed and disconcerted by his results. There are references to a Haunter of the Dark awaked by gazing into the Shining Trapezohedron, and insane conjectures about the black gulfs of chaos from which it was called. The being is spoken of as holding all knowledge, and demanding monstrous sacrifices. Some of Blake's entries show fear lest the thing, which he seemed to regard as summoned, stalk abroad; though he adds that the streetlights form a bulwark which cannot be crossed.

Of the Shining Trapezohedron he speaks often, calling it a window on all time and space, and tracing its history from the day it was fashioned on dark

Yuggoth, before ever the Old Ones brought it to earth. It was treasured and placed in its curious box by the crinoid things of Antarctica, salvaged from their ruins by the serpent-men of Valusia, and peered at eons later in Lemuria by the first human beings. It crossed strange lands and stranger seas and sank with Atlantis before a Minoan fisher meshed it in his net and sold it to swarthy merchants from nighted Khem. The Pharaoh Nephren-Ka built around it a temple with a windowless crypt, and did that which caused his name to be stricken from all monuments and records. Then it slept in the ruins of that evil fane which the priests and the new Pharaoh destroyed, till the delver's spade once more brought it forth to curse mankind.

Early in July the newspapers oddly supplement Blake's entries though in so brief and casual a way that only the diary has called general attention to their contribution. It appears that a new fear had been growing on Federal Hill since a stranger had entered the dreaded church. The Italians whispered of unaccustomed stirrings and bumpings and scrapings in the dark windowless steeple, and called on their priests to banish an entity which haunted their dreams. Something, they said, was constantly watching at a door to see if it were dark enough to venture forth. Press items mentioned the longstanding local superstitions, but failed to shed much light on the earlier background of the horror. It was obvious that the young reporters of today are no antiquarians. In writing of these things in his diary, Blake expresses a curious kind of remorse, and talks of the duty of burying the Shining Trapezohedron and of banishing what he had evoked by letting daylight into the hideous jutting spire. At the same time, however, he displays the dangerous extent of his fascination, and admits a morbid longing—prevading even his dreams—to visit the accursed tower and gaze again into the cosmic secrets of the glowing stone.

Then something in the *Journal* on the morning of July 17 threw the diarist into a veritable fever of horror. It was only a variant of the other half-humorous items about the Federal Hill restlessness, but to Blake it was somehow very terrible indeed. In the night a thunderstorm had put the city's lighting-system out of commission for a full hour, and in the black interval the Italians had nearly gone mad with fright. Those living near the dreaded church had sworn that the thing in the steeple had taken advantage of the street lamps' absence and gone down into the body of the church, hopping and bumping around in a viscous, altogether dreadful way. Toward the last it had bumped up to the tower, where there were sounds of the shattering of glass. It could go wherever the darkness reached, but light would always send it fleeing.

When the current blazed on again there had been a shocking commotion in the tower, for even the feeble light trickling through the grime-blackened, louver-boarded windows was too much for the thing. It had bumped and slithered up into its tenebrous steeple just in time—for a long dose of light would have sent it back into the abyss whence the crazy stranger had called it. During the dark hour praying crowds had clustered round the church in the rain with lighted candles and lamps somehow shielded with folded paper and umbrellas—a guard of light to save the city from the nightmare that stalks in darkness. Once, those nearest the church declared, the outer door had rattled hideously.

But even this was not the worst. That evening in the *Bulletin* Blake read of what the reporters had found. Aroused at last to the whimsical news value of the scare, a pair of them had defied the frantic crowds of Italians and crawled into the church through the cellar window after trying the doors in vain. They found the dust of the vestibule and of the spectral nave plowed up in a singular way, with pits of rotted cushions and satin pew-linings scattered curiously around. There was a bad odor everywhere, and here and there were bits of yellow stain and patches of what looked like charring. Opening the door to the tower, and pausing a moment at the suspicion of a scraping sound above, they found the narrow spiral stairs wiped roughly clean.

In the tower itself a similarly half-swept condition existed. They spoke of the heptagonal stone pillar, the overturned Gothic chairs, and the bizarre plaster images; though strangely enough the metal box and the old mutilated skeleton were not mentioned. What disturbed Blake the most—except for the hints of stains and charring and bad odors—was the final detail that explained the crashing glass. Every one of the tower's lancet windows was broken, and two of them had been darkened in a crude and hurried way by the stuffing of satin pew-linings and cushion-horsehair into the spaces between the slanting exterior louver-boards. More satin fragments and bunches of horsehair lay scattered around the newly swept floor, as if someone had been interrupted in the act of restoring the tower to the absolute blackness of its tightly curtained days.

Yellowish stains and charred patches were found on the ladder to the windowless spire, but when a reporter climbed up, opened the horizontally-sliding trap-door and shot a feeble flashlight beam into the black and strangely fetid space, he saw nothing but darkness, and an heterogenous litter of shapeless fragments near the aperture. The verdict, of course was charlatanry. Somebody had played a joke on the superstitious hill-dwellers, or else some fanatic had striven to bolster up their fears for their own supposed good. Or perhaps some of the younger and more sophisticated dwellers had staged an elaborate hoax on the outside world. There was an amusing aftermath when the police sent an officer to verify the reports. Three men in succession found ways of evading the assignment, and the fourth went very reluctantly and returned very soon without adding to the account given by the reporters.

From this point onward Blake's diary shows a mounting tide of insidious horror and nervous apprehension. He upbraids himself for not doing something, and speculates wildly on the consequences of another electrical breakdown. It has been verified that on three occasions—during thunder-storms—he telephoned the electric light company in a frantic vein and asked that desperate precautions against a lapse of power be taken. Now and then his entries show concern over the failure of the reporters to find the metal box and stone, and the strangely marred old skeleton, when they explored the shadowy tower room. He assumed that these things had been removed—whither, and by whom or what, he could only guess. But his worst fears concerned himself, and the kind of unholy rapport he felt to exist between his mind and that lurking horror in the distant steeple—that monstrous thing of night which his rashness had called out of the ultimate black spaces. He seemed to feel a constant tugging at his will, and callers of that period remember how he would sit abstractedly at his desk and stare out of the west window at that far-off spire-bristling mound beyond the swirling smoke of the city. His entries dwell monotonously on certain terrible dreams, and of a strengthening of the unholy rapport in his sleep. There is mention of a night when he awakened to find himself fully dressed, outdoors, and headed automatically down College Hill toward the west. Again and again he dwells on the fact that the thing in the steeple knows where to find him.

The week following July 30 is recalled as the time of Blake's partial breakdown. He did not dress, and ordered all his food by telephone. Visitors remarked the cords he kept near his bed, and he said that sleep-walking had forced him to bind his ankles every night with knots which would probably hold or else waken him with the labor of untying.

In his diary he told of the hideous experience which had brought the collapse. After retiring on the night of the 30th he had suddenly found himself groping about in an almost black space. All he could see were short, faint, horizontal streaks of bluish light, but he could smell an overpowering fetor and hear a curious jumble of soft, furtive sounds above him. Whenever he moved he stumbled over something, and at each noise there would come a sort of answering sound from above—a vague stirring, mixed with the cautious sliding of wood on wood.

Once his groping hands encountered a pillar of stone with a vacant top, whilst later he found himself clutching the rungs of a ladder built into the wall, and fumbling his uncertain way upward toward some region of intenser stench where a hot, searing blast beat down against him. Before his eyes a kaleidoscopic range of fantasmal images played, all of them dissolving at intervals into the picture of vast, unplumbed abyss of night wherein whirled suns and worlds of an even profounder blackness. He thought of the ancient legends of Ultimate Chaos, at whose center sprawls the blind idiot god Azathoth, Lord of All Things, encircled by his flopping horde of mindless and amorphous dancers, and lulled by the thin monotonous piping of a demoniac flute held in nameless paws.

Then a sharp report from the outer world broke through his stupor and roused him to the unutterable horror of his position. What it was, he never knew—perhaps it was some belated peal from the fireworks heard all summer on Federal Hill as the dwellers hail their various patron saints, or the saints of their native villages in Italy. In any event he shrieked aloud, dropped frantically from the ladder, and stumbled blindly across the obstructed floor of the almost lightless chamber that encompassed him.

He knew instantly where he was, and plunged recklessly down the narrow spiral staircase, tripping and bruising himself at every turn. There was a nightmare flight through a vast cobwebbed nave whose ghostly arches reached up to realms of leering shadow, a sightless scramble through a littered basement, a climb to regions of air and street lights outside, and a mad racing down to a spectral hill of gibbering gables, across a grim, silent city of tall black towers, and up the steep eastward precipice to his own ancient door.

On regaining consciousness in the morning he found himself lying on his study floor fully dressed. Dirt and cobwebs covered him, and every inch of his body seemed sore and bruised. When he faced the mirror he saw that his hair was badly scorched, while a trace of strange, evil odor seemed to cling to his upper outer clothing. It was then that his nerves broke down. Thereafter, lounging exhaustedly about in a dressing-gown, he did little but stare from his west window, shiver at the threat of thunder, and make wild entries in his diary.

The great storm broke just before midnight on August 8th. Lightning struck repeatedly in all parts of the city, and two remarkable fireballs were reported. The rain was torrential, while a constant fusillade of thunder brought sleeplessness to thousands. Blake was utterly frantic in his fear for the lighting system, and tried to telephone the company around one A.M., though by that time service had been temporarily cut off in the interest of safety. He recorded everything in his diary—the large, nervous, and often undecipherable hieroglyphs telling their own story of growing frenzy and despair, and of entries scrawled blindly in the dark.

He had to keep the house dark in order to see out the window, and it appears that most of his time was spent at his desk, peering anxiously through the rain across the glistening miles of downtown roofs at the constellation of distant lights marking Federal Hill. Now and then he would fumblingly make an entry in his diary, so that detached phrases such as "The light must not go"; "It knows where I am"; "I must destroy it"; and "It is calling to me, but perhaps it means no injury this time" are found scattered down two of the pages.

Then the lights went out all over the city. It happened at 2:12 A.M. according to power-house records, but Blake's diary gives no indication of the time. The entry is merely, "Lights out—God help me." On Federal Hill there were watchers as anxious as he, and rain-soaked knots of men paraded the square and alleys around the evil church with umbrella-shaded candles, electric flashlights, oil lanterns, crucifixes, and obscure charms of the many sorts common to southern Italy. They blessed each flash of lightning, and made cryptical signs of fear with their right hands when a turn in the story caused the flashes to lessen and finally to cease altogether. A rising wind blew out most of the candles, so that the scene grew threatening dark.

Someone roused Father Merluzzo of Spirito Santo Church, and he hastened to the dismal square to pronounce whatever helpful syllables he could. Of the restless and curious sounds in the backened tower, there could be no doubt whatever.

For what happened at 2:35 we have the testimony of the priest, a young, intelligent, and well-educated person; of Patrolman William I. Monohan of the Central Station, an officer of the highest reliability who had paused at that part of his beat to inspect the crowd; and of most of the seventy-eight men who had gathered around the church's high bank wall—especially those in the square where the outward façade was visible. Of couse, there was nothing which can be proved as being outside the order of nature. The possible causes of such an event are many. No one can speak with certainty of the obscure chemical processes arising in a vast, ancient, ill-aired, and long-deserted building of heterogeneous contents. Mephitic vapors— spontaneous combustion—pressure of gases born of long decay—any one of numberless phenomena might be responsible. And then, of course, the factor of conscious charlatanry can by no means be excluded. The thing was really quite simple in itself, and lasted less than three minutes of actual time. Father Merluzzo, always a precise man, looked at his watch repeatedly.

It started with a definite swelling of the dull fumbling sounds inside the black tower. There had for some time been a vague exhalation of strange, evil odors from the church, and this had now become emphatic and offensive. Then at last there was a sound of splintering wood, and a large, heavy object crashed down in the yard beneath the frowning easterly façade. The tower was invisible now that the candles would not burn, but as the object neared the ground the people knew that it was the smoke-grimed louvered-boarding of that tower's east window.

Immediately afterward an utterly unbearable fetor welled forth from the unseen heights, choking and sickening the trembling watchers, and almost prostrating those in the square. At the same time the air trembled with a vibration as of flapping wings, and a sudden east-blowing wind more violent than any previous blast snatched off the hats and wrenched the dripping umbrellas of the crowd. Nothing definite could be seen in the candleless night though some upward-looking spectators thought they glimpsed a great spreading blur of denser blackness against the inky sky—something like a formless cloud of smoke that shot with meteor-like speed toward the east.

That was all. The watchers were half numbed with fright, awe and discomfort, and scarcely knew what to do, or whether to do anything at all. Not knowing what had happened, they did not relent their vigil; and a moment later they sent up a prayer as a sharp flash of belated lightning, followed by an earsplitting crash of sound rent the flooded heavens. Half an hour later the rain stopped, and in fifteen minutes more the street lights sprang on again, sending the weary, bedraggled watchers relievedly back to their homes.

The next day's papers gave these matters minor mention in connection with the general storm reports. It seems that the great lightning flash and deafening explosion which followed the Federal Hill occurrence were even more tremendous farther east, when a burst of the singular fetor was likewise noticed. The phenomena was most marked over College Hill, where the crash awaked all the sleeping inhabitants and led to a bewildered round of speculations. Of those who were already awake only a few saw the anomalous blaze of light near the top of the hill, or noticed the inexplicable upward rush of air which almost stripped the leaves from the trees and blasted the plants in the gardens. It was agreed that the lone, sudden lightning-bolt must have struck somewhere in this neighborhood, though no trace of its striking could afterward be found. A youth in the Tau Omega fraternity house thought he saw a grotesque and hideous mass of smoke in the air just as the preliminary flash burst, but his observation has not been verified. All of the few observers, however, agree as to the violent gust from the west and the flood of intolerable stench which preceded the belated stroke; whilst evidence concerning the momentary burned odor after the stroke is equally general.

These points were discussed very carefully because of their probable connection with the death of Robert Blake. Students in the Psi Delta house, whose upper rear windows looked into Blake's study, noticed the blurred white face at the westward window on the morning of the ninth, and wondered what was wrong with the expression. When they saw the same face in the same position that evening, they felt worried, and watched for the lights to come up in his apartment. Later they rang the bell of the darkened flat, and finally had a policeman force the door.

The rigid body sat bolt upright at the desk by the window, and when the intruders saw the glassy, bulging eyes, and the marks of stark convulsive fright on the twisted features, they turned away in alarmed dismay. Shortly afterward the coroner's physician made an examination, and despite the unbroken window reported electrical shock, or nervous tension induced by electrical discharge, as the cause of death. The hideous expression he ignored altogether, deeming it a not improbable result of the profound shock as experienced by a person of such abnormal imagination and unbalanced emotions. He deduced these latter qualities from the books, paintings, and manuscripts found in the apartment, and from the blindly worded entries in the diary on the desk. Blake had prolonged his frenzied jottings to the last, and the broken-pointed pencil was found clutched in his spasmodically contracted right hand.

The entries after the failure of the lights were highly disjointed, and legible only in part. From them certain investigators have drawn observations differing greatly from the materialistic official verdict, but such speculations have little chance for belief among the conservative. The case of these imaginative theorists has not been helped in the action of superstitious Doctor Dexter, who threw the curious box and angled stone—an object certainly self-luminous as seen in the black windowless steeple where it was found—into the deepest channel of Narragansett Bay. Excessive imagination and neurotic unbalance on Blake's part, aggravated by knowledge of the evil bygone cult whose startling traces he had uncovered, form the dominant interpretation given those final frenzied jottings. These are the entries—or all that can be made of them.

"Lights still out—must be five minutes now. Everything depends on lightning. Yaddith grant it will keep up! . . . Some influence seems beating through it. . . . Rain and thunder and wind deafen. . . . The thing is taking hold of my mind. . . .

"Troubled with memory. I see things I never knew before. Other worlds and other galaxies. . . . Dark! . . . The lightning seems dark and the darkness seems light. . . .

"It cannot be the real hill and church that I see in the pitch-darkness. Must be retinal impression left by flashes. Heaven grant the Italians are out with their candles if the lightning stops!

"What am I afraid of? Is it not an avatar of Nyarlathotep, who is antique and shadowy Khem even took the form of man? I remember Yuggoth, and more distant Shaggai, and the ultimate void of the black planets. . . .

"The long, winging flight through the void . . . cannot cross the universe of light . . . re-created by the thoughts caught in the Shining Trapezohedron . . . send it through the horrible abysses of radiance. . . .

"My name is Blake—Robert Harrison Blake of 620 East Knapp Street, Milwaukee, Wisconsin. . . . I am on this planet. . . .

"Azathoth have mercy!—the lightning no longer flashes—horrible—I can see everything with a monstrous sense that is not sight—light is dark and dark is light . . . those people on the hill . . . guard . . . candles and charms . . . their priests. . . .

"Sense of distance gone—far is near and near is far. No light—no glass—see that steeple—that tower—window—can hear—Roderick Usher—am mad or going mad—the thing is stirring and fumbling in the tower—I am it and it is I—I want to get out . . . must get out and unify the forces. . . . It knows where I am . . .

"I am Robert Blake, but I see the tower in the dark. There is a monstrous odor . . . senses transfigured . . . boarding at that tower window cracking and giving way. . . . Iä . . . ngai . . . ygg. . .

"I see it—coming here—hell-wind—titan blur—black wings—Yog Sothoth save me—the three-lobed burning eye. . . ."

SOUTH CAROLINA

Song of the Slaves
by Manly Wade Wellman

GENDER PAUSED at the top of the bald rise, mopped his streaming red forehead beneath the wide hat-brim, and gazed backward at his forty-nine captives. Naked and black, they shuffled upward from the narrow, ancient slave trail through the jungle. Forty-nine men, seized by Gender's own hand and collared to a single long chain, destined for his own plantation across the sea. . . . Gender grinned in his lean, drooping mustache, a mirthless grin of greedy triumph.

For years he had dreamed and planned for this adventure, as other men dream and plan for European tours, holy pilgrimages, or returns to beloved birthplaces. He had told himself that it was intensely practical and profitable. Slaves passed through so many hands—the raider, the caravaner, the seashore factor, the slaver captain, the dealer in New Orleans or Havana or at home in Charleston. Each greedy hand clutched a rich profit, and all profits must come eventually from the price paid by the planter. But he, Gender, had come to Africa himself, in his own ship; with a dozen staunch ruffians from Benguela he had penetrated the Bihé-Bailundu country, had sacked a village and taken these forty-nine upstanding natives between dark and dawn. A single neck-shackle on his long chain remained empty, and he might fill even that before he came to his ship. By the Lord, he was making money this way, fairly coining it—and money was worth the making, to a Charleston planter in 1853.

So he reasoned, and so he actually believed, but the real joy to him was hidden in the darkest nook of his heart. He had conceived the raider-plan because of a nature that fed on savagery and mastery. A man less fierce and cruel might have been satisfied with hunting lions or elephants, but Gender

539

must hunt men. As a matter of fact, the money made or saved by the journey would be little, if it was anything. The satisfaction would be tremendous. He would broaden his thick chest each day as he gazed out over his lands and saw there his slaves hoeing seashore cotton or pruning indigo; his forty-nine slaves, caught and shipped and trained by his own big, hard hands, more indicative of assured conquest than all the horned or fanged heads that ever passed through the shops of all the taxidermists.

Something hummed in his ears, like a rhythmic swarm of bees. Men were murmuring a song under their breath. It was the long string of pinch-faced slaves. Gender stared at them, and mouthed one of the curses he always kept at tongue's end.

"Silva!" he called.

The lanky Portuguese who strode free at the head of the file turned aside and stood before Gender. *"Patrao?"* he inquired respectfully, smiling teeth gleaming in his walnut face.

"What are those men singing?" demanded Gender. "I didn't think they had anything to sing about."

"A slave song, *patrao.*" Silva's tapering hand, with the silver bracelet at its wrist, made a graceful gesture of dismissal. "It is nothing. One of the things that natives make up and sing as they go."

Gender struck his boot with his coiled whip of hippopotamus hide. The afternoon sun, sliding down toward the shaggy jungle-tops, kindled harsh pale lights in his narrow blue eyes. "How does the song go?" he persisted.

The two fell into step beside the caravan as, urged by a dozen red-capped drivers, it shambled along the trail. "It is only a slave song, *patrao,*" said Silva once again. "It means something like this: 'Though you carry me away in chains, I am free when I die. Back will I come to bewitch and kill you.'"

Gender's heavy body seemed to swell, and his eyes grew narrower and paler. "So they sing that, hmm?" He swore again. "Listen to that!"

The unhappy procession had taken up a brief, staccato refrain:

"Hailowa—Genda! Haipana—Genda!"

"Genda, that's my name," snarled the planter. "They're singing about me, aren't they?"

Silva made another fluid gesture, but Gender flourished his whip under the nose of the Portuguese. "Don't you try to shrug me off. I'm not a child, to be talked around like this. What are they singing about me?"

"Nothing of consequence, *patrao,*" Silva made haste to reassure him. "It might be to say: 'I will bewitch Gender, I will kill Gender.'"

"They threaten me, do they?" Gender's broad face took on a deeper flush. He ran at the line of chained black men. With all the strength of his arm he slashed and swung with the whip. The song broke up into wretched howls of pain.

"I'll give you a music lesson!" he raged, and flogged his way up and down the procession until he swayed and dripped sweat with the exertion.

But as he turned away, it struck up again:

"Hailowa—Genda! Haipana—Genda!"

Whirling back, he resumed the rain of blows. Silva, rushing up to second him, also whipped the slaves and execrated them in their own tongue. But when both were tired, the flayed captives began to sing once more, softly but stubbornly, the same chant.

"Let them whine," panted Gender at last. "A song never killed anybody."

Silva grinned nervously. "Of course not, *patrao*. That is only an idiotic native belief."

"You mean, they think that a song will kill?"

"That, and more. They say that if they sing together, think together of one hate, all their thoughts and hates will become a solid strength—will strike and punish for them."

"Nonsense!" exploded Gender.

But when they made camp that night, Gender slept only in troubled snatches, and his dreams were of a song that grew deeper, heavier, until it became visible as a dark, dense cloud that overwhelmed him.

The ship that Gender had engaged for the expedition lay in a swampy estuary, far from any coastal town, and the dawn by which he loaded his goods aboard was strangely fiery and forbidding. Dunlapp, the old slaver-captain that commanded for him, met him in the cabin.

"All ready, sir?" he asked Gender. "We can sail with the tide. Plenty of room in the hold for that handful you brought. I'll tell the men to strike off those irons."

"On the contrary," said Gender, "tell the men to put manacles on the hands of each slave."

Dunlapp gazed in astonishment at his employer. "But that's bad for blacks, Mr. Gender. They get sick in chains, won't eat their food. Sometimes they die."

"I pay you well, Captain," Gender rumbled, "but not to advise me. Listen to those heathen."

Dunlapp listened. A moan of music wafted in to them.

"They've sung that cursed song about me all the way to the coast," Gender told him. "They know I hate it—I've whipped them day after day—but they keep it up. No chains come off until they hush their noise."

Dunlapp bowed acquiescence and walked out to give orders. Later, as they put out to sea, he rejoined Gender on the after deck.

"They do seem stubborn about their singing," he observed.

"I've heard it said," Gender replied, "that they sing together because they think many voices and hearts give power to hate, or to other feelings." He scowled. "Pagan fantasy!"

Dunlapp stared overside, at white gulls just above the wavetips. "There may be a tithe of truth in that belief, Mr. Gender; sometimes there is in the faith of wild people. Hark ye, I've seen a good fifteen hundred Mohammedans praying at once, in the Barbary countries. When they bowed down, the touch of all those heads to the ground banged like the fall of a heavy rock.

And when they straightened, the motion of their garments made a swish like the gust of a gale. I couldn't help but think that their prayer had force."

"More heathen foolishness," snapped Gender, and his lips drew tight.

"Well, in Christian lands we have examples, sir," Dunlapp pursued. "For instance, a mob will grow angry and burn or hang someone. Would a single man do that? Would any single man of the mob do it? No, but together their hate and resolution becomes—"

"Not the same thing at all," ruled Gender harshly. "Suppose we change the subject."

On the following afternoon, a white sail crept above the horizon behind them. At the masthead gleamed a little blotch of color. Captain Dunlapp squinted through a telescope, and barked a sailorly oath.

"A British ship-of-war," he announced, "and coming after us."

"Well?" said Gender.

"Don't you understand, sir? England is sworn to stamp out the slave trade. If they catch us with this cargo, it'll be the end of us." A little later, he groaned apprehensively. "They're overtaking us. There's their signal, for us to lay and wait for them. Shall we do it, sir?"

Gender shook his head violently. "Not we! Show them our heels, Captain."

"They'll catch us. They are sailing three feet to our two."

"Not before dark," said Gender. "When dark comes, we'll contrive to lessen our embarrassment."

And so the slaver fled, with the Britisher in pursuit. Within an hour, the sun was at the horizon, and Gender smiled grimly in his mustache.

"It'll be dark within minutes," he said to Dunlapp. "As soon as you feel they can't make out our actions by glass, get those slaves on deck."

In the dusk the forty-nine naked prisoners stood in a line along the bulwark. For all their chained necks and wrists, they neither stood nor gazed in a servile manner. One of them began to sing and the others joined, in the song of the slave trail:

"Hailowa—Genda! Haipana—Genda!"

"Sing on," Gender snapped briefly, and moved to the end of the line that was near the bow. Here dangled the one empty collar, and he seized it in his hand. Bending over the bulwark, he clamped it shut upon something—the ring of a heavy spare anchor, that swung there upon a swivelhook. Again he turned, and eyed the line of dark singers.

"Have a bath to cool your spirits," he jeered, and spun the handle of the swivel-hook.

The anchor fell. The nearest slave jerked over with it, and the next and the next. Others saw, screamed, and tried to brace themselves against doom; but their comrades that had already gone overside were too much weight for them. Quickly, one after another, the captives whipped from the deck and splashed into the sea. Gender leaned over and watched the last of them as he sank.

"Gad, sir!" exclaimed Dunlapp hoarsely.

Gender faced him almost threateningly.

"What else to do, hmm? You yourself said that we could hope for no mercy from the British."

The night passed by, and by the first gray light the British ship was revealed almost upon them. A megaphoned voice hailed them; then a shot hurtled across their bows. At Gender's smug nod, Dunlapp ordered his men to lay to. A boat put out from the pursuer, and shortly a British officer and four marines swung themselves aboard.

Bowing in mock reverence, Gender bade the party search. They did so, and remounted the deck crestfallen.

"Now, sir," Gender addressed the officer, "don't you think that you owe me an apology?"

The Englishman turned pale. He was a lean, sharp-featured man with strong, white teeth. "I can't pay what I owe you," he said with deadly softness. "I find no slaves, but I smell them. They were aboard this vessel within the past twelve hours."

"And where are they now?" teased Gender.

"We both know where they are," was the reply. "If I could prove in a court of law what I know in my heart, you would sail back to England with me. Most of the way you would hang from my yards by your thumbs."

"You wear out your welcome, sir," Gender told him.

"I am going. But I have provided myself with your name and that of your home city. From here I go to Madeira, where I will cross a packet bound west for Savannah. That packet will bear with it a letter to a friend of mine in Charleston, and your neighbors shall hear what happended on this ship of yours."

"You will stun slave-owners with a story of slaves?" inquired Gender, with what he considered silky good-humor.

"It is one thing to put men to work in cotton fields, another to tear them from their homes, crowd them chained aboard a stinking ship, and drown them to escape merited punishment." The officer spat on the deck. "Good day, butcher. I say, all Charleston shall hear of you."

Gender's plantation occupied a great, bluff-rimmed island at the mouth of a river, looking out toward the Atlantic. Ordinarily that island would be called beautiful, even by those most exacting followers of Chateaubriand and Rousseau; but, on his first night at home again, Gender hated the fields, the house, the environs of fresh and salt water.

His home, on a seaward jut, resounded to his grumbled curses as he called for supper and ate heavily but without relish. Once he vowed, in a voice that quivered with rage, never to go to Charleston again.

At that, he would do well to stay away for a time. The British officer had been as good as his promise, and all the town had heard of Gender's journey to Africa and what he had done there. With a perverse squeamishness beyond Gender's understanding, the hearers were filled with disgust instead

of admiration. Captain Hogue had refused to drink with him at the Jefferson
House. His oldest friend, Mr. Lloyd Davis of Davis Township, had crossed
the street to avoid meeting him. Even the Reverend Doctor Lockin had
turned coldly away as he passed, and it was said that a sermon was
forthcoming at Doctor Lockin's church attacking despoilers and abductors
of defenseless people.

What was the matter with everybody? savagely demanded Gender of
himself; these men who snubbed and avoided him were slave-holders. Some
of them, it was quite possible, even held slaves fresh from raided villages
under the Equator. Unfair! . . . Yet he could not but feel the animosity of
many hearts, chafing and weighing upon his spirit.

"Brutus," he addressed the slave that cleared the table, "do you believe
that hate can take form?"

"Hate, Marsa?" The sooty face was solemnly respectful.

"Yes. Hate, of many people together." Gender knew he should not
confide too much in a slave, and chose his words carefully. "Suppose a lot of
people hated the same thing, maybe they sang a song about it—"

"Oh, yes, Marsa," Brutus nodded. "I heah 'bout dat, from ole gran-pappy
when I was little. He bin in Affiky, he says many times dey sing somebody to
deff."

"Sing somebody to death?" repeated Gender. "How?"

"Dey sing dat dey kill him. Afta while, maybe plenty days, he die—"

"Shut up, you black rascal!" Gender sprang from his chair and clutched at
a bottle. "You've heard about this somewhere and you dare to taunt me!"

Brutus darted from the room, mortally frightened. Gender almost
pursued, but thought better and tramped into his parlor. The big,
brown-paneled room seemed to give back a heavier echo of his feet. The
windows were filled with the early darkness, and a hanging lamp threw rays
into the corners.

On the center table lay some mail, a folded newspaper and a letter.
Gender poured whisky from a decanter, stirred in spring water, and dropped
into a chair. First he opened the letter.

"Stirling Manor," said the return address at the top of the page. Gender's
heart twitched. Evelyn Stirling, he had hopes of her . . . but this was written
in a masculine hand, strong and hasty.

> "Sir:
> "Circumstances that have come to my knowledge compel me,
> as a matter of duty, to command that you discontinue your
> attentions to my daughter."

Gender's eyes took on the pale tint of rage. One more result of the
Britisher's letter, he made no doubt.

> "I have desired her to hold no further communication with you,
> and I have been sufficiently explicit to convince her how

unworthy you are of her esteem and attention. It is hardly necessary for me to give you the reasons which have induced me to form this judgment, and I add only that nothing you can say or do will alter it.

"Your obedient servant,

"JUDGE FORRESTER STIRLING."

Gender hastily swigged a portion of his drink, and crushed the paper in his hand. So that was the judge's interfering way—it sounded as though he had copied it from a complete letter-writer for heavy fathers. He, Gender, began to form a reply in his mind:

"Sir:

"Your unfeeling and arbitrary letter admits of but one response. As a gentleman grossly misused, I demand satisfaction on the field of honor. Arrangements I place in the hands of . . ."

By what friend should he forward that challenge? It seemed that he was mighty short of friends just now. He sipped more whisky and water, and tore the wrappings of the newspaper.

It was a Massachusetts publication, and toward the bottom of the first page was a heavy cross of ink, to call attention to one item. A poem, evidently, in four-line stanzas. Its title signified nothing—*The Witnesses*. Author, Henry W. Longfellow; Gender identified him vaguely as a scrawler of Abolitionist doggerel. Why was this poem recommended to a southern planter?

In Ocean's wide domains,
Half buried in the sands,
Lie skeletons in chains,
With shackled feet and hands.

Once again the reader swore, but the oath quavered on his lips. His eye moved to a stanza farther down the column:

These are the bones of Slaves;
They gleam from the abyss;
They cry, from yawning waves . . .

But it seemed to Gender that he heard, rather than read, what that cry was.

He sprang to his feet, paper and glass falling from his hands. His thin lips drew apart, his ears strained. The sound was faint, but unmistakable—many voices singing.

The Negroes in his cabins? But no Negro on his plantation would know that song. The chanting refrain began:

"*Hailowa—Genda! Haipana—Genda!*"

The planter's lean mustaches bristled tigerishly. This would surely be the refined extremity of his persecution, this chanting of a weird song under his window-sill. It was louder now. *I will bewitch, I will kill*—but who would know that fierce mockery of him?

The crew of his ship, of course; they had heard it on the writhing lips of the captives, at the very moment of their destruction. And when the ship docked in Charleston, with no profit to show, Gender had been none too kindly in paying them off.

Those unsavory mariners must have been piqued. They had followed him, then, were setting up this vicious serenade.

Gender stepped quickly around the table and toward the window. He flung up the sash with a violence that almost shattered the glass, and leaned savagely out.

On that instant the song stopped, and Gender could see only the seaward slope of his land, down to the lip of the bluff that overhung the water. Beyond that stretched an expanse of waves, patchily agleam under a great buckskin-colored moon, that even now stirred the murmurous tide at the foot of the bluff. Here were no trees, no brush even, to hide pranksters. The singers, now silent, must be in a boat under the shelter of the bluff.

Gender strode from the room, fairly tore open a door, and made heavy haste toward the sea. He paused, on the lip of the bluff. Nothing was to be seen, beneath him or farther out. The mockers, if they had been here, had already fled. He growled, glared, and tramped back to his house. He entered the parlor once more, drew down the sash, and sought his chair again. Choosing another glass, he began once more to mix whisky and water. But he stopped in the middle of his pouring.

There it was again, the song he knew; and closer.

He rose, took a step in the direction of the window, then thought better of it. He had warned his visitors by one sortie, and they had hidden. Why not let them come close, and suffer the violence he ached to pour out on some living thing?

He moved, not to the window, but to a mantelpiece opposite. From a box of dark, polished wood he lifted a pistol, then another. They were duelling weapons, handsomely made, with hair-triggers; and Gender was a dead shot. With orderly swiftness he poured in glazed powder from a flask, rammed down two leaden bullets, and laid percussion caps upon the touchholes. Returning, he placed the weapons on his center table, then stood on tiptoe to extinguish the hanging lamp. A single light remained in the room, a candle by the door, and this he carried to the window, placing it on a bracket there. Moving into the gloomy center of the parlor, he sat in his chair and took a pistol in either hand.

The song was louder now, lifted by many voices:

"*Hailowa—Genda! Haipana—Genda!*"

Undoubtedly the choristers had come to land by now, had gained the top of the bluff. They could be seen, Gender was sure, from the window. He felt perspiration on his jowl, and lifted a sleeve to blot it. Trying to scare him, hmm? Singing about witchcraft and killing? Well, he'd show them who was the killer.

The singing had drawn close, was just outside. Odd how the sailors, or whoever they were, had learned that chant so well! It recalled to his mind the slave trail, the jungle, the long procession of crooning prisoners. But here was no time for idle revery on vanished scenes. Silence had fallen again, and he could only divine the presence, just outside, of many creatures.

Scratch-scratch-scratch; it sounded like the stealthy creeping of a snake over rough lumber. That scratching resounded from the window where something stole into view in the candlelight. Gender fixed his eyes there, and his pistols lifted their muzzles.

The palm of a hand, as gray as a fish, laid itself on the glass. It was wet; Gender could see the trickle of water descending along the pane. something clinked, almost musically. Another hand moved into position beside it, and between the two swung links of chain.

This was an elaborately devilish joke, thought Gender, in an ecstasy of rage. Even the chains, to lend reality . . . and as he stared he knew, in a split moment of terror that stirred his flesh on his bones, that it was no joke after all.

A face had moved into the range of the candlelight, pressing close to the pane between the two palms.

It was darker than those palms, of a dirty, slaty deadness of color. But it was not dead, not with those dull, intent eyes that moved slowly in their blistery sockets . . . not dead, though it was foully wet, and its thick lips hung slackly open, and seaweed lay plastered upon the cheeks, even though the flat nostrils showed crumbled and gnawed away, as if by fish. The eyes quested here and there across the floor and walls of the parlor. They came to rest, gazing full into the face of Gender.

He felt as though stale sea-water had trickled upon him, but his right hand abode steady as a gun-rest. He took aim and fired.

The glass crashed loudly, and fell in shattering flakes to the floor beneath the sill.

Gender was on his feet, moving forward, dropping the empty pistol on the table and whipping the loaded one into his right hand. Two leaping strides took him almost to the window, before he reeled backward.

The face had not fallen. It stared at him, a scant yard away. Between the dull, living eyes showed a round black hole, where the bullet had gone in. But the thing stood unflinchingly, somehow serenely. Its two wet hands moved slowly, methodically, to pluck away the jagged remains of the glass.

Gender rocked where he stood, unable for the moment to command his body to retreat. The shoulders beneath the face heightened. They were bare and wet and deadly dusky, and they clinked the collar-shackle beneath the lax chin. Two hands stole into the room, their fish-colored palms opening toward Gender.

He screamed, and at last he ran. As he turned his back, the singing began yet again, loud and horribly jaunty—not at all as the miserable slaves had sung it. He gained the seaward door, drew it open, and looked full into a gathering of black, wet figures, with chains festooned among them, awaiting him. Again he screamed, and tried to push the door shut.

He could not. A hand was braced against the edge of the panel—many hands. The wood fringed itself with gleaming black fingers. Gender let go the knob, whirled to flee into the house. Something caught the back of his coat, something he dared not identify. In struggling loose, he spun through the doorway and into the moonlit open.

Figures surrounded him, black, naked, wet figures; dead as to sunken faces and flaccid muscles, but horribly alive as to eyes and trembling hands and slack mouths that formed the strange primitive words of the song; separate, yet strung together with a great chain and collar-shackles, like an awful fish on the gigantic line of some demon-angler. All this Gender saw in a rocking, moon-washed moment, while he choked and retched at a dreadful odor of death, thick as fog.

Still he tried to run, but they were moving around him in a weaving crescent, cutting off his retreat toward the plantation. Hands extended toward him, manacled and dripping. His only will was to escape the touch of those sodden fingers, and one way was open—the way to the sea.

He ran toward the brink of the bluff. From its top he would leap, dive and swim away. But they pursued, overtook, surrounded him. He remembered that he held a loaded pistol, and fired into their black midst. It had no effect. He might have known that it would have no effect.

Something was clutching for him. A great, inhuman talon? No, it was an open collar of metal, with a length of chain to it, a collar that had once clamped to an anchor, dragging down to ocean's depths a line of shackled men. It gaped at him, held forth by many dripping hands. He tried to dodge, but it darted around his throat, shut with a ringing snap. Was it cold . . . or scalding hot? He knew, with horror vividly etching the knowledge into his heart, that he was one at last with the great chained procession.

"Hailowa—Genda! Haipana—Genda!"

He found his voice. "No, no!" he pleaded. "No, in the name of—"

But he could not say the name of God. And the throng suddenly moved explosively, concertedly, to the edge of the bluff.

A single wailing cry from all those dead throats, and they dived into the waves below.

Gender did not feel the clutch and jerk of the chain that dragged him alone. He did not even feel the water as it closed over his head.

SOUTH DAKOTA

The Eagle-Claw Rattle
by Ardath Mayhar

IT WAS a shackledy old scaffold. You'd never catch a white man doing such a sorry job, particularly if he was planning to stick the body of one of his great men on top of it. The Sioux, though . . . what can you expect from a bunch of heathen Injuns who think that's the only proper way to do the dead? Closer to the Great Spirit—hah! Any white man can tell you that the only place to put a dead man is in the ground. This scaffold business is just unsanitary, if not downright sinful.

Anyway, it was the devil and all to climb. Particularly in the dark. Even out there in the back of beyond, you never knew if one of those red-tailed varmints was there in the rocks, watching. A cautious man doesn't rob Injun graves, mind you, but of those that do, the most wary live longest. I've been at it (and other things) all over the Dakota Territory for a long time, and I've still got my hair to prove it.

There was a tad of moon—just a toenail-trimming's worth. A low and lonesome wind was whishing along the ground, stirring up enough dust to fog up the landscape a bit, which suited me fine. If it was also moaning and hissing around the scaffold and its burden, well, that was fine, too. I figured that the day had come and gone when old Thunder-on-the-Mountain could give me any hassle.

I could see the dark, oblong shape against the stars, whenever I'd look up. Mighty long and thin . . . of course, he'd been a big cuss, from what I'd heard. Likely the desert air had dried the juices out of him and thinned him down. Even with all the bundled wraps they'd put around him, he looked mighty narrow. Still, I'd never seen one yet that'd rotted away to bones, not in this climate. When I first started taking orders for "Indian artifacts," I unwrapped one or two, just to see what I was dealing with. They were just like old, stiff leather. Not much different from what the really old 'uns look like when they're alive.

This one was the top of the line, though. The red devils think old Thunder helped hang the moon, from what you hear around the campfires at night. Said he could shake up storms out of the mountains with that painted rattle of his. Could make the ground shake so hard it split open and let whole rivers get lost and never come out again.

I laughed. Now here he hung, with the wind singing through his teeth, not even able to spit out a mouse-sized curse at the white man who was going to make off with his fourteen-karat, hundred-proof magic rattle. And sell it, what's more, to an Eastern fella who was fool enough to offer *two hundred dollars* for it.

The wind seemd to pick up, the higher I got. Or maybe I was going above the shelter of the ridge of rocks that curved away to the east. I could see eagle feathers fluttering, now, tied onto the scaffolding in untidy bunches. They were all but worn down to the nub by the wind and the dust, but they still spun round and round or else flittered away at the ends of thongs.

Funny, the way your imagination will rise to any occasion. I'd have sworn that I heard that corpse shift, just the way a man does when he's been lying down too long and needs to ease his bones. It was the wind moving the deer hide wrappings, of course, but it gave me an almighty start until I figured it out.

When I came out on the narrow platform, it seemed almost light, for the moon had pulled out from behind the thin mare's tails that were misted across the sky to the east. I could see the way the outer wrap was tied. It was buffalo hide, weathered to the toughness of wood, and the bindings had been knotted for so long that there was no way on God's green earth you could have untied them.

I got out my boot-knife and began cutting. I knocked down a couple of pots and what must have been a bundle of lances while I was moving around the edge of the platform, trying to get everything cut before I opened it up. They made a godawful clatter and crash, and I stopped for a minute and listened. Injuns have an unchancy habit of going out to forsaken places like this to sit and meditate and wait for their heathen gods to talk to them.

Still and all, if there'd been one around, I'd know it by now, I figured, and got busy again. Then the cutting was all done, and I carefully pulled back the buffalo robe. It cracked in a long split, and the section I'd lifted caught the wind and went sailing away. That left a shell shaped something like a long narrow boat, and in it was Thunder-on-the-Mountain, in person.

They'd tanned deer hide so fine that it was silky. Even in the dark I could see the beadwork twinkling in the moonlight, as I unfolded the top layer. Underneath that was a pair of dark hands. They were so well-preserved that they still looked strong enough to strangle a bear. Big, tough, long-fingered hands, they were, and they were clasped like grim death around the handle of a big gourd rattle.

And that was what I'd come for. A gourd that old, mind you, can be brittle as paper, so I tried to ease it out of those hands. It was as if they'd been glued together. I stood up for a minute to ease my back, and as I did, I looked up at the end where the face would have been, if it hadn't been covered with deerskin.

The wind fluttered the layer of hide just a bit. Just enough so it looked like somebody was breathing underneath it. And I felt like two hot black eyes were blazing away under there, fit to burn twin holes in the pale skin.

I shook my head and laughed. Robbing graveyards—even heathen graveyards—was no business for a man who let himself get fanciful. I laughed again and went back to work.

Now it's not that I'm squeamish. I've handled more than my share of dead bodies, both fresh and mummified, and I've never thought a thing of it. But those hands were another matter. First off, they looked alive. They looked as if, when I laid hand to them, they just might grab hold of my wrists and throw me down off the scaffold.

As I stood there considering, it suddenly dawned on me that he didn't *smell* right, either. All the others had had a faint, musty, nasty odor, not strong but mighty noticeable. This one didn't, and it wasn't just that the wind was carrying it off. The only smell there was was tanned deer hide and old buffalo robe. Not the best of stinks, but better than mummified Injun.

The moon was way up by now, and I wasn't done with my job, so I shook my head to get the foolishness out of it and went about my business. If the hands wouldn't turn loose of the rattle, then, by George, they'd just have to go along with it, at least until I could figure out a way to get them off without busting my two hundred dollars all to flinders.

My boot-knife was just the ticket, and I had them off at the wrists in no time. Even then, they held onto that rattle as it they'd grown to it. And I couldn't see that fella buying a pair of dead hands. Easterners have weak stomachs.

I cut off a bit of hide and tied it around the whole thing, rattle and all, making a loose bundle of it. As I lifted it, the eagle claws fastened to the rattle clicked sharply against its painted sides. It was shuddery—worse than a rattlesnake in a dark room.

I put things back as well as I could, for it's just as well to avoid any trouble you can. The piece of robe that had blown away was long gone, but I fixed the deer hide back together and tied some of the fringes to keep it in place. I'll admit that it was a relief to hide those dark wrist stumps, too.

I went back down with the bundle slung over my shoulder, the rattle clashing gently away at every move. The wind was picking up, too, whipping my coattails and pushing and prying at my bundle. As I reached the ground, the moon went under a cloud, and I looked up to see that the mare's tails had moved together into a black mat that covered half the sky.

My horse was dancing around, whinnying that wild way they do when a storm is coming, and it was all I could do to calm him down enough to get mounted. I hadn't more than got my feet settled into the stirrups when a pure wall of wind and dust and rain, all mixed up together, came whooping down on me.

I kneed Gray over against the rock outcrop to knock off part of the wind, and we just hunched down to wait it out. The lightning came, then, sizzling down so close that I could hear the little pop that comes before the big crack. Thunder rolled down over us like a giant walking on drums, and I glanced out from under my hatbrim to see if the rain was slacking off any.

It wasn't. It was, if anything, harder, and the continuous lightning lit it into silver sheets.

In the midst of it stood a big man. He was dressed in fine-tanned deerskin, and the rain hadn't wet an inch of it. He was standing four paces away, just looking at me, and his eyes were big dark holes in his face. The thunder boomed right above us, shaking the air and the ground and even the rock my elbow was touching.

The Injun didn't move. He stood there, waiting and watching, and I stared back, knowing what he wanted but still too stubborn to admit that I had to do it.

The rain got harder; the lightning danced around us like mad fireworks, and the thunder sounded fit to shake down the sky. In a little bit, that Injun stepped forward one pace. I shrunk down into my coat, wet as it was, but I couldn't look away.

He raised his head toward the sky, and he held up his arms. His hands were gone, but as if he had called on further powers, the storm got worse. A lot worse.

So I slowly got down from my shivering horse and tied him securely to a knob of rock. I took the bundle and put it over my shoulder again. Then I waited. I wasn't going a bit closer to that big Injun than I was, and he sensed it right off.

Between one wink of lightning and the next, he was gone.

I sighed; then I gritted my teeth. To think a white man, a Christian, could be maneuvered by a heathen Injun made my blood boil . . . but quietly.

I climbed the scaffold again, and the rain was ending as I reached the top. The long form lay there, and the wind hadn't stirred a fold of its wrappings. I untied the strings, then the bundle I carried. Carefully, I fitted the hands back to the stumps of the wrists. Before I could take my fingers away, I felt . . . I felt the damn things *flex*.

The lightning, dying away to westward, lit the place by flashes. The hands lay still and dark, grasping the rattle. I shook my head and looked at the bundled shape. Might as well do the thing right, I thought.

Sighing, I went down and got my buffalo robe from my bedroll. It was two jobs to get it back up, with the wind still blowing in gusts, but I managed. Then I lifted and shifted and maneuvered until I had it around old Thunder-on-the-Mountain, and I tied it down good and proper.

He lay there, quiet as death, but I still had the feeling that those eyes were wide open and seeing through to *my* bones. I went down the scaffold for the last time in one rush, got on my horse and lit out.

The lightning had stopped, now, but I could hear some sort of low, grumbling sound that hadn't any direction that I could fix. Then, over the rumbling and pounding of Gray's hooves, I could hear the sharp, clear sound of that eagle-claw rattle.

Gray screamed and shuddered, rearing and turning as the ground opened in front of us. It unseated me, and I fell, my boots sliding out of the stirrups as if they were greased. I seemed to fall forever, with the sound of that rattle clashing and laughing in my ears all the way down.

I felt bones snap all over me when I hit bottom. My teeth were full of grit, and I think my jaw was busted. I went out for a long time.

When I came to, old Thunder was sitting there beside me. The rattle was shushing away in a soft rhythm, and the old bastard was saying something long and complicated in his heathenish lingo. Now and again he'd stand up and shake his hands at the sky. They were back on, good and tight.

He's waiting for me to die. He's making Injun magic right now, and it'll trap me down here, with the walls of the crack already beginning to sag back together. As soon as I die, he's going to bury me, body, soul, and all, in all this rock and dirt, and I'll never get to heaven. I'll turn to old boot leather, just like he did, instead of rotting away like a Christian corpse to bones.

Damn him. He's going to make me a mummy, too.

TENNESSEE

Our Town
by Jerome Bixby

A JET bomber and four fighters had appeared low over Bald Ridge, out of the east. They'd curved up as one to clear Lawson's Hill, their stubby wings almost brushing the treetops, their hiss and thunder rolling back and forth between the valley walls like a giant's derision; they'd dipped into the valley proper, obviously informed that Smoky Creek, Tennessee (population 123) had no anti-aircraft installations, and circled the town at about five hundred feet. They circled and looked down—broad slavic faces with curious expressions, seen through plexiglass, as if thinking: *So this is an American small town.*

Then they took altitude and got to work. The first bomb was aimed at the big concrete railway bridge spanning the upper end of the valley; that was the main objective of the attack. The bomb exploded four hundred yards north of the bridge, at about six hundred feet altitude—the ideal point from which to flatten Smoky Creek. Low altitude bombing can be tricky, of course, especially in mountain country. A-bombs were cheap though, turned out by the carload; not like 20 years before, when they were first developed. So it was likely the bombardier tripped a bomb over the town just for the hell of it.

The next bomb got the bridge. The next tore up a quarter mile of track. The next tore up a quarter mile of road. That was the mission. The bomber circled, while the fighters strafed Smoky Creek for good measure; and then they roared away past Lawson's Hill over Bald Ridge, into the east toward their invasion-coast base.

Everybody died. The bombs were midget A's, designed for tactical use; so

Smoky Creek wasn't reduced to dust—just to sticks. There wasn't much heat from the bomb and there was hardly any residual radiation. But everybody in town died. Concussion. Smoky Creek had been comprised of one main street and three cross streets, and that's not much area—the wave had thumped down from right above, like a giant fist. Everybody died, except twenty-one old men and women who had been off in the woods at the far end of the valley, on their annual Grandfolk's Picnic. They didn't die, except inside.

Three months later, an enemy jet came out of the sky and over the valley. A scoop arrangement under its belly was sniffing Tennessee and Alabama air for radioactive particles. It sniffed low over the town, and then again—a ruined town might hide an underground lab and converter—and then it barrel-rolled and crashed. Nine rifle bullets had hit the motor; straight back through the jet intake, into the blades.

A year after that another jet came low over the town, and it crashed too. Only three bullets this time; but a jet motor's like a turbine—you get a blade or two, and it goes crazy.

Two years after that, Ben Bates (no longer Mayor Ben, because a mayor has to have a town; but still the man in charge) knocked off playing horseshoes in what had been the Town Hall. Now the building served as a recreation hall; there were horseshoe pits at one end of the long room, there were tables for checkers and cards, and a short tenpin alley along one wall. Three years ago the alley had been twice as long as it was now; but then there were young men around who could peg the length of it without tiring every time. Overhead the roof sagged, and in one place you could see quite a piece of sky—but under the hole the old men had rigged a slanted board watershed that led to a drainage ditch; and scattered through the room were a lot of supporting posts and timber braces. Actually the building was about as safe as it had ever been.

There were other buildings like it; buildings that the bomb hadn't pounded flat or made too risky. They were propped up and nailed together and buttressed and practically glued so they'd stay up. From outside you'd think they were going to crumble any minute—walls slanted all cockeyed, boards peeled off and hanging, and roofs buckling in. But they were safe. Fixed up every which way—from the inside. All from the inside; not an inch of repair on the outside. It had to be that way, because the town had to look like a dead town.

After the men had finished propping, the women had come along with all the furniture and things they'd salvaged and they swept and scrubbed and did a hundred jobs the men never would have thought of; and so the old people ended up with half a dozen buildings to live in, secretly and comfortably, in the town that had to look dead.

"Arthritis is bad," Ben Bates told his teammates and opponents. "Hell, I'm just giving away points. Maybe next week. I'll rest up, and kick you all around next week."

He lit a cigar, a big grey man with long legs and a good-humored mouth, and he watched Dan Paray throw one short; then he strolled over to kibitz at the checker game between Fat Sam Hogan and Windy Harris, at one of the tables near the door. Late morning sunlight slanted in through the window by the table and struck light off Windy's glasses as he leaned across the board, thumped a checker three times and said triumphantly, "King me, Sam. You're getting blind, I swear. Or dumber."

Behind his back Ben Bates heard a shoe ring against the stake; then he heard it spin off, and he grinned at Owen Urey's bullfrog cussing.

Tom Pace was saying urgently, "Look—look, Jim, damn it, you didn't no more shoot down that plane singlehanded than I did. We was all shooting. Godamighty—where you get off claiming *you* brung it down?"

Ben turned and sat down at the table next to the checker game, and stretched his legs in the sunlight. He raised thick brows like clumps of steel-wool at Tom and at old Jim Liddel, who sat in his pillowed armchair like a thin, scowling, bald, mansized spider.

"You keep talking so high and mighty," Tom said, "we'll carry you out o' here and take you and dump you in the creek. You can tell the fish about who got the plane."

"Still arguing over who planted the shot, huh," Ben grinned. "Regular feud, you two."

"Well, hell, Ben," Tom said, and bit down on his gums so his whiskers almost hid the end of his hose. "I just get filled up on this old windbag hollering how he—"

"You go call me a windbag once more, Tom Pace," Jim Liddel said, and he stirred his all but helpless body in the armchair, "you're gonna have a sore eye, you seventy year old whippersnapper. *I* brung it down."

"In a hog's behind, you brung it down, Mister Dan'l Boone!"

"It 'us just after I let loose it started smoking," old Jim snarled, "and nobody else was shooting right then! You're gonna get a sore eye, I swear—tobacco in it. I can spit to where you sit, and I can spit faster'n you can move, I bet, unless you're faster'n a fly, and you ain't. You just ask anybody who was there . . . it 'us just after I shot it started—"

Tom Pace thumped the table. "*I* was there, you old . . . now, now, Jim, don't spit, for Godsake! Hold on. What I mean, I was there too, and maybe somebody's shot from a second or two before was what done the trick. Maybe even my shot! Takes a plane a while to know it's hurt, don't it? Ever think o' that?"

"Maybe," Ben Bates said. "Maybe, maybe. And maybe. Let it go, you two. It ain't important who done it; we oughta just be grateful we got it."

"Grateful *I* got it," Jim Liddel grunted.

Tom Pace said, "Now, looky here, Jim—" Ben Bates nudged Tom's leg under the table; and then slowly, fingering his jaw he said, "Well, now, Jim . . . I figure maybe you did, at that. Like you say, it smoked and crashed right after you shot, so I always kind o' figured it *was* you brought it down. But that's a hard thing to prove."

Jim snorted. "Can't prove it! But I got it, all right. A man knows when he sunk a shot."

"In a varmint, maybe," Tom Pace objected, "or a man. But you claiming to know where to hit a plane the worst?"

"We was *all* shooting at the front, up where they put the motor," Jim said nastily. "Don't know about planes, but I know my aim. I got it square-on."

"Well," Ben said, "why don't you just let it lay, eh, Tom? Jim's got a lot on his side." He looked sidewise at old Jim, and saw that Jim was still scowling at Tom. Old Jim was ninety eight, and some set in his notions.

"Mm. Hell," Tom said reluctantly, after a second, "I ain't saying you *didn't*, Jim. That ain't my intent. I just get burned when you yell you did, like no man dared say you was wrong. Sure, maybe you're right. But ain't you willing to admit you might be wrong too?"

"*No,*" Jim Liddel yelled, and from the checker table came Windy Harris's encouraging, "You tell 'em who got that plane, Jim!"

Ben Bates scraped an inch of ash off his cigar against the table-edge, sighed and got up. He looked down at the glowering pair and said, "Well, come the next plane, if there is one, we'll shove a rifle in your hand, Jim, and see how good your eye is. You too, Tom. Till that time, reckon this is no place for a reasoning man."

"Sit down, Ben Bates," old Jim snarled. "If you're a reasoning man, sit down. Be glad to talk to one, after Tom here goes away."

"You go to hell. *I* ain't going no place," Tom said, and he picked up the cards and started shuffling them in his stiff hands.

Ben sat down and stretched out his legs again.

After a second, old Jim said wistfully, "You know, I wish I *could* still handle a rifle, Ben. Or do anything but sit. No way for a man to live, to have dead legs and dying arms." He shifted in his cushions. "You know, I reckon when I start to really die—die all over— I'm gonna get up out o' this chair. I'll stand up, somehow, even if it kills me faster. A man oughta fall when he dies, like a tree, so they know he stood up in his time. A man oughtn'ta die sitting down."

"Sure, Jim," Ben said. "You're right about that."

"Never had a sick day in my life, until they dropped that bomb. Why, I could outpitch and outcrop and outshoot any of you whippersnappers, until they . . ." Old Jim walloped the chair arm. "Damn, I made up for it, though! Didn't I? *They* put me in a chair, I sat in it and *I* got me an airyplane, and that's more'n they could do to me, by golly, they couldn't kill me!"

"Sure, Jim," Ben said.

"And when my time comes, I'll be up and out o' this chair. Man oughta fall and make a noise when he dies."

"Sure, Jim," Ben said. "But that's a long ways off, ain't it?"

Jim closed his eyes, and his face looked like a skull. "You squirts always think a man lives forever."

From outside came the late morning sounds: the murmuring of Smoky

Creek at the edge of town, under its cool tunnel of willows; the twittering of a flock of robins circling above; the constant soft rustle of the trees that crowded the green hills around. From the warehouse down by the tracks came the faint sounds of livestock—and the voices of the men whose job it was to look after them this week: to feed them, turn them out into the big pens for an hour's sunlight, then drive them back into the warehouse again.

Lucky the warehouse had stood the bomb—it was perfect for the use.

"Wonder how the war's going," Tom Pace said. He dropped some cards and bent painfully to retrieve them; his voice was muffled: "I just wonder how it's going, you know? Wonder who's killing more than who today."

"Maybe," Tom continued, coming up, "it's all over. Ain't seen no planes for couple years now. Maybe somebody won."

Ben shrugged. "Who knows. Don't matter none to us. We're ready as we can be if another plane comes around. Other than that, it ain't our concern."

"Darn tootin'," Tom said, and pushed the cards together and started shuffling again.

Jim Liddel said, "War!" and looked like he'd bit into spoiled meat. "Never settled nothing . . . just makes the biggest dog top-dog for a while, so he can get his way. Man, I wish I could still lift a rifle, if an airyplane come around! I'd love to get me another one." He put his thin back against the cushions and pushed at the edge of the table with his hands. Jim's fingers didn't move so well any more; some were curled and some were straight out, and the joints were different sizes, and now they were trembling a little. "Sometimes when I think o' Johnny and Helen and all the kids—when I think o' that day, and those damn bombs, and that white tower o' smoke up over the town, I . . . oh, godamighty, I'd love to see another airyplane! I'd shout and yell and pray; I'd pray almighty God for you to get it!"

Ben pulled on his cigar with stiff lips, and said slowly, "Well, we might, Jim. We just might. Two out o' seven ain't bad." He puffed out smoke. "We been running in luck, so far, what with nobdy ever coming back loaded for bear. Reckon that means the other five didn't see us, low as they was; probably didn't even know they was being shot at."

"They musta found bulletholes, though," Tom Pace said. "Afterwards. Not a chance we'd all miss—" he bobbed his beard at old Jim—"'specially with Dan'l Boone here plugging away. They'd know they was shot at, all right. Might even find rifle bullets."

"Maybe they did," Ben said. "Nobody ever come snooping back though."

"Wouldn't know where to, would they?" Windy Harris said. He and Fat Sam Hogan had stopped playing checkers, and had been listening. "Smoky Creek looks dead as Sodom. Buildings all down, and stuff knee-deep in the streets. Bridge down, and the road out. And the valley is way the hell out o' the way . . . no call for them to suspect it more'n anyplace else. Less, even. They'd likely figure somebody took a potshot from a hill . . . and there's a pack o' hills between here'n outside."

"Looks like," Ben said. "We just got to keep it that way. We got a good plan: if the plane's up high we just freeze under cover; if it comes down low a time or two, we figure we're likely spotted and start shooting. We shoot, and maybe it shoots too, and we pray."

"It's a good plan," Jim Liddel said, looking out the window. "We got two."

Windy Harris got up and stretched out his arms.

"Two ain't *enough*," old Jim said bitterly.

"Well," Windy said, "I hope we keep on getting 'em—them as sees us, anyway. Hope nobody *ever* knows we're here. It's peaceful here. Way off by ourselves, nothing to do but get up and go to bed, and do what we want in between." He sent tobacco juice into the cuspidor by the door. "Right now, me, I guess I'll go fishing down by the creek—promised Maude I'd bring home a cat or two for supper. Anybody come along?"

Tom Pace shook his head, and old Jim looked like he'd like to go, if he only could—and Ben said, "Maybe I'll be down a little while later, Windy. Keep to the trees."

Windy left, and Tom Pace shuffled the cards and looked over at Jim Liddel. "You going to play with Ben and me, you old windbag, or you going to keep bragging so loud a man can't stand your company?"

"Why, you whippersnapper," Jim growled, "you just go ahead and run 'em. Reckon a reasoning man and a nitwit's about the best I can do right now."

Tom dealt out two cards, and said, "War!" without dealing out the rest. He looked at Ben, his eyes cloudy. "Got a cigar, Ben?"

Ben handed one over and held a match, and Tom got it going, puffing longer than he had to, like he didn't want to talk yet.

Then he said, "It didn't have to happen." He worked the cigar over to the corner of his mouth and settled it in the nest of stained whiskers there. "None of it had to happen—what happened here, and whatever happened outside the valley. It just didn't have to happen."

"'Course it didn't," Ben said. "Never has to. It just always does. Some people got reasons to let it happen, and some ain't got the sense not to."

Fat Sam Hogan said, "I don't figure there's anything in the world a man can't sit down and talk out, instead o' reaching for a gun. Don't know why that oughtn'ta hold for countries."

Ben Bates looked at one of two cards Tom Pace had dealt—his hole card. It was a four, and he lost interest. "Yup," he said, "it holds all right . . . they'll just both reach half the time anyway. One war on top of another. Even one right after this one, ten years or so, if this one's over. I just bet. Every country wants a piece out o' the next one's hide—or his poke—and they won't give an inch except in talk; they won't really buckle down to stop a war. Never. Not if they can't get what they want by talk." He looked at the card again, just in case—a four, sure enough. "Only time there's never a war is when everybody has what they want, or figure they can get it without killing somebody. But the second they see that's the only way, then it's war. War, war, war. It's a rotten way to run a world, killing to decide who's right or wrong . . . 'specially killing people who got damn little say about it. But I seen three-four wars now, and they don't look to stop soon, judging." He shook his head wonderingly. "Put half the money they spend on killing toward curing, instead, and helping them that wants, and finding out all about diseases and such . . . why, shucks, it'd be a brand-new world."

"I seen five," Jim Liddel said. "I seen wars come and go. I fought in one. Afterwards, every time, they say everything's fine. The war to save this or that's over, and things are fine. Then somebody wants something somebody else has, and they're at it again, like two bulls trying to hump the same heifer. Bulls don't have enough sense to know there's enough cows to go around; but people ought. It's a big enough world." He worked those hands of his together until they were clasped, and he pushed them that way against the table-edge until the overgrown knuckles looked like chalk. "When I think o' that noise, and that cloud, . . . how we come running and screaming back here into all the dust and mess, and all them bodies . . . I . . . Ben, I . . ."

"You lost heavy, Jim," Ben said. He let smoke out of his lungs, and it curled off into the broad beam of sunlight that came through the window, and it looked like the smoke that had shadowed a murdered town. "Heavy. You lost heavier'n any of us."

"You can't count it," old Jim said, and the chalk was whiter. "We all lost the same; I just had more of it. Our kids and their kids—and *their* kids . . . lost heavy? What can a man lose more'n his life? . . . And if you're as old as us, what's your life except the family you made out o' your own flesh? What else's a man got when he's eighty or a hundred?"

Tom Pace said, "Ruth and Dave and their kids. I remember little Davey. He called me Tom Peach. I bought him a toy plane for his birthday. That was a couple days before the real planes come. I buried it with him . . . I think. I think it was him I put it with. It mighta been Joey . . . they looked alike."

"A man ain't nothing, when he's as old as us," Jim Liddel said, his skull sockets closed, "except what he done. *He* ain't much any more, himself; he's mostly what he done with his life, whatever he done and left around that he can point to and say, 'I did that,' that's all. And what's he got left if they take that away? We can't make it again. We made Smoky Creek; built it; wasn't a thing here that didn't come out o' us or ours. We made the valley, after God give it to us; wasn't a thing here we didn't let live or help live or make live. We made our families, and watched 'em fit into the town and the valley, like the valley fits into the world, and we watched 'em go on doing what we done before them: building and working and planting and raising families—going on, like people got to go on. That's the way it was. That's what we had. Until they dropped the bomb and killed it—killed all we done that made us men." Tears were squeezing out of the skull sockets, and Ben Bates caught Tom Pace's eye and looked away, out the window, at the green walls of the valley that was a coffin.

"I just wish an airyplane would come around again," old Jim said. "*I—just—wish*. You know, Ben?"

Ben tried to talk and had to clear his throat; he put out his cigar in the ashtray, as if that was what was wrong with his throat, and said, "I know, Jim. Sure. And maybe you'll get your wish." He pushed back his chair and tried to grin, but it came out sour. "Maybe you will, you old fire-eater—and what if one comes and we get spotted and it shoots us up or goes back and tells everybody we're here? That's one wish we don't want the good Lord to grant, ain't it? Ain't it, now?"

Jim didn't say anything.

Ben got up and said, "'Bout noon. Guess I'll go home for a bite and then go down and fish with Windy."

Jim said, thinly, "I meant, I wish one would come and we'd *get* it."

"Well maybe one will," Ben said, turning toward the door. "They built a slew o' them. And maybe *we* will, if it does."

He stopped by the door of the Town Hall to listen carefully, his sharp old eyes half-shut. Behind him, at the far end of the room, somebody made a ringer, and Dave Mason said, "Nice, Owen," in his reedy voice. Ben listened and didn't hear what he was listening for. He stepped past the rifle that leaned beside the door and made his way to the end of the porch, walking close to the wall. The summer sun stood at noon, and the porch was in shadow; beyond, the street was a jumble of boards and broken glass, its canyon walls of leaning building-fronts and sagging porches, its caverns of empty windows and doorways shimmering in the heat. You couldn't see much dirt along the way; where the debris didn't come to your knees, it reached over your head.

At the end of the porch Ben stopped and listened again; heard nothing. He stepped down and walked as fast as he could—damn arthritis again—to the porch of the next building.

This had been Fat Sam Hogan's Hardware Store, and about all that was left of it was the porch; the rest was a twisted mess of wood that slumped away to the ground at the rear. The porch had been down too, right after the bombing—but the old men, working at night, had raised it and braced it up. Something to walk under.

A Springfield stood, oiled and waiting, against the wall. Ben paused and touched the barrel—it was his own. Or rather it had once been his own; now it was the town's, strictly speaking, to be used by whoever was nearest it when the time came. It was a good gun, a straight-shooter, one of the best—which was why it was here instead of at his house. A man could get a better shot from here.

He went on, hugging the wall.

He passed a rifle wedged up between the fender and hood of Norm Henley's old Model A, and he remembered how the bomb had flipped the car right over on its top, and how the car must have protected Norm from the blast—just a little. Enough so they found him two blocks up the street, in front of his mashed house, trailing blood from every hole in him, to get to his family before he died.

Ben passed rifles leaned against walls and chairs on porches, rifles standing behind trees, leaned in the cracks between what buildings still stood to provide cracks, even old Jim's carbine lying under the ledge of the pump-trough in front of Mason's General Store. All of them in places where they were protected from rain or snow, but where they were easy to get at.

He passed sixteen rifles—walking, as everybody walked when they were out of doors, as close to the walls of the buildings as possible. When you had to cross open spaces you ran as fast as your seventy or eighty year old legs would take you—and if you couldn't run, you walked real fast. And always you listened while you walked; particularly you listened before you went out. For planes. So you wouldn't be spotted from the air.

At the end of the porch of the last building on the street, Ben paused in the shade and looked out across the creek to where the first plane they'd shot down had crashed—the one Jim claimed to have got by his lonesome. They'd buried what they found of the pilot, and cleared away every last bolt and nut and scrap of aluminum, but the long scar in the ground remained. Ben looked at it, all broken up by rocks and flowers and bushes the old people had transplanted so it wouldn't show from the air; and he looked at the cemetery a hundred feet beyond at which the scar pointed like an arrow—the cemetery that wasn't a cemetery, because it didn't have headstones; just bodies. A town that was dead shouldn't have a lot of new graves—the dead don't bury themselves. A pilot might see a hundred graves he hadn't seen before and wonder—and strafe.

So Ben looked at the flat ground where those hundred bodies lay, with only small rocks the size of a man's fist with names scratched on them to mark who lay beneath; and he thought of his daughter May, and Owen Urey's son George who'd married May, and their three kids, and he remembered burying them there; he remembered their faces. The blood from eyes, nose, ears, mouth—*his* blood it was, part of it.

Then Ben looked up. "We ain't looking for trouble," he said to the empty blue bowl of sky. "But if you do come, we're ready. Every day we're ready. If you stay up high, we'll hide. But if you come down low, we'll try to get you, you crazy murderers."

His house was only a few yards farther on; he got there by sticking under the trees, walking quickly from one to the next, his ears cocked for the jetsound that would flatten him against a trunk. Way off to his left, across a long flat of sunflowers and goldenrod, he saw Windy Harris down on the creekbank, by the bridge. He yelled, "They biting?"—and Windy's faint "Got two!" reminded him of all old Jim had said, and he shook his head. He left the trees and walked fast up his front path.

His house was in pretty good shape. All four houses on the outskirts had come off standing—his and Windy's and Jim's and Owen Urey's. They'd needed just a little bracing here and there, and they were fine—except Owen's. Owen had stomped around in his, and listened to the sounds of it, and said he didn't trust it—and sure enough, the first big storm it had gone down.

Now Ben and his wife Susan lived downstairs in his house; Joe Kincaid and his wife Anna lived on the second floor; and Tom Pace lived in the attic, claiming that climbing the stairs was good for his innards.

Anna Kincaid was sitting on the porch-swing, peeling potatoes. Ben said, "Afternoon, Anna," and saw her pale bright eyes flicker up at him, and that scared smile touched her mouth for just a second; then she hunched her shoulders and kept on with the potatoes, like he wasn't even there.

Ben thought, *It must be lonely to be that way*—and he attracted her attention again, his voice a little louder: "Hope you're feeling fine, Anna."

Again the flicker of eyes. "Just fine, Ben, thanks," she said, almost in a whisper. "Peeling spuds."

"I see."

Her knife sped over a potato, removing a spiral of skin. She popped out an eye with a twist of the point. "Think Keith'll be back from the war today, Ben? It's been so long . . . I hate to think o' my boy fighting out there so long. Will they let him come home soon, Ben?"

"They will, Anna. I think they will, real soon. Maybe tomorrow."

"Will they?"

"Sure."

Keith Kincaid was under one of those fist-sized rocks, out in the cemetery that wasn't a cemetery—next to his wife, June Hogan, and their four kids. But Anna Kincaid didn't know that. Since the bomb, Anna hadn't known much of anything except what the old people told her, and they told her only things that would make her as happy as she could be: that Keith was in the Army, and June was off with the kids having a nice time in Knoxville; and that they'd all be back home in a day or so.

Anna never wondered about that "day or so"—she didn't remember much from day to day. Joe Kincaid sometimes said that helped a little, as much as anything could. He could tell her the same nice things every day, and her eyes would light up all over again. He spent a lot of time with her, doing that. He was pretty good at it, too . . . Joe Kincaid had been Doctor Joe before the bomb. He still doctored some, when he could, but he was almost out of supplies; and what with his patients being so old, he mostly just prayed for them.

In the kitchen, Susan had lunch ready and waiting—some chicken from last night, green beans, boiled potatoes and a salad from the tiny gardens the women tended off in the weedy ground and around the bases of trees where they wouldn't be seen.

On the way in Ben had noticed that the woodbox was about empty—he'd have to bring home another bag of charcoal from the "general store"—

which was Windy's barn, all braced up. Into it the old people had taken every bit of clothing, canned food, hardware, anything at all they could use in the way of housekeeping and everyday living, and there it all stood; when somebody needed something, they went and took it. Only the canned foods and tobacco and liquor were rationed. Every week or so, around midnight, Fat Sam Hogan and Dan Paray went into the big cave in Lawson's Hill, right near where the second plane had crashed, and set up a lot of small fires, back where the light wouldn't be seen; they made charcoal, and when it cooled they brought it down to the "store," for cooking and such—a charcoal fire doesn't give off much smoke.

Over coffee, Ben said, "Reckon I'll fish some this afternoon, honey. How's a cat or two for supper sound?"

"Why, goodness, Ben, not for tonight," Susan smiled. "You know tonight's the Social; me and Anna are fixing a big dinner—steaks and all the trimmings."

"Mm," Ben said, draining his cup. "Forgot today was Sunday."

"We're going to have some music, and Owen Urey's going to read Shakespeare."

Ben pursed his lips, tasting the coffee. It was rationed to two cups a day; he always took his with his lunch, and sometimes he'd have sold a leg to dive into a full pot. "Well . . . I might as well fish anyway; take in some fun. Fish'll keep till tomorrow, won't it?"

"You can have it for breakfast." She sat down across the table and picked up the knitting she'd been on when Ben came home; he had a hunch it was something for his birthday, so he tried not to look interested; too early to tell what it was, anyway. "Ben," she said, "before you go—the curtain pole in the bay window come down when I was fixing the blankets over it for tonight. The socket's loose. You better fix it before you go. You'll maybe get home after Anna and me want to light the lamps, and we can't do it till it's fixed."

Ben said, "Sure, hon." He got the hammer and some nails from the toolbox and went into the parlor, and dragged the piano bench over in front of the bay window. The iron rod was leaning by the phonograph. He took it up with him on the chair and fitted the other end of it into the far socket, then fitted the near end into the loose socket, and drove nails around the base of the socket until the thing was solid as a rock. Then he got the blanket from the couch and hung it down double over the rod, and fitted the buttonholes sewn all along its edge over the nails driven around the window casing, and patted it here and there until not a speck of light would escape when the lamps were lit.

He inspected the blankets draped over the other windows; they were all right. The parlor was pretty dark now, so he struck a match to the oil lamp on the mantel, just so Susan and Anna could see to set the table. When the others arrived, they'd light the other lamps; but not until; oil was precious. The only time anybody in town ever lit a lamp was on Social night: then the old people stayed up till around midnight for eats and entertainment; otherwise everybody got to bed at eight or so, and climbed out with the dawn.

He went back into the kitchen and put away the hammer, and said, "My second cup still hot, honey?"

She started to put down her knitting and get up, and he said, "Just asking," and pressed her shoulder till she sat again. He went around her and filled his cup at the stove.

"Ben," she said, when he sat down again, "I wish you'd take a look at the phonograph too. Last time the turntable made an awful lot of noise. . . . I wish it could sound better for tonight."

"I know, honey," Ben sighed. "That motor's going. There ain't much I can do about it, though. It's too old. I'm scared to take it apart; might not get it back together right. When it really quits, then I guess I'll fool around and see what I can do. Heck, it didn't sound too bad."

"It rattled during the soft parts of the music."

Ben shook his head. "If I try, I might ruin it for good." He smiled a little. "It's like us, Suse—too old to really fix up much; just got to keep cranking it, and let it go downhill at its own pace."

Susan folded her knitting and got up. She came around the table, and he put an arm around her waist and pulled her into the chair beside him.

"It'll go soon, won't it, Ben?" she said softly. "Then we won't have any music. It's a shame . . . we all like to listen so much. It's peaceful."

"I know." He moved his arm up and squeezed her thin shoulders. She put her head on his shoulder, and her grey hair tickled his cheek; he closed his eyes, and her hair was black and shining again, and he put his lips against it and thought he smelled a perfume they didn't even make any more.

After a moment he said, "We got so much else, though, Suse . . . we got peaceful music you can't play on a machine. Real peace. A funny kind of peace. In a funny-looking town, this one—a rag town. But it's ours, and it's quiet, and there's nothing to bother us—and just pray God we can keep it that way. Outside, the war's going on someplace, probably. People fighting each other over God knows what—if even He knows. Here, it's peaceful."

She moved her head on his shoulder. "Ben—will it ever come here, what's going on outside? Even the war, if it's still going on?"

"Well, we were talking about that this morning down at the hall, Suse. I guess it won't. If rifles can stop it, it won't. If they see us from the air, we'll shoot at 'em; and if we get 'em we'll clean up the mess so if anybody comes looking for a missing plane, they won't give Smoky Creek a second look. That's the only way anything can come, honey—if they see us from the air. Nobody's going to come hiking over these mountains. There's noplace they'd want to get to, and it's sure no country for fighting."

"If the war *is* over, they'll likely be around to fix up the bridge and the road. Won't they?"

"Maybe so. Sooner or later."

"Oh, I hope they leave us alone."

"Don't worry, hon."

"Ben—about the phonograph—"

"Suse . . . " He turned his head to look at her eyes. "It's good for longer'n we are. That motor. So's the bridge, the way it is, and the road . . . we'll be gone first. Before they get around to fix 'em. Before the phonograph gives out. What we want is going to last us—and what we don't want will come too late to hurt us. *Nothing's* going to hurt our peace. I know that somehow. We got it, and it'll be like this for as long as we're here to enjoy it . . . I *know.*"

"Ben—"

"If I want to go fishing," Ben said, and pressed her head against his shoulder again, "I go. If I want to relax with the men, I do it. If I want to just walk and breathe deep, I do it—keeping to the trees, o' course. If I want to just be with you, I do it. It's quiet. It's real quiet in our rag town. It's a world for old people. It's just the way we want it, to live like we want to live. We got enough gardens and livestock, and all the canned stuff in the store, to last us for a . . . for as long as we got. And no worries. About who's fighting who over what. About who won. About how the international mess is getting worse again, and we better make more bombs for the next one. About who's winning here and losing there and running neck-and-neck someplace else. We don't know any things like that, and we don't want to know. It don't matter none to us . . . we're too old, and we seen too much of it, and it's hurt us too bad, and we know it just don't matter at all."

"Ben . . . I got to crying today. About May and George and the children. I was crying, and thinking about that day . . ."

"So did I think. None of us ever forgets for a minute. For a second." His lips thinned. "That's part of why we do what we do. Rest is, we just want to be left alone."

They sat in silence for a moment, his arm around her shoulders, his other hand holding hers. Then he released her hand and thumped his own on the table, grinned at her and said, "Life goes on, now! Reckon I'll go down and get that cat—or go walking—or just go soak in some sun. What time are the folks showing up for—"

Jetsound slammed across the peaceful valley.

Ben got up and walked as fast as he could to the door, picked up the rifle leaning there, cocked it. Looking toward town he saw that Tom Pace had been on his way home, and the sound had caught him between trees. Tom hesitated, then turned and dived toward the tree he'd just left—because a rifle was there.

Ben saw men pour out of the doorways of the two habitable buildings on Main Street; they stuck close to the walls, under the porches, and they picked up rifles.

Motionless, hidden, in shadows, under trees, in doorways, behind knotholes, they waited. To see if the plane would buzz the town again.

It did.

It came down low over Main Street while the thunders of its first pass still echoed and rolled. Frightening birds out of trees, driving a hare frantically along the creekbank, blotting out the murmur of the creek and the tree-sounds, driving away peace.

They saw the pilot peering through the plexiglass, down at the buildings . . . he was past the town in four winks; but in two they knew that he was curious, and would probably come back for a third look.

He circled wide off over the end of the valley, a vertical bank that brought a blinding flash of sunlight from one wing, and he came back.

Ben leveled his rifle and centered the nose of the plane in his sights. For some reason—probably because the valley walls crowded the town on both sides—the planes always lined up with Main Street when they flew low over the town.

The plane grew at startling speed in Ben's sights—it loomed, and the oval jet intake was a growling mouth—and he waited till it was about two seconds and a thousand feet from him; then he sent his bullet up into that mouth: a bullet aimed by a man who'd handled a rifle for sixty years, who could pop the head off a squirrel at a hundred feet. A running squirrel.

That was the signal, Ben's shot.

From under the tree Tom Pace's rifle spoke.

The jet was past town then, and he wheeled to follow it with his eyes; its whining thunder lashed down and pressed his ears, lowering suddenly in pitch as it receded; and though he couldn't hear them for the thunder, he knew that nineteen rifles had roared before it completed its turn, each aimed head-on at the plane. Aimed by men and women who could shoot with Ben, and even outshoot him.

The plane coughed. Lurched. It had time to emit a fuzzy thread of black smoke before it nosed down and melted into the ground and became a long ugly smear of mounds and shreds and tatters of flame.

The sounds of the crash died. Ben heard men shouting; loudest of all was old Jim Liddel's, "Got him . . . by God, I prayed, and we got him!"

Behind him Susan was crying.

Ben saw men and women head for the crash-site; immediately they'd start to carry away what debris wasn't too hot to handle. Then they'd wait, and as soon as anything was cool enough it would be carried off and hidden.

And there'd be a burial tonight.

Ben saw that some of the men had carried old Jim's chair out onto the porch of the Town Hall; and he saw that Jim was half-standing out of his cushions, propped up on his fists and still shouting; and Ben wondered if the Maker wasn't on the porch there with Jim, waiting for Jim to fall and make his noise.

He turned away—at seventy you don't want to see a man die—and went inside and put his rifle on the kitchen table. He crossed to the cabinet under the sink to get his reamer and oiling rag. Every rifle was taken care of that way. Right now Tom Pace and Dan Paray were hurrying around gathering rifles to clean them, load them. No rifle must miss fire, or throw a bullet an inch off aim—because that might be the rifle whose aim was right.

"Lucky we got that one," he said. "I think he saw us, Suse . . . he come in low and sudden, and I think he saw us."

"Was—was it one of theirs, Ben . . . or one of ours?"

"Don't know. I didn't even look. I can't tell 'em apart. Owen'll be around to tell me when they find out . . . but I reckon it was one of ours. If he saw us and didn't shoot then I reckon it was one of ours. Like the last one."

"Oh, *Ben,*" Susan said. "Ben, ain't it against God?"

Ben stood looking out the window over the sink; watching a cloud of yellow dust settle over the wreckage of the plane, and a cloud of black smoke rising from the wreckage to darken the yellow. He knew some of the men would be passing buckets from the well, and spading dirt on the flames where they weren't too hot to get to.

"That's the way it is," he said. "That's how we decided. God didn't stop the bomb dropping, Suse . . . for whatever reasons He had. It don't seem He'd deny us the right to shoot rifles, for the reasons we got. If we get turned away at the Gates, we'll know we was wrong. But I don't think so."

Quiet was returning to the valley; and birds had already started singing again. You could hear the trees. From the direction of the creek came Windy Harris, running, and he broke the quiet with a shout as he saw Ben by the window: "Got it, huh, Ben?"

"Sure did," Ben said, and Windy ran on.

Ben looked toward the porch of the Town Hall. Old Jim had sunk back into his pillowed chair, and he was shaking his fist, and Ben could hear him yelling, "Got it . . . *got* it, we did!"

He'll be around for a while yet, old Jim, Ben thought, and turned back to the table. He sat down and listened to the sounds of the valley, and his eyes were the eyes of the valley—they'd seen a lot, and understood enough of it.

"It don't matter whose it was," he said. "All of a cloth." He slid the reamer into the barrel of the rifle, and worked it. "The hell with the war. Even if it's over, the hell with it. With any war. Nothing's ever going to give us back what we lost. Let 'em stay away, all them that's to blame. Them and their planes and wars and bombs . . . they're *crazy!*" His lips curled as he worked the reamer. "Let 'em stay out o' what they left us for lives. Don't want to hear what they're doing, or *how* or *why*, or *who*. . . don't want to hear about it. It'd be *crazy*. The hell with 'em. *All* o' them. *The hell with the whole Twentieth Century.*"

TEXAS

Perverts
by Whitley Strieber

FRANK WAS sick of living only after dark, sick of always being dirty and afraid and so godawful tired. And hungry. As usual he needed something more than the single doughnut he had been able to afford. He needed a hamburger or a steak or a Chateaubriand—or even more, the softest of caresses. He sipped his coffee, watching the waitress move back and forth behind the long white counter. She was as pale as the marble countertop, her hair ash-blonde, her eyebrows made visible only by the droplets of sweat gleaming in the hairs. When the screen door creaked she glanced up for an instant. A smile of recognition flickered across her face and she tossed a curl out of her eyes with a carefully manicured finger. "Hiya, Becky," she said to the tall woman who had entered.

Small town people. Everybody knows people. Frank looked down into his cup. He knew that the two deputy sheriffs at the corner table were aware of him, and that they'd jump at any excuse to put a dirty hobo on the county gang for a couple of weeks. One of the two men had an elaborately bandaged upper lip, and eyes as hard and bright as ball bearings.

The waitress came and went, flashing like a shaft of sunlight up and down the counter. Two prim little girls sat together drinking Postum. They also knew the waitress, and nodded to the tall woman as she pulled up to the counter. Funny that kids would be allowed out this late and nobody seeming to mind.

The tall woman, not quite young, her face dense with makeup, her fingernails cracked by hard work, ordered sausage and eggs. The waitress was also the chef, and she slung the meal together over the grill, adding plenty of home fries and even a half of a tomato. Frank knew he wouldn't get

571

extras if he ordered a meal. When the plate was put in front of her the tall woman hung over it, eating steadily.

For midnight in the middle of the dust bowl this was a pretty lively place. But around it, in the dark, Frank knew that there was nothing but vast, dark Texas space, miles of weevil-ridden cotton and houses with rattling shutters, sweaty beds and wind, wind without end.

Frank mourned. There had been a time when he wouldn't even have glanced at such a girl as this waitress. He had been made so rich by the 1928 runup in shares that he had gone to the continent on the Berengaria, the world's most luxurious liner. The hiss of the water, the icy, tinkling chatter of Rebecca Landauer, the roses and the whispering sheets . . .

Rebecca Landauer, dark where this girl was light, her eyes full of fire and complication. What did the waitress offer? Lust, for her friends. For the likes of a hobo, absolutely nothing.

Which was okay by him. He understood. He didn't want to make trouble. He had come in here to rest his bones and take advantage of the endless coffee pot, and that was all.

"Hey, kid." He nodded toward his mug.

"You got it." She swung past, gave him his refill. He watched the faint blue veins on the back of her hand as she poured, then looked up into her eyes. He was startled by something unexpected there, a fierceness that confused him, and he quickly glanced away. Her full lips, slightly parted, were touched by a complex smile.

A man with a dollar and seven cents in his pocket does not come on to a decent woman, not even a counter girl. He pushed his old porkpie back on his head and wished for roses and calling cards and his enormous car. But life is loss, the green becomes brown, the dancers go home.

And Octobers come, like for example, the October of two years ago when men strutting in broadcloth one day were penniless the next. He had known what it was to take his last ride in his Dusenberg, to smell the maroon leather interior for a final time, to cancel his massage at the Athletic Club and his last date with Rebecca Landauer, to leave his splendid apartments in the Majestic and find himself, blinded by tears, clumsily learning in the middle of the night the trick of hopping a freight.

Rebecca Landauer. If only, only, only she had not convinced him to put so very much money in the Commercial Solvents pool. If only. She had murdered him with her innocent tip.

The Depression was a boon for Rebecca Landauer. She had gone short a few days before the crash.

And she had said: "the race goeth to the swift, Frankie." Her indifference was so vast that it was a kind of affliction, like a withered limb or the inability to laugh.

He had discovered how dark the land gets after moonset, and the way hobos in boxcars smell, and the taste of the truncheon and the rifle stock. He had been beaten and threatened and made to crouch for two days in a cell that had been a chicken coop. The freights and the other 'bos and the bulls had become too much for him, and he had abandoned the rails in Waco, and taken to the road. He was just another Oakie now, and he had learned all there is to know about dust and getting left behind and wishing to almighty God that you would just keel over and die.

Frank was a man who had given a girl a two-thousand-dollar necklace on her birthday, but now he cared only for the lingering taste of his doughnut and this steaming mug of java.

He had listened to wind in prairie grass, and found that night was his best time, because darkness is the friend of desperate men. He had walked the roads, stopping to examine Hershey wrappers and corn shucks, and longing for just five minutes of riding in one of the old flivvers that occasionally chugged by. He had slept away this past afternoon in a culvert because he didn't dare enter Waco during daylight hours. If he did he would end up doing a stretch chained to other stinking unfortunates, backing at roadside brush with a sickle or hauling shoulder gravel.

Two weeks ago a woman had given him three dollars to tear down a barn. He had slaved ten hours a day for five days, and finally gotten the job done—and in the process learned a lot about how to use sledgehammer and crow bar with hands that had touched little more than narrow waists and bearer bonds and silver service.

The front door of the diner slammed as the two deputy sheriffs left. They started up their Ford and drove off, their single tail light glowing red beyond the diner's dark windows.

Frank was halfways finished with his second mug of coffee. He sipped it slowly. The overhead fans cooled him, and the smell of bacon and steak and eggs brought back creamy memories. He contemplated yet again the ten cent breakfast, but dared not drop below that critical dollar that kept him from committing the crime of vagrancy. He could not face jail again. Men died on the chain gangs all the time.

"You kids better get goin', y'all're up so late," the waitress said to the prim little girls. "Y'all sure you know what to do, now?"

"Yes ma'am," said the eldest of the girls, a child of sullen and extraordinary beauty. There was about her, with her straw-blonde hair pulled back into a bun, a sense of severe energy. And her eyes were cold.

As the girls got up the middle-aged woman suddenly stretched and yawned expansively. "Now you got me yawnin', Pearl. I think maybe I'll turn in." She glanced in Frank's direction and he knew that her eyes were asking the waitress if she felt safe alone with the hobo.

Pearl laughed. "You go on. I'm gonna close down in about fifteen minutes. Ain't nobody else comin' in now you vaudevilles and the sheriffs're done."

Frank watched the waitress set about cleaning the counter with a big gray cloth. The whirring of the fan and the snapping of the cloth were the only sounds until she spoke. "Give you one more cup, 'bo, then you're off. And don't you go sleepin' out behind this place. There's a fella comes in on the mornin' shift killed a 'bo back there last month. Stove in his head. Don't like you 'bos."

He thought: my name is Franklin Waring III. I am the grandson four times removed of General Augustus Waring of the Continental Army, who ate his boots at Valley Forge.

And then, as the fall of rain from an October sky, he was crying. The sobs poured out of him. When he fought them they became hacking, choked snarls of sound, but they would not stop.

She put her hand under his chin and raised his face. He did not want her to see the distortion of his tears and tried to turn away. "No," she said, "you got a right, 'bo." And he revealed the humble truth of his grief to her. When he looked into her bland country prettiness he saw there something that had no limit and no end.

She asked, "You ridin' or walkin'" and his heart began to pound.

He thought to ask, to beg her—deliver me from the evil poem of my life. But he said only: "Walkin'."

"Me, I'd ride. The freights are slow coming around Eight-Mile Bend and there's no bulls. Easy hop, if you want to do it. Get you to LA in eight days."

"The Katy Railroad is safe. But you've got to change to the Sante Fe in San Antonio, and Santa Fe bulls shoot to kill."

"You aren't a regular 'bo. You talk too nice."

"I'm from back East."

She leaned across the counter to pick up his doughnut plate, and he thought she might have the most milk-white cleavage that had ever been granted mortal woman. He scented the promise of the breasts, and saw little jewels of sweat. "You want that coffee, Back East? Last chance."

"Frank."

"Hi, Frank. I'm Pearl."

"'Lo, Pearl."

"I come from the Garden of the Gods, Frank. I'm an actress. This is just fill-in work."

"Nightclub hereabouts?"

"Not the Garden of the Gods. It's vaudeville. Runs real late night. They got a place down along the Brazos. People come in all the way from New York and places to see the Garden of the Gods."

"Roadhouse? I'd like to go in one of those places and just say to the waiter, you give me the biggest and the best steak you've got. I'd eat myself to death and die a happy man."

"You won't die of overeating." Their eyes connected, and Frank felt almost as if she were touching him, but in a place so intimate that it didn't even have a name. He was repelled, like the time in the boxcars when the little boy had offered to "help him get to sleep" for a nickel. The kid had evoked this same cloying uneasiness, as if he had been stroked in a way that he could not bear, but could not resist. "I have the second sight," Pearl said. She took his hand and opened his palm. "You'll die in a fire. And not long from now. Not long at all."

Her words affected him as a sudden flash where no light should be. He laughed, of course. "You've got a lot to learn about fortune telling. Nobody'll ever pay you for news like that."

"It's what I see."

"I've suffered enough!" The vehemence of his own words astonished him. It was not his practice to speak intensely to women. When she smiled saucy and confident, he felt an urge to hit her, to slam his knuckles into that pale skin. He suddenly knew how men came to commit murder, and why they had to be executed for it.

"Gawd, Gawd," a tremendous black man had said in a Kansas holding tank—big catchall cage in the Perry County Jail—"Gawd, Gawd, they gonna 'lectrocute me." He had just come back from his sentencing and was on his way to the state prison. A big illiterate man, with a Kirk fountain pen he conceived of as a kind of magic wand, he stood at the edge of the cage and fingered the bars.

You could get fifteen years for stealing a nickel, life for robbing a storekeeper of a dollar, or death for threatening a woman, if you were a 'bo.

Little places do not like wanderers, they bring too much of the tang of the road with them. For the crime of having less than a dollar to his name Frank had broken rocks on the Perry County gang for a month, watched by an indifferent trusty and hounded by summer-bored kids who liked to torture the convicts by tossing stones at their heads.

"You're remembering," Pearl said. "You left a fine life. And you miss it awful bad." She had come around the counter and now stood behind him.

"Not much to remember. Losing all my money. Hitting the road. Breaking rocks."

Her eyes seemed almost to haze. "Look, if you need a place to get some shut-eye—"

She lapsed to silence, slowly and carefully placing her coffee pot on the counter. Afraid even to whisper such wild, improbable, dangerous hopes, Frank questioned her with his eyes. When she smiled his heart started once more to pound. "Miss, if you've got a bed I could lie down in, I'll do anything in the world to get to it."

Her hand came and touched his temple, a gentle, motherly gesture. The night wind moaned around the corner of the diner. "Well, you can come along with me."

He felt stirring in his loins. "Thank you," he managed to breathe. Gratitude rushed over him, surged as a drowning tide, forcing more tears and downcast eyes.

Once again her hand lifted his chin. "There's no shame in hard times, Frank."

She cut off the fans one by one, then the grill and the coffee pot and she emptied the till into the floor safe. She looked around, sighed. "Diners are a hard business." Then she regarded Frank, who was still seated at the counter. If he got up his body was going to reveal his desire. His overalls were thin. He had no underwear to contain him. Her eyes became warmer, and she turned out the lights. "Might as well get going," she said. "The place is a little ways off from here."

He followed her stiffly down the unpaved street, watching her white uniform glowing like a baleful lantern ahead. They moved down toward the Brazos, in among the dark shacks of the poor, until they came to an enormous bulk of a house surrounded by huge China trees. The Brazos muttered in the blackness, the stars gave only enough light to edge the shadows. Frank was aware of their feet crunching on gravel and then tapping on granite pavements. He was a little perplexed in his mind, but his blood sang: woman, woman, woman. Along with the fragrance of laurel, the wind brought the dense perfume of her sweat.

Inside the house was steaming hot, the air absolutely still, absolutely black. There was a sense of large, dense space. And there were more perfumes here, even some he remembered: Arpege, Lanvin, and Rebecca's favorite, La Nuit.

He could no longer see even Pearl's uniform.

Then her hands touched both his cheeks, with such assurance that he knew she could see, and see well. For a moment she pressed her body against his and he felt what a full, strong woman she was, not fragile like the fashionable girls of Manhattan. His flesh was tense with desire for these heavy cornbread hips. Her finger touched his lips. "You're scared," she said. Then a giggle came out of the darkness. "I think that's the bee's knees."

He heard the hiss of cotton against skin and thought she might be undressing. Then her hand came around his wrist. "Come," she said and her tone seemed odd, as if she were calling a pet. "Come." Her fingers were too firm. Had he not been certain that this was the hand of a kind and gentle woman he would have recoiled.

She drew him through the house to a back room. He had an impression of curtained hallways, and once he thought he might have heard a whisper. "What is this place?"

"An abandoned mansion. Joringel, it's called. It belongs to a bankrupt cotton planter. Lots of those in this part of Texas."

He heard a faint click. She had locked the door. The darkness was absolute and impalpable. He couldn't see even the suggestion of a shape. When she laid his hand against her own cool thigh, he knew that she was indeed naked. "Come on over here," she said, "the bed's right here." There was a creak. "Lemme get you naked, 'bo, then you lie right down." He did not resist her quick fingers, and soon felt the intimacy of night air against his own stone skin. "Whatever I do, 'bo, you just lie still."

"I won't move, Pearl." No indeed. He felt her weight as she straddled him, and thought he must be beneath the very body of kindness.

She spoke to him in a voice that recalled the comforts of childhood. The bed was narrow and hard but she was neither, and he lay in the luxurious pillows of her flesh, and remembered how blonde she was, and kissed her where he could, on her belly. She swung off him, then took his head and guided it down to the unknown regions of her body, where he grazed as contentedly as a herded steer.

As he touched and held and kissed her soft skin, he sensed that he was close to the border of passion, that this might very well become his deepest entry yet into love.

They rode on through the night, steaming in a sweated jungle of their own limbs and lips, while the heavens changed and the tiny room grew close with more breath than their own.

Then things changed. A sense of largeness came into the air, and it grew subtly cooler. He was confused. What was this greater dark, this soft, huge movement as if the wall itself was rising? "I told you, 'bo, just keep right on."

"Holy God, we're on stage!"

"'Bo, I'm gonna give you whatfor if you don't shut up." Her voice was shrill, excited. "Right in front of all these people. You won't like it, 'bo."

One of the little girls from the diner was lighting candles around the bed, candles that burned with low, red flames.

Beyond the proscenium Frank could just see the first rows of the audience, their faces as rigid as wax.

"Welcome, ladies and gentlemen," said a voice that sounded very much like one of the deputies from the diner, "to the Garden of the Gods, where we offer you the spectacle of love and death, ladies and gentlemen, for your delight and your enlightenment."

Frank had heard of this place before, and what he had heard made his mouth go dry. He remembered rumors spoken in hushed whispers in the parlor car of the Century, in the smoking room of the Union Club . . . of a house somewhere in the South where frightful things were done, where it was possible to be witness to love, and to death. Rebecca had known of it. "Reality is the final entertainment there," she had said. "The farthest outpost of civilization, where art is death." Rebecca Landauer could be pompous. But she had also lured Frank into the extraordinary pleasures of absinthe and opium, on long, languid afternoons in her rooms at the Astor. Afternoons of nakedness, while Rebecca whispered all the twists of her imagination, then spoke them aloud: astonishing perversions, games of tasting what must not be tasted and touching what could not bear caress, of pleasure so extreme that it was harder to endure than pain.

He realized that she must have been to the Garden of the Gods. In a sense, perhaps, she had lured him here, not with artifice, but with a spider's patience.

"Rebecca," he called into the rows of uplifted faces. But of course she did not answer.

Pearl lay flat upon him as the quick-fingered girls from the diner tied his wrists to the bedframe.

"Let them," Pearl said, "you could get hurt if you resist."

He was surprised at how little afraid he was.

The deputies, in evening dress now, stood like sentinels at the edges of the stage. High above a skylight was cranked open. Night air flowed down, cool and rich. Frank fixed his gaze on the stars, and tried to notice what Pearl was doing to him.

But his body noticed, and flexed with the pleasure her hands brought it. Each gasping spasm brought a flurry of applause from the audience.

The world was a very different place from what it seemed. The rows of houses, the Fords, the men in straw hats, the cherry phosphates of summer and the hot toddies of winter were not real at all, nor the mothers in their shawls, nor the Princeton crew, nor the trimotor airplane, nor the Graf Zeppelin, nor the old general store at Cox's Corner in Maine, where he and Rebecca had stopped for spoons to prepare opium, and she had said, "It deserves doing in silver."

And then his body noticed how very rough she was being with him. In a reedy voice the deputy said, "The crime of the Hindoo priestess Lopash-long!" The laughter came like knives, and a sudden white torment between his legs left him stunned and choking.

The trophy, his own self, was laid on a silver tray and taken through the aisles by the deputy with the wounded lip.

When it came back the bloody flesh was covered with tips: fifty dollar gold pieces, hundred dollar bills, jewelled trinkets, even the keys to a car. Pearl jangled the keys at the audience and then left the girls to pick the other tips from the bloody pile.

Frank supposed that he must be in shock. He understood the disaster that had befallen him, and felt the agony, but he was curiously unmoved by it all. He gazed at the stars, and listened to his own blood trickling into a can. Pearl caressed his face with a moist cloth. "You could kiss me," he said.

"My brother got his lip bitten off that way last week, kissing a client. She lost a breast, and she was madder than you."

"I'm not mad." He stared into the pale, soft features and longed for this one more touch of sex, this last meaningful contact of lip to lip. But she withdrew from him, lightly touching her fingers to his mouth. "Pearl, is this how everybody dies?"

She smiled. "Don't you trouble yourself about that. You just close your eyes now, 'bo."

"I want to look at the stars."

"If you see what we're about to do, you'll suffer. You've earned a peaceful death, 'bo."

"Who are the people in the audience?"

"Hush now, 'bo." Something scratched and flickered. Then she was cradling a match. Almost lazily, Frank tested his bonds. His hands and feet were tight to the bedframe.

The girls cuddled Frank tightly in the sheets as Pearl knelt down beside the bed. She leaned far under it and busied herself there for a few moments.

He could see the fire she had set flickering on the faces of the audience.

A needle seemed to penetrate his left thigh, then another, then another.

UTAH

The Goddess of Zion
by David H. Keller

IT WAS my first trip to the Zion National Park and as I slowly drove through it, pausing now and then to obtain a better view of the multicolored cliffs I was impressed with its grandeur and majesty. The canyon was rather wide when I drove into it but rapidly narrowed until finally the high walls were so close together that they barely left space for the road and the rushing mountain stream, which ran through it like a miniature Colorado River. The rock walls were all colors and where the sun hit them, sparkled like gigantic jewels.

The last week in August found few tourists in this waste place of great beauty. Now and then an automobile would pass, but for minutes at a time I had a sense of loneliness and isolation from the world. I found myself regretting that my dog was not with me; she would not have appreciated the scenery, but, at least, she would have relieved my loneliness. At last I came to the end of the road. There was nothing to do but to turn around and go back, or leave the car and walk a few miles further up the trail. The shadows were now deep, almost twilight at the bottom of the canyon though it was only midafternoon. As I stopped the car and left it by the side of the road I looked to the left and saw the great white throne. A huge mountain with almost smooth sides, rearing its terrific mass upward some thousands of feet to end against a background of blue sky. A mountain of peculiar whiteness, bare of trees or any form of vegetation. And at the very top a circular opening so perfect in shape that it seemed to have been bored there by a gigantic auger.

I made a statement, "What a place to build a temple to worship a God!" and I asked myself a question, "What is on the other side of that hole? Has anyone ever been through it to find out?"

Before I had time to even think of the answer, a car parked in back of mine and the driver walked over and joined me. He was a young man, large, yellow hair and blue eyes. Even before he spoke I mentally classified him as someone like a Greek God. Not Jove or Vulcan but rather Apollo or Mercury.

"Rather fine," he commented, as he looked at the white mountain.

"More than fine," I replied. "It has a mysterious way of asking me questions I cannot, at least so far, find answers to."

"You wonder at it?"

"I do. For example, what is on the other side of that circular hole? Has anyone been back of it to find out? Was it made by water, wind or some long-forgotten race?"

"I judge," he commented, "that this is your first visit to Zion. You have never been up to the top?"

"Never, and it is my first visit. Have you been there?"

"Yes,—at least I think I have, but it was a long time ago—a very long time ago. Would you like to climb it?"

"Not this afternoon," I replied, looking at my watch. "I have no desire to spend the night halfway up. But I might consider the trip tomorrow."

"You really will go with me tomorrow?" he asked eagerly.

"Yes. If you think we can reach the top, and find out something more about that opening, I will accept your invitation. How long ago were you there?"

"I will tell you tomorrow. Suppose we have supper and a night's rest, and then meet here at dawn. We will see a lot of each other tomorrow, so it would be just as well to see little of each other today. I think it will be light soon after four in the morning, and we can leave our cars right here. Better bring some food with you, chocolate and sandwiches, or whatever you want. It will be a long walk."

"Dangerous?"

"Not especially. Slippery in spots, and you'd better wear rubber-soled shoes, but no need of ropes. If you have done any mountain climbing at all you will have no difficulty. Of course it has been some years since I was there, and there may have been changes in the path. If you find it too much for you, I will go on by myself. In fact I have to. I promised to be there."

There was no suitable reply to make to that statement. I did not want to be too inquisitive; so I told him I would meet him, and started my car. That night I spent at the small Lodge in the Canyon. After supper I looked up all the available literature, especially historical facts, but found nothing except that the canyon had been discovered by the Mormons, and had only recently been made a National Park and accessible to tourists through the building of a road.

Before going to bed I asked the desk clerk whether anyone had ever been to the top of the white mountain.

"Not that I know of," he said laughingly. "I do not know why anyone would want to go there for except to brag about having been there. Of course I do not know what there is on the back side, but as far as I can see a man would have to be a human fly to climb it."

I dressed, had breakfast, brought some food and was in my car by three-thirty the next morning. At the end of the four-mile drive I saw the tail lights of another car. There was a little light but not much. The man was standing by his car, evidently waiting for me. We exchanged greetings, and he expressed his pleasure and slight astonishment that I had kept the appointment.

"Hardly expected you. Before we do anything else suppose we become acquainted. My name is Lief Larson and lately I have been living in Wyoming."

"And I am John Erickson, from Boston," I replied.

"Educated?"

"You might call it that, if a few degrees mean education."

"Not at all sensitive to the occult?"

"Hardly, though I do not know what you mean; that is, I do not know just how you use the word," I replied.

"Just now it does not make any difference. Not very light, but I guess you can see if you follow me."

"You know the trail?"

"I ought to."

For three hours I followed him along a winding and slightly upward narrow path. He walked rapidly, with the ease and grace of a deer or a mountain lion. Often he had to wait for me. At nine he sat down and I was glad to rest. We were surrounded by sharp sides of what seemed to be a secondary canyon. The walls were high and the rock black and vermilion. He pulled out of his pocket a large piece of chalk.

"Better mark the path from now on. You may be coming back by yourself."

"I am lost already," I remarked with an uneasy laugh.

"No. From here on back just take the easiest way downhill and it will take you back to the road. But as we go ahead just make a cross mark or an arrow every fifty feet on the rocks."

Without any further conversation he started, and now we entered a crack in the rock that was just wide enough for one person, and the walls were white.

"Once you are in here," Larson explained, "there are only two ways to go; forward or backward. The path widens considerably later on, but there are no side trails till we reach the top of the great white throne. It has been some time since I was here last, but it has not changed any. There are some wall pictures around the next turn."

He was right. On the white rock, painted in startling blacks, reds and yellows the pictures rose twenty feet above the bottom of the path. Some day they will be found and copied and a book written about them. All I can say now is that there were at least three hundred figures, life size, rather artistically done, and with the colors hardly faded. Men, women and animals. The men and women were fighting, working, loving and apparently worshiping. The animals? I recognized the mammoth with downward-curving tusks, the buffalo, deer and perhaps the beavers. Others seemed to go back hundreds of thousands of years, perhaps millions of years. There were figures, such as the cross, the swastika and the crescent moon. The men and women were brown and red, but high above all other pictures on the wall was a white woman with golden hair. She had been painted against a background of black, and in one hand she held a writhing snake and in the other an ear of corn.

I had been walking slowly, but when I saw with sharply twisted neck this white woman's picture, I paused and sat down. My companion joined me.

"This is a most remarkable group of wall paintings," I exclaimed. "Do not pretend to be an expert in such matters but know enough about it to realize that these are as fine as anything in America. What I cannot understand is that no one has ever found them before. There should be a trail up here with satisfactory signs, and everyone who comes to Zion should come here."

"I am afraid that such publicity would spoil it. Can you imagine a stand here for food and drink? With postal cards, and booklets telling all about it? I am afraid that She would not like it."

"You mean that the lovely woman high on the wall would not approve? After all it is just a painted woman."

"I am not so sure about that. Are you? Do you suppose that she was just a dream placed on the rocks by those primitive artists? Or did they have such a woman in their lives?"

There did not seem to be any answer. Perhaps he did not want his questions answered. At least not at that time. We walked on and now came to steps carved out of the rock, and the steps were worn, either with water or the feet of men long dead. At times we went through long tunnels. Larson had brought a flashlight. He pointed it upwards and showed me the blackened ceiling.

"They used torches in those days," he explained.

I could tell by my ears that we were going up rather rapidly, and at last we came out through a short tunnel into brilliant daylight. We were on top of a mountain. I looked around. On all sides were great depths. And on one side was a circular hole. Without a word I climbed into it and looked down. Below was the cement road. I could even see our two automobiles, like little beetles, by that road, and going up and down were other little car-bugs. All around us were other mountains. But we were above them.

"I told you," cried Larson, in quiet exhaltation, "that I would bring you to the top and show you the circular opening and there it is. From the bottom of the canyon it looks rather small, but up here you see it is rather large and the base of it is level with the floor of the mesa. I think that it was originally carved out by water, but as we see it now it shows smoothing by human tools. See that large circular stone in back of it? That is the Queen's throne. During the ceremony of sacrifice she sits on it. There is sacrifice of men and women but no blood up here, because the offerings to the Goddess are hurled down into the canyon by a mammoth. They must have landed in the river. It was much larger in those days and their dead bodies were washed out of the canyon and finally eaten by the crows."

I looked at him. He was saying it all rather casually. In fact his matter-of-fact tone roused some resentment in me. I said:

"You seem to know a lot about it. Putting it on rather thick, are you not? Must think I am a tenderfoot, willing to believe anything you say."

"No. I presume you think I am a liar or insane or had a bad dream last night. Suppose we sit down and have something to eat, and while we are eating I am going to tell you a story. But first I want to give you the keys to my car. Tomorrow night there is going to be a full moon. At exactly twelve you stand just where the cars are parked. In my car you will find, in the glove compartment, a rather fine set of binoculars. You keep looking at the circle. The moon will help you and then I think there will be fires back of the circle that will help you to see a little of what is happening. You can report the affair to the Park Police, call it an accident. No use notifying my family, because I have no one who cares. We will sleep up here tonight, and early tomorrow I want you to start for the bottom as fast as you can."

I was sure now that there was something wrong with his mind. Of course you cannot tell a man bluntly that he is insane, but I thought it might be best to humor him and try to take him down to civilization. Evidently, for some reason or other, he was thinking of killing himself by jumping through the hole. Must have had it all arranged for and even wanted someone to witness his curving leap through the air.

"Suppose we eat, and then go back together," I suggested.

"No. A promise is a promise. Listen to the story. I came out here the first time about seven hundred years ago, one of a party of Norsemen. I do not know what urge kept us going, but we followed the setting sun, west and still further west. I have a map in my car with our course marked on it as well as I can remember. We came to Niagara Falls and then followed the Great Lakes to the end of Lake Superior, and then west and south from there. Not in one year, you understand, because there were no automobiles then and no horses. We traveled in spring and summer, and in the fall we built huts and gathered firewood and provisions for the winter.

"We kept time by the number of winters. None of us could write; we were warriors and not scholars. Hardships? Plenty of them. Fighting? Plenty of that also. At times we were treated as Gods and at other times hunted like wild beasts. One by one my comrades died. At last I was left alone by the Great Salt Lake. I remember swimming in it. From there I went South and at last came to this Canyon. It was summer and the hunting was good. The river was nearly three times as large as it is now. I saw for the first time this white mountain with the circular opening, and that night I was captured by the brown people."

"Not Indians?" I asked.

"No. At least not like any Indians I have ever seen since. They were little people, none over five feet tall and a peculiar brown, not copper-colored and not black. Had it been daylight I might have escaped but they overpowered me before I was awake. I have to laugh when I think of it. Lief the Fearless, hero of a hundred sea battles, a man who never knew defeat, helpless and the captive of a group of little men I could have brushed aside like so many flies had I met them in the daylight.

"They did not want to hurt me. In fact they gave me food, and tried by signs to show that they wished to be friendly to me. But they had my armor and my sword, and their lances were long and sharp even though the spearheads were of stone. It seemed that all they wanted me to do was to go with them. There was nothing else I could do so I went.

"They were cave people. I never was able to find just where they lived, because they covered my eyes. Not many of them. Perhaps not more than a hundred, counting the women and children. A dying race! At one time there must have been thousands of them because their bone heaps were large. And now I come to the part that will be hard for you to believe. They had a mammoth up here, a very old and large elephant and every day they brought him grass and grain up this path we have just taken. You saw a picture of one of them on the rocks. Remember? With the tusks turned downward?"

"Now listen to me," I interrupted, "I do not want to be discourteous to you. I am willing to believe all the rest of your story but I draw the line at that elephant. I am willing to admit that there were such animals here at one time but not on top of this mountain. Not if he walked up the way we did. There were places where the space between the rock walls was so narrow he could not have possibly squeezed through."

"I thought you would say something like that. I had the same idea when I saw him for the first time. I said to myself, 'He is up here, but how did he get here?' I found out after I learned to talk to the Queen. They caught him when he was just a baby, took him up to the top and kept him there. Made a pet of him, taught him tricks; and when he grew full size he just stayed there because he could not get down."

"So they made a pet of the elephant?" I asked.

"Yes. Almost considered him as a God. And every year when they had their sacrifices he took a leading part. He would stand near the edge of this circle, and they would bring an offering to him and he would curl his trunk around the man and raise him in the air and then throw him over into the canyon."

"You saw him do that?"

"Yes. For five years. The brown people would go hunting and bring back Indian captives. They would wash them and feed them and take the best of care of them and then once a year they would all gather up here, light their fires, sing their songs and worship their Goddess, and then one at a time the Indians would be brought to the mammoth."

"But of course they never threw you over?" I remarked casually.

"No. I suppose they would have done so, but the Queen took a fancy to me and told them I was a God from the skies, just as she was, and as they worshiped her, they believed her—at least for awhile."

"And you did not try to escape?"

"Why should I try to? Did you see her picture on the rocks? Can you imagine a normal man trying to escape from a woman as beautiful as she was? I tell you that we acted like Gods in the daytime, but at night she was just a woman and I was very much of a man. The brown people worshiped her and because of that they tolerated me. We learned to talk to each other though at first we only used signs. But pantomime is very effective when a man and woman love each other.

"Once a year we all gathered here, right where we are now, for the yearly sacrifice. She would sit on this rock, almost nude, covered only with gold ornaments, anklets, bracelets, armlets, her snake in one hand and a ripe ear of corn in the other. I would sit near her. The brown people would build the fires and sing and dance, and when they beat on their drums the mammoth would sway in time with the music, and at the last, one at a time he would hurl the Indians to their death over two thousand feet below. And then the fires would fade and the brown people one by one leave us, and finally dawn would come and only the Queen and I would be there. And she would kiss me and tell me how happy she was that one more year had passed and I was still alive and able to love her.

"At times when she talked to me I thought she was immortal and would never die, but she said that this was not true. The brown people had had many Queens. I never was able to find out where they came from. My love looked like a Norsewoman, but she knew nothing about her childhood. Though her people worshiped her she was, in a way, as much of a captive as I was. She thought that somewhere in the caves there was another white girl, growing into womanhood, tenderly cared for and educated to become the next Queen. At the first sign of old age the Queen simply disappeared and a new one took her place. She remembered the day when she had become Queen.

"I tried to persuade her to escape with me. But she felt that it was useless to try. I suppose she really did not want to. She had lived as a Goddess so long that perhaps she could not have lived as a woman had she wanted to. I can see now that she was rather tangled as far as her thinking about life was concerned."

"I suppose you know that this is all rather hard for me to believe," I said. "I have no doubt that you think you are telling me the truth, but, at the same time, this is 1938 and you talk as though this experience happened yesterday instead of seven hundred years ago."

"I realize how you feel. But I have to go on with the story. The thing that we feared happened. She became sick. Knowing that if she died the brown people would probably sacrifice me, she thought of a compromise with her worshipers. The new Queen was to take her place and she was to be the grand sacrifice to their spirit God. I was to be given my liberty, but some day, when they sent for me, I was to come back, and in my turn be hurled through the hole. She told them that she would come back, sit on the stone, once again hold the sacred snake and the ripe ear of corn. They believed her. I gave my promise to return when I was sent for. She told me that for long years I would live on, in different bodies but with the same soul. After my final death we would live through eternity united and unseparated. Did you ever love a woman?"

"Yes."

"Then you know how I felt that last day we spent together. It seemed we could not be close enough together. But night came and the full moon. All that day we had been alone up here with the mammoth. She gave me one of her gold bracelets. Night came and the little people built their fires, sang their songs and sacrificed their captives. Then she walked over to the opening in the rock and started to take off all of her golden jewelry. The little people produced, as though by magic, the new Goddess, a beautiful young girl, and on her they placed all the ornaments, the feathered head-dress and the robe of white deerskin. And then something very unusual and unexpected happened. My beloved stood, nude and beautiful, in spite of her illness, waiting for the elephant to pick her up and hurl her through space. Instead he turned, rushed toward the new Queen, picked her up with his trunk, walked over to the edge of the opening and threw her into space."

"I did not expect that ending," I exclaimed.

"No one did," he replied. "It had a terrifying effect on the brown people. You see the elephant was one of their Gods. Whatever he did was right. Now he had refused the sacrifice. Leaving us they fled down the path, leaving us alone. I went over to my beautiful one and took her in my arms. We simply held each other close till the dawn came. I told you she was sick. When the sun rose I knew she was very sick. And so was the mammoth. He walked around us as though he wanted to help in some way but did not know just what to do. At last he rushed against the rocks, deliberately broke off his tusks and then hurled himself through the circular opening.

"My Goddess knew she was dying. She said she was not afraid of death if only she could meet me afterwards. She asked me to hold her close till she died and then throw her body down into the river, and her last words were:

"'You will live on and on till the time appointed, and then, when I send for you, I want you to come up here and join me.'

"I did as she requested. Not easy but it had to be done. And now after all these centuries I have come back."

"I am sorry," I said, "but I cannot believe your story."

"I cannot blame you. The next day I left, and the brown people made no effort to detain me. After that, part of my memory is not clear. I suppose I married and had a son, and he married and had a son, but through the generations my soul lived in the oldest son of the family and that soul never forgot what happened and the promise given. My descendants mated but though we had children the love for this Goddess of Zion remained. They went back finally to Norway. And at long last this body that is called Lief Larson was born.

"From my boyhood I had dreams of the long past. I never married but lived and loved a dream woman, the white Queen of Zion."

"I still do not believe you," I insisted.

"I am going to make you believe me. After my beloved died I took the mammoth's tusks and the gold bracelet and buried them under a cairn of stones. See that pile of rock over there? Under it are the ivory and the gold. I am going to uncover them."

I told myself that this was 1938 and such a story could not be true. But he threw stone after stone to this side and that and at last pulled out two tusks, over six feet long, and a massive piece of gold.

"We will sleep here tonight," he said softly. "Tomorrow you will go back by yourself. At midnight use the binoculars. The brown people may come back. Even the mammoth may be reincarnated. And you will see what you will see."

"Don't do it, Larson," I urged, putting my hand on his shoulder. "You are sick, very ill, more so than you think. Rest awhile and then go back with me, Let me take you to a hospital where you can recover from this wild delusion."

He shook his head.

"I love her, Mr. Erickson. For centuries I have waited for her. This time, if we are united, we will never be separated. We will live happily, lovingly through the ages. I tell you she is waiting for me. How can I fail her? Would you disappoint the woman you loved?"

"Perhaps you will feel better tomorrow morning."

"I will feel better but no different. But it has been a hard day for both of us. Suppose we go to sleep."

I slept in spite of the hard stone bed, in spite of my nervousness. It was the sleep of utter exhaustion and with it came dreams. I thought I saw Larson with a wonder woman in his arms. The mammoth stood beside them. Little men came carrying firewood. Drums beat! But when I woke with the dawn Larson and I were alone on the rock. He told me to go and take the flashlight and his car keys. He made me promise I would watch the circular opening at midnight. And he thanked me for coming with him and listening to his story and ended by saying that he was very happy because he had spent the night with the Goddess of Zion, and knew that the end was going to be a glorious one. The last thing he did was to give me the gold bracelet to keep in memory of his wonder woman and their great love.

It was much easier going down the mountain than coming up it. I had little difficulty finding the way. When I came to the rock pictures I sat down for over an hour, making copies of some of the pictures in my notebook. The colors seemed more brilliant than they had the day before. Had I been an artist I would have drawn the Goddess of Zion.

It was nearly dark when I finally arrived at the two automobiles. I opened Larson's car, found the binoculars, locked it and drove back to the lodge in my own automobile. There I ate a much needed supper.

By eleven that night I was back to the place by the road where Larson's car was parked. There was a full moon and a wonderfully clear star-studded sky. The white mountain loomed high in the air and at the top was a circle of red. "A forest fire back in the mountains!" I whispered to myself. The rolling throb of drums came to me. "Thunder from the clouds," I said. All the time I was trying to think clearly, to tell myself that it just simply was not true, that such things could not happen in 1938. Then I took the binoculars and focussed on the circular opening and saw a mammoth against a background of flame and in front of him stood a man, holding in his arms a woman with feathers in her hair and they seemed to be kissing each other.

And then the mammoth took the two of them in the circle of his trunk and threw them into space.

I found the crushed body of Larson near the river bed the next day. The authorities believed the story I told them, which I fabricated simply because I knew they would not believe the real one. They identified him from papers in his pocket, located his car and the coroner decided that it was suicide. Perhaps it was. But I still have the binoculars and the gold bracelet and the pictures in my notebook. Some day when I recover from my mental confusion I am going back and try to find the trail and the rock pictures.

Unless I do find them I think it would be best to simply think that it was all a dream.

VERMONT

Alannah
by August Derleth

I WAS never one to be hasty in my judgment of others, but I *do* think that Mrs. Stewart might have paid a little more attention to Maurice, she might have given him the kind of affection he needed. Now that everything is over, there can be no harm in setting down what I know about what happened at that house. Mr. Stewart could not have done any more than he did; he had his work, and sometimes he came out from the city pretty tired. Mrs. Stewart was the one. She was that kind of woman—lived for herself too much, and not enough for others. I don't say that a person shouldn't live for himself—but not alone that. My grandmother used to say that it is much better and richer to love than to be loved. I thought of that often about Mrs. Stewart; I always felt that she never knew what it was to love. Yet I wouldn't want to say that she didn't love her son; nobody knows what love is, and love is a great many things to different people. Sometimes love is the most enriching thing in the world, and sometimes it is not; sometimes it is good and wholesome, and sometimes it is possessive and destructive and evil. Sometimes it is strong enough to live after death, and if love lives after it, then surely hunger and terror and all the emotions of man, made strong enough and great enough, live afterward, too.

The Stewarts had taken the house in the Vermont hills when I joined them. That is, they had moved in for the summer, and they had been there for almost a month when I answered their advertisement for a governess. A great many women simply did not want to take positions so far from the city, which meant, really, that they wanted to be in the city, because the Stewart house was only about twelve miles from the nearest city, where Mr. Stewart had his law offices, and from which he came home almost every night to work over his briefs. Mrs. Stewart was not the type of woman I would have thought satisfied with such a place; she was one of those women who, because they think always of themselves, are apt to get very lonely if there is not someone before whom they can perform all their little vanities.

I know it sounds as if I were prejudiced against Mrs. Stewart, but I do not think I was. It's only that if she had been a different kind of person, I don't think anything would have happened—at least, things would not have happened as they did there. I ought to say that the very first time I saw the house, I had the feeling that there was something *wrong* about it. I know people will say, "Isn't that just like a woman!" but it is true, all the same. After I got to know Mrs. Stewart I naturally thought that she was what was wrong about the house. That was a mistake, I know now. Sometimes I wonder if the house was not responsible for some of the things Mrs. Stewart did—or rather, didn't do. I really don't have any prejudice against her, poor woman; she is what she is, just as I am what I am, and Mr. Stewart is what he is, and Maurice . . .

It was really a beautiful house. It was old, a low two-story stone building, with a charming roof on which the moss grew green. The house was yellow, but *wet*—actually wet outside; that I thought was due to the brook that flowed past, for there was a brook, a real Vermont brook, and if you've even seen those crystal streams, with their green-blue water, you will know what I mean. The brook came flowing down from the hills, and right in the center of the grounds around the house, though, a little off to one side, beyond the north end and so behind the house, its former owner had built a deep pool, with a fine brick-and-stone rim curving in an arc toward the brook from both banks; the brook flowed in at one end and out the other. And there were trees all along the brook, so that the pool was always shadowed and dark, and one would have thought that there would be fish in plenty there, but, strangely enough, there were fish above the pool in the brook, lying under the grassy banks, and there were fish below, but there was not a fish or a frog or even a water spider in the pool, though lilies grew there, and their green leaves and yellow flowers made the water seem all the blacker, and there was a curious illusion of bottomlessness about it when you loked into the water.

They told me—that is, Mr. Stewart, who interviewed me—that Maurice was a "problem" child, and I came prepared to deal with something like a thoroughly spoiled youngster. Maurice was then five, or a little older, and he was a singularly beautiful child, with his grave blue eyes, which could sometimes be as merry as the blue water of the brook racing over the sunlit sand and the rocks in its course, and curly blond hair, and a sensitive, full-lipped mouth; his skin was fair, with a good color, and he had an innate understanding of neatness. All that first day I kept waiting for him to explode into mischief, but he did nothing of the sort; he was quiet, a little shy, he looked into books—he was precocious for his age, they told me—and he behaved very well. I thought it would come the next day, but it did not, and finally, somewhat mystified, I went to Mrs. Stewart and asked her bluntly in what way Maurice was a "problem" child.

Mrs. Stewart was a dark-eyed, thin-faced woman. She seemed to be always a little remote from the present, but she was clearly a most passionate type of woman, for she held her husband absolutely, and many times he deferred his better judgment to hers, though he never condoned error. She carried on a great deal of correspondence, and telephoned friends in the city all day long, and what I held and still hold against her was that she never seemed to find much time for Maurice, even if he was her son. When I asked her, she seemed to be annoyed at once, just as if she should not have had the duty of telling me.

"Oh, didn't Wayne tell you?"

"No, Madam, he did not. I expected a lively, mischievous lad, but I have not found Maurice at all mischievous."

"No, if it were only mischief!" she sighed. "But it is something much worse—I suppose the best way to say it is to tell you that he is endowed with an overabundance of imagination."

I said nothing.

"It is quite distressing for us, but he has fallen into the habit of telling the most bare-faced lies, and Mr. Stewart and I feel that he must be broken of it. It is embarrassing for us all to hear him speak before those of our friends who weekend with us, and the worst of it all is that there is no explanation for it."

"What kind of lies, if I may ask?"

She waved one hand about half vaguely, half in a gesture of dismissal. "Oh, all kinds of lies, Miss Kerlsen."

I must admit that I have never liked people who tell lies, though one expects a certain amount of it in children. It was a shock to me to hear that Maurice was addicted to lying; somehow we are always prone to associate goodness and all the virtues with beauty, especially in children; and I resolved that I would do all in my power to break Maurice of prevaricating. The next day I even went so far as to test him. I saw him break a little dish in the kitchen, and carefully pick up the pieces to discard them in the ash-can; so I asked him quite casually about an hour later what had become of the little dish, as if I wanted to use it for something.

"I broke it, Miss Kerlsen," he said candidly.

That puzzled me. I reasoned that if he were the bare-faced liar his mother said he was, he would certainly have lied about the dish; he did not know I had seen him. It was very mystifying, and it grew more so as the days slipped by. Until the sixth day—that was Saturday, for I came on the Monday of that week. That day Maurice came over to where I was resting on the low verandah on the south side of the house and said that Alannah wanted to see me. Though I had never seen Maurice with a playmate, I assumed that Alannah was someone from one of the farms nearby.

"Bring her here," I said.

"Oh, no. You've got to go to her," answered Maurice, and held out his hand confidently.

"Very well," I said, laughing, and took his hand.

He led me around the house quite proudly. I thought his playmate would be out in back, that is, on the up-slope of the hill, but there was no one there. Nevertheless, Maurice led the way straight across the yard; I looked all around quickly, but I could see no one. Then we came to the pool, where Maurice was accustomed to spend long hours dreaming, and Maurice pulled at my hand, and sat down, indicating that I was to sit down, too.

"But where is she?" I asked.

"Do not say anything, please, Miss Kerlsen."

His fair face was flushed with excitement, and I thought his pulse had quickened a little. I put up my hand to touch his forehead, to discover whether he had a fever, but I had barely touched his skin before the most extraordinary thing happened. I felt as if my hand had been brushed aside. The impression was only momentary, it is true, and at the same time Maurice leaned away a little to look into the water; so that in a few seconds I decided that the illusion had been caused by the boy's movement. I looked around to where the woods came down at the far end of the lawn, half expecting to see a little girl come running out; but there was no sign of anyone. Maurice continued to gaze into the pool, with a little smile on his lips. His eyes, though, were somewhat anxious.

Suddenly, without a word, he stood up, offered me his hand, and hurried me back to the verandah. He smiled quickly at me, and then hastened back around the house. I was astonished by his action, and took the trouble to walk out from the verandah until I could look back into the lawn there to see where he had gone. Just as I suspected, he was sitting on the rim of the pool once more, looking into that dark water, reaching down with one hand.

That evening, as I stood beside his bed, I asked him, "And where was your Alannah this afternoon, Maurice?"

"You didn't see her," he answered in a curiously flat tone of voice, as if he were disappointed.

"No, I didn't," I answered. "How does she look?"

"Oh, she's pretty."

"Is she as pretty as Mother?"

"Yes."

"Where does she live?"

"In the pool."

So at last I understood what the Stewarts meant by saying that Maurice was a "problem" child, that he told bare-faced lies. It was not true that he told lies of all kinds; of that I was certain. He had probably told his parents about Alannah, and they had not understood that a sensitive, imaginative child lives in a world of make believe, and, lacking companions in the flesh, is very apt to conjure up imaginary companions. At the moment I did not say anything; I only smiled at Maurice, but I was instantly resentful that his parents should not have taken a little more trouble to find out that what Maurice needed more than anything else was companionship. There was no one—only his mother, the cook, an old gardener who came over from a nearby farm, and myself, with his father in the evenings, all far older than the boy—no one his own age. And since there was no likelihood of there being anyone his own age here for the summer, I knew that I would have to enter into his play-world with him as much as possible.

I went right down to where Mr. and Mrs. Stewart sat, in a screened-off porch on the west side of the living room, and asked them whether the boy's imagination was the thing that had caused them to think of him as a problem child.

"It is lies," said Mrs. Stewart stubbornly.

"I would not call them lies," I answered, just as stubbornly. "The boy is just lonely, and he makes up these things."

Mr. Stewart loked up from his papers and observed that it was not a healthy sign. He seemed genuinely concerned.

"I don't know what you mean by healthy, but it's certainly normal enough."

"No, no it is not," said Mrs. Stewart.

"That is just not my opinion alone, Mrs. Stewart," I replied.

"I don't care whose opinion it is. Maurice has got to be stopped from telling those—those tales or whatever you want to call them." Her eyes flashed at me. "We are depending on you to do what you can."

"I shall do what I can, but I think it is the worst thing in the world to treat the boy as if he were a liar. I will not do that."

"We expect you to do things in your way, Miss Kerlsen," said Mr. Stewart.

The issue, you see, was not cleanly forced. It never was; Mrs. Stewart remained emotional about it, and annoyed; Mr. Stewart was too far from its daily manifestations, obviously. And I—well, I suppose you might say that if I had a more common-sense attitude, I lacked imagination in almost the same proportion as Maurice had an overabundance of it. I suppose if I had had a little more of it, what happened would not have had to happen.

As I was coming up the stairs considerably later that night, I saw Maurice coming down the hall. The hour was almost midnight, though it was a clear night, with a moon shining, and I wondered what he was doing up at that hour. He could have got himself a drink in the bathroom next to his room; so it was not that. I concealed myself and watched him go by. He went down and out of the house, and I went after him, not making a sound.

He went right over to the pool and crouched down on the rim in his white nightgown, and I heard his whispered voice calling, "Alannah! Alannah!" in hushed tones. And then suddenly a little rippling came on the water, a vapor that was not there before. How it startled me! I felt chilled at the sight of it, but it was gone again just as quickly as it had come; there was nothing there, and I began to think my eyes had played a trick on me when Maurice came along with his hand held out and up, just as if he were holding someone's hand, the hand of an older person, and he kept looking up from time to time, as if he were listening to someone walking at his side.

I cannot describe my feelings as I saw that. It was uncanny. I saw him quite clearly in the moonlight, but there was absolutely nothing else moving across the lawn—only that curly-headed lad in his white nightgown. But when he went past me, where I stood in the shadow of an old tree near the house, I felt his passage as if a cold wind had brushed me, and once again that feeling of unutterable chill, and something of terrible emotional intensity rose up and seemed to cling to me, like something alive; so that I was frightened, almost terrified, by something I could not see or hear, something less tangible than the wind. That feeling lingered until after Maurice had gone into the house, and it was some moments before I could bring myself to follow him.

I went straight to the stairs—he had to go upstairs to his bed—and the moment I put my hand on the stair-rail, I withdrew it as if I had touched ice. I might as well have done so, for the rail was *wet*, wet and *cold*, oh, how cold! And the moment I touched it, I felt the most awful loneliness I ever knew, I felt the most dreadful solitude, as if I were isolated in a place far, far from any human touch or voice, and I felt invaded by the most tearing longing, the most moving desire for someone to hold close to me, someone to possess, *to love*!

It was awful!

I wrenched my hand away and fell back against the wall, shaking and trembling. I put on the light, and, though I would not touch the stair-rail again, I saw the wet gleaming on it all the way up, and I followed it; I saw the wet along the hall and the wall and I saw it on the knob of the door to Maurice's room. I did not want to touch it again, but I had to know that he was all right. So I leaned forward, bracing myself, and quickly opened the door.

The instant I touched the wetness, I felt it again—oh, the most heart-rending despair, the most pitiful agony, the most utter desolation! Oh, the terrible wanting for someone, someone near, someone to love and adore, someone to belong to and to belong to me! I clung to the door and looked in; but he was there, safe in his bed; and I pulled the door shut and drew away from it, shuddering and gasping, for such a tearing emotion I had never known, such a cold isolation of the spirit, such a dread and terror and *emptiness*. It was just as if all the sorrows and griefs of a lifetime had come to life anew and taken away all the memories of compensating pleasures, as if someone were forever doomed to live out his years far from his kind—oh, it is impossible to describe it, it was terrible!

Whatever they may say of me, I am not a coward. I knew then that there was something horribly wrong about the house. Despite the crying out of every instinct against it, I forced myself to go back downstairs, back out across the lawn to the pool. I sat down on the rim, and looked into that black water, where now the moonlight lay like silver, and I could see my face there looking up at me out of that dark, moonlit water, spectrally. It was beautiful there, with the moonlight all around, and the brook talking above and below the pool, and occasionally the sound of a fish splashing. I sat there looking into the pool for five minutes—I do not know what I expected to see there. Certainly it was not what I saw just as I got up to go—that other thin face, a woman's face, with dark where her eyes should have been, and light hair flowing wetly down beside her head, so sharp and strong that I thought it was someone looking over my shoulder into the water, and turned, but there was no one there, no one at all. And then there was nothing in the water either, nothing but my own face looking down. But there was something inside me again—once more that terrible loneliness, that poignant longing, that incredible, hurtful wanting, that agonized desolation which shook me and tore me and sent me staggering away from that pool and brought me to my knees in tears, that strong it was, that terrible and moving.

I fled to the house and was glad to be in my room, myself once more, save for the trembling and the pity I felt for whatever it was in such desperation out there.

I think it was two days later that I found the letter. It was stuck in an old album, put into where a photograph should have been, and left in a closet off my room. It was ten years old, in a man's handwriting, and it was addressed to Mrs. Luella Withers. It was not a nice letter.

> Lu Alannah,
>   I have tried all week to talk myself into coming back and starting over, but it's no use. I'm too weak to do it, I never was much on the noble side of things anyway. So I've taken passage on a tramp steamer for Singapore and the Malay States, which makes it easy for you to get a divorce on the grounds of desertion. I want you to have the house; it is really yours—you planned it and all. I am sorry there never was a youngster to share it with us for the little while we were there together. It was rotten luck, but it was our luck.
>
>   Jack.

I put it back where I found it and went down to talk to Mrs. Stewart. I asked her who had lived in this house before.

"A Mrs. Luella Withers, Miss Kerlsen."

"What kind of woman was she?"

She shrugged. "I have no idea. She's dead, of course. The house belongs to some relative and we leased it through an agent."

She knew nothing at all about Mrs. Withers. I was half of a mind to point out to her that it was a curious coincidence to discover that Mr. Withers had called his wife by the same pet name that Maurice called his friend. I should not have asked Mrs. Stewart at all; she said she thought it was not "proper" to inquire into the habits and the life of the previous tenant of the house. I should have talked to someone else right away. As it was, it was three days after that before I managed to take a few hours one afternoon while Maurice was asleep to walk down the country road and pay a visit to one of the neighbors.

Mrs. Warren was a farmer's wife, well along in years, but still a big, strong woman. She was canning strawberries that day, and I sat in the kitchen with her, after telling her who I was. Like most country people, once they have no reason to be suspicious of you, she was very friendly with an ease of manner that made it very pleasant to talk to her. She took me for just what I was, and only asked about the Stewarts in the most casual way, not prying at all, but just wanting to know something about her neighbors, so that it was easy for me, at last, to come around to the subject of Mrs. Luella Withers.

"Oh, yes, I knew her," said Mrs. Warren. "Poor, poor woman!" She shook her head, and an expression of sympathy appeared in her warm brown eyes.

"Was she unhappy here?"

"Unhappy's not in it. She was terrible lonesome. I never saw a woman—nor a man, either—that lonesome. She would set and eat her heart out. Her husband got lost on a steamer somewhere. Nobody knows what made him up and take the trip in the first place. They didn't have any children; so she was left alone. And how she wanted a child! I don't know what it was, but I think she was the one couldn't have children. Anyway, if a body took a boy or a girl up along with her visiting there, she never wanted the child to leave, she used to try to keep him there or coax him back—why, it was something awful the way she carried on! They said the lonesomeness just went to her head. It made her thin and hungry-looking, and I reckon in the end it would have killed her."

"She is dead, then?"

"Oh, yes. Couldn't stand it any more. I guess he left her the house, but there wasn't much money; she tried to sell it, but she couldn't; and she couldn't go anywhere else—no money, you see—so one fine day she up and drowned herself."

"In the pool," I said almost involuntarily.

"Yes. They say it's deeper than a body thinks."

It gave me a queer helpless feeling to listen to Mrs. Warren tell about Mrs. Withers. "Tell me," I said at last, "did you ever hear her called *Alannah?*"

"That was *his* name for her. I reckon it's a sweetening name. It's not a name that's in the books, but he would say it the way a man would talk to his sweetheart, and she would smile and her eyes would shine—so I reckon that's what it was."

After that, I felt that the best thing for Maurice would be to get him away from there. I thought it all over the night, and the next morning, before Mr. Stewart left, I went downstairs and talked to them both at the breakfast table. Maurice was still asleep. I said that I had been thinking everything over, and I felt that Maurice was not lying at all, that his loneliness was responsible for his queer fancies. Perhaps I should have said that I was not sure they were fancies, but I knew that if I had, they would have discounted everything I recommended; so I could not; I had to hold back part of the truth. They were somewhat put out, but I convinced them.

Then I said, "If I may make a further suggestion, I would most strongly recommend that Maurice be not told of your intention to leave until it is time to go, or else he may brood about it."

"That is going too far," said Mrs. Stewart. "I will not have the boy growing up a mollycoddle. He will have to learn now that life never gives anybody his way all the time."

I said that the principle was a sound one, but in this case I felt its application would work adversely, and I begged them to reconsider, with such earnestness that Mr. Stewart said finally they would think it over, and there the matter rested—until the day before they left.

Mrs. Stewart had her way after all. True, they compromised. Mr. Stewart thought I was right, but Mrs. Stewart thought she was right; so they compromised by not telling Maurice until the morning of the day before they planned to return to town, and then they told him.

We were all sitting at the table that morning, and when they told him, I saw his face; he went all white, and one hand clenched tightly around his fork.

"I'm not going," he said in a low voice.

"What was that?" asked Mrs. Stewart.

"I'm not going," he said again.

"I don't think you need more than a day to say good-bye to your friend," said Mrs. Stewart coldly.

Mr. Stewart coughed.

Maurice put down his fork precisely and sat back.

"Eat your breakfast, Maurice," said Mrs. Stewart warningly.

"I'm not hungry."

"Eat."

"I won't."

Mrs. Stewart looked up with flashing eyes. "You see, first it is lies and then it is disobedience," she said to no one in particular. "It goes from bad to worse, and if he is this way now, what will he be a few years from now?"

Maurice got up and went away from the table.

"Come back here!" cried Mrs. Stewart in a voice that was shrill with anger.

Maurice never said a word but simply walked out of the room.

Mrs. Stewart would have got up and gone after him, but Mr. Stewart held her back. He said brusquely that telling Maurice had been a shock, and it was better to let it work itself out of him without any unnecessary pressure. I was grateful for that, and Mrs. Stewart, after brooding about Maurice's behavior for a few minutes, resumed her breakfast and grew quite cheerful again, as if she had forgotten the entire incident.

But I did not forget it. I watched Maurice carefully all that day, and I watched him especially at the pool. I was short with his lessons that day because I knew he would want to go around and bid his favorite haunts good-bye. He did not say very much, but I could see that he had something on his mind. People often think, particularly adults who have grown far away from their own childhood, that a child's world is dependent upon the world of the adults; but this was never so and will never be true, for a child always lives in his own world, no matter what his circumstances, and a sensitive child never completely forgets that world in his adulthood.

I was glad when Maurice fell asleep that night. He had spent a long time at the pool during the late afternoon, and I felt sure that he had been bidding Alannah good-bye; so I asked him gently that evening whether he had.

"Yes. She doesn't want me to go, and I don't want to go. Miss Kerlsen, I like her better than Mum. Is that wrong?"

"I don't think so if you keep it your secret." It was a difficult question to answer.

"Alannah loves me."

"Yes," I said, with a catch in my throat. "Yes, I'm sure she does. But you can come back sometimes and see her again."

He looked at me gravely and smiled. "They always tell me I'm lying when I talk about Alannah, but you don't, Miss Kerlsen."

"I believe you, Maurice," I said.

"Thank you," he answered.

I did not leave him until he had fallen asleep. And then I sat up until one o'clock in the morning.

As it turned out, I did not sit up long enough. I was very tired, for I had helped with the packing, and I fell asleep. It was about two o'clock when I awoke, and the waning moon had just reached about tree height in the sky. I do not know what woke me, unless it was the movement of something before my eyes, closed as they were; that is an experience far more usual than is commonly supposed. I had fallen asleep before the window that looked down to the lawn and the brook; the pool lay within easy sight, and the object which had crossed before my eyes was Maurice in his nightgown on his way to the pool.

I was fully awake right away. I came out of my chair to my knees at the window and called to him.

"Maurice! Maurice! Come back!"

But he did not turn. He went straight over to the pool and he sat down on the rim of it, and I heard his voice, low and soothing, as if he were comforting someone, and then I saw that vapor again, like a long, white woman's arm come up out of the water and take his hand a pull him into the pool.

I screamed, stumbled to my feet, and ran out of the room as fast as I could—down the stairs and across the lawn.

But it was too late. Maurice had gone under and he did not come up again until he had drowned.

Even while the others came running from the house, there was something else. While I knelt there at that dark pool I felt something come out of it and go past me toward the stone house behind, and I saw the grass move in the moonlight as if two people walked there. And what I felt was not cold, it was not any more that terrible, despairing loneliness—no, it was warm and fulfilling, ineffably beautiful, as if the heart and soul of love itself had become briefly, briefly tangible there and touched me in passing by.

VIRGINIA

His Coat So Gay
by Sterling E. Lanier

THERE HAD been a big spread in the newspapers about a British duke going through bankruptcy proceedings and his third divorce simultaneously. The divorce was contested, the evidence was sordid and those giving it equally so. The nobleman in question came out of the whole thing very badly, it being proved, among other things, that he had run up huge debts to tradesmen, knowing damn well he couldn't hope to pay. There was lots more, though, including secret orgies, which seem to have been dirty parties of the sort to have passed quite unnoticed in Los Angeles.

One of the members tapped his newspaper. A few of us were sitting upstairs in the library after dinner. It was a hot night in New York, but the club was air-conditioned and very pleasant.

"Good thing," said the man with the paper, "that Mason Williams isn't here to shout about this. He'd love to give General Ffellowes a hard time. Can't you hear him? 'Rotten bunch of degenerates! Lousy overbearing crooks and cadgers! Long line of aristocratic bums and swindlers!' It would be the best opportunity he's had in years for trying to annoy the Brigadier."

"I notice you were smart enough to say 'trying,'" said someone else. "He's never managed to annoy Ffellowes yet. I doubt if this would do it either."

"Who wants to annoy me, eh?" came the easy, clipped tones of our favorite English member. He had come up the narrow back stairs at the other end of the room and was now standing behind me. He always moved silently; not, I feel certain, out of a desire to be stealthy, but from a lifetime's training. Ffellowes' years in (apparently) every secret as well as public branch of Her Majesty's service had given him the ability to walk like a cat, and a quiet one at that.

603

I jumped and so did a couple of the others and then there was a moment of embarrassed silence.

Ffellowes is very quick. He saw the newspaper headline in my neighbor's lap and began to chuckle.

"Good heavens, is that supposed to offend me? What a hope! I suppose someone thought our friend Williams might make use of it to savage the British Lion, eh?" He moved from behind my chair and sat in a vacant seat, his eyes twinkling.

"Item," he said, "the man in question's a Scot, not English. Most important distinction. A lesser and unstable breed." This was said with such dead-pan emphasis that we all started to laugh at once. Ffellowes' smooth, ruddy face remained immobile, but his blue eyes danced.

"If you won't be serious," he said, when the laughter died away, "I shall have to explain why Chattan's little peccadilloes are unlikely to move me to wrath. Or anyone else with any real knowledge, for that matter.

"You know, Richard the Lion Heart was a bad debtor on a scale that makes anyone modern look silly. All the Plantagenets were, for that matter. Richard seems to have been a quite unabashed queer as well, of course, and likewise William the Second, called Rufus. When, at any rate, one asked those lads for monies due, one had better have a fast horse and a waiting ship ready. They cancelled debts rather abruptly. There are thousands more examples, but I mention the kings as quite a fairish sample. Now Chattan's an ass and his sexual troubles are purely squalid, fit only for headlines in a cheap paper. But there are other cases no paper ever got to print. Not so long ago, one of your splashier magazines ran a purely fictional piece about an aged nobleman, Scots again, who was sentenced never to leave his family castle, as a result of an atrocious crime, not *quite* provable. The story happens to be quite true and the verdict was approved by the Lords in a closed session. The last Pope but two had a South Italian cardinal locked up in his own palace for the remainder of his life on various charges not susceptible of public utterance. The old man died only ten years ago. So it goes, and there are dozens more cases of a similar nature.

"The fact is, persons in positions of power often abuse that power in the oddest and most unpleasant ways. The extent of caprice in the human mind is infinite. Whenever public gaze, so to speak, is withdrawn, oddities occur, and far worse than illicit sex is involved in these pockets of infection. Once off the highways, if you care for analogies, one finds the oddest byways. All that's needed is isolation, that and power, economic or physical." He seemed to brood for a moment.

Outside the windows, the haze and smog kept even the blaze of Manhattan at night dim and sultry-looking. The garish electricity of New York took on something of the appearance of patches of torch and fire light in the heat and murk.

"Haven't you left out one qualification, Sir?" said a younger member. "What about time? Surely, to get these Dracula castle effects and so on, you have to have centuries to play with a complaisant bunch of peasants, hereditary aristocrats, the whole bit. In other words a really *old* country, right?"

Ffellowes stared at the opposite wall for a bit before answering. Finally he seemed to shrug, as if he had come to a decision.

"Gilles de Rais," he said, "is perhaps the best example known of your Dracula syndrome, so I admit I must agree with you. In general, however, only in general. The worst case of this sort of thing which ever came to my personal—and very personal it was—knowledge took place in the early 1930's in one of your larger Eastern states. So that while time is certainly needed, as indeed for the formation of any disease, the so-called modern age is not so much of a protection as one might think. And yet there was great age, too."

He raised his hand and the hum of startled comment which had begun to rise died at once.

"I'll tell you the story. But I'll tell it my way. No questions of any sort whatsoever. There are still people alive who could be injured. I shall cheerfully disguise and alter any detail I can which might lead to identification of the family or place concerned. Beyond that, you will simply have to accept my word. If you're interested on that basis . . . ?"

The circle of faces, mine included, was so eager that his iron countenance damned near cracked into a grin, but he held it back and began.

"In the early days of your, and indeed everyone's, Great Depression, I was the most junior military attache of our Washington embassy. It was an agreeable part of my duties to mix socially as much as I could with Americans of my own age. One way of doing this was hunting, fox-hunting to be more explicit. I used to go out with the Middleburg Hunt and while enjoying the exercise, I made a number of friends as well.

"One of them was a man whom I shall call Canler Waldron. That's not even an anagram, but sounds vaguely like his real name. He was my own age and very good company. He was supposed to be putting in time as a junior member of your State Department.

"It was immediately obvious that he was extremely well off. Most people of course, had been at least affected a trifle by the Crash, if not a whole lot, but it was plain that whatever Can's financial basis was, it had hardly been shaken. Small comments were revealing, especially his puzzlement when, as often happened, others pleaded lack of funds to explain some inability to do a trip or to purchase something. He was, I may add, the most generous of men financially, and without being what you'd call a 'sucker,' he was very easy to leave with the cheque, so much so one had to guard against it.

"He was pleasant-looking; black-haired, narrow-faced, dark brown eyes, a generalized North European type and as I said about my own age, barely twenty-six. And what a magnificent rider! I'm not bad, or wasn't then, but I've never seen anyone to match Canler Waldron. No fence ever bothered him and he always led the field, riding so easily that he hardly appeared to be

606 STERLING E. LANIER

conscious of what he was doing. It got so that he became embarrassed by the attention and used to pull his horse in order to stay back. Of course he was magnificently mounted; he had a whole string of big black hunters, his own private breed he said. But there were others out who had fine 'cattle' too: no, he was simply a superb rider.

"We were chatting one fall morning after a very dull run and I asked him why he always wore a black hunting coat of a nonhunt member. I knew he belonged to some hunt or other and didn't understand why he never used their colors.

"'Highly embarrassing to explain to you, Donald, of all people,' he said, but he was smiling. 'My family were Irish and very patriotic during our Revolution. No pink coats ('pink' being the term for hunting red) for us. Too close to the hated Redcoat Army in looks, see? So we wear light green and I frankly get damned tired of being asked what it is. That's all.'

"I was amused for several reasons and said, 'Of course I understand. Some of our own hunts wear other colors, you know. But I thought green coats were for foot hounds, beagles, bassetts and such?"

"'Ours is much lighter, like grass, with buff lapels,' he said. He seemed a little ill at ease for some reason, as our horses shifted and stamped under the hot Virginia sun. 'It's a family hunt, you see. No non-Waldron can wear the coat. This sounds pretty snobby, so again, I avoid questions by not wearing it except at home. Betty feels the same way and she hates black. Here she comes now. What did you think of the ride, Sis?'

"'Not very exciting,' she said quietly, looking around so that she should not be convicted of rudeness to our hosts. I haven't mentioned Betty Waldron, have I? Even after all these years, it's still painful.

"She was nineteen years old, very pale and no sun ever raised so much as a freckle. Her eyes were almost black, her hair midnight and her voice very gentle and sad. She was quiet, seldom smiled and when she did my heart turned over. Usually, her thoughts were miles away and she seemed to walk in a dream. She also rode superbly, almost absent-mindedly, to look at her."

Ffellowes sighed and arched his hands together in his lap, his gaze fixed on the rug before him.

"I was a poor devil of an artillery subaltern, few prospects save for my pay, but I could dream, as long as I kept my mouth shut. She seemed to like me as much, or even more, than the gaudy lads who were always flocking about and I felt I had a tiny, the smallest grain of hope. I'd never said a thing. I knew already the family must be staggeringly rich and I had my pride. But also, as I say, my dreams."

"'Let's ask Donald home and give him some real sport,' I suddenly heard Can say to her.

"'When?' she asked sharply, looking hard at him.

"'How about the end of cubbing season? Last week in October. Get the best of both sports, adult and young. Hounds will be in good condition and it's our best time of year.' He smiled at me and patted his horse. 'What say, Limey? Like some real hunting, eight hours sometimes?'

"I was delighted and surprised, because I'd heard several people fishing rather obviously for invitations to the Waldron place at one time or another and all being politely choked off. I had made up my mind never to place myself where such a rebuff could strike me. There was a goodish number of fortune-hunting Europeans about just then, some of them English, and they made me a trifle ill. But I was surprised and hurt too, by Betty's reaction.

"'Not this fall, Can,' she said, her face even whiter than usual. 'Not—this—fall!' The words were stressed separately and came out with an intensity I can't convey.

"'As the head of the family, I'm afraid what I say goes,' said Canler in a voice I'd certainly never heard him use before. It was heavy and dominating, even domineering. As I watched, quite baffled, she choked back a sob and urged her horse away from us. In a moment her slender black back and shining topper were lost in the milling sea of the main body of the hunt. I was really hurt badly.

"'Now look here, old boy,' I said. 'I don't know what's going on, but I can't possibly accept your invitation under these circumstances. Betty obviously loathes the idea and I wouldn't dream of coming against her slightest wish.'

"He urged his horse over until we were only a yard apart. 'You must, Donald. You don't understand. I don't like letting out family secrets, but I'm going to have to in this case. Betty was very roughly treated by a man last year, in the fall. A guy who seemed to like her and then just walked out, without a word, and disappeared. I know you'll never speak of this to her and she'd rather die than say anything to you. But I haven't been able to get her interested in things ever since. You're the first man she's liked from that time to this and you've got to help me pull her out of this depression. Surely you've noticed how vague and dreamy she is? She's living in a world of unreality, trying to shut out unhappiness. I can't get her to see a doctor and even if I could, it probably wouldn't do any good. What she needs is some decent man being kind to her in the same surroundings she was made unhappy in. Can you see why I need you as a friend so badly?' He was damned earnest and it was impossible not to be touched.

"'Well, that's all very well,' I mumbled, 'but she's still dead set against my coming, you know. I simply can't come in the face of such opposition. You mentioned yourself as head of the family. Do I take it that your parents are dead? Because if so, then Betty is my hostess. It won't do, damn it all.'

"'Now look,' he said. 'Don't turn me down. By tomorrow morning she'll ask you herself, I swear. I promise that if she doesn't the whole thing's off. Will you come if she does and give me a hand at cheering her up? And we are orphans, by the way, just us two.'

"Of course I agreed. I was wild to come. To get leave would be easy. There was nothing much but routine at the embassy anyway and mixing with people like the Waldrons was as much a part of my duties as going to any Fort Leavenworth maneuvers.

"And sure enough, Betty rang me up at my Washington flat the next morning and apologized for her behavior the previous day. She sounded very dim and tired but perfectly all right. I asked her twice if she was sure she wanted my company and she repeated that she did, still apologizing for the day before. She said she had felt feverish and didn't know why she'd spoken as she had. This was good enough for me and so it was settled.

"'Thus, in the last week in October, I found myself hunting the coverts of—well, call it the valley of Waldrondale. What a glorious, mad time it was! The late Indian summer lingered and each cold night gave way to a lovely misty dawn. The main Waldron lands lay in the hollow of a spur of the Appalachian range. Apparently some early Waldron, an emigrant from Ireland during the 1600's, I gathered, had gone straight west into Indian territory and somehow laid claim to a perfectly immense tract of country. What is really odd is that the red men seemed to feel it was all fine, that he should do so.

"'We always got along with our Indians,' Canler told me once. 'Look around the valley at the faces, my own included. There's some Indian blood in all of us. A branch of the lost Erie nation, before the Iroquois destroyed them, according to the family records.'

"It was quite true that when one looked, the whole valley indeed appeared to have a family resemblance. The women were very pale and both sexes were black-haired and dark-eyed, with lean, aquiline features. Many of them, apparently local farmers, rode with the hunt and fine riders they were too—well-mounted and fully familiar with field etiquette.

"Waldrondale was a great, heart-shaped valley, of perhaps eight thousand acres. The Waldrons leased some of it to cousins and farmed some themselves. They owned still more land outside the actual valley, but that was all leased. It was easy to see that in Waldrondale itself they were actually rulers. Although both Betty and Can were called by their first names, every one of the valley dwellers was ready and willing to drop whatever he or she was doing at a moment's notice to oblige either of them in the smallest way. It was not subservience exactly, but instead almost an eagerness, of the sort a monarch might have gotten in the days when kings were sacred beings. Canler shrugged when I mentioned how the matter struck me.

"'We've just been here a long time, that's all. They've simply got used to us telling them what to do. When the first Waldron came over from Galway, a lot of retainers seemed to have come with him. So it's not really a strictly normal American situation.' He looked lazily at me. 'Hope you don't think we're too effete and baronial here, now that England's becoming so democratized?'

"'Not at all,' I said quickly and the subject was changed. There had been an unpleasant undertone in his speech—almost jeering, and for some reason he seemed rather irritated.

"What wonderful hunting we had! The actual members of the hunt, those who wore the light green jackets, were only a dozen or so, mostly close relatives of Canler's and Betty's. When we had started the first morning at dawn I'd surprised them all for I was then a full member of the Duke of Beaufort's pack, and as a joke more than anything else had brought the blue and yellow-lapelled hunting coat along. The joke was that I had been planning to show them, the Waldrons, one of our own variant colors all along, ever since I had heard about theirs. They were all amazed at seeing me not only not in black, but in "non-red" so to speak. The little withered huntsman, a local farmer named McColl, was absolutely taken aback and for some reason seemed frightened. He made a curious remark, of which I caught only two words, "Sam Haines," and then made a sign which I had no trouble at all interpreting. Two fingers at either end of a fist have always been an attempt to ward off the evil eye, or some other malign spiritual influence. I said nothing at the time, but during dinner asked Betty who Sam Haines was and what had made old McColl so nervous about my blue coat. Betty's reaction was ever more peculiar. She muttered something about a local holiday and also that my coat was the 'wrong color for an Englishman,' and then abruptly changed the subject. Puzzled, I looked up, to notice that all conversation seemed to have died at the rest of the big table. There were perhaps twenty guests, all the regular hunt members and some more besides from the outlying parts of the valley. I was struck by the intensity of the very similar faces, male and female, all staring at us, lean, pale and dark-eyed, all with that coarse raven hair. For a moment I had a most peculiar feeling that I had blundered into a den of some dangerous creatures or other, not unlike a wolf. Then Canler laughed from the head of the table and conversation started again. The illusion was broken, as a thrown pebble shatters a mirrored pool of water, and I promptly forgot it.

"The golden, wonderful days passed as October drew to a close. We were always up before dawn and hunted the great vale of Waldrondale sometimes until noon. Large patches of dense wood had been left deliberately uncleared here and there and made superb coverts. I never had such a good going, not even in Leicestershire at its best. And I was with Betty, who seemed happy, too. But although we drew almost the entire valley at one time or another there was one area we avoided, and it puzzled me to the point of asking Can about it one morning.

"Directly behind the Big House (it had no other name) the ground rose very sharply in the direction of the high blue hills beyond. But a giant hedge, all tangled and overgrown, barred access to whatever lay up the slope. The higher hills angled down, as it were, as if to enclose the house and grounds, two arms of high rocky ground almost reaching the level of the house on either side. Yet it was evident that an area of some considerable extent, a smallish plateau in fact, lay directly behind the house, between it and the sheer slopes of the mountain, itself some jagged outlier of the great Appalachian chain. And the huge hedge could only have existed for the purpose of barring access to this particular piece of land.

"'It's a sanctuary,' Canler said when I asked him. 'The family has a burial plot there and we always go there on—on certain days. It's been there since we settled the area, has some first growth timber among other things, and we like to keep it as it is. But I'll show it to you before you leave if you're really interested.' His voice was incurious and flat, but again I had the feeling, almost a sixth sense if you like, that I had somehow managed to both annoy and, odder, amuse him. I changed the subject and we spoke of the coming day's sport.

"One more peculiar thing occurred on that day in the late afternoon. Betty and I had got a bit separated from the rest of the hunt, a thing I didn't mind one bit, and we also were some distance out from the narrow mouth of the valley proper, for the fox had run very far indeed. As we rode toward home under the warm sun, I noticed that we were passing a small, white, country church, wooden, you know, and rather shabby. As I looked, the minister, parson, or what have you, appeared on the porch, and seeing us, stood still, staring. We were not more than thirty feet apart, for the dusty path, hardly a road at all, ran right next to the church. The minister was a tired-looking soul of about fifty, dressed in an ordinary suit but with a Roman collar, just like the C. of E. curate at home.

"But the man's expression! He never looked at me, but he stared at Betty, never moving or speaking, and the venom in his eyes was unmistakable. Hatred and contempt mingled with loathing.

"Our horses had stopped and in the silence they fidgeted and stamped. I looked at Betty and saw a look of pain on her face, but she never spoke or moved either. I decided to break the silence myself.

"'Good day, Padre,' I said breezily. 'Nice little church you have here. A jolly spot, lovely trees and all.' I expected I sounded half-witted.

"He turned his gaze on me and it changed utterly. The hatred vanished and instead I saw the face of a decent, kindly man, yes and a deeply troubled one. He raised one hand and I thought for a startled moment he actually was going to bless me, don't you know, but he evidently thought better of it. Instead he spoke, plainly addressing me alone.

"'For the next forty-eight hours this church will remain open. And I will be here.'

"With that, he turned on his heel and re-entered the church, shutting the door firmly behind him.

"'Peculiar chap, that,' I said to Betty. 'Seems to have a bit of a down on you, too, if his nasty look was any indication. Is he out of his head, or what? Perhaps I ought to speak to Can, eh?'

"'No,' she said quickly, putting her hand on my arm. 'You musn't; promise me you won't say anything to him about this, not a word!'

"'Of course I won't, Betty, but what on earth is wrong with the man? All that mumbo-jumbo about his confounded church bein' open?'

"'He—well, he doesn't like any of our family, Donald. Perhaps he has reason. Lots of people outside the valley aren't too fond of the Waldrons. And the Depression hasn't helped matters. Can won't cut down on the high living and of course hungry people who see us are furious. Don't let's talk any more about it. Mr. Andrews is a very decent man and I don't want Canler to hear about this. He might be angry and do something unpleasant. No more talk now. Come on, the horses are rested, I'll race you to the main road.'

"The horses were *not* rested and we both knew it, but I would never refuse her anything. By the time we rejoined the main body of the hunt, the poor beasts were blown, and we suffered a lot of chaff, mostly directed at me, for not treating our mounts decently.

"The next day was the thirty-first of October. My stay had only two more days to run and I could hardly bear to think of leaving. But I felt glorious too. The previous night, as I had thrown the bedcloths back, preparatory to climbing in, a small packet had been revealed. Opening it, I had found a worn, tiny cross on a chain, both silver and obviously very old. I recognized the cross as being of the ancient Irish or Gaelic design, rounded and with a circle in the center where the arms joined. There was a note in a delicate hand I knew well, since I'd saved every scrap of paper I'd ever received from her.

"*'Wear this for me always and say nothing to anyone.'*

"Can you imagine how marvelous life seemed? The next hunt morning was so fine it could hardly have been exceeded. But even if it had been terrible and I'd broken a leg, I don't think I'd have noticed. I was wearing Betty's family token, sent to *me*, secretly under my shirt and I came very close to singing aloud. She said nothing to me, save for polite banalities and looked tired, as if she'd not slept too well.

"As we rode past a lovely field of gathered shocks of maize, your 'corn,' you know, I noticed all the jolly pumpkins still left lying about in the fields and asked my nearest neighbor, one of the younger cousins, if the local kids didn't use them for Hallowe'en as I'd been told in the papers.

"'Today?' he said and then gobbled the same words used by the old huntsman, 'Sam Haines,' or perhaps 'Hayne.'

"'We don't call it that,' he added stiffly and before I could ask why or anything else, spurred his horse and rode ahead. I was beginning to wonder, in a vague sort of way, if all this isolation really could be good for people. Canler and Betty seemed increasingly moody and indeed the whole crowd appeared subject to odd moods.

"*Perhaps a bit inbred,* I thought. *I must try and get Betty out of here.* Now apparently I'd offended someone by mentioning Hallowe'en, which, it occurred to me in passing, was that very evening. 'Sam Haines' indeed!

"Well, I promptly forgot all that when we found, located a fox, you know, and the chase started. It was a splendid one and long and we had a very late lunch. I got a good afternoon rest, since Canler had told me we were having a banquet that evening. 'A farewell party for you, Donald,' he said, 'and a special one. We don't dress up much, but tonight we'll have a sort of hunt ball, eh?'

"I'd seen no preparations for music, but the big house was so really big that the London Symphony could have been hid somewhere about.

"I heard the dinner gong as I finished dressing and when I came down to the main living room, all were assembled, the full hunt, with all the men in their soft emerald green dress coats, to which my blue made a mild contrast. To my surprise, a number of children, although not small ones, were there also, all in party dress, eyes gleaming with excitement. Betty looked lovely in an emerald evening dress, but also very wrought up and her eyes did not meet mine. Once again, a tremendous desire to protect her and get her out of this interesting but rather curious clan came over me.

"But Can was pushing his way through the throng and he took me by the elbow. 'Come and be toasted, Donald, as the only outsider,' he said, smiling. 'Here's the family punch and the family punchbowl too, something few others have ever seen.'

"At a long table in a side alcove stood an extraordinary bowl, a huge stone thing, with things like runes scratched around the rim. Behind it, in his 'greens' but bareheaded, stood the little withered huntsman, McColl. It was he who filled a squat goblet, but as he did so and handed it to me, his eyes narrowed and he hissed something inaudible over the noise behind me. It sounded like 'watch.' I was alerted and when he handed me the curious stone cup I knew why. There was a folded slip of paper under the cup's base, which I took as I accepted the cup itself. Can, who stood just behind me, could have seen nothing.

"I'm rather good at conjuring tricks and it was only a moment before I was able to pass my hand over my forehead and read the note at the same instant. The message was simple, the reverse of Alice's on the bottle.

"'*Drink nothing.*' That was all, but it was enough to send a thrill through my veins. I was sure of two things. McColl had never acted this way on his own hook. Betty, to whom the man was obviously devoted, was behind this.

"I was in danger. I knew it. All the vague uneasiness I had suppressed during my stay, the peculiar stares, the cryptic remarks, the attitude of the local minister we had seen, all coalesced into something ominous, inchoate but menacing. These cold, good-looking people were not my friends, if indeed they were anyone's. I looked casually about while pretending to sip from my cup. Between me and each one of the three exits, a group of men were standing, chatting and laughing, accepting drinks from trays passed by servants, but *never moving*. As my brain began to race overtime, I actually forgot my warning and sipped from my drink. It was like nothing I have had before or since, being pungent, sweet and at the same time almost perfumed, but not in an unpleasant way. I managed to avoid swallowing all but a tiny bit, but even that was wildly exhilarating, making my face flush and the blood roar through my veins. It must have showed, I expect, for I saw my host half smile and others too, as they raised their cups to me. The sudden wave of anger I felt did not show, but now I really commenced to think.

"I turned and presented my almost full goblet to McColl again as if asking for more. Without batting an eye, he *emptied* it behind the cover of the great bowl, as if cleaning out some dregs, and refilled it. The little chap had brains. As again I raised the cup to my lips, I saw the smile appear on Can's face once more. My back was to McColl, blocking him off from the rest of the room and this time his rasping penetrating whisper was easy to hear.

"'After dinner, be paralyzed, stiff, frozen in your seat. You can't move, understand?'

"I made a circle with my fingers behind my back to show I understood, and then walked out into the room to meet Canler who was coming toward me.

"'Don't stand at the punch all evening, Donald,' he said, laughing. 'You have a long night ahead, you know.' But now his laughter was mocking and his lean, handsome face was suddenly a mask of cruelty and malign purpose. As we moved about together, the faces and manners of the others, both men and women, even the children and servants, were the same, and I wondered that I had ever thought any of them friendly. Under their laughter and banter, I felt contempt, yes and hatred and triumph too, mixed with a streak of pure nastiness. I was the stalled ox, flattered, fattened and fed, and the butchers were amused. They knew my fate, but I would not know until the door of the abbatoir closed behind me. But the ox was not quite helpless yet, nor was the door quite slammed shut. I noticed Betty had gone and when I made some comment or other, Can laughed and told me she was checking dinner preparations, as indeed any hostess might. I played my part as well as I could, and apparently well enough. McColl gave me bogus refills when we were alone and I tried to seem excited, full of *joie de vivre*, you know. Whatever other effect was expected was seemingly reserved for after dinner.

"Eventually, about nine I should think, we went in to dinner; myself carefully shepherded between several male cousins. These folk were not leaving much to chance, whatever their purpose.

"The great dining room was a blaze of candles and gleaming silver and crystal. I was seated next to Betty at one end of the long table and Canler took the other. Servants began to pour wine and the dinner commenced. At first, the conversation and laughter were, to outward appearances, quite normal. The shrill laughter of the young rose above the deeper tones of their elders. Indeed the sly, feral glances of the children as they watched me surreptitiously were not the least of my unpleasant impressions. Once again and far more strongly, the feeling of being in a den of some savage and predatory brutes returned to me, and this time, it did not leave.

"At my side, Betty was the exception. Her face never looked lovelier— ivory white in the candle glow, and calm, as if whatever had troubled her earlier had gone. She did not speak much, but her eyes met mine frankly, and I felt stronger, knowing that in the woman I loved, whatever came, I had at least one ally.

"I have said that as the meal progressed, so too did the quiet. I had eaten a fairish amount, but barely tasted any of the wines from the battery of glasses at my place. As dessert was cleared off, amid almost total silence, I became aware that I had better start playing my other role, for every eye was now trained at my end of the table.

Turning to the girl, an unmarried cousin, on my right side, I spoke slowly and carefully, as one intoxicated.

"'My goodness, that punch must have been strong! I can scarcely move my hand, d'you know. Good thing we don't have to ride tonight, eh?'

"Whatever possessed me to say *that*, I can't think, but my partner stared at me and then broke into a peal of cold laughter. As she did so, choking with her own amusement, the man on her far side, who had heard me also, repeated it to his neighbors. In an instant the whole table was aripple with sinister delight, and I could see Can at the far end, his white teeth gleaming as he caught the joke. I revolved my head slowly and solemnly in apparent puzzlement, and the laughter grew. I could see two of the waiters laughing in a far corner. And then it ceased."

"A great bell or chime tolled somewhere, not too far off and there was complete silence as if by magic. Suddenly I was aware of Canler who had risen at his place and had raised his hands, as if in an invocation.

"'The hour returns,' he cried. 'The Blessed Feast is upon us, the Feast of Sam'hain. My people, hence to your duties, to your robes, to the sacred park of the *Sheade*! Go, for the hour comes and passes!'

"It was an effort to sit still while this rigamarole went on, but I remembered the earlier warnings and froze in my seat, blinking stupidly. It was as well, for four of the men-servants, all large, now stood behind and beside my chair. In an instant the room was empty, save for these four, myself and my host, who now strode the length of the table to stare down at me, his eyes filled with anger and contempt. Before I could even move, he had struck me over the face with his open hand.

"'You, you English boor, would raise your eyes to the last princess of the Firbolgs, whose stock used yours as the meat and beasts of burden they are before Rome was even a village! Last year we had another one like you and his polo-playing friends at Hicksville are still wondering where he went!' He laughed savagely and struck me again. I can tell you chaps, I learned real self-control in that moment! I never moved, but gazed up at him, my eyes blank, registering vacuous idiocy.

"'The mead of the *Dagda* keeps its power,' he said. 'Bring him along, you four, the Great Hour passes!'

"Keeping limp, I allowed myself to be lifted and carried from the room. Through the great dark house, following that false friend, its master, we went, until at last we climbed a broad stair and emerged under the frosty October stars. Before us lay the towering, overgrown hedge, and now I learned the secret of it. A great gate, overgrown with vines so as to be invisible when shut, had been opened and before me lay the hidden place of the House of Waldron. This is what I saw:

"An avenue of giant oaks marched a quarter mile to a circular space where towered black tumuli of stone rose against the night sky. As I was borne toward these monoliths, the light of great fires was kindled on either side as I passed, and from them came an acrid, evil reek which caught at the throat. Around and over them leapt my fellow dinner guests and the servants wearing scanty, green tunics, young and old togerher, their voices rising in a wild screaming chant, unintelligible, but regular and rhythmic. Canler had vanished momentarily, but now I heard his voice ahead of us. He must have been gone longer than I thought, for when those carrying me reached the circle of standing stones, he was standing outlined against the largest fire of all, which blazed, newly-kindled, behind him. I saw the cause of the horrid stench, for instead of logs, were burning white dry bones, a great mountain of them. Next to him stood Betty and both of them had their arms raised and were singing the same wild chant as the crowd behind me.

"I was slammed to the ground by my guards but held erect and immovable so that I had a good chance to examine the two heirs of the finest families in the modern United States.

"Both were barefoot and wore thigh-length green tunics, his apparently wool, but hers silk or something like it, with her ivory body gleaming through it almost as if she were nude. Upon her breast and belly were marks of gold, like some strange, uncouth writing, clearly visible through the gauzy fabric. Her black hair was unbound and poured in waves over her shoulders. Canler wore upon his neck a massive circular torque, also of gold and on his head a coronal wreath, apparently of autumn leaves. In Betty's right hand was held a golden sceptre, looking like a crude attempt to form a giant stalk of wheat. She waved this in rhythm as they sang.

"Behind me the harsh chorus rose in volume and I knew the rest of the pack, for that's how I thought of them, were closing in. The noise rose to a crescendo, then ceased. Only the crackling of the great, reeking fire before me broke the night's silence. Then Canler raised his hands again in invocation and began a solitary chant in the strange harsh tongue they had used before. It was brief and when it came to an end, he spoke again, but in English this time.

"'I call to Sam'hain, Lord of the Dead, I, Tuathal, the Seventieth and One hundred, of the line of Miled, of the race of Goedel Glas, last true *Ardr'i* of ancient Erin, Supreme Vate of the *Corcou Firbolgi*. Oh, Lord from Beyond, who has preserved my ancient people and nourished them in plenty, the bonefires greet the night, your sacrifice awaits you!' He fell silent and Betty stepped forward. In her left hand she now held a small golden sickle, and very gently she pricked my forehead three times, in three places. Then she stepped back and called out in her clear voice.

"'I, Morrigu, Priestess and Bride of the Dead, have prepared the sacrifice. Let the Horses of the Night attend!'

"D'ye know, all I could think of was some homework I'd done on your American Constitution, in which Washington advocated separation of church and state? The human mind is a wonderful thing! Quite apart from the reek of the burning bones, though, I knew a stench of a spiritual sort. I was seeing something old here, old beyond knowledge, old and evil. I felt that somehow not only my body was in danger.

"Now I heard the stamp of hooves. From one side, snorting and rearing, a great black horse was led into the firelight by a half-naked boy, who had trouble with the beast, but still held him. The horse was saddled and bridled and I knew him at once. It was Bran, the hunter I'd been lent all week. Behind him, I could hear other horses moving.

"'Mount him,' shouted Canler, or Tuathal, as he now called himself. With that, I was lifted into the saddle, where I swayed, looking as doped and helpless as I could. Before I could move, my hands were caught and lashed together at the wrists with leather cords, then in turn tied loosely to the headstall, giving them a play of some inches but no more. The reins were looped up and knotted. Then my host stepped up to my knee and glared up at me.

"'The Wild Hunt rides, Slave and Outlander! You are the quarry, and two choices lie before you, both being death. For if we find you, death by these . . . and he waved a curious spear, short and broad in the blade.

"'But *others* hunt on this night, and maybe when those Who Hunt Without Riders come upon your track, you will wish for these points instead. Save for children's toys, the outside world has long forgotten their Christian Feast of All Hallows. How long then have they forgot that which inspired it, ten thousand and more years before the Nazarene was slain? Now—ride and show good sport to the Wild Hunt!'

"With that someone gave Bran a frightful cut over the croup, and he bounded off into the dark, almost unseating me in the process. I had no idea where we were going, except that it was not back down the avenue of trees and the blazing fires. But I soon saw that at least two riders were herding me away at an angle down the hill, cutting at Bran's flanks with whips when he veered from the course they had set. Twice the whips caught my legs, but the boots saved me from the worst of it.

"Eventually, we burst out into a glade near the southern spur of the mountain and I saw another, smaller gate had been opened in the great hedge. Through this my poor brute was flogged, but once through it I was alone. The big house was invisible around a curve of the hill, and no lights marked its presence.

"'Ride hard, Englishman,' called one of my herdsmen. 'Two deaths follow on your track.' With that, they turned back and I heard the gate slam. At the same time, I heard something else. Far off in the night I heard the shrill whinnying of a horse. Mingled with it and nearer was the sound of a horn, golden and clear. The horse cry was like that of no horse I have ever heard, a savage screaming noise which cut into my ear drums and raised the hackles even further on my back. At the same time I made a new discovery.

"Some sharp thing had been poking into my left thigh ever since I was placed on the horse. Even in the starlight I now could see the reason. The haft of a heavy knife projected under my leg, apparently taped to the saddle! By stretching and bending my body, I could just free it and once free I cut the lead which tethered my wrists to the head stall. As I did so, I urged Bran with my knees downhill and to the right, keeping close to the trees which grew unclipt at the base of the mountain spur. I knew there was little time to waste, for the sound of galloping horses was coming through the night, far off, but drawing nearer by the instant! It might be the twentieth century outside the valley, but I knew it would be the last of me if that pack of green-clad maniacs ever caught up with me. The Wild Hunt was not a joke at this point!

"As I saw it I had three secret assets. One, the knife, a sturdy piece of work with an eight-inch blade, which I now held in my teeth and tried to use to saw my wrists apart. The other was the fact that I have a good eye for ground and I had ridden the length and breadth of the valley for a week. While not as familiar with the area as those who now hunted me over it like a rabbit, I was, nevertheless, not a stranger and I fancied I could find my way even at night. My third ace was Betty. What she could do, I had no idea, but I felt sure she would do something.

"The damned leather cords simply could not be cut while Bran moved, even at a walk, and I was forced to stop. It only took a second's sawing, for the knife was sharp, and I was free. I was in deep shadows, and I listened intently, while I unknotted the reins.

"The sound of many horses galloping was still audible through the quiet night but it was no nearer, indeed the reverse. It now came from off to my left and somewhat lower down the valley. I was baffled by this, but only for a moment. Canler and his jolly group wanted a good hunt. Drugged as I was supposed to be, it would never do to follow directly on my track. Instead, they were heading to cut me off from the mouth of the valley, after which they could return at leisure and hunt me down. All of this and much more passed through my mind in seconds, you know.

"My next thought was the hills. In most places, the encircling wall of mountain was far too steep for a horse. But I could leave Bran behind and most of the ground ought to be possible for an active chap on foot. By dawn I could be well out of reach of this murderous gang. As the thought crossed my mind, I urged Bran toward the nearest wall of rock. We crossed a little glade and approached the black mass of the slope, shrouded in more trees at the base, and I kept my eye peeled for trouble. But it was my mount who found it.

"He suddenly snorted and checked, stamping his feet, refusing to go a foot forward. I drew the knife from my belt, also altered—and by a sudden awakening of a sense far older than anything merely physical. Ahead of us lay a menace of a different sort than the hunters of Waldrondale. I remembered my quondam host threatening me that something else was hunting that night, and also that the men who had driven me through the hedge called after me that *two* deaths were on my track.

"Before me, as I sat, frozen in the saddle, something moved in the shadows. It was large, but its exact shape was not easy to make out. I was conscious of a sudden feeling of intense cold, something I've experienced once or twice. I now know this to mean that one of what I'll call an Enemy from Outside, a foe of the spirit, is about. On my breast there was a feeling of heat as if I'd been burnt by a match. It was where I wore Betty's gift. The cross too was warning me. Then, two dim spots of yellow phosphorescence glowed at a height even with mine. A hard sound like a hoof striking a stone echoed once.

"This was enough for Bran! With a squeal of fright which sounded more like a hare than a blood horse, he turned and bolted. If I had not freed my hands I would have been thrown off in an instant, and as it was I had the very devil of a time staying on. He was not merely galloping, but bounding, gathering his quarters under him with each stride as if to take a jump. Only sheer terror can make a trained horse so forget himself.

"I did my best to guide him, for through the night I heard the golden questing note of a horn. The Wild Hunt was drawing the coverts. They seemed to be quite far down the valley and fortunately Bran was running away across its upper part, in the same direction as the big house.

"I caught a glimpse of its high, lightless gables, black against the stars as we raced over some open ground a quarter mile below it, then we were in the trees again, and I finally began to master the horse, at length bringing him to a halt. Once again, as he stood, sweated and shivered, I used my ears. At first there was nothing, then, well down the vale to my right front came the sound of the questing horn. I was still undiscovered.

"You may wonder, as I did at first, why I had heard no hounds. Surely it would have been easy for this crew to keep some bloodhounds, or perhaps smear my clothes or horse with anise and use their own thoroughbred fox hounds. I can only say I don't know. At a guess, and mind you, it's only a guess, there were other powers or elements loose that night which might have come into conflict with a normal hunting pack. But that's only a guess. Still, there were none, and though I was not yet sure of it, I was fairly certain, for even the clumsiest hound should have been in full cry on my track by now. The Wild Hunt then, seemed to hunt at sight. Again the clear horn note sounded. They were working up the slope in my direction.

"As quietly as possible, I urged Bran, who now seemed less nervous, along the edge of the little wood we were in and down the slope. We had galloped from the hill spur on the right, as one faced away from the house, perhaps two thirds of the way across the valley, which at this point was some two miles wide. Having tried one slope and met—well, whatever I *had* met, I would not try the other.

"My first check came at a wooden fence. I didn't dare jump such a thing at night, as much for the noise as for the danger of landing badly. But I knew there were gates. I dismounted and led Bran along until I found one, and then shut it carefully behind me. I had not heard the mellow horn note for some time and the click of the gate latch sounded loud in the frosty night. Through the large field beyond I rode at a walk. There was another gate at the far side, and beyond that another dark clump of wood. It was on the edge of this that I suddenly drew rein.

"Ahead of me, something was moving down in the wood. I heard some bulky creature shoulder into a tree trunk and the sound of heavy steps. It might have been another horse from the sound. But at the same moment, up the slope behind me, not too far away, came the thud of hooves on the ground, many hooves. The horn note blew, not more than two fields away, by the sound. I had no choice and urged Bran forward into the trees. He did not seem too nervous, and went willingly enough. The sound ahead of me ceased and then, as I came to a tiny glade in the heart of the little wood, a dim shape moved ahead of me. I checked my horse and watched, knife ready.

"'Donald?' came a soft voice. Into the little clearing rode Betty, mounted on a horse as dark as mine, her great black mare. I urged Bran forward to meet her.

"'I've been looking for you for over an hour,' she whispered, her breath warm on my cheek. I was holding her as tightly as I could, our mounts standing side by side, amiably sniffing one another. 'Let me go, Donald, or we'll both be dead. There's a chance, a thin one if we go the way I've thought out.' She freed herself and sat looking gravely at me. My night vision was good and I could see she had changed into a simple tunic of what looked like doeskin and soft, supple knee boots. Socketed in a sling was one of the short, heavy spears and I reached over and took it. The very heft of it made me feel better. The glimmering blade seemed red even in the dim tree light and I suddenly realized the point was bronze. These extraordinary people went in for authenticity in their madness.

"'Come on, quickly,' she said and wheeled her horse back the way she had come. I followed obediently and we soon came to the edge of the forest. Before us lay another gentle slope, but immediately beneath us was a sunken dirt road, which meandered away to the left and downhill between high banks, their tops planted with hedge. We slid down a sandy slope and our horses began to walk along the road, raising hardly any dust. Betty rode a little ahead, her white face visible as she turned to look back at intervals. Far away a cock crowed, but I looked at my watch and it was no more than 3 A.M. I could hear nothing uphill and the horn was silent. We rode through a little brook, out path crossing it at a pebbly ford only inches deep. Then, as we had just passed out of hearing the gurgle of the stream, a new sound broke the quiet night.

"It was somewhere between a whinny and a screech and I remembered the noise I had heard as the two riders had driven me through the hedge. If one could imagine some unthinkable horse-creature screaming at the scent of blood—eagerly, hungrily seeking its prey, well, that's the best I can do to describe it.

"'Come on, we have to ride for our lives!' Betty hissed. 'They have let the Dead Horse loose upon us. No one can stand against that.'

"With that, she urged her mount into a gallop and I followed suit. We tore along the narrow track between the banks, taking each twist at a dead run, always angling somehow downhill and toward the valley mouth.

"Then, the road suddenly went up and I could see both ahead and behind. Betty reined up and we surveyed our position. At the same time the horn blew again, but short, sharp notes this time and a wild screaming broke out. Three fields back up the long gentle slope the Wild Hunt had seen our black outlines on the little swell where we paused. I could see what looked like a dozen horsemen coming full tilt and the faint glitter of the spears. But Betty was looking back down along our recent track.

"From out of the dark hollows came a vast grunting noise, like that of a colossal pig sighting the swill pail. It was very close.

"Betty struck her horse over the withers and we started to gallop again in real earnest. Bran was tired, but he went on nobly, and her big mare simply flew. The Hunt was silent now, but I knew they were still coming. And I knew too, that something else was coming. Almost, I felt a cold breath on my back, and I held the spear tightly against Bran's neck.

"Suddenly, Betty checked, so sharply her horse reared, and I saw why as I drew abreast. We had come very close to the mouth of the valley and a line of fires lay before us, not three hundred yards away on the open flat. Around them moved many figures, and even at this distance I could see that a cordon was established and from the hats and glint of weapons, I knew not by the Waldrons of their retainers. Apparently the outside world was coming to Waldrondale, at least this far. We had a fighting chance.

"Between us and the nearest fire, a black horseman rode at us, and he was only a hundred feet off. The raised spear and the bare head told me that at least one of the valley maniacs had been posted to intercept me, in the unlikely event of my getting clear of the rest.

"I spurred the tired hunter forward and gripped the short spear near its butt end, as one might a club. The move was quite instinctive. I knew nothing of spears but I was out to kill and I was a six-goal polo player. The chap ahead, some Waldron cousin, I expect, needed practice, which he never got. He tried to stab at me overhand, but before our horses could touch I had swerved and lashed out as I would on a long drive at the ball. The heavy bronze edge took him between the eyes and really, that was that. His horse went off to one side alone.

"Wheeling Bran, I started to call to Betty to come on and as I did saw that which she had so feared had tracked us down.

"I am still not entirely certain of what I saw, for I have the feeling that part of it was seen with what Asiatics refer to as the Third Eye, the inner 'eye' of the soul.

"The girl sat, a dozen yards from me, facing something which was advancing slowly upon us. They had called it the Dead Horse, and its shifting outlines indeed at moments seemed to resemble a monstrous horse, yet at others, some enormous and distorted pig. The click of what seemed hooves was clear in the night. It had an unclean color, an oily shifting, dappling of grey and black. Its pupilless eyes, which glowed with a cold, yellow light, were fixed upon Betty, who waited as if turned to stone. Whatever it was, it had no place in the normal scheme of things. A terrible cold again came upon me and time seemed frozen. I could neither move nor speak, and Bran trembled, unmoving between my legs.

"My love broke the spell. Or it broke her. God knows what it must have cost her to defy such a thing, with the breeding she had, and the training. At any rate, she did so. She shouted something I couldn't catch, apparently in that pre-Gaelic gibberish they used and flung out her arm as if striking at the monster. At the same instant it sprang, straight at her. There was a confused sound or sounds, a sort of *spinning*, as if an incredible top were whirling in my ear and at the same instant my vision blurred.

"When I recovered myself, I was leaning over Bran's neck clutching him to stay on and Betty lay silent in the pale dust of the road. A yard away lay her horse, also unmoving. And there was nothing else.

"As I dismounted and picked her up, I knew she was dead, and that the mare had died in the same instant. She had held the thing from Outside away, kept it off me, but it had claimed a price. The high priestess of the cult had committed treason and sacrilege and her life was the price. Her face was smiling and peaceful, the ivory skin unblemished, as if she were asleep.

"I looked up at the sound of more galloping hoofbeats. The Wild Hunt, all utterly silent, were rounding a bend below me and not more than a hundred yards away. I lifted Betty easily, for she was very light, and mounted. Bran still had a little go left and we headed for the fires, passing the dead man lying sprawled in his kilt or whatever on the road. I was not really afraid any longer and as I drew up at the fire with a dozen gun barrels pointed at me, it all felt unreal. I looked back and there was empty hill, a barren road. The riders of Waldrondale had vanished, turned back apparently at the sight of the fires and the armed men.

"'He's not one; look at the gal! That crowd must have been hunting *him*. Call the parson over or Father Skelton, one of you. Keep a sharp lookout, now!'

"It was a babble of voices and like a dream. I sat down, staring stupidly and holding Betty against my heart until I realized a man was pulling at my knees and talking insistently. I began to wake up then, and looking down, recognized the minister I had seen the previous day. I could not remember his name but I handed Betty down to him when he asked, as obediently as a child.

"'She saved me, you know,' I said brightly. 'She left them and saved me. But the Dead Horse got her. That was too much, you see. She was only a girl, couldn't fight *that*. You do see, don't you?' This is what I am told I said at any rate, by Mr. Andrews, the Episcopal minister of the little Church of the Redeemer. But that was later. I remember none of it.

"When I woke, in the spare bed of the rectory the next day, I found

Andrews sitting silently by my bed. He was looking at my bare breast on which lay the little Celtic cross. He was fully dressed, tired and unshaven and he reeked of smoke, like a dead fireplace, still full of coals and wood ash.

"Before I could speak, he asked me a question. 'Did she, the young lady, I mean, give you that?'

"'Yes,' I said. 'It may have saved me. Where is she?'

"'Downstairs, in my late wife's room. I intend to give her Christian burial, which I never would have dreamed possible. But she has been saved to us.'

"'What about the rest of that crowd?' I said. 'Can nothing be done?'

"He looked calmly at me. 'They are all dead. We have been planning this for three years. That Hell spawn have ruled this part of the country since the Revolution. Governors, senators, generals, all Waldrons, and everyone else afraid to say a word.' He paused. 'Even the young children were not saved. Old and young, they are in that place behind the house. We took nothing from the house but your clothes. The hill folk who live to the west came down on them just before dawn, as we came up. Now there is a great burning; the house, the groves, everything. The State Police are coming but several bridges are out for some reason, and they will be quite a time.' He fell silent, but his eyes gleamed. The prophets of Israel were not all dead.

"Well, I said a last good-bye to Betty and went back to Washington. The police never knew I was there at all, and I was apparently as shocked as anyone to hear that a large gang of bootleggers and Chicago gangsters had wiped out one of America's first families and gotten away clean without being captured. It was a six-day sensation and then everyone forgot it. I still have the little cross, you know, and that's all."

We sat silent, all brooding over this extraordinary tale. Like all of the Brigadier's tales, it seemed too fantastic for human credibility and yet—and *yet*.

The younger member who had spoken earlier could not resist one question, despite Ffellowes' pre-story ban on such things.

"Well, Sir," he now said. "Why this means that one of the oldest royal families in the world, far more ancient than King Arthur's, say, is only recently extinct. That's absolutely amazing!"

Ffellowes looked up from his concentration on the rug and seemed to fix his gaze on the young man. To my amazement he did not become irritated. In fact, he was quite calm.

"Possibly, possibly," he said, "but of course they all appear to have been Irish or at least Celts of some sort or other. I have always considered their reliability open to considerable doubt."

WASHINGTON

Bigfish
by Edward D. Hoch

AFTER I took an early retirement from the aircraft industry, my wife, Matty, and I decided we liked the area around Puget Sound too much to move south as we'd always planned. California beckoned—we had a married daughter in Santa Barbara, after all—but our hearts were in the forests and mountains and waterways of Washington. We were even willing to put up with the dreary, rainy winters in order to revel in the sheer delights of the rest of the year.

Our retirement home was the vacation cabin on the western edge of the Sound that I'd added to so diligently over the years. It was not far from a state park, in a wooded area that seemed infinitely remote—even though a half-hour's drive would have taken us into Winslow or Bremerton, where the ferry to Seattle left several times each day.

Matty and I were both in our mid-fifties, but we jogged every morning and kept in good shape. One of the reasons I'd retired early was to spend more time with Matty, and here in our wooded retreat we were away from the city's tensions and temptations. Our few neighbors, retired people like ourselves, were out of sight down the road. If we stayed around the cabin we were unlikely to see anyone except the mailman passing during the course of the day.

"I do miss Ellen," Matty would say occasionally, referring to our daughter in California. "And our grandchild. I wish we could go visit them."

"Now, Matty, you know that's impossible right now. We're just relaxing, enjoying our retirement. Maybe in the winter we can take a trip down."

"That's what you said last year, but we never went."

This day, a warm August afternoon when it felt good to be alive, we were walking back to the house after strolling a fair distance when a little Japanease car with Oregon plates appeared suddenly over the crest of the hill. A man and woman and two children were crowded into it with suitcases and other vacation gear. As they reached us the car paused and the woman stuck her head out the window. "We're looking for Bigfish," she announced. "This the way to see Bigfish?"

"What?" Matty and I looked at each other, uncomprehending.

"Bigfish—you know, that giant salmon they're exhibiting in a van."

"Haven't heard about it," I admitted. "Once in a while there's talk of Bigfoot, but never Bigfish." Bigfoot, the legendary Yeti of the Himalayas or the Sasquatch of the Canadian Rockies, had been sighted and even photographed in several northwestern states. A great furry creature that walked upright like a man, Bigfoot was always good for newspaper space on days when the news was slow. But Bigfish was a new one on me.

"It's supposed to be on route 305, north of Winslow."

"You got sidetracked," I explained. "You should have taken the left fork instead of the right."

The man, who was driving, leaned over past his wife to say, "That's what I told her. My name's Russ Caulkins and this is my wife Freda. It's mostly the kids want to see Bigfish. I can think of other ways to spend my vacation." He glanced back at the two boys.

"You'd better turn around and get back on the paved road," I suggested. "Then turn right. That should get you there."

"Thanks a lot."

The idea of a giant salmon made Matty chuckle. "Maybe we should get in the car and go see it ourselves," she said.

I studied her, trying to determine if she meant it. "OK," I decided. "Maybe tomorrow."

"What's wrong with right now? It might not be there tomorrow."

So we got in the car and drove out the way the family of tourists had gone, following our dirt road until it connected with route 305. I made a sharp right turn and we headed south toward Winslow. There was a ferry from nearby Eagle Harbor to Seattle, and a suburban development of commuting businessmen had grown up among the wooded hills and inlets overlooking Puget Sound. Sometimes I worried about these new families getting too close to our little retirement cabin.

Before long I spotted the large camper pulled off the road with a sign on the side:

BIGFISH! SEE THE WORLD'S LARGEST SALMON! OVER SIX FEET LONG! ADMISSION ONE DOLLAR.

"There's that Japanese car," Matty observed. "I guess the Caulkinses found it all right."

"Yes." I pulled up behind them and we got out. There were no other cars around.

"We were met at the door by a jolly bearded man of indeterminate age." "Greetings, folks. I'm Captain Bob Showcroft, but you can just call me Captain Bob. Bigfish is right through here. That'll be a dollar each, please."

Russ and Freda Caulkins and their two boys were already inside, gaping at the huge chinook salmon that lay stretched out across three card tables. "Hello there," Freda said, seeing us enter. "Decided to come along for a look at Bigfish?"

"He certainly is a big fellow," I agreed.

Captain Bob followed us in, using a wooden pointer to deliver a short lecture on his prize. "This here's a chinook salmon. It's six feet, one inch long and weighs a hundred and five pounds."

"Did you catch it?" the smaller of the two boys asked.

"Quiet, Tommy!" the woman nudged him. "Let the captain tell his story."

"Well, I didn't exactly catch it myself," the bearded man answered patting the small boy on the head, "but I know the fella who did. And this fish gave him quite a tussle."

"Where was it caught?" I asked.

"Kelp Bay, in Alaska. Biggest one they ever took there. Biggest in the world, far as we know."

He went on with a lecture about the life cycle of the salmon that seemed to bore even the two boys. After touching Bigfish a bit tenuously, the older one drifted away, followed by little Tommy. Captain Bob wound up his talk and asked perfunctorily, "Any questions?"

Freda Caulkins noticed the boys had slipped out of the camper and went in search of them. Matty followed, leaving me with Russ Caulkins. "It's stuffed, isn't it?" he asked Captain Bob.

"Oh, sure. You don't eat a baby like this. You keep it to show off. I been touring the northeast with Bigfish all year. Probably donate it to a museum someday."

"Would you consider selling it?" I asked.

A shrewd look came into his eyes. "Well, sure, if the price was right. You don't find a fish like this every day, though. Worth a lot of money. You interested in buying?"

"No," I said with a laugh. "I just wondered."

"Guess I'll be closing up now," he decided. "It's getting dark and I want to make the last ferry over to Seattle."

Freda Caulkins came to the door and called to her husband. "Russ, the boys were playing in the woods and now I can't find Tommy."

He sighed and started outside. "All right, I'm sure he's around somewhere."

It had grown dark quickly among the tall trees that lined both sides of the road, and I could see Matty standing over by our car, anxious to get back home. Still, I felt I should remain until the boy was found. Russ went up to the bigger boy and asked, "Bill, where's your brother? Where's Tommy?"

"I don't know. I think he went back inside. He wanted another look at Bigfish."

"We just came out of there," Russ Caulkins said.

"There's a door at the other end," his wife pointed out. She called to Matty. "Did you see anything of him?"

"Not a thing. Perhaps he's still in the woods playing."

We all headed for the woods, calling his name, but there was no answer. "He couldn't just disappear," Russ said, turning to his other son. "Weren't you watching him?"

"Not every second," Bill answered. "Maybe bigfoot got him."

"Let's look inside," I suggested, a growing apprehension building in the pit of my stomach. "Maybe he sneaked in the other door."

But the entrance to the camper was locked now, and Captain Bob was up front, in the driver's seat. "Gotta be going, folks," he called out.

"Just a minute!" Freda shouted, running to him. "You have to open up! Our little boy is missing. We think he's inside!"

"He's not in there."

"Can't you open up and look?" her husband asked, his voice sharpening.

"He's not in there. What more can I tell you? Hell, you just came out five minutes ago. Nothing in there but Bigfish."

"Open it up so we can see."

He sighed and climbed out of his seat, going back to unlock the door. We crowded inside, but he'd been telling the truth. There was no sign of the missing boy.

"Where could he be?" Freda Caulkins asked, close to hysteria.

"Afraid I can't help you. How old is he?"

"Six," the father answered, "but he's small for his age. I'd hate to think of him in those woods with night coming on."

"He'd never go off by himself," Freda said. "He must have fallen down, or else someone took him."

"Don't say crazy things," her husband reproved. "No one's in the woods, and he was only out of sight a couple of minutes. He'll turn up."

"He's in here, in this camper!" Freda Caulkins suddenly insisted, her voice wild with panic. She confronted Captain Bob. "What have you done with my child?"

"Lady, you're as crazy as they come. I didn't touch the little brat!"

Russ Caulkins grabbed the bearded man's shirt before I could intervene. "If you've harmed Tommy—"

"God, man—look for yourself! Where's there room to hide him in here?"

Caulkins and his wife went quickly through the camper, looking in the bunk bed and the toilet. There was no sign of the missing boy, but with each frustration the woman's hysteria seemed to grow. "You've got him here someplace—I know it! He came back to see the fish again."

"Lady—"

Her breath was coming faster. She stared down at the stuffed salmon stretched across its card tables and said very softly, "He's inside the fish."

Her husband got a grip on her shoulders. "Freda, Freda, you can't—"

"*He's inside the fish!*" It was a scream now, torn from the very heart of her.

"Help me get her outside," Caulkins said to me. "We'd better search the woods again and then phone the state police."

"Make him open the fish! Make him open it up before Tommy dies!"

I tried to grip one arm, but she shook me off. "We'll find him," I told her. "We'll get the police."

"The fish! Tommy's in the fish!"

We were back outside when I saw a state police car cruising in the distance. He stopped when we flagged him down, and radioed for more assistance. The officer's name was McBride, and he listened to the hysterical woman with a look of helplessness. "Lady, I'm sure your son just wandered off into the woods. We'll find him."

"The fish. Make him open the fish!"

Captain Bob's face was flushed with rage. "I was only in there alone for five minutes! I didn't touch the kid, and I certainly didn't put him inside that salmon! Why would I do a crazy thing like that?"

"Was the boy small enough to have fit inside the fish?" the officer asked Caulkins.

"Oh, yes. Tommy is only six, and that's a big fish."

Officer McBride went into the camper with the rest of us following. He stared at Bigfish and asked, "What's inside it?"

Captain Bob wet his lips nervously. "You understand stuffed fish are usually painted synthetic models, using only the fins and tail from the actual creature. In this case, though, the whole fish was used. The insides were cleaned out and filled with excelsior."

"Can we turn it over?"

"I—I suppose so."

Officer McBride glanced up. "The ladies had better wait outside."

Caulkins took his wife and Matty outside, while I remained with Captain Bob. We managed to flop the fish over onto its other side, and the bearded man reluctantly cut through the line of stitching. The salmon was filled with excelsior. There was no child inside.

I went outside and told them. Another police car had arrived on the scene, and already the officers were making plans to search the nearby woods. Freda Caulkins had collapsed, sobbing, against her husband's shoulder and was being led to the car.

"It's time for us to be getting along," I told Matty.

I gave Officer McBride our address and told Russ I hoped his son would be found. As we drove away, Captain Bob was rolling up his Bigfish poster.

It was night by the time we reached our familiar dirt road, and as I turned onto it I summoned up the courage to speak to Matty at my side. "What did you do with the body, dear?" I asked calmly.

Even in the darkness I knew the wild look would be back in her eyes, that look I'd been dreading, hoping and praying against, for almost a year. "In the trunk," she answered, nodding toward the rear of the car. "This one was easy, he died so quickly. Not like the others."

"Matty—"

Then there was a tremor in her voice, a sudden note of fear. "Does this mean you won't take me to visit our grandson again this year?"

WEST VIRGINIA

Lonely Road
by Richard Wilson

THE HUM of the tires and the throb of the heater had made him sleepy. He realized that when the hum became a squeal. He had taken a sharp curve unconsciously, at full speed. Time for a coffee stop, he decided.

He had been driving half the night. Another twelve hours to go. He could do it without sleep, if he didn't doze himself into a ditch. Coffee every three hours would help.

The red neon sign said EAT and the smaller one below it said *Dan's Diner, Truckers Welcome*. But no trucks were parked there, and no cars. Maybe Dan's coffee wasn't good. He'd have to take the chance. He stretched his cramped legs and breathed the good cold air, then went in and sat at the long blue counter.

No one came. He picked up a cardboard menu, though he knew what he was going to have. Coffee and a hamburger, and a piece of pineapple cheese pie if they had it. If not, then apple.

Still no one came. He rapped on the counter with the menu. Then he noticed that there was no fire under the grill and that no coffee was being kept hot.

He went behind the counter to a door that stood ajar.

Behind it was a little storeroom, empty. He tried another door at the end of the diner. A washroom, also empty. Where was Dan?

There was a coke machine—caffein was caffein—but he wanted something hot. He went behind the counter again, prepared to apologize if Dan appeared, and took down a vacuum tin of coffee. He put water in the bottom of a glass coffee maker.

The coffee, as he brewed it, was foul. But he drank it, washing down a cold

629

sandwich he'd made from meat and cheese in the refrigerator. He had a piece of pie—apple—and drank a glass of water.

He computed the cost of the meal. He meant to leave the money on the counter but he had nothing smaller than a five. Feeling guilty, he went to the cash register, rang up $.65 and made change.

He'd eaten too fast and the food lay heavy in his stomach. He breathed several lungfuls of cold air, got in the car and drove away fast, headlights stabbing through the blackness.

He needed gas. The luminous needle was uncomfortably close to the luminous E. Another dial told him it was 2:15. He'd passed a filling station a while back. The gas pumps had been lighted but the gas wasn't his brand. Any brand would do now. He found a station whose pumps were aglow and whose little office was lighted. He honked.

No one came.

He couldn't risk going on to the next one. He got out impatiently and went to the office. It was empty.

Where was everyone tonight? Now that he thought about it, he hadn't passed any cars for some time, in either direction. He couldn't remember how long it had been. Since dark? Nonsense. Still, he couldn't recall having dimmed his country beams for an oncoming car.

Then he remembered the sudden rain in the late afternoon which had darkened the sky and blurred his windshield. Other cars had turned on their headlights, he recalled now, and so had he. But his windshield wipers had refused to work and for a time he'd driven slowly, unwilling to get out into the rain to fix them. He'd come to a wide underpass then, pulled over and stopped. Sheltered from the downpour by the mass of concrete, he'd got out of the car and given the wipers a push. They immediately took up their click-click. They'd been stuck, that was all.

He'd been standing for a moment, stretching, when he noticed two pools of water near a catch basin. They'd reminded him of his son, dead these seven years. Among the last things he and Joan had bought for the boy were two fishbowls Bobby wanted for his experiment. He stared at the two pools in the underpass, thinking of the boy and of Joan waiting at home at the end of his drive. He got back in the car. He couldn't remember having seen another car after that.

Now, at the gas station, there was no response to his *Hallo*. He shrugged and went to the pumps. Self-service night, he thought.

He filled his tank and went back to the office. He took out the four singles he'd taken in change from the diner and looked for a place to leave them. There was no cash register here. Greasy papers, catalogs and small tools littered the top of a battered desk. He put the bills down in a clear spot and weighted them with a pair of pliers.

After he'd driven on for some minutes he became acutely aware of the fact that he'd seen no one else on the highway. It wasn't a U.S. highway, true, but it was a good state road, usually well-traveled.

Puzzled now and beginning to feel lonely, he switched on the radio. But button after button yielded only the static of dead air. That was strange. Ordinarily, even if he could get nothing else, he could bring in WWVA. The powerful station in Wheeling blanketed the eastern seaboard in the night hours, playing its hillbilly records and hawking its patent medicines and illustrated Bibles.

The luminous clock said 3:10. He switched off the radio and hummed to himself, nervously.

He came to the outskirts of a town. Street lights hung over the road and there was an occasional light in a house. Cars were parked along the curbs. He began to feel better.

A traffic light turned from green to amber as he approached it, then red. He stopped. A block ahead was what looked like an all-night drug store. The traffic light turned green and he went ahead in low and parked. It was a drug store and it was open.

He pushed through the door and rapped on the counter. He'd buy a pack of cigarettes, though he had plenty, and mention jovially to the night clerk that he'd begun to feel that he was all alone in the world. He'd tell him about the empty diner and the unattended gas station. The clerk might have an explanation.

No one answered his rap.

The store lay bright around him, a clutter of magazines, school supplies, candies, tobacco products, a soda fountain. He looked over the top of a frosted glass partition, back to where prescriptions were compounded. No one was there.

He hungered for someone; anyone.

There was a telephone booth he hadn't noticed before and he went to it with relief. He'd been getting himself into a state. The voice of the operator would snap him out of it. He dropped a dime in the slot, got a dial tone and dialed Operator. He would tell her about the empty drug store and ask if she thought the police should know about it. He'd wait till the police came, he'd say.

He heard the ringing at the other end. At the tenth ring he pulled on the hook, got his dime back, reinserted it and dialed Operator again. After ten more rings he was beginning to sweat.

He unfolded the door of the booth and dialed 411, for Information. There was no answer.

He dialed 211, for Long Distance. No answer.

He dialed 611, for Repair Service. No answer.

He dialed seven times at random. No answer.

He fled out of the booth and out of the store. He roared the car away from the curb and through the town until he was again on the highway. It was more normal to be alone on the road. But his hand shook as he lit a cigarette. The clock on the dashboard said 4:55.

At dawn he turned off the headlights and rubbed his caking eyelids. His back and neck ached. He would have to stop and sleep. When he woke up maybe it would have been all a dream.

He found a tourist court. There was no one in the first cabin, marked *Office*. He signed the book, Clarence R. Spruance, and put a five-dollar bill between its pages. He noticed that he had left his car where it would block the way for others. So, to avoid anything that would jeopardize a return to normal when he woke up, he parked the car carefully in front of the cabin he chose.

He let himself in, locked the door behind him, washed the grit from his eyes, undressed to his underwear, prayed on his knees for the first time since childhood, eased under the covers and slept immediately.

When he awoke it was daylight again—or still. He stretched and scratched the bristles on his face. He would need a shave.

Then he remembered, all at once and in complete detail. And he knew it was no dream.

But perhaps it had changed. Maybe it was all right again—the people back, the noise and bustle and other cars on the highway. If they were, he would accept them. As a sort of bargain with himself, he would ask no questions. He would pretend they'd never been away.

But when he looked he saw nothing, heard nothing.

He was tempted to go back to bed, to try to sleep again, to give it another chance. For a long time he stood in his bare feet, looking out dully. Then he went into the bathroom and shaved.

He drove slowly, looking for a place to have breakfast. He didn't see any immediately and he drove faster. Then with a little laugh, he crossed to the far left lane and accelerated to 65 miles an hour, then 70. He held steady at 70, hugging the left edge of the concrete, laughing as he roared blindly around curves, bracing himself inwardly for a sudden head-on-crash. His heart pounded at each left-hand curve and he had to force himself to keep his foot on the accelerator and hold the needle at 70.

But after a while he was taking the curves without panic and it began to seem normal to drive on the left. He felt depressed again, after his momentary exhilaration, and let the car decelerate to 40 as he eased across the road to the right.

He drove till he came to a gas station. He filled his tank, left some money in the office and drove on.

He noticed that he had only a few singles and some change remaining. There was really no reason for him to pay for anything but he felt that he must. If he did not, he would be accepting what was apparent—that he was the only person left. He would not accept that, and he determined that he would pay for what he took as long as he was able. It was a kind of insurance that the rest of humanity would return eventually from wherever it had gone.

So at the next town he went into a bank. At a teller's window he made out a check to cash, for two hundred dollars, signed Clarence R. Spruance, and pushed it under the grill. But there was no money within reach. He found his way to the back of the teller's cages, went into the one he had picked from the other side and pulled open the drawer.

An alarm bell clanged, and continued to clang.

He stepped back in shock. Apparently there was a button that had to be touched so the drawer would open silently. The clanging unnerved him.

He made himself count out two hundred dollars, then count it again to be sure, and put the check in a slot where there were other checks. He shut the drawer but the harsh clanging continued. He made himself walk, not run, back around the cages and out the door. Another alarm was sounding outside with a terrible insistence.

The sound followed him through the empty town. He was glad to reach the open road again. He felt indignant about that alarm. It was unfair of it to have gone off that way, after he had been scrupulously ethical.

The tires hummed on the smooth road. The heater throbbed unnoticed. He didn't need the heater now, with the sun high and warm, but he'd neglected to turn it off. He became drowsy. His cigarette burned down and the heat of it on his knuckles roused him. He tossed out the butt and switched off the heater. Comfortable now but not sleepy, he drove for hours, automatically.

He slowed to read a sign. Forty-eight miles to go. As close as that.

He recognized the road now. The river was ahead, with a bridge. The toll bridge. He wondered if he'd be able to reach out and put a quarter on the counter inside the toll booth without leaving the car. He'd continue to pay as he went, people or no people.

He drove onto the bridge approach. You paid at the far end, he remembered. He slowed, took the quarter from his change pocket, transferred it to his left hand and coasted toward the booth.

A man in a gray uniform, with a badge, wearing a visored cap, stepped halfway out of the booth, hand extended, looking bored.

Spruance jammed on his brakes. The car bucked to a stop. The engine stalled. He sat, gripping the steering wheel, the quarter hard in his palm.

"Twenty-five cents, please," the uniformed man said.

Spruance held the coin out to him automatically.

"Twenty-five cents. Of course. That's right, isn't it?" He stared at the officer, felt the man's fingers pick the coin out of his palm. Stared at him. "You're back," he said.

"What?"

"I mean everything's the same. It's not—"

"Twenty-five cents," the officer said. "A quarter. That's what it's been as long as I can remember. You had it right."

"Yes, I did, didn't I? It's right, isn't it? It's all right again. The way it was before."

"Look, mister, you paid your toll. Now will you move along? Other people want to use the bridge, too, you know."

Spruance looked in his rear-view mirror. A car was behind him, waiting, and another car behind that one. Still other cars were moving along the highway at the end of the bridge.

The car behind him honked.

Spruance started his engine and went ahead slowly in first. The officer looked after him for a moment, then turned to take a coin from the next driver. Spruance shifted, then joined the road that ran south along the river bank. The car behind him made the same turn, honked again, then roared past. Other cars whizzed by from the opposite direction.

There was a sign, *POPULATED AREA*.

Then a town. A normal town, with people in it.

He found a parking space near a newsstand. He bought a metropolitan afternoon daily dated the 19th.

"Is this today's?" he asked the newsdealer.

"Yeah, sure."

He scanned the headlines but saw nothing unusual. He folded the paper under his arm and went into a lunchroom. Over coffee and scrambled eggs he looked at the paper from front to back, reading the first paragraph of each story. There was no hint in any of them that the major and minor crises of the world had been interrupted in any unusual way.

He beckoned to the counterman for a second cup of coffee. As he poured the cream in this time he noticed that it curdled slightly, as if it were a couple of days old.

"This cream isn't fresh," he said.

The counterman looked sullen. "I only work here," he said. "If you want to complain I'll get the manager."

"Never mind," Spruance said. He got up, leaving the second cup of coffee untouched. He put down some coins and left.

He went back to the newsstand. "You wouldn't have a copy of yesterday's paper, would you? For the 18th?"

The newsdealer mumbled, not looking at him: "No. Sorry."

"Well, does this town have a daily paper?"

"Yeah, but it's not out yet."

"I see. Where's its office?"

"Two blocks down, turn right half a block. But—" The newsdealer looked up at him, then down again, quickly.

"But what?"

"Nothing. Nothing."

Spruance thanked him and went on down the street. The people he passed either avoided his glance or looked at him with—hostility? That couldn't be right. It wasn't such a small town that a stranger would be noticed or resented. He paused in front of the five and ten cent store and pretended to look in the window. Several people passed, some in couples. He noticed that the hostility was general. Everyone was being distant with everyone else.

At the newspaper office he told the girl at the reception desk he'd like to look at some back issues.

"How far back?"

"Yesterday and the day before."

She looked troubled. "I'll have to call the morgue. The library, I mean."

"I know," he said, smiling.

She said into the phone: "That's right, the 17th and 18th. . . . Oh. . . . Okay, I'll tell him. . . . Yes, I know." She turned to Spruance again. "I'm sorry. They haven't been filed yet."

"That's all right. I'll look at loose copies."

"No, sir, you can't. We don't—we can't make an exception."

"I see." She seemed almost frightened, so he added: "It doesn't matter. Thank you anyway. Goodby."

It was beginning to get dark.

His wife answered the phone on the ninth ring. While it was ringing he'd had the lonely feeling again and had to look out of the booth to assure himself that the people were still back. So he spoke almost sharply to his wife when she answered.

"Where were you?" he asked.

"I was in the attic. How are you, Clare? Will you be home soon?"

"Yes. I'm in Hayesville. I'm all right, I guess. How do you feel, Joan?"

"Fine. Are you sure you're all right? How was your trip?"

"I'll tell you about it later. What were you doing in the attic?"

"I'll tell *you* later. It's a bit odd."

Joan had fixed coffee and a tray of sandwiches. "I thought we'd have a snack now and dinner later," she said. He nodded and kissed her absently.

"It's good to be back," he said. "I'm also glad you're back," he added with a little laugh. Then he told her what he meant.

She heard him out, frowning a little. "The check you left at the bank," she said. "That will come back in your statement."

"That's the only proof I have. If it proves anything. How about you? Are there two days you can't account for? Everybody I've spoken to seems to feel something's wrong but they won't talk about it. Will you?"

"I was in the attic when it happened," she said slowly. "I'd gone up to look at Bobby's aquarium."

Bobby, their son, had died when he was nine. They'd had no other children but kept the big house anyway, with its attic full of memories.

"The aquarium," he said. "Two of them, identical, for Bobby's experiment."

"There were two," Joan said. "There's only one now."

She'd gone up to the attic late in the afternoon. Bobby's things lay under the eaves, dim in the light of the naked electric bulb near the top of the stairs. The tricycle he'd outgrown. The two-wheeler he'd just learned to ride when he became ill. His stack of books. A first baseman's glove. The aquariums.

Bobby had been very good about his illness. He became a tropical fish enthusiast, spending hours watching the gaily-colored creatures dart among the water plants and in and out of the pottery castle in the sand at the bottom of the big tank.

Then one day Bobby had asked for another aquarium, exactly like the first, down to the last plant and the castle. They had bought it for him, of course, and set it beside the other near his bed. Bobby made adjustments in the slope of the sand, the angle of the castle and the spacing of the plants.

His mother wanted to know about the twin aquariums but he wouldn't tell her anything except that it was an experiment. Later, when she'd left the room, closing the door at his request, he'd transferred the fish from the old tank to the new one.

Bobby died not long after that. Later the fish died, too, and they'd emptied the two aquariums and put them in the attic.

"That afternoon," Joan said, "I picked up one of the aquariums and was holding it in both hands. I'd forgotton how heavy it was.

"Then I felt as if I was being *moved*. Not lifted or pushed—but *moved* in some positive way. The light flickered for an instant, then the feeling stopped. I was still holding the aquarium. I put it down. Everything seemed the same. Only it wasn't. There were *three* aquariums now."

"Three?" her husband asked softly.

"Yes. It was as if I'd been taken out of my own house—my world—and transferred to one that duplicated the old one down to the last smudge on the wallpaper. The way Bobby transferred the fish for his experiment. But they didn't fool me completely—just as the fish must have known their new aquarium was different."

"Who are 'they'?"

"I don't know. Whoever moved me and everybody else in the world— except you—to another tank, to study us for a while."

"And then transferred you back again?"

"Yes, this afternoon. I had the same feeling of being *moved*. I was here in the living room, dusting, wearing my yellow dust mitt. The feeling came and I recognized it. Then it passed and everything was familiar again. *Old* and familiar. I went to the broom closet to put the dust mitt away—and it was there already."

"You mean there were two dust mitts?"

"Yes. The one I'd been using—the duplicated one from the other world—and the one that had been in our own closet. So, after I thought about it for a while I went up to the attic."

He smiled. "To count the aquariums?"

"That's right. And there was only one. I'd taken one of them into that other world, and later I brought back an extra dust mitt."

"So they put you all in a new tank and studied you for a while and then brought you back. But why not me?"

"Yes," Joan said. "Why everybody *except* you?"

"Maybe I was overlooked, like the snail."

"The snail?"

"Yes. Remember how proud Bobby was after he'd transferred the fish to the new tank? He thought he'd done a thorough job till I pointed out that the snail was still in the old tank, hiding inside the castle. It was like me, fixing my windshield wiper in the underpass."

"Perhaps," his wife said. "I remember Bobby was annoyed because he'd missed the snail. But then he said: 'It was only an experiment. And not a very important one.' And, instead of putting the snail in the new tank too, he put all the fish back in the old tank. He said he thought they liked it better there."

WISCONSIN

Beyond the Threshold
by August Derleth

I

THE STORY is really my grandfather's.

In a manner of speaking, however, it belongs to the entire family, and beyond them, to the world; and there is no longer any reason for suppressing the singularly terrible details of what happened in that lonely house deep in the forest places of northern Wisconsin.

The roots of the story go back into the mists of early time, far beyond the beginning of the Alwyn family line, but of this I knew nothing at the time of my visit to Wisconsin in response to my cousin's letter about our grandfather's strange decline in health. Josiah Alwyn had always seemed somehow immortal to me even as a small child, and he had not appeared to change throughout the years between: a barrel-chested old man, with a heavy, full face, decorated with a closely clipped mustache and a small beard to soften the hard lines of his square jaw. His eyes were dark, not over-large, and his brows were shaggy; he wore his hair long, so that his head had a leonine appearance. Though I saw little of him when I was very young, still he left an indelible impression on me in the brief visits he paid when he stopped at the ancestral country home near Arkham, in Massachusetts—those short calls he made on his way to and from the remote corners of the world: Tibet, Mongolia, the Arctic regions, and certain little-known islands in the Pacific.

I had not seen him for years when the letter came from my cousin Frolin, who lived with him in the old house grandfather owned in the heart of the forest and lake country of northern Wisconsin. "I wish you could uproot yourself long enough from Massachusetts to come out here. A great deal of water has passed under various bridges, and the wind has blown about many changes since last you were here. Frankly, I think it most urgent that you come. In present circumstances, I don't know to whom to turn, grandfather being not himself, and I needing someone who can be trusted." There was nothing obviously urgent about the letter, and yet there was a queer constraint, there was something between the lines that stood out invisibly, intangibly to make possible only one answer to Frolin's letter—something in his phrase about the wind, something in the way he had written *grandfather being not himself*, something in the need he had expressed for *someone who can be trusted.*

I could easily enough take leave of absence from my position as assistant librarian at Miskatonic University in Arkham and go west that September; so I went. I went, harassed by an almost uncanny conviction that the need for haste was great: from Boston by plane to Chicago, and from there by train to the village of Harmon, deep in the forest country of Wisconsin—a place of great natural beauty, not far from the shores of Lake Michigan, so that it was possible on days of wind and weather to hear the water's sound.

Frolin met me at the station. My cousin was in his late thirties then, but he had the look of someone ten years younger, with hot, intense brown eyes, and a soft, sensitive mouth that belied his inner hardness. He was singularly sober, though he had always alternated between gravity and a kind of infectious wildness—"the Irish in him," as grandfather had once said. I met his eyes when I shook his hand, probing for some clue to his withheld distress, but I saw only that he was indeed troubled, for his eyes betrayed him, even as the roiled waters of a pond reveal disturbance below, though the surface may be as glass.

"What is it?" I asked, when I sat at his side in the coupe, riding into the country of the tall pines. "Is the old man abed?"

He shook his head. "Oh, no, nothing like that, Tony." He shot me a queer, restrained glance. "You'll see. You wait and see."

"What is it then?" I pressed him. "Your letter had the damnedest sound."

"I hoped it would," he said gravely.

"And yet there was nothing I could put my finger on," I admitted. "But it was there, nevertheless."

He smiled. "Yes, I knew you'd understand. I tell you, it's been difficult—extremely difficult. I thought of you a good many times before I sat down and wrote that letter, believe me!"

"But if he's not ill? I thought you said he wasn't himself."

"Yes, yes, so I did. You wait now, Tony; don't be so impatient; you'll see for yourself. It's his mind, I think."

"His mind!" I felt a distinct wave of regret and shock at the suggestion that grandfather's mind had given way; the thought that the magnificent brain had retreated from sanity was intolerable, and I was loath to entertain it, "Surely not!" I cried. "Frolin—what the devil is it?"

He turned his troubled eyes on me once more. "I don't know," he said. "But I think it's something terrible. If it were only grandfather! But there's the music—and then there are all the other things: the sounds and smells and—" He caught my amazed stare and turned away, almost with physical effort pausing in his talk. "But I'm forgetting. Don't ask me anything more. Just wait. You'll see for yourself." He laughed shortly, a forced laugh. "Perhaps it's not the old man who's losing his mind. I've thought of that sometimes, too—with reason."

I said nothing more, but there was beginning to mushroom up inside me now a kind of tense fear, and for some time I sat at his side, thinking only of Frolin and old Josiah Alwyn living together in that old house, unaware of the towering pines all around, and the wind's sound, and the fragrant pungence of leaf-fire smoke riding the wind out of the northwest. Evening came early to this country, caught in the dark pines, and, though afterglow still lingered in the west, fanning upward in a great wave of saffron and amethyst, darkness already possessed the forest through which we rode. Out of the darkness came the cries of great horned owls and their lesser cousins, the screech owls, making an eerie magic in the stillness otherwise broken only by the wind's voice and the noise of the car passing over the comparatively little used road to the Alwyn house.

"We're almost there," said Frolin.

The lights of the car passed over a jagged pine, lightning-struck years ago, and standing still with two gaunt limbs arched like gnarled arms toward the road: an old landmark to which Frolin's words called my attention, since he knew I would remember it as but half a mile from the house.

"If grandfather should ask," he said then, "I'd rather you said nothing about my sending for you. I don't know that he'd like it. You can tell him you were in the midwest and came up for a visit."

I was curious anew, but forebore to press Frolin further. "He does know I'm coming, then?"

"Yes. I said I had word from you and was going down to meet your train."

I could understand that if the old man thought Frolin had sent for me about his health, he would be annoyed and perhaps angry; and yet more than this was implied in Frolin's request, more than just the simple salving of grandfather's pride. Once more that odd, intangible alarm rose up within me, that sudden, inexplicable feeling of fear.

The house loomed forth suddenly in a clearing among the pines. It had been built by an uncle of grandfather's in Wisconsin's pioneering days, back in the 1850's: by one of the sea-faring Alwyns of Innsmouth, that strange, dark town on the Massachusetts coast. It was an unusually unattractive structure, snug against the hillside like a crusty old woman in furbelows. It defied many architectural standards without, however, seeming ever fully free of most of the superficial facets of architecture circa 1850 making for the most grotesque and pompous appearance of structures of that day. It suffered a wide verandah, one side of which led directly into the stable where, in former days, horses, surreys, and buggies had been kept, and where now two cars were housed—the only corner of the building which gave any evidence at all of having been remodeled since it was built. The house rose two and one-half stories above a cellar floor; presumably, for darkness made it impossible to ascertain, it was still painted the same hideous brown; and, judging by what light shone forth from the curtained windows, grandfather had not yet taken the trouble to install electricity, a contingency for which I had come well prepared by carrying flashlight and electric candle, with extra batteries for both.

Frolin drove into the garage, left the car and, carrying some of my baggage, led the way down the verandah to the front door, a large, thick-paneled oak piece, decorated with a ridiculously large iron knocker. The hall was dark, save for a partly open door at the far end, out of which came a faint light which was yet enough to illumine spectrally the broad stairs leading to the upper floor.

"I'll take you to your room first," said Frolin, leading the way up the stairs, surefooted with habitual walking there. "There's a flashlight on the newel post at the landing," he added. "If you need it. You know the old man."

I found the light and lit it, making only enough delay so that when I caught up with Frolin, he was standing at the door of my room, which, I noticed, was almost directly over the front entrance and thus faced west, as did the house itself.

"He's forbidden us to use any of the rooms east of the hall up here," said Frolin, fixing me with his eyes, as much as to say: You see how queer he's got! He waited for me to say something, but since I did not, he went on. "So I have the room next to yours, and Hough is on the other side of me, in the southwest corner. Right now, as you might have noticed, Hough's getting something to eat."

"And grandfather?"

"Very likely in his study. You'll remember that room."

I did indeed remember that curious windowless room, built under explicit directions by great-uncle Leander, a room that occupied the majority of the rear of the house, the entire northwest corner and all the west width save for a small corner at the southwest, where the kitchen was, the kitchen from which a light had streamed into the lower hall at our entrance. The study had been pushed part way back into the hill slope, so that the east wall could not have windows, but there was no reason save Uncle Leander's eccentricity for the windowless north wall. Squarely in the center of the east wall, indeed, built into the wall, was an enormous painting, reaching from floor to ceiling and occupying a width of over six feet. If this painting, apparently executed by some unknown friend of Leander's, if not by my great-uncle himself, had had about it any spark of genius or even of unusual talent, this display might have been overlooked, but it did not; it was a perfectly prosaic representation of a north country scene, showing a hillside, with a rocky cave opening out into the center of the picture, a scarcely defined path leading to the cave, an impressionistic beast which was evidently meant to resemble a bear, once common in this country, walking toward it, and overhead something that looked like an unhappy cloud lost among the pines rising darkly all around. This dubious work of art completely and absolutely dominated the study, despite the shelves of books that occupied almost every available niche in what remained of the walls in that room, despite the absurd collection of oddities strewn everywhere—bits of curiously carven stone and wood, strange mementoes of great-uncle's seafaring life. The study had all the lifelessness of a museum and yet, oddly, it responded to my grandfather like something alive, even the painting on the wall seeming to take on an added freshness whenever he entered.

"I don't think anyone who ever stepped into that room could forget it," I said with a grim smile.

"He spends most of his time there. Hardly goes out at all, and I suppose, with winter coming on, he'll come out only for his meals. He's moved his bed into that room, too."

I shuddered. "I can't imagine sleeping in that room."

"No, nor I. But, you know, he's working on something, and I sincerely believe his mind has been affected."

"Another book on his travels, perhaps?"

He shook his head. "No, a translation, I think. Something different. He found some old papers of Leander's one day, and ever since then he seems to have got progressively worse." He raised his eyebrows and shrugged. "Come on. Hough will have supper ready by this time, and you'll see for yourself."

Frolin's cryptic remarks had led me to expect an emaciated old man. After all, grandfather was in his early seventies, and even he could not be expected to live forever. But he had not changed physically at all, as far as I could see. There he sat at his supper table—still the same hardy old man, his moustache and beard not yet white, but only iron gray, and still with plenty of black in them; his face was no less heavy, his color no less ruddy. At the moment of my entrance he was eating heartily from the drumstick of a turkey. Seeing me, he raised his eyebrows a little, took the drumstick from his lips and greeted me with no more excitement than if I had been away from him for but a half hour.

"You're looking well," he said.

"And you," I said. "An old war horse."

He grinned. "My boy, I'm on the trail of something new—some unexplored country apart from Africa, Asia, and the Arctic regions."

I flashed a glance at Frolin. Clearly, this was news to him; whatever hints grandfather might have dropped of his activities, they had not included this.

He asked then about my trip west, and the rest of the supper hour was taken up with small talk of other relatives. I observed that the old man returned insistently to long-forgotten relatives in Innsmouth: what had become of them? Had I ever seen them? What did they look like? Since I knew practically nothing of the relatives in Innsmouth, and had the firm conviction that all of them had died in a strange catastrophe which had washed many inhabitants of that shunned city out to sea, I was not helpful. But the tenor of these innocuous questions puzzled me no little. In my capacity as librarian at Miskatonic University, I had heard strange and disturbing hints of the business at Innsmouth. I knew something of the appearance of Federal men there, and stories of foreign agents had never had about them that essential ring of truth which had made a plausible explanation for the terrible events which had taken place in that city. He wanted to know at last whether I had ever seen pictures of them, and when I said I had not, he was quite patently disappointed.

"Do you know," he said dejectedly, "there does not exist even a likeness of Uncle Leander, but the old-timers around Harmon told me years ago that he was a very homely man, that he looked like something that had been thrown up by the sea, as he was, and one old woman said a curious thing: that he reminded her of a *frog*." Abruptly, he seemed more animated, he began to talk a little faster. "Do you have any conception of what that means, my boy? But no, you wouldn't have. It's too much to expect. . . . "

He sat for a while in silence, drinking his coffee, drumming on the table with his fingers and staring into space with a curiously preoccupied air until suddenly he rose and left the room, inviting us to come to the study when he had finished.

"What do you make of that?" asked Frolin, when the sound of the study door closing came to us.

"Curious," I said. "But I see nothing abnormal there, Frolin. I'm afraid—"

He smiled grimly. "Wait. Don't judge yet; you've been here scarcely two hours."

He went to the study after supper, leaving the dishes to Hough and his wife, who had served my grandfather for twenty years in this house. The study was unchanged, save for the addition of the old double bed, pushed up against the wall which separated the room from the kitchen. Grandfather was clearly waiting for us, or rather, for me, and, if I had had occasion to think cousin Frolin cryptic, there is no word adequate to describe my grandfather's subsequent conversation.

"Have you ever heard of the Wendigo?" he asked.

I admitted that I had come upon it among other north country Indian legends: the belief in a monstrous, supernatural being, horrible to look upon, the haunter of the great forest silences.

He wanted to know whether I had ever thought of there being a possible connection between this legend of the Wendigo and the air elementals, and, upon my replying in the affirmative, he expressed a curiosity about how I had come to know the Indian legend in the first place, taking pains to explain that the Wendigo had nothing whatever to do with this question.

"In my capacity as librarian, I have occasion to run across a good many out of the way things," I answered.

"Ah!" he exclaimed, reaching for a book next his chair. "Then doubtless you may be familiar with this volume."

I looked at the heavy black-bound volume whose title was stamped only on its backbone in goldleaf: *The Outsider and Others,* by H. P. Lovecraft.

I nodded. "This book is on our shelves."

"You've read it, then?"

"Oh, yes. Most interesting."

"Then you'll have read what he has to say about Innsmouth in his strange story, *The Shadow Over Innsmouth.* What do you make of that?"

I reflected hurriedly, thinking back to the story, and presently it came to me: a fantastic tale of horrible sea-beings, spawn of Cthulhu, beast of primordial origin, living deep in the sea.

"The man had a good imagination," I said.

"Had! Is he dead, then?"

"Yes, a year ago."

"Alas! I had thought to learn from him. . . . "

"But, surely, this fiction," I began.

He stopped me. "Since you have offered no explanation of what took place in Innsmouth, how can you be so sure that his narrative is fiction?"

I admitted that I could not, but it seemed that the old man had already lost interest. Now he drew forth a bulky envelope bearing many of the familiar three-cent 1869 stamps so dear to collectors, and from this took out various papers, which, he said, Uncle Leander had left with instructions for their consignment to the flames. His wish, however, had not been carried out, explained grandfather, and he had come into possession of them. He handed a few sheets to me, and requested my opinion of them, watching me shrewdly all the while.

The sheets were obviously from a long letter, written in a crabbed hand, and with some of the most awkward sentences imaginable. Moreover, many of the sentences did not seem to me to make sense, and the sheet at which I looked longest was filled with allusions strange to me. My eyes caught words like *Ithaqua, Lloigor, Hastur*; it was not until I had handed the sheets back to my uncle that it occurred to me that I had seen those words elsewhere, not too long ago. But I said nothing. I explained that I could not help feeling that Uncle Leander wrote with needless obfuscation.

Grandfather chuckled. "I should have thought that the first thing which would have occurred to you would have been similar to my own reaction, but no, you failed me! Surely it's obvious that the whole business is in a code!"

"Of course! That would explain the awkwardness of his lines."

My grandfather smirked. "A fairly simple code, but adequate—entirely adequate. I have not yet finished with it." He tapped the envelope with one index finger. "It seems to concern this house, and there is in it a repeated warning that one must be careful, and not pass beyond the threshold, for fear of dire consequences. My boy, I've crossed and recrossed every threshold in his house scores of times, and there have been no consequences. So therefore, somewhere there must exist a threshold I have not yet crossed."

I could not help smiling at his animation. "If Uncle Leander's mind was wandering, you've been off on a pretty chase," I said.

Abruptly grandfather's well-known impatience boiled to the surface. With one hand he swept my uncle's papers away; with the other he dismissed us both, and it was plain to see that Frolin and I had on the instant ceased to exist for him.

We rose, made our excuses, and left the room.

In the half-dark of the hall beyond, Frolin looked at me, saying nothing, only permitting his hot eyes to dwell upon mine for a long minute before he turned and led the way upstairs, where we parted, each to go to his own room for the night.

II

The nocturnal activity of the subconscious mind has always been of deep interest to me, since it has seemed to me that unlimited opportunities are opened up before every alert individual. I have repeatedly gone to bed with some problem vexing me, only to find it solved insofar as I am capable of solving it, upon waking. Of those other, more devious activities of the night mind, I have less knowledge. I know that I retired that night with the question of where I had encountered my Uncle Leander's strange words before strong and foremost in mind, and I know that I went to sleep at last with that question unanswered.

Yet, when I awoke in the darkness some hours later, I knew at once that I had seen those words, those strange proper names in the book by H. P. Lovecraft which I had read at Miskatonic, and it was only secondarily that I was aware of someone tapping at my door, and called out in a hushed voice.

"It's Frolin. Are you awake? I'm coming in."

I got up, slipped on my dressing gown, and lit my electric candle. By this time Frolin was in the room, his thin body trembling a little, possibly from the cold, for the September night air flowing in through my window was no longer of summer.

"What's the matter?" I asked.

He came over to me, a strange light in his eyes, and put a hand on my arm. "Can't you hear it?" he asked: "God, perhaps it *is* my mind."

"No, wait!" I exclaimed.

From somewhere outside, it seemed, came the sound of weirdly beautiful music: flutes, I thought.

"Grandfather's at the radio," I said. "Does he often listen so late?"

The expression on his face halted my words.

"I own the only radio in the house. It's in my room, and it's not playing. The battery's run down, in any case. Besides, did you ever hear *such* music on the radio?"

I listened with renewed interest. The music seemed strangely muffled, and yet it came through. I observed also that it had no definite direction; while before it had seemed to come from outside, it now seemed to come from underneath the house—a curious, chant-like playing of reeds and pipes.

"A flute orchestra," I said.

"Or Pan pipes," said Frolin.

"They don't play them any more," I said absently.

"Not on the radio," answered Frolin.

I looked at him sharply; he returned my gaze as steadily. It occurred to me that his unnatural gravity had a reason for being, whether or not he wished to put that reason into words. I caught hold of his arms.

"Frolin—what is it? I can tell you're alarmed."

He swallowed hard. "Tony, that music doesn't come from anything in the house. It's from outside."

"But who would be outside?" I demanded.

"Nothing—no one human."

It had come at last. Almost with relief I faced this issue I had been afraid to admit to myself must be faced. *Nothing—no one human.*

"Then—what agency?" I asked.

"I think grandfather knows," he said.

"Come with me, Tony. Leave the light; we can make our way in the dark."

Out in the hall, I was stopped once more by his hand tense on my arm. "Do you notice?" he whispered sibilantly. "Do you notice this, too?"

"The smell," I said. The vague, elusive smell of water, of fish and frogs and the inhabitants of watery places.

"And now!" he said.

Quite suddenly the smell of water was gone, and instead came a swift frostiness, flowing throuth the hall as of something alive, the indefinable fragrance of snow, the crisp moistness of snowy air.

"Do you wonder I've been concerned?" asked Frolin.

Giving me no time to reply, he led the way downstairs to the door of grandfather's study, beneath which there shone yet a fine line of yellow light. I was conscious in every step of our descent to the floor below that the music was growing louder, if no more understandable, and now, before the study door, it was apparent that the music emanated from within, and that the strange variety of odors came, too, from that study. The darkness seemed alive with menace, charged with an impending, ominous terror, which enclosed us as in a shell, so that Frolin trembled at my side.

Impulsively I raised my arm and knocked on the door.

There was no answer from within, but on the instant of my knock, the music stopped, the strange odors vanished from the air!

"You shouldn't have done that!" whispered Frolin. "If he . . ."

I tried the door. It yielded to my pressure, and I opened it.

I do not know what I expected to see there in the study, but certainly not what I did see. No single aspect of the room had changed, save that grandfather had gone to bed, and now sat there with his eyes closed and a little smile on his lips, some of his work open before him on the bed, and the lamp burning. I stood for an instant staring, not daring to believe my eyes, incredible before the prosaic scene I looked upon. Whence then had come the music I had heard? And the odors and fragrances in the air? Confusion took possession of my thoughts, and I was about to withdraw, disturbed by the repose of my grandfather's features, when he spoke.

"Come in, then," he said, without opening his eyes. "So you heard the music, too? I had begun to wonder why no one else heard it. Mongolian, I think. Three nights ago, it was clearly Indian—north country again, Canada and Alaska. I believe there are places where Ithaqua is still worshipped. Yes, yes—and a week ago, notes I last heard played in Tibet, in forbidden Lhassa years ago, decades ago."

"Who made it?" I cried. "Where did it come from?"

He opened his eyes and regarded us standing there. "It came from here, I think," he said, placing the flat of one hand on the manuscript before him, the sheets written by my great-uncle. "And Leander's friends made it. Music of the spheres, my boy—do you credit your senses?"

"I heard it," I said. "So did Frolin."

"And what can Hough be thinking?" mused grandfather. He sighed. "I have nearly got it, I think. It only remains to determine with which of them Leander communicated."

"Which?" I repeated. "What do you mean?"

He closed his eyes and the smile came briefly back to his lips. "I thought at first it was Cthulhu; Leander was, after all, a sea-faring man. But now—I wonder if it might not be one of the creatures of air: Lloigor, perhaps—or Ithaqua, whom I believe certain of the Indians call the Wendigo. There is a legend that Ithaqua carries his victims with him in the far spaces above the earth—but I am forgetting myself again, my mind wanders." His eyes flashed open, and I found him regarding us with a peculiarly aloof stare. "It's late," he said. "I need sleep."

"What in God's name was he talking about?" asked Frolin, in the hall.

"Come along," I said.

But, back in my room once more, with Frolin waiting expectantly to hear what I had to say, I did not know how to begin. How could I tell him about the weird knowledge hidden in the forbidden texts at Miskatonic University—the dread *Book of Eibon,* the obscure *Pnakotic Manuscripts,* the terrible *R'lyeh Text,* and, most shunned of all, the *Necronomicon* of the mad Arab Alhazred? How could I say to him with any conviction at all the things that crowded into my mind as a result of hearing my grandfather's strange words, the memories that boiled up from deep within—of powerful Ancient Ones, elder beings of unbelievable evil, old gods who once inhabited the earth and all the universe as we know it now, and perhaps far more—old gods of ancient good, and forces of ancient evil, of whom the latter were now in leash, and yet ever breaking forth, becoming manifest briefly, horribly to the world of men. And their terrible names came back now, if before this hour my clue to remembrance had not been made strong enough, had been refused in the fastnesses of my inherent prejudices—Cthulhu, potent leader of the forces of the waters of earth; Yog-Sothoth and Tsathoggua, dwellers in the depths of earth; Lloigor, Hastur, and Ithaqua, the Snow-Thing, the Wind-Walker, who were the elementals of air. It was of these beings that grandfather had spoken; and the inference he had made was too plain to be disregarded, or even to be subject to any other interpretation—that my great-uncle Leander, whose home, after all, had once been in the shunned and now deserted city of Innsmouth, had had traffic with at least one of these beings. And there was a further inference that he had not made, but only hinted at in something he had said earlier in the evening—that there was somewhere in the house a threshold, beyond which a man dared not walk, and what danger could lurk beyond that threshold but the path back into time, the way back to that hideous communication with the elder beings my Uncle Leander had had!

And yet somehow, the full import of grandfather's words had not dawned upon me. Though he had said so much, there was far more he had left unsaid, and I could not blame myself later for not fully realizing that grandfather's activities were clearly bent toward discovering that hidden threshold of which Uncle Leander had so cryptically written—*and crossing it!* In the confusion of thought to which I had now come in my preoccupation with the ancient mythology of Cthulhu, Ithaqua and the elder gods, I did not follow the obvious indications to that logical conclusion, possibly because I feared instinctively to go so far.

I turned to Frolin and explained to him as clearly as I could. He listened attentively, asking a few pointed questions from time to time, and, though he paled slightly at certain details I could not refrain from mentioning, he did not seem to be as incredulous as I might have thought. This in itself was evidence of the fact that there was still more to be discovered about my grandfather's activities and the occurrences in the house, though I did not immediately realize this. However, I was shortly to discover more of the underlying reason for Frolin's ready acceptance of my necessarily sketchy outline.

In the middle of a question, he ceased talking abruptly, and there came into his eyes an expression indicating that his attention had passed from me, from the room to somewhere beyond; he sat in an attitude of listening, and, impelled by his own actions, I, too, strained to hear what he heard.

Only the wind's voice in the trees, rising now a little, I thought. A storm coming.

"Do you hear it?" he said in a shaky whisper.

"No," I said quietly. "Only the wind."

"Yes, yes—the wind. I wrote you, remember. Listen."

"Now, come, Frolin, take hold of yourself. It's only the wind."

He gave me a pitying glance, and, going to the window, beckoned me after him. I followed, coming to his side. Without a word, he pointed into the darkness pressing close to the house. It took me a moment to accustom myself to the night, but presently I was able to see the line of trees struck sharply against the starswept heavens. And then, instantly, I understood.

Though the sound of the wind roared and thundered about the house, nothing whatever disturbed the trees before my eyes—not a twig, not a leaf, not a treetop swayed by so much as a hair's-breath!

"Good God!" I exclaimed, and fell back, away from the pane, as if to shut the sight from my eyes.

"Now, you see," he said, stepping back from the window, also. "I have heard all this before."

He stood quietly, as if waiting, and I, too, waited. The sound of the wind continued unabated; it had by this time reached a frightful intensity, so that it seemed as if the old house must be torn from the hill-side and hurtled into the valley below. Indeed, a faint trembling made itself manifest even as I thought this: a strange tremor, as if the house were *shuddering*, and the pictures on the walls made a slight, almost *stealthy* movement, almost imperceptible, and yet quite unmistakably visible. I glanced at Frolin, but his features were not disquieted; he continued to stand, listening and waiting, so that it was patent that the end of this singular manifestation was not yet. The wind's sound was now a terrible, demoniac howling, and it was accompanied by notes of music, which must have been audible for some time, but were so perfectly blended with the wind's voice that I was not at first aware of them. The music was similar to that which had gone before, as of pipes and occasionally stringed instruments, but was now much wilder, sounding with a terrifying abandon, with a character of unmentionable evil about it. At the same time, two further manifestations occurred. The first was the sound as of someone walking, some great being whose footsteps seemed to flow into the room from the heart of the wind itself; certainly they did not originate in the house, though there was about them the unmistakable swelling which betokened their approach to the house. The second was the sudden change in the temperature.

The night outside was warm for September in upstate Wisconsin, and the house too, had been reasonably comfortable. Now, abruptly, coincident with the approaching footsteps, the temperature began to drop rapidly so that in a little while the air in the room was cold, and both Frolin and I had to put on more clothing in order to keep comfortable. Still this did not seem to be the height of the manifestations for which Frolin so obviously waited; he continued to stand, saying nothing, though his eyes, meeting mine from time to time, were eloquent enough to speak his mind. How long we stood there, listening to those frightening sounds from outside, before the end came, I do not know.

But suddenly Frolin caught my arm, and in a hoarse whisper, cried, "There! There they are! Listen!"

The tempo of the weird music had changed abruptly to diminuendo from its previous wild crescendo; there came into it now a strain of almost unbearable sweetness, with a little of melancholy to it, music as lovely as previously it had been evil, and yet the note of terror was not completely absent. At the same time, there was apparent the sound of voices, raised in a kind of swelling chant, rising from the back of the house somewhere—as if from the study.

"Great God in Heaven!" I cried, seizing Frolin. "What is it now?"

"It's grandfather's doing," he said. "Whether he knows it or not, that thing comes and sings to him." He shook his head and closed his eyes tightly for an instant before saying bitterly in a low, intense voice, "If only that accursed paper of Leander's had been burned as it ought to have been!"

"You could almost make out the words," I said, listening intently.

There were words—but not words I had ever heard before: a kind of horrible, primeval mouthing, as if some bestial creature with but half a tongue ululated syllables of meaningless horror. I went over and opened the door; immediately the voices seemed clearer, so that it was evident that what I had mistaken for many voices was but one, which could nevertheless convey the illusion of many. Words—or perhaps I had better write *sounds,* bestial sounds—rose from below, a kind of awe-inspiring ululation:

"*lä! lä! Ithaqua! Ithaqua cf'ayak vulgtmm lä! Ugh! Cthulhu fhtagn! Shub-Niggurath! Ithaqua naflfhtagn!*"

Incredibly, the wind's voice rose to howl even more terribly, so that I thought at any moment the house would be hurled into the void, and Frolin and myself torn from its rooms, and the breath sucked from our helpless bodies. In the confusion of fear and wonder that held me. I thought at that instant of grandfather in the study below and, beckoning Frolin, I ran from the room to the stairs, determined, despite my ghastly fright, to put myself between the old man and whatever menaced him. I ran to his door and flung myself upon it—and once more, as before, all manifestations stopped; as if by the flick of a switch, silence fell like a pall of darkness upon the house, a silence that was momentarily even more terrible.

The door gave, and once more I faced grandfather.

He was sitting still as we had left him but a short time before, though now his eyes were open, his head was cocked a little to one side, and his gaze was fixed upon the overlarge painting on the east wall.

"In God's name!" I cried. "What was that?"

"I hope to find out before long," he answered with great dignity and gravity.

His utter lack of fear quieted my own alarm to some degree, and I came a little further into the room, Frolin following. I leaned over his bed, striving to fix his attention upon me, but he continued to gaze at the painting with singular intensity.

"What are you doing?" I demanded. "Whatever it is, there's danger in it."

"An explorer like your grandfather would hardly be content if there were not, my boy," he replied crisply, matter-of-factly.

I knew it was true.

"I would rather die with my boots on than here in this bed," he went on. "As for what we heard—that's something for the moment not yet explicable. But I would call to your attention the strange action of the wind."

"There was no wind," I said. "I looked."

"Yes, yes," he said a little impatiently. "True enough. And yet the wind's sound was there, and all the voices of the wind—just as I have heard it singing in Mongolia, in the great snowy spaces, over the shunned and hidden Plateau of Leng where the Tcho-Tcho people worship strange ancient gods." He turned to face me suddenly, and I thought his eyes feverish. "I did tell you, didn't I, about the worship of Ithaqua, sometimes called Wind-Walker, and by some, surely, the Wendigo, by certain Indians in upper Manitoba, and of their beliefs that the Wind-Walker takes human sacrifices and carries them over the far places of the earth before leaving them behind, dead at last? Oh, there are stories, my boy, odd legends—and something more." He leaned toward me now with a fierce intensity. "I have myself seen things—things found on a body dropped from the air—just that—things that could not possibly have been got in Manitoba, things belonging to Leng, to the Pacific Isles." He brushed me away with one arm, and an expression of disgust crossed his face. "You don't believe me. You think I'm wandering. Go on then, go back to your little sleep, and wait for your last through the eternal misery of monotonous day after day!"

"No! Say it now," I said. "I'm in no mood to go."

"I will talk to you in the morning," he said tiredly, leaning back.

With that I had to be content; he was adamant, and could not be moved. I bade him goodnight once more and retreated into the hall with Frolin, who stood there shaking his head slowly, forbiddingly.

"Every time a little worse," he whispered. "Every time the wind blows a little louder, the cold comes more intensely, the voices and the music more clearly—and the sound of those terrible footsteps!"

He turned away and began to retrace the way upstairs, and, after a moment of hesitation, I followed.

In the morning my grandfather looked his usual picture of good health. At the moment of my entrance into the dining room, he was speaking to Hough, evidently in answer to a request, for the old servant stood respectfully bowed, while he heard grandfather tell him that he and Mrs. Hough might indeed take a week off, beginning today, if it was necessary for Mrs. Hough's health that she go Wausau to consult a specialist. Frolin met my eyes with a grim smile; his color had faded a little, leaving him pale and sleepless-looking, but he ate heartily enough. His smile, and the brief indicative glance of his eyes toward Hough's retreating back, said clearly that this necessity which had come upon Hough and his wife was their way of fighting the manifestations which had so disturbed my own first night in the house.

"Well, my boy," said grandfather quite cheerfully, "you're not looking nearly as haggard as you did last night. I confess, I felt for you. I daresay also you aren't nearly so skeptical as you were."

He chuckled, as if this were a subject for joking. I could not, unfortunately, feel the same way about it. I sat down and began to eat a little, glancing at him from time to time, waiting for him to begin his explanation of the strange events of the previous night.

Since it became evident shortly that he did not intend to explain, I was impelled to ask for an explanation, and did so with as much dignity as possible.

"I'm sorry," he said, "if you've been disturbed. The fact of the matter is that that threshold of which Leander wrote must be in that study somewhere, and I felt quite certain I was onto it last night, before you burst into my room the second time. Furthermore, it seems undisputable that at least one member of the family has had traffic with one of those beings—Leander, obviously."

Frolin leaned forward. "Do you believe in them?" he asked.

Grandfather smiled unpleasantly. "It must be obvious that, whatever my abilities, the disturbance you heard last night could hardly have been caused by me."

"Yes, of course," agreed Frolin. "But some other agency."

"No, no—it remains to be determined only which one. The water smells are the sign of the spawn of Cthulhu, but the winds might be Lloigor or Ithaqua or Hastur. But the stars aren't right for Hastur," he went on. "So we are left with the other two. There they are, then, or one of them, just across that threshold. I want to know what lies beyond that threshold, if I can find it."

It seemed incredible that my grandfather should be talking so unconcernedly about these ancient beings; his prosaic air was in itself almost as alarming as had been the night's occurrences. The temporary feeling of security I had had at the sight of him eating breakfast was washed away; I began to be conscious again of that slowly growing fear I had known on my way to the house last evening, and I regretted having pushed my inquiry.

If grandfather was aware of anything of this, he made no sign. He went on talking much in the manner of a lecturer pursuing a scientific inquiry for the benefit of an audience before him. It was obvious, he said, that a connection existed between the happenings at Innsmouth and Leander Alwyn's nonhuman contact *outside*. Did Leander leave Innsmouth originally because of the cult of Cthulhu that existed there, because he, too, was becoming afflicted with that curious facial change which overtook so many of the inhabitants of accursed Innsmouth?—those strange batrachian lineaments which horrified the Federal investigators who came to examine into the Innsmouth affair? Perhaps this was so. In any event, leaving the Cthulhu cult behind, he had made his way into the wilds of Wisconsin and somehow he had established contact with another of the elder beings, Lloigor or Ithaqua—all, to be noted, elemental forces of evil. Leander Alwyn was apparently a very wicked man.

"If there is any truth to this," I cried, "then surely Leander's warning ought to be observed. Give up this mad hope of finding the threshold of which he writes!"

Grandfather gazed at me for a moment with speculative mildness; but it was plain to see that he was not actually concerning himself with my outburst. "Now I've embarked upon this exploration, I mean to keep to it. After all, Leander died a natural death."

"But, following your own theory, he had traffic with these—these things," I said. "You have none. You're daring to venture out into unknown space—it comes to that—without regard for what horrors might lie there."

"When I went into Mongolia, I encountered horrors, too. I never thought to escape Leng with my life." He paused reflectively, and then rose slowly. "No, I mean to discover Leander's threshold. And tonight, no matter what you hear, try not to interrupt me. It would be a pity, if after so long a time, I am still further delayed by your impetuosity."

"And, having discovered the threshold," I cried. "What then?"

"I'm not sure I'll want to cross it."

"The choice may not be yours," I said.

He looked at me for a moment in silence, smiled gently, and left the room.

III

Of the events of that catastrophic night, I find it difficult even at this late date to write, so vividly do they return to mind, despite the prosaic surroundings of Miskatonic University where so many of those dread secrets are hidden in ancient and little-known texts. And yet, to understand the widespread occurrences that came after, the events of that night must be known.

Frolin and I spent most of the day investigating my grandfather's books and papers, in search of verification of certain legends he had hinted at in his conversation, not only with me, but with Frolin even before my arrival. Throughout his work occurred many cryptic allusions, but only one narrative at all relative to our inquiry—a somewhat obscure story, clearly of legendary origin, concerning the disappearance of two residents of Nelson, Manitoba, and a constable of the Royal Northwest Mounted Police, and their subsequent reappearance, as if dropped from the heavens, frozen and either dead or dying, babbling of *Ithaqua*, of the *Wind-Walker*, and of many places on the face of the earth, and carrying with them strange objects, mementoes of far places, which they had never been known to carry in life. The story was incredible, and yet it was related to the mythology so clearly put down in *The Outsider and Others*, and even more horribly narrated in the *Pnakotic Manuscripts,* the *R'lyeh Text,* and the terrible *Necronomicon*.

Apart from this, we found nothing tangible enough to relate to our problem, and we resigned ourselves to waiting for the night.

At luncheon and dinner, prepared by Frolin in the absence of the Houghs, my grandfather carried on as normally he was accustomed to, making no reference to his strange exploration, beyond saying that he had now definite proof that Leander had painted that unattractive landscape on the east wall of the study, and that he hoped soon, as he neared the end of the deciphering of Leander's long, rambling letter, to find the essential clue to that threshold of which he wrote, and to which he alluded increasingly now. When he rose from the dinner table, he solemnly cautioned us once more not to interrupt him in the night, under pain of his extreme displeasure, and so departed into that study out of which he never walked again.

"Do you think you can sleep?" Frolin asked me, when we were alone.

I shook my head. "Impossible. I'll stay up."

"I don't think he'd like us to stay downstairs," said Frolin, a faint frown on his forehead.

"In my room, then," I replied. "And you?"

"With you, if you don't mind. He means to see it through, and there's nothing we can do until he needs us. He may call . . . "

I had the uncomfortable conviction that if my grandfather called for us, it would be too late, but I forebore to give voice to my fears.

The events of that evening started as before—with the strains of that weirdly beautiful music welling flute-like from the darkness around the house. Then, in a little while, came the wind, and the cold, and the ululating voice. And then, preceded by an aura of evil so great that it was almost stifling in the room—then came something more, something unspeakably terrible. We had been sitting, Frolin and I, with the light out; I had not bothered to light my electric candle, since no light we could show would illumine the source of these manifestations. I faced the window and, when the wind began to rise, looked once again to the line of trees, thinking that surely, certainly, they must bend before this great onrushing storm of wind; but again there was nothing, no movement in that stillness.

And there was no cloud in the heavens; the stars shone brightly, the constellations of summer moving down to the western rim of earth to make the signature of autumn in the sky. The wind's sound had risen steadily, so that now it had the fury of a gale, and yet nothing, no movement disturbed the line of trees dark upon the night sky.

But suddenly—so suddenly that for a moment I blinked my eyes in an effort to convince myself that a dream had shuttered my sight—in one large area of the sky the stars were gone! I came to my feet and pressed my face to the pane. It was as if a cloud had abruptly reared up into the heavens, to a height almost at the zenith; but no cloud could have come upon the sky so swiftly. On both sides and overhead stars still shone. I opened my window and leaned out, trying to follow the dark outline against the stars. *It was the outline of some great beast, a horrible caricature of man, rising to a semblance of a head high in the heavens, and there, where its eyes might have been, glowed with a deep carmine fire two stars!*—Or were they stars?

At the same instant, the sound of those approaching footsteps grew so loud that the house shook and trembled with their vibrations, and the wind's demoniac fury rose to indescribable heights, and the ululation reached such a pitch that it was maddening to hear.

"Frolin!" I called hoarsely.

I felt him come to my side, and in a moment felt his tight grasp on my arm. So he, too, had seen; it was not hallucination, not dream—this giant thing outlined against the stars, and moving!

"It's moving," whispered Frolin. "Oh, God—it's coming!"

He pulled frantically away from the window, and so did I. But in an instant, the shadow on the sky was gone, the stars shone once more. The wind, however, had not decreased in intensity one iota; indeed, if it were possible, it grew momentarily wilder and more violent; the entire house shuddered and quaked, while those thunderous footsteps echoed and re-echoed in the valley before the house. And the cold grew worse, so that breath hung a white vapor in air—a cold as of outer space.

Out of all the turmoil of mind, I thought of the legend in my grandfather's papers—the legend of *Ithaqua*, whose signature lay in the cold and snow of far northern places. Even as I remembered, everything was driven from my mind by a frightful chorus of ululation, the triumphant chanting as of a thousand bestial mouths—

"Iä! Iä! Ithaqua, Ithaqua! Ai! Ai! Ai! Ithaqua cf'ayak vulgtmm vulgtlagln vulgtmm. Ithaqua fhatagn! Ugh! Iä! Iä! Ai! Ai! Ai!"

Simultaneously came a thunderous crash, and immediately after, the voice of my grandfather, raised in a terrible cry, a cry that rose into a scream of mortal terror, so that the names he would have uttered—Frolin's and mine—were lost, choked back into his throat by the full force of the horror revealed to him.

And, as abruptly as his voice ceased to sound, all other manifestations came to a stop, leaving again that ghastly, portentous silence to close around us like a cloud of doom.

Frolin reached the door of my room before I did, but I was not far behind.

He fell part of the way down the stairs, but recovered in the light of my electric candle, which I had seized on my way out, and together we assaulted the door of the study, calling to the old man inside.

But no voice answered, though the line of yellow under the door was evidence that his lamp burned still.

The door had been locked from the inside, so that it was necessary to break it down before we could enter.

Of my grandfather, there was no trace. But in the east wall yawned a great cavity, where the painting, now prone upon the floor, had been—a rocky opening leading into the depths of earth—and over everything in the room lay the mark of Ithaqua—a fine carpet of snow, whose crystals gleamed as from a million tiny jewels in the yellow light of grandfather's lamp. Save for the painting, only the bed was disturbed—*as if grandfather had been literally torn out of it by stupendous force!*

I looked hurriedly to where the old man had kept Uncle Leander's manuscript—but it was gone; nothing of it remained. Frolin cried out suddenly and pointed to the painting Uncle Leander had made, and then to the opening yawning before us.

"It was here all the time—the threshold," he said.

And then I saw even as he; as grandfather had seen too late—*for the painting by Uncle Leander was but the representation of the site of his home before the house had been erected to conceal that cavernous opening into the earth on the hillside, the hidden threshold against which Leander's manuscript had warned, the threshold beyond which my grandfather had vanished!*

Though there is little more to tell, yet the most damning of all the curious facts remain to be revealed. A thorough search of the cavern was subsequently made by county officials and certain intrepid adventurers from Harmon; it was found to have several openings, and it was plain that anyone or *anything* wishing to reach the house through the cavern would have had to enter through one of the innumerable hidden crevices discovered among the surrounding hills. The nature of Uncle Leander's activities were revealed after grandfather's disappearance. Frolin and I were put through a hard grilling suspicious county officials, but were finally released when the body of my grandfather did not come to light.

But since that night, certain facts came into the open, facts which, in the light of my grandfather's hints, coupled with the horrible legends contained in the shunned books locked away here in the library of Miskatonic University, are damning and damnably inescapable.

The first of them was the series of gigantic footprints found in the earth at that place where on that fatal night the shadow had risen into the starswept heavens—the unbelievably wide and deep depressions, as of some prehistoric monster walking there, steps a half mile apart, steps that led beyond the house and vanished at a crevice leading down into that hidden cavern in tracks identical with those found in the snow in northern Manitoba where those unfortunate travelers and the constable sent to find them had vanished from the face of the earth!

The second was the discovery of my grandfather's notebook, together with a portion of Uncle Leander's manuscript, encased in ice, found deep in the forest snows of upper Saskatchewan, and bearing every sign of having been dropped from a great height. The last entry was dated on the day of his disappearance in late September; the notebook was not found until the following April. Neither Frolin nor I dared to make the explanation of its strange appearance which came immediately to mind, and together we burned that horrible letter and the imperfect translation grandfather had made, the translation which in itself, as it was written down, with all its warnings against the terror beyond the threshold, had served to summon from *outside* a creature so horrible that its description has never been attempted by even those ancient writers whose terrible narratives are scattered over the face of the earth!

And last of all, the most conclusive, the most damning evidence—the discovery seven months later of my grandfather's body on a small Pacific island not far southeast of Singapore, and the curious report made of his condition: perfectly preserved, *as if in ice*, so cold that no one could touch him with bare hands for five days after his discovery, and the singular fact that he was found half buried in sand, *as if "he had fallen from an aeroplane!"* Neither Frolin nor I could any longer have any doubt; this was the legend of Ithaqua, who carried his victims with him into far places of the earth, in time and space, before leaving them behind. And the evidence was undeniable that my grandfather had been alive for part of that incredible journey, for if we had had any doubt, the things found in his pockets, the mementoes carried from strange hidden places where he had been, and sent to us, were final and damning testimony—the gold placque, with its miniature presentation of a struggle between ancient beings, and bearing on its surface inscriptions in cabalistic designs, the placque which Dr. Rackham of Miskatonic University identified as having come from some place beyond the memory of man; the loathsome book in Durmese that reveals ghastly legends of that shunned and hidden Plateau of Leng, the place of the dread Tcho-Tcho people; and finally, *the revolting and bestial stone miniature of a hellish monstrosity walking on the winds above the earth!*

WYOMING

The Monster of Lake LaMetrie
by Wardon Allan Curtis

Being the narration of James McLennegan, M.D., Ph.D.
Lake LaMetrie, Wyoming
April 1st, 1899

Prof. William G. Breyfogle,
University of Taychobera.

Dear Friend—Inclosed you will find some portions of the diary it has been my life-long custom to keep, arranged in such a manner as to narrate connectedly the history of some remarkable occurrences that have taken place here during the last three years. Years and years ago, I heard vague accounts of a strange lake high up in an almost inaccessible part of the mountains of Wyoming. Various incredible tales were related of it, such as that it was inhabited by creatures which elsewhere on the globe are found only as fossils of a long vanished time.

The lake and its surroundings are of volcanic origin, and not the least strange thing about the lake is that it is subject to periodic disturbances, which take the form of a mighty boiling in the centre, as if a tremendous artesian well were rushing up there from the bowels of the earth. The lake rises for a time, almost filling the basin of black rocks in which it rests and then recedes, leaving on the shores mollusks and trunks of strange trees and bits of strange ferns which no longer grow—on the earth, at least—and are to be seen elsewhere only in coal measures and beds of stone. And he who casts hook and line into the dusky waters, may haul forth ganoid fishes completely covered with bony plates.

All of this is described in the account written by Father LaMetrie years ago, and he there advances the theory that the

659

earth is hollow, and that its interior is inhabited by the forms of
plant and animal life which disappeared from its surface ages
ago, and that the lake connects with this interior region.
Symmes' theory of polar orifices is well known to you. It is amply
corroborated. I know that it is true now. Through the great holes
at the poles, the sun sends light and heat into the interior.

Three years ago this month, I found my way through the
mountains here to Lake LaMetrie accompanied by a single
companion, our friend, young Edward Framingham. He was led
to go with me not so much by scientific fervor, as by a faint hope
that his health might be improved by a sojourn in the mountains,
for he suffered from an acute form of dyspepsia that at times
drove him frantic.

Beneath an overhanging scarp of the wall of rock surrounding
the lake, we found a rudely-built stone-house left by the old cliff
dwellers. Though somewhat draughty, it would keep out the
infrequent rains of the region, and serve well enough as a shelter
for the short time which we intended to stay.

The extracts from my diary follow:

April 29th, 1896.

I have been occupied during the past few days in gathering
specimens of the various plants which are cast upon the shore by
the waves of this remarkable lake. Framingham does nothing but
fish, and claims that he has discovered the place where the lake
communicates with the interior of the earth, if, indeed, it does,
and there seems to be little doubt of that. While fishing at a point
near the centre of the lake, he let down three pickerel lines tied
together, in all nearly three hundred feet, without finding
bottom. Coming ashore, he collected every bit of line, string,
strap, and rope in our possession, and made a line five hundred
feet long, and still he was unable to find the bottom.

May 2nd, Evening.

The past three days have been profitably spent in securing
specimens, and mounting and pickling them for preservation.
Framingham has had a bad attack of dyspepsia this morning and
is not very well. Change of climate had a brief effect for the better
upon his malady, but seems to have exhausted its force much
sooner than one would have expected, and he lies on his couch of
dry water-weeds, moaning piteously. I shall take him back to
civilization as soon as he is able to be moved.

It is very annoying to have to leave when I have scarcely begun
to probe the mysteries of the place. I wish Framingham had not

come with me. The lake is roaring wildly without, which is strange, as it has been perfectly calm hitherto, and still more strange because I can neither feel nor hear the rushing of the wind, though perhaps that is because it is blowing from the south, and we are protected from it by the cliff. But in that case there ought to be no waves on this shore. The roaring seems to grow louder momentarily. Framingham—

May 3rd. Morning.

Such a night of terror we have been through. Last evening, as I sat writing in my diary, I heard a sudden hiss, and, looking down, saw wriggling across the earthen floor what I at first took to be a serpent of some kind, and then discovered was a stream of water which, coming in contact with the fire, had caused the startling hiss. In a moment, other streams had darted in, and before I had collected my senses enough to move, the water was two inches deep everywhere and steadily rising.

Now I knew the cause of the roaring, and, rousing Framingham, I half dragged him, half carried him to the door, and digging our feet into the chinks of the wall of the house, we climbed up to its top. There was nothing else to do, for above us and behind us was the unscalable cliff, and on each side the ground sloped away rapidly, and it would have been impossible to reach the high ground at the entrance to the basin.

After a time we lighted matches, for with all this commotion there was little air stirring, and we could see the water, now half-way up the side of the house, rushing to the west with the force and velocity of the current of a mighty river, and every little while it hurled tree-trunks against the house walls with a terrific shock that threatened to batter them down. After an hour or so, the roaring began to decrease, and finally there was an absolute silence. The water, which reached to within a foot of where we sat, was at rest, neither rising nor falling.

Presently a faint whispering began and became a stertorous breathing and then a rushing like that of the wind and a roaring rapidly increasing in volume, and the lake was in motion again, but this time the water and its swirling freight of tree-trunks flowed by the house toward the east, and was constantly falling, and out in the centre of the lake the beams of the moon were darkly reflected by the sides of a huge whirlpool, streaking the surface of polished blackness down, down, down the vortex into the beginning of whose terrible depths we looked from our high perch.

This morning the lake is back at its usual level. Our mules are drowned, our boat destroyed, our food damaged, my specimens and some of my instruments injured, and Framingham is very ill. We shall have to depart soon, although I dislike exceedingly to do so, as the disturbance of last night, which is clearly like the one described by Father LaMetrie, has undoubtedly brought up from the bowels of the earth some strange and interesting things. Indeed, out in the middle of the lake where the whirlpool subsided, I can see a large quantity of floating things; logs and branches, most of them probably, but who knows what else?

Through my glass I can see a tree-trunk, or rather stump, of enormous dimensions. From its width I judge that the whole tree must have been as large as some of the California big trees. The main part of it appears to be about ten feet wide and thirty feet long. Projecting from it and lying prone on the water is a limb, or root, some fifteen feet long, and perhaps two or three feet thick. Before we leave, which will be as soon as Framingham is able to go, I shall make a raft and visit the mass of driftwood, unless the wind providentially sends it ashore.

May 4th, Evening.

A day of most remarkable and wonderful occurrences. When I arose this morning and looked through my glass, I saw that the mass of driftwood still lay in the middle of the lake, motionless on the glassy surface, but the great black stump had disappeared. I was sure it was not hidden by the rest of the driftwood, for yesterday it lay some distance from the other logs, and there had been no disturbance of wind or water to change its position. I therefore concluded that it was some heavy wood that needed to become but slightly waterlogged to cause it to sink.

Framingham having fallen asleep at about ten, I sallied forth to look along the shores for specimens, carrying with me a botanical can, and a South American machete, which I have possessed since a visit to Brazil three years ago, where I learned the usefulness of this sabre-like thing. The shore was strewn with bits of strange plants and shells, and I was stooping to pick one up, when suddenly I felt my clothes plucked, and heard a snap behind me, and turning about I saw—but I won't describe it until I tell what I did, for I did not fairly see the terrible creature until I had swung my machete round and sliced off the top of its head, and then tumbled down into the shallow water where I lay almost fainting.

Here was the black log I had seen in the middle of the lake, a monstrous elasmosaurus, and high above me on the heap of rocks lay the thing's head with its long jaws crowded with sabre-like teeth, and its enormous eyes as big as saucers. I wondered that it did not move, for I expected a series of convulsions, but no sound of a commotion was heard from the creature's body, which lay out of sight on the other side of the rocks. I decided that my sudden cut had acted like a stunning blow and produced a sort of coma, and fearing lest the beast should recover the use of its muscles before death fully took place, and in its agony roll away into the deep water where I could not secure it, I hastily removed the brain entirely, performing the operation neatly, though with some trepidation, and restoring to the head the detached segment cut off by my machete, I proceeded to examine my prize.

In length of body, it is exactly twenty-eight feet. In the widest part it is eight feet through laterally, and is some six feet through from back to belly. Four great flippers, rudimentary arms and feet, and an immensely long, sinuous, swan-like neck, complete the creature's body. Its head is very small for the size of the body and is very round and a pair of long jaws project in front much like a duck's bill. Its skin is a leathery integument of a lustrous black, and its eyes are enormous hazel optics with a soft, melancholy stare in their liquid depths. It is an elasmosaurus, one of the largest of antediluvian animals. Whether of the same species as those whose bones have been discovered, I cannot say.

My examination finished, I hastened after Framingham, for I was certain that this waif from a long past age would arouse almost any invalid. I found him somewhat recovered from his attack of the morning, and he eagerly accompanied me to the elasmosaurus. In examining the animal afresh, I was astonished to find that its heart was still beating and that all the functions of the body except thought were being performed one hour after the thing had received its death blow, but I knew that the hearts of sharks have been known to beat hours after being removed from the body, and that decapitated frogs live, and have all the powers of motion, for weeks after their heads have been cut off.

I removed the top of the head to look into it and here another surprise awaited me, for the edges of the wound were granulating and preparing to heal. The colour of the interior of the skull was perfectly healthy and natural, there was no undue flow of blood, and there was every evidence that the animal intended to get well and live without a brain. Looking at the interior of the skull, I was struck by its resemblance to a human skull; in fact, it is, as nearly as I can judge, the size and shape of the brain-pan of an ordinary man who wears a seven-and-an-eighth hat. Examining the brain itself, I found it to be the size of an ordinary human brain, and singularly like it in general contour, though it is very inferior in fibre and has few convolutions.

May 5th, Morning.

Framingham is exceedingly ill and talks of dying, declaring that if a natural death does not put an end to his sufferings, he will commit suicide. I do not know what to do. All my attempts to encourage him are of no avail, and the few medicines I have no longer fit his case at all.

May 5th, Evening.

I have just buried Framingham's body in the sand of the lake shore. I performed no ceremonies over the grave, for perhaps the real Framingham is not dead, though such a speculation seems utterly wild. To-morrow I shall erect a cairn upon the mound, unless indeed there are signs that my experiment is successful, though it is foolish to hope that it will be.

At ten this morning, Framingham's qualms left him, and he set forth with me to see the elasmosaurus. The creature lay in the place where we left it yesterday, its position unaltered, still breathing, all the bodily functions performing themselves. The wound in its head had healed a great deal during the night, and I daresay will be completely healed within a week or so, such is the rapidity with which these reptilian organisms repair damages to themselves. Collecting three or four bushels of mussels, I shelled them and poured them down the elasmosaurus's throat. With a convulsive gasp, they passed down and the great mouth slowly closed.

"How long do you expect to keep the reptile alive?" asked Framingham.

"Until I have gotten word to a number of scientific friends, and they have come here to examine it. I shall take you to the nearest settlement and write letters from there. Returning, I shall feed the elasmosaurus regularly until my friends come, and we decide what final disposition to make of it. We shall probably stuff it."

"But you will have trouble in killing it, unless you hack it to pieces, and that won't do. Oh, if I only had the vitality of that animal. There is a monster whose vitality is so splendid that the removal of its brain does not disturb it. I should feel very happy if someone would remove my body. If I only had some of that beast's useless strength."

"In your case, the possession of a too active brain has injured the body," said I. "Too much brain exercise and too little bodily exercise are the causes of your trouble. It would be a pleasant thing if you had the robust health of the elasmosaurus, but what a wonderful thing it would be if that mighty engine had your intelligence."

I turned away to examine the reptile's wounds, for I had

brought my surgical instruments with me, and intended to dress them. I was interrupted by a burst of groans from Framingham and turning, beheld him rolling on the sand in an agony. I hastened to him, but before I could reach him, he seized my case of instruments, and taking the largest and sharpest knife, cut his throat from ear to ear.

"Framingham, Framingham," I shouted and, to my astonishment, he looked at me intelligently. I recalled the case of the French doctor who, for some minutes after being guillotined, answered his friends by winking.

"If you hear me, wink," I cried. The right eye closed and opened with a snap. Ah, here the body was dead and the brain lived. I glanced at the elasmosaurus. Its mouth, half closed over its gleaming teeth, seemed to smile an invitation. The intelligence of the man and the strength of the beasts. The living body and the living brain. The curious resemblance of the reptile's brain-pan to that of a man flashed across my mind.

"Are you still alive, Framingham?"

The right eye winked. I seized my machete, for there was no time for delicate instruments. I might destroy all by haste and roughness, I was sure to destroy all by delay. I opened the skull and disclosed the brain. I had not injured it, and breaking the wound of the elasmosaurus's head, placed the brain within, I dressed the wound and, hurrying to the house, brought all my store of stimulants and administered them.

For years the medical fraternity has been predicting that brain-grafting will some time be successfully accomplished. Why has it never been successfully accomplished? Because it has not been tried. Obviously, a brain from a dead body cannot be used and what living man would submit to the horrible process of having his head opened, and portions of his brain taken for the use of others?

The brains of men are frequently examined when injured and parts of the brain removed, but parts of the brains of other men have never been substituted for the parts removed. No injured man has ever been found who would give any portion of his brain for the use of another. Until criminals under sentence of death are handed over to science for experimentation, we shall not know what can be done in the way of brain-grafting. But the public opinion would never allow it.

Conditions are favorable for a fair and thorough trial of my experiment. The weather is cool and even, and the wound in the head of the elasmosaurus has every chance for healing. The animal possesses a vitality superior to any of our later-day animals, and if any organism can successfully become the host of a foreign brain, nourishing and cherishing it, the elasmosaurus with its abundant vital forces can do it. It may be that a new era in the history of the world will begin here.

May 6th, Noon.

I think I will allow my experiment a little more time.

May 7th, Noon.

It cannot be imagination. I am sure that as I looked into the elasmosaurus's eyes this morning there was expression in them. Dim, it is true, a sort of mistiness that floats over them like the reflection of passing clouds.

May 8th, Noon.

I am more sure than yesterday that there *is* expression in the eyes, a look of troubled fear, such as is seen in the eyes of those who dream nightmares with unclosed lids.

May 11th, Evening.

I have been ill, and have not seen the elasmosaurus for three days, but I shall be better able to judge the progress of the experiment by remaining away a period of some duration.

May 12th, Noon.

I am overcome with awe as I realise the success that has so far crowned my experiment. As I approached the elasmosaurus this morning, I noticed a faint disturbance in the water near its flippers. I cautiously investigated, expecting to discover some fishes nibbling at the helpless monster, and saw that the commotion was not due to fishes, but to the flippers themselves, which were feebly moving.

"Framingham, Framingham," I bawled at the top of my voice. The vast bulk stirred a little, a very little, but enough to notice. Is the brain, or Framingham, it would perhaps be better to say, asleep, or has he failed to establish connection with the body? Undoubtedly he has not yet established connection with the body, and this of itself would be equivalent to sleep, to unconsciousness. As a man born with none of the senses would be unconscious of himself, so Framingham, just beginning to establish connections with his new body, is only dimly conscious of himself and sleeps. I fed him, or it—which is the proper designation will be decided in a few days—with the usual allowance.

May 17th, Evening.

I have been ill for the past three days, and have not been out of doors until this morning. The elasmosaurus was still motionless when I arrived at the cove this morning. Dead, I thought; but I soon detected signs of breathing, and I began to prepare some mussels for it, and was intent upon my task, when I heard a slight, gasping sound, and looked up. A feeling of terror seized me. It was as if in response to some doubting incantations there had appeared the half-desired, yet wholly-feared and unexpected apparition of a fiend. I shrieked, I screamed, and the amphitheatre of rocks echoed and re-echoed my cries, and all the time the head of the elasmosaurus raised aloft to the full height of its neck, swayed about unsteadily, and its mouth silently struggled and twisted, as if an attempt to form words, while its eyes looked at me now with wild fear and now with piteous intreaty.

"Framingham," I said.

The monster's mouth closed instantly, and it looked at me attentively, pathetically so, as a dog might look.

"Do you understand me?"

The mouth began struggling again, and little gasps and moans issued forth. "If you understand me, lay your head on the rock."

Down came the head. He understood me. My experiment was a success. I sat for a moment in silence, meditating upon the wonderful affair, striving to realise that I was awake and sane, and then began in a calm manner to relate to my friend what had taken place since his attempted suicide.

"You are at present something in the condition of a partial paralytic, I should judge," said I, as I concluded my account. "Your mind has not yet learned to command your new body. I see you can move your head and neck, though with difficulty. Move your body if you can. Ah, you cannot, as I thought. But it will all come in time. Whether you will ever be able to talk or not, I canot say, but I think so, however. And now if you cannot, we will arrange for some means of communication. Anyhow, you are rid of your human body and possessed of the powerful vital apparatus you so much envied its former owner. When you gain control of yourself, I wish you to find the communication between this lake and the under-world, and conduct some explorations. Just think of the additions to geological knowledge you can make. I will write an account of your discovery, and the names of Framingham and McLennegan will be among those of the greatest geologists."

I waved my hands in my enthusiasm, and the great eyes of my friend glowed with a kindred fire.

June 2nd, Night.
The process by which Framingham has passed from his first

powerlessness to his present ability to speak, and command the use of his corporeal frame, has been so gradual that there has been nothing to note down from day to day. He seems to have all the command over his vast bulk that its former owner had, and in addition speaks and sings. He is singing now. The north wind has risen with the fall of night, and out there in the darkness I hear the mighty organ pipetones of his tremendous, magnificent voice, chanting the solemn notes of the Gregorian, the full-throated Latin words mingling with the roaring of the wind in a wild and weird harmony.

To-day he attempted to find the connection between the lake and the interior of the earth, but the great well that sinks down in the centre of the lake is choked with rocks and he has discovered nothing. He is tormented by the fear that I will leave him, and that he will perish of loneliness. But I shall not leave him. I feel too much pity for the loneliness he would endure, and besides, I wish to be on the spot should another of those mysterious convulsions open the connection between the lake and the lower world.

He is beset with the idea that should other men discover him, he may be captured and exhibited in a circus or museum, and declares that he will fight for his liberty even to the extent of taking the lives of those attempting to capture him. As a wild animal, he is the property of whomsoever captures him, though perhaps I can set up title to him on the ground of having tamed him.

July 6th.

One of Framingham's fears has been realised. I was at the pass leading into the basin, watching the clouds grow heavy and pendulous with their load of rain, when I saw a butterfly net appear over a knoll in the pass, followed by its bearer, a small man, unmistakably a scientist, but I did not note him well, for as he looked down into the valley, suddenly there burst forth with all the power and volume of a steam calliope, the tremendous voice of Framingham, singing a Greek song of Anacreon to the tune of "Where did you get that hat?" and the singer appeared in a little cove, the black column of his great neck raised aloft, his jagged jaws wide open.

That poor little scientist. He stood transfixed, his butterfly net dropped from his hand, and as Framingham ceased his singing, curvetted and leaped from the water and came down with a splash that set the whole cove swashing, and laughed a guffaw that echoed among the cliffs like the laughing of a dozen demons, he turned and sped through the pass at all speed.

I skip all entries for nearly a year. They are unimportant.

June 30th, 1897.

A change is certainly coming over my friend. I began to see it some time ago, but refused to believe it and set it down to imagination. A catastrophe threatens, the absorption of the human intellect by the brute body. There are precedents for believing it possible. The human body has more influence over the mind than the mind has over the body. The invalid, delicate Framingham with refined mind, is no more. In his stead is a roistering monster, whose boisterous and commonplace conversation betrays a constantly growing coarseness of mind.

No longer is he interested in my scientific investigations, but pronounces them all bosh. No longer is his conversation such as an educated man can enjoy, but slangy and diffuse iterations concerning the trivial happenings of our uneventful life. Where will it end? In the absorption of the human mind by the brute body? In the final triumph of matter over mind and the degradation of the most mundane force and the extinction of the celestial spark? Then, indeed, will Edward Framingham be dead, and over the grave of his human body can I fittingly erect a headstone, and then will my vigil in this valley be over.

Fort D. A. Russell, Wyoming,
April 15th, 1899.

Prof. William G. Breyfogle.

Dear Sir—The inclosed intact manuscript and the fragments which accompany it, came into my possession in the manner I am about to relate and I inclose them to you, for whom they were intended by their late author. Two weeks ago, I was dispatched into the mountains after some Indians who had left their reservation, having under my command a company of infantry and two squads of cavalrymen with mountain howitzers. On the seventh day of our pursuit, which led us into the wild and unknown part of the mountains, we were startled at hearing from somewhere in front of us a succession of bellowings of a very unusual nature, mingled with the cries of a human being apparently in the last extremity, and rushing over a rise before us, we looked down upon a lake and saw a colossal, indescribable thing engaged in rending the body of a man.

Observing us, it stretched its jaws and laughed, and in saying this, I wish to be taken literally. Part of my command cried out that it was the devil, and turned and ran. But I rallied them, and thoroughly enraged at what we had witnessed, we marched down to the shore, and I ordered the howitzers to be trained upon the murderous creature. While we were doing this, the thing kept up a constant babbling that bore a distinct resemblance to human speech, sounding very much like the jabbering of an imbecile, or a drunken man trying to talk. I gave the command to fire and to fire again, and the beast tore out into the lake in its death-agony, and sank.

With the remains of Dr. McLennegan, I found the foregoing manuscript intact, and the torn fragments of the diary from which it was compiled, together with other papers on scientific subjects, all of which I forward. I think some attempts should be made to secure the body of the elasmosaurus. It would be a priceless addition to any museum.

Arthur W. Fairchild
Captain U.S.A.